To my parents, with love.

To Stephen - Happy Reading! (:))

THE SECRETS OF KELMAR

KELMAR TRILOGY
BOOK II

By

Laura Sepesi

Spellbound Press

Copyright © 2011 by Laura Sepesi
Cover design by Laura Sepesi
Cover art by Doug Axmann

ISBN-13: 978-1463776961

ISBN-10: 1463776969

Printed in the United States of America

Published August 2011

Spellbound Press

CONTENTS

PROLOGUE
THE BLAZING PORTENT

It was shortly before sunset on a warm, mid-September day when the ceremony began. The long-awaited wedding of Reoc Haidar and Renalda Camersley was taking place on the grass of a rocky cliff on Amera Island, overlooking the shimmering crystal sea. The sky was painted in fiery shades of orange and red as the fifty invited guests took their seats in anticipation of the entrance of the Sarcan Commander and his bride.

Carmen Fox sat in the first row of white chairs on the right side of the aisle beside her Souls of Destiny—Blaze, Stellar, Glamis, and Anubis. Around her neck, Carmen wore the gray claw belonging to Dagtar, her fifth and final Soul—the Dragon who had been the Partner of Merlin Cloud, the creator of Kelmar. On this day, Dagtar's claw gave off a pleasant warmth against Carmen's skin. She could feel the deceased Dragon's presence with her as she sat before the white wedding trellis, which was adorned with lilac and yellow flowers.

The fact that Carmen was here to celebrate her instructor's wedding in the magical world of Kelmar was amazing in and of itself. Carmen Fox was a sorcerer—and no ordinary sorcerer at that. Just over a year ago, Carmen had arrived in Kelmar as a quiet and naïve girl who would train in Thunder Academy under Commander Haidar to develop her magical strengths and take her place as the chosen Guardian of Kelmar. Along the way, she had met her Souls of Destiny, who helped her to battle and eventually defeat the evil Desorkhan and his Magicon followers.

Carmen was a sixteen-year-old girl with golden-brown hair and green eyes. All of her friends sitting next to her were magical creatures native to Kelmar. Her best friend and Partner, Blaze, was a creature called a Sarcan. He had golden fur with blue, flame-shaped markings, and he wore a navy bandana around his neck. He also possessed bat-like wings, large blue eyes, and a yellow lightning bolt-shaped horn. Together, he and Carmen had journeyed across Kelmar and fought by each other's sides to combat Desorkhan and his Sarcan, Singe. Blaze, as well as the rest of Carmen's friends, was unique, and what made *Carmen* unique was that she was not *just* a sorcerer but the one whose very destiny, and her fulfillment of her duties as Guardian, made her a legend in Kelmar.

Days after Carmen's birth, a Dark sorcerer named Lucifer Mondalaus had found her in the non-magical realm. Under the orders of the Dark Master, Desorkhan, Mondalaus had set fire to the printing factory owned by Carmen's parents in an attempt to murder their infant daughter—the one chosen in an ancient prophecy as the child who would lead the Kelmarians over the Magicon. Carmen's parents had been killed in the fire, but her grandfather had rescued her and raised her from that day forward.

Though Blaine loved Carmen, and gave her everything that he could, Carmen had lived her life as a virtual outcast in the non-magical realm, unable to make friends, and always feeling as if she didn't belong. She would spend countless long and lonely hours in her grandfather's secondhand bookshop searching for her true purpose.

That was Carmen's life, until just over a year ago, when her grandfather presented her with the gift of a magical golden key on her fifteenth birthday, shortly before she found an enchanted book called *The Book of Kelmar*, which imprisoned the soul of Desorkhan. It was on that day that Carmen's world changed in nearly every way imaginable.

She traveled to Kelmar and learned of her story, taking the journey of a lifetime through a world that, at the time, knew only war. Most of its inhabitants lived in fear of the Dark Master, who desired to take control of Kelmar, and killed anyone who stood in his way. Just prior to the conclusion of her formal training that year, Carmen and her friends found themselves in battle against Desorkhan and his Magicon fighters. Carmen defeated and ultimately killed Desorkhan and his followers by stabbing *The Book of Kelmar* with a magical saber called the Dark Sword—realizing her destiny as the Guardian of Kelmar.

At the moment, Carmen's grandfather, Blaine Fox, was sitting to her left. Blaine was tall and had caring blue eyes, wispy white hair, and a lined face. Though he was older than most of the sorcerers present here tonight, he was quite strong and sharp-witted.

To Blaine's left was Alazar Friar, a friend of both the bride and the groom. Alazar was seated beside his Partner, Redge—a small, furry brown creature with a long tail called a Lenkin. Renalda's Frelark, Enn, was sitting next to him. With a body resembling that of a koala, Enn had violet fur and bright eyes.

The sorcerer named Alazar was middle-aged, with silvery russet hair and friendly green eyes. He walked with a limp from an injury he had sustained in battle decades prior, but he was as active and wise as he ever was. The eccentric inventor was absentmindedly fiddling with his camera while he waited for the start of the ceremony. Alazar had modified his bulky black box camera to produce pictures that, when tapped with a wand, would change to also feature the person who took the photo.

"You never know. A meteor could strike the island, and there would be no one else around to take the picture," Alazar had explained earlier, as he proudly showed off his newest gadget to Carmen and her friends. "If that were the case, I

3

couldn't possibly snap the photo and be in it at the same time. This type of scenario is just what this little device is for. It's also much more convenient than taking another picture to include the person behind the camera."

As Alazar tinkered with his camera's controls, the other guests talked quietly with one another about the coming arrival of Haidar and Renalda. The two had been engaged to marry nearly twenty years prior, but Haidar had decided to call off the ceremony and the marriage at the last minute, feeling that he would not be able to take care of Renalda the way he should. At the time, he needed to focus his attention on his Unit and students during the Magicon War. But now that the war was finally over, Haidar had had a change of heart.

Two months after the final battle, Haidar had returned to visit Renalda on Amera Island to propose to her once again. Renalda, who had lived for many years only seeing him every so often when he would come to the island for Army-related duties, accepted his proposal on one condition. Haidar had to agree that he would lighten up a bit. This pledge included Haidar's attendance at a party, which Alazar offered to throw for him and Renalda the night before the wedding.

Alazar had reserved a chamber in Crystal Hall for the rehearsal dinner, and provided his friends with a fitting party, whose guests included many of Haidar's past and current students, as well as friends and relatives of both Renalda and the Sarcan Commander.

Haidar kept his promise by dancing and celebrating with Renalda and their friends at the informal affair. Carmen and her Souls of Destiny had had a great time—eating and dancing with the other guests until late into the evening. Among the numerous people that they met for the first time were Haidar's mother and father.

Upon first impression, Sanoria Haidar appeared nothing like her son. A relatively short and stocky older woman, Sanoria wore silk Kelmarian scarlet robes and a smile as bright as the sun spread across her gentle, round face when she approached Carmen.

"Carmen Fox, the Guardian of Kelmar!" Sanoria wrapped her arms tightly around Carmen as she hugged her. "Reoc always tells me what fine students you and Blaze are, and coming from him, that's saying something!"

Ganvan Haidar, on the other hand, looked very much like an older version of Reoc. His crew cut hair was silver and white, and his face was lined. He shook Carmen's hand with a firmness and strength that was reminiscent of that of his son. Prior to his retirement, Ganvan had also been a Sarcan Master in the Kelmarian Army before his promotion to General. He had returned to service for the Magicon War, and had been stationed in South Kelmar fighting Dark rebels, returning home just in time to attend his son's wedding.

"This is a big step for Reoc," Ganvan remarked. "But the time is finally right, and I'm proud of him for making this decision. Renalda is a wonderful person. There is no one else that I could see him with."

Sanoria and Ganvan sat on the left side of the aisle along with other members of Haidar's family on this night of the wedding. Scattered throughout the rest of the seats on both sides were the recently graduated Sarcan Captains, and quite a number of older former students. Other notable guests included Renalda's parents, and her two sisters, both of whom were younger than Renalda by a few years.

The marriage was to be performed by a Kelmarian Parliament officiator named Alardan Tiyagar, who stood beneath the white trellis with *The Kelmarian Code of Law* tucked under his arm. He was an older, pasty-faced man with a narrow nose, white hair, and rectangular framed glasses. He was dressed in the scarlet and gold robes that Kelmarian Parliament Members always wore.

After making his formal entrance to the ceremony area, Commander Reoc Haidar now stood next to him, clad in formal black and white robes. The tall and trim, dark-skinned man had deep brown eyes and a crew cut. His usually composed and confident face held the slightest hint of nervousness as he gazed out at the forest, waiting for Renalda to appear.

Blaine's Partner, Thunderbolt, began the procession by flying up the aisle carrying a small wooden box in his paws. Nestled safely inside the Sarcan's box were the bride and groom's rings.

Cherub the Sarcan came next, flying gracefully up the aisle, dropping armfuls of red flower petals in the grass as she went. The waves were tumbling up onto the sand of the beaches far below the cliff on which the ceremony was taking place, the rumble of the powerful ocean carrying across the island with the sea breeze. The late summer air held only remnants of the heat that had filled the days leading up to this one.

Finally, the moment that they had all been waiting for had come. From somewhere out of view of the guests, lovely, harmonious music began playing, and Renalda stepped out of the trees.

Carmen hardly recognized her. The sorceress had always been pretty, but tonight, she looked nothing less than beautiful. Renalda was tall and thin, with brown eyes, fair skin, and some subtle wrinkles. For this occasion, her long black hair was pinned back in an elegant bun.

Renalda promptly began her walk across the supple grass of the ocean cliff. Her sweeping white dress was simple, yet stunning. Rhinestones were sprinkled throughout the silky fabric, which flowed and shined in the orange light of the sunset. She carried a bouquet of lavender and white flowers.

As she moved slowly up the aisle, the flashes from the cameras illuminated her teary eyes, which held nothing but long overdue happiness. The always-serious Haidar couldn't stop smiling at her. It was a sight that Carmen was sure she would never forget.

Renalda reached the trellis and stood beside Reoc, the cool ocean breeze rushing past her face as she beamed at her groom. Tiyagar waited for the singing of the plum-feathered birds flying over the cliff to finish before he began the ceremony. Then he smiled at the bride and groom before speaking to everyone present.

"Ladies and gentlemen…we are gathered here on this day to join together this man and this woman in matrimony," he said, in a deep, calm voice. "True love is a rare and precious gift. From the beginning to the end of time, it is forever. Tonight, we bring together two people, who in finding each other, found friendship, trust, and a connection that will stay with them for the rest of their lives and beyond…."

As Carmen watched Reoc and Renalda's service, she felt exceptionally happy for the both of them. Reoc had always been strong and independent, but now he would finally have someone to lean on as a partner in life—someone for whom he cared deeply, and for whom he would sacrifice anything to protect. Renalda, meanwhile, had waited for Reoc for decades, and she deserved to finally be with the man whom she loved and with whom she wanted to spend the rest of her years.

Carmen had never been to a wedding prior to this one, and this ceremony was more special than any she could have imagined. The warmth of the sunset washing over the cliff, the cerulean ocean sparkling in the night, the singing of the birds that flew through the skies above, the sweet aroma of the flowers…. All of it came together effortlessly to create a magnificent ceremony—one that would undoubtedly always hold a special place in her heart.

"…. Do you, Reoc Haidar, take this woman as your wife?" Tiyagar asked, turning to the groom.

"I do," Haidar answered.

Tiyagar then gazed at Renalda.

"And do you, Renalda Camersley, take this man as your husband?"

"I do," Renalda said softly.

"Then by the power vested in me by the Kelmarian Statute of Authority…I now declare you united as one for all of eternity."

The blazing orange sun disappeared beneath the ocean as Haidar and Renalda shared their first kiss as husband and wife. The flowers decorating the trellis around them magically transformed into white and silver Incadoves, which fluttered through the air, circling gracefully around Haidar and Renalda as they embraced in a symbol of love and everlasting unity.

The guests burst into applause as Haidar, Renalda, Thunderbolt, and Cherub proceeded down the aisle, their faces aglow with smiles. Hand-in-hand, Renalda and Reoc Haidar walked off into the night, the stars shining brightly down on them as they began what would be the start of the rest of their lives together.

The reception following Reoc and Renalda's ceremony consisted of a marvelous dinner inside a spacious white tent, which stood on the grass farther in from the cliff where the ceremony had taken place. After everyone had eaten, the guests made their way outside to dance to music performed by a band of sorcerers dressed in silver robes.

Carmen was standing off to the side with her Souls, listening to the music and watching as several of the guests danced together. She was wearing a long, billowy sapphire dress and a pair of matching heels, which she had purchased just for the occasion. She closed her eyes and felt the cool breeze against her face…. A couple of minutes later, she felt a tap on her shoulder.

Carmen opened her eyes and glanced to her right. Her classmate, Shea Garnett, was looking more anxious than usual as he stood before her. A sandy-haired boy with kind blue eyes, he was noticeably sweaty as he tugged restlessly at the collar of his formal black and white robes. He had trouble maintaining eye contact with Carmen as he spoke.

"Hi, Carmen," he said quietly.

"Hi, Shea," Carmen replied politely. "What's going on?"

"Uh...well, I was wondering...wou-would you like to dance with me?" he asked timidly.

"Oh...umm, well...."

Surprised by the question, Carmen bit her lip. This was the first time that she had ever been asked to dance. She wasn't even sure that she knew *how* to dance with another person, and was scared at the thought of making a fool out of herself. Carmen momentarily gazed beyond Shea to see their classmate, Kamie Lonvan—a tall, pretty girl with long brown hair—approaching the two of them from the other side of the lawn. She had just finished dancing with fellow Sarcan Master, Max Wychnor.

"Hey, guys!" she said, as she walked up to Carmen and Shea. She was dressed in a sleek, bright pink gown. "Come out and dance with everyone!"

"Uh, I don't know, Kamie," Carmen replied, her gaze falling between her and Shea. "I'm not a very good dancer."

Kamie persisted. "Oh come on, anybody can do it," she said. "Just give it a try."

"Err...I'm not sure I can."

"Carmen, you defeated Desorkhan!" Kamie reminded her impatiently. "Dancing should be pretty easy compared to the things that *you've* done."

"She has a point, Car," Blaze said, as he flew over his Master's shoulder. "Go have fun. You deserve to have a good time."

9

Carmen sighed.

"All right, fine," she decided, willing to sacrifice her comfort to make Shea and the others happy. She grinned as Cherub flew over from the sea of dancers and begged Blaze to join her.

"Let's go, Shea."

Without another word to each other, Carmen and Shea walked across the grass to the center of the dancing sorcerers and creatures. Carmen felt awkward and out of place as she stood with Shea amongst the other couples. Still a quiet person by nature, Carmen had a hard time feeling relaxed in doing something like this, which was so far from what she knew. As she readied herself to begin dancing with her classmate, she decided that learning to master her magical powers and defeating the Dark Master seemed much easier.

The band, whose members were standing on a stage to the north of the dancers, began to play a slow, melodious song. Gently, Carmen laid her left hand on Shea's shoulder as he put his right hand on her waist. They held each other's opposite hands—and they danced.

After a few minutes, it seemed to get easier. As Carmen and Shea danced, carefully, so as to avoid stepping on their respective partner's feet, it gradually became more natural, less forced. Blaze and Cherub, together with several other Sarcans, danced cheerfully in the skies above. Renalda somehow persuaded Reoc to dance to nearly every song with her, and he did so, not grudgingly, but with grace.

As Carmen looked over Shea's shoulder, she spotted Stellar chatting with Glamis. The Boarax was munching on some insects that had the misfortune of scuttling through the grass at his feet. Carmen and Shea circled around the entire dance space step by step, occasionally brave enough to look into each other's eyes and smile in spite of their earlier apprehension.

After searching for him since she had begun to dance, Carmen finally found Anubis toward the end of the third song. The black Jackal with the golden ribbon collar was standing north of the band and the dancers, near the edge of the cliff, not far from the white trellis. He had his back to most of the other guests as he looked out over the ocean. The light of the stars was shining in his golden eyes.

Carmen continued to dance and twirl with Shea as the distinct sounds of the rushing ocean and the peaceful music carried through her ears. It was unexpectedly blissful and serene—one of the most carefree nights that Carmen had experienced following the conclusion of the Magicon War. Dancing with Shea was a surprisingly enchanting experience for her, and as the minutes passed by without notice by either of them, Carmen and Shea enjoyed the rest of the evening's dances together.

Carmen felt warm all over as the night wore on. She was utterly happy and at peace here with her friends. The chirping Harkleflies sang throughout the evening as an ocean of stars twinkled in the island sky.

Sometime close to midnight, faraway thunder rumbled across the cliff. Moments later, someone screamed.

The music stopped abruptly as everyone looked out toward the ocean. A blinding bolt of lightning cut through the dark sky and struck the cliff, inches from where Anubis was standing. The grass of the hill instantly ignited in flames.

"ANUBIS!"

Her heart suddenly racing, Carmen ran with her other Souls and the rest of the guests over to the edge of the cliff.

What's happening? she thought, panic-stricken.

When Carmen and her stunned friends reached the spot where the lightning had struck, they peered down into the fire.

A series of words were burned into the grass of the hill, the flickering flames illuminating the black fur of Anubis's face as he read the message aloud.

The legend has come to life,
and with it, the destructive clash of the Worlds Triad.
Beware, for the balance of power has shifted.
Unlock the Secrets, and restore the harmony,
or Kelmar will experience the storm.

CHAPTER ONE

THE GREAT STORM

Carmen and Blaze shuffled into Blaine's house behind Glamis, out of the storm. It had rained every day for a week following Reoc and Renalda's wedding and the appearance of the troubling warning in the grass, which spoke of a disruption in the balance of forces in Kelmar. The Kelmarian Parliament had not taken the occurrence lightly. Upon receiving notice of the bizarre incident, its Members had launched a full investigation into what the message could indicate, devoting numerous resources to discovering the meaning behind the mysterious portent that had come from the skies over Kelmar.

Carmen left her rain-soaked boots by the door and hung up her jacket on the coat hook. Her magical blue robes with gold trim, which had the golden Great Seal of Kelmar stitched into the back, had done a decent job of keeping her dry.

Carmen's grandfather, Stellar, Anubis, Reoc, and Renalda were all sitting in the cozy living room, which was home to two plush green sofas, a coffee table, a lamp, a fireplace, and a hand carved rocking chair that had once belonged to Carmen's grandmother. Newlyweds Reoc and Renalda Haidar had returned from their honeymoon spent on Amera Island earlier this evening and had come to visit Carmen in her home in the scenic Mortrock Forest.

The banging of cast-iron pots and the smell of sizzling Arakives wafting out from the kitchen meant that Blaze's father, Thunderbolt, was busy preparing dinner. Carmen walked to the closet and retrieved a thick towel with which she helped Glamis dry his saturated fur.

"How is it out there, Carmen?" Blaine asked, as he looked up from his Kelmarian newspaper. "Did you sense anything when you were out on your walk?"

"It's raining pretty hard again," Carmen answered, as she rubbed the towel vigorously through Glamis's black fur. It would take almost ten minutes to dry off his bulky body.

Glamis possessed a bright orange nose, a pair of white tusks, and a long, tufted tail. As the king of his Boarax herd, he wore a spiked red collar, a scarlet cape, and a golden, jeweled crown.

"It was clear this morning, so the ground had just started to dry up," Carmen told Blaine as she worked on drying Glamis's fur. "But now that it's raining again, there's probably going to be some flooding. I didn't sense anything out of the ordinary...so I'm not sure what's up."

"Parliament also claims to know little of what's going on," Blaine commented, peering over the top of the newspaper from where he sat in his rocking chair dressed in his favorite scarlet and gold robes. Splashed across the front page of *The Kelmarian Review* that he was holding were large, bold letters, the headline reading:

THE MYSTERY OF THE BLAZING PORTENT REMAINS UNSOLVED

"I'm sure that they have *some* idea as to the meaning of it," Carmen said. "They're just not saying what it is yet so that nobody panics if it's bad."

Blaze flew over to Stellar, who was lying on the hardwood floor in front of the fireplace gnawing on the bone of a feathered Verdden that he had eaten a couple of hours ago. The Keinen resembled a large cat with brown fur. He also had saber teeth, a barbed tail, and emerald green armor that ran down his back. Blaze shook the rain out of his wet fur, showering Stellar in cold water.

Stellar dropped his bone and jumped up to get away from him.

"You did that on purpose!" Stellar yelled, indignant. He was now wet as well.

"You needed a bath anyway," Blaze said, grinning mischievously. "The last time that I saw you wetter than this was when you swam across Calmic Lake. Even *you* have to admit that was a long time ago."

"Fair enough. But from now on, if I want a shower, I'll ask you for it," Stellar replied, glaring at Blaze as he shook the water out of his fur.

"Here you go, Stell." Carmen tossed the Keinen the partially damp towel that she had used to dry off Glamis. She then crossed the room with Blaze to sit on the green squishy couch beside Anubis. The black Jackal was staring pensively into the flames dancing in the fireplace. The unnaturally cold temperatures for September had forced Blaine to use the fireplace much earlier in the year than he normally would.

"There is unrest in Kelmar," Anubis stated, as he watched the flames flicker and skip across the hearth. *"I have felt very strange for the past few days…yet I can't identify the exact reason."*

There was a sharp squeak of metal springs straining as Glamis plopped down onto the sofa opposite Anubis and Carmen, next to Reoc and Renalda.

"The conditions are highly unusual," the Boarax King remarked. "I would expect us to be receiving news from the government any day now."

The rain pattered against the glass of the windows, the wind rattling the wooden frames as Carmen and her friends talked.

"There is reason to be concerned about these recent weather patterns," Reoc said darkly, gazing at Carmen and

Blaze. "While there have been several uncharacteristically fierce rainstorms across North Kelmar, the other sectors of our world are also experiencing abnormal phenomena. In the South and West, for example, there have been exceedingly high temperatures reported. East Kelmar, meanwhile, has been feeling the effects of sleet and snowfall—weather patterns rarely experienced outside of the winter months. It is very disturbing…particularly as it comes after the portent that we received a week ago. I believe that the connection between the words of the message and the timing of the bizarre weather is no coincidence."

"What could it mean?" Carmen asked. "Do you have any ideas?"

"Regrettably, I do not," Reoc said in a dull voice. "I fear for the future…. I do not know what these events could be foretelling."

Renalda rubbed Reoc's hand for comfort. She had to keep pushing away her rain and wind-tousled hair, which was falling down into her eyes.

"Well, we know one fact is for certain," Renalda said, gazing steadily at Carmen. "Kelmar is in a strange phase of transition…and until we get further information from Parliament, all that we can do is wait to see where it's going."

Just as Renalda said this, a clap of thunder sounded through Mortrock Forest. The pouring sheets of rain beat against the stone roof. The unsettling feeling was shared amongst Carmen and her friends as they listened to the storm blowing outside.

A little while later, Thunderbolt called Carmen and the others for dinner. They left the living room together and sat down at the long table in Blaine's welcoming kitchen. Blaine had made all of the antique wooden cabinets around the walls decades ago, but with some polish and hard work, the dark wood looked just as exquisite as it had when the cabinets were first installed.

In addition to the cabinets and table, there was also a counter and sink, and a stove and a refrigerator that stood next to each other in the space. The beige tiled floor had been cleaned after Carmen moved in late in the spring. Over the summer, she and all of her Souls had helped Blaine to bring warmth and hominess to the fifty-year-old cottage.

Blaine pointed his long red wand with its silver blade at the wooden table and used a lengthening spell to extend it just a tad longer for Reoc and Renalda to fit. He also conjured two additional chairs so that everyone was able to sit comfortably together. Carmen and Blaze helped Thunderbolt to pass around the large bowls of mashed Bocanores, which looked and tasted similar to potatoes; the Qwethral that Stellar had stuffed and carved; seasoned Orkafish; and fresh, green Kelmarian vegetables.

As Carmen and her friends ate, the bright white flashes of lightning that lit up the kitchen grew more and more frequent, and the bursts of thunder continued to intensify with each passing minute. Carmen feared for Cherub, the Sarcan that she and her friends had rescued as a baby during her Third Challenge to gain acceptance into Thunder Academy. She hoped that the Sarcan had gone back to Sarcanian Valley for shelter from the dangerous winds and lightning.

"This is one of the worst storms I've ever witnessed," Blaine said, worried. He stared out through the small window above the sink at the rain and lightning that illuminated the dark sky before gazing across the table at Renalda and Reoc. "You both must stay here until the storm quiets down," he insisted. "We have plenty of room if you need to spend the night. I can sleep on the couch in the living room so that you can have my bed upstairs."

"Thank you, Blaine," Commander Haidar said gratefully, as he cut through his slice of Qwethral with his knife. "We may need to stay if the storm doesn't begin to weaken."

Suddenly, a loud crash of thunder shook the small home, the pots and pans piled near the sink clattering with the force that traveled through the house.

Everybody at the table exchanged troubled glances. More than slightly distressed by the storm, Carmen and her companions resumed their meal, but it was becoming increasingly difficult to ignore the storm that was raging just outside.

"Carmen, I have some news from Thunder Academy to share with you," Reoc told his student, who was seated next to her grandfather, across from him.

Carmen finished hungrily shoving a forkful of Bocanores into her mouth and looked up at her Commander with interest.

"The new Sarcan Council has hired an additional Sarcan instructor to teach Basic Training," Reoc said. "Her name is Faelyn Sheridae. She's a Sarcan Officer, and an excellent Master. I'm sure that she will make a fine instructor. And since the war is over, the Council has also made the decision to provide Advanced Master and Sarcan Training to graduates of the Basic Training program. In the years prior to the Magicon rebellion, there had been such a course offered, but after the uprising began, all trained Sarcan Captains were needed to fight. They've now decided to bring the program back, and I will serve as an instructor to only the advanced students.... That means that I will be your teacher once again."

"Great," Carmen said, pleasantly surprised. "So everyone who was in our class will be there. What about the Sarcan Captains who graduated before us?"

"Right now, Thunder Academy is offering the training only to the most recent class of Captains," Reoc explained. "But if the program is successful, in the future, the Sarcan

Councilors will probably open the course up to older students to give them the option to build upon their skills and gain additional knowledge. The term starts next week. The Council has already sent out letters to the rest of the Captains to inform them about the new course, which they will all be required to attend."

"How do the new Councilors seem?" Blaze asked. "Do you think that they'll do well?"

"Yes. I am in complete agreement with Parliament's selections for the Council," Reoc said with a nod. "And Seth has been helping them to get acquainted with the school and its procedures."

"Former Councilors Kantour, Jesslyn, and Novalis are going to be held in the Pyramid City Prison for the time being, pending their trial," Blaine informed Blaze. "According to *The Kelmarian Review*, the new Council intends to undertake the task of forming a new review committee to look into the practices of elected officials…. Their objective is to discourage corruption and dishonesty amongst our politicians."

"That's always a good thing," Carmen remarked.

She remembered quite well how three of the five Sarcan Councilors who were in office last year had used her to gain more power for themselves in the Kelmarian government, while the fourth Councilor, Sylvine Yokaro, had committed an even worse crime in having been a spy for Desorkhan. As Desorkhan's Secret Guard, she had attempted to have Carmen killed on more than one occasion, and later died in the final battle against the Kelmarians, along with the Dark Master and the rest of the Magicon. Councilor Peruveus Seth had been the only one of the five Councilors on Carmen's side, and had worked to keep her safe from the others throughout her first term at Thunder Academy.

Carmen and her friends enjoyed Cornathid cream pie for dessert, courtesy of the baking skills of Glamis. The Boarax King had spent a good part of the day creating the insect-filled pastry, and proudly served it to the others when it came time. As he ate, Stellar pulled bunches of Cornathid legs from his teeth and placed them on his plate—when it was not of notice to Glamis.

The storm continued to gust outside as Blaine's guests retired to the living room. Carmen stayed behind in the kitchen to help Thunderbolt and Blaze clean the dishes. Blaine, meanwhile, chatted with Reoc, Renalda, and the rest of the Souls of Destiny. Throughout the night, the intense lightning surges constantly flashed through the windows as thunder roared out in the forest.

Carmen used a washing spell to assist Blaze and his father. With a twirl of her wand, she was able to make the scrubbing brush near the sink come to life and scour the dishes clean all by itself.

Once they had finished washing and putting away the dishes, Carmen, Blaze, and Thunderbolt joined the others in the living room.

"That message from the sky was a forewarning to all of these storms," Anubis told Blaine, as Carmen and her friends sat down. *"According to the portent, these storms are the result of an imbalance in the forces controlling Kelmar.... It is wise to assume that if the balance is not corrected, these peculiar weather patterns will continue to wreak havoc in our world."*

"The portent mentioned a legend," Carmen said. "Do you know what that could be referring to?"

"After much thought...I have determined that the portent was referencing the Legend of the Worlds Triad," Anubis replied. *"It is an ancient myth that tells the tale of Kelmar's creation, as well as that of the two realms of the afterlife. Together, the three magical worlds make up what is known as the Worlds Triad. The conclusion of the story discusses what would happen if life ever ended in Kelmar.... The story implies that if Kelmarsia and Keltan ever went to war, Kelmar as we know it would cease to exist.*

This is what the message from the sky was trying to direct our attention to."

From what Carmen knew of Kelmarsia and Keltan, Kelmarsia was the world in the sky where deceased sorcerers and creatures who had lived honorable lives existed as spirits in the heavenly eternal afterlife; Keltan was Kelmarsia's counterpart realm, inhabited by departed Dark sorcerers and creatures who were to be punished for the misdeeds that they had committed while alive.

"The worlds of the afterlife going to war...." Carmen said, dazed. "You think that that's what's happening?"

"I am not completely certain of anything," Anubis said. *"All I know is that when there is a problem in nature, I can usually sense it before most other kinds of creatures. And I can tell you that there is most definitely something sinister taking place here—and possibly elsewhere—in the Kelmarian spirit realms."*

"If this keeps up, we're in trouble," Stellar said, sounding nervous. "The damage from all of these storms could be catastrophic if they persist for much longer. There's already been a lot of flooding, and fires from lightning strikes."

"That's true. The storms need to die down, and soon," Thunderbolt said. "I can't see how Kelmar will survive unless conditions return to normal.... I received a letter from Noel earlier today; she said that many of the Sarcans living around Dormien's Rock have had to move into the caves of the mountain or travel north to escape the water rising from the lakes and rivers."

"What should we do?" Carmen asked. ".... Is there anything that we *can* do?"

"Let's hope that things improve," Blaze said, in a perturbed voice. "Otherwise...we may have a very serious situation on our hands."

Carmen's eyes flew open as a flash of light flooded her room. She had been fast asleep in her bed later that night before the sounds of booming thunder and violent winds outside stirred her back to consciousness. She turned over and switched on the lamp on her bedside table. Blaze, who had been sleeping beside her, was now wide-awake as well. He sat up, and both he and Carmen gazed out through the window next to their bed.

The sky beyond the forest was black but had transitioned to a gloomy gray color over the house. Carmen felt her insides tighten up. All around the cottage, trees and bushes were blowing, breaking, snapping, and being ripped out from the ground. An aggressively spinning tornado was moving rapidly through the woods...lifting massive trees from their roots as though they were nothing at all, sending them flying through the air as the storm plowed through the forest. Wind and loud crashes were causing the walls of the house to shake. The cottage was in the direct path of the twister.

"CARMEN, WAKE UP!" Blaine shouted from out in the hall, rapping frantically on the bedroom door.

Carmen and Blaze scrambled out of bed. Blaine rushed into the room, still in his pajamas and terrycloth robe, holding his wand. Anubis, Stellar, and Glamis were looking uneasy as they got up off the floor where they had been sleeping.

"We've got to leave right now," Blaine told all of them, trying to keep his voice steady. "Carmen, bring your wand and the Light Sword and meet me downstairs in the living room. I need to place Protections on the house...but we can't afford to stay here should the Protections fail against the wrath of this storm."

Lightning flashed outside the window of the room. The crash of thunder that followed was even louder than the one that had awakened Carmen and her Souls. The light from Carmen's bedside lamp, as well as all of the other lights in the house, extinguished as the house shook. Blaine and his granddaughter exchanged restless glances. Blaine then dashed out of the room and hurried downstairs.

Carmen hastened over to her closet to grab the sword that had been given to her by Senior Parliament Member Fellathor Foronte following her victory over Desorkhan. She swiftly attached the saber in its scabbard onto her belt, which she threw on over her blue and gold robes. An endless array of thoughts spinning in her mind, she grabbed her black boots from near the door and slipped them on before rushing out of her bedroom with her four Souls of Destiny, the claw of Dagtar swinging haphazardly from its chain around her neck as she ran.

A third of the way down the stairs, Carmen pulled out the Key of Kelmar and summoned her wand, all the while trying not to stumble in the darkness as she bolted down the steps, her friends bringing up the rear.

"Come forth the magic of Kelmar.... Wand, reveal thyself to me!"

The enchanted golden key, which was crowned with Carmen's winged magic circle and engraved with the initials of the names of her Souls, lengthened in her hand to become a shining gold staff with which she could use her magic at a moment's notice to cast spells.

Carmen lit her wand and pointed it down into the living room. Renalda stood in the center of the space in her nightclothes with her arms folded, looking restlessly toward the front door as she rocked back and forth on the balls of her feet. When she saw Carmen and her Souls coming down the stairs, she made an effort to appear much less worried than she actually was.

"Blaine, Thunderbolt, and Reoc are outside casting the Protections," she told them, her voice trembling slightly. "We're going to use the Zohar Complex to go to my parents' home in East Kelmar. I have a Vanishing Point right here."

Renalda picked up a silver quill that was lying on the coffee table. Carmen was quite familiar with this method of travel. A Vanishing Point was a magical object, which a sorcerer or creature could use to transport him or herself to a pre-selected destination. Renalda walked over and hugged Carmen.

"Don't worry.... We'll be fine," she promised.

Then, without warning, the front door of the house burst open. Reoc, Blaine, and Thunderbolt swept into the living room, the wind and rain blustering in behind them as they crossed over the threshold, all of them rain drenched and windblown. Thunderbolt shut the door.

The three of them quickly made their way to the center of the room and gathered around Renalda, who held the Vanishing Point quill in her hand. Renalda hastily removed her golden necklace to summon her wand, whose crown became that of the teardrop-shaped orange stone that had adorned her piece of jewelry.

Renalda laid the silver quill pen down on the carpet in the center of everyone so that they could all reach to touch it. After everyone had a hand, a paw, a hoof, or a claw around the quill, Renalda swished her wand through the air in a *Z* pattern in front of her, and a large, golden circle of light drew itself on the ground at her feet.

"Kelmar, I ask you to grant us passage through this Zohar Complex I command," she ordered. *"To the Cadriach Mountains!"*

All of them waited, anticipating finding themselves inside a home within a small mountain range in East Kelmar a split second later...but nothing happened. The light faded away.

Renalda waved her wand and stated the Zohar incantation once more. And again...to their dismay, they remained huddled in Blaine's small cottage, the winds tearing through the forest just outside the walls that surrounded them.

"The severe weather is interfering with the Zohar Complex," Reoc said, as his wife glanced fretfully around her. "There would be no reason for anyone to block the system, so the weather is the only logical explanation."

"*Now* what?" Stellar asked, rather hopelessly.

At that exact moment, there was an abrupt pounding on the front door. Renalda crossed the room to the home's entryway. She cracked open the door, careful to hold on tight to prevent it from flying wide-open in the winds, and peered outside.

Her eyes widened. She immediately turned back to her friends.

"Everyone, come quick!" she cried.

Startled, Reoc and the others hustled over to the door and followed Renalda's eyes upward. It took Carmen a few seconds to realize that Alazar Friar was flying hundreds of feet over the forest, pedaling a small, two-man airship. The craft consisted of a basic wooden frame with two sets of metal handlebars, two cushioned seats, one in front of the other, pedals to power the ship, and a single white sail at the back. Alazar's Lenkin, Redge, and Renalda's Frelark, Enn, were perched on opposite shoulders.

"Hello!" Alazar waved down to Carmen and her friends through the rain and wind. He was wearing aviation goggles, and his azure robes blew out behind him as he flew his bizarre-looking airship down to them.

Less than a minute after he had appeared, he landed gently down in front of Blaine's cottage, where Carmen's group had come out to meet him.

"Some weather, huh?" Alazar asked, raising his voice to be heard over the winds. "You'll never get to the Cadriach Mountains through Zohar in these conditions, so I've come to take you there myself."

Renalda and her friends gaped at him.

"But Alazar, there's a tornado!" Renalda shouted, even though he was just inches away from her. Her long hair was whipping wildly across her face. "We can't fly through *this!*"

"You always underestimate my resources, Renalda!" Alazar yelled back, as he showed her the contraption upon which he was riding. "This manual airship is capable of flying through almost any kind of weather activity you can think of. I should know," he declared. "I invented it! So you, Glamis, Stellar, and Anubis can ride with me. Redge and Enn can go with Carmen and Reoc."

"You're mad!" Renalda yelled, as a fresh round of thunder crashed through the woods. "There's *no way* that this will work!"

"Trust me, Renalda!" Alazar said, sounding confident.

Renalda stared at him for a moment, and then turned back to Reoc and her friends. Carmen wasn't sure what to make of Alazar's plan, but there was no other immediate solution. The tornado was racing closer to them every second, and there was no point in arguing about a better way out of their dire situation.

"We must go," Reoc decided. "We don't have any choice. If we stay here, we risk losing our lives to this storm. If we leave, we have a much better chance of making it through in one piece."

Renalda nodded tersely. Despite her uncertainty, she crossed the grass with haste and situated herself into the second seat of Alazar's airship. Redge scurried down off of Alazar's right shoulder and over to Carmen. Enn nuzzled Renalda's face and then climbed down from the ship to scamper over to Reoc.

Anubis, Glamis, and Stellar each gave Carmen a reassuring smile as they got aboard Alazar's ship. Even though it had a relatively long frame, it was still extremely challenging to fit twelve riders onto a craft that was designed to carry only a pair. Anubis was forced to lean awkwardly against Renalda's back, laying his front paws over her shoulders. Stellar was squeezed between the rear and front seats, and Glamis sat uncomfortably atop the front handlebars, his red velvet cape blowing back into Alazar's face.

"READY?" Alazar called back to the other riders. "Okay, everyone follow me!"

Alazar pedaled rapidly; Renalda did the same, and the manual airship rose up into the air.

Carmen, Reoc, and Blaine summoned their wings, and together with Blaze and Thunderbolt, they flew up alongside the magical airship as the wind gusted around them. Carmen struggled to remain upright as the storm's winds pulled her in every direction. She shivered. The freezing rain was penetrating through her robes and biting at her skin.

"Grab a hold of the ship!" Alazar shouted to Carmen and the rest of the fliers. "Hold on tight!"

With Redge and Blaze on her shoulders, Carmen reached out and wrapped her hand around one of the handlebars. Reoc, Enn, Blaine, and Thunderbolt followed suit.

"OFF WE GO, THEN!" Alazar bellowed. *"EUREK-CANSU!"*

Alazar pushed a round button in the middle of his handlebars—and suddenly they were speeding away from the storm, the violent winds stinging their faces as they flew off to the Cadriach Mountains of East Kelmar.

CHAPTER TWO

THE GHOST OF DAGTAR

Carmen screamed. She couldn't help it. She was holding on to the handlebar of Alazar's airship with one hand and gripping her wand in the other, her wings blowing back behind her. She and her friends were soaring through the skies at an unnaturally high rate of speed. Colors, sights, and sounds rushed past her, but it was difficult for her to distinguish where she and the others were at any given moment. As all of this was happening, the rains and thunder were lessening the farther away from Mortrock Forest they flew.

It took only a half an hour for Carmen and her companions to reach the Cadriach Mountains of East Kelmar, which were more than a hundred miles from Mortrock Forest. Beneath the warmth of a late afternoon sun, a picturesque mountain range came into view through the passing, translucent clouds. Rows of small wooden houses with sharply sloping roofs were built along the rocky landscape, offering an extraordinary view of Haziran Forest, which lay in the shade of the mountains.

"That's it—just down there!" Alazar pointed down at a home with a green roof situated on one of the peaks, where an older couple had just walked out through a back door and were waving up at them.

Alazar and Renalda slowed down their pedaling. Carmen was shocked to see that neither one appeared to be out of breath after having to use so much physical energy to bring her and her fellow travelers here. The journey had been a long one, but magic had evidently assisted them in their flight.

Alazar and Renalda directed the airship downward, and the group touched down smoothly on the grassy ground behind the Camersleys' home. Renalda climbed off of the wooden craft, and Stellar, Anubis, and Glamis were then able to clamber down as well.

After initially standing back to give her visitors plenty of room to land, Mrs. Camersley rushed forward to embrace Renalda.

"Renalda, thank goodness you're safe," she said, as she wrapped her arms around her daughter, who was a mirror image of her in many ways.

Mrs. Camersley wore ginger robes and had a head of long black and silver hair. It was plain to see that Renalda had inherited her gentle brown eyes and sharply pointed nose.

"I was so worried," Mrs. Camersley said, sighing. "There were reports of tornadoes and dreadful rainstorms in several places."

"We were just able to escape one of them, thanks to Alazar here," Renalda said, gesturing toward her friend. "Zohar didn't work. Reoc believes that the bad weather is responsible."

"He's likely right," Mr. Camersley said, walking up to his daughter and her friends. He was tall, with thinning auburn hair, cool brown eyes, and glasses. He wore olive-colored robes that were noticeably shabby. "These storms are to blame for the failure of numerous means of magical transportation. Word is that most all community airships traveling to North and West Kelmar have been grounded until further notice."

Carmen and her Souls had met Renalda's mother, Tedra, and her father, Adelin, back at the rehearsal dinner that Alazar had thrown for Renalda and Reoc. Adelin and Tedra owned a small magical artifact and relic shop in the nearby town of Brandec. Their store sold all sorts of unusual and fascinating items that dated back thousands of years. Carmen had never been to the shop herself, but her grandfather had told her that it was a remarkably interesting place to visit.

"Come on inside, everyone," Mr. Camersley suggested, motioning toward the house. "You must've had a tiring trip. I hear that the weather in parts of North Kelmar has destroyed forests and knocked down some older buildings there."

Carmen and the others gladly followed Mr. and Mrs. Camersley inside their home. The dwelling turned out to be a humble one, but it was kept very clean and organized. They entered through the back door into the den, which had twin skylights that allowed the sun's rays to cascade into the room and warm the space. The den had dark red carpeting and was occupied by a couple of worn, gray couches; a round table and lamp; and tall bookcases lined with Kelmarian historical volumes. There was a small kitchen off of the den and a staircase that led to the bedrooms and baths on the second floor.

Renalda's mother hurried off to the kitchen to remove a boiling pot of water that was squealing loudly on the stove. Her husband showed Carmen and her friends around while she used her wand to direct a set of china teacups to fly out of the cabinets and land on the table in the study.

After completing a short tour of the downstairs, Mr. Camersley and the others sat down on the couches in the den. Mrs. Camersley came strolling in about five minutes later with her teapot in hand, and poured Perterale tea into everyone's teacups. The Kelmarian tea was sweet and refreshing—a common drink in the households of sorcerers.

"I hate to be the one to have to tell you this, but something awful has happened," Mr. Camersley informed his visitors in a forlorn voice, as his wife filled her guests' cups with steaming tea. "Yesterday, Tedra was out gathering Harmony Berries for a friend of ours who had been hurt during one of the storms in West Kelmar, when she came upon an injured

Lathra in the forest.... The creature had been viciously attacked with a sword and was close to death."

Mr. Camersley looked both disgusted and uncomfortable as he spoke. Renalda gasped.

"We were fortunate that the Lathra allowed Tedra to feed it some of the berries that she had picked," Mr. Camersley said, "and the creature's wounds were then healed."

"Who could have done that?" Renalda asked, in a highly agitated voice. Her Frelark, Enn, was on her shoulder, chewing on the skin of an Aprapome fruit. "Lathra are a protected species," she said. "It's against the law to harm or kill them. In fact, I'm almost certain that the punishment for that kind of crime is—"

"Execution," her father finished. "But what makes the situation most disturbing is that this incident is not the first of its kind. Quite a few episodes similar to this one have taken place in recent weeks in our area...innocent beings being attacked for no reason. No creatures have been killed yet, but it's no longer a question of *if* it will happen but rather *when* it will happen."

"How is it that Parliament hasn't caught anyone yet?" Carmen asked. "They must have some thoughts as to who's behind these attacks."

"One would like to believe that they do, but as of yet, they haven't made their knowledge public," Mr. Camersley said, as he sipped his tea. "They do have a lot on their hands with these wacky weather occurrences, and now the attacks.... I wouldn't be shocked if there are a fair number of empty seats in the assembly once all of this is over. I'm convinced that none of them anticipated these kinds of problems following the disbandment of the Magicon."

"That's just the question, isn't it?" Blaze said. "With the Magicon eliminated, who would have the motive and the power to carry out these acts of violence?"

"No one seems to have a clue," Mr. Camersley replied, putting down his tea. "We'll just have to be careful for now."

"The new term begins in only a week for the Sarcan Captains and Cadets," Reoc said. "If the weather doesn't improve by then, I don't see how the Council can open the school for classes. Pending the circumstances stabilizing, it's likely that Thunder Academy will delay opening its doors this year until this most recent predicament is resolved."

"There is far too much risk in allowing young sorcerers and Sarcans to practice magic outdoors with the current state of affairs taken into account," Anubis concurred. *"Someone could get hurt."*

Stellar muttered in agreement.

"I don't suppose that the new Councilors have anything to say about these incidents?"

"I have a meeting scheduled with the Council next week," Reoc said. "If I learn of anything, I will, obviously, inform all of you. I'm afraid that if we don't get an answer relatively soon, trying days may very well lie ahead for us."

"Until they catch those responsible, all of those here should stay alert and remain extra aware of what's happening around them," Mrs. Camersley said, as she lowered herself down onto the couch next to her husband. "It's scary out there right now…especially so for most of those in this room." She looked around at all of them. Her eyes fell on Carmen last.

"Carmen, be mindful of your surroundings," she told her, in a somber tone. "Out of all of us, *you* should be the most wary…. If any of what's happening now is tied into the Dark Master's defeat, you could become a target."

"Tedra's right you know, Carmen," Alazar said, placing his empty teacup down on the table. "Our world isn't a safe place right now, especially for you, as the Guardian of Kelmar."

Redge the Lenkin curled his long, brown striped tail around the handle of his china teacup and raised it to his mouth, holding the cup in his paws as he drank. From his perch upon his Master's shoulder, he looked at Carmen, his eyes wide with worry.

"I'll be fine," Carmen assured Alazar and Redge. "I've got the best friends in the world to protect me." She smiled proudly. "Anyway, we can't go on being afraid all of the time…. It's okay to be cautious, but we need to stand strong if we're going to get through this, just like we did when we defeated the Magicon."

"You're right, Carmen," Blaine said. "But your safety and well-being are far more essential than taking any unwise risks. That being said, you and your Souls should stay here where it's safe for right now, at least until the circumstances change."

"Assuming that *our* house is standing, we can go back and get anything that we need after the storms pass through," Thunderbolt said, before Carmen could protest. "If conditions in Kelmar are still the way they are right now when the school term is scheduled to begin, you won't need to worry about missing any classes. There's no chance that Thunder Academy will open under the present skies."

"Fair enough," Carmen said. "But I'm trying not to worry too much. There *must* be an explanation for what's happening. The reason just needs to be discovered…and then our problems will be solved. Whatever it is can't be worse than what we've already gone through, right?"

"Right as always, Guardian," Glamis said, sounding confident. "The real unsettled issue here is this: what is everyone having to eat? Following that trip, I'm famished!"

"I'll have food ready for you in no time at all, Glamis," Mrs. Camersley kindly promised him. "You are welcome to stay as long as you like. Adelin's already placed a number of Protections on the house, and we have ample room for everyone."

"Excellent, excellent," Glamis said, laughing. "Thank you so *very* much."

Following a generous meal, during which Mr. and Mrs. Camersley's guests gathered around a magically extended table and exchanged stories and accounts of the storms, Carmen and her friends separated off into three separate upstairs bedrooms to get some much desired sleep. Each of the three rooms had once been occupied by Renalda or one of her two sisters when they were young. Renalda, Reoc, and Enn slept in Renalda's old room; Alazar, Blaine, Redge, and Thunderbolt took Nerien Camersley's room; while Carmen, Blaze, Stellar, Anubis, and Glamis took the final and largest room, which had belonged to the youngest Camersley child, Rachel.

Carmen lay on her back on the feathered mattress, listening to Glamis's deep snoring as he slept on the carpet beside her bed. Her tired mind worked hard to ponder what the following day would bring. The uncertainties concerning the conditions in Kelmar worried her considerably more now than they had during the day. It seemed to her that many hours had passed before the stars that glittered in the black sky outside the window faded from her vision, and Carmen slowly felt herself pulled into unconsciousness....

"Carmen, I need to speak with you...."
"What?"

Carmen was suddenly standing in a great shadow, in the middle of an empty green field that she didn't know, beneath a bright blue sky. She looked up at the impressive Dragon flying over her. He had a spiked head, crystal eyes, and a long body covered in sparkling emerald scales. There was a striking brown sail running down his back, and smaller fins on the backs of his legs. His leathery wings were so huge that Carmen wondered how he didn't block out the sun altogether. She recognized him right away as her fifth Soul of Destiny, alive and well. But how could he be here?...wherever here was?

"Carmen, you must listen to me," the Dragon said. "There is little time. Kelmar is in great danger, and mayhem is at hand in the worlds of Kelmarsia and Keltan. I'm waiting for you in Haziran Forest. I must see you before the night is over.... Listen to your heart, and the claw will lead your way to me."

"What are you talking about?" Carmen asked. "Can't you tell me what's going on right now?"

"Visitation dreams are too limited for all that I must tell you," Dagtar replied. "Yes, Carmen, this is a dream. You must awaken now. I will see you again before the night expires."

Dagtar vanished as the world around Carmen liquefied and blurred.

"Wait, don't go!"

Carmen opened her eyes and sat up in bed. Dagtar's claw around her neck was warm, and a gentle breeze was blowing through the curtains of the open window to the left of her bed. She gazed out into the dark forest behind the Camersleys' home. For a moment, she thought that she saw something white and wispy floating behind the trees. But the form swiftly vanished into the blackness of the woods.

"Blaze." Carmen hurriedly roused the Sarcan sleeping next to her. "Blaze, wake up."

Blaze turned over to face her.

"What's going on?" he asked.

"Dagtar spoke to me in a dream," Carmen whispered fervently. "He said that he's outside in Haziran Forest.... We have to go find him."

Blaze stared at her, bewildered.

"Carmen, Dagtar is dead," he reminded her, as though she could have forgotten. "He can't be out there. His spirit lives in Kelmarsia."

"He said that we're in danger," Carmen told him, disregarding the idea of how irrational she must have sounded. "There's some kind of turmoil in Kelmarsia and Keltan.... We need to talk to him."

Blaze looked alarmed, to say the least.

"Okay. Let's go then," he said resolutely. "Let's not wake up the others though.... If Dagtar only needs to talk to you, then we should let everybody else sleep."

Carmen grabbed the Key necklace, which was lying on the nightstand, and slipped the chain over her head. She then put on her boots before silently creeping over to the window, with Blaze close behind her. She had to be particularly cautious as she stepped over Glamis, Anubis, and Stellar's sleeping forms. When she was at the window, she murmured the flight incantation.

Carmen's large Sarcan wings magically appeared on her back. She folded them in just enough so that she could squeeze out through the small bedroom window behind Blaze. Once outside, Carmen and Blaze flew quietly down to the ground. The cool, late summer air was refreshing as it brushed against their faces.

After she touched down on the grass, Carmen summoned her wand and muttered, *"Illumina,"* causing the crown of her wand to glow brightly.

Unexpectedly, Carmen heard someone running from around the side of the Camersleys' home. She pointed her lit wand in the direction of the approaching footsteps and saw Renalda in her pale pink nightgown hastening toward her and Blaze, her unkempt black hair billowing out behind her. She was also carrying her luminous staff, and her fair face was filled with fear.

"Carmen, what are you doing?" she said, struggling to keep her voice at a whisper as she strode over to her. "I got up to get a glass of water, and when I checked in on you on my way downstairs, you were gone! You can't imagine what a fright you gave me."

"Sorry, Renalda," Carmen said. "Does anyone else know that we're out?"

"No, but you had better have a good explanation as to why you're sneaking off, or they *will* find out," Renalda said, scolding her. "You can't just go wandering outside in the middle of the night with all that's been going on. You could get hurt, and nobody would be able to find you."

"I had a visitation dream," Carmen explained quickly. "Dagtar told me that he's out in the forest and needs to talk to me.... He seems to know why Kelmar has become unstable."

Renalda raised an eyebrow.

"The Dragon of Merlin?" she questioned. "That's impossible.... He's gone."

"I can sense his presence," Carmen said, staring off into the trees behind her. "His claw is warm," she muttered, as she rubbed the Dragon's nail on its chain.

"I can feel it, too," Blaze said. "There's a definite unusual aura coming from the forest. I didn't feel it inside, but out here, I do."

Renalda sighed.

"I do believe both of you," she said, her face softening a little. "*I* can't feel it, but that doesn't mean that it's not there. You're not going into that forest alone though; I'm coming with you."

So with that, Carmen, Blaze, and Renalda walked off into Haziran Forest, Carmen and Renalda holding out their wands to light their path. The stars hanging in the black sky above provided little assistance, as the trees of the dark woods were so dense and tall that little light was able to escape down to the forest floor.

"This forest is one of the oldest in all of Kelmar," Renalda noted, as they passed through the trees. "It's also one of the biggest. Dozens of different Kelmarian species inhabit these woods."

"I'm not sure if that makes me feel better or worse about being here," Carmen murmured, thinking back to her experiences in wooded areas similar to this one. She had encountered everything from giant Gorfelrods to the hundreds of tiny insects that Glamis enjoyed so much in other forests across Kelmar.

"Wait here," Carmen told Blaze and Renalda, after about ten minutes of walking.

She closed her eyes and tried to get an idea of where Dagtar was. His spirit was definitely here somewhere. If only she could pinpoint the precise location....

Carmen took three steps forward, attempting to feel whether the magical aura was becoming any more pronounced.

Dagtar, please tell me where you are.... she pleaded silently. The claw around her neck abruptly grew warmer.

"I am not far from you, Guardian," came Dagtar's voice in Carmen's head. *"Keep following your heart, and you will find me."*

Carmen led Blaze and Renalda deeper into the trees, focusing her energies on discerning Dagtar's presence from those of the forest's various living creatures. She and her friends kept walking through the dark and twisting maze of foliage, occasionally stopping when Carmen felt that they should change their direction.

"It's getting stronger," she said, feeling closer to the Dragon every minute as they drew farther into the woods.

But then, without warning, a large creature walked out from the brush not far ahead of them and collapsed onto the forest floor.

"A Lathra!" Renalda shouted, horrified.

She ran to the creature's side with Carmen and Blaze on her heels. The beautiful white animal with russet markings and antlers had a huge gash in its flank, the blood soaking into its fur and dripping into the grass, where it glistened in the moonlight.

Renalda dropped to her knees and quickly began to tend to the Lathra. Muttering a Healing spell, Renalda traced her wand over its injured body. Carmen's mind was racing. This was the same type of creature that had been attacked just days ago.... Why was this happening?

"Carmen!"

Without warning, Dagtar's claw ignited with a searing heat that nearly caused Carmen to rip it off of her neck. Without a second of hesitation, Carmen ran to where she heard Dagtar's voice, with Blaze following right behind her. She heard Renalda yell after them, but she could not stop running. Dagtar was calling out to her so strongly that she knew if she didn't reach him tonight, surely more trouble would follow.

Carmen raced through the forest, her lungs swallowing up great gulps of the cool night air as she galloped to find the Dragon of Merlin. She could feel Dagtar's spirit.... She was getting closer to him. The energy radiating from the claw around her neck was blistering.

"We're almost there!" Carmen yelled, as she dashed around a bush. Then she abruptly tripped over a raised tree root sticking up out of the ground.

"Arghhh!" She stumbled and fell awkwardly to the ground, her ankle twisting beneath her. A sharp pain shot through her as she fell, and all of her weight then came crashing down on her ankle.

"Carmen!"

Blaze was right there when it happened, and came swiftly to his Master's aid. The Sarcan looked down at her, concerned. She was wedged uncomfortably between the tree and a large boulder.

"Do you think that it's broken?" he asked her at once.

Carmen grimaced in agony, breathing heavily both from the run and the fall. Her ankle felt like a thousand pounds of bricks had been dropped on it.

"No...but I definitely can't walk on it right now."

Blaze flew down to the boulder and leaned over Carmen. He closed his eyes and gently touched the tip of his lightning bolt-shaped horn to her injured ankle. Blaze's body began to glow as he cast the Healing spell.

"Healio Ingatia."

The pain radiating from Carmen's throbbing ankle was noticeably dulled within a couple of minutes. Carmen carefully stood back up and walked gingerly away from the tree and the boulder to discover that she was perfectly fine again.

Carmen smiled at her best friend, more than grateful.

"Thanks, Blaze."

Just then, a brilliant burst of light from behind Carmen made her whirl around, half-expecting to see the morning sun. But it was not the light of day; it was the wispy, silvery ghost of Dagtar shimmering in the moonlight.

The dazzling, brightly shining silver-white Dragon drifted toward Carmen and Blaze, his enormous wings and glowing eyes unmistakably familiar even in his ghostly form. Distinguishable warmth emanated from Dagtar as he flew down to them, the light from the stars sparkling off of his resplendent scales.

"My friends, I have been waiting for you," the Dragon said, with a bow of his grand spiked head. Though he was now standing on the ground, none of the leaves beneath Dagtar's feet had crunched when he landed.

"There is much that needs to be said, and not much time. I come to you for help, as my home of Kelmarsia is on the verge of collapse. Triedastron, the ruthless Master of Keltan, has become too powerful, and his realm, the World of Darkness, threatens to conquer the World of Light."

Carmen gaped at him.

"Does this have anything to do with the strong storms that we've been having here in Kelmar?"

Dagtar nodded.

"Yes, the storms are a result of the unending struggles between Kelmarsia and Keltan, as are the attacks on the innocent creatures of Kelmar," he said, looking toward the trees, beyond which Renalda still remained with the injured Lathra. *"The more severe that the fighting in the afterlife becomes, the more intense the storms that are felt down here. Coincidently, the creatures that are being attacked have been targeted specifically by Triedastron to join him in Keltan. He selects gifted sorcerers and creatures to add to his forces against Kelmarsia. Triedastron becomes stronger with every human and creature that dies and is sent to Keltan. Until the spirit worlds are in harmony with each other again, the storms and attacks in Kelmar will not end.... This is why I sent you the portent—to warn you that the Legend of the Worlds Triad was coming true."*

"That was *you?*" Carmen asked, her mind flashing back to the words burned into the grass by the lightning strike during Haidar's wedding reception. "Why is this happening? I thought that once Desorkhan was defeated, everything would go back to normal around here."

Dagtar looked at Carmen with the most serious of expressions.

"Carmen, the reason that things are the way that they are is because *the Dark Master is dead."*

"What?"

"Everything in nature lives in the state it does because all of the forces in and around it are balanced," Dagtar explained. *"From the smallest insect's relationship with the greatest creature, to the connection between good and evil, the key to their coexistence is balance. If that balance is ever lost, chaos ensues. The spirit worlds of Kelmarsia and Keltan are at peace when the balance be-*

tween Light and Dark is perfect. It is when that stability fails, and one world becomes stronger than the other, that there is strife. The balance of good and evil in the afterlife has shifted so that the evil now outweighs the good. Because Desorkhan and his Magicon followers have moved on to Keltan for the rest of eternity, Keltan has become more dominant than Kelmarsia.... The World of Darkness obtained a significant accumulation of new members with the conclusion of the Magicon War, and not just any members, but those who are among the most powerful Dark sorcerers and creatures who have ever lived. They have all joined together with Triedastron to create the single greatest union of Dark beings that has ever come to be, and they are currently preparing to take control of Kelmarsia and its inhabitants."

Carmen felt like she had just been swept up into one of the tornadoes that had ripped through North Kelmar. Desorkhan and his followers were gone from *this* world, and yet even in death they somehow had the ability to overthrow another....

"Unless you can restore the balance between Kelmarsia and Keltan, Kelmar shall be lost forever," Dagtar said, his crystal eyes fixed on Carmen. *"The storms will continue to destroy this world and everyone in it until the Worlds of Light and Darkness are back at peace with each other. Carmen, it is* you *who must restore the harmony amongst the realms of the Worlds Triad."*

"Me?" Carmen asked, her heart beating loudly in her ears. "Why me? What can I do?"

"You are the Guardian of Kelmar," Dagtar reminded her, *"and it is your responsibility to defend this world against anything that threatens it. Your duties as Guardian didn't end when you defeated Desorkhan. That was only the beginning. The promise that you made to protect Kelmar holds true for as long as you live."*

A nervous trembling traveled from Carmen's head down to her feet. She was well aware of the vow that she had taken, and she had every intention of keeping to her word. But she had no idea how she would go about doing what was asked of her this time…. What could she do to stop an entire afterworld of Darkness from devastating the heavens, and Kelmar itself?

"How will I be able to do this?" Carmen asked her fifth Soul of Destiny. "I don't even know where to start…."

Dagtar gazed patiently at her.

"You will need to unlock the Secrets of Kelmar," he told her. *"The Secrets of Kelmar hold the key to reinstating peace in Kelmar's spirit worlds. Discover the Secrets, and you will have learned how to balance Light and Dark."*

"The Secrets?" Carmen asked, her thoughts jumbled. "…. And just who knows of the Secrets?"

Dagtar's eyes twinkled.

"There is but a single individual who knows of them—the creator of the Secrets himself. And in order for you to speak with him, you must travel to Kelmarsia."

"But what happens if I can't correct the imbalance?" Carmen asked, not even beginning to think about how she could possibly travel to the afterlife. "What will become of all of this?"

"If the problem is not resolved before Keltan captures Kelmarsia, the resulting storms in Kelmar will most certainly destroy this world," Dagtar said. *"It is up to you, Carmen. Together with your Souls, you are Kelmar's one and only hope."*

Carmen and Blaze exchanged determined glances. Carmen gripped her wand tightly. She knew that she had a challenging task ahead of her, but it was not one from which she would run. The destiny of Kelmar had once again found itself in her young hands. The difference this time, however, was that she had had more than a full year of experience fighting the forces of evil to preserve what she loved and believed in— and both her magic and her confidence were stronger because of it.

"Okay. We'll do it," Carmen promised Dagtar, sounding resolute. "Just tell us what actions we have to take to achieve the restoration…and we'll prepare ourselves as best as we can."

Dagtar appeared to be very satisfied with her response.

"You will need to travel to Kelmarsia, the World of Light," he said. *"I suggest that you speak with Anubis about this. He has the means to travel to the afterlife, and he will be able to tell you how you and the others can do this as well. After you arrive in Kelmarsia, I will meet you and help you to find the person from whom you will learn more about the Secrets of Kelmar. For the moment, this is all I can tell you, as I must now return to my home in Kelmarsia."*

The light radiating from Dagtar's form gradually began to extinguish…. Then came the sound of tree limbs snapping and bending back as Renalda burst out of the brush behind Carmen and Blaze, not at all anticipating what she was about to see.

"Carmen!" she said breathlessly. "What happened to…?"

She stopped mid-sentence, her mouth gaping open as she saw the spirit of the deceased Dagtar rising through the air. She stepped out of the trees, mesmerized and unable to take her eyes off of the radiant silver Dragon.

Carmen and her friends watched Dagtar float slowly up into the black night sky, which was speckled with millions of glowing white stars.

"Blaze, Carmen, look after each other," the Dragon asked of them as he drifted higher into the darkness. *"I will see you in Kelmarsia. The fates of the magical worlds of both the living and the deceased now rest with you."*

And at those parting words, the sparkling ghost of Dagtar faded from sight. The stars over Haziran Forest seemed to glitter brighter than before as the legendary Dragon returned to the mystical heavens of Kelmar.

CHAPTER THREE
THE OPENER OF THE WAY

To Carmen's immense relief, she, Blaze, and Renalda returned to the Camersleys' home late that evening to find it the same as they had left it. With their friends and family sound asleep upstairs, Carmen and the others were able to sneak back inside without so much as a stir from any of their companions. On the return trip to the house, Renalda had wasted no time in engaging Carmen and Blaze in a hushed but rather frenzied conversation about what she had just witnessed in the forest.

"I was able to heal the Lathra well enough, and I placed a Protective spell on it to prevent any more Dark attacks," she told them quickly, as she swept through the woods holding her lit wand out in front of her, her pale pink nightgown swishing in the breeze. "Then all of a sudden I look up, and the two of you are off running! What happened to you guys?"

"I felt Dagtar's presence stronger than I ever had," Carmen explained, walking swiftly to keep up with Renalda. "I knew that if I didn't run, I would miss the opportunity to talk to him.... I sensed that it was urgent that I speak with him...and I was right."

"You were, indeed," Blaze agreed, flying just over her right shoulder. "For the spirit of one who has passed on to come back and be able to communicate with a living soul, a considerable amount of magic is required on both sides of the connection. It's not a very common occurrence.... The magical beings must have a strong bond, in addition to great power shared between them."

"What exactly did he say?" Renalda asked, as she and her friends hastened through the trees. "When I found you, he had nearly gone. What did he mean when he said that he would see you in Kelmarsia? He expects you to go to the World of Light?"

"Yeah, we need to travel there to help stop the fighting between Kelmarsia and Keltan," Carmen told her. "Their war is what's been causing the storms and the attacks in Kelmar."

Renalda abruptly stopped walking, nearly causing Carmen to run into her. She looked almost as dazed as she had when she saw the late Dragon of Merlin appear in the middle of Haziran Forest.

"The Worlds of Light and Darkness combating each other...." Renalda said slowly, and then a thought seemed to strike her. She cupped her hand over her mouth and practically shouted, "The Magicon! The imbalance is because Desorkhan and his followers have made Keltan stronger than Kelmarsia!"

"Exactly," Carmen said. "Dagtar said that the balance of power between the two spirit worlds needs to be corrected before the storms will end down here, but to figure out how to do that, we need to find the Secrets of Kelmar. One individual knows what they are...and we need to go to Kelmarsia to find that person."

Renalda looked dumbfounded.

"The Secrets of Kelmar?" she wondered, as she and her friends stepped out of the forest and began to cross the lawn behind the house. "I've never heard of anything like that before.... In any case though, at least we're now aware of the reason for all of the problems here. But how will you get to Kelmarsia? It was my understanding that only the spirits of those who have passed on are allowed to journey there."

"This is true," Blaze confirmed. "I'm not entirely sure how we would do this.... It's something that we need to address with Anubis. Dagtar believes that he has the means to get us there."

"Let's hope that he's right," Carmen said wearily, as she, Blaze, and Renalda ambled up the sloping grass hill that was the backyard of the Camersleys' home. "I can't think of anyone else who would know more than him," she concluded, recalling the times when Anubis had allowed her and her friends to see into the past and future—acts that ultimately helped her to find the way to defeat the Dark Master.

"In any event, he'll undoubtedly have a better idea than we do."

Carmen and the others slipped into the house through the back door. Carmen realized how lucky she had been that Renalda had discovered her and Blaze leaving, as only *she* knew the spell that would allow them to pass through the Protections that her father had placed on the house earlier in the day.

They tiptoed up the stairs and went their separate ways to their bedrooms. Renalda extinguished the light from her wand and whispered a muted "Goodnight" to Carmen and Blaze as she creaked open her door and disappeared inside.

Carmen and her Partner soon arrived at their room a few doors down the hall and managed to lie down on their bed without disturbing their friends, all of whom were lying scattered on the floor around the room. Carmen was more than grateful for Glamis's loud snoring on this night, his grunts and the intermittent rumbling sound emitting from deep within his throat covering up any noise produced by the squeaking floorboards and whiny mattress springs.

Carmen and Blaze went to sleep quickly, not wanting to risk waking the others with any hushed discussion of what they had seen. They decided instead to hold such talks until the following morning, when it could be a conversation shared by all of those staying in the Camersleys' home.

The next morning, Carmen was able to help Blaine clean and stack the breakfast dishes using magic, even organizing them by size as Mrs. Camersley had had them stored in the cupboards. As Carmen put away the pink and green floral ceramic plates, Blaze continued to tell the story of the previous night, which Carmen had started at the beginning of the meal. Their tale fascinated everyone from Carmen's other Souls, to Blaine, Alazar, and the Camersleys—all of them listening with rapt attention to what the Dragon of Merlin had spoken about. Commander Haidar had initially worn a stern and disapproving frown when he learned that Carmen and Blaze had attempted to leave the house without telling anyone else where they were going. But he hesitated to reprimand them for their dangerous actions when he heard that they would have to make the voyage to Kelmarsia in order to save Kelmar.

"It all makes sense," the Sarcan Commander remarked. "The portent from the sky, the storms, the attacks.... I don't know why I didn't see the connection before. Regardless, we cannot wait for this disclosure to find its way to Parliament through whispers and circulating rumors. We must inform them of the news before the situation gets any worse."

"Reoc is right. Someone has to go to Pyramid City," Renalda said, though her face held a twinge of apprehension as she gazed around the table. "Which one of us is going to go?"

"It really should be Carmen who goes," Alazar reasoned, as he handed Redge a piece of bacon that he had saved from his breakfast. "But seeing as that she'll need time to figure out how she will make the voyage to Kelmarsia, I think that it would be a good idea to send someone else in her place—someone who has the means to gain access to Parliament and have a closed-door meeting with its Members without issue.... Out of those of us here...I would say that the best person to do that would be Reoc."

Reoc nodded.

"It should be no problem for me to see them," he agreed, in an even tone. "Fortunately, the storms in North Kelmar have calmed down for the moment. I can take an airship from Brandec to Pyramid City this afternoon. Depending on what happens there, I should be back in a couple of days or so."

"Thank you, sir," Carmen said, as she put away the last of the dishes. Then she glanced over at the Jackal sitting beside Glamis. He had been quiet through most of the meal as he listened to her and Blaze speak. He now had his eyes closed, appearing to be deep in thought.

"Anubis, have you thought of any way that we'll be able to travel to Kelmarsia?" Carmen asked him hopefully.

Anubis opened his eyes.

"I have," he replied calmly. *"But I alone do not possess the means of getting us there. That power rests with my father, Inpu. If we are to journey to Kelmarsia, we must go to see him. When he is in Kelmar, he lives in the South, in the Tashana Deserts. Once we are there, I believe that he will be able to assist us."*

"Sounds good to me," Stellar said optimistically. "So how is it done exactly…traveling to the afterlife?"

"I know one truth about it that is absolute," Anubis said. *"No one alive enters the World of Light, or the World of Darkness, for that matter. Only spirits of those who have died can pass through Kelmarsia's gates…. Or to put it another way…it is not possible that we will be going on to Kelmarsia in our living states."*

"Whoa, hold on there a minute," Stellar said, interrupting, a nervous expression on his face. "You're saying that we're going to have to…die in order to save the world?"

"That is correct," Anubis answered, as Stellar's mouth dropped open. Carmen felt her throat dry up.

"There is no way around it," he told Stellar and the others. *"It is simply a matter of* how *we will go about dying, and then being able to return to our living forms once we are through in*

Kelmarsia. That is why we are going to see my father. If there is a way that it can be done, he would be the one who would know it."

"What makes you so sure that he can help us?" Stellar asked, after getting over the shock of being told that he would have to voluntarily depart this life for the cause of rescuing Kelmar. "Has your father done this before?"

"Oh, he has done much more than that," Anubis said, with a confident glint in his golden eyes. *"He is known as the Opener of the Way—the one who guides the spirits of those who have died to the next life. He also protects the spirits, prepares them for the trials to come, and assists in their final judgment that determines to which of the two afterworlds they will be sent."*

Carmen wasn't the only one staring at Anubis in awe following this revelation. She had no idea that his father was such a special being…the very one who leads the spirits of sorcerers and creatures who pass on to the realms of the afterlife…how much power he must possess to hold such an important responsibility.

"Remarkable," Glamis said, his voice alive with wonder. "I've read stories about this amazing creature before, but never did I think I would have the opportunity to meet him…. How superb!"

"This should be quite a trip for you, Carmen," Blaine said, his blue eyes shining. "And you should be able to use Zohar to get to Cardell City in South Kelmar."

"Your grandfather is right," Mr. Camersley said, smiling as he gazed across at Carmen. "I used to do a lot of traveling back and forth from here to the South for business, and so I set up a Complex there that's still open. The Tashana Deserts are just outside the borders of the town. As long as the weather holds up, you should be able to travel there without any problems."

"That would be terrific," Carmen said, feeling grateful for his help.

"Would we be able to go today?" Blaze asked him. "It's urgent that we visit with Inpu at once."

"I don't see why not," Mr. Camersley said warmly. "Whenever you're ready, just give me the word—" he retrieved a small bronze compass that was his Vanishing Point from the pocket of his russet robes, "—and I'll get you there."

Carmen and her friends decided that they would depart for South Kelmar later that evening, after Commander Haidar had left for Pyramid City. As they stood in the shadow of the great stone archway at the end of Brandec with Renalda, Reoc, Blaine, Alazar, and the Camersleys just before sunset, Carmen and her Souls observed the countless airships that landed and took off from beyond a tall, metal fence with a huge gate.

The largest flight terminal in the East, the Brandec Airfield was a long, paved runway that was home to about half of the Kelmarian airships in East Kelmar. Carmen watched dozens of winged wooden airships, in all sizes and shapes, rise up into the silky clouds of the stunning crimson and orange sky. Handfuls more were making their descent to the station.

Hundreds of sorcerers and creatures, many of them with suitcases or other bags, climbed down out of the ships and crossed the terminal, where they then filtered out into the small and narrow streets of Brandec. Mrs. Camersley explained to Carmen that the storms raging throughout several other parts of Kelmar were the main reason for the influx of visitors to the city. Most of them had come here to escape the poor weather and dangerous conditions back home.

Finally, a good-sized wooden airship with sweeping white and red sails and strong, feathered Verdden-like wings landed near the front of one of the two lines of carriers. Scrawled in silver letters across the bow of the ship was the vessel's name: *The Steadfast*. A wooden ladder slid down from the starboard side of the craft to allow its next passengers, bound for Pyramid City, on board.

"That's the one." Reoc pointed it out to the others as he lifted his plain leather suitcase up off of the ground. "Hopefully, by the time I get back, everything will have been sorted out in the capital."

He gave Renalda a quick kiss on the cheek and then looked over at his students.

"Good luck, Carmen, Blaze," he said, with a salute to her and her Sarcan, which they returned. "I shall see you again soon."

He marched ahead to the gate, giving one final wave back to his friends.

"Goodbye, everyone."

The others waved back as Reoc turned and passed through the gate with a yellow ticket in hand, headed toward the magical ship that would take him hundreds of miles north to Kelmar's capital city. Carmen and her friends waited while the aircraft filled up with robed travelers and their creatures. Then they watched the ladder ascend and the door of the vessel shut before the ship glided up into the air, soaring off to its destination.

"He'll be fine," Alazar assured everyone, breaking the silence that had fallen over the group following Reoc's departure. He then pulled up one of the sleeves of his lilac robes to see his watch.

Even though she was standing right beside him, Carmen still could not make sense of Alazar's outlandish timepiece. Only the item's unconventional sorcerer inventor could read the crooked and twisted Roman Numerals that appeared in a random order on the face of the watch, which was a smiling full moon with crystal eyes.

"Ah, the hour is growing late, even though it is still quite early," Alazar remarked, gazing up at the darkening sky. "Are you ready to go, Carmen?"

Blaine rested his hands on his granddaughter's shoulders. Carmen turned and gazed up at him in the ginger light of the sunset, trying to imagine what he must be thinking. The two of them hadn't been far apart since they had reunited in the dawn of Desorkhan's defeat. Carmen knew that her grandfather would worry about her leaving—especially in the midst of the serious issues that Kelmar was experiencing. But she was also sure that he would not fear for her nearly as much as he would if she were going alone. With Blaze, Stellar, Glamis, and Anubis at her side, Carmen had the greatest friends that she could ever ask for. The unfailing faith in her grandfather's misty blue eyes told her that he was quite conscious of this.

"Be careful, Carmen," Blaine said, as he hugged her tightly. "Remember, you have all of our support, and even though we won't always be together...we're forever here for you."

Then he pushed aside her hair and whispered into her ear.

"You're about to embark on a whole new adventure, but I know that after it's over, you'll be an even stronger person than you already are.... And if you ever feel sad or defeated, remember how proud I am of you, and how much I love you."

"Thanks, Pop," Carmen said in a tight voice, fighting back the tears that were burning in the back of her eyes. With her grandfather's profound words, the reality of what she was about to do finally hit her. She didn't know when she would see her grandfather again, or what would happen as she began what would most definitely be a long and challenging journey. She had her face buried briefly in his scarlet and golden robes before looking up into his eyes.

"I love you, too. I promise, I won't forget."

Renalda, Alazar, and the Camersleys each embraced Carmen and wished her good luck. Then Mr. Camersley reached into his pocket and passed Carmen his compass. Carmen clutched it securely in her left hand as she drew the golden Key of Kelmar and summoned her wand.

Carmen knelt down, with the compass lying flat in her palm, so that each of her four Souls of Destiny could touch it. The magical bronze mariner's compass was a small round object with a glass cover, containing a revolving needle on a pin. Once Carmen and her Souls were all touching the outer portion of the compass, Carmen pointed her wand at the center of the glass.

"Kelmar, I ask you to grant us passage through this Zohar Complex I command," she recited. *"To Cardell City!"*

The needle of Mr. Camersley's compass suddenly began to spin wildly. A gusting wind blew up around Carmen and her friends, and the crown of the golden wand shimmered. Carmen was forced to shout her goodbye to the others to be heard over the spinning, enchanted winds. She heard her grandfather yell something back to her, but within moments, the town of Brandec and the sight of Blaine, Alazar, Renalda, and the Camersleys standing together vanished. She and her friends were now traveling through a perpetually dark tunnel at what must have been an extremely accelerated speed.

Carmen remembered experiencing this strange but extraordinary form of travel once before—alone on the first day that she had come to Kelmar, more than a year ago. It had been how she had gotten here to this amazing place that she now called home, though at the time she had no way of knowing what was happening, or all that she would experience when she emerged on the other side of that magical portal. How long ago that seemed now…. She had grown and learned so much since that momentous birthday that it seemed like she had become a whole new person. That day had been the start of her new life, the life to which she had always belonged.

A small dot of light in the eternal darkness ahead of her told Carmen that she and her friends were almost to Cardell City. Within seconds, the light expanded to a view of a shadowy, dusty old town surrounded by the sands of a vast desert.

The darkness around them dissolved, and Carmen and her friends were standing in the center of Cardell City—a small town comprised of umber adobe buildings linked together by narrow, unpaved streets. There were a few sorcerers passing through the town, as well as some Zahartas flying overhead. These black-feathered and skeletal vulture-like scavengers called out to one another as they flew on toward the desert to hunt for food.

Far off beyond the borders of the sleepy town, the faint silhouettes of outlying mountains cut through the pale twilight sky. There was a light breeze rustling across the barren landscape—a gentle wind that provided the inhabitants of this typically scorching dry place with much-needed relief after the heat of the day had passed.

Carmen observed a couple of Hetscopes scurrying about, darting in and out of cracks in the lower bricks of buildings, trying to avoid becoming the prey of the hungry Zahartas circling above. The large-eared desert mice had short olive fur. Their beady brown eyes enabled them to see distinct forms in the dark—a feature that proved to be their greatest defense against their dominant predators.

Then there were the scaly, spotted Lirkoes, which looked like overgrown lizards, crawling about the streets and surrounding deserts, burrowing beneath the sands to escape the high temperatures during the daylight hours.

Carmen slipped Mr. Camersley's compass into her pocket. Then she and her friends began to examine their surroundings, trying to determine the best way to go. The only one of them who was familiar with this area of Kelmar was Anubis, having lived here with his father until he joined Carmen as her fourth Soul of Destiny. And so it was he who would lead the others to Inpu, the Opener of the Way.

"The Tashana Deserts are all around us," Anubis said in a dreamy voice, as the rest of them followed him down the main street of the town. *"This city was built nearly two hundred years ago, in the middle of the great deserts of South Kelmar. It was the first time that this area was colonized by humans...."*

Anubis gazed around at the brick buildings with fascination. He had not been here in quite a while, and he seemed to be captivated by the way it currently looked.

"For the longest time, this part of the South was an isolated place that very few creatures could inhabit," he explained to his friends. *"My parents lived in the desert for decades before sorcerers began to settle here and develop the lands. Now there are a number of cities in these deserts; the nearest one being the town of Wodane, about fifty miles west of where we are."*

"Do you think that your father will be surprised to see you?" Carmen asked the black Jackal. "A lot's happened since you left. I'm sure that he's missed you."

"You are right," he acknowledged. *"Much has happened, but I have no doubt that my father is aware of this, and will not be at all taken aback upon seeing me.... I know that he is quite cognizant of the fact that we are on our way to him."*

"He knows that we're coming?" Stellar inquired. "How could he? We just found out that we were leaving this morning.... You must know of an awfully fast messenger bird in Brandec."

"I did not use the mail system to contact him," Anubis said quietly. *"I reached out to him using my mind. Because we can both use telepathy, I was able to tell him that we were coming to see him even though I was not in his direct presence."*

"That's convenient," Stellar replied. "It must be nice to be able to carry on a conversation with someone hundreds of miles away without even having to open your mouth."

"So how are you feeling, Carmen?" Blaze asked his Master, as he rode atop her shoulder. "We're about to meet the one responsible for guiding Kelmarian spirits into the next life.... He's one of the most powerful creatures in our world."

"I'm kind of nervous *and* excited," Carmen said, after some thought. "I really hope that he'll be able to help us.... If he can't, I don't know what will happen."

"It will be all right," Glamis assured her, nudging the side of her leg with his nose. "I have a feeling that Inpu holds the very answer that we're searching for."

Carmen and her Souls reached the end of the small town a short while later. By this time, the lights of most of the homes had been turned on, and the first stars were plainly observable in the calm, blue-gray desert sky. Anubis directed the others out through the city's western gates and into the Tashana Deserts.

With Anubis leading the way, the group trekked through the sands. The lands of the desert supported little vegetation, and the handful of creatures that lived here were sparse in number and hard to see in the mounting darkness. Carmen and her Souls walked up and down countless sand dunes and across enormous ergs as the night wore on. Luckily for all of them, the evening air in South Kelmar was pleasantly cool, with a recurrent breeze.

As they journeyed deeper into the desert, Carmen silently questioned how Anubis knew where he was going when their surroundings hardly changed. Just by glancing up at the sky every so often, the Jackal seemed to have no trouble in finding his way to his father. As the remaining daylight vanished beneath the horizon and the stars sparkled vibrantly overhead, Carmen cast the *Illumina* spell to light their way into the night.

An hour or so after they had begun the hike through the sands, Carmen began to feel an unfamiliar tingling sensation grow inside of her, a sense that a powerful force was reaching out to her from somewhere distant. The farther she walked, the stronger the feeling became. She could sense a unique existence unlike any that she had ever felt before.... It was mysterious, mystical, and all-knowing. She knew that the others could surely feel it as well. Blaze muttered to Carmen that they were getting close to Inpu.

Anubis took Carmen, Blaze, Stellar, and Glamis up to the peak of a tall sand hill. When they stood at the top of the dune, they gazed around at the endless desert of sands and shadowy, far-away mountains. Of all of the places that she had traveled in Kelmar, Carmen had never been to a more desolate and lonely spot than this. These deserts were almost part of an entirely new world within itself.

She and her friends stood atop the dune for a few minutes, the sounds of the wind shifting sands and the distant howling of Skelyotes hunting in the outskirts of the desert echoing through the night air. Anubis looked up into the sky, where a slender white crescent moon was suspended high in the black velvet darkness over South Kelmar.

With immense concentration, he continued to gaze upward into the heavens, his golden eyes staring into the eternal night. Then, before Carmen could anticipate something unusual happening, she peered down and across the desert to see a massive black form standing a few hundred feet away from them. It had appeared seemingly out of nowhere...but from where she was, Carmen couldn't tell what this gigantic creature could be.

Suddenly, the tremendous shadow began to move rapidly in the direction of her and her friends. Carmen pointed her lit wand down at the giant, mysterious shape. As it drew closer, she realized that this was not *one* creature; it was a large pack of black Jackals running toward them.

The Jackals all had dark eyes, in contrast to those of Anubis. There were easily twenty of them, each of them racing with swift speed across the sands. As they came nearer, Carmen quickly realized that these were no ordinary Jackals. Their forms were blurred and almost ghostly. As they ran, it was almost as though she were watching them on a slow-motion film rather than in real life. The hazy creatures left a vaporous black trail behind them that gradually evaporated into the air, and their paws left no prints in the sand. These Jackals were not living, breathing beings; they were spirits.

Carmen and her Souls were so engrossed with the approaching Jackals that they nearly missed all that was happening in the sky over their heads. Had it not been for the spectacular magical warmth that overcame each and every one of them, they just might have missed one of the most amazing spectacles one could witness in the enchanting world of Kelmar.

With a brilliant burst of light that illuminated the dark sky, brighter and greater than any lightning ever seen, a spiraling whirlwind blew down from the heavens over the desert sand dune. As the sky opened up, the Jackal spirits became golden and raced up and over the hill, past Carmen and her friends as they stared with fascination up into the miraculously twisting and billowing storm, rushing by them in a blaze of divine energy.

And then, down through the center of the gusting storm, there drifted a creature whose body was swathed in a sheath of translucent magical light, a prodigious energy that was rivaled only by the intensity of his powerful gaze.

Carmen couldn't look away from the sight of the fantastic beast soaring down to her and her friends. The black Jackal wore a golden, jewel-encrusted ribbon around his neck that glimmered in the starlight, and he possessed a burning and captivating energy that utterly mesmerized her. As he was lowered slowly and elegantly down to the ground by the heavenly winds, Carmen hardly failed to notice how much he reminded her of his son, with whom she had journeyed many miles and experienced more than a few incredible moments.

Inpu stood before them at the peak of the sandy embankment, his form still basking in the soft but radiant Kelmarsian glow. The amazing storm blowing all around him vanished, as did the shining Jackal spirits. By the light of her wand, Carmen could see Inpu clearly as he looked at her and the others with interest. He was only a tad greater in stature than Anubis, and his golden eyes were quite reminiscent of those of the creature who Carmen had come to know so well. She also noticed that the numerous precious stones inlaid upon the gold ribbon around Inpu's neck included five large jewels in the colors of green, red, yellow, blue, and white—each representing one of the five Kelmarian Elements of Land, Fire, Lightning, Water, and Sky.

Following several tranquil moments of pure silence, Inpu bowed his head to Carmen and her four Souls.

"Good evening, everyone," Inpu said, in a smooth and mystical voice. Then he addressed the Jackal created in his image standing opposite him. *"Anubis, my son."*

"Father," Anubis said, with a respectful bow. *"I have missed you."*

"I have also missed you, very much," Inpu replied, gazing over his son with pride. Then he turned to the others.

"Carmen, Blaze, Stellar, Glamis—" he recognized each of them individually, *"—I'm quite pleased to be meeting you after all this time. I am aware of what you've gone through to get here...and I must tell you how appreciated your sacrifices are in Kelmarsia. Had it not been for your efforts, Kelmar would have*

collapsed upon itself during the Magicon War, and everything that we live for would have been lost."

It took Carmen almost a minute to gather the courage to speak to him.

"Inpu...we need your assistance," she finally said. "Last night, Blaze and I talked with Dagtar, the Dragon of Merlin.... He told us that we needed to go to Kelmarsia to bring an end to the fighting between the Worlds of Light and Darkness, but the problem is that we have no means of getting there...unless you can help us."

Inpu nodded slowly as Carmen spoke.

"Yes, I am well aware of what has transpired in the Worlds of Light and Darkness," he said sadly. *"And as the Opener of the Way, I can certainly be of help to those wishing to travel into the realms of the afterlife. However, I am obligated to inform you that this is not accomplished without the strong will of the travelers.... Journeying to the worlds beyond is no simple task, particularly for souls who wish to return to the world of the living. As you would expect, the trip to the afterlife is intended to be a one-way crossing. Very few individuals make the passage with the intention of coming back to the living world.... Death is one of the inescapable places to which we all must one day venture, and so it is that even those with the objective of leaving, for the most noble of reasons, don't make it back."*

"So you mean...if we go...we might not be able to come back to Kelmar?" Carmen asked, her stomach tight. She was almost too sure of what the most likely answer would be.

"The prospect is great that you and the others will not return," Inpu said, bowing his head for a moment in sadness. *"If this should happen, Kelmar will lose its greatest defenders. But should you decide not to take the risk...Merlin help us get through these difficult times."*

Inpu gazed pensively up into the dark sky before looking across at Carmen again.

61

"The choice is ultimately yours. If you choose to go, I will make it my promise to guide you safely to the World of Light."

Carmen felt a complex mixture of conflicting emotions stirring inside of her.... Before coming to the desert, she had secretly wished that Inpu would have a way for her and her Souls to securely travel to Kelmarsia at the same time that she pushed the idea of an unfeasible return out of her mind. Now that she looked back, Carmen felt rather foolish for having thought that she would be able to cheat death by coming back from a place that no one *ever* came back from. If it were that simple to return to life, her parents would be here with her now....

It was in that last thought that Carmen grasped at something much bigger than herself—something that she had been certain for the longest time to be an unattainable dream....

"Inpu..." she said slowly, trying not to get excited over an unlikely scenario. "If we went to Kelmarsia...would we be able to see my parents?"

Inpu's eyes glistened.

"I was waiting for you to ask me that, Child of Destiny," the Jackal said calmly. *"And it is with great pleasure that I tell you the truth."*

He smiled at her.

"Yes, you will see them, as well as others connected to you and your Souls who have passed on. All of you have family, friends, and even those you might not have expected waiting for you to come to the World of Light.... You will see ancestors from generations long before yours, and you will learn the answers to questions that you had whilst you were living. That is what the spirit world entails. And as the Opener of the Way, it is my responsibility to lead you there. But while I cannot guarantee *your return, know that I will do everything within my power to see that you do make it back to Kelmar once your time in Kelmarsia is over."*

Carmen couldn't believe it.... Upon Inpu's words, the scar left in her heart by the loss of parents that she thought would never heal, was unexpectedly feeling less painful for the first time. Carmen had never felt the way that she did in this moment. To be reunited with her parents, who had been taken from her sixteen years ago.... It was as if someone had just told her that the rest of everything that she had ever wanted besides all that Kelmar had given to her was about to come to pass. The thought of seeing her family, destroyed by the most powerful Dark sorcerer to ever live, after all these years was so overwhelming and unbelievable that it left Carmen feeling like crying and rejoicing right there on the sand dune in the middle of the Tashana Deserts.

She stood there, speechless, allowing the emotions to wash over her like a tidal wave of the greatest joy that one could ever experience. Then the tears started before she could do anything to stop them. Carmen fell to her knees in the sand and cried—cried in the purest happiness of realizing that the very thing she had dreamed about ever since she was a little girl was now so close to coming true.

Blaze flew down onto Carmen's shoulder and hugged her tightly. Carmen couldn't bear to look at him, knowing that the sight of her best friend would only make her sob harder. She felt Glamis's enormous body supportively lean up against her.... And though she was looking watery-eyed down into the crystal sands, she saw Stellar and Anubis standing before her, each of them nuzzling the sides of her face. Dagtar's claw was warm against her skin.

Carmen finally wiped the tears from her face with the backs of her hands and glanced up at her Partner.... Blaze's large blue eyes were sparkling. She would never forget how fortunate she was to have these extraordinary creatures as companions.

Inpu was watching the five friends patiently. He took a couple of steps toward them and lowered his head to speak to Carmen.

"What is it that you would like to do, Guardian?" he asked her gently. *"You must know that this decision is yours alone, and no matter what you choose, you will always have the love and friendship of all those you've touched."*

Carmen swallowed hard.

With quivering lips, she muttered, "I know.... And I know what I have to do."

Carmen stood up gradually, using her wand to steady herself. Then she gazed up into the sky's glittering stars.... She understood why she had been chosen to make the voyage to Kelmarsia—to preserve the goodness and purity that Kelmar held, a sense of duty to save a world and its inhabitants who were so very dear to her heart. Should this obligation mean finding her parents again, then that would be only one more reason to take the risk that she was already willing and ready to accept.

Carmen looked unwaveringly into Inpu's eyes.

"I'm going to go to Kelmarsia," she said slowly. "I know that I might not come back, that I might die...but I also know that I can't live without having done what I was meant to do."

She looked over at Blaze and the rest of her friends before facing Inpu again.

"I'm not afraid of death...." she said with resolve, spreading her arms out around her Souls. "I'm afraid of losing *this*."

Inpu stared at Carmen thoughtfully. Then he inclined his head to her.

"This comes as no surprise to me," he said softly. *"You are a wise and courageous young woman, Carmen Fox. And you will go far in this life for the bravery and righteousness that will forever be a part of your legacy. I have knowledge of all that you have already*

done up until this point, and I trust that you will only become greater as the churning sands of time spur us forward."

A cool wind whispered across the arid Tashana Deserts, carrying with it a sense that everything they had known was about to change.

CHAPTER FOUR

THE LEGEND OF THE WORLDS TRIAD

Remind me again why we have to go all the way back to Brandec?" Stellar asked irritably, as he pawed his way through the coarse sands of the desert. "And why don't we just use Zohar to return to Cardell City? It would be a lot faster than walking."

"Is complaining all that you know how to do?" Blaze replied sharply. "First of all, we're going back to Brandec to find out more about the Legend of the Worlds Triad, just as Inpu asked us to do. The Camersleys have a collection of ancient books in their antique shop. I'm sure they have one that contains that story...and once we find it, it may give us some insight as to what Carmen will have to do to quell the fighting in Kelmarsia and Keltan," he said evenly. "And as to your second harebrained remark, traveling by way of the Zohar Complex requires a considerable amount of magic. Seeing as we'll need to use it to get back to East Kelmar, there's really no logical sense in utilizing it to save us a few steps and risk not having enough strength to get us to Brandec."

When Blaze wasn't looking, Stellar opened and closed his mouth in playful mockery of the Sarcan as he spoke. Carmen hardly listened to her friends' conversations during the hike to Cardell City. Her mind was still racing endlessly with thoughts of seeing her parents in Kelmarsia.

Would they recognize her? Was there a chance that they would know of everything that had happened to her in Kelmar? Would she be able to speak with them? What would they be like? Her restless mind swirled with a boundless assortment of questions to which she desperately wanted answers. She would continue to eagerly ponder the thrilling possibilities as the night progressed.

Carmen used her wand for light to help Anubis lead her and the others back to Cardell City. After a wearing day, they would need to leave for Brandec near to the place where they had arrived in order to preserve energy for the lengthy trip back through Zohar. The farther away they were from the original spot to which they had been brought, the more magic that would be necessary. And so Carmen and her Souls had unanimously chosen to revisit Cardell City to depart for the northeastern town of Brandec.

Inpu had left them to return to Kelmarsia, departing from Kelmar in as grand a fashion as he had come. Carmen, Blaze, Glamis, and Stellar had watched as Anubis bid goodbye to his father, and then saw the lustrous Inpu rise up into the swirling clouds of the magnificent night sky. As he disappeared into the darkness, Inpu promised Carmen and her friends that he would see them again shortly. With his ability to communicate with Anubis worlds away, and their need to travel with him to Kelmarsia, Carmen was sure that they *would* in fact meet again before time had the chance to part them for very long.

Carmen and the others traveled on through the desert night, finally arriving back in the peaceful Cardell City late in the evening. Once they had passed through the city gates, Carmen retrieved Mr. Camersley's magical compass from the pocket of her robes. Then she knelt down to allow all of her Souls to touch it.

Hungry and tired from the long walk across the desert, Carmen closed her eyes and called upon all of the strength she had left to take her and her friends back to Brandec.

"Kelmar, I ask you to grant us passage through this Zohar Complex I command," she recited, as she pointed her wand at the needle of the compass. *"To Brandec!"*

The adobe buildings of the quiet town around them melted away, unbounded blackness engulfing their vision as the carnivorous cries of the flying Zahartas were replaced by absolute silence. Carmen and her friends remained joined together in the darkness by the binds of the compass, as it steered them thousands of miles away to the small town that stood in the shadows of the Cadriach Mountains.

In only seconds, Carmen and the others had arrived back outside the tall metal fence that surrounded the Brandec Airfield. Though the hour was late, the landing strip for the airships remained brightly illuminated by half a dozen lofty air traffic control towers and lights that ran along the asphalt runways home to ships that would be coming and going all throughout the night.

They walked beneath the stone archway at the end of town and trooped back to the Camersleys' house by the light and safety of Carmen's wand, as well as that of the street lamps that lined Brandec's winding, cobblestone streets. Carmen's Souls remained close to her as they marched up the sidewalk of the main street. At the end of the road, they took a few sharp turns and hiked up a hill to the high-roofed Camersley home, which had a couple of steps leading up to the porch.

When she knocked on the front door at the top of the stairs, Carmen hardly expected to be met with the pale and distraught face of Renalda's father, who greeted her when it was cracked open seconds later. When he saw who was there, Mr. Camersley looked to be tremendously relieved.

"Carmen! Are you hurt? Is everyone all right?" he asked in a raspy whisper, as he opened the door wider. He was wearing a loose, faded blue robe over his pajamas.

Momentarily startled by the fear etched upon his face, Carmen assured him that everyone was fine. Mr. Camersley then looked instinctively out into the darkness beyond her, as though concerned that someone had followed them.

"Come inside, quickly," he said, as he hastily ushered Carmen and her friends in off of the porch, shutting and locking the door behind them.

The lights were dimly lit in the den when Carmen and her Souls entered. Renalda was looking tense as she sat in her nightgown on one of the two gray couches. There were noticeable puffy, dark circles under her eyes from lack of sleep. Her Frelark, Enn, was hanging over the back of the sofa, her ears perked up. She seemed to be much more on edge than usual. Mrs. Camersley was leaning halfway out of the kitchen doorway, dressed in her periwinkle robe, her arms folded across her chest. Her face was creased with lines of worry. Carmen was afraid to ask what was happening, fearing the worst.

Mr. Camersley directed her over to the nearest sofa, where she, Blaze, and the others sat down. None of them said anything, but all of them were thinking the same thing; something must have happened to Commander Haidar. Mr. Camersley sat on the couch across from Carmen's group, taking off his glasses and rubbing his eyes despairingly.

"We received some news a couple of hours ago," he said, in a weary but alert voice. "Reoc encountered difficulties in Pyramid City.... Blaine, Thunderbolt, Alazar, and Redge left for the capital shortly after Reoc arrived to assist him. We're still waiting for the latest word, but from Blaine's most recent message, it sounded as though they had gotten the situation under control."

"What kind of difficulties?" Carmen pressed quickly. "What happened?"

Mr. Camersley readjusted his glasses.

"From what we've been told, Reoc was met with resistance from one of the most outspoken members of the assembly upon trying to set up a meeting with Parliament," he said darkly. "Reoc was speaking out in the entrance hall with Danuvius Dorvai, the Head of State, when Maidak Kalvaro emerged from within the chambers, demanding to know why his meeting had been interrupted."

"Maidak Kalvaro...." Carmen said slowly. "Is he related to the boy in my class, Draven? What was he doing there?"

"Maidak is Draven's father. He's also a prominent Parliament Member," Blaze reminded her. "He's been in the legislature for a while now.... Though, as I'm sure you remember, he was a Magicon for several years prior to that."

"Right, how could I forget?" Carmen said, frowning.

"Before Reoc got there, I'm told that Maidak had been pushing for a bill that would grant Senior Parliament Members sovereignty in selecting how many days notice would have to be given to Parliament before Kelmarian subdivisions could request government financial assistance," Mr. Camersley informed her. "As if they didn't already have enough jurisdiction in that department," he added, with a derisive roll of his eyes.

"So, according to Reoc, Kalvaro came storming out of one of the chambers, and Dorvai proceeded to explain to him the urgency of Reoc's call for an emergency session of Parliament to brief the other Members on the recent developments that Dagtar spoke about." Mr. Camersley shook his head. "Maidak scoffed at the idea. He said that the storms and the attacks have been on the decline recently, and so there was no need to rush to such impulsive action."

"Maidak is a pretentious, arrogant dirtbag," Renalda said, her uncombed black hair falling down into her face. "He's so full of himself that he's blind to what's really happening, even though it's taking place right in front of his eyes."

Mrs. Camersley remained in the doorway of the kitchen. "Reoc sent us a Herald Guard just before all of you got back," she said, looking drained. "It said that after Alazar and Blaine got to the hall and confirmed Reoc's story, Maidak finally gave in, and they were able to hold a special session of Parliament to address the issue. Alazar, Blaine, and the others then decided to stay in Pyramid City with Reoc for the night.... They should be returning tomorrow afternoon."

Carmen frowned, her brow wrinkling in confusion.

"A Herald Guard is a magical messenger that allows sorcerers to communicate back and forth with each other," Mr. Camersley clarified, seeing her perplexed look. "It's useful for urgent messages and maintaining secure contact. The Guard spell takes the form of the Master's Partner, and is able to pass on messages to whomever the sorcerer wishes to reach out to."

"So, how did the meeting go?" Carmen asked, concerned. "What is Parliament going to do now that they know the truth?"

Mr. Camersley sighed. "For the moment, it appears that the fate of all of us once again rests on your shoulders, Carmen," he said. "They'll do what they can to protect the citizens of Kelmar from the wrath of the feuding afterworlds, and the effects felt here. Ultimately, the portent calls out to *you*. Nobody can halt the advance of this war but the chosen Guardian of Kelmar."

Carmen nodded stiffly. She was numbly aware of all that she was up against.

"I understand.... I just hope they take the appropriate measures to defend those here from the repercussions Kelmar's been feeling as a result of the fighting in the afterlife," she said. "As long as I can be sure that everyone's safe here...I'll be able to do my best to make things better out in the other worlds."

Renalda got up from her chair and placed her hand on Carmen's shoulder. When she looked down at her, she was on the verge of tears.

"We'll do everything that we can to protect one another," Renalda pledged. "And you must promise us that you'll be careful.... You're far too precious to us to risk losing you."

"I promise I'll be careful," Carmen vowed, meeting her gaze. "And you make sure that you and the others remain safe. I'm not sure what's going to happen from here on out...but I know how important it is to stay together."

"Yes, most definitely," Renalda said, with quiet determination. But Carmen could sense that there was something she wasn't telling her.

"I just fear for your safety," Renalda admitted, noticing Carmen's troubled expression. "I know that *we'll* be fine, but...you're going to be doing something that's never been done before. And...you might not come back from it." Her voice cracked.

"That kind of challenge is nothing new to us," Blaze said, trying to sound reassuring. His inner strength and fortitude were now especially present in his bright blue eyes. "We've been confronted with struggles against the odds before...and I believe that Carmen and the rest of us are prepared to face this one."

"But that's not all that's happening," Mr. Camersley interjected, confirming Carmen's suspicions that there was much more going on here than what she and the others had already been told. "Reoc was able to find out from Parliament that Triedastron, the Master of Keltan, has become so powerful that he now has the ability to send Phantom Warriors into our world." He nodded toward the windows, and then spoke his next words in a noticeably lower voice. "This information isn't being released to the public for obvious reasons. Merlin knows Kelmar would be thrown into pandemonium."

"Phantom Warriors...?" Carmen asked. "What are they?"

"They are member spirits of Keltan who fight under the command of Triedastron," Mr. Camersley explained, still keeping his voice low. "They are deceased sorcerers and creatures who have crossed over into our world to cause destruction and recruit new fighters."

"But why does Triedastron need more fighters?" Carmen pursued, more than perturbed at the thought of vengeful demon spirits running rampant throughout Kelmar. "What exactly are he and his followers planning?"

"Parliament believes that Triedastron is trying to expand his military for the cause of taking over Kelmarsia," Mr. Camersley said. "He needs all the help that he can get to gain control of the World of Light, so he's sent his Phantom Warriors to Kelmar to enlist sorcerers and creatures into joining them in Keltan. The average Phantom Warrior is usually not strong enough to kill living things on his or her own, but they can *all* take living beings to Keltan to be slain by Triedastron and join in his militia."

Carmen sat there, too horrified to speak. The Phantom Warriors were the ones who had attacked the Lathra and all of the other creatures to gather additional forces for Triedastron....

"We've got to put a stop to this," she said, her voice steady. Then she stood up.

"I need to leave now," she declared. "There's no time.... I've got to get to Kelmarsia before things get any worse."

"Carmen, wait." Mr. Camersley stood up as well. "You just got back from Cardell City, you've had nothing to eat for hours, and by now your magic is very weak. Even if Triedastron were standing at the front door, you cannot leave in the condition that you're in now. You must eat and rest before you can go anywhere...so get some sleep, and wait until morning. You can leave after dawn if you wish, but I won't let you go without giving your magic and your body time to restore themselves."

Carmen came to realize that he was right, and even if she were fine physically, she knew that she wasn't going anywhere until morning. Still, she wished more than anything that she could leave tonight.... She shuddered at thinking about evil spirits roaming through the forests of Kelmar, hunting for innocent souls to prey upon....

"I'll make a good, hearty meal up for you now," Mrs. Camersley said tenderly. "We had some leftover Qwethral for dinner that I can warm up."

Mrs. Camersley disappeared into the kitchen to retrieve the food from the refrigerator. Meanwhile, Mr. Camersley crossed the room and walked over to the steps leading upstairs. Once he was standing at the base of the staircase, he whistled up into the darkness of the upper floor.

In a matter of seconds, a pair of creatures appeared at the top of the stairs. They were turquoise in color, and had it not been for their brightly colored fur and long, trim tails that were each tipped with a golden star, at first glance, they would have appeared to resemble Siamese cats. The two slender creatures slinked down the steps side-by-side, their olive-shaped yellow eyes glowing in the muted light of the den. Both cats possessed triangular patches of dark purple on their faces and star-shaped markings throughout their fur. One of the animals carried a tattered brown book in its jaws.

"Starclaws," Mr. Camersley said proudly. "Excellent Partners...among the most loyal of all Kelmarian creatures in my opinion. The one on the right is Coyan, my wife's Partner." The Starclaws reached the bottom step. "And the one to the left with the book is my Partner, Loric."

The Starclaw duo bowed their heads to Carmen and her Souls, who got up to meet them.

"Our Masters wanted you to have this," Coyan said in a smooth voice, motioning to Loric, who approached Carmen with the old book.

Carmen reached out and accepted the book from the Starclaw, and then looked down at the cover.

Forenthal's Book of Fables was the title scrawled across the front of the old hardback. The relic was so ancient that the maroon letters were faded and barely legible. Beneath the title was an illustration of a young, female sorcerer engaged in a magical duel with what looked like some kind of giant, grotesque demon. The horned, brown-red creature had a long barbed tail and gargantuan bulging muscles. The book that Carmen held was only slightly taller than *The Book of Kelmar,* and noticeably thinner.

She flipped through the worn but still intact pages, leafing through more than a dozen short narratives, each one containing its own illustrations below and around the text. Near the end of the book she came to a frayed bookmark placed at the first page of a story that featured an image of a storm cloud releasing a bolt of lightning. Above the drawing sat the title, *The Legend of the Worlds Triad.*

Carmen's eyes widened; this was just the story that she needed to read to get information about restoring the balance in the Kelmarian afterworlds. She was so excited to have it in her hands that it took her a minute to realize something that didn't make sense to her.

"Mr. Camersley?" Carmen asked, looking up from the book. "How did you know that we needed this story? We only just decided to look for it before we came back to Brandec."

Mr. Camersley's lips curled into a small smile.

"You're quite thoughtful and clever for such a young sorceress," he said calmly. "I spoke with your grandfather about the portent shortly after you left, and I got the feeling that you would eventually come searching for this story in hopes of getting yourself some answers. So while you were still in South Kelmar, I dug through the shop's book collection and was fortunate enough to find this for you. It did cost some time, and a few broken trinkets that had been stuffed into the bookshelves, but I think you'll agree that it was well worth it."

"Thank you so much for getting it," Carmen said, grinning. "This is excellent…. I'm going to read it tonight."

"Not until you've had something to eat first," Mrs. Camersley corrected, as she marched in from the kitchen. "Dinner's ready, dear," she said in a gentler voice. "Come, come, you must be famished."

Mr. and Mrs. Camersley went to bed just after Carmen and her Souls got seated, leaving them to eat their filling supper of Qwethral, sweet Bocanores, bread, and Caluyptus juice with Renalda and Enn, who stayed up to sit and talk with them at the kitchen table.

"It just doesn't seem right what Kalvaro was doing," Renalda said, halfway through the meal. "Trying to stop Reoc from requesting an emergency meeting...how ridiculous. He *knows* that Reoc wouldn't have made the trip to Pyramid City unless there was sufficient proof that Triedastron was on the warpath. It just makes me question whether he's up to something.... In all honesty, I still don't trust him," she disclosed. "He was a Magicon for the longest time, and even though he's gone so far as to become a Senior Parliament Member, I've always had my reservations about him...and I'm not the only one."

"Draven always defends him," Carmen recalled, putting down her drink. "I confronted him about it once...and I don't think that he says what he does just because he's his son, but because he genuinely believes in him. That's what I think anyway, but there's no way to know for sure."

"One can never really tell, can they?" Renalda concurred, in a faraway voice. "You might be right though.... I guess I'm just a little biased toward him based on his past." She turned thoughtful. "As long as he doesn't get in the way of what you're trying to do here, Carmen, I have nothing against him."

Enn swallowed the skin of a Bocanore that she had been munching on.

"I don't believe that we should be bothered by him unless he threatens us in some way," Enn said, in a pleasant yet resolute voice. "And for right now, he's not. Besides, we are greater than he is. So for now, let's concentrate on making sure that everyone is rested for the trip. We can't lose sight of all that's at stake.... If we do, Kelmar will pay the ultimate price."

Renalda nodded. "You're right." She gazed out through the glass door of the kitchen into the dark forests that were home to the enduring Keltan attacks. "I just hope we're not too late."

Carmen and her Souls of Destiny retired to their room after dinner. Though the hour was late, and they had promised Renalda that they would be going to sleep straight away, they instead huddled closely together on Carmen's bed, looking over the open *Forenthal's Book of Fables* by the light of Carmen's wand. Unsure of how much time they would have to read *The Legend of the Worlds Triad* the following morning, Carmen and her friends chose to study the story tonight to at least get some kind of idea as to what they would be met with once they crossed over to the next world.

Having had to turn off the lights to convince Renalda that they were sleeping, Carmen and her Souls had to rely on her wand's power to provide them with adequate reading light. They squeezed tightly together to block the light from escaping out into the hall, as well as to see the pages of the very old book. Carmen ran her fingers over the drawing of the lightning strike at the beginning of the story and thought back to the one that had occurred just over a week ago—what had started all of this unrest...the portent from Kelmarsia....

The legend has come to life, and with it, the destructive clash of the Worlds Triad.... Beware, for the balance of power has shifted. Unlock the Secrets, and restore the harmony…or Kelmar will experience the storm.

Carmen snapped herself back into the present to read along with the others. The room would remain still as they read silently to themselves, the only noise being the occasional rustle of paper as Carmen turned each page of the story.

There once lived a man named Merlin Cloud. He was a sorcerer who possessed tremendous wisdom, as well as great power. Merlin used his magic for good, and helped to better the lives of the people and creatures he met throughout his time. With his powers, he would cure the sick, heal the injured, and protect the weak. And though he had more magic at his command than any other sorcerer at the time, Merlin always saw himself as a champion for those who were going through severe personal struggles. In countless ways, Merlin was the strongest defender and the greatest example of magical honor in his lifetime.

During Merlin's early life in the non-magical realm, however, he existed as an outcast. Sorcerers were shunned and secluded from the rest of the human population. A human child born of magic would be sent away to live amongst others like him or herself, never to enjoy the company of those who did not possess the same gifts. As one of the strongest of these individuals, Merlin was forced into isolation at an early age to practice magic out of sight of anyone different from him. So Merlin grew up to become an independent and original thinker, and as he aged, he never lost his burning desire to learn more—whether it was lessons in magic or experiences in life. Merlin Cloud always wanted to become more than what he was at any given moment. It was the very passion he had for gaining knowledge that led him to become the true master of his own destiny.

One fateful day, Merlin decided that he would use his powers to create a new world—one that would embody all of what he stood for and everything that he desired in a place where sorcerers could live in harmony with one another; a place that would come to be called Kelmar. Merlin spent the remaining years of his life building this realm of his own, in which he and other magical beings could freely coexist without fear of oppression or attack. As the Master of Kelmar, Merlin also established two afterworlds in which would live the spirits of Kelmarian creatures yet to be born, as well as sorcerers and creatures who had passed on. Kelmarsia would be the sky world in which would live the unborn and the spirits of beings who had lived virtuous lives in Kelmar. Keltan was made to be the afterworld that was the domicile of immoral and corrupt souls. Together, the three interconnected magical worlds became known as the Worlds Triad.

After his death, Merlin went on to become the Master of Kelmarsia, and appointed a gifted deceased sorcerer named Triedastron as the Master of Keltan. Their roles were equivalent; each one would have complete control over their respective afterworld, and be responsible for keeping their realm and its inhabiting spirits secure. Though Merlin knew Triedastron to be an influential Dark sorcerer, he believed that he could contain his powers enough as the Master of Kelmarsia to allow him to rule over Keltan devoid of trouble.

Thousands of years passed following the creation of the Worlds Triad, and though strife and conflict surfaced, dissipated, and resurfaced now and then, the worlds rebuilt and always overcame, surviving for years of peace with one another. That remarkable resiliency, which came to be a trait of Kelmarians through the generations, held true until the day that the sun didn't rise—the day that the Worlds Triad reached an untimely end.

There came a morning that brought with it an improbable fate—a fate that while unforeseen by most, was one shared by all born holding the gift of magic. Keltan welcomed through its gates that day one of the most powerful Dark sorcerers to have ever lived, and while his death was a hard-fought blessing for many, brought about by the efforts of the tireless Kelmarians young and old, De-

sorkhan arrived in Keltan equipped to begin his rise to the side of Triedastron at the helm of the World of Darkness. As the two great Dark Masters stood in command, Keltan set forth to declare war on Kelmarsia—a war with what they saw as the grandest of all prizes at stake: domination of the World of Light and the consequential destruction of Kelmar.

With the fate of Kelmar, the central realm in the Worlds Triad, hanging in the balance, the kingdoms of Kelmarsia and Keltan battled one another in the most intense magical conflict to ever transpire, the storms of their quarrel felt throughout the farthest reaches of Kelmar. As the fighting grew more severe, Triedastron's army expanded ever larger, eventually becoming so dominant that even with the worlds of Kelmar and Kelmarsia united against it, Keltan would sweep victory over its counterparts in the Worlds Triad.

The war reached its fiery conclusion in the final hours of a darkened day, with Keltan as the winner; Kelmarsia, the fallen; and Kelmar, the ruined. Under the rule of Triedastron, the World of Light became a haven of Darkness, and the overpowered Kelmar fell into nonbeing—destined to join its sister realm in converting to a Dark empire.

The collapse of the Worlds Triad was one that history shall forever look back upon as the end of a tremendous magical era of Light, and the beginning of a Dark and grim age in which magic would be utilized only as a means to satisfy the desires of the most feared and powerful among us.

Whilst that very authoritarian party now controls most every aspect of our lives, like Merlin Cloud, we retain the power to decide upon our own fates, and the side to which we choose to align ourselves. There comes a point in each of our lives when we must determine the path that we will travel down, and it is that choice, not the consequences of that choice, that tells us who we really are.

Carmen looked up when she reached the end of the story. Anubis was sitting across from her, his golden eyes sparkling in the light of her wand. Even after all of them had finished reading, there remained an overwhelming silence. There had been no mention made of a hero anywhere in the story, nobody rising from the ashes to defeat Triedastron and the Dark Master and bring Kelmar back to peace.

"Well, according to this story, we don't stand a chance," Carmen said half-sarcastically, closing the book and setting it on the bedside table. "Or I should say, we *didn't* stand a chance. Because if we follow what the book said, we already lost."

"Yes, I'm a little disappointed myself," Blaze muttered, looking over at the ancient volume. "It didn't even refer to the Secrets of Kelmar that Dagtar talked about.... I'm not even sure that this was really worth coming back for."

"Reading this legend was a waste of our time," Stellar mumbled. "The only thing that it told us was that we and the rest of the magical population are doomed to a cruel and unpleasant fate."

"Now, let's not be so downbeat," Glamis said, in a much more optimistic tone. "At least we are now aware of what Dagtar's portent was speaking of. We also know much better than this myth that Carmen has the strength and ability to correct the imbalance in the Worlds Triad before it reaches the stage of impossibility that the tale focuses on."

"I would have to agree with Glamis," Anubis said quietly. *"I have known of the message of this myth for a long time, and though it is not as positive as we would prefer, I still feel it was important for us to read together as a group. I think of this story as one that we should keep in the backs of our minds as we press onward with our journey.... It just might prove to be more than an interesting read someday."*

There was a murmuring of agreement amongst the group before Carmen flicked her wand through the air and whispered, *"Dor"* to extinguish the light.

"Let's try to get some rest," she said. "Tomorrow will probably be a long day."

The mattress bounced slightly as Glamis and Anubis jumped down to sleep on the floor. But much to Blaze's disappointment, Stellar chose to curl up into a ball near the foot of the bed to snooze.

"He'd better not snore. If he does, he's going to get a silencing spell put on him," Blaze grumbled to his Master, as she pulled the quilt over the two of them.

"Come to think of it...." he said slowly, "that kind of spell would keep him quiet during the *day,* too...."

Carmen smiled, her overactive mind finally relaxing, at least for a moment.

"That's it. I've decided," Blaze said. "I'm definitely going to use it on him one of these days when he's talking too much. I really don't know why I never tried it before now."

Carmen chuckled at the thought of seeing Stellar unable to speak for an entire day. Then she decided that she had better close her eyes for the night.

"I'm going to sleep now," she told Blaze, as she rolled over onto her side, still smiling for no real reason at all. "Goodnight, Blaze."

It seemed as though she had only been asleep for ten minutes or so when Carmen was abruptly awakened by Renalda's shouts.

"Carmen! Carmen! Wake up!"

There was a sharp banging on the bedroom door. Carmen hurriedly sat up in bed and rubbed her eyes just as Renalda burst into the room, still in her nightgown, clutching her wand

and breathing as though she had just run a long marathon. Enn was clinging to her shoulder, her eyes wide with fear. Everyone in the room had been roused by the loud and frantic commotion.

"You need to get out of here," Renalda said in a shaken voice. "They've come for you...the Phantom Warriors."

"What?"

There was instant confusion as Carmen jumped out of bed with Blaze and Stellar, and Glamis and Anubis scrambled to their feet.

"They're here right now?" Carmen asked, her heart pounding loudly in her ears.

Renalda nodded.

"My parents are downstairs trying to hold them off and give you time to escape. You need to follow me out the back door so that they won't see you," she said urgently. "Kelmar has gotten too dangerous for you to stay.... If they find you, they'll take you to Keltan, and Triedastron will kill you. You've got to get to Kelmarsia, where they can't get to you."

With her mind working overtime, Carmen clumsily slipped on her boots and reached under the bed for her backpack, which contained her most valuable possessions. She was instantly grateful that her grandfather had brought it back from the cottage in Mortrock Forest earlier that day.

As she threw on her belt, which was fitted with the Light Sword in its scabbard, Carmen took a final glance around the room for anything that she could have forgotten. She spotted *Forenthal's Book of Fables* lying on the bedside table. Without thinking, she wrenched open her bag and stuffed the tattered old book inside.

"Hurry, Carmen!" Renalda shouted.

Belongings in hand, Carmen and her Souls rushed swiftly out of the room and followed Renalda up the hall to the staircase leading down to the den. They could hear the shouting of incantations and curses and the sounds of struggle coming from the front of the house as Mr. and Mrs. Camersley fought off the Phantom Warriors. There were several male voices that Carmen didn't recognize yelling and attempting to force their way into the home. With no idea where she and her friends were going, Carmen could do nothing but wait for instructions from Renalda as all of them hastened down to the rear of the den and crossed the darkened room in a flash to the back door.

"Go into town and make your way to my parents' shop as quickly as you can," Renalda said, with a sideways glance through the glass of the door into the woods. "Tedra and Adelin's Artifacts and Ancient Relics on the corner of Mooncross and Spire Streets. Hide inside the store and wait for Inpu. I sent him a Herald Guard to find you. In the meantime, stay out of sight. Phantom Warriors can see through invisibility spells," she said, as Carmen opened her mouth to suggest that they use that very approach.

"I'm going to stay here and help my parents," Renalda told her. She tried her best to sound determined, but her voice quivered with fear. "Hopefully we'll be able to drive them away…. But we can't be sure they won't come back. That's why you've got to get on your way to Kelmarsia. The Phantoms can't survive there for extended periods of time."

A crash sounding somewhere near the kitchen jolted the group. An instant later, a tall sorcerer drifted out of the darkness across the way, his glassy scarlet wand pointed at Carmen and the others. He was wearing a gleaming metallic mask and was dressed in a long, black hooded cloak. Two devilish horns rose up from the crown of his head. His form didn't look entirely solid; instead, it was vaporous and ghostly.

"Go!" Renalda shouted at her friends, even though they were right beside her. "I'll take care of him! Go now!"

"Keltania Transtarna!" the Phantom Warrior hissed.

A searing hot jet of red light fired from his sharpened staff across the dark room at Renalda, who stood with her wand held defensively out in front of her.

"Illumina Hesquel!" she shouted back.

Resisting the strong urge to stay and fight, Carmen threw open the back door and rushed out into the night, her Souls of Destiny at her side.

CHAPTER FIVE

THE SEER'S AMULET

Without looking back, Carmen and her friends raced down the grassy hill and around the side of the house. The light of the late evening stars guided their way through the cool night as they galloped across the lawn; the echoes of spells and shouts carried through the thin air and cut across the moss-covered mountain like a blade through stone.

Carmen sprinted through the grass alongside the flying Blaze and the rest of her Souls running on foot. Her throat was dry, and she was perspiring, but she couldn't afford to slow down. She and the others had to find Inpu and get to Kelmarsia or risk losing all that they had fought for over the past year.

Suddenly, a shrill scream rang out of the darkness. Carmen's heart skipped a beat, and she skidded to a halt, forced to catch her balance as her shoes slipped on the dew-sodden grass. Her friends all stopped dead in their tracks as well, exchanging frozen looks of fear. Judging from the high pitch of the painful cry, all of them knew that either Renalda or her mother had been attacked.

Carmen and her Souls turned at once and stared back up at the darkened house. Stationed on the crest of the backyard hilltop were half a dozen Phantom Warriors, the moonlight illuminating the black cloaks of the masked men. Standing at attention at the side of each of the sorcerers was a fiendish black Keinen. Every one of them had sharp, blood red eyes and saber teeth. The armor on their backs was a deep scarlet color.

The fighters remained silent on the top of the hill before a seventh ghostly Master and Keinen pair joined them, floating across the grass from the direction of the house.

Carmen felt her stomach muscles tighten as a swell of horror engulfed her. The sorcerer who had joined the group was carrying the limp body of Mrs. Camersley in his arms, a long, bleeding sword wound clearly visible on her forearm, which dangled freely below her robe. The unconscious outline of her Starclaw Partner could be seen trapped in the jaws of the Keinen that marched beside his Master.

A man's shout came from inside the house. An instant later, Blaine Fox burst out of the back door and charged toward the horde of Phantom Warriors with his wand outstretched. His Partner, Thunderbolt, flew out right behind him.

"Instundo!" Blaine bellowed, sending a potent jet of orange light racing across the lawn at the bloodthirsty demons.

One of the human Phantoms nearer to Blaine reacted immediately by leaving the others and sending a curse flying back in his foe's direction. But despite his age, Blaine was quick to respond with a defensive shield. The curse bounded off of the magical shield that grew out from his wand and melted away into nothing.

Another Phantom then emerged through the back door of the house. Even from a distance, Carmen could see his ashen, withered, skeletal fingers curled around his wand. Before she could do anything to stop it, the sorcerer fired a *Body Snare* curse at Blaine's back.

"POP!" Carmen cried.

Blaine could not turn around fast enough. The *Body Snare* curse hit him and knocked him to the ground. Blaine struggled to free himself as enchanted ropes conjured out of thin air and wrapped themselves around his body.

After having been frozen mid-retreat by the sight of the bedlam ensuing before her eyes, Carmen could stand by no longer.

"Follow me!" Carmen told her Souls, as she raced up the hill.

The cold air rushing past her face, Carmen unsheathed the Light Sword, which had a gold hilt encrusted with red stones. She pointed its blade in the direction of the ghostly sorcerers and creatures. When she was within striking distance of her enemies, she released her spell.

"Sword of Light!" she shouted.

Almost instantly, Carmen could feel an intense energy radiate from the golden hilt of the sword up through the blade. Slashing her saber through the air, she set free an explosion of blinding white light that fired toward the Phantoms and sent the swarm of sorcerers and creatures scattering.

Having accomplished just what she wanted to do, Carmen hurried over to tend to her grandfather. She promptly used the *Eiruk* spell to destroy the ropes that had tied him up, and then helped Blaine to his feet.

"Are you okay?" Carmen asked him, as he hastily brushed the dirt from his robes. "What are you doing here?"

"Yes, yes," he replied, meeting her gaze. "Reoc, Alazar, and Redge are inside helping Renalda and Enn…. We had a feeling that there was trouble, and it looks like we got back here just in time. Thanks, Carmen."

"I wouldn't be so quick to say that," hissed a bitter voice off to their right.

The Phantom Warriors had regrouped at the top of the hill. A single armed sorcerer had stepped out of the line and begun to make his way over to Carmen and her friends. Mrs. Camersley and Coyan were still out cold, held prisoner by the other Phantoms.

Carmen maintained a steady grip on her sword as the masked man approached her and her grandfather. She was quite conscious of the fact that at any moment, disaster could strike. Her Souls positioned themselves protectively around her. Blaine had his wand drawn, ready to defend himself. The

Phantom sorcerer stopped walking when he stood no more than five feet away from them.

"Pleasant night for a recruitment, I'd say," the man said, as though he were speaking of a stroll through a park on a summer evening. Then he glanced back at his Kelmarian captives. "Normally, acquiring two like these would be adequate for one evening, but we came here not for such weaklings. We came for the ones who would put up more of a fight."

"Release them," Blaine ordered, gesturing with his wand at Mrs. Camersley and her Starclaw.

Though the Phantom had a mask on, Carmen was certain that his eyes were glued on her and Blaze. She could hear Renalda and the others fighting inside the house with the rest of the Phantoms. She didn't know how many were here now...but she knew that they were hungry for blood—just as Mr. Camersley had warned....

"It sounds like they think they have a choice, Xoncarg," one of the other sorcerers called to the first, as a handful of others laughed.

Xoncarg shook his head.

"You have no say in this matter," he told Blaine. "Now...I will be so kind as to give you a choice regarding how you will travel to Keltan...dead or nearly dead. Should you decide upon the latter, you can be assured of just as painful a slaying when you get there. We would never allow you to be deprived of that experience."

Carmen took a bold step toward Xoncarg so that their faces were mere centimeters apart. She would not allow his threats to scare her away.

In a voice that was just loud enough for everyone present to hear, she whispered, "We're not going anywhere...not without a fight."

Within a split second, there was an explosion of movement on both sides. Xoncarg raised his wand. Carmen flung up her sword and blocked the curse that the sorcerer fired at her. The Phantom Warriors who stood behind Xoncarg broke out of their formation and began shooting their own curses across the lawn at Carmen and the others, and Xoncarg's black Keinen broke free from his pack and ran toward his opponents.

Opening his mouth, the Keinen sent a vicious *Poisonous Knives* curse in Blaze's direction. As Carmen dueled with Xoncarg, her other Souls, her grandfather, and Thunderbolt rushed into battle with the rest of the Phantom Warriors. Blaine purposely went after the duo of Phantoms who held Mrs. Camersley and Coyan before challenging any of the others.

Carmen and Xoncarg dueled for some time, each of them firing powerful attacks at each other but neither one able to cause any severe harm to the other. Their Partners, meanwhile, exchanged magical blows of their own. At one point, Blaze was able to slash Xoncarg's Keinen across his jaw with his claws. As the Keinen tried to get away, the Sarcan used his *Lightning Strike* spell to weaken him further—hitting him with a sharp bolt of lightning that exploded out of his horn.

In the midst of their struggle, Xoncarg ordered a *Nazakus* curse at Carmen. The violet eruption of energy that burst from his wand caught her by surprise, and the curse hit her squarely in the chest.

Carmen screamed as the curse ripped through her body. It felt like someone was burning her all over with a searing hot iron. The sensation lasted only seconds, but in that time, its excruciating pain made her feel nearly overcome. Her knees gave way from beneath her, and she buckled to the ground. The Light Sword slipped from her hand and fell to the grass at her side.

"So much for the great Guardian of Kelmar!" Xoncarg declared, as Carmen lay in agony across from him.

Xoncarg peered around him to make sure that he had gotten enough of his comrades' attention, even though many of them were still fighting. Blaine shouted something to Carmen, but she couldn't hear him over the sounds of the struggle around her. Blaze tried to fly down to his Master, but the drove of Keinen that now obstructed his path prevented him from getting to her.

When Xoncarg had turned his head to see his fellow fighters' progress against the Kelmarians, Carmen reached for her sword.

Xoncarg strode over to where she lay and stood over her, gazing down with hatred.

"There's no Dragon or magical shield for you to hide behind now, Fox. You're finished here."

Ignoring the unbearable heaviness in her limbs, and perhaps her better judgment, Carmen pointed her sword up at Xoncarg's mask. Now inches from death, she just had to see the face of the man who was working so unrelentingly to have her destroyed.

"Revealio!"

With that spell, Xoncarg's silver mask was blasted off of his face and fell to the ground with a heavy thud. Carmen gasped as she found herself staring up into a pair of black eyes on the face of a young man with straggly brown hair. Their eyes locked, and for some reason, Carmen found herself frozen. Even more than his dark eyes, she was shaken by how young he appeared.... Xoncarg couldn't be more than two years older than she was.... How could *he* be a Phantom Warrior?

"I appear to have rendered you speechless," Xoncarg remarked, as if he could read her thoughts, his black eyes blazing into hers. "As much as I've enjoyed it, I think that it's time that we end this game for the night."

He pointed his wand down at her face.

"You never gave me an answer as to how you'd like to go to Keltan, so I've chosen for you," he said callously. "You'll be much easier to deal with once you're dead."

"You can't kill me," Carmen was quick to reply, being sure to keep a tight grip on her sword. "You're not strong enough.... So I would give up the act if I were you."

A vein pulsed in Xoncarg's pale temple.

"Not strong enough?" he repeated, in a malicious whisper, edging the crown of his black, twisted wand even closer to her face. He smiled as he stared down at her.

"I've just decided that I won't be saving the final goodbye for Triedastron, Carmen Fox," he said, as he raised his wand. "Oh no, that pleasure will rest with me alone. *Lei Ruza!*"

"*Tolth Lumicatia!*" came Blaine's voice from the other side of the lawn.

Before the white-blue beam of Xoncarg's curse could materialize at the crown of his wand, the faster of the two spells rocketed down from the sky over Xoncarg and Carmen—the lightning striking the lead Phantom Warrior in a bright burst of light. Carmen hurried to stand up as Xoncarg hollered and collapsed to his side, his face twitching and his body convulsing.

Carmen made a brave dash across the grass to Blaze, firing spells at unsuspecting Phantoms as she ran, all the while trying to make sense of the mayhem that was playing out all around her. Alazar, Redge, Reoc, Renalda, Enn, Loric, and Mr. Camersley had all joined in the battle that had spilled out onto the lawn behind the house. Each of them was dueling their own assemblage of Dark opponents.

Blaine had succeeded in sending four pairs of the Phantoms back to Keltan with the blade of his wand, including those who had been holding Mrs. Camersley and Coyan. He was now engaged in a duel with one of the few remaining Dark sorcerers. Coyan and her Master lay beneath a magical domed shield that Mr. Camersley had conjured out on the opposite end of the lawn. Three Phantom Keinen remained in battle with Anubis, Stellar, Glamis, and Blaze.

As she galloped toward them, Carmen slashed her sword through the air in a fiery sweep to frighten off the cluster of enemy Keinen with the *Karsthra Murtog* spell. The Keinen vanished into the darkness when they dispersed back to Keltan, as did each of the defeated sorcerers.

Blaze turned toward his Master. "How are you doing?" he asked, as the last of the creatures disappeared.

"Just fine," Carmen answered, stopping to catch her breath.

Upon hearing his granddaughter's voice, Blaine launched an *Arickio* attack spell on his opponent, smashing the sorcerer in the stomach and weakening him enough to make him retreat. Blaine then glanced back over his shoulder at Carmen and shouted, "GET GOING! WE CAN HANDLE THE REST OF THEM!"

"But we—"

"JUST GO, CARMEN!" he ordered, as another Phantom sorcerer ran toward him. "DON'T LOOK BACK! KEEP GOING!"

There was just a handful of Phantoms who remained now, and so Carmen decided to take his advice and leave for town with her Souls before more of them came. Though she wanted to help him, or at least thank him for assisting her, it did seem that Blaine was putting up a strong fight, along with the others. She thought better of going against his wishes.

"Let's go!"

With her mind made up, Carmen slipped the Light Sword back into its scabbard, and she and her Souls turned on their heels and sprinted back across the sloping lawn. Spells and shouts continued to fly back and forth through the damp night air as they raced down the grassy knoll.

Just as they reached the bottom of the hill, Carmen heard Xoncarg's screech of rage far behind her. From Haidar's shouts of attack, she knew that he was the one now dueling with Xon-carg.

"YOU CAN'T RUN FROM DEATH, GUARDIAN!" Xoncarg roared down at Carmen. "MARK MY WORDS, THE FIRES OF KELTAN THAT SEEK YOU SHALL BRING YOU TO YOUR END! WE *WILL* KILL YOU!"

Haidar ordered a *Thunder Ray* spell, and the ensuing crash of thunder drowned out anything else that Xoncarg might have said. Making the conscious effort not to look back, Carmen kept running with her friends, the perspiration on her brow dripping down into her eyes as she rushed onward. She knew that they could not slow down. They had to get to the Camersleys' shop, and quickly, at all costs.

As Carmen, Blaze, Stellar, Glamis, and Anubis entered the small town of Brandec, they noted that despite the battle that was taking place back at the house, the streets of the city appeared to be calm. Carmen lit her wand to scan the street signs in search of Mooncross or Spire Street, and within fifteen minutes, she and her Souls came upon Tedra and Adelin's Artifacts and Ancient Relics on the corner of the two streets, just before the center of town.

Carmen and her friends cautiously approached the small shop's darkened storefront window and peeked through the glass. Carmen used her wand to illuminate the interior of the shop.

The store was filled with numerous magical antiques, including everything from battle items like wands, shields, and swords to more everyday items, such as dinnerware, furniture, and old knick-knacks.

Even with just the light of her wand, Carmen and her friends could see that almost everything in the store had a sufficient layer of dust on it. The only items that didn't appear to be dusty were the knives and other tools that were behind glass below the counter off to the right. A small room at the back of the central store space was dark, just as the rest of the shop was.

"It doesn't look like anyone's here," Stellar observed, turning to Anubis. "Can you call out to your father?"

"I attempted to reach out to him when we got into town, and again just now," Anubis replied softly. *"There was no response, but there could be a number of reasons for this.... He may already be inside."*

"Let's go in," Blaze decided. "If he's not there, we'll wait for him."

Carmen nodded in agreement. She tapped her wand to the door and murmured, *"Lockstra."*

The bronze doorknob turned and clicked, and the five of them went inside, Carmen shutting the door quietly behind them.

Carmen cast *Illumina* again so that her wand would continue to emit light as she and the others moved through the shop, each of them understandably concerned that someone or something unwelcome and unpleasant might be waiting for them, lurking in the shadows and dark corners of the store. The building smelled musty and appeared deserted, but the group knew better than to let down their collective guard.

Carmen gazed around at the old wooden cabinets that were standing throughout the space. They held a variety of objects—collections of early encyclopedias on relevant subjects like spells, potions, and magical creatures among them. Holding her wand against the glass, Carmen read the years on a number of the books and found volumes in that small selection alone that dated back as far as six hundred years ago. She still marveled at collections such as this, and for a brief time, she was brought back to the years when she had worked in her grandfather's old bookshop in the non-magical realm. She was appreciative now of the many hours that she had spent alone

95

there reading about distant places, the art of swordsmanship, and fascinating people who changed history. But even all those years could never have prepared her for what she found in coming here to Kelmar, and the countless adventures that she had experienced since. How little she knew back then....

"Carmen...Carmen," Blaze's voice in her ear and his tug on her robes snapped her back to the present.

"Wha—oh, sorry," she muttered. "I was just thinking about something from the past...."

Carmen moved away from the book cabinets as she and her Souls crept over to the doorway at the rear of the shop. With caution, they crossed the threshold into the back room. Carmen held her wand high to light up the entirety of the area.

The store's back room was a long space, but it was fairly cramped due to the fifteen or so ancient stone sarcophagi that were lined up around the walls. Some were standing vertically, while others were lying down on the floor. Other than a pile of dusty cardboard boxes in a corner, these were the only objects in the room. Glancing upward, Carmen noticed a wrought iron chandelier hanging from the ceiling. She utilized a Fire spell to light the candles and better illuminate the space.

The light from the candles cast a soft glow on the coffins and highlighted their more distinguishing qualities. The light revealed each of the sarcophagi to be painted in gold and decorated with tiny inscriptions written in Keltongue. The upper portion of each casket was carved to resemble a particular Kelmarian creature.

"These are *exceptional*," Glamis said, as he stood before one of the standing caskets. "These date back at least 2,000 years, and yet they're nearly perfectly preserved. They must have had Protective spells placed on them when they were created to prevent the ravage of time.... Unbelievable."

"Why would there be a need for coffins if all Kelmarians move on to Kelmarsia or Keltan when they die?" Carmen asked.

"Oh, these tombs were purely ceremonial," Glamis explained, the enthusiasm in his voice characteristic of his great appreciation for history. "No one would be buried in these certainly, as Kelmarians need their bodies to pass into the afterlife. Sarcophagi were created in ancient times as a way of honoring deceased leaders, but the practice eventually lost its appeal. Most of them were destroyed in the Magicon War over the years…. To find ones like these in such pristine condition is quite significant."

"Hey, guys!" Stellar called from across the room. "Take a look at this."

Carmen and the others crossed the room over to where Stellar stood at the foot of another standing sarcophagus. The top of the coffin he was looking at was sculpted and painted in the form of a black Jackal's head.

"This one looks just like you," Stellar said to Anubis.

Carmen and her friends leaned in close and stared at the intricacies of the elaborate coffin. Carmen couldn't read the message that was engraved into the stone, but the Jackal did indeed look very much like Anubis….

Silence fell over the room as Carmen and her Souls admired the beautiful old sarcophagus. Now that they looked more closely at it, they could see what a superlative piece it truly was.

Stellar turned his head to try to read the message written in the Kelmarian language of Keltongue, which was inscribed around the side of the coffin. Suddenly, there was a great BANG!

Stellar and the rest of them immediately jumped back at the sound, which seemed to have come from behind the ancient coffin, the Keinen yelling in surprise as he nearly fell backwards on top of Glamis. Carmen held back a scream. She pointed her wand steadily at the sarcophagus as she and her

Souls slowly backed away from it.... The coffin shook, and the lid slowly slid itself to the side.

The sound of the stone lid scraping against the box was the sole sound that could be heard as Carmen and the others steadied themselves and prepared for a Phantom ambush. It seemed to take an eternity for the lid to completely slide away from the rest of the box. Her heart beating rapidly and her hands trembling, Carmen raised her wand.

A hunched over old man dressed in a blue, hooded robe stepped out of the coffin. His eyes hidden beneath his hood, he reached for something in an inner pocket of his robe. Carmen was just about to use her *Stun* spell on him when a familiar voice from behind the man said, *"Good evening, Carmen."*

Carmen peered around the man to see Anubis's father emerging from a hidden passageway at the back of the coffin's interior.

"Inpu?" she asked blankly. "What's going on? Who is he?" she asked of the thin, elderly man.

"This is Eli Elezar," the Jackal said politely, as the man removed a small round object from inside his robe. *"He is a dear friend of mine."*

Upon seeing Carmen and her friends gaping at the sarcophagus, Inpu added, *"This casket is a Gateway of Truth from my home in the Tashana Deserts."*

A Gateway of Truth was a secret magic tunnel that sorcerers and creatures could use to travel between different places, arriving at their destination much quicker than they could by air or by foot. Eli lowered his hood to reveal a head of thinning white hair. He had a short nose, and his face was wrinkled into a small smile. He appeared rather harmless.

"Please forgive me for frightening you," he said quietly, his glassy blue eyes glistening.

"Not at all," Stellar replied, the hair on his back still standing up from the scare.

"Inpu asked me to come with him to see you off to Kel-marsia," Eli explained. "I have an object in my possession Inpu thought might be of better use to you than it is to me."

"Eli is a Seer," Inpu informed Carmen and her friends. *"He can glimpse into the future, and his visions are often even clearer than those that can be observed by Jackals and other Seeing creatures."*

"Earlier today, I had a vision of you, Guardian," he said, respectfully bowing his head to her. "You were in Kel-tan...dueling with a Dark sorcerer, and struggling to defend yourself in the horrendous Darkness of that realm."

"You see, Carmen, the atmospheres of the afterlife are far different from that of Kelmar," Inpu said, to clarify. *"As of right now, we intend to travel only to Kelmarsia, but if you are to ever challenge Triedastron, eventually, we will need to journey to Kel-tan. Keltan is a vile, oppressive, and ghastly place.... And while its foul effects are felt by all magical beings present there, they are especially straining on humans—particularly so on those unaccustomed to the feeling."*

"But I've dueled a lot of Dark sorcerers and creatures in the past," Carmen argued. "I've become stronger in fending off Dark influences over time."

"Surviving the horrors of Keltan has nothing to do with strength," Inpu said sharply. *"Likewise, being unable to fight it says naught of a weakness. The purpose of the realm is to make all those in it suffer for the offenses of the inhabitants, and so its powers are not limited only to the deceased.... Keltan was never intended to be a place for good sorcerers and creatures like you and your Souls. But we have reached a point where* not *venturing into the World of Darkness could mean the end of all of us."*

"Yes," Carmen acknowledged. She was now feeling especially unwise for having believed that she would have no trouble in fighting back against the Dark forces that ruled over Keltan.

Eli shuffled forward.

"If I may," he said, extending his empty hand to Carmen. "Take my hand, and you will temporarily be afforded my foresight.... You'll be able to see the prospect of the future should you not be protected with something stronger than just your own magic when you cross over into Keltan."

Carmen glanced over Eli's shoulder at Inpu to get his approval. Once she got it, she reached out and placed her left hand in Eli's right. There was a gush of white light...and then, Carmen's vision abruptly went black.

Gradually, an image of a shadowy world of dark caverns and fiery trenches came into Carmen's sight. The outlines of two dueling figures appeared soon after, firing spells back and forth at each other, as though she were watching some kind of bizarre movie in her head. Both sorcerers were clearly casting the spells verbally, but Carmen couldn't hear either of their voices.... All of a sudden, she recognized one of the people in the duel as herself, but the features of the other were cloaked too deeply in shadow for her to identify who they belonged to.

The sorcerers battled until Carmen's figure unexpectedly dropped her wand and flung her hands to her neck, as though she were choking. She crumpled to the ground, her body shivering violently. The real Carmen's eyes widened, and her hands trembled as the enemy sorcerer raised his wand. All at once, she was feeling lightheaded.

"MOVE!" she shouted at her fallen self, trying hard to stay conscious as she watched. "GET UP, NOW!"

A torrent of scarlet light hit the shivering Carmen, and she became motionless. The real Carmen then felt an intense cold come over her, a bitter chill that sliced through her skin and numbed her to the bone. Eli's vision became hazy...slowly rotating and distorting into nothingness again.

"NO!" Carmen heard herself shout.

A second sea of white light washed over Carmen's sight, and she was back in the present.

Carmen blinked repeatedly to try to see around her. She was lying on her back on the floor of the antique shop, looking up into the faces of her anxious Souls, Inpu, Eli, and the tops of the sarcophagi that stood behind them.

"Carmen, are you all right?" Blaze asked, lightly touching her cheek with his paw. "You were screaming…and you tried to run toward something. We laid you down so that you wouldn't hurt yourself."

Carmen sat up slowly and shook her head, trying to clear the image of her own death from her mind. Her forehead was moist with perspiration, and her hands were still shaking, but she was fully awake and aware. She picked up her wand, which she had dropped at some point during the vision.

"I…just saw…Keltan," she told Blaze and the others, gazing up at them. "It wasn't good," she muttered, unable to think of any words to accurately describe the horror of what she had seen.

"I would have to agree with that," Eli said sadly. "The sensations that you felt in seeing the vision were mere vibrations of what the real experience will be like if you do not have proper protection against the Dark elements of Keltan. We cannot allow what you just saw to happen."

Carmen gingerly got up off of the ground and brushed the dust from her robes. Eli leaned in toward her and opened his left hand to reveal a gleaming silver and gold amulet on a long chain. The charm was circular, with a golden triangle inside of it and a shining, round black opal at the center. Streaks of cobalt, emerald, yellow, and violet sparkled inside the precious stone.

"The Seer's Amulet," Eli said fervently, stroking his thumb over the opal. "It provides the wearer with powerful protection against Dark elements and influences…. There are only three of these known to exist in all of Kelmar. I had the good fortune of coming across this one five years ago in my travels. Thank Merlin I did, because now I can pass it on to you."

Carmen stared down at the glittering amulet in Eli's hand. Its opal was the most perfect stone that she had ever laid eyes on. The rock was polished so smoothly that she could see her own weary face looking back at her as she gazed into it. The gold and silver metals around the stone sparkled in the light of the candles. It was both weird and wonderful for Carmen to think that this small amulet alone could help shield her from the controlling Darkness of Keltan....

"How do you know that this amulet is potent enough for where we'll be going?" she inquired further, staring at Eli. "And what about my friends? They need to be protected as well."

"Upon request, the amulet's magic can extend to others connected to the one who wears it," Eli assured her. "This amulet is the most effective of its kind in defending against outside Dark forces. Inpu will tell you that I've been around for a while...and this find was one of the greatest I ever made."

"Besides being a Seer, Eli is also a well-known magical treasure hunter," Inpu told Carmen and her friends. *"He's uncovered some of the most valuable relics from ancient Kelmarian history. He works as a magical historian and archeologist."*

"So I would wear the amulet the entire time that I'm in Keltan?" Carmen asked the Seer. "Are there any negative effects from wearing it?"

"That's right," Eli answered. "And no, there is nothing wrong with wearing it for all of the time you are in the afterlife.... In fact, I would advise you to. The instant that you remove it, the magical Protections that guarded you from the Darkness will expire, and you will not be safe again until you put it back on."

Eli seemed genuinely trustworthy, but this didn't stop Carmen from double-checking with Anubis's father before she accepted his offer of protection. If her time in Kelmar had taught her anything, it was to be very careful about who she believed.

"Are you certain about this, Inpu?" Carmen asked the Jackal, in a more casual voice, so as not to offend Eli.

Inpu nodded his head.

"I have known Eli for years, and he is a sincere and caring friend. He is worthy of your trust."

Carmen looked to her Souls of Destiny. One by one, they all acknowledged their agreement. Finally content with where she stood, Carmen accepted the gift of the Seer's Amulet.

Eli gently placed the enchanted charm in Carmen's hand. The metal was cool against her skin, and the black opal glimmered mysteriously. The room was eerily hushed when Carmen closed her fingers around the mystical object—the shifting colors of the opal reflecting the uncertainty that was in the eyes of all of those present as they gazed down at the amulet in the candlelight.

CHAPTER SIX

THE VOYAGE TO THE WORLD
OF LIGHT

How will we travel to Kelmarsia?" Carmen asked Anubis's father.

"Eli will put you and your Souls into an enchanted sleep," Inpu answered, *"and I will perform the ritual of lifting your spirits from your bodies and escorting you up to the World of Light."*

Evidently, he had planned it all out before coming to the shop.

"Whilst you are in Kelmarsia, your physical forms will sleep here, perfectly safe until your spirits reunite with your bodies and you awaken."

Inpu walked over to one of the standing sarcophagi.

"The reason that I told Renalda we would leave from here is because of the genius of the location's features," he explained, as he gazed around the room. *"The sarcophagi are where your bodies will remain hidden when your spirits cross over into the afterlife. Renalda will pass on the word to everyone who needs to know where you'll be. Likewise, there will be virtually no chance for anyone looking to do harm to you to locate where you are."*

"Don't you think that we'll be needing our bodies to get anything done in Kelmarsia?" Stellar asked.

"Only deceased spirits need their bodily forms to exist in Kelmarsia," Inpu clarified. *"Just as the unborn spirits of creatures yet to be paired with their Masters live in Kelmarsia while their physical beings exist in Kelmar, your spirits can also survive in Kelmarsia without your bodies. Unless you plan on spending an eternity in the World of Light, you will not want your body there*

with you. If your spirit inhabits your body in the afterlife, there is no going back. Your spirit will need to be free to return to your body in Kelmar once your work in the spirit realms is complete."

Carmen had a hard time coming to terms with what she was about to do. She was essentially going to temporarily surrender to death in an attempt to rescue herself and the rest of Kelmar from a permanent demise. As difficult and perplexing as this entire task was, the aspect of it that scared Carmen the most was that this venture was one of incredibly vast unknowns. For as much as she and the others had done in Kelmar, none of them had ever taken part in anything like this…and it was quite probable that they would not make it back alive. Even Anubis, the son of the great Inpu, had not visited the afterworlds in his lifetime.

Though she ardently longed to see her parents, Carmen was beginning to feel distressed—the magnitude of the moment seeming to truly hit her for the first time. As she stood in the silence of the Camersleys' shop with her friends, surrounded by the sarcophagi in which their outwardly lifeless bodies would lie until their spirits returned to Kelmar, Carmen felt as though she were about to walk straight through a supernatural door into an inescapable, uncharted world from which there was no turning back.

Perhaps it was Eli's vision of the prospective future, or purely the idea of embarking on such a dangerous voyage, that made Carmen second-guess what she was getting herself into. Regardless of the reason, Carmen felt an uneasy gnawing at the pit of her stomach that probably wasn't going away anytime soon. It also didn't help that she had to make such a tiring effort to keep her emotions in check during all of this.

From the taste of blood on her tongue, Carmen knew that she was biting her lip fairly hard. She was tense all over…. Her muscles were tight, and she could feel her pulse pounding loudly in her ears. She wanted to scream in anticipation, and cry for both the happiness and the dread that she was feeling now. A part of her even felt like running away from this adventure all together.

"Carmen, calm down," Blaze said gently.

Carmen glanced up at the Sarcan perched on her shoulder. He was gazing back at her through his large blue eyes as he spoke. Through his connection to her, he could clearly sense her terrible apprehension and felt the need to calm his best friend's nerves.

"Listen, I know that you're scared; I am, too," he admitted. "With everything new that we face in life, there is to be some trepidation. But remember that you are the Guardian of Kelmar. You have bravely faced and conquered challenges that few would ever dare to meet. You never turn down such tests, and your courage inspires others—that's the Carmen Fox I know. This expedition is merely one more trial that has come before you that will allow you to shine. You're never alone in this either.... I'm not going anywhere without you, and all of us have faith in you."

"Thank you, Blaze," Carmen said, forcing a smile. She was very grateful for his reassuring words, but at the moment, she was largely unable to express it. "I know that everything will be fine...."

"We can look at this as one more journey," he said, with a small smile, sounding very much like her grandfather. "We'll make it through, and before it's all over, we'll realize that it will have been worth everything that we put into it. You'll see."

"Are you ready, Carmen?" Inpu asked, gazing over at her with curiosity. *"We should be getting off.... The protection of the night will shortly part with the morning sun, and we must be gone."*

"I'm ready," Carmen replied, feeling considerably less nervous after her brief but reassuring conversation with Blaze. "Let's go."

In keeping with Inpu's carefully thought out plan, Carmen and her Souls came to situate themselves into four separate sarcophagi—Carmen and Blaze in one of the ornamental standing coffins, and Glamis, Stellar, and Anubis each lying down in their own horizontal stone casket. Carmen had the Seer's Amulet on its chain around her neck, along with the Key and Dagtar's claw. She would leave her backpack behind in the sarcophagi when she traveled to the afterlife.

Inpu and Eli stood at the center of the group of coffins, prepared to help Carmen and the others complete the departure.

Eli would be casting the *Death's Eternal Sleep* spell to place Carmen and her Souls into the enchanted sleep. *("I do not need to be put to sleep, as I am free to travel between the three worlds as the Opener of the Way,"* Inpu had reminded them.) Once Carmen and her friends fell asleep, Inpu stood ready to perform *the Opener's Sacred Duty* of lifting their spirits from their bodies and guiding them to Kelmarsia. Once they had gone, Eli would slide the lids over the respective caskets to conceal the bodies from view, and then use the Gateway of Truth to get back home before daybreak to avoid attracting attention out in the streets of Brandec.

Carmen leaned against the back of the sarcophagus's interior, with Blaze sitting atop her shoulder, looking out at the rest of her friends in the other coffins. The next time she would see the room from this perspective, she would be waking up from a conscious out-of-body experience.

Eli muttered a sequence of inaudible words and proceeded to make his way around the room—using his jade, opal encrusted wand to draw an outline of golden magical light around the exterior of each of the sarcophagi that contained one of Carmen's Souls.

After he had traced the line around every casket, he instructed all of the creatures to close their eyes. He performed the action on Carmen and Blaze's box last, and then returned to his place at the center of the room with Inpu.

Utilizing a spell requiring deep concentration, Eli lifted his staff into the air with one hand and began to speak the incantation for *Death's Eternal Sleep.*

"Death be not the final separation in the tale of one's life, but the start of life renewed and made whole," he recited, in a clear voice. *"And while each of us is inevitably bound to experience loss by death's hand, in living we are without limits in exploring the frontiers of death in sleep.... The waters in the realms of the departed are not sailed by those of flowing blood and breath-filled lungs, but by those who invite death to their own being, and those who give way to death. With this hand, I grant you death's impermanent form, but keep you of sound mind and body to one day return to your worldly existence. I hereby bestow my magic on thee to cast you into Death's Eternal Sleep!"*

In the stillness of the space, for a few tranquil minutes, all that Carmen could hear was Blaze's breathing close beside her. Then she felt a wave of somnolence fall over her like a velvet sheet, and she drifted into oblivion.

An indeterminable amount of time had passed from the instant that Carmen drifted off, to the moment when she first felt herself floating.... She could hear Inpu's voice somewhere near, but she could not comprehend his words.... She desperately wanted to open her eyes, yet her sight remained black. Her mind was foggy, her thoughts and memories jumbled and indistinct....

Carmen had no idea where she was or how she had gotten there, but she was aware enough to know that something had happened—but just what it was remained uncertain. She lingered in that state of semi-deliriousness for what seemed to her like hours, but was actually only seconds, before a hazy white light tore through the blackness obscuring her vision.

Carmen blinked. She could see across to the other side of the Camersleys' back room just as she could before, only now, the tops of the sarcophagi were at her eyelevel.... She then gazed downward to observe herself still lying asleep with Blaze in the standing gold casket. The rest of her Souls were also resting peacefully several feet below. Eli was pointing his wand at the nearest coffin lid and directing it to slide over Glamis's box, and he went on to do the same with the rest of the caskets.

Carmen received a jolt when she held her own vaporous hands out in front of her face and found that they were more or less transparent. As she floated close to the ceiling, she examined her ghostly body from head to toe—even touching her arm, and staring in stunned fascination as her hand passed right through her wispy blue robes, feeling nothing. Being apart from her body was an amazingly freeing experience. It was as though she could travel anywhere and do anything that she wanted without fear of physical harm. So this was what being a spirit was like....

"Well, this is different," Stellar remarked, his voice sounding as though he were in an echo chamber.

"Indeed! This is unbelievable!" Glamis said.

"I always wondered what it felt like to exist as a spirit," Anubis mused. *"This is much like I imagined it would be. We are essentially ghosts, but otherwise look like ourselves."*

Following a thorough inspection of her own condition, Carmen looked over to her left, where the spirits of Stellar, Anubis, and Glamis floated about five feet away. Like her, they really did look just as they always had, aside from the fact that they were silvery, translucent ghosts of their worldly forms. Blaze's spirit was hovering just above his Master's shoulder, in the Sarcan's usual manner, but Carmen had been so preoccupied with her own state of being that she hadn't noticed him there before now.

"Some transformation, huh, Car?" Blaze said, his voice also sounding very far away.

Suddenly, a strong wind picked up—gusting from the front of the shop to the back. The heavy chandelier overhead swung violently back and forth in the powerful breeze. Understandably anxious, the five friends glanced around them. Carmen suppressed a cry of panic as a spiraling, otherworldly tornado swallowed them up in its winds.

"Do not fear, for you are safe," came Inpu's tranquil, distant voice from above.

Carmen and her friends fixed their eyes up on the elegant black Jackal wearing the gold, jeweled ribbon collar. He was floating just beneath the wrought iron chandelier hanging from the ceiling. His brilliant golden eyes were shining as he gazed down at them, and his body was bathed in sparkling, divine light.

"I have freed your spirits from the binds of your physical forms, which rest beneath us," he told them, his magical voice unmistakably clear and penetrating through the winds. *"It is now time for us to move on to Kelmarsia. Relax your senses...and allow me to escort you to the World of Light."*

Inpu turned his attention aloft, and Carmen and her Souls felt themselves float weightlessly up to him.

Quite gracefully, Inpu soared up and out through the ceiling of the room. Carmen cringed as she felt herself rise up alongside her friends after him, certain that they were going to crash head-on into the stone roof. But just as Inpu had done, they glided right through the ceiling and out into the late summer night air—the view of the antique shop disappearing from sight beneath them as they climbed higher into the starry sky.

Carmen gazed in wonder down at the twinkling lights of the homes and stores far below. On this cloudless, cool evening, the view from high above the city was breathtaking. Streetlamps lined the narrow, winding streets, casting vibrant light upward. The high rooftops of the buildings and the tall mountains that surrounded the city were reduced to crinkles and ridges leaping across the landscape.

The spirits of Carmen and the others floated higher and higher, farther and farther away from the town of Brandec, at a speed unmatched by any living creature. Though Carmen knew from being outdoors just minutes ago, in her body, that the night air was cool and crisp, she could feel neither the cold, nor the bite of the wind as a spirit. Without her physical form, exterior forces had no effect on her.

Carmen and her friends followed Inpu up into the outer reaches of the atmosphere, higher than Carmen had ever flown when she was alive. She was almost sure that any moment, she could reach out and touch one of the millions of glowing stars that danced around them.

Carmen watched as the buildings, mountains, forests, and rivers shrank to minuscule speckles of light and faint silhouettes. Before she knew it, the world beneath her had vanished on the other side of the clouds as she and her companions soared farther on into the night. For the better part of the trip, all that could be seen out ahead of them was the blackness of the heavens.

But then, just when Carmen thought that they could go no farther, a thin golden line of light cut through the dark, spanning out before them like a shimmering beacon in the cold, ceaseless nighttime sky.

When it first appeared, Carmen thought the line to be an illusion to her tired eyes, but as she and the others drew nearer to it, the line grew brighter and more real, and a soft but distinct sound found its way to her ears. It sounded like…music….

"We are about to pass through the magical barrier that divides Kelmar from the World of Light," Inpu reported, the hauntingly beautiful music growing louder from somewhere beyond. *"The moment has nearly arrived. Brace yourselves, for you are about to enter a place upon which few have ever laid eyes."*

As he said this, Inpu and his company approached the golden light, which was glorious and welcoming, just as the melodious music reached a peak. Inpu jumped forward through the light first, his body disappearing from sight as he crossed over to the other side.

Carmen and her Souls were then magically lifted to the light. As though a pair of great hands reached down from Kelmarsia and lifted them higher, Carmen and Blaze, followed by Stellar, Glamis, and Anubis, rose up and through the light— the enchanted music ringing in their ears.

Upon passing through the border into Kelmarsia, Carmen and her friends found themselves underwater and gazing up at the bottom of a long wooden ferryboat, decorated with carvings and ornate circular designs. The mystical, harmonious music continued to play, though it sounded mellow and echoed beneath the blue-green water. It was now especially difficult to tell if this music had been produced with instruments, or if people were singing, but even underwater…the tune was the most peaceful and captivating sound Carmen had ever heard.

Sorcerers and creatures of all ages and kinds swam past— each of them staring up at the ship above them. These were the spirits of those who had just died and passed over from Kelmar….

"This is the River of the Departed Spirits," Inpu informed Carmen and her Souls. *"All Kelmarian spirits must pass through here before they are formally accepted into this realm."*

Because they did not breathe as the living did, no bubbles came from any of the spirits' noses as they floated beneath the sparkling, cerulean water. Similarly, the waters of the river passed through the vaporous spirits' forms without their notice.

Carmen watched as the ghostly beings drifted upward, and right through the bottom of the stationary ship, vanishing from sight one at a time.

She couldn't grasp how deep or how wide this river was, but as she floated up to the ship behind Inpu, Carmen could only dream of what they would find on board the grand ferryboat.... She braced herself for what was certain to be another dramatic sight.

As Carmen and her friends passed through the ship's hull, a fantastic azure sky shone through the glassy water far above their heads. They emerged from the enchanted water and stood aboard the deck, together with thirty or so other spirits near the front of the ship. The wondrous chorus of heavenly music that they had been hearing all along greeted them now with warm clarity. Her eyes wide and bright, Carmen felt her jaw drop at the sight of the world that lay before her.

The river in which the ferryboat of spirits sat sliced through a lush green valley. The sun sparkled off the stone walls that encircled the gorge beyond the surrounding forests. Glistening spirits of hundreds of creatures, representing each and every Kelmarian species, stood watching the newly arrived spirits from high, mossy ledges of rock along the two walls of the ravine. Their mouths moved in time with the music that was continuously playing here, and although the words were incomprehensible, it was apparent that they were the ones singing this moving, divine melody....

Not far ahead, the mouth of the enormous river opened up to a sea. There, a towering white castle stood atop a tree-covered mountain. The peak sat at the center of a sweeping, blossoming island whose forests and beaches glittered with unsurpassed brilliance.

Standing at the bow of the ferryboat, Inpu tapped his right front foot three times to the wooden deck, and then turned to meet his travelers' awestruck faces as the ship sailed ahead.

"My friends…welcome to Kelmarsia."

CHAPTER SEVEN
THE PRINCESS OF KELMARSIA

Carmen continued to gape alongside everyone else on board, wishing that her eyes were ten times larger to take everything in as the ship drifted slowly through the water. In this single staggering moment, she was instantly brought back to the way she had felt when she first arrived in Kelmar. She remembered seeing the untouched beauty of the forests, the meadows, the rivers, the mountains, and the valleys. How splendid, mystical, and absolutely magical everything had seemed.... And now, witnessing the indescribable realm of Kelmarsia made Kelmar seem almost ordinary in comparison. In many ways, this place looked very much *like* Kelmar, except that every surface, object, and entity glistened in a golden light of heavenly goodness and purity.

"My.... It is *beautiful,*" Glamis said, marveling at his surroundings.

"I'll say," Stellar agreed, an enthralled smile on his face. He looked as at peace as he had ever been in his life.

"Kelmarsia has always been thought of as a perfect world," Anubis said, gazing up into the blue sky. *"It looks just as I always imagined...incredible beyond words."*

In addition to the sheer beauty of the realm, there was also a distinct feeling in the air here that was not of Kelmar, or anywhere else in the existence of the living...a sense of endless, undeniable warmth that embraced all who existed here. And the farther Inpu's ferryboat of spirits sailed upriver toward the castle, the more Carmen noticed the warmth, which filled her, and made her feel safe and amazingly happy.... She recalled experiencing a similar sensation when she and her friends met

Inpu in the Tashana Deserts, yet by some means it seemed one hundred times more powerful here....

The welcoming chorus of the Kelmarsian creatures continued to sing as the ferryboat paddled ahead, the soft beating of the enchanted oars in the water muted by their gracious song. The other spirits on board were whispering happily with one another, several of them pointing out sights that they found particularly wondrous to the spirits close to them. Carmen noticed that some had tears in their eyes.

Inpu had to do nothing physically to steer the gleaming boat that carried the Kelmarian spirits onward toward the island. But as he stood ahead of the others with his golden eyes fixed on the majestic pearl white castle, it was evident to Carmen that this was where they were headed. Inpu was quite accustomed to this ritual of ferrying the departed spirits across the central river of Kelmarsia as a part of his obligations as the Opener of the Way. Carmen couldn't even venture a guess as to how many times he had made this trip in his lifetime, but she was sure that for as phenomenal as it was for her and the others, the voyage was nothing but routine to him.

It took only ten amazement-filled minutes for the ferryboat to reach the shore of the forested island. As the spirits neared the beach, it was plain to see that the mountain upon which the castle sat covered the greater part of the island. Straight ahead of them stood an arched gold tunnel that was carved into the base of the peak. Inpu's ferryboat glided unhurriedly into the tunnel, the mountain's shadow falling over the boat as it sailed ahead.

Thousands of glowing crystals were inlaid on the brown stone walls of the long tunnel, illuminating the etched walls of the mountain passageway, which were carved with images of flying Dragons and swirling clouds. The melodic music from beyond, which echoed off of the tunnel's walls, was the only sound in the unnaturally quiet channel. The ferryboat leisurely wound its way up the mountain, through the river's waters, which magically flowed upward to the summit of the peak.

Within less than half an hour, the passengers aboard the boat rounded the final corner of the mountain before they would reach the top. They could see a serene white light coming from the end of the tunnel ahead of them.... Where were they going?

Carmen and the others strained to see beyond Inpu as they floated closer to the exit. In the distance, they could make out the faint outline of a lofty white castle wall, and the imposing towers that stood beyond it....

They continued to drift forward, and soon the ferryboat and those aboard basked in the radiant sun's light as they passed through a second golden archway and sailed into a canal that cut through the castle's square, grassy courtyard.

The ship docked at the base of a tall stone monument of three figures, which Carmen didn't immediately recognize. The first statue was that of a beautiful young woman with long hair, cradling a baby Dragon in her arms. She was standing between the statues of two men who appeared slightly older than she was, and looked to be related to her. They both had their arms draped around her shoulders, and all three of the humans were smiling affectionately down at the small Dragon. The sculpture was easily ten feet tall, and looked especially lovely as it sparkled in the sunlight.

Inpu used his mind to order the door on the starboard side of the ferryboat to open. He then directed the spirits to disembark onto the grass. Carmen and her Souls were the last ones off the boat, with Inpu stepping out right behind them.

While she could not feel the lawn beneath her as a spirit, Carmen quickly became aware by the way that the grass glistened and reflected the sun's rays that it was special. For a short time, she and the rest of the spirits stood on the lawn with Inpu, gazing around with excited anticipation at the undisturbed courtyard.

This open space was at the very center of the castle atop the mountain, and it was lined with white stone columns that stood around the entire perimeter of the fortress's inner walls. As they observed their surroundings, the spirits waited as patiently as they could for something to happen…and in the next moment, it did.

First came the sound of beating wings from somewhere overhead. Carmen was startled to feel the Dragon claw around her neck grow warm, letting her know that her fifth Soul of Destiny was calling out to her. It was the first change in temperature that she had felt as a spirit since experiencing the enchanted warmth upon entering Kelmarsia.

"Look at *that!*" she heard one of the other spirits exclaim.

Carmen gazed upward and witnessed a magnificent green Dragon soaring gracefully down through the blue sky. He was carrying a female rider who was dressed in flowing, white-silver robes.

The spirits on the ground watched as the two fliers made an aerial circle around the perimeter of the courtyard. Then the young woman braced her legs against the Dragon's sides and hugged his neck as she guided him downward. They descended with poise onto the grass, about twenty feet away from where Inpu's spirits were situated.

The Dragon lowered his body to the ground, allowing the fair-skinned woman to dismount. The emerald creature possessed sparkling blue eyes, a spiked head, a great brown sail, and leathery wings.

"Thank you, Dagtar," his rider said, in a serene and kindly voice, gently touching her palm to his face as she climbed down from his back.

118

"You are very welcome," the Dragon replied, with a bow of his head.

The woman rider was slender and had very smooth and fair skin. She also possessed smoky gray-blue eyes, and long blonde hair that was so light it looked almost white in the sun, though she appeared to be in her early twenties. Her youthful face was caring and peaceful, her features soft and easy to look at. She wore a gold tiara that was inlaid with rubies, and she carried a sleek silver wand with her as she walked toward Inpu and the others. It didn't take Carmen very much time to realize that she was the woman portrayed in the stone sculpture beside the river. But for as stunningly beautiful and seemingly delicate as this girl was, Carmen got the sense that she was someone of immense significance...someone with a great deal of power.

As the young woman approached the newly arrived spirits, Carmen observed that her silver staff was crowned with the Great Seal of Kelmar. This woman, who was clearly of royalty, had a distinct air of righteousness and sovereignty about her that felt ever more real as she drew nearer…. It was so unique that it indefinitely maintained the attention of everyone present. Who was she?

The sorceress smiled as she laid eyes on this fresh group of spirits, her mild yet penetrating gaze capturing all of their awareness. It was as though she could see right through them to each of their standards of decency—evaluating their worthiness to be here. Carmen thought that she saw the woman's eyes flicker approvingly when she spotted her present amongst the crowd of sorcerers and creatures.

"Welcome to the World of Light." The sorceress greeted the spirits with a cordial bow as she stood beside Inpu. "My name is Kelmari. I serve as Primary Judge of Morality here in Kelmarsia. You are standing before me now because Inpu and I have deemed you pure of heart and virtuous in your deeds. And so…in recognition of the honorable life that you led in Kelmar, you are henceforth free to live with us in this paradise that is Kelmarsia for the rest of eternity."

Kelmari spread her arms out wide, and both she and Inpu looked skyward. They closed their eyes as a soft glow emitted from their bodies, and a tremendously bright white light from high above washed over the spirits.

Carmen and her Souls watched as those standing around them shed their ghostly exteriors...and changed into more solid beings. Although Carmen herself wasn't experiencing what her fellow spirits were, she could tell by their heavenly, smiling faces that this magical transition was extremely enjoyable.

When the process was finally complete, every sorcerer and creature from the ship but Carmen and her Souls had made the transformation into their final physical forms. Kelmari opened her eyes and lowered her arms, causing the spiritual light above them to fade and disappear.

"We have returned your bodily forms to you so that you may experience all that this world has to offer and take pleasure in living out your time in the afterlife to the fullest," Kelmari told the spirits. "Now, before we part ways...I wish to reintroduce you to the loved ones of your past."

And with that, Kelmari turned and beckoned toward a set of heavy wooden doors in the castle behind her. The doors slowly opened to reveal a blinding white light.... From beyond that light came the outline of a large group of humans and creatures.

These spirits, who were also solid and distinct, walked out to meet the newly transformed souls, all of them grinning the most loving and peaceful smiles that Carmen had ever seen. Her heart was beating loudly in her chest.... Her parents must be here, too.

One by one, the relatives and ancestors of the other spirits reunited with their family members—embracing and crying tears of joy. Carmen craned her neck in search of her parents in the giant crowd that formed as deceased Partners found their way back to their Masters, young children leapt into the arms of their parents, and older couples found themselves back together at last. It was a genuinely beautiful sight for all who witnessed it....

As the minutes passed, not a single spirit came to meet Carmen. It was painfully clear to her that neither *her* ancestors nor those of her Souls were among those here.... Was this some kind of cruel trick?

Kelmari smiled and remained patiently at Inpu's side as the old and new spirits reconnected and reflected on memories, conversing loudly and energetically with one another. Eventually, Kelmari raised her right hand, and before long, she had magically regained everyone's attention.

"I pray that you find Kelmarsia to be as magnificent as your greatest dreams and more," she said quietly, tapping the base of her staff to the grass. "And until we meet again...I bid you all the fondest farewell."

One by one, the Kelmarsian sorcerers and creatures floated slowly upward into the azure sky—until they were high in the air above the tallest towers of the castle.

Kelmari watched them with care and blew a regal kiss up to them. Then the new members of Kelmarsia, joined with their families and friends, flew off in their own directions, each of them no doubt traveling to the part of the realm that they desired to call home.

Kelmari laid her hand on Inpu's back and absentmindedly stroked his fur. She then turned and motioned for Dagtar to come to her, brushing her other hand against his scaly neck when he arrived. And with Carmen, Blaze, Stellar, Glamis, and Anubis as the only visiting spirits remaining in the courtyard, Kelmari's eyes fell intentionally on them for the first time.

"We've been waiting for you," she said thoughtfully, her gray-blue eyes glittering. "I wish for you to join Inpu and me in the castle. There are many things that need to be done…and so much that you have to learn. Because of these circumstances, we have gathered together those in Kelmarsia who we wish for you to meet separately from the others, and they are waiting for you inside the Castle of Merlin."

"Who's there?" Carmen asked, before she could stop herself. "Are my parents…?"

"You will see soon enough," Kelmari said, in a calm but firm voice. "Now, please follow me. This is a very busy time."

Dagtar bid a passing greeting to Carmen and her friends before taking off into the sky once again. With his sturdy wings carrying him swiftly up and away from the castle, his imposing yet nimble form gradually faded from sight as he soared into the distant heavens.

Knowing better than to ask any more questions of Kelmari, Carmen and her Souls silently followed her and Inpu across the lawn and through the set of open doors at the rear of the castle.

Stepping inside the Castle of Merlin was like walking into a great king's palace. Gold-framed oil paintings of past Kelmarian leaders and dignitaries hung on the white walls, all of which glinted unnaturally bright. The furniture on this floor, and surely all of the others, was of the finest quality.

A series of white marble archways led to a sweeping staircase, which took them nearly ten minutes to climb, even at the quickened pace in which they walked. The group reached the landing, and a single gold door lay at the end of the long, windowed hallway before them. Kelmari directed her visitors down the corridor, her wand in hand and her white-silver robes swishing as she walked.

As they approached the end of the hall, Carmen's sense that something incredible waited for them beyond that door grew ever stronger. When Kelmari raised the golden Dragon doorknocker, her mouth dried up, and her pulse was beating so loudly in her ears she was sure that they would explode.

Kelmari knocked twice, and stood back. No more than fifteen seconds passed…and then the heavy door gradually swung open. Kelmari and Inpu walked inside first, followed by Carmen and her four Souls.

At the center of the ornate, golden room was a large, red and gold throne. A trio of stained glass windows on either side of the room brought in a beautiful rainbow of light that cascaded over the marble floor and caused the throne to sparkle. The high ceiling was painted with images of angelic Kelmarian creatures and clouds.

Carmen and her friends gazed around. There was nobody here in the room but them. Carmen was just about to ask Inpu what was going on when a hidden gold door at the back of the space creaked open.

A handsome man, who possessed tousled auburn hair and Carmen's green eyes, emerged. Walking out behind him was a tall woman with soft blue eyes and Carmen's shoulder length golden-brown hair. Both were dressed in royal blue and silver robes. Their beaming eyes met those of their daughter, and had Carmen been in possession of her body at the time, her heart just might have stopped.

For several seconds, Carmen remained rooted to the spot, paralyzed and struggling to speak as she held their gaze…. Could this *possibly* be real? She felt a strong burning sensation behind her eyes as her parents crossed the room to her.

Without a word, the three of them embraced one another tight…and it was like an explosion of love and happiness that transcended time and memory.

As if someone had released a switch, Carmen lost control and burst into tears, as the meeting that she had dreamed of ever since she was a small child came to be just like that. Her parents were crying, too, and for a number of minutes, they remained sheltered in one another's arms, their tears falling without notice or care—the world forgotten for everything gained in that one extraordinary moment.

When she had finally gathered the composure to meet her parents' eyes, Carmen smiled wider than she ever had, and in their glowing faces she saw herself reflected, and everything that she wanted to be. It was as though she and her parents had always been together, separated only by the physical boundaries of their own worlds.

Her father placed his hand to her cheek, and though she was only a spirit, somehow she could feel his comforting touch, just as she had his warm embrace.

"Carmen...." he said softly, his kind face just inches from hers. "You can't imagine how happy we are to see you.... You've grown up so beautifully."

"I *can* imagine," Carmen replied, past a lump in her throat. "Because I've been searching for *you* all this time...."

"My baby girl," Isabella said, through her misty eyes, running her hand lovingly through her daughter's wispy hair. She looked so very much like her daughter that Carmen herself marveled at seeing her face in person for the first time. "We are so proud of you.... I can't believe that you're finally here with us."

"I see that Blaze is here, too," William said warmly of the Sarcan, who had been watching all of this unfold with a smile as wide as Carmen's. William and Isabella moved toward him and hugged their daughter's Partner with loving affection.

"Thank you for protecting our Carmen," Isabella said, her eyes filled with tears of gratitude as she embraced him.

William then approached Stellar, Anubis, and Glamis, crouching down to gaze into their eyes.

"And thank you all as well," he said, kindly stroking each of their heads. *The Blaze of Fire and four more...bring together all five of the Guardian's Souls of Destiny,"* he recited, in a voice just above a whisper. "And we're not the only ones who have been waiting for you," he said, as he rose.

He walked back to Carmen and placed his hands on her shoulders, showing her and the others the open door through which he and his wife had come.

"Just look there...."

Their eyes wide, Carmen and her friends stared with astonishment.... A grand parade of people and creatures were marching in through the door.

First came a pair of flying golden Sarcans—the Foxs' Partners, Flare and Airian. Behind them were Blaine's wife, Ellynor, who had died before Carmen was born, and her Sarcan...and then Isabella's parents and *their* Sarcans, whom Carmen also never knew. They all gathered around the Guardian of Kelmar and embraced her—each ancestor's hug and kind words reminding her of what a truly unbelievable experience this was.

Yet out of her momentary shock and continuing appreciation for what was happening...there were unanswered questions that Carmen just needed to know suddenly eating at her, regarding the woman who had brought her here.

After spending several precious and unforgettable minutes joyously reconnecting with her family, Carmen moved a few steps toward the pretty young woman, who was smiling beside Inpu in the doorway. Carmen had sensed from the beginning that there was something remarkably different about her...and now was as good a time as any to find out just what it was.

"Kelmari?" Carmen began, her heart beating restlessly, "...what exactly is your connection to Kelmar?"

Kelmari closed her eyes for a few moments, and then gave Carmen a sincerely blissful look that suggested she had been expecting this question for a long time.

"I am the one for whom the world of Kelmar was created and named after," she said, in an earnest voice. "…. I am the sister of Merlin and Desorkhan Cloud."

CHAPTER EIGHT
THE UNTOLD TALE OF KELMAR

I f not for the ceaseless chorus of the welcoming creatures outside, the drop of a feather on the marble floor could have
shattered the silence in the room following Kelmari's revelation. It was unquestionably obvious by the unnatural lull in
conversation, as well as the entire group's abrupt focus on the
young Kelmarsian, that nobody present had been expecting
such an announcement.

Carmen's head was spinning.... Desorkhan *Cloud?* No, it
couldn't be.... He just couldn't be Merlin's brother.... There
was simply no way that this could be so.

"I told you there was much that you had to learn," Kelmari murmured to the stunned Carmen. "And it is about time
that you know my story, because *my* story is *your* story as well."

Kelmari looked past Carmen and nodded to her deceased
relatives.

"I'm going to take Carmen and her Souls on a little tour
around the castle," she informed them. "I'll bring them up to
Essence Chamber in time for dinner, where you're welcome to
join us for a grand meal to celebrate their arrival."

"That sounds excellent," William said, though his face
still held a hint of surprise. His wife was standing agreeably at
his side. "Thank you."

With a contented smile, Kelmari turned and gestured for
Carmen and her friends to follow her back out of the throne
room. But Carmen hung back, not wanting to leave her parents
now that she had come all this way. She yearned to talk with
them about every subject imaginable, to get to know them the

way she had always wanted to…. There was just so much catching up that they had to do after sixteen long years.

Kelmari gazed pensively at her.

"You and your Souls will return in a couple of hours for dinner, and then you can have all the time that you want with your ancestors," she promised. "There is a reason for this temporary separation. I assure you that what I have to tell you is of dire importance."

Taking her word for it, Carmen reluctantly agreed to go. She and her Souls quietly shuffled past her family on their way out the door. Inpu stayed behind, acknowledging that he would see them later.

Before her parents were out of sight, Carmen glanced back at them, nonsensically fearing that they would vanish as nothing more than a sensational illusion the moment she left them. Her nerves settled only when she saw them waving and smiling to her. She felt a grin slide over her own face as she walked back up the sunlit corridor. Her mind, meanwhile, continued to swirl with thoughts regarding what Kelmari had said about her relationship with Merlin and Desorkhan.

"So, Carmen, I'm sure you have a lot of questions for me," Kelmari said nonchalantly, as she escorted her guests toward the stairs. "But before I tell you anything, I have a question for *you*."

"Um…sure," Carmen replied, a little taken aback. "What is it?"

Kelmari led the line of spirits down the staircase.

"As the Guardian of Kelmar," she began, as she descended the stairs, "are you prepared to risk everything that you've gained over the past year for the cause of preventing your world from falling into Darkness?"

"Absolutely," Carmen said, following Kelmari down the steps with her Souls. She was surprised that she would even be asking her such a question. "That's the commitment that I made after all."

Kelmari threw Carmen a satisfied glance over her shoulder. "I'm glad to hear you say that," she said, with a small smile, "because your path is not an easy one. There will be times along your journey when you may find yourself questioning your gifts, as well as your destiny.... But I want to remind you that following your heart will always lead you to the answers that you search for."

As Carmen contemplated Kelmari's words, she and the others reached the bottom of the stairs, and Kelmari began talking about the more characteristic elements of the castle. The building was relatively vacant now, aside from a handful of passing spirits, but Kelmari promised Carmen and her Souls that by tonight, the castle would be filled to near capacity for the feast in their honor. As she talked, Carmen got the sense that Kelmari wished to refrain from discussing the matter of her future any further for now, forcing her to keep her thoughts about the sorceress's mysterious words to herself, and ask no questions until Kelmari gave her permission to.

The Castle of Merlin had one hundred staircases—tall and wide ones, narrow spiraling ones, and others that were hidden behind suits of armor and paintings, accessible only with the correct password. Carmen also guessed that there were a number of secret passageways located throughout this legendary white castle with its numerous towers and snaking tunnels.

The building had an inner bailey, as well as a fortified outer bailey, complete with battlements to protect the castle from attack. Red and golden flags that were stationed atop a selection of the towers, as well as the banners that hung in the halls throughout the castle, were all decorated with the Great Seal of Kelmar and its representative symbols for the five Kelmarian Elements.

Kelmari told Carmen how Merlin himself had built the castle not long after he created Kelmar, and that it served as the capital building of Kelmarsia. It remained the crown jewel of the World of Light, as the realm's standing symbol of strength and internal fortitude—two qualities that Merlin greatly admired in others. Among the countless magical Protections safeguarding the castle was the pair of stone Dragon statues flanking either side of the front drawbridge. Should any unwanted guests attempt to enter the building, the Dragons would spring to life and defend the castle using their snapping jaws and releasing magical bursts of fire on command. Their spiked, thrashing tails could crush with impressive force.

Carmen and her friends followed Kelmari outside to the rear grounds of the castle. They walked through a beautiful pergola that was shaded with climbing green plants, and then out onto a cobbled path that snaked through a large square of hedged gardens.

In the gardens, bright and radiant tropical flowers in nearly every color of the rainbow were growing—all of them appearing to be in full bloom beneath the warmth of the sun. Carmen had never observed such unique and fascinating plants.

There were short, mushroom-like plants with purple and orange speckles, as well as snaking vines and giant flowers with vibrant petals the size of dessert plates. And then there was the amazing smell.... Carmen and her Souls were only spirits, but the indescribably stupendous floral scent of the Kelmarsian vegetation still filled their noses and cast each of them into a dreamy state.

Once the castle visitors had gotten used to the distinctive blend of natural aromas, Kelmari walked them over to a flower with diamond-shaped pink and red glassy petals, and encouraged all of them to smell it.

Carmen bent down and sniffed the flower along with the others, and a delightfully fruity scent drifted upward, instantly making her feel calm and serene.

"The Samantre Flower," Kelmari said. "It's only found here in Kelmarsia.... We extract a magical substance from its petals that can be used to heal the hurts of emotional scars. It's used very selectively, on spirits who come from lives so tragic and sad that passing into Kelmarsia alone does not free them of the pains that they suffered while alive."

Carmen looked up at Kelmari with curiosity.

"Usually, when Inpu and I reunite spirits with their individual bodies, all of the human or creature's past wounds—both physical and emotional—leave them, and in turn, they gain forgiveness for those who hurt them, and are granted the liberty to live in Kelmarsia in happiness and peace forever," Kelmari explained. "But sometimes, we use the magical properties of this plant to help ease them through the transition."

It now made sense to Carmen why the spirits who had been on the ferryboat with her and her friends looked so happy and at ease when making Kelmari's official passage into Kelmarsia.... Healing one's self of the scars left by past hurts surely must be one of the most liberating experiences possible. But because Carmen was still alive, it was hard for her to conceive of herself ever feeling forgiveness toward someone like Desorkhan, the murderer of her parents. Perhaps it was the emotional damage suffered by an act as heinous as their murders that would cause one to need the healing powers of the Samantre Flower in order to experience all of Kelmarsia's wonders.

Kelmari showed Carmen and her friends the way to an arched white trellis at the end of the path. They passed beneath the shadow of the arch and found themselves standing before a sprawling green garden flourishing with life. The tops of great blue and pink eggs could be seen peeking out of the ground, in row upon row of tilled soil. Overhead, young silver and white

Incadoves fluttered about, just as colorful, winged Talsonca puppies barked playfully and chased one another through the sky.

"Welcome to the Garden of Spiritual Birth," Kelmari said, showing Carmen and the others around the garden. "This is where the unborn spirits of Kelmarian creatures reside in safety and warmth until their chosen Masters arrive in Kelmar. The blue eggs are males, and the pinks are females."

Kelmari knelt down near a pale blue egg, which was roughly the size of a child's backpack. The egg was trembling a little in the dirt. Kelmari leaned over so that her ear was just a hair's length away from the smooth surface, and gently tapped the egg with her fingertips.

She listened intently for a short time...and then, apparently satisfied with what she heard inside, began to speak.

"Fate ultimately chooses what human each creature will be paired with," Kelmari told Carmen, though she was looking down at the egg as she spoke. "Not every creature that is to be born is assigned to a human Master, but the lucky few who are each serve as their human's guardian angel here in Kelmarsia until the day that the human comes to Kelmar. And the creature's spirit is then sent down to meet them."

She finally looked up at Carmen, but Carmen was staring over her shoulder at Blaze.

"Guardian angel...." she said slowly. "That means...you were protecting me before I came to Kelmar and knew that I was a sorcerer?"

"That's right," Blaze said, with a knowing smile.

"And he saved your life a handful of times before he was born," Kelmari added, as she stood up. "Do you remember the snowstorm that some parts of the non-magical realm experienced a few years ago? You were nearly killed the next day, when you walked outside your grandfather's bookshop and the ice and snow fell down from the overhang, but Blaze came through just in time."

It didn't take Carmen more than a minute to remember that very unusual happening. She gasped.

"The ice on the roof of my grandfather's shop…." she recalled vividly. "I was about to open the door when I saw a bolt of lightning touch down across the street…. Because I stopped and watched it, I stayed inside a couple of extra seconds. If I had gone out when I was originally going to…I would have gotten hit with the huge slab of ice and snow that fell down just before I opened the door."

Carmen gaped at Blaze, dumbfounded.

"That was *you?*"

"You've got it." Blaze grinned. "I could not come through into the non-magical realm entirely…but I *could* send you that signal to stop you from opening the door. I helped you out some other times before that, too, but nothing that serious," he said, with a lighthearted wink.

"Kelmarian creatures love their Masters unconditionally," Kelmari said, after Carmen delivered Blaze a long overdue thank you. "They are loyal and faithful from the moment they are born until the day they die." She smiled warmly at Blaze.

Kelmari and her visitors then watched as the blue egg at her knees shook itself free from the upper layer of dirt, and a thin crack began to make its way around the outside of the shell. It took only seconds for the single crack to break into a spider web of surface fractures.

The egg quivered sharply—and then a small, fuzzy head burst through a hole in the shell and shattered the rest of it. In place of the broken egg now sat a baby Komozale with large yellow eyes. The brown-furred lizard issued a high chirping noise…and within minutes, his mother emerged from the forest of trees beyond the garden to come care for her son.

The long, female Komozale, whose scaly body was covered in brown and beige striped fur, carefully scooped the baby up in her powerful jaws and carried him back to the woods. As her large form lumbered away into the deeper forest, Kelmari led Carmen and the others off in that same direction.

After walking through a dense maze of trees and shrubbery, alive with many different species of Kelmarsian creatures, they finally reached a wooden bench that sat beside a brook with an arched footbridge. It was a peaceful little spot, shaded by giant, ancient trees and fairly well hidden from the castle. Sunlight streamed in through the tree branches and made the cool, clear water of the brook glisten.

Kelmari sat down on the bench and requested that her guests do the same. Carmen and Blaze sat on the bench next to her. Anubis, Glamis, and Stellar made themselves comfortable on the ground at their feet.

Laying her wand across her lap, Kelmari closed her eyes and exhaled deeply.

"Isn't it beautiful here?" she asked, to nobody in particular. "I just love this world so much."

Carmen was watching her restlessly.

"Kelmari…" she said anxiously, unable to wait any longer for an explanation as to what the sorceress had said back in the castle. "Please tell us more about who you are…. I don't think I understand where you fit into all of this."

Kelmari opened her eyes and looked over at her and her friends.

"It is time that you know the truth about Kelmar," she said, speaking slowly and with intention. "Some of what you are about to hear will most likely come as a shock…but there is a history that you must be aware of as the Guardian of Kelmar and the Souls of Destiny. It is a story that few are aware of, and those who are do not speak of often."

Kelmari straightened up and fixed her gaze somewhere in the distance, beyond the brook.

"It begins with my eldest brother, Merlin Cloud. Without his struggles and sacrifices, we would not be sitting here having this conversation."

A quiet breeze rustled through the trees as a faint, whispering backdrop to Kelmari's silky voice.

"Merlin was a gentle, kind, and caring man, and he loved his family very much. He would always do whatever he could to keep us together…. When our parents would argue, as they often did when we were young, it was always Merlin who would remind them of how important it was for us to stay united as a family…. He had a calming presence about him that brought harmony and love back to where there had been only discord and strife. I still believe this to be his greatest gift."

At that point, Kelmari focused her eyes on Carmen and Blaze.

"All of the magic in the world cannot replace the gift of love," she said. "Even if he'd had no powers, Merlin knew how precious love was, and how taking it for granted would be the biggest mistake that he could ever make. He would always remind us of this, not always in words, but in what he did…and in the kind of life that he led."

Kelmari closed her eyes again as she thought back.

"Then there was my second eldest brother, Desorkhan," she continued.

A sharp jolt of cold ran up Carmen's spine.

"He and Merlin were best friends when we were young," Kelmari revealed. "They had the most fun any two brothers could have, playing together and casting harmless spells on each other…. I remember one particular day in which Merlin and Desorkhan were playing with a group of their friends on the playground. I was six, Desorkhan was ten, and Merlin was twelve. Our mother was shopping for a couple of things in town and was going to come pick us up at the park when she was finished. Desorkhan had taken his shoes and robes off to swim in the river with three friends. So while he was swimming, Merlin snuck out from behind the bushes and used a spell to make Desorkhan's shoes and clothes disappear when he and the rest of the children weren't looking. When Desorkhan tried to find his things later, Merlin told him that someone had stolen them. Desorkhan was then forced to wear his undergarments for the rest of the time at the park until our mother came to get us, much to the amusement of the other kids."

A nostalgic smile came over Kelmari's face as she relived what was evidently one of her fondest childhood memories.

"Well, our mother could see right through Merlin's innocent grin," she went on to say. "She screamed at him and ordered him to bring back Desorkhan's clothes at once. She then made sure to give Merlin a scolding for what he had done...but it was all in good fun. And I'll never forget Desorkhan chasing Merlin around the park for making him look so silly in front of the other children—until my mother got the both of them under control."

Carmen didn't know how to react to these things that Kelmari was telling her. She was having a very difficult time picturing a young Desorkhan engaging in such child's play.

"Even though we were living in the non-magical realm with our fellow sorcerers, in a desolate, isolated community called Eirech, we had our untroubled times," Kelmari said, before her voice took on a more serious tone. "Those days came to an end when we grew older.... The tight family unit collapsed. We never had much money, and when I was eleven, our parents separated. Merlin, Desorkhan, and I were sent to live with our aunt, Madora, until my mother had saved up enough money to let us move back in with her. Though Madora was a sorceress herself...she would not permit us to use magic under any circumstance. She had a horrible fear of being discovered by non-magic persecutors and being sent to jail for practicing magic, which was seen as a terrible crime back in those days.... During the years that we spent with our aunt, sorcerers were seen as a threat to the rest of humanity, and they were usually locked away in prisons or executed. That is why, to this day, children born of magic are not allowed to reveal their powers to anyone in the non-magical realm outside of their immediate families."

Carmen nodded thoughtfully as Kelmari spoke. If ordinary people knew of the things that sorcerers could do with their magic, there would always be those who would seek them out for immoral reasons.... They could use sorcerers in war against their will; they would experiment on them, and perhaps even kill them, just as they had hundreds of years ago.

"We were not allowed to attend school with the other magical children in our town," Kelmari recalled. "Our aunt was very strict, and she made us do all of our academic studying at home, after our chores were finished. We were essentially bound to the house. She did not allow us to leave unless she was with us, and she watched us like a hawk all hours of the day. Desorkhan grew frustrated with the constant supervision and lack of freedom, and he desperately desired to develop his powers to the fullest extent. He, Merlin, and I all studied magic in secret—using ancient textbooks and literature belonging to our parents, which we had snuck in with our other belongings when we first moved in."

Kelmari paused briefly, considering what she was going to tell Carmen and her Souls next.

"Merlin was the smartest of the three of us—and he studied all of his subjects much more intensely than Desorkhan and I," she finally said. "He would sit in the corner of his room for hours on end, poring over stacks of books and notes that he had taken…. Desorkhan was a little jealous of him, I'd say. Merlin always seemed to receive more attention, greater praise, and less severe punishments when he got in trouble. So after a while, Desorkhan began studying harder…determined to gain more magical knowledge and skill than his brother. The two of them would end up practicing advanced spells out of sight of the other, and the sibling rivalry grew more and more pronounced over the years."

"Didn't your aunt suspect that something was going on?" Carmen asked. "How did you hide the fact that you were studying magic from her all that time?"

"We made sure to do our studying late at night, and we would hide our things if we heard her coming up the stairs to check on us," Kelmari explained. "So our aunt was practically oblivious to everything that was happening, and the three of us made sure to keep it that way. Though there were instances when my brothers were tempted to fire spells at each other during dinner table disputes, Merlin and Desorkhan kept their bickering clean for the preservation of their secret undertakings in magical learning."

Kelmari lowered her eyes.

"We had been living with our Aunt Madora for two years when our mother became gravely ill and passed away…. That was when the family grew apart even more. Merlin tried his best to keep us together, but the loss of our mother was just too much for everyone to bear. Our father moved away to the countryside, and our aunt became bitter and depressed—crying nearly every night for a year over the death of her only sister. Desorkhan was especially affected by her death…more so than anyone else…. It changed him in ways that we never anticipated. He withdrew even further into his studies, and over time, he spoke with us less and less. In his despair and heartache, he found a zealous passion for Dark Magic, which seemed to distract him from his pain and somehow made him feel more powerful and in control of his own life. He secretly began to learn the ways of Dark sorcerers who lived in the community. He became highly skilled in the use of their spells and curses, and eventually decided that that was the path he wanted to take."

"Did you and Merlin ever try to talk him out of it?" Blaze asked.

"Oh yes...especially Merlin," Kelmari said. "The confrontations and the near-constant fighting were terrible.... And it didn't end until Desorkhan moved out when he was eighteen...to pursue the life that he believed he wanted, outside of our secluded little town and free of the obligations of his family."

But then...in spite of everything, Kelmari chuckled.

"Desorkhan had always been exceptionally protective of me...and so when I got sick six years later with a rare disease, he returned to Eirech to be with me," she said, her voice growing more solemn. "Our aunt had since died, and I was living in a small home with Merlin on the outskirts of town. I had been feeling weak and ill for some time...and the doctor in Eirech confirmed that I would die within a year from this unforgiving condition, for which there was no cure. When Merlin's letter reached Desorkhan, informing him of the bad news, I was bedridden, losing my sight, and barely able to speak. Merlin and I hadn't spoken with Desorkhan since he left, and so we were staggered when he walked into our home two weeks after Merlin had sent the letter. Merlin had been compassionately caring for me since I had fallen ill, and all the while, he had also been working on something very secret as I rested during the long days and nights."

Kelmari idly rested her left arm on the Great Seal of Kelmar atop her wand.

"After Desorkhan came in, he reached down to hold my hand at my bedside, and Merlin walked over to the closet.

When he returned to my bed, Merlin had a baby Dragon curled up in his arms.... The creature was no larger than a six-month-old puppy then. With great care, he leaned over and placed the handsome green Dragon into my hands and whispered to me that his name was Dagtar. Merlin then sat down on the edge of my bed and told me that he had another gift for me—a gift that he called...Kelmar."

Carmen shivered in amazement.

"Merlin told me that he had created a new world—one where I could live without pain or suffering," she said calmly. "I would be cured of my sickness...and I could be free to do whatever I wanted and not have to fear sorrow, disease, or death. That place that he spoke of was the Kelmar that you now know so well."

Kelmari smiled at Carmen, and then gazed pensively into the forest.

"It had taken him years to envision this magical realm, and then become powerful enough to make it a reality," she explained. "But it wasn't quite ready yet.... In order to bring Kelmar and the subsequent worlds of the afterlife to fruition, he needed more magic. He had already surrendered half of all of his magic to create Kelmar, and he needed Desorkhan to relinquish half of *his* magic as well in order to complete the world."

Kelmari carelessly stroked the crown of her wand before going on.

"Desorkhan agreed for my sake, and within days...the world of Kelmar was born. Merlin knew of a spell that would enable me to walk for a day, and that was when he took me there for the first time. When I saw Kelmar for myself...I couldn't believe it.... It was just so amazing," she said, in a faraway voice. "In my new, magically healed state, I led Kelmar for a short time as one of its many rulers. But the pure elation that I had first felt in walking through the fields of flowers with

Merlin and Desorkhan was only a fantasy…because soon after, my brothers began to fight again. Desorkhan wanted total control of Kelmar; not just half, and Merlin wouldn't allow it. In time, they both formed armies that battled each other without end—the hatred and bloodshed nearly destroying Kelmar all together. I just couldn't bear to see my brothers fighting because of me, and so I returned to the non-magical realm without their knowledge. I foolishly thought that if I died, their conflict would cease, and Kelmar would survive for new generations of sorcerers and creatures who would live together in peace, just as Merlin had always wanted. I passed away at the age of twenty-one—and have lived here in Kelmarsia ever since."

Kelmari gazed contemplatively at the peaceful splendor around her.

"Despite my death…the fighting between my brothers did not end. Instead, it escalated into a war beyond measure," she said, deep sadness in her voice. "My passing was the final dagger that pierced Desorkhan's heart and drove him into madness, plunging him ever deeper into the darkness that already consumed him. He blamed Merlin for my death, saying that his carelessness was what had caused me to leave and ultimately die. In his uncontrolled rage, Desorkhan vowed to claim Kelmar as his own. So blinded by torment and anger, he murdered his own brother to try to secure control of Kelmar, and gain revenge for the cruelties with which life had burdened him."

It was then that there was a heavy break in Kelmari's speech. By this point, Carmen was so engrossed in the tale that her hands were clenched tightly around the edge of the bench upon which she sat. So when Kelmari turned and looked her way, she instantly met her eyes, which were reflective and shining in the sunlight that peeked through the trees.

"When Merlin died, Desorkhan's soul was sealed inside *The Book of Kelmar,*" Kelmari finished. ".... And I believe you know the rest of the story."

There was a hushed stillness in that tranquil corner of the woods as Kelmari reached the end of her tale. It would take a while for everything that she said to permanently sink into Carmen's mind, but as she sat on the bench beside Blaze and her four other Souls, she could feel Dagtar peacefully calling out to her from somewhere distant—content with her new-found awareness.

Carmen's thoughts slowly found their way back to the statue of the three Cloud siblings standing together in the scenic courtyard beneath the light of the afternoon sun. It was in this moment that she came to realize how everybody who lives is connected to one another, and how each of their stories was but only a single chapter in a much greater story.

CHAPTER NINE
A NOBLE MASTER'S TASK

W"ith the defeat of Desorkhan, we thought that we had seen the end of war," Kelmari said, rising from her seat. "But alas, with his death has come a new war—one that threatens both Kelmar *and* the World of Light," she declared, as she stared out toward Merlin's castle, the evening breeze gently blowing through her long, white-blonde hair. "We stand in the midst of a struggle that has the potential to abolish 3,000 years of history."

Carmen stared at Kelmari's silhouette in the shadows of the fiery orange sun. The pure blue sky was beginning to transition into the striking reds and purples of sundown as daylight sank beneath the horizon.

"You're probably wondering how I can say that we are at war when Kelmarsia looks as beautiful and peaceful as it does now," Kelmari muttered, capturing one of the numerous thoughts currently speeding through Carmen's mind.

"Keltan fighters cannot enter or survive in Kelmarsia in the light of day," she explained, turning around to face Carmen and her Souls. "They invade only after the sun has set, and arrive with the objective of capturing the Castle of Merlin and claiming control over the whole of Kelmarsia. All of the combat between the Keltan and Kelmarsian fighters here happens at night...and by sunrise, the Keltan fighters leave Kelmarsia in a state of chaos and ruin and return to the World of Darkness. Kelmarsia magically renews itself each morning, and looks just as it did before the Keltans attacked. But our resources are not unlimited. Eventually, Kelmarsia will run out of the magic that it needs to sustain itself because of all of the energy that must be devoted to fighting this war."

"That happens every night?" Stellar asked, unable to comprehend that so much violence could take place in a heaven such as this.

"How do the Keltans pass through the magical barrier that separates the spirit worlds from each other?" Anubis added.

"The fighting has been taking place with greater and greater consistency lately. It's occurring nearly each night now," Kelmari replied, sounding disgusted at the thought. "The state of Kelmarsia at any given time determines the weather in Kelmar, and so your world feels the repercussions of the struggle in the form of vicious storms, just as the fighting is happening up here. The more brutal the battles in the afterlife are, the harsher the storms in Kelmar become."

Kelmari held up her wand so as to allow the sun's rays to shine through the cavities in the Great Seal of Kelmar crowning the staff. The light flowed through the spaces dividing the golden sun from the moon, the clouds, the water, the fire, the lightning, and the trees that were interlocked by crisscrossing straight and twisting lines.

"Desorkhan's strength is what has enabled the Keltan armies to breach the Impassable Barrier that divides Kelmarsia, Kelmar, and Keltan," Kelmari explained. "Triedastron had been trying for years to break through the border and take over the World of Light…and Desorkhan and his followers gave him that last surge of power that he needed to do it. We have worked repeatedly to reseal the barrier with more effective Protective spells and enchantments, but for the most part…we've been unsuccessful. Triedastron has found ways around most of the Protections, and has even reversed some of them."

Kelmari suddenly took notice of her guests' disconcerted expressions.

"As of today, we feel that the most recent Protections implemented at the Impassable Barrier will be sufficient enough to hold off Triedastron, at least until we can create a more permanent solution," she said. But the lack of conviction in her voice was palpable.

"Can't Kelmarsia engage in diplomatic relations with Keltan?" Glamis suggested, his golden crown glinting in the light of the sunset. "Perhaps a ceasefire or a peace treaty of some kind can be devised."

"Oh how I wish that were possible," Kelmari said, sounding disappointed. "We have tried, Glamis…and our attempts at diplomacy have failed miserably. Triedastron has his mind set on conquering the World of Light just as the Legend of the Worlds Triad predicts—and he will allow no one to hinder his plans. And with Desorkhan at his side, he is endowed with more power than he's ever had. He truly believes that he can achieve his greatest desires now that he has such a large and able army."

Kelmari shook her head unhappily.

"Triedastron was one of Desorkhan's first teachers in Dark Magic," she disclosed. "Desorkhan trained under him for many years during his rise to power, and now the two greatest Dark Masters have joined forces. Their combined militaries represent the most expansive assemblage of Dark sorcerers and creatures currently in existence."

"Just when we thought that it couldn't get any worse," Stellar mumbled bitterly, staring out into the trees. "We find out that there's *another* Dark Master…and the one who we defeated is posing even more of a threat dead than he did when he was alive."

"There must be a way that we can solve this crisis before it escalates any further," Carmen concluded.

She looked up at Kelmari.

"Before we came here, Dagtar mentioned something about the Secrets of Kelmar holding the key to what we seek—an end to this new war," Carmen said. "Do you know anything about the Secrets of Kelmar?"

Kelmari switched her staff to her other hand, looking contemplative.

"I do not, but I know of the one who does," she answered, leaning in closer to Carmen.

"Following dinner tonight, you and Blaze will meet Dagtar in the courtyard," she whispered. "He will take you to where you need to go."

Then, slowly straightening up, Kelmari glanced into the orange and red sky. After a brief moment, she looked back at Carmen and her friends.

"Come," she said, tapping the base of her staff to the ground. "We must return to the castle, lest the Keltan forces break through the barrier tonight. You are safe within the castle walls, but if you venture outside past nightfall…you must be very careful."

With the skies growing darker, Carmen, Blaze, Glamis, Anubis, and Stellar followed Kelmari back through the forest and the neighboring gardens to the Castle of Merlin. They could hear the nocturnal creatures living in the woods beginning to stir as the day transitioned to night. The creatures standing on the rocky ledges bordering the River of the Departed Spirits continued to sing on into the evening. As Carmen and her friends passed through the gardens, the scent of the countless flowers growing there carried through with the calm night breeze, enlivening their senses.

Once back inside the castle, Kelmari and her accompanying spirits marched up a tall staircase off the central corridor of the first floor, and then down a hallway to a set of grand doors inlaid with multicolored gemstones and carved with beautiful swirling designs. Essence Chamber, the spacious gathering place of Kelmarsian bureaucrats and other carefully selected individuals, stood behind those doors. Upwards of five hundred humans and creatures could fill the chamber at any given time, according to Kelmari, though it was only on a very rare occasion that so many actually would.

"Technically, spirits don't need to eat, or even sleep, for that matter," Kelmari told her company, shortly before they reached the doors. "But we're still able to enjoy the food in our spirit forms if we so desire."

On this night, the muffled clamor of hundreds of voices carried out into the corridor from the assembly room's crowded interior. Just when Kelmari and her guests were close enough to walk in, the double doors magically swung open—and a wall of sound and colors swallowed them up.

The vast hall was filled to near capacity with hundreds of Kelmarsian humans and creatures, seated together in plush Dragon-footed chairs at five long tables that ran all the way from the doors to the tall, stained glass windows at the back of the room. Dozens of colored banners featuring the Great Seal of Kelmar and symbols of each of the Kelmarian species were hanging from the arched white ceiling. The space was illuminated with light from the dozens of candles that were suspended from ornate chandeliers high above, glinting off the gold plates that were piled high with fresh food at all of the tables.

The young and old Kelmarsians' enthusiastic chatter quickly died down when Kelmari and the others entered the hall. All of the eyes in the room suddenly turned to them....

Then, after a brief silence, the chamber unexpectedly ruptured into applause.

"The Guardian of Kelmar!" someone shouted eagerly.

Kelmari smiled at Carmen's momentarily stunned look.

"They're aware of everything that you've done for Kelmar," she said. "All of us in Kelmarsia are tremendously appreciative of your bravery.... This dinner tonight is to honor your efforts, and to embrace you as the true hero that you are to so many."

Feeling embarrassed and somewhat undeserving of the attention, especially considering everything that was going on now with the recent war, Carmen sheepishly acknowledged the Kelmarsians' ovation, which carried on for nearly five minutes straight. Then she gazed around the room for somebody she knew in the huge sea of magical beings. She hadn't been searching for more than fifteen seconds when she heard her mother elatedly call out, "Carmen, over here!"

Standing up and clapping at the farthest table to the right were Carmen's mother, Isabella, and her father, William, their smiling faces glowing in the candlelight. Flare and Airian were also applauding, seated in chairs next to their Masters. Five chairs directly opposite them had been reserved for Carmen and her Souls. Inpu and the rest of their ancestors were sprinkled throughout the same table—all of them beaming proudly.

Kelmari smiled, too, pointing toward the table with her wand, indicating to Carmen and her friends that they were finally free to speak with their family members. Without needing to be told twice, they made their way over to the table, Carmen more than happy to escape the attention of the rest of the hall. Stellar, Anubis, and Glamis sat down across from Carmen's parents and began to chat excitedly with the Kelmarsians seated near them, which included Stellar's father, Inpu, and Glamis's grandfather. Carmen hugged her parents tightly, and cheerfully joined them at the table. Blaze started to talk with Flare and Airian, as well as his own grandparents, who were sitting not far away from him.

In only minutes, Carmen and her friends and family were all together, sharing stories and partaking in the generous feast that Kelmari had provided. Among the wide selection of food were braised Qwethral, grilled and seasoned Iyderfish, baked potato-like Bocanores, and a variety of steamed fruits and vegetables native to Kelmarsia.

All of the spirits sipped Perterale tea, which was made from the dried and prepared leaves of a magical shrub called a Perterale, and munched on a desert of frozen, fruity Caluyptus ice cream as they laughed and talked amongst themselves. The night was filled with the sounds of clattering dishes and friendly, familiar voices. Carmen wished that her grandfather could be here with her to experience all of this.... Surrounded by her friends, and family members with whom she never thought she would have the opportunity to reconnect, truly made this evening the happiest one that she had ever enjoyed.

Carmen learned countless things about her family and her heritage as she talked with her parents and grandparents. She was also highly relieved and delighted to find her parents to be every bit as kind and wonderful as she had hoped they would be, and so much more. In a relatively short period of time, she recognized that her compassion and determination had come from her mother. And through her father's entertaining tales of his adventures during his youth in Kelmar, she was reminded of those she had gone on herself, and was unable to stop laughing as he described his first attempt at flying, which reminded her so much of her own.

"It was dreadful!" William said, lightly slapping the wooden table in front of him. "I would swear that I nearly got myself killed when I first tried.... If I could have provided you with any words of advice before you went to Kelmar, Carmen, they would have been this: Don't ever try to take off from a high cliff your first time out. I don't care how good you think you'll be at flying. It never ends well."

William pulled his Sarcan, Flare, into a playful, one-armed hug.

"I'm telling you, if it weren't for Flare, I would have ended up here in Kelmarsia a lot sooner than I did."

"And if it weren't for *me* warning you to watch out for trees the rest of the time after we met, you'd be in far worse straits than that," Isabella corrected, as she used her knife to cut a piece of her Qwethral. "Kelmari and Inpu would have sent you down to Keltan just to keep you from causing trouble up here."

"That's a very good point," William admitted, laughing. He wrapped his other arm affectionately around his wife's shoulder. "You did keep me out of danger most of the time. And when we *were* in danger, you were always there to remind me of how it was my fault, and that you knew all along that those guys who were chasing us were Magicon in disguise."

William and Isabella's respective Partners, Flare and Airian, were equally as charming as their Masters. Flare had deep golden fur, luminous umber eyes, and red and orange markings, while the appealing blue-eyed Airian possessed lighter golden fur with small plum and ruby colorations. Flare was a friendly jokester with a kindly persona; Airian was a gracious and charismatic lady.

"There was one time when William and some of our friends tricked Haidar into believing that all of the Cadets were going to skip training the following day because it was the Commander's birthday," Flare recalled with fondness. "So when Haidar came looking for the Cadets at sunrise the next morning, we were all waiting for him in Thunder Stadium. When he finally found us, you can imagine the look of fury on his face…. But then when he saw the two-dozen of us flying above the stands, holding up a giant banner that wished him a happy birthday, his anger quickly turned to gratitude. He was especially appreciative of the cake that we made for him. But most importantly, we *did* get to skip training for the day!"

Carmen and Blaze laughed heartily.

"Flare and William would play these kinds of jokes all the time," Airian told them. "They were quite the daring duo. The day that Isabella and I met them, the four of us went on a hike together through the mountains after class. There, we had the misfortune of coming across a noticeably irritable Gorfelrod, and Flare and William assured us that they'd handle it."

Airian shot Flare a look that suggested she knew better.

"Well, as expected, their plan to divert the Gorfelrod's attention so that Isabella and I could escape didn't go so smoothly," Airian said.

"We ended up saving them from being the Gorfelrod's dinner," Isabella finished. "And that was just the start of what would be a lifetime of adventures with these two."

The time that Carmen spent with her Kelmarsian ancestors felt like a precious dream come true. Despite their years of separation, none of their conversations were forced, awkward, or odd in any way. On the contrary, the interactions that she and her relatives shared were unexpectedly natural and pleasurable, and it was just the same for her Souls and *their* family members. They talked about their lives and exchanged stories for nearly four hours, eating and taking delight in one another's company, until Kelmari stood up at her table on the opposite side of the room and tapped her glass chalice with her knife to get her guests' attention.

Once she could see the eyes of everyone in the hall, she lowered her glass and began to speak.

"Thank you for joining us this evening," Kelmari said, her voice echoing throughout the chamber.

She then raised her chalice, prompting the rest of the dinner's attendees to do the same. When Carmen attempted to raise hers, her father gently lowered her hand and shook his head.

"I would like to bring tonight's feast to a close with a toast to our newest Kelmarsians at heart," Kelmari proposed, her gray-blue eyes shining in the light of the chandeliers. "To Carmen Fox, her Partner, Blaze, and the rest of the Souls of Destiny present: Stellar, Glamis, and Anubis."

Kelmari tipped her glass in their direction.

"Thank you for everything that you've done, and for all you've sacrificed for the good of Kelmar's inhabitants," she said, with genuine appreciation. "We will forever be grateful for your courage and resolve in the face of darkness and terror."

Kelmari recognized each of them, and then tipped her glass toward the windows.

"We also toast Dagtar, Carmen's fifth Soul and beloved member of Kelmarsia."

At the conclusion of the toast, Kelmari and the others drank from their glasses. Moments later, the hall rang with the fervent applause of the assembled Kelmarsians.

The ovation continued for nearly two minutes before Kelmari made a settling motion with her hands, like an entering judge indicating for her courtroom to sit. Dagtar's claw was warm against Carmen's neck.

"Regrettably, we in Kelmarsia are currently confronting our own challenges following the Magicon War's conclusion," Kelmari announced, in a much more somber tone. "I have no doubt that many of you present are aware of the battles with Keltan forces that take place on an almost nightly basis here," she said grimly. "Triedastron and his armies have breached the Impassable Barrier, and threaten the security and well-being of both the World of Light and Kelmar. And should the fighting carry on…"

Kelmari's voice trailed off for a moment. She seemed hesitant to allow her next words to pass through her lips.

"…It's likely that Kelmarsia surrenders to an untimely demise."

The relatively serene atmosphere of Essence Chamber stiffened with a perceptibly heightened level of unease at Kelmari's warning.

"While we will not be thrown into a state of despondency by an ancient legend that no one knows to be truth or pure fantasy," Kelmari began slowly, "we cannot consent to close our eyes to the disorder of the present. The fact of the matter is that we are on the brink of a war that spans the three magical realms, and there shall be no rest within the Worlds Triad until the magic that reigns supreme in Keltan is brought back under control."

Kelmari gazed off in the direction of Carmen's table, and then looked out at the rest of the room.

"To conclude, my fellow Kelmarsians, I wish for you not to live each day in fear of what has yet to come, but at the same time, I must urge caution for the foreseeable future. The Kelmarsian Military is armed and prepared to protect us from the menace that is Keltan...but in keeping with the honesty that I vowed to always maintain with my people, I urge you to hold your dear ones close. Unlike in times past, I can no longer promise you peace in the eternal hereafter. But I can tell you that love *is*...and *always will be*...undying—it holds everlastingly strong, particularly in times of darkness, and it sees us through when we have lost all other guidance."

Carmen could have sworn that she saw Kelmari's eyes look into hers.

"Follow your heart," Kelmari declared to her guests, "and you shall never lose your way."

An uncomfortable silence, superseding any and all lightness and amusement from earlier in the evening, followed Kelmari's rather ominous speech. Out of all of the tables, the members of Carmen's appeared the least outwardly apprehensive, perhaps because most of them had had significant first-hand dealings with Dark sorcerers and creatures, and so were less easily intimidated than the others at the mention of them. But even so, there was a noticeably sobering shift in the mood and tone for the remainder of the meal, until Kelmari came over to meet Carmen and Blaze at the table.

"Dagtar's waiting for you out in the courtyard," she said, in a hushed voice. "He'll fly you to where you'll learn more about the Secrets of Kelmar.... When you're done, he'll bring you back to the castle. The rest of your friends will be sleeping here as well."

"Can they come with us?" Carmen asked hopefully.

Kelmari shook her head.

"I'm sorry, but only the two of you can go. Once again, there is a reason for it," she said, before Carmen could question her separating her from her friends and loved ones.

"Don't worry. I'll make certain of their safety until you get back," Kelmari promised.

Carmen and Blaze left shortly after that—making as inconspicuous an exit as they could through the chamber's entry doors as the first Kelmarsians were pushing in their chairs to return home for the night. Carmen's parents had told their daughter that Kelmari had invited them to stay in the castle tonight, and so they could meet up with her again in the morning. The halls were empty as Carmen and Blaze strode back up the corridor, down the many stairs, and out into the starlit courtyard.

They came to find that all was quiet in the verdant castle square. Dagtar was lying patiently on his stomach in the grass, the mellow light from the glowing half-moon high over the courtyard glinting off of his emerald scales. The crystal river that had carried the ferryboat with the newly arrived spirits flowed calmly past him.

Dagtar's blazing sapphire eyes were sparkling much like the stars above him as his friends approached.

"It fills me with such joy to see you again," he said, bowing his great spiked head.

Carmen reached up and stroked Dagtar's face, able to feel his cool and smooth scales against her ghostly skin, her smile reflecting his same sentiments.

"We've missed you in Kelmar," she said quietly. "They built a statue of you in Pyramid City...so no one will ever forget what you did to save our world."

"Well, that was silly of them, wasn't it?" Dagtar remarked, catching Carmen off guard. *"That should have been a statue of a young girl, not a Dragon. She's* the true hero of Kelmar," he said of his friend. *"I suppose that they will eventually realize their mistake, and erect your statue there in my place."*

"Kelmari told us the true story of Kelmar's beginnings," Blaze told the Dragon. Then he realized, to his slight embarrassment, that Dagtar was likely aware of this by now. "Well, you probably already know that she did...right?" he added.

Dagtar grinned as he nodded.

"One of the more amazing aspects of Kelmarsia is the knowledge that one gains of their friends and family. I was always able to communicate with you in Kelmar through my claw, even when I wasn't with you, but every spirit who lives here in Kelmarsia has a nearly unlimited ability to glimpse into the lives of their loved ones, no matter what realm they reside in."

Dagtar looked toward Carmen.

"This is how your parents know nearly everything of what has happened to you in Kelmar. They witnessed your final duel with Desorkhan from up here...and though they didn't have the power to help you, they were always *watching over you. So in that sense, they were with you all along, and will forever continue to be."*

"I would say that *is* rather amazing," Blaze agreed.

Dagtar flicked his long tail.

"Did you have a pleasant dinner?" he asked politely.

"Oh yes, it was excellent," Carmen said brightly. "We had such a good time."

Dagtar smiled.

"I'm so pleased that you enjoyed it."

Then he gazed up at the luminous moon behind him.

"Well, I believe that the time has come for us to depart for our destination," he said. *"Kelmari lent me her saddle for your use,"* he said of the pale suede saddle strapped onto his back.

Dagtar bowed his neck, allowing Carmen and Blaze to climb up. Carmen lifted her foot into the stirrup, and then took a hold of the saddle's horn with one hand as she used her other to hoist herself up onto his scaly back. Once she was situated comfortably at the base of the Dragon's neck with Blaze, Dagtar rose slowly to his feet.

"Hang on," he said, spreading his impressive wings.

Carmen hugged her body tightly against Dagtar's neck— and the Dragon glided up into the sky. The gusting wind from his beating wings blew through her ghostly hair.

Dagtar was climbing steadily higher each moment. Carmen could feel his muscles working to raise them up through the starry sky...and soon the three of them were speeding upwards at a sharp angle, like an ascending shooting star slicing through the darkness.

Carmen had to hold on with all of her strength to keep from slipping off of Dagtar's back as the Dragon raced higher still. She could see nothing but fuzzy smears of the forms around her. Dagtar had never flown this fast with her aboard before.... She almost wanted to close her eyes to stop the barrage of dizzying colors and shapes rushing past her eyes, but she was afraid of what that would feel like.

But then, just when Carmen was sure that they couldn't go any faster…Dagtar slowed and turned his head back to her and Blaze.

"We are going down now," he told his disheveled and windblown passengers. *"This is reasonably dangerous, so keep a steady grip."*

Carmen didn't even have the chance to ask where they were going before Dagtar made a sudden nosedive downward. They were traveling so fast that had she been screaming, she probably wouldn't have been able to hear herself over the wind. As Dagtar neared the Castle of Merlin, gathering greater momentum and speed each second, he took a quick turn, leveled out again, and flew his passengers toward the tallest tower, where soft candlelight glowed from behind the colored windows.

Dagtar was within a few hundred feet of the tower when one of the uppermost colored windows facing them creaked open. Squinting through into the window, Carmen could make out the golden walls of the throne room where she had met her parents.

"Is that…?"

Dagtar sailed toward the side of the tower, gradually slowing down as he neared it.

"When I get there, I will let you off," he said, *"and I will be back for you when you are finished."*

They soon arrived at the windowsill, and Dagtar lined his body up against the building so that Carmen and Blaze could safely climb through the open window.

"I apologize for the difficult trip," he said ruefully. *"This room has a special enchantment on it that only allows in visitors who know how to get here in their predetermined, designated manner. For me, that means flying in the set pattern that I just did. Had I flown in a more logical way, the window would not*

have opened.... The spell's purpose is to keep out uninvited, and possibly sinister, company."

Dagtar remained as still as he could to permit Carmen to crawl from his back onto the windowsill.

"*I shall return for you shortly,*" the Dragon promised, as Carmen and Blaze jumped down from the windowsill and into the room.

Without another word, Dagtar flew away from the tower and soared off into the night, leaving his two friends standing alone in the very same golden throne room where they had first met Carmen's ancestors. Though the room was otherwise empty now, it had a far different feel to it than it had that afternoon. There was a definite variation in the ambiance that made Carmen shiver, a feeling of profound power.... It was entirely different than the atmosphere in the rest of the castle.

Carmen was busy studying the high ceiling in the space, which was decorated with painted clouds and winged, angelic magical creatures, trying to figure out what the presence was that she was sensing here, when the gold door at the back of the room clicked open.

A moment later, a tall and thin silver-haired sorcerer with shining blue eyes swept into the room. His face was lined with deep-set wrinkles, yet somehow, he looked both wise *and* youthful. He was dressed in flowing red, white, and gold robes, and his head was crowned with a red pointed sorcerer's hat. In his right hand, he held a long golden wand inlaid with colored jewels representing the Kelmarian Elements, and topped with the Great Seal of Kelmar. Carmen was thankful that she was a spirit, for it was likely that she would have otherwise fainted from shock as he walked toward her.

"And so...we meet at last," Merlin said, his eyes sparkling as he reached out and shook Carmen's limp hand. "Carmen Fox, the Guardian of Kelmar, how honored I am to have you here."

Then he reached above her shoulder and stroked Blaze's fur.

"I am equally privileged to be in the presence of the legendary Blaze of Fire," he said graciously. "I am Merlin Cloud. Welcome to my sanctuary."

Still as taken aback as ever, Carmen and Blaze exchanged congenial bows with the renowned sorcerer, who possessed an all-knowing aura of power and revered prestige that was tangible to anyone in his company. The Master of Kelmar and Kelmarsia...the man who had created everything in this world, and the one from which they had come. Carmen couldn't believe or fathom that this was where she found herself now—standing face-to-face with the greatest sorcerer who ever lived. Standing before Merlin Cloud was like standing before the most powerful king in the entire universe. It was the most fantastic and surreal of feelings that Carmen had ever experienced.... Even when considering everything else that had happened since she and her friends had come to Kelmarsia, this improbable encounter was still especially hard to take in.

Carmen continued to stand there, unable to formulate any words as she thought about Kelmari's story and nearly a million other things. Merlin turned and walked over to his extravagant throne. He smiled at Carmen and Blaze's spellbound stares as he lowered himself down into his seat, leaning his staff against the arm of the chair.

"Surprised?" he asked warmly.

"Uh...a little," Carmen replied. She felt tremendously awkward, and her heart was pounding in her chest. "We're honored to meet you, Master Cloud," she said, with another bow.

Merlin raised his hand to stop her from going any further.

"Please," he said, "call me Merlin.... I hope that your visit to Kelmarsia has so far been gratifying."

"Oh, absolutely, yes," Carmen said at once. "It's been wonderful.... Thank you so much."

"I believe that you've already met your parents and other ancestors. Am I correct?" Merlin asked with polite interest, even though Carmen was positive that he already knew the answer.

"That's right," Carmen said. "I've had such a great time here.... All of us have."

"Ah, I'm delighted to hear that," Merlin replied. "I also rest more soundly knowing that you have an increased awareness of how and why Kelmar began.... It was important for you to know the truth, and I knew that Kelmari would tell it much better than I could."

He leaned forward with a small smile.

"Truth be told, I've never been much of a storyteller."

"Umm...sir," Carmen began, her mind practically bursting with questions, "how is it that Desorkhan can be your brother? He's one of the most...evil sorcerers to ever exist, and *you're* the good creator of Kelmar."

"Funny isn't it, how vastly different two siblings can be?" Merlin remarked, scratching his chin thoughtfully.

Funny wasn't the first word to come to Carmen's mind in describing the situation, but Merlin's astoundingly benevolent and considerate manner prompted her to listen even more carefully to his next thoughts on the matter.

"My relationship with Desorkhan is representative of the truth that evil is not born within the blood, but rather brought into being by human weakness, fear, and the sinister side of ambition. It was Desorkhan's own faults and frailties that led him to become the atrocious man that he became," Merlin said, a flicker of wistfulness in his ocean-blue eyes.

"I understand how difficult it is for you to come to terms with the idea of Desorkhan feeling concern toward someone other than himself. If I didn't know him as well as I do, I would feel the same way," he continued. "But there was no deceit behind the love that he felt toward our only sister, even in his darkest days. Throughout her short life, Kelmari was kind, innocent, and unassuming—qualities I believe he admired, and secretly wished that he also possessed. And for years after her death, in the refuge of Desorkhan's own mind, her death ate away at him like a debilitating disease, tearing him apart bit by bit. Though he would never confess to it...I know that he blamed himself for losing her, even while he outwardly blamed *me* to somehow make him feel less blame inside. I would even say that a better part of the rage that manifested itself in his immoral actions was due, at least in part, to his anguish over Kelmari's early passing."

Carmen paid close attention to every word of Merlin's speech. It was trying for her to understand all of Desorkhan's complexities, but clearly there was a significant piece of his history that she had never known before coming to Kelmarsia, and she now had a better understanding as to the reasons behind his wrathful path to becoming the most powerful and feared Dark sorcerer in Kelmar. There was still no justifying what he had done in his years as the murderous Dark Master, and the damage and pain that he had caused to so many throughout the Magicon War, but in a bizarre way, Carmen could almost identify with his pain and insecurities.

Desorkhan was so tortured by the untimely deaths of both his sister and his mother that any goodness and decency that he'd once had, had been slowly destroyed—and this was his greatest weakness. On the other hand, following her own parents' deaths, Carmen had rebounded from her desolation to heights that far exceeded her own expectations of herself. The defining difference between the two of them was that which separates the strong from the weak—the ability to rise from a tragedy as hopeful and more compassionate than before, and that was just what Carmen had done, and Desorkhan had failed at.

As a new thought came into Carmen's mind, she opened her mouth to ask Merlin yet another question, but the kindly old sorcerer spoke first.

"Why do I appear so much older than my sister even though I'm just six years her elder, when she appears to be the same age as when she died?" Merlin asked, accurately reading Carmen's questioning look.

"It is because I choose to," he said, matter-of-factly. "You see, Carmen, when sorcerers and creatures move on to the afterlife, they can choose to be any age that they were at any one point in their existence in Kelmar. Most people would likely desire their youth and innocence back, and thus elect to be of that age again.... However, eternal youth has its drawbacks. The age that one decides to be in Kelmarsia leaves them with only the knowledge and experiences they had up until that age when they were alive. So the younger one is here, the fewer memories and wisdom they will have, especially when compared to someone who lived for many years, and has decided to remain at their oldest for the rest of time." Merlin winked. "Kelmari died when she was only twenty-one; whereas I lived for much, much longer. I don't mind a couple of wrinkles in exchange for the understanding and perception that I acquired over my lifetime."

Merlin looked across at Carmen with great respect.

"Your parents were sensible in deciding to remain the age that they were when they passed away," he said. "But I would expect nothing less of such outstandingly intelligent people."

A crackle of thunder growled in the remote Kelmarsian mountains. Merlin didn't so much as glance outside before flicking his wand in that direction, prompting the only open stained glass window in the room to blow shut in the magical breeze. Then he gestured for Carmen and Blaze to come closer to him.

"There is no easy way for me to tell you this...but the need has arisen for me to call on you yet again to save Kelmar," he said. "The Worlds Triad teeters on the edge of collapse—and it is you who our people depend on to prevent that from happening. As a Kelmarsian, my powers over Kelmar are restricted. So, as the protectors of Kelmar, *you* must be the ones to restore the balance of power between the magical realms before it is too late for us."

"We'll do what needs to be done," Carmen promised, with a respectful bow.

"Yes, we will," Blaze added.

"Thank you," Merlin said, sincere gratitude glistening in his eyes.

He then leaned down to retrieve his wand. After requesting that Carmen and Blaze each get down on one knee, he ceremoniously placed the crown of his wand to their shoulders, like a king knighting two of his soldiers.

"The fates of our three worlds now rest with you," he said steadily. "Please hold out your hands, Carmen."

She did as she was asked. The legendary sorcerer closed his eyes and whispered a long and inaudible phrase in Keltongue before waving the crown of his wand over the palms of Carmen's vaporous hands.

A couple of seconds later, a thin disk—not much larger than a dinner plate—materialized in Carmen's hands. The disk was made up of two concentric circular wooden plates mounted one on top of the other. Carved into the smaller central circle was the Great Seal of Kelmar, surrounded by a ring of randomized letters. The outer edge of the larger disk was inscribed with the alphabetic sequence in regularly divided cells along the circumference of the circle. The object was also precisely engraved with intricate patterns and looping designs that traced around everything from the Kelmarian seal to the letters running along the edges of the circles.

"Have you ever seen one of these before?" Merlin asked Carmen, as she stared at the object.

Carmen looked up at him and shook her head.

"This is a cipher disk. It is used to decipher hidden messages," Merlin told her. "To reveal a message, the operator locates the first letter of a ciphertext message on the inner disk and then finds the corresponding plaintext letter on the outer disk that lines up with it," he said, pointing to the ring of letters around the outside of the object. "The operator then locates the *second* ciphertext letter of the message on the inner disk and takes note of the matching plaintext letter…and so on."

"What is the purpose of this cipher disk?" Blaze asked.

"Well, if this were my real cipher disk, it would be used to decipher the messages of the Secrets of Kelmar and enable their implementation," Merlin explained. "But this one is a fake. I created the real cipher disk hundreds of years ago with a spell that permits only one person to unlock it. Its intent was to make sure that no single person knew *all* of Kelmar's Secrets. As such, the person who was chosen could not be one of the heads of the three magical realms—yet he or she still had to be someone with the courage and wisdom of one," he said.

His eyes peered into Carmen's.

"And so, that person…is *you.*"

Merlin watched as Carmen and Blaze looked over the disk.

"Triedastron stole the real one from me a few weeks ago to try to prevent the restoration of the balance of power amongst the spirit worlds," he told them. "It serves no purpose to him other than this, especially being that he does not have the ciphertext messages that the disk deciphers. The key to discovering the locations and meanings of those messages lies with you, Carmen."

Carmen felt her robes…. There was suddenly the bulge of a small, rolled up piece of parchment in her inner pocket. She was beginning to feel nervous…. She had never used a cipher disk, or anything like it, before…but at the very least, she was glad to finally know what she had to do to utilize the Secrets of Kelmar.

"You do not need to look at the map that I have just given you now, but you *do* need to keep it safe," Merlin said sharply. "Without the ciphertext messages, and the map that will lead you to them, the real cipher disk is useless, and vice versa. And the *false* cipher disk does not work *even with* the ciphertext messages. Triedastron was fortunate enough to find the real cipher disk…but the maps that he stole along with it were a set of fakes, which were created just in case the cipher disk was ever lost. Therefore, they will not direct him anywhere near to where the true Secrets are hidden."

Merlin lowered his voice as he leaned toward Carmen and Blaze.

"I need you to go to Triedastron's fortress in Keltan and swap the fake cipher disk for the real one," he said, in a most urgent voice. "Take the real one back to Kelmar with you, and work there to find and decipher the hidden messages of the Secrets of Kelmar that my map will lead you to…. Once you crack the code, you will know how to end this war."

"What if we can't figure it out on our own?" Carmen asked, thinking about her lack of experience working with ciphers and secret messages. "Is there anyone that we can ask for help?"

Merlin's eyes flickered in a mysteriously confident way.

"I believe you will eventually find all of the resources you'll need to carry out this task," he said. "It is also of vital importance that you keep the ciphertext messages and the real cipher disk safe after you find them. I would think better of letting either one fall into enemy hands, as once Triedastron realizes that the cipher disk, as well as the maps that he currently possesses, are all fakes, he will undoubtedly seek out the *real* items to keep you from unlocking the Secrets and bringing back the balance between Light and Darkness."

Merlin laid his wand aside as he rose from his throne and placed his hands on Carmen's shoulders.

"We in Kelmarsia have the utmost confidence that you will succeed," he said nobly. "You just need to have faith in your powers, and trust your intuitions…. The Secrets of Kelmar won't reveal themselves unless you believe in yourself, and in your gifts."

Carmen felt Dagtar's claw on her necklace. She recalled her fifth Soul reminding her of this very principle just before she defeated Desorkhan in their last duel…. She would need to possess that same kind of conviction for triumph in *this* undertaking that she did back then.

"We'll do our best," Carmen vowed to the Master of Kelmarsia, meeting his eyes with the same courage that he valued so highly in her.

Merlin smiled.

"I know you will."

He pointed his wand at the sanctuary's stained glass windows, causing all of them to fly open with a *snap*. There was a stormy wind blowing in from the west—a sign that conflicting forces were once again at war in the Worlds Triad.

Merlin walked over to the nearest window and stared out into the darkness, his forehead creased with lines of concern.

"Time is just one of the enemies forged against us," he said gravely. "And unfortunately for you, Carmen, this fight is far from over."

CHAPTER TEN

THE CHIMERA AT THE GATE

It was a strangely quiet trip back to the room where Carmen and her friends would be spending the night in Merlin's castle. Dagtar had flown Carmen and Blaze down from the tower and directed them to a bedroom on the first floor, none of them speaking much about what had been discussed back in the Master of Kelmar's sanctuary. Though he didn't ask specifically what Merlin had said, Carmen knew that Dagtar was surely mindful of the duty with which he had entrusted her.

With Merlin's map secure in the pocket of her robes, Carmen carried the imitation cipher disk at her side as she and Blaze made their way to their room.

Halfway down the corridor, they slipped into the unlocked bedroom. It was a relatively small but comfortable room, containing one bed with a wooden headboard sitting opposite a closet. There was also a nightstand, a leather armchair in the corner, and a pair of tall windows on the back wall that granted a lovely view of the courtyard.

Carmen was glad to see that Anubis, Stellar, and Glamis were asleep when she and Blaze came in. She wanted to wait to tell them the important news until morning. The day in Kelmarsia had been mentally and emotionally draining, and Carmen longed to lie down and sleep away the conflicting worries and thoughts that afflicted her. Though for as many uncertainties as she had…she still couldn't believe that she had just met the Master of Kelmar! For someone who possessed so much power and depth of understanding, he had been incredibly kind and relatable…. It was an experience that she would not soon forget.

Dizzy with thoughts, Carmen crossed the room to her bed. While Kelmari had said that spirits didn't need to sleep, she nevertheless wanted nothing more tonight than to escape into the nothingness of slumber.

Carmen managed to find her way to the bed in the darkness without stepping on any of her Souls, thanks to the light from the stars, which passed in through the windows at the back of the room. Carmen got into bed and pulled the soft covers over Blaze and herself. She quickly fell asleep, and thought no more.

"So...that's the story," Carmen said, at the conclusion of her tale the next morning. She was sitting in the armchair in the corner of the bedroom, surrounded by Glamis, Anubis, and Stellar, who were listening on the floor. Blaze was sitting on the back of the chair, looking down at Carmen as she spoke. She had just finished recounting Merlin's new assignment for them, and had laid the replica cipher disk on the floor so that all of her friends could see it.

The reaction to her speech was mixed, at best. Throughout her report, Glamis made a nervous clucking noise in his throat, and at this moment, Anubis was pushing the cipher disk across the floor with his nose as he studied the inner pattern of letters. Stellar, meanwhile, was rattling off all of the reasons why it would be impossible for them to switch the false cipher disk with the real one.

"Triedastron's fortress is probably guarded with all sorts of Dark Protective spells, and who knows what else," Stellar pointed out. "We don't know what we're going to find there.... Doesn't Merlin have some kind of army that he can send to protect us?"

"We *are* the army," Blaze said crisply. "Merlin seems to think that we can handle it just fine.... Anyway—"

"That's easy for *him* to say," Stellar interrupted. "He'll be safe up here in his castle while we're down there risking our lives to get back some old wooden disk that we can't even read."

"We're the only ones who *can* do it," Blaze asserted. "Unless you want to see Kelmar destroyed, we have no choice but to go to Keltan, and then gather and decipher the messages of the Secrets. It's the only way we're going to bring Triedastron to defeat."

Stellar still looked skeptical.

"I just don't see how we're going to sneak into the Fortress of Darkness, by some miracle find the cipher disk, *and* get back to Kelmar without being caught," he said.

"I don't want to sound like a worrywart, but I would have to agree with Stellar," Glamis said. "This does seem like a rather unfeasible task."

"*Yes, Glamis, but let us think this through more carefully,*" Anubis said, looking up from the cipher disk. "*There is obviously a reason why Merlin chose this responsibility for us.... It is not a question of if we are able. We need to do this in order to save our world.*"

"Merlin didn't say that it would be easy," Carmen said. "But it's what needs to be done nonetheless. As for finding the cipher disk inside the fortress...there's got to be some way for us to get a better idea of exactly where it is—"

The sudden warmth that was now emanating from Carmen's necklace caught her by surprise. It indicated that Dagtar was calling out to her.

She caught a glimpse of movement out of the corner of her eye. Dagtar was outside, on the grass of the courtyard, lumbering over to the bedroom windows.

Carmen sprang out of the chair and rushed over to open the pair of sunlit windows. Dagtar bowed his neck and slid his huge, barbed head into the room.

"Good morning, everyone," he said, greeting them affably. *"Carmen, I couldn't help overhearing your dilemma regarding the cipher disk. May I ask if you've gotten a chance to look at the paper that my Master gave you last night? If you haven't...I suggest that you take a peek at it. It may help you with your predicament."*

Carmen reached down into the pocket of her robes and pulled out the small, rolled up piece of parchment, which was tied closed with a red silk ribbon. Looking through the parchment, Carmen could see an image scrawled in black ink across the surface. She removed the ribbon and unrolled the paper.

Drawn on the parchment was a comprehensive diagram of a pythonic castle containing mazes of hallways, trapdoors, hidden passageways, and secret rooms. An imposing fence with a gate surrounded the building and prohibited intruders from entering the Dark stronghold.

"The map that is currently displayed on the parchment is that of Triedastron's Fortress of Darkness in Keltan," Dagtar said. *"It will change later on, once you have located the cipher disk and are ready to hunt for the Secrets themselves. I also wanted to tell you that I would be coming with you to Keltan. My powers of invisibility, which can temporarily be extended to each of you, should be of value."*

Carmen felt as though a huge weight had just been lifted off of her shoulders. If her arms were long enough to reach around his body, she would have hugged Dagtar at that moment.

"This is fantastic!" she exclaimed. "I knew that Merlin wouldn't send us in alone."

Dagtar beamed at her.

"You're welcome to breakfast in Essence Chamber before we leave," he said. *"If I'm not mistaken, your family and the families of the others are already there, awaiting your company."*

There was a significantly lighter mood amongst Carmen and her friends following Dagtar's visit as they walked upstairs to the chamber. It was reassuring to know that the fifth Soul of Destiny would be escorting them to Keltan. The voyage seemed much more doable now.

Earlier, Anubis had reached the conclusion that even after they got the real cipher disk back, finding the Secrets of Kelmar might not be as clear-cut as just reading the map. *"Such treasured secrets are likely protected by something powerful that the straightforward map won't show us. We must keep this in mind when we leave to search for them."*

But all the same, Carmen and her friends reveled in having a breakfast of fried Parksla eggs, toast, and sweet Snotree juice with Carmen's parents and loved ones. The talk during the meal was still relatively cheerful considering the looming departure of Carmen and her friends.

Carmen waited until they were nearing the end of their breakfast to inform her parents of the mission that Merlin had delegated to her. But much to her amazement, they already knew about it.

"Inpu told us last night after dinner," Isabella said. Her voice was unconvincingly jovial as she tried to cover up the sadness she was feeling. "Your father and I know that you'll be fine…. You'll have Dagtar and everyone else there with you, and before you know it, you'll be safe and sound back in Kelmar."

It was at that point that the reality of time struck Carmen. She had been trying to put it out of her mind since last night, but there was no ignoring it anymore…. After today, she didn't know when, or even if, she would see her parents in this life again. It could be days, months, or even years. She did not belong here; she belonged in Kelmar.

Carmen knew that it was likely she wouldn't be back here until she deciphered the Secrets of Kelmar, and she might not be able to return even when she did. The crossing into Kelmarsia was not a trip that could be made for desire alone.... The risks involved in embarking on the journey were far too great.

"We're always with you, Carmen. You know that," William reminded her, though his voice was heavyhearted as well. "You must perform your responsibilities as Guardian.... All of us here and in Kelmar are counting on you."

Carmen nodded but kept her eyes down, carelessly picking at the remaining eggs on her plate with her fork while her mind wandered elsewhere. Kelmari and Inpu entered the hall a little while later, just as she and the others were quietly finishing eating. Following a pleasant greeting, Kelmari asked Carmen, her Souls, her parents, and Flare and Airian to meet her and Inpu out by the archway leading from the connecting corridor out to the courtyard.

Carmen's group left Essence Chamber at the conclusion of breakfast, the rainbow of sunlight entering through the stained glass windows glittering off of the gold plates and utensils. The remaining members of Carmen and her Souls' families waved goodbye as the heavy hall doors magically closed behind them.

The spirits marched up the long hallway, and then made a left turn down another corridor that ended in a lofty stone archway, beyond which stretched the emerald green grass and pure azure sky of Merlin's courtyard.

Kelmari and Inpu stood attentively in the shadow of the arch. They directed the attention of Carmen and the other spirits to the center of the lawn, where Dagtar lay in the sun-drenched grass, Kelmari's suede saddle strapped securely to his back.

"Inpu will be going with you and Dagtar to guide you back to Kelmar after you are finished in Keltan," Kelmari informed Carmen and her Souls. She seemed to notice Carmen's gloomy face.

"This goodbye is not forever," she said, a glimmer of hope in her voice as she placed her hand delicately on Carmen's shoulder. "You will be back again someday—perhaps even sooner than you think."

Kelmari didn't need to tell Carmen that it was time for her goodbyes; she just knew.

A heavy feeling in her chest, she looked up at her parents...the parents that she didn't want to leave behind again. The fleeting hours she had spent with them had been among the most wonderful in her life...and at this moment, she wished for nothing else but one more day, or even just one more hour, to be with them. Temporarily unable to speak, Carmen hugged her parents tight—longing to never let go again.

Despite how hard she tried, her eyes were bleary with the tears that she could not hold back. Her mother was also fighting off her own tears, and William's face was strained. As his wife and daughter shared their words of farewell, William turned and motioned for Blaze to come over and join them. Within seconds, Flare and Airian had also drifted into the group hug.

The six of them remained there, locked in one another's embrace for several precious moments as Kelmari and Inpu looked on, their faces sad but peaceful. Stellar, Anubis, Glamis, and Dagtar watched sadly as their friends bid their Kelmarsian ancestors goodbye.

"I don't want to go," Carmen said over her mother's shoulder, before pulling back to look into her eyes. "I want to stay here with you."

Isabella brushed Carmen's tousled golden hair away from her face.

"I know, Carmen," she said soothingly. "But you know that you are destined for greater things. You have so much more to experience in your life, and so many memories you have yet to make. I promise you that one day, you will look back and treasure every moment."

"Your mother is right," William said, gently lifting Carmen's chin and wiping her tearstained face with his fingers. "You can only imagine all that's awaiting you in your bright and limitless future.... You'll make mistakes along the way, just like everyone else, but have no regrets...because every one of those mistakes makes you a better person. You have the power to make your life, and your destiny, anything that you want them to be."

William looked as loving in that moment as Carmen had ever seen him.

"The most important piece of wisdom that I can give you as your father is to be kind to yourself, your Souls, and everyone else you love," he said. "For without love, life has no meaning, and certainly, no significance."

Carmen took a step back from her parents. Though her eyes were still red and puffy from crying...her lips parted into a wide smile.

"Thank you for everything..." she said, her voice wavering with emotion. "...I'll never forget what you've told me."

William had his arm around Isabella's shoulder as she wiped away the last of her tears with a silk handkerchief.

"Say 'Hi' to your Pop for us," William said, beaming at his daughter. "Be sure to tell him that we're well and that we miss him."

Carmen nodded.

"I will," she assured him.

Carmen glanced across at Dagtar and the rest of her Souls patiently waiting for her out in the grass. Now much more at peace, she shared one last brief but adoring hug with her parents.

"I love you," she whispered.

"We love you, too, Carmen," Isabella and William said, their eyes shining with unconditional affection.

Blaze quietly flew down onto Carmen's right shoulder. Carmen felt happier and stronger than she had in a long time as she turned and walked across the lawn to stand in Dagtar's giant shadow.

Once at the center of the courtyard, she peered up at the Dragon, took a deep breath, and told him through thought that she was ready to go.

Carmen got a steady grip on Dagtar's saddle and carefully mounted herself atop his back, swinging her right leg over the Dragon's flank as Blaze clung to her shoulder. Stellar and Anubis bravely stood against the Dragon's side and allowed Glamis to climb over them to get onto Dagtar's back, since he was incapable of jumping up so high.

Once Glamis was seated behind Carmen, Stellar leapt up and positioned himself behind the Boarax. Inpu had wandered over to Dagtar while his friends climbed onto the Dragon's back. He stood beside his son.

"Go ahead," Inpu told Anubis.

Anubis looked up at Dagtar—and then jumped upward to situate himself just in front of Carmen and Blaze.

Now that Anubis was aboard, Inpu leapt up in front of him to sit at the base of Dagtar's neck.

With all of the passengers finally in place, Dagtar stood up and gazed back down at Kelmari, who raised a steady hand in goodbye.

Dagtar lifted his lofty wings and began his ascent into the sky.... In only seconds, he and his friends were more than fifty feet off of the ground.

Carmen took a long, final look back at her parents, their Sarcan Partners, and Kelmari waving farewell to them. She could still hear the chorus of Kelmarian creatures singing joyously in the outlying mountains.

Carmen waved back to her magical family—and within moments, she was soaring once more into Kelmarsia's brilliant, never-ending sky, leaving the World of Light behind as she and her friends glided away into the clouds.

"How much time will we have to use your invisibility after we get to Keltan?" Carmen asked Dagtar, midway through the trip. The Dragon was flying higher and faster the farther away from Kelmarsia he and the others got.

"Like most any other magical ability, the power of invisibility is not intended to be permanent," Dagtar explained carefully. *"You'll be endowed with my powers so long as you need them and I have the strength to provide them. To put it another way, you'll use invisibility only when you need it...and no longer. The spell will help to protect you from the Darkness of Keltan that causes all who inhabit the realm to suffer. We shall hope that my magic will sustain each of your visual concealments for the length of time that we are there.... Regardless, we don't intend to be in Keltan for any longer than it takes to find the real cipher disk and swap the false one in its place."*

It seemed almost immediate that Dagtar and his passengers got to within sight of the golden line of light slicing through the blue sky. They had reached the Impassable Barrier that separated Kelmarsia and Keltan. Dagtar communicated to his riders that the World of Darkness laid just beyond that border, and that he would proceed to cast them into invisibility.

Not more than a minute later, a great, wispy magical sheath draped itself over Dagtar and all of his passengers as they flew up to the light. Though each of them could still see the others, they knew that to outsiders, they were no longer visible.

Carried up with the breeze, Dagtar flew through the golden barrier...and on into the World of Darkness.

In sharp contrast to entering Kelmarsia, passing into Keltan felt like crossing under a cascade of freezing water. A shock of cold worse than any winter chill ripped through Carmen as she and the others descended through a sea of blackness.

They emerged on the other side of the barrier to find themselves floating down into a vast and darkened cavern, cut through by flowing red rivers of magma that bubbled and hissed. Rusting lit torches made eerie shadows dance across the gray, crumbling stone walls. Countless tunnels and grottos snaked off of the central cavern, whose yawning ceiling was comprised purely of ominous-looking stalactites that dripped murky water down into the pools of magma below, adding to the dark and foreboding ambiance. The outlines of shadowy mountains rose up in the distance.

All throughout the cavern, masked sorcerers carrying leather whips were directing lines of black hooded and cloaked figures away through the tunnels in chains and shackles. It was evident from the wear on the head sorcerers' whips that they were used often. Inpu communicated to Carmen that those sorcerers being shuffled away were Keltan's latest arrivals. The spirits were being taken to Triedastron for judgment. There, the punishment they would have to endure for the crimes they had committed in their former lives would be determined.

Carmen watched as their shadows disappeared into the tunnels. Their departing footsteps echoed throughout the cavern as the looming stalactites continued to drip water into the fiery magma. Carmen wrinkled her nose at the stench of the molten rock, which was akin to that of hundreds of rotting eggs that had been decomposing for more than a year.

There was an assortment of Dark creatures living throughout the caverns of Keltan—nearly all of them horned, barbed, or in some other way frightening to look at.

Keltan's collection of demonic beings included yellow-furred creatures called Sharops that almost made Carmen think of what a full-grown tiger and horse would look like if they were combined in some kind of bizarre scientific experiment. Their eyes were red and catlike. They had black stripes running through their fur, as well as wispy tails and retractable claws. Two great spikes ran along the Sharops' backs, and they all possessed a pair of gnarled horns atop their long heads. A group of them were gathered around a pool of magma in the corner, communicating with one another in their own growling language.

There were also smaller, green flying creatures swarming about that Blaze identified as Deltsows. They were wicked sprites with horns, barbed tails, and beady yellow eyes. And only slightly larger than the Deltsows were the Rezsels—scarlet devilish creatures that screeched and scampered up the walls of the central cavern. These and several other fiendish beings were among the hordes of frightening Keltans lurking in the area.

"Look over there!" Blaze whispered to Carmen.

Carmen followed his pointing claw across the huge cavern to a monumental and sinister dark castle that was home to countless towers and surrounded by a silver spiked fence and an elaborate iron gate. Candles glowed behind the dingy windows of the ancient building known as the Fortress of Darkness. But even more intimidating than the castle itself was the menacing beast guarding the gate.

She had the body and head of a powerful lioness, with a second head of a gray goat growing out of her back, at the center of her spine. Her long tail was the body of a green serpent. She had a ruff that was quite prominent, and almost like a mane, but her brown body was both sleek and strong. She was a Chimera.

"She is the Partner of Triedastron," Dagtar told his friends. *"She can breathe fire, and she is a swift-footed creature."*

"Will she be able to see us?" Carmen asked him, aware that some creatures possessed the ability to see through spells of invisibility.

"Chimeras cannot sense invisible beings," he assured her, as he flew her and their friends toward Triedastron's fortress, being careful to fly as near as he could to the ceiling of the cavern without being grazed by the stalactites, so that those sorcerers and creatures below wouldn't feel the wind from his wings as he soared overhead.

They were only a few hundred feet away from the fence when the Chimera raised her lioness head and began to sniff the air. Carmen's stomach churned nervously. There was no way that she could *smell* them, could she? Carmen tried to shake the possibility out of her head as they flew onward, hoping that adrenaline was the only reason for her uneasiness.

Dagtar flew down lower as they approached the gate. Having studied the map of the fortress before they left, Dagtar planned to drop Carmen and the rest of her Souls off on the rooftop, and they would then enter the castle through one of the tower doors or windows. From there, the Kelmarians would make their way down the stairs and into the heart of the castle, in search of Triedastron's study—the first room on their devised list of possible hiding places for the real cipher disk. Dagtar and Inpu, in the meantime, would wait outside for them to emerge with the object, and take them back to Kelmar afterward. The plan made every ounce of sense in their minds, but whether it would go so smoothly in its execution would be another matter.

Dagtar was nearing the air over the gate. The Chimera was still furiously sniffing the air, when suddenly she released a deafening roar.

Carmen was positive that anyone within a thousand-foot radius had surely heard the noise. She gulped, trying to temper her racing heart. Then, without warning, Dagtar bucked forward, as though he had unexpectedly crashed into an invisible boundary.

Carmen and her fellow riders were dangerously close to being jostled off of his back, but managed to hang on to one another and Dagtar's body just tight enough. The Chimera spit a breath of fire up at them—and Dagtar took an abrupt turn upwards.

"What is it?" Carmen immediately asked the Dragon, as he evaded the flames.

"There's an Entrance by Conquest Protective spell over Triedastron's fortress that I was not aware of," he told her. *"The only way that it can be broken is if we defeat the guarding Chimera in a duel."*

Carmen felt a surge of panic overtake her.

"How are we supposed to do *that?*" she asked, highly disturbed at the thought of battling the angry beast. "She has three heads!"

"And we have seven," Dagtar reminded her, as he turned to avoid another Chimera fireball that was hurled up into the air from the back of the beast's throat. *"So on that count alone, we have an advantage. And while the Chimera can smell us, she cannot see us. I am faster in the air than on land, so you will fire your spells from atop my back.... Brace yourselves, all of you. I'm going to fly lower so that Carmen can get a clearer shot at her."*

Carmen's mind was working at warp speed as she summoned her wand. She knew nothing about this creature other than that she breathed deadly fire and was quick on her feet.

How was she supposed to defeat her when she didn't even know any of her weaknesses?

With virtually no time to construct any sort of sound battle plan, Carmen leaned over Dagtar's flank as he glided within range of the Chimera. Then she pointed her wand at her and cast a *Lightning Strike* spell. There was an ensuing clap of thunder as Carmen's lightning bolt raced from the ceiling down through the air.

With astoundingly gifted reflexes and timing, the Chimera leapt out of the lightning's path just as it struck the ground where she had been standing just milliseconds earlier.

The beast didn't miss a beat when it came to her response. The veins in her largest neck throbbing rapidly, the Chimera's lioness head snorted a bright blast of red fire up in Carmen's direction.

Dagtar yet again succeeded in straying far enough away to dodge the flames, but Carmen knew that time was of the essence. Dagtar's powers of invisibility would only hold out for so long, and to keep up with the Chimera, he had to exert extra energy that he could not afford to waste.... She had to discover what the Chimera's weakness was, and find a way to capitalize on it—fast.

Carmen watched the enemy creature carefully as Dagtar flew her and the others higher. The Chimera's serpent tail was hissing angrily, the lioness's head was watching them, and had they been close enough, the goat's head would have gladly lanced them with her horns. There had to be some way to defeat all three of them in one fell swoop.... They were all parts of the same body, Carmen reasoned, so if she could only figure out how to weaken the lioness's body, maybe she could bring the whole of the creature to defeat.

Dagtar turned and soared downward once more to allow her another attempt to hit the Chimera. Slightly more prepared this time, Carmen held her wand steady as she pointed it down at her target, waiting until the very last moment to cry out, *"Firejolt!"*

Carmen's lightning-infused fire spell cut down through the air in a flash of scarlet and gold light. The Chimera roared her own breath of fire back up at the oncoming spell.

The two attacks collided midway between them in a fiery blast, negating each other.

It took a few more failed tries before Carmen started to grow frustrated. As Dagtar flew her back away from the Chimera's ferocious flames one more time, she finally came up with an idea that she had formulated after studying her opponent's fighting pattern.

The Chimera's lioness head was clearly the strongest of the three—and it seemed to work independently of the other two. The serpent hissed irritably and lashed out at Dagtar when he flew over, even though the fire from the lioness's throat was more than enough to force the Dragon back. The horned goat had also tried to challenge them a number of times by this point.

Keeping all of that in mind, Carmen decided that she would ask Blaze to distract the snake and goat heads while *she* moved in to attack the lioness. She would attempt a risky move, but one that she thought just might bring the creature down. She would shoot her *Lightning Arrow* spell into the gaping mouth of the Chimera as she opened it to release her fire, and then hope that the lightning would be enough to weaken her and break the Protective spell over Triedastron's Fortress of Darkness.

Carmen quickly ran through her plan with Blaze, and then whispered it to Dagtar. Dagtar stayed high enough above the Chimera to be out of her detectable scent range while the invisible Sarcan flew down to her by himself.

As soon as she caught on to Blaze's scent, the Chimera's serpent tail thrashed about, and the goat's head aimed her horns up in his direction. Blaze flew in a zigzag pattern around the beast to maintain her attention—the Chimera spitting fuming fireballs at him as he darted through the air.

The serpent snapped her jaws, trying ineffectively to sink her teeth into Blaze's fur when he flew by, but Blaze had the edge over the creature in that he was both visually undetectable, and faster than the snake. The goat, for the moment, was repeatedly attempting to attack her irritatingly agile foe with her sharp pair of curling horns. The lioness head was still heatedly sniffing out the rest of her enemies—quite aware that they were all still in her territory.

Carmen visualized her strike on the Chimera while Blaze fluttered around the beast's deadly trio of heads. At just the right point, she gave Dagtar a nudge in his flank with her heels to indicate that she was ready to attack.

Dagtar nimbly soared downward toward the Chimera. With one tense hand clutched around the horn of the Dragon's saddle, Carmen gazed around Anubis and Inpu and over Dagtar's shoulder as she held on to her wand.

Feeling the movement in the winds from Dagtar's wings, and smelling each of the riders' distinct scents, the Chimera sent a gust of fire upward. Carmen and the others leaned with Dagtar as he tilted his gigantic body to steer clear of the flames.

Blaze continued to divert the attention of the goat and serpent by constantly flying in circles and taking shots at them with his own fire. Close enough now to her opponent, Carmen leaned over as far as she could without slipping off of Dagtar's back, and pointed her wand at the Chimera.

Her focused gaze met the Chimera's steely black eyes. The Chimera opened her wide jaws one more time to exhale her lethal breath—and Carmen fired the *Lightning Arrow* spell into the great hollow that was her mouth.

In a flash of dazzling light, the bright, electrically charged arrow shot from the crown of Carmen's wand and pierced the inside of the Chimera's throat. The creature howled as the spell crippled her. And just as Carmen had imagined it would, the lightning energy raced through her to flood her entire body—including the other two adjoining heads.

The Chimera struggled to keep herself standing, but within a minute, she fell to her side, her breathing somewhat erratic.

When the serpent tail was finally limp, and the other two heads both had their eyes closed, Blaze flew back up with Dagtar and his riders, all of them looking down at the defeated Chimera to be sure that they had weakened her enough to unlock the *Entrance by Conquest* Protection on the fortress.

Sure enough, Dagtar was promptly able to fly his friends beyond the gate and the silver pointed fence, up to the sharply angled castle rooftop.

Once he had lowered himself to a height that was just above the surface of the roof, Dagtar allowed his passengers to safely climb down.

Anubis, Carmen, Blaze, Glamis, and Stellar all dismounted the Dragon's back one at a time. They were now standing at the center of the polished, black tiled roof of the Fortress of Darkness. Inpu remained sitting at the base of Dagtar's neck.

"We'll be here when you are finished," Dagtar promised Carmen and the rest of her Souls. *"We won't stray outside of the Protective boundary, should the Chimera awaken before you return."*

"Be safe," Inpu said calmly, gazing at each of the Kelmarians through his peaceful golden eyes. *"Try your best to stay out of trouble."*

Carmen had to suppress a laugh at that last remark. She had somehow been able to survive all of the trouble that had come before her so far, yet more trouble always seemed to be on the horizon. If she could have figured out a way to avoid it before now, there was no way that she would be where she currently was—standing atop the roof of a fortress in the World of Darkness, armed with not much more than a cryptic map and an old wooden disk, which she would discreetly attempt to exchange for another.

No, the potential for trouble never seemed to be far from Carmen Fox and her friends. So it was not of much surprise when they heard the Chimera tentatively rise to her feet and begin to prowl the nearby grounds at the base of the fortress gate far below. They could only hope that whoever happened to be inside the fortress on this night hadn't heard her fall the first time.

CHAPTER ELEVEN
CIPHERS AND SIEGES

Carmen pointed her wand at a nearby tower. She and her friends would have to discreetly enter the fortress through a window of any one of the many towers that sprang up from the tiled roof.

"Let's start with Triedastron's study," she decided, glancing down at Merlin's map. "If I'm reading this right, we should only have to go down one floor."

Carmen and her four Souls crossed the roof, careful not to slip on the gleaming black tiles, and peered through one of the stone tower's windows. The room was dark, but there didn't appear to be anyone moving inside. Deciding that they should take a chance and try to sneak in through here, Carmen used *Lockstra,* and then pulled open the wooden window. She lit her wand to illuminate the room and gazed cautiously inside.

The space turned out to be a tiny storage room lined with shelves of sinister-looking green and gray bottles containing magical potions, elixirs, and other concoctions. But judging by the thick layer of dust coating the bottles, Carmen was practically certain that this room was rarely used.

Feeling confident that it was safe to enter the castle through this secluded room, Carmen and her Souls crawled down through the window, squeezing into the narrow aisle of the shadowy closet. Carmen shut the window behind them.

Blaze moved to the front of the closet and pressed his ear to the door.

"I don't hear anything," he whispered, after almost an entire minute of listening. "We should be clear to go."

Blaze grabbed the doorknob and slowly opened the door, and he and the rest of his invisible friends walked out into the hallway.

The floor of the corridor was covered with a long maroon carpet, and the dark gray walls were lit with flaming torches. There were countless framed paintings hanging throughout the castle fortress, but none that were of anything even remotely pleasant. One painting, for example, showed a pack of ravenous Skelyotes feasting on the decomposing carcass of a red Leafox. Another painting was a portrait of a deceased Dark sorcerer with whom Carmen was glad she wasn't familiar. The man in the portrait had a gaunt face, dark eyes, and a black goatee. He wore dark green robes and a twisted smile as he pointed his blood-soaked sword out at the viewer.

Carmen extinguished her wand's light as she and her friends walked across the hall to a grand stone staircase that led down to the next floor. They made sure to tread lightly as they made their way down the steps. Off to the right on the lower floor lay a series of doors through which Carmen and the others could hear muffled voices. *Their* destination though was Triedastron's study, which was located in a corridor off to the left.

Carmen and her Souls reached the landing, their eyes continuously scanning around them for signs of movement. This hall was lined with suits of armor covered in spikes and holding jagged swords at their sides, as well as stone statues of grotesque gargoyles. As Carmen's group crossed the torch-lit hall, they heard a door on the other side of the stairway creak open.

Instantly more alert, they turned and watched one of the hooded sorcerers whom they had seen outside tramping toward the far door, where the hushed voices were coming from. His heavy steps made the sound of his steel-toe boots echo loudly through the hall.

As the sorcerer disappeared into the room, Carmen tried to see beyond him to what was inside, but he was quick to shut the door behind him. She and her Souls then decided to keep moving. Without delay, they crossed the hall to Triedastron's dimly lit corridor. His study was one of six doors located in this particular passageway, and it was difficult to determine just which one it was from Merlin's somewhat complicated map.

In the flickering light of the torches, Carmen squinted to read the tiny cursive writing that labeled each of the rooms on the map. She finally spotted the one marked *Triedastron's Study,* and pointed her friends toward the last door at the end of the hall.

"I'm pretty sure that this is it," she said, tucking the map away in her pocket as they walked to the dark wooden door. When they reached the study, she pointed her wand at the bronze doorknob.

"Lockstra."

Carmen opened the door and lit her wand. The room was completely dark. She and her friends crept quietly into the study, softly closing the door after them. Carmen pointed her wand up at the ceiling, where a wrought iron chandelier was hanging. Blaze flew up and lit the candles with a breath of fire.

Triedastron's study was a spacious library. The room contained several rows of wooden bookcases that were lined with hardcover books. There was also a mahogany desk off to the left, and a couple of burgundy armchairs sitting in the back corners of the room. In addition to the books on the shelves, there were a number of books opened and facedown scattered around the study, and a tall stack of parchment stood atop the desk, upon which also sat a quill pen and inkwell. With no windows to light the space, Blaze had to light various sets of candles that were placed throughout the room to provide them all with the adequate means to see.

Carmen and her Souls then initiated their search of the room. Blaze rummaged through the contents of the desk drawers while Stellar, Glamis, and Anubis explored the areas near the bookshelves. Carmen wandered over to the very last row of shelves and noticed that nearly all of the volumes there were historical reference encyclopedias.

She stared at the books that occupied the shelves at the back wall of the study, trying to see if she could find the cipher disk inconspicuously hiding amongst the hardbacks. She slowly ran her fingers along the spines of the books that were at her eyelevel as she moved down the aisle. She was trying to think of possible places that Triedastron might consider hiding the cipher disk, which was a fairly large object to conceal, when one of the volumes near the middle of the bookcase felt strangely cold to her touch.

She instantly stopped walking and stared at the book, which had a dark red cover and no title. She reached up to feel the tops of the pages.... They were cold and smooth. This object was not a book at all; it was only a replica of a hardback, made purely out of metal and painted to look like a real one. Why in the world would Triedastron have a fake book in his study?

Carmen decided to feel the volume next to this one, only to find that it, too, was unnaturally cold...another fake. She then felt the book next to that one.... This one was real.

With a combination of bewilderment and excitement, Carmen leaned her wand against the shelves and pushed the two imitation books away from each other, almost as though she were pulling back a set of curtains.

Carmen suppressed a gasp. There was a long, thin hole cut out of the back of the bookcase. Staring into the darkness, she carefully slid her hand inside the hole and felt engraved wood beneath her fingertips.

"Guys, come here!" she whispered. "I think I found something!"

Blaze and the others hastily dropped what they were doing and rushed over to her. They gathered together around Carmen just as a broad smile spread across her face. She pulled the cipher disk out of the crack in the back of the bookcase....

SNAP.

Carmen didn't even feel the floor drop out from beneath her feet before she realized that she was falling down a cold, metal shaft.

"AHHHHHHHHHHHHH!!!!"

Their screams echoed through the chute as Carmen and her friends crashed down onto a spiraling, slick metal slide and descended sharply downward into pure darkness. Lying on her back in front of her Souls, Carmen could see nothing but black as she and the others glided down the dizzying slide, continuously increasing speed, into the depths of Triedastron's fortress. The cold, dank air ripped past their faces as they slid farther and farther down. Their noses were burning with the heavy stench of mold.

But then, abruptly, the slide dropped off, and Carmen and her Souls of Destiny continued to fly forward for a couple of feet—until they fell hard onto an earthen floor, which was coated in a thick layer of green and brown grime.

Carmen was lying on the filthy floor, the two cipher disks on top of her, her mind spinning from the ride down the spiraling slide. She couldn't think straight.... What had just happened?

"Ugh..." Stellar grumbled, as he shakily got to his feet behind Carmen and looked around the space. "Where are we?"

Carmen sat up, and then illuminated her wand, flooding the cramped, windowless space with light.

The stone ceiling was too low to permit her to stand. Cinderblock walls surrounded them on three of four sides.... It seemed that they were trapped in a narrow crawl space between floors. The only way out was through an aluminum air duct that lay about five feet out in front of them.

"That bookcase was a trap," Blaze said, staring back up the slide into the darkness. "Triedastron must have installed it to prevent someone from stealing the cipher disk."

Carmen brushed some dust from her robes as she got onto her hands and knees. She placed the two wooden cipher disks side-by-side on the floor in front of her.

Complete with two intricate circular pieces of wood containing both random and consecutive letters, as well as the golden Great Seal of Kelmar, the two cipher disks were virtually identical.

"Luckily the trap was a little slow...because we got away with the real one," Carmen said, as her Souls came together around her. "But we still have to put the fake one in its place."

"Perhaps we can get back through there," Glamis said. He picked up his gold crown, which had fallen on the floor, and pointed toward the air shaft.

"Before we go, we should put a mark on the real cipher disk so that we know which one is which," Stellar suggested, observing that there was currently no way to tell one from the other just by sight. "I can put a small scratch on the genuine one, so it will be easy to tell them apart."

Nodding, Carmen handed Stellar the authentic cipher disk, and he marked the back of it with a noticeable claw mark.

Carmen then passed Blaze the false cipher disk to hold for her as she proceeded to crawl over to the metal tunnel that lay ahead of her and the others, which was just wide enough to allow two of them through at a time.

She could hear an unrecognizable man's voice echoing through the shaft as she and her Souls approached it...but the sound was too far away to distinguish what was being said.

Carmen pointed her lit wand into the duct. There was no telling how long the shaft was, or where it would lead them, but for now, it represented their only means of escape.

"Should we see where this goes?" Carmen turned and asked her companions. "I think that it's safer than trying to fly back up...and the trapdoor that we fell through is probably closed anyway."

"I believe this to be our only viable option," Anubis said. *"Let us go and see where it takes us."*

The others all agreed, and so Carmen and Blaze crawled through first. Stellar, Glamis, and Anubis followed behind them.

Once he was inside the air duct, Blaze flew as high as he could and held Carmen's wand for her, pointing it ahead of them for light.

The smooth aluminum felt as cold as ice beneath Carmen's hands as she and her friends made their way straight ahead through the narrow passageway.... The farther inward they advanced, the more complete pieces of muffled conversation they could hear carrying through the air shaft. Somewhere in the fortress, men and women were speaking in low voices.

"...new Protections at the Barrier."

"It matters not. The Kelmarsians are running out of options."

A man cleared his voice.

"Without the cipher disk, they can only stall for so long.... Their attempts at resistance shall not be detrimental to our capture of the Kelmarsian capital."

Carmen's heart instantly began to beat faster. She and the others continued to follow the voices through what became a startlingly complex maze of tunnels and turns in the ventilation system. The air shaft gradually sloped upward as they crawled as fast as they could through the ductwork, listening hard.

"What about Merlin's Dragon? Did you take him into consideration?"

"The beast will be taken care of in good time, along with the rest of them. He and his little friends are no threat to us."

Carmen and her Souls rounded a corner, and came upon an opening in the bottom of the vent, which let light up into the otherwise dark tunnel; so they moved with haste toward it.

Cautious, they peered down through the ventilation duct and observed the scene below them through the metal bars of the opening.

They were in the ceiling of a meeting room lit by a wrought iron chandelier similar to the one in Triedastron's study. Carmen's heart skipped a beat when she saw who was present.

Several Dark sorcerers and creatures were seated around a long table, at the head of which sat a middle-aged man with dark gray hair. His face was cloaked in the veil of the shadows at the far end of the room.

The tall, lean man seated to his right had a tanned, pointed face, slick black hair, black eyes, and a thin scar that ran from his temple down to his cheek. His Sarcan had black fur with red markings, a yellow lightning bolt-shaped horn, and a sharply angled tail. Their names, which were synonymous with evil, were Desorkhan and Singe.

Seated beside them were Lucifer Mondalaus—a pale man with blonde hair and sharp blue eyes, and his Zelthrel, Narcista—who was an acid green, Dragon-like creature with yellow eyes, a slimy, scaly body and large wings.

Next were Sevadia Nankarsa and her Syntor, Syth. Nankarsa was thin, and possessed long black hair and piercing purple-blue eyes. She had worked as a Dark Agent under Desorkhan in his Magicon army for years. Her Partner was a tall, sleek and slender, electric blue creature. He had luminous, scarlet eyes that were both cat and snake-like, and dark blue markings on his face. His head was crowned with two sharply pointed ears that were tipped with red.

The line of familiar Magicon members continued until it finally reached Sylvine Yokaro, who was seated at the opposite end of the table as Desorkhan. She was a short, older woman with shoulder length black and gray hair, and icy blue eyes. Her lined face was tense and unforgiving.

Mixed in between the rest of the deceased Magicon fighters were the young Phantom Warrior, Zorlan Xoncarg, and accompanying sorcerers and creatures of Keltan unknown to Carmen. All of the humans, except for the silver-haired man sitting at the head of the table, were dressed in long black robes decorated with orange and red flames; *he* was dressed in burgundy robes.

"There is little that Kelmarsia can do to halt this latest invasion," the commanding sorcerer announced, in a calm, silky voice. "They are attempting to buy time, but no matter how numerous or creative their desperate efforts to hold us off become…we will go ahead with our siege of Merlin's castle as planned."

"I certainly hope that you are not mistaken, Triedastron," Desorkhan said, folding his arms and leaning back in his chair. "Rumor has it that Merlin has formulated a new spell involving the Secrets…the likes of which none born of magic blood have ever seen."

"Don't tell me that you're buying into the Kelmarsians' dismal attempts to deter us from our destiny," Triedastron said. His relaxed tone abruptly turned cruel. "Just because *you* could not stand against a teenager and a Sarcan doesn't mean that *I* possess similar weaknesses."

There was a strained silence before any of the others at the table spoke. Embarrassed, Desorkhan looked away from Triedastron, a vein pulsing in his forehead. Carmen brushed away a layer of perspiration from her brow. For some reason, she was suddenly beginning to feel shaky and weak.... Her knees were aching from the long crawl through the air ducts.

Syth muttered into his Master's ear. Sevadia Nankarsa brushed her long black hair away from her eyes and then looked down at Triedastron.

"What *about* the child, Master?" she inquired, at last breaking the quiet of the room. "Should we not be concerned now that she has been chosen to find and decipher the Secrets?"

Mondalaus, as well as many of the others, gazed toward Triedastron for his response. Triedastron didn't seem fazed in the slightest by the question.

Carmen had no idea how the Keltans were aware of Merlin choosing her to acquire and implement the Secrets...and it disturbed her to think of what else they could possibly know about her.

"I must say, even when considering *all* of the many thoughts presently consuming my exceptional mind, Carmen Fox fails to appear," Triedastron replied curtly.

"You seem very confident, Triedastron," Yokaro observed, almost suspiciously. "What do you know that we don't?"

The head sorcerer leaned forward and delivered a cool smile to his closest confidants.

"Let's just say that it's a matter of foresight," Triedastron said quietly. He calmly pressed his index finger to his temple and closed his eyes.

The other sorcerers and creatures seated around Triedastron carried on muted conversations with those near to them as he sat there in silence for more than a full minute. What was he doing?

Carmen gasped as the genuine cipher disk briefly illuminated in her hands. A few seconds later, Triedastron tapped his finger to the table to regain the attention of his associates. His nails were grotesquely long and yellow, and he spoke in a louder voice than perhaps he had to.

"My Partner, Lucia, has just brought to my attention that some uninvited guests have joined us this evening," Triedastron said evenly, causing Carmen to shudder. But then his face suddenly broke into a disingenuous smile. "It would be rude not to invite them in, would it not?"

Triedastron removed a tarnished gold necklace from around his neck. It was fashioned with an elaborate circular charm carved with demonic images of fire, horns, a serpent, and a lion.

"Come forth the magic of Keltan…. Wand reveal thyself to me!"

Blaze grabbed a hold of Carmen's arm. Thanks to Triedastron's Chimera, their unwelcome presence was no longer a secret. The Master of Keltan pointed his sinister-looking gold staff upward as he gazed in the direction of the ceiling vent. His forehead was deeply lined, his eyes, dark and devious.

"Revealio!"

With a thunderous crack, the floor of the ventilation shaft burst open. Carmen screamed as she and her Souls of Destiny crashed down through the air, collapsing onto the table in a painful heap.

For a moment, there was only silence and shock…. And then mayhem erupted.

As Carmen and her friends scrambled to get up, Desorkhan and the rest of the Dark sorcerers and creatures at the table were on their feet in a flash—summoning their wands and staring at their foes, vengeance gleaming in their eyes.

"She has the cipher disk!" Nankarsa hissed, pointing at the wooden disk in Carmen's hand.

Carmen and her Souls were standing in the middle of the long table, surrounded on all sides by their enemies. Carmen spotted the lone door leading out on the other side of the room.

"Get her!"

Carmen whirled around as Mondalaus lunged forward, throwing himself across the table to seize her.

"Eurorkaisia!"

The burst of blue light that shot from Carmen's staff knocked Mondalaus back, and she and the others made a frenzied dash to the opposite end of the polished table, dodging a deluge of spells and curses that were firing at them from every direction.

Carmen summoned an *Invisible Shield* as she and her friends jumped off of the table and ran toward the only exit. But just as they neared the door, Desorkhan shouted, *"Rovenlock!"*

There was the click of a bolt sliding into place as the door in front of Carmen and her Souls sealed itself shut. Desorkhan laughed as Carmen wildly tried to break off the doorknob with her bare hands before attempting a sequence of failed *Lockstra* spells to try to unlock it.

"Carmen!" Blaze cried.

A split second later, Carmen felt the cold metal of Desorkhan's wand pressed against her throat. Desorkhan seized her from behind and dragged her back to the center of the room, even as her friends remained protectively around her.

When they were near the table, the Dark Master turned Carmen around so that she was facing the entire assemblage of Keltans. His long fingers were wrapped over her shoulder like horrible bony claws, his other hand still clutching the silver staff pressed to her neck.

Carmen was shaking; beads of cold sweat were pouring down her face as she stood restrained by Desorkhan before Triedastron and his huge collection of Dark sorcerers and creatures.... Her legs were numb, and she felt abnormally weak…as though she had been fighting for far longer than she had.

"This is it, Fox," Desorkhan whispered into Carmen's ear. "Don't move…or I will destroy you."

Triedastron murmured something to Yokaro, absent-mindedly running his fingers through his black and silvery hair. Then he strutted across the room to Carmen and Desorkhan.

Triedastron was a tall man, whose brocade burgundy robes swept the floor. His glare was so vindictive that it seemed to suck the air right out of the room.

As he laid his dark brown eyes upon the Guardian of Kelmar, Triedastron sneered.

"Well, well, what exactly do we have here?" he asked softly, his merciless gaze passing onto each of Carmen's friends. "I'm touched that you wanted to visit me, but regrettably for you, Lucia informed me of your presence before you could pull off another one of your infamous escapes."

Triedastron feigned an expression of sadness, before his coldhearted stare returned.

"You must think very highly of yourselves—managing to wrestle your way past a full-grown Chimera…. She doesn't take kindly to enemy intruders, and neither do I."

Carmen could feel her hands trembling. She couldn't think of anything to say or do that would get her out of this awful position…. Feeling lightheaded, she stared at Triedastron's wand. It was a tall and twisted dark gold staff crowned with the same cursed charm that had adorned his necklace. In the center of the magic circle was a sharply warped K, no doubt standing for Keltan.

When Carmen didn't respond to his question, Triedastron frowned, accentuating the creases in his gaunt forehead.

"You seem to be at a loss for words," he said, glaring at Carmen through his dark, anger-filled eyes. "Let me help you with that."

Suddenly, Triedastron snatched Carmen's wand out of her hands.

"Step away, Desorkhan," Triedastron ordered, pointing his own wand at Carmen while he held hers steadily at his side.

Desorkhan promptly followed orders and slipped away into the horde of Dark sorcerers behind him.

Carmen's mind was hazy.... Without her wand, she was virtually helpless in defending herself. She could hear the rapid pounding of her heart. Something was blocking her thoughts.... She couldn't think to reach for the Light Sword in its scabbard on her belt.

"Zarsketska!"

A red blast of energy erupted from Triedastron's wand and struck Carmen straight on, sending a rush of searing pain throughout her body. Carmen screamed out as the power of the curse overtook her, blinding her senses and disorienting her further.

"Ahhhhhiiieeee!!!!"

"Carmen, fight back!" Blaze shouted, his voice sounding very distant, even though he was right beside her.

Carmen tried desperately to reach for the gold hilt of the Light Sword. Her numb hand was shaking so much that she couldn't get a grip on her saber.

"I...I can't do it.... Something's wrong!"

The sight of her attackers standing before her started to spin.... Carmen's vision was quickly growing dark. She felt herself falling forward.... The cipher disk slipped from her limp hand and clattered to the floor. Anubis ran in front of her.

"Carmen!"

There was a burst of sinister laughter from Triedastron and his assembly as Carmen collapsed onto Anubis's back, barely conscious of what was happening around her. Anubis remained standing, strong enough to support her weight. Through her limited vision...Carmen saw Blaze hurry to snatch up the authentic cipher disk before the Keltans could get to it.

The Sarcan then darted toward Triedastron. He bit him hard on the arm and grabbed Carmen's wand from him. Triedastron shouted, furious, as he flew away, but before he could go after his foe, Glamis threw himself into the action.

There was the sound of pounding hooves behind Carmen as the Boarax unexpectedly broke free from the others and galloped toward his enemies, running swiftly through the legs of the Keltans and avoiding the numerous curses that they fired at him.

When he was at the back of the room, Glamis took a deep breath…before charging back the way he came, his body aglow in a pale green light.

"Instundo!"

"Body Snare!"

"Siayetha!"

Unremitting eruptions of colored light exploded from the Keltans' wands as they attempted to impede Glamis's charge. Blaze cast his own *Thunder Shield* Protection to keep himself safe, and soared across the room to deflect many of the oncoming curses being fired at the Boarax.

Glamis continued on his blazing path to the door, with most of the Keltans eventually diving to get out of the way of the powerfully built creature wearing the spiked collar and the golden crown. The green light encasing the Boarax grew brighter as he sprinted toward the exit, the power of the *Rushing Stampede* spell building with each step.

The door was now within reach. Glamis issued an impressive roar and lifted his head. Then, in an intense blast of emerald green light, the Boarax King crashed through the wooden door, sending it flying open and nearly knocking it off of its hinges.

"Get Carmen out of here!" Stellar shouted to Anubis. She lay draped over his back, semi-conscious. The Keinen jerked his head toward the exit. "Glamis and I can handle things from here."

"Are you sure?"

"Yes, just go!"

Anubis silently cast a spell that would allow him to safely carry Carmen on his back as he ran, with no chance of her slipping off. Blaze followed Anubis as he bolted from the room, the angry shouts of the Keltans carrying out into the hall after them.

Anubis and Blaze hurried across the hall with Carmen, leaving Stellar and Glamis behind to buy them time to escape. They soon found an empty corner and laid Carmen down on the floor to try to heal her.

Struggling to stay alert to her surroundings, Carmen stared up into Anubis's golden eyes.... Blaze was flying right next to him. Though they were spirits, both of them looked extra blurry around the edges to her, surely due to whatever ailment was weakening her and causing her to lose her vision. Anubis rubbed his nose gently across her face.

"She's been poisoned by something powerful," he concluded.

Blaze carefully brushed Carmen's disheveled hair off of her face.... He looked more afraid for her life than he had in a long time. She desperately wanted to smile at him to give him comfort that she would be all right, even though she didn't know if she really would be. But as hard as she tried to deliver him that reassuring grin...she couldn't do it. She just didn't have the strength.

"You're going to be fine, Carmen," Blaze promised her softly, holding her cold hand in his paw, his blue eyes wide with worry.

"I cannot free her body of this poison without a strong antidote.... All that I can do is give her a boost of strength that will

temporarily make her strong enough to get back home," Anubis said, after some thought. "Dolen's Heart is an impermanent Healing spell that can mask and partially limit poison's effects."

"I'll help you," Blaze said at once, still holding Carmen's hand. "That way you won't lose too much of your energy. We'll do it together."

Anubis laid his paw on Carmen's other hand. He then nodded to Blaze...and each of them spoke the incantation through thought.

Blaze and Anubis's outlines glowed in a soft pink light.... Just seconds later, Carmen felt an astonishing warmth travel from her hands...up to her arms...and through the rest of her body. The heat stopped her hands from shivering, and little by little brought her mind back to full consciousness. The sight of Blaze and Anubis above her soon came back into focus.

The light and warmth faded a couple of minutes after it had materialized, and a smile finally broke across Carmen's face. She sat up.

Not feeling fully back to normal...but much better than she had just ten minutes earlier...Carmen exhaled deeply. With the lightheaded feeling gone, she could finally think coherently.

"Thank you, guys," she said, stroking Blaze and Anubis's fur. Blaze handed her back both of the cipher disks and her wand. "I don't know what came over me...."

"You were poisoned, but by what we don't know," Anubis said, as Carmen Returned her wand and drew the Light Sword from its scabbard. "But we've restored you enough so that you are able to fight...if need be. We need to return to Kelmar as soon as possible to get you fully healed."

"Stellar and Glamis are still—"

A sudden crash from inside the meeting room down the hall echoed through the corridor before Blaze could finish his sentence. Carmen quickly rose to her feet.

"Hurry! We have to get back to the rooftop!" Anubis said, nodding toward the staircase. *"I told my father to have Dagtar meet us there."*

"But what about Stellar and Glamis?" Carmen asked. "We can't leave them behind!"

"Stellar asked that we do just that," Anubis reminded her, blocking her from running back to Triedastron and the others. *"We will return for them with Dagtar and my father.... We're not strong enough without them."*

"We can't wait that long!" Carmen persisted, trying to get around him. "We need to fight back *now!*"

BOOM!

There was more shouting from the meeting room, and then Carmen heard Stellar cry, "Stay back, Glamis!"

When Anubis had turned in the direction of the noise, Carmen ran past him to go help her two Souls who were in danger.

"Carmen, wait!"

Blaze and Anubis ran down the hall after her. As they rounded the corner of the staircase, they saw that the front doors of the fortress were wide open. They realized then that much of the noise was actually coming from outside, but they couldn't spare the extra moment to look out and see what it was.

Stellar and Glamis were fighting off Sevadia Nankarsa, Syth, and Dezra Razok just outside the meeting room. A thin cloak of smoke hung over them, and the stench of burning fibers lingered in the air. Stellar stood protectively in front of Glamis. The Keinen was breathing heavily and looking guarded, his brown fur matted with soot.

"Come now, Stellar, why don't you show us what you've *really* got?" Nankarsa said, mocking him in her high, screechy voice, carelessly throwing her black hair over her shoulder. In her left hand, she held her staff, which was a bright blue saber crowned with a magic circle containing the Magicon symbol inside a ring of rubies. "I'm sure that all those years with the Magicon taught you *something*."

"He's too weak," Syth said, glaring at Stellar through his scarlet, cat-like eyes as he flexed his sharpened blue claws. He was floating a couple of inches off the ground beside his Master. *"Without the Guardian, he is defenseless."*

Stellar growled and tightened up. He hadn't noticed Carmen, Blaze, and Anubis standing only three yards off to his right. Nankarsa's gaze flashed to them momentarily when they burst onto the scene, and her lips formed into a dreadful smile. But she chose to keep most of her attention centered on the Keinen.

"So let's see you get angry, Stellar," Razok said, jabbing his serrated silver wand toward him. "Or has being with the Kelmarians for so long softened you?"

Stellar glowered at him.

"It better prepared me for challenging you darkhorts," he said evenly.

Nankarsa scowled. "This is taking far too much time, traitor."

She turned toward the scrawny sorcerer to her right. "Just kill him already, Razok."

"Redentum!"

As a dark jade flash of light released itself from Razok's wand, Stellar raised his head and issued a roar like Carmen had never heard from him before.

"Cerkatra—a powerful attack spell used by creatures born of the Land," Blaze muttered.

A beam of orange, sparkling light erupted from the back of Stellar's throat and fired toward his trio of enemies. The spell blazed through the light of Razok's curse and continued on its way toward the Magicon.

"Arhhhhhhhhhh...."

Nankarsa, Syth, and Razok scattered, running in three different directions down the hall. The spell followed them and hit each one consecutively, slamming them to the floor and draining much of their physical strength.

Carmen, Anubis, and Blaze rushed over to Stellar and Glamis as the Magicon lay weakening on the floor around them.

"Stellar, that was great!" Carmen said, excited. "Now we've got to get out of here."

"I don't think so, Guardian," Desorkhan said coldly.

With a sick feeling in their stomachs, Carmen and her Souls looked behind them, where the Dark Master was walking slowly down the grand staircase, his silver and black wand pointed directly at them. A gang of Dark sorcerers followed behind him, their wands also raised.

"You've got to be kidding me," Carmen said, as a sinking feeling settled in her chest.

Stellar didn't wait another minute. Not saying a word, he edged in front of his friends and closed his eyes. Then he slashed his paw through the air in an arch-like motion.

A small, golden arch of light conjured itself at Stellar's feet and grew progressively upward into a seven-foot-tall archway.

"The Keinen's Arch!" Blaze said in surprise. "It protects everyone on the spell caster's side of the arch by preventing Dark forces from coming through it!"

"Come on!" Stellar ordered, ushering everyone toward the front doors of Triedastron's fortress.

Carmen and her friends ran to the entranceway, and then outside onto the grounds of Keltan...but they abruptly came to a standstill only a few feet away from the Dark castle's entrance. The chaos that was ensuing inside the fortress was nothing more than mild disorder when compared to the warfare that was taking place just outside of it.

Carmen stood before the gate of the Fortress of Darkness and gaped. Dozens of Kelmarsians and Keltans were battling one another all across the barren landscape of Keltan…. The gray and rocky ground was barely visible beneath the feet of the Magicon and Kelmarian spirits fighting over the better portion of the land…. Sorcerers and creatures alike were engaged in fierce duels, none of which showed any signs of slowing down. The roar of shouting, spells flying, and the clashing of swords stung Carmen's ears as she watched the massive battle unfold. The air above her head was filled with all sorts of flying creatures, from Dragons to Skelyotes and Verdden hawks.

Her mind racing, Carmen could do nothing but stare at the outlandish, out of control scene playing out in front of her eyes. She didn't know anything of what was going on…how it had happened…or what she should do now. She searched the skies for any sign of Dagtar and Inpu…. Suddenly, Dagtar's cry rose from somewhere in the smoky air.

Carmen and her Souls watched as Dagtar's colossal, emerald green body soared over Triedastron's fortress. Carmen sighed with relief…a smile finding its way to her face. He was coming for them.

But then she heard the unmistakable sound of running footsteps behind her. Carmen whirled around. Lucifer Mondalaus was charging toward her and her friends, his sword drawn. Carmen pointed the Light Sword back at the approaching Magicon Officer.

"Verestrosa!"

"Lightning Spark!"

Carmen and Mondalaus's spells shot toward each other from the blades of their swords. The Magicon's spell was a black, cursed serpent. Carmen's was a bolt of golden electricity. At the very same time, Carmen saw another figure rushing toward her from the corner of her eye…. It was Sylvine Yokaro.

The two attacks collided in an explosion of purple smoke, but a weakened form of Mondalaus's curse still continued on its path to Carmen. Yokaro raised her wand—a brown and purple staff topped with her magic circle—and seized the opportunity to launch her own running assault on the group of Kelmarians.

"Fortozan!"

A blast of fiery darkness burst from Yokaro's staff.

"Illumina Hesquel!"

Carmen kept both of her hands tight around the hilt of her saber as she skillfully crisscrossed it through the air. With that motion, the blade instantly expelled torrents of blinding white light. The interlocking light wrapped itself into a protective domed shield that would come to encase her and her Souls.

The flaming curses of Mondalaus and Yokaro struck Carmen's *Light Shield* together in a blistering explosion.

Carmen struggled against the combined power of the Dark Magic…. Her weakened arms shook as the curses tore through her magical defense.

Blaze flew in circles around Carmen and the others, his horn expelling brilliant golden light ribbons that reinforced his Master's. But even Carmen and Blaze's united front was not enough to completely destroy their enemies' attack…. Lucifer and Sylvine's spells struck Carmen's group in a flaming blast that instantly ignited the ground around them, encircling them in a ring of flames that shot up six feet into the air.

Mondalaus laughed from the other side of the inferno as he and Yokaro watched Carmen and her friends search restlessly for any escape from the fiery entrapment. Yokaro's stare was hostile—fury surpassed only by that of the man now approaching the circle of fire from behind his comrades.

Desorkhan, his cold, black eyes ablaze, marched toward Carmen and the Souls of Destiny. The dark silhouette of his Sarcan, Singe, was visible over his shoulder.

Not uttering a word to either of his fellow Magicon, Desorkhan strode past them to stand just inches from the flames that encircled his Kelmarian foes.

Desorkhan reached his wand inside the ring of fire, magically parting the curtain of flames and bringing Carmen and her Souls into sight.

"What's the matter, Fox?" the Dark Master asked cruelly, smiling at Carmen's fatigued appearance. "You're looking a little pale. Perhaps you should take a rest...a *permanent* one," he said, his smile twisting into a scowl. "I can certainly be of assistance with that."

"I think I'll be okay, thanks," Carmen replied.

Desorkhan slowly shook his head.

"I'm sorry to disappoint you...but you are not leaving here with that cipher disk." His eyes fell on the pair of wooden disks Carmen was holding at her side. "The Secrets belong to Triedastron alone. And if you plan to be alive thirty seconds from now, you will surrender to us."

Yokaro and Mondalaus were slowly sidestepping around the outside of the flaming circle, their weapons pointed at the trapped Carmen and her Souls.

Carmen was thinking fast.... The ground around her and the others continued to smolder, and the fire was gradually inching inward. She had to come up with a way to escape the ring of fire before it consumed them....

"Carmen, I'm here!" an invisible Dagtar called out to her, from beyond Desorkhan and his followers. *"The Kelmarsians are trying to stop Keltan reinforcements from coming to the aid of those who were inside the fortress. Break away from the curse and run to me."*

The Invisible Shield! Carmen thought. She considered her plan for a minute...and then mentally asked Anubis to intercept her thoughts.

"Anubis, I'm going to cast Invisible Shield over all of us," she told him. *"Tell everyone to run the moment that it's conjured.... We're going to make a break for Dagtar. He's here, behind Desorkhan."*

There was a brief pause, during which Anubis passed Carmen's message on to the rest of her Souls.... When he was finished, Anubis nodded.

"It is done."

"Great."

Desorkhan was barely able to hide his impatience.

"As much as you're enjoying the conversation that you're having with yourself right now, I just can't help interrupting," he said callously.

Then he raised his wand.

"Farewell, Carmen Fox."

In a flash of silver, Desorkhan shouted, *"Toxulana!"*

"Invisible Shield!"

As the Dark Master's *Toxic Strike* curse materialized, Carmen used the Light Sword to cast a glowing, transparent sphere around her and her friends. Within only seconds, Stellar, Anubis, and Glamis broke free from the circle of fire, running through the flames and dashing past the trio of Magicon.

Carmen and Blaze charged out of the fire next. Carmen swung her sword at Desorkhan, the blade slicing through his smoky curse. Desorkhan Returned his wand and drew his sword. Blaze flew after Singe and took swipes at him with his claws.

Carmen attacked Desorkhan with a *Lightning Blade* spell as Blaze dueled with Singe. The Dark Master easily blocked Carmen's attack, laughing maliciously as his opponent continued on her offensive against him. Her magic just didn't seem to be as effective as it was in Kelmar....

"IS IT JUST ME, OR DO THE CURSES HERE SEEM TO HAVE MORE POWER?" Carmen shouted to Blaze over the noise of the battle, as she dueled with Desorkhan.

"DARK SPELL CASTERS POSSESS A MAJOR ADVANTAGE OVER LIGHT SPELL CASTERS IN KELTAN!" Blaze yelled back, shooting a lungful of fiery air in Singe's direction. "IN KELMARSIA, THE OPPOSITE IS TRUE. THE ENVIRONMENT FAVORS ITS INHABITANTS!"

Carmen glanced beyond Desorkhan to see Glamis, Stellar, and Anubis battling Mondalaus and Yokaro. She was relieved that Mondalaus's Partner was nowhere in sight at the moment. She knew that she and her Souls had to escape before Mondalaus summoned her.

Carmen ducked to avoid a powerful strike from Desorkhan's sword. Desorkhan was clearly enjoying the fact that his longtime opponent was struggling to keep up with him.

"You appear to have lost your touch, Guardian," Desorkhan said, taunting Carmen as he thwarted another one of her attacks. "Not so confident without all of your precious Souls of Destiny, are you?"

"What?"

Carmen glanced over Desorkhan's shoulder. Glamis and Anubis had disappeared somewhere. Stellar was running away from Mondalaus and Yokaro, who were firing nonstop curses at him.

"STELLAR!"

Stellar looked back over his shoulder and met Carmen's gaze as he continued to run.

"THROW THE CIPHER DISK TO ME!" he shouted to her, dodging the Dark spells flying through the air at him. "I'LL CATCH IT!"

Carmen shielded herself against another one of the Dark Master's attacks.

"You wouldn't *dare*," Desorkhan snarled, as their swords clashed violently in a shower of blue sparks. "I'll kill you faster than you can take a breath."

"THE KEINEN IS MINE!" Mondalaus shouted at Yokaro, firing a *Dark Wrath* curse after Stellar.

"It's like I'm reliving the same nightmare over and over again!" Carmen exclaimed, as she continued to fight off Desorkhan. *"Fires of the Sarcan!"*

The fiery Sarcan immediately burst from her sword and chased Desorkhan back, just as she wanted it to do. Utilizing the only free moments that she would have, Carmen slipped her saber back into its scabbard and called out to Stellar.

Stellar glanced over his shoulder at her before opening his mouth to shoot a blinding *Sun Ray* spell back at Mondalaus and Yokaro.

As his pursuers screamed in surprise at the approaching spell, the Keinen pulled to a stop, turning around and locking eyes with Carmen. The immense heat of the spell tore through the bodies of the temporarily blinded Magicon, and they collapsed to the ground thirty feet behind him.

"NOW!" Stellar shouted.

Carmen took the cipher disk with the claw mark in her right hand and held it to her opposite shoulder. As though it were a flying disk, she threw the magical object as hard as she could across the battlefield to him.

Stellar galloped toward the oncoming cipher disk, not taking his eyes off of the spinning object as he ran through the crowds of fighters. Carmen quietly prayed that he would get to it in time....

With a leap through the air, Stellar caught the wooden disk smoothly in his jaws. Carmen exhaled, but it was only seconds later that Desorkhan thrust his sword at her side. Carmen drew her sword and guarded against Desorkhan's strike all in one motion, but the force of impact when the two sabers crashed together made her stumble. She nearly lost her balance.

Blaze and Singe continued to fight in the sky overhead. Singe fired a bolt of lightning at Blaze, but Blaze was able to shield himself from it with his wings.

"Is that really your best effort, Blazey?" Singe asked sarcastically, as he evaded a blast of fire from his Sarcan opponent. "Is your Master's poor performance rubbing off on you?"

"Humor me and keep your mouth shut for a change," Blaze snapped, eluding Singe's own flames.

Trying to regain her breath, Carmen snuck a glance beyond Desorkhan.... Stellar had disappeared, but so had Mondalaus and Yokaro, at least for right now.

"This can go on for as *long* as you want, Fox," Desorkhan declared bitterly, spreading out his arms. "Though you do know that your pitiful attempts to resist us are only delaying the inevitable, do you not? There is no chance whatsoever that you and your Souls will depart from the World of Darkness alive."

As tired and weakened as she was, Carmen shook her head in defiance.

"Sorry, but I'm not going to make this easy for you," she said calmly. "I'm not giving in just yet."

Desorkhan threw back his sword to bring it down on her, but Carmen was faster.

"Tolth Lumicatia!"

In mere moments, the imposing shadow of storm clouds fell over the land...cloaking the two teams of combatants in darkness. Then a burst of lightning illuminated the clouds above Carmen.

She pointed her saber up into the air, gasping as she found herself staring up at Dagtar, who was invisible to all of the Magicon, flying above her. The *Swift Lightning* spell whizzed down from one of the clouds in a blaze of golden light and struck Carmen's sword.

"Grab my tail! We'll pull you up!" Dagtar called down to her.

Carmen dropped the imitation cipher disk and reached up to feel Dagtar's cool scales beneath her fingertips. Then she cut her lightning-imbued sword down through the air and pointed it at Desorkhan. The lightning raced on toward the Dark Master, who flung up his sword to block the attack.

"Flaming Shield!"

Leaving Singe lost in a cloud of smoke, Blaze flew back to Carmen. Carmen slid her saber back into its scabbard and reached up to grab on to Dagtar's tail with both hands. Aboard the back of the regal green Dragon were Inpu, Anubis, Glamis, and finally, Stellar, who held the real cipher disk securely in his mouth.

As the closest to Dagtar's tail, Stellar reached down to Carmen and helped her to climb up onto the Dragon's back.

After she and Blaze were both safely seated on Dagtar's saddle, the Dragon released a thundering roar, and became visible.

Desorkhan parted the flames that had shielded him from Carmen's attack. Staring savagely up at his adversaries soaring higher into the air, he cursed at them as they escaped yet again.

Carmen gazed down over the Dragon's flank at the ongoing battles of the Kelmarsians and Keltans.... She was sure that Triedastron was down there fighting somewhere, in the midst of all of the turmoil.

It appeared that the Kelmarsians were closing in on his fortress, but just what would come of this siege, and that which was planned for Merlin's castle, Carmen could no longer ponder. As Dagtar approached the southern entrance of Keltan and the golden Impassable Barrier dividing the spirit worlds, she felt her eyes drifting closed.... Her head felt heavier than it ever had.

"This is only the beginning, isn't it?" Blaze asked Anubis's father, as they crossed over into Kelmar.

"Yes, I'm afraid so," Inpu replied, his voice sounding distant. *"Our battle has just begun.... Yet with this victory, we draw one step closer to an ending that would bring peace."*

A bright, white light flooded Carmen's eyes, and she slipped from consciousness.

CHAPTER TWELVE
THUNDER ACADEMY

Carmen awoke some time later to the sight of the familiar stone walls of her bedroom in Thunder Academy. The space was wide and rectangular, decorated with royal blue trim around the walls.

A round, wooden table with matching chairs sat in the middle of the space, in the center of an ornate blue rug with gold fringe. The room held three beds: one sitting against a window at the back, and one more against each of the two side walls. There was also a wooden dresser in one corner of the room, and a tall grandfather clock in the opposite corner. A stone fireplace, which was used only in the winter, stood against the right-hand wall.

Carmen was lying in the softness of her bed at the rear of the room, beneath the sunlight pouring in through her window. Commander Haidar was looking over her, his deep brown eyes staring down with concern. Also watching her nervously were Blaze, Glamis, Stellar, and Anubis, who were standing on the other side of the bed.

"How are you feeling, Carmen?" Haidar asked.

Carmen blinked, trying to get used to the bright light, which had been nonexistent in Keltan. She was feeling genuinely well for the first time since traveling to the Kelmarian afterlife.... She sat up, causing her friends to jump.

"I'm…feeling really good," she said, with a small smile.

Upon seeing her reflection in the glass of the grandfather clock across the room, Carmen hastily tried to tame her messy hair, embarrassed to be looking so dreadful in front of her Commander.

"That's excellent to hear," Haidar replied, the light from the sun glittering off of the countless badges that adorned his scarlet and gold Kelmarian Army uniform. "We were all quite worried about you."

Haidar reached into his pocket. "I cured you of the effects of *this*."

Haidar opened his hand. He was holding a circular silver and gold charm on a gleaming chain. The charm had a golden triangle with a shining, round black opal in the center of it—the Seer's Amulet, belonging to Eli Elezar.

"The amulet was slowly poisoning you, and it eventually would have killed you had we not been so fortunate," Haidar told Carmen, who stared wide-eyed at the magical charm that she had worn around her neck for supposed protection from Dark elements in Keltan.

"We've been in touch with Inpu, and we think that Eli was unknowingly operating under the control of a sinister curse known as *Devious Manipulation* when he presented you with the amulet. The curse allows the spell caster to take control of one individual's thoughts and actions for a brief period of time."

Haidar slipped the glittering object back into his pocket.

"In his right mind, Eli would never have intentionally given you a poisoned amulet," he said. "He is well respected by many Kelmarian leaders, Inpu and I among them. The object that he gave you was likely tampered with by a Dark influencer...and Eli's behavior since the incident appears to have confirmed our suspicions. Once its effects wear off, the curse is known to cause the victim temporary mind impairment, and Eli has since developed amnesia and suffered some impermanent brain damage.... I am told that he is currently under the care of a Kelmarian Healer; in time, he will recover completely."

"But who cursed him?" Carmen asked, though she could think of quite a few people who would do most anything that it took to kill her.

"We don't know just yet," Haidar said. "Inpu is working to trace the amulet's path to you as we speak, and I presume that if and when he discovers its origins, he will send word to us. Based purely on the potency of the poison though, I can tell you that whoever it was, was trying to take your life, and quickly…. If Anubis and Blaze had not healed you in Keltan, you likely wouldn't have made it back to us."

Carmen closed her eyes and groaned, pressing her fingers to her forehead. At one time, she and her friends had thought that the days of having to fret about being attacked by an entire army of relentless enemies had passed. Evidently, those days were still very much upon them.

"How did we get here?" Carmen asked Haidar, even though it was likely irrelevant at this point. "Our bodies were back in the Camersleys' shop in Brandec."

"Your grandfather and I brought you and your friends' bodies back here once we heard from Inpu of the siege in Keltan," Haidar explained. "We knew that it would be far safer for you to come straight here than to have to journey all the way from Brandec, especially after everything that you had been through in the World of Darkness. So when you got back from the afterlife, Inpu returned your spirits to your bodies. Blaine and I fetched your possessions for you as well," he said, motioning toward Carmen's canvas backpack, which was sitting in the corner of the room.

"Thank you…." Carmen said quietly. "Is my grandfather okay?"

Haidar sighed.

"He was deeply concerned for you, as you could imagine that he would be for his only granddaughter," he replied. "But he was assured that he would be leaving you in good hands.

Even so, I think that it would be a fine idea to write to him and let him know that you're sound, once things settle down. He's currently staying with Renalda's parents. Your home in Mortrock Forest was damaged in the storms, and until he finishes the repairs, he cannot move back in."

Carmen nodded.

"I'll write to him," she promised. "And how is Renalda doing?"

Haidar clapped Carmen on the shoulder.

"Renalda is living back on Amera Island for right now, until the storms die down," he said. "I advised her to go back, because the storms never seem to get as intense there as they do on the mainland. But in the meantime, you should continue to rest. Monday is the first day of training for Sarcan Captains and Cadets. And on top of this, you and your friends now have the difficult task of finding and deciphering the Secrets of Kelmar before it's too late to rescue the World of Light. The Captains will train during the week, and have the weekends to themselves. We will meet each day at dawn out on the grounds of Sarcanian Valley for Advanced Training."

Haidar paused, gazing out through the window before speaking again.

"I don't think that any of us imagined, even just weeks ago…that we in the valley would be training to save ourselves from succumbing to a new evil…one that knows no limits."

Haidar bid Carmen and her Souls goodbye a little while later. Carmen got up to stretch and have a bite to eat. A hearty lunch of oatmeal, vegetables, juice, and bread had been delivered while she was asleep, and sat waiting for her on the round table. As Carmen ate, Blaze and the others, who had eaten while Carmen rested, filled her in on what they had learned from Inpu.

"When Lucia, Triedastron's Chimera, alerted him that we were inside his fortress, Dagtar communicated back to Kelmarsia that reinforcements were needed to help us escape with the real cipher disk," Blaze said, watching as Carmen finished her meal. "Merlin took the request one step further by requesting that his Kelmarsians attempt an all-out siege of the Fortress of Darkness. The Kelmarsian fighters arrived quickly, and they worked to isolate the fortress from outside help.... The Kelmarsian forces were instructed to surround the fortress and attack when necessary to reduce the Keltans' resistance."

"Wow, they did all of that?" Carmen asked, before swallowing a mouthful of warm oatmeal. "And what's happened since we left?"

"Inpu said that the Kelmarsians eventually retreated back to the World of Light, but they had accomplished their primary goals of weakening the Keltan front and allowing us to safely escape," Blaze explained. "But as Kelmari told us, the fighting in the afterworlds resumes most every night. Until we locate the Secrets of Kelmar and decipher them, it will continue without end."

Carmen swallowed the last of her food.

"I need to take a look at the cipher disk," she said, putting down her spoon.

"I'll get it." Stellar jumped down off of his chair and made his way over to Carmen's bed, reaching under it to retrieve the wooden disk. Grabbing it in his jaws, he walked it back to his friend.

"That was a great catch back there, by the way," Carmen said, smiling as she took the cipher disk from Stellar's mouth and placed it up on the table.

"It wasn't a bad toss either," Stellar replied, grinning.

"Okay, let's see what we have here...." Carmen ran her fingers over the grooves and markings on the etched surface. "Some of these symbols along the edge of the disk look like those of the Kelmarian Elements if you squint your eyes a little...."

Carmen reached into her pocket and pulled out the scrap of parchment that Merlin had given her back in his castle. It had so far served her very well in providing a map that successfully led her to Triedastron's study, where the genuine cipher disk had been hidden. When she wasn't using it, Carmen would keep this essential document tucked securely in the pocket of her robes so that it never left her possession. She unrolled the small piece of parchment, expecting it to contain the map of Triedastron's fortress, but instead, Carmen found herself staring at a blank piece of paper.

"What's wrong, Carmen?" Blaze asked. There was instant unrest in his eyes. "What does it say?"

"There's nothing here," she said, looking up at him. "The paper's blank."

"Blank?" Blaze's brow wrinkled. He flew over Carmen's shoulder to get a look at the parchment. "Check the other side," he suggested.

Carmen flipped over the parchment. Here was a new map drawn with black ink. It was not a single map, but rather, three smaller maps, separated by vertical black lines that ran down the sides of each one. The maps contained beautiful drawings of towns, mountains, bodies of water, and forests.

"I don't understand...." Carmen said slowly. "How do we know which one of these we're supposed to use?"

"Perhaps all three," Blaze reasoned. "Maybe you could ask Dagtar. Remember, you can communicate with him through his claw."

"That's an idea," Carmen said, nodding her head.

She reached up and touched Dagtar's claw on the gold chain around her neck.... She had never called out to him directly this way, but she could see no harm in trying.

Carmen closed her eyes…and tried to clear her thoughts before reaching out to him.

"Dagtar, can you hear me? Are you able to talk?"

There was silence for thirty seconds…and then,

"Yes, Carmen. I am here."

Carmen smiled at hearing Dagtar's calm and ageless voice in her head. The claw was pleasantly warm beneath her fingers.

"Are you okay?" she asked. *"I didn't know what happened after we left Keltan."*

"Everyone is fine," Dagtar assured her. *"We Kelmarsians have returned to the World of Light for right now, but we are happy to have assisted you in your mission."*

"Thank you," Carmen said. Then she hesitated for a moment.

"I…I need your help again," she admitted. *"I just looked at the parchment that Merlin gave me, and—"*

"It has three maps," Dagtar finished.

"How did you know?"

"Merlin showed it to me once. I promised him that if asked, I would explain it only to you," Dagtar said gently. *"Each of the three maps represents one realm of the Worlds Triad. Hence, the one in the center is of Kelmar, to the left of that is Kelmarsia, and the one to the right is Keltan. There are three Secrets of Kelmar— one found in each of the three magical worlds. Together, the deciphered Secrets will grant you the power to restore harmony to the realms of Light and Dark. In order to find them, you and the others must travel through the three worlds and discover the ciphertext Secret belonging to each. You will use the maps to help you find your way, and then decipher the Secrets into plaintext using the cipher disk."*

Carmen took a couple of minutes to formulate a response that didn't sound nearly as overwhelmed as she now felt.

"I understand. I will do as you say…and hopefully I'll succeed…. Will you be able to come with us?"

"In Kelmar, I shall be with you in spirit, as I've always been," Dagtar vowed. *"In Kelmarsia and Keltan, I will be able to join you in body."*

Dagtar paused. *"I am unable to speak with you much longer, as my Master has summoned me to his quarters. But before I go, I wish to offer you the following advice: Begin your search with the Secret in Kelmar. After you find it, ask Anubis to summon Inpu here to help you travel to the other two realms."*

"I will," Carmen pledged. *"Thank you for your help. Good luck."*

"It is always my pleasure, Guardian," Dagtar said warmly, his voice becoming more distant. *"Fear not the challenges that lie ahead of you, for you are more ready than you know."*

With that, Dagtar's claw became cold again, and Carmen opened her eyes to her other Souls of Destiny.

"So what did he say?" Anubis inquired.

"He said that the maps are our guides to finding three Secrets of Kelmar," she told him and the rest of her friends. "There's one located here, one in Keltan, and one in Kelmarsia. Once we acquire each of them, we have to decipher them."

"Well, that's fairly clear-cut," Glamis said, sitting back in his chair. "We can certainly handle that."

Stellar sighed. "Somehow I have a feeling that it's not going to be that easy."

"What would make you think that?" Blaze quipped. "Haven't these sorts of things always been simple for us?"

Carmen grinned.

"If only, Blaze. If only."

The five friends slept well each night leading up to Monday, when Carmen and Blaze rose well before the sun to get ready for their first class in Advanced Master and Sarcan Training with Commander Haidar.

After she got up, Carmen dug through her backpack to retrieve her blue and gold training uniform only to find that a new patch had been sewn onto the upper arm of the right sleeve. The patch was that of a Sarcan-winged saber sitting just above the words, *Sarcan Captain*. The other sleeve was embroidered with a single Sarcan wing patch.

Also decorating the royal blue jumpsuit, which had gold padding at the knees and elbows, was a small, golden lightning bolt stitched into the chest. The final item decorating the uniform was the Silver Medal of Honor for Bravery, which had been awarded to Carmen for her efforts in the final battle in the Magicon War.

Blaze waited patiently as Carmen finished eating breakfast, and then the two of them left the castle for the grounds of Sarcanian Valley. It had been months since Carmen had walked through the arched stone corridors of Thunder Academy. Being back here now after the summer made her better appreciate the striking medieval architecture and the beauty of the sun showing through the tall windows and reflecting off of the suits of armor that lined the halls like polished, stationary guards.

Carmen and Blaze walked down the central corridor, which was lined with stone statues of Masters and Sarcans and lit with thousands of lighted crystals installed in the high ceiling. Soon, they reached the school's pair of wooden entry doors. They walked outside and looked out at the darkened grounds of Sarcanian Valley.

Because it was not yet sunrise, the stunning red sandstone that comprised the mountainous valley could not be seen in its full glory. Come dawn though, the valley's sweeping rock formations would transform into a breathtaking view of nature's splendor.

Sarcanian Valley was a huge gorge encircled by the Barahir Mountains and Mortrock Forest, in the heart of North

Kelmar. A long, winding river known as the Eldron Canal sliced across the basin and through an arched tunnel at the back of the valley. A massive stone sculpture of a Sarcan sentinel stood at either side of the tall archway. Thunder Academy, the ancient school that housed both the Sarcan Council and the Sarcan Masters and their Partners, was a great stone castle with many towers and spires, whose roof was crowned by a giant gold lightning bolt. It was built into the mountain high above the archway of the canal.

The castle overlooked the whole of Sarcanian Valley, and had a tall staircase that led up to it. In the valley below the castle, there were six giant rectangles painted with white paint and spaced equally apart on the red stone ground. These were the dueling fields that Sarcan students and castle visitors used for outdoor classes and practice.

Near the front of the valley was the grand Thunder Stadium, which held quite a few levels of tiered seating and enclosed a central rectangular field where Masters would duel each other. And just beyond the borders of the valley off to the west was a vast, circular canyon with high cliffs known as Thunder Canyon. Its red sandstone walls were lined with the same Sarcan sentinel figures that stood at the tunnel of the Eldron Canal.

Most of Carmen and Blaze's twenty-two classmates were standing out on the dueling fields in the center of the valley. The sorcerers were all dressed in identical blue and gold training uniforms. At the present, they and their Sarcans were busy getting reacquainted with one another.

With a cautiously optimistic attitude for the coming months, Carmen and Blaze marched down the tall staircase of Thunder Academy to join them. It was a mildly cool morning, with a light breeze and some passing clouds that drifted over the valley. Carmen breathed in the wonderful smelling air, which always carried the pure scent of the neighboring mountains and forests.

She and Blaze met their peers with hugs and warm greetings. They found most of the students to be in high spirits…yet there remained a shared sense of unease concerning the matter of Kelmar's instability. Kamie pulled Carmen aside from the rest of the group.

"What are your thoughts on what's happening?" she asked, in a voice hardly above a whisper. "Do you know anything about all of these mysterious things that have been going on? I got a letter from my aunt the other day saying there was a blizzard in South Kelmar…. And that's just the start of it."

"I know. I've seen some pretty disturbing stuff myself," Carmen replied, thinking how Kamie couldn't know the half of it. "I'll let Haidar fill you in on what we know so far. I'm sure he'll explain it better than I could."

"Do you think he'll really tell us?"

"Certainly he will," Carmen said, without a moment of hesitation. "He's our Commander. Why wouldn't he?"

"Well…from what I've heard, Parliament is trying to keep some things under wraps," Kamie said, folding her arms across her chest. Her long brown bangs were falling down into her green eyes. She glanced to her right, where Draven Kalvaro was standing, before lowering her voice even more.

"There are rumors about upheaval among the Members," she whispered. "Supposedly, Draven's father is vying for Danuvius Dorvai's job as Head of State." Her eyes flashed to their classmate, who was standing just out of earshot. "Dorvai's up for reelection next year, and Maidak is trying to get himself into office without even an election."

"He couldn't get away with that," Carmen said, frowning. "The other Members wouldn't let such a thing happen."

"I hope you're right," Kamie muttered, with a shrug. "We have enough problems around here as it is."

Kamie turned at the sound of her classmate, Jayden Maewin, calling her over from several yards away.

"Kamie, wait." Carmen reached out for her arm before she could leave. "Where did you hear those things about Kalvaro?"

"Oh…it was in *The Kelmarian Review,*" Kamie replied. "Everyone's talking about it…. If you want to read it, you can send in a request to have the paper delivered to you here in the valley."

"Okay, thanks. I'll look into that," Carmen said.

As Kamie walked away, Carmen gazed over at Draven.

His hands in his pockets and his back to the others, he appeared unusually subdued. The tall, brown-haired, fair-skinned boy with dark brown eyes was looking out in the direction of Thunder Canyon, where the new class of Sarcan Cadets was currently assembling. Carmen wondered what he could be thinking about, but thought better of approaching him.

Blaze was busy catching up with the other Sarcans when Carmen noticed Shea Garnett, Naomi Yao, and Akira Melkor talking together in the corner of one of the dueling fields.

Carmen made her way over to them, a grin breaking across her face as she got reacquainted with her friends. Though she had seen all of them at Renalda and Reoc's recent wedding, it seemed like much longer after everything that had happened since. They'd had no idea then that that joyous night would usher in the start of a new chapter in Kelmarian history.

"How are you and Blaze doing?" Shea asked Carmen. "Everyone's a bit on edge these days."

"Tell me about it. We're doing very well though, thanks." Carmen smiled. "And you and Gia?"

"Oh, we're both just super," he replied, his friendly blue eyes twinkling.

"That's good to hear."

It was then that Carmen noticed something different about her classmate. She remembered Shea being slightly shorter than she was last year, but over the summer, he had grown taller, as he now stood at her height.

Akira pushed a few strands of her dark brown hair behind her ear. A petite girl with a gentle face and large brown eyes, she was one of Carmen's closest friends in Sarcanian Valley.

"I'm looking forward to this class," Akira said cheerfully. "I was so thrilled when I got the letter from Haidar about the Advanced Training.... I wonder what kinds of things he'll be teaching us this year."

"Me, too," Naomi chimed in. "These must be some really important lessons!"

Naomi was a quiet girl with soft brown eyes and a polite manner about her. Her Sarcan, Tyr, was one of those talking with Blaze.

"Let's hope that it's nothing that involves climbing," Shea said warily.

They all laughed at that comment, remembering quite well what it had been like scaling the wall of Thunder Canyon each day with Haidar and their fellow Cadets. During their first attempt at it last year, Carmen and Blaze had helped Shea to overcome his fear of heights, and gotten him to climb the wall with the others. In turn, Shea had saved Carmen from falling off of the wall when she slipped on that first trip up. Those long and painful days were ones that all of them were more than glad to have behind them.

A pair at a time, the remaining Sarcan Captains arrived. Carmen and her peers watched the rest of their classmates walk down from the castle, and chatted with one another as they waited for Haidar to come meet the class.

With a couple of minutes to dawn, the castle doors opened once more. As all of the Captains had already arrived at the dueling fields by this time, everyone expected to see Commander Haidar emerge from within the school. But it was not the wise leader who stepped outside into the valley. Instead, it was an unfamiliar boy dressed in a Sarcan Captain's uniform.

Carmen and the rest of the class stared at the boy, who was tall and had black hair. As he walked down the front steps, his dark brown eyes were focused straight ahead of him. He appeared to be their age, yet none of them had ever seen him before now.

The boy had a pale complexion, a sharp nose, and a lean build. His facial features looked oddly familiar to Carmen, and she couldn't help staring as he drew nearer to them. She thought hard to remember the person whom he resembled.... When he got to within a few feet of her and the others, she noticed that his nails were yellowed.

No one seemed to know quite what to make of the newcomer, who had no Sarcan with him. He seemed different somehow...almost otherworldly. He said nothing to any of the other Captains, and when he approached, the group almost seemed to take a collective step back from him. The conversations had hushed, and all eyes were on the outsider as he swept over to where Carmen and Blaze stood between Shea and Akira.

The corners of his mouth curled into a slight smile as he stared at Carmen.... It was hard for her to continue looking at him. There was a coldness in his dark eyes that made her very uncomfortable. Though he was smiling, just barely, he looked more like he wanted to destroy something.

"Hello, Carmen," the boy said, in a silky, somewhat inhuman voice. "It's nice to see you again."

Carmen bit her lip, unsure of how to respond. She didn't know this boy, and though he looked vaguely familiar, she was certain that she had never met him before now.

"Blaze." The boy nodded his head to Carmen's Sarcan, who was sitting on her shoulder. "What a pleasure it is to see you, too."

Blaze said nothing. He stared at the boy with distrust.

"Why, don't you remember me?" the boy asked calmly. "I certainly remember *you*."

The tense silence that followed that strange remark was broken when a horn sounded somewhere off toward the castle. Everyone's attention shifted to the northern end of the valley.

Commander Reoc Haidar was standing on the arched rooftop of Thunder Academy, beneath the grand golden lightning bolt that crowned the school. How long he had been there, none of them knew, but he was watching his new class of Sarcan Captains with the intensity of a hawk looking over its young. He was wearing his scarlet and gold Kelmarian Army uniform, which always immediately afforded him respect from others. It also symbolized his strength and courage.

Haidar spread his wings and flew down to the valley, a graceful dive and descent that took only moments. When he touched down at the edge of one of the nearest dueling fields, about ten feet away from his students, he ordered them to line up side-by-side in a horizontal line at the center of the painted white line drawn across the field.

The twelve pairs of Sarcan Masters and Sarcans and the new boy all did as they were told and marched toward him. Carmen was able to slip a few people away from the new arrival as she and her classmates assembled into formation.

Just as they had been trained to do, they stood at attention and waited quietly for instruction. Haidar bowed to his students, who then bowed back respectfully.

Commander Haidar observed his students closely. Carmen tried to catch his eye and direct his attention to the odd student standing amongst them, though he was eventually bound to notice him himself. Gazing down the line, Haidar finally met Carmen's gaze for only a brief moment.

He nodded to her, but so subtly that it could have easily been mistaken for an involuntary twitch. Carmen knew that this meant that the stranger's presence was not unexpected to him, so she tried to quiet her unsettling thoughts as her instructor began to speak.

"Welcome back to Thunder Academy, Sarcan Captains," Haidar said. "As you've probably noticed, we have a new face here with us today." He motioned toward the additional boy. "This is Natlek Foretsam. He is the nephew of Remnor Foretsam, a Senior Kelmarian Parliament Member. Natlek is not a Sarcan Master, but he longs to learn the ways of the esteemed Sarcans and Masters of Thunder Academy. He fought in the Magicon War, and has been given special permission by the Sarcan Council to join us in our training for a few weeks. So, I ask all of you to make him feel welcome during his time here."

Some of the Captains exchanged wary expressions. Haidar kept his attention focused on the entire group.

"You are all here because you have successfully completed Basic Master and Sarcan Training, and served Kelmar with honor and grace in the Magicon War as Sarcan Cadets," he said proudly. "You stand before me now as deserving Sarcan Captains, and today marks the beginning of your course in Advanced Training. I look forward to being your instructor once again, and to watching your growth and helping you to reach your newfound potential."

Haidar placed his hand on the center of his chest.

"I believe that there is a light that shines within each of us," he began. "With guidance and care, that light can grow brighter and stronger to lead the way for others. But if that light is not fostered, it can fade...and eventually extinguish. Do not allow your flame to expire. Instead, from this point forward, you must release yourself from the binds of insecurities that hold you back.... Only when you believe in yourself and what you do will your light be free to shine as a symbol of hope in these hours of darkness."

Commander Haidar began to walk slowly past the row of Captains, his hands folded behind his back as he talked.

"I know that many of you are understandably disturbed by the dark activity that has been taking place in our world lately," he said, in a clear voice. "You're wondering what's happening, and why.... And you have the right to know."

Haidar paused to make eye contact with all of his students before continuing.

"The Kelmarian Parliament does not wish for you to be aware of what I am about to tell you, but as your instructor and your Commander, I will not keep secrets from you to appease others," he declared. "The abnormal weather patterns and the attacks that Kelmar has been experiencing are not by men or creatures of this world; they are the work of a much more sinister kind.... I speak of course of the inhabitants of Keltan—the World of Darkness."

Several gasps broke out amongst the class of Captains.

"After the Magicon War, the afterworld of Keltan saw an abundance of new members come its way—members of number and strength that outmatched those who currently live in Kelmarsia, thus causing the shift in the balance of power between the Worlds of Light and Darkness," Haidar said. "Triedastron, the leader of Keltan, together with the Dark Master, has plotted to capture Kelmarsia and turn it into a second World of Darkness that he alone would command. Until the situation in the afterlife stabilizes, the storms that we feel down here as the product of the enduring battles between the two spirit worlds will continue, and have the strength to destroy Kelmar if the fighting intensifies to a severe level.... So should Keltan acquire the knowledge and the means to defeat Kelmarsia...we in Kelmar will lose everything."

An uneasy silence followed Haidar's last statement. Carmen knew that her classmates were surely as shocked as she had been when first learning of what was happening in the Worlds Triad.

"As for the attacks on innocent Kelmarians that you've heard about," Haidar said, finally breaking the silence, "Triedastron has sent an army of his Phantom Warriors into Kelmar in search of new fighters to grow his military even larger, so that he may complete his takeover of Kelmarsia. The Phantoms are the spirits of deceased Dark sorcerers and creatures who travel from the afterlife into our world to spread destruction and capture humans and creatures for Triedastron's cause."

Shea flinched.

"Fortunately though, we have been able to defeat the Phantoms who have gotten through the Impassable Barrier, which divides the worlds of the afterlife from Kelmar. Parliament has also just instituted a new Protective spell at the barrier to safeguard us from future attacks," Haidar said, much to the relief of his students. "The Protection is being closely monitored, so should the Phantoms find a way around it, we can work quickly to head them off before they get far into Kelmar."

A sharp breeze rippled across Sarcanian Valley as Haidar spoke.... Carmen noticed Natlek clench his fist, and then release it again. He was staring straight ahead of him.

There was an air about Natlek that gave Carmen chills. She was sure that she couldn't be the only one who sensed it.

"I do not tell you these things to frighten you into pursuing your training further," Haidar assured his students, breaking Carmen's train of thought. "I keep you informed for your own safety and well-being.... You are still young, but this does not mean that you should be shielded from the truth."

Haidar paused, his expression softening somewhat.

"Rest assured, Captains, that our crisis is not without hope," he said, in a more optimistic tone. "Your classmate, Carmen Fox, has traveled to Keltan with her Souls of Destiny, and recovered the object central to Kelmarsia's victory...the cipher disk that will help them to decipher the Secrets of Kelmar."

Again, there was a brief silence.

"What are the Secrets of Kelmar?" Akira asked, speaking for nearly the entire class.

"According to the portent, and those in Kelmarsia, the Secrets are the three keys to restoring the balance between Light and Darkness that keeps the spirit worlds at peace," Haidar patiently explained. "In order to carry out the Secrets' solution, Carmen and Blaze have the grueling chore ahead of them of locating the Secrets, and then deciphering them using an enchanted cipher disk belonging to Merlin Cloud. They were chosen for this endeavor by Merlin himself...but they will not be alone in their quest to save Kelmar."

Haidar looked down toward Carmen and Blaze, his gaze confident and reassuring.

"We will stand by you, and do everything in our power to help you," he promised. "We are a Unit, first and foremost."

Grateful, Carmen bowed. Commander Haidar then turned toward Thunder Academy.

"Yesterday, I met with the Sarcan Council concerning the matters that I just spoke about, and how they will affect our training. There were concerns that perhaps it has become too dangerous to train the advanced students," he revealed, to the surprise of many of them. "But following much thought and consideration...we unanimously decided to move ahead with our plans to offer Advanced Training to our newest class of Captains."

Haidar removed the curled tooth that hung on a golden chain around his neck. Placing the tooth in his palm, he summoned his wand—a tall, braided bronze and golden staff crowned with his lightning-infused magic circle.

"With our current trials taken into account, we have adapted our Advanced Training program to meet the present-day needs of Masters and Sarcans," Haidar said, standing with his wand at his side. "In this class, you will be learning advanced Kelmarian magic, as well as Kelmarsian magic. You will also learn how to defend yourself against Keltan curses…. I ask all of the Masters to now summon their wands."

Commander Haidar's students complied with his order. One at a time, the sorcerers' wands appeared in their hands.

After summoning her own wand, Carmen snuck a quick look at Natlek to see him holding a deep golden staff crowned with a magic circle containing symbols of mountains and fire.

"All sorcerers and creatures with ancestors living in Kelmarsia are able to cast selected Kelmarsian spells here in Kelmar and in the World of Light," Haidar explained. "The use of Kelmarsian magic will be central to our efforts against the Keltans, as it is more powerful than Kelmarian magic when executed in either of the two spirit realms."

Amaris Fletcher raised his hand. He was a tan young man with olive-colored eyes and a long nose. He was one of Draven's friends.

"Yes, Master Fletcher?" Haidar asked.

"Does this mean we'll be doing battle in the afterworlds?" he inquired. "I thought that only spirits of the deceased could do that."

"There are ways for living beings to exist for brief periods of time in the afterworlds," Haidar answered. "It *has* been done before…and should the need arise for the undertaking, we will take the necessary steps to make the voyage to the afterlife at that time. Is it dangerous? Yes. But as of right now, I see no other option," he said frankly. "Regardless of whether we like the idea, at some point, we *will* be fighting in Kelmarsia and Keltan."

There were no other questions as of that moment, so Commander Haidar continued on with the day's lesson.

"Kelmarsian spells are typically more complicated to cast, and require more magical energy here than they do if they are cast in one of the two spirit worlds," Haidar said. "But with practice, you'll get as accustomed to using *them* as you are of using Kelmarian spells."

The Sarcan Commander extended his wand arm out to the side of his body as far as he could, holding his staff upright.

Haidar then closed his eyes and abruptly threw his wand sideways over his head.

"Eternal Gates!"

Haidar's wand slowed down in midair…and a pair of white, ghostly wrought iron gates materialized from the arc of the wand's path. The elaborate and vaporous gateway promptly grew taller and wider to shield Haidar from any potential attack. The Sarcan Commander caught the wand in his other hand.

The Captains watched, slack-jawed, as Haidar tapped the gates with his staff, allowing them to swing open. He stepped out through the gates and used his wand to wave them away.

"That was a basic Kelmarsian Protective spell," Haidar said. *"Eternal Gates* will guard against physical attacks and most Keltan curses. It is one of the most effective and useful defenses to have in your arsenal."

Commander Haidar tapped the base of his wand to the ground three times. A five-foot by five-foot square carved itself in the rock at his feet.

A wooden box slowly rose up from the center of the square. The box was filled to the top with leather and steel helmets sized for humans and Sarcans.

"Now it's your turn to try," Haidar announced, as he reached into the box and proceeded to hand out a helmet to each Master and Sarcan. "I will walk you through it step-by-step," he promised. "I have no doubt that you will all have this spell mastered before we break for lunch."

The strong leather helmets featured steel plating and a locking chinstrap. Carmen and the others nervously strapped on their helmets as they received them, and then spread out across the dueling fields at Haidar's request.

The teams of Captains gave each other plenty of space, positioning themselves a safe distance away from one another and so that they could all see Haidar, who was now standing in the center of the dueling fields.

"So, the first step in casting *Eternal Gates* is for each of the Masters to extend their wand arm parallel to the side of his or her body as far as they can. Sarcans, each of you must remain flying just above your Master's opposite shoulder," Haidar advised, raising his voice so that every student could hear.

After everyone was in position, Haidar continued with the second stage.

"Next, Masters and Sarcans, you must close your eyes and visualize a set of perfectly white wrought iron gates.... Wait to see the gateway in your mind before you make your next move."

Carmen closed her eyes and tried to envision a set of gates similar to those that she had seen Haidar conjure. She breathed in deeply, and then exhaled—in an attempt to release herself from further thought.

"When the Master and Sarcan are both confident of their visualization, the Master will hold his or her wand at its center before pitching it in a parallel motion over their head," Haidar instructed. "The helmets are to protect you from potential injury. It often takes a few tries to get the throw just right."

Carmen's vision of the flawless white gates momentarily changed into the thought of her throwing the metal wand and it dropping down onto her head.

"As soon as your wand escapes your grasp, you must order the incantation, *Eternal Gates,*" Haidar said. "You may then open your eyes.... If you cast the spell correctly, your wand will expel the gates, which will afford you protection from attack. Your staff will come down more slowly to permit you to catch it with your non-dominant hand."

Haidar allowed all of the students the time to take in all of his instructions and to voice any concerns. In less than ten minutes, he granted the signal to start.

"If there are no more questions, please begin."

Carmen kept her eyes closed as she thought hard to imagine the sight of the beautiful white gateway.

"Take your time, Carmen," Blaze said. "Don't rush, or we may have to be *carried* back up to the castle."

Carmen laughed. Blaze's comment served its purpose of actually making her relax a little. She held her wand at its center, and waited.

"Can you see the gates?" she asked her Sarcan.

"Yes...I see them," Blaze replied.

When the image of the gateway was seared into her own mind, Carmen gave her wand an upward and sideways toss.

"Eternal Gates!" she shouted.

Carmen and Blaze both held their breath as the golden staff soared over Carmen's head. When they opened their eyes, the wand was slowing down in mid-flight.

A surge of misty white light broke free from the crown of Carmen's wand and transformed into a set of grand, pearl-colored gates.

At that same moment, a cascade of white light shot from Blaze's horn, wrapping itself around the outer edges of the gate in front of them. The light quickly expanded into a glittery fence that wrapped itself around Carmen and Blaze on all sides as an extra layer of protection.

Carmen caught her wand in her left hand and sighed with relief. A huge smile lit up her face as she turned to Blaze.

"That wasn't too stressful, right?" she asked.

"Not at all," Blaze said, also looking relieved. "The helmets certainly helped though."

Curious, Carmen peeked over the top of the magical fence that surrounded her and Blaze to see how their classmates were doing. From the looks of things, not all of them were managing nearly as well as they were.

Shea and his Sarcan, Gia, were running out of the way of Shea's wayward wand, which was about to drop down on them. Arianna Quagel, a fair girl with black hair and blue eyes, had removed her helmet to check for a dent after her wand had fallen during her execution of the spell. Naomi failed to catch her wand on its way down, and this caused her gateway to disappear. She had to pick up the staff and try again.

Most of the other Masters and Sarcans were in similar states of confusion. Not counting Carmen and Blaze, only Draven and Flint, and Jayden Maewin and Rose had been able to execute the spell correctly on the first try.

Carmen looked around for Natlek, and it didn't take her long to spot him. He was standing at the end of the dueling field straight ahead of her, staring at both her and Blaze. He had not cast the *Eternal Gates* spell; still holding his wand, the twisted smile on his face seemed to suggest that he had more sinister intentions.

"Why is he looking at us like that?" Carmen muttered to Blaze, not taking her eyes off of Natlek.

"I haven't got a clue," Blaze admitted, staring back at the boy. "But I *will* find out. I don't know who he is…but I sense a dark aura coming from him. It feels like he's trying to conceal it, but it's definitely there."

"Yeah, I get that same feeling," Carmen said, still looking at him.

She was thankful when Haidar came over to inspect her and Blaze's work and take her mind off of the unwanted visitor. The Sarcan Commander was more than pleased with their spell's implementation, and so he asked the two of them to walk out from behind the gates as he had done earlier.

Carmen rapped lightly on the gates with her wand, causing them to swing open.

After she and Blaze walked out, she waved her wand and dissolved the gateway into a misty white fog that gradually vanished.

"Fantastic work, both of you," Haidar said. "Needless to say, I would expect no less."

"Thank you," Carmen said, somewhat absentmindedly. She had to put a great deal of effort into shaking off the uncomfortable feeling generated by Natlek's constant presence.

Haidar left shortly after that to check on the progress of the other students, and Carmen and Blaze could choose to continue practicing or go help some of their classmates. The instructor might have said something to that effect to Carmen, but she was too distracted with her own thoughts to hear him. So when Blaze asked her if she wanted to go help Akira and her Sarcan, Keko, it took her a moment to think of what they could possibly want help with.

"Sorry…I'm kind of off today," Carmen murmured, as she and Blaze walked over to Akira's dueling field.

"I can't imagine why," Blaze said sarcastically, shooting a sideways glance at Natlek. "But no need to worry. We'll figure him out soon enough."

Akira and Keko were in the midst of casting *Eternal Gates* when their friends approached them. Carmen watched as Akira's wand soared over her head.

The pale pink staff, which was decorated with cascading gold chains, reached the peak of its flight, and Akira waited for the light of the spell to escape from the crowning pair of wings and turn into a set of gates.

But the light did not appear. Akira's eyes were suddenly wide with her fear of the wand falling. Carmen felt that now was the time to help.

"Focus, Akira, focus!" She shouted encouragement from across the way. "Don't lose the image of the gates!"

A split second later, Akira's wand began to tremble over her head. Knowing that they had not a moment to spare, Carmen and Blaze raced across the field to stand behind their classmates.

Then, without much thought to it, Carmen dropped her wand and laid her hands atop Akira's shoulders. Blaze did the same with Keko.

Carmen and Blaze stared intensely up at Akira's staff—blocking out all other thoughts to see only a set of the iron gates in their minds.

The wand stopped shaking at once—and then blinding white light burst from both the crown and Keko's horn. A magical breeze blew back against the students' faces. The spell's light swelled, and began to transfigure into an enormous set of white *Eternal Gates*. Carmen and Blaze grinned as the glowing gateway and accompanying wrought iron fence came into being around them.

The winds slowly subsided, and the four Captains found themselves effectively guarded all around by the stunning Protective spell. Akira caught her wand and turned to Carmen, her face aglow with both the surrounding light and the release of the tension that she had been feeling before her friends stepped in.

"How did you do that?" Akira asked, breathless.

"Uh…I don't know, actually," Carmen confessed, smiling as she shrugged her shoulders. "I just wanted to help you. Luckily, it worked out."

They heard clapping coming from no more than thirty feet away. Haidar was walking slowly toward them, a satisfied smile on his face. Carmen's classmates, Max Wychnor and Kai, Neal Oskavar and Vix, and Luke Harren and Zay were all walking alongside him. The rest of the Captains soon joined them.

Akira and her friends emerged from behind the gateway to the sight of their classmates and their Commander. The gates disappeared behind them in a gust of white smoke.

"Well done!" Haidar said, still applauding. "What a great team effort!"

"Can you explain exactly what we did?" Carmen asked, as he approached. "Because I'm not even really sure myself…."

Haidar laughed, turning to look briefly back at his other students as they gathered around Carmen, Akira, and their Sarcans.

"Captains, what Carmen and Blaze just did is called an Energy Transfer," the Sarcan Commander said. "It is a way to reassign power and concentration from one magical being to another. The technique doesn't require an incantation, or even a wand. It is merely a way to assist another human or creature in need…. There's no formal way that it has to be carried out, but the energy is always transferred through the hands of the person or creature providing the aid. One just has to possess the desire and strength to perform the spell."

"I read about it in a book late last term," Carmen said, remembering back. "But I never tried it before now."

"Well, the intent and proper application were there, so we come out of this in a positive way," Haidar said. "I think Master Melkor and Keko would agree."

Then he looked over the rest of the class.

"An act such as that is something that I will expect from each and every one of you, should the time come," Haidar declared, his tone more solemn. "Unconditional collaboration is how we succeed as a Unit, and as living beings. Should we ever fail to remember that…we may never get the chance to forget again."

Carmen and her classmates continued to practice *Eternal Gates* for a little while before Haidar taught them a few more Kelmarsian spells. Aside from some infrequent stumbles along the way—including Shea accidentally throwing his wand too hard and nearly hitting four nearby Captains—Haidar's students did exceptionally well with the new spells. The Commander called his class together around midday.

"Normally, Captains would break for lunch, and then come back for the second half of the day," Haidar said, as the students gathered into formation. "But after watching you work so hard today, on this first day of class, I'm pleased to tell you that you need not return for the second half. Tomorrow, we'll resume our lesson on Kelmarsian defenses before moving on to attack spells."

Haidar saluted them.

"Class dismissed."

Carmen and Blaze stayed behind as the other Sarcan Captains happily made the trip back up to the castle. Natlek left with them, but walked a considerable distance behind the rest of the students. From what Carmen had seen of him, he hadn't cast a single spell all morning. And it was for this reason and many others that Carmen hung back to voice her concerns to Haidar.

"Yes, Master Fox?" Haidar asked, as Carmen walked up to him with Blaze.

"Sir, what is Natlek Foretsam really doing here?"

Haidar's eyebrows rose slightly at the question.

"He's here for the reasons that I discussed during class," he replied, in an even voice. "He holds none of the responsibilities or expectations that the rest of you do, as it is his *choice* to be here. He merely wishes to observe and learn the ways of the Sarcans and their Masters, so I am told."

"Who sent him here?" Carmen asked, trying not to cross the line of confidentiality that separated students and teachers.

"Remnor, his uncle in Parliament," Haidar answered. "But regardless of that, I am watching him closely. Trust is not simply passed down through the regal bloodline; it is something that must be earned."

He was right, of course. Carmen thanked him for talking to her before lowering her gaze. She knew that Haidar was obligated to have Natlek here even if he didn't want him; Senior Parliament Members had jurisdiction over the school and its instructors.

Carmen turned to leave, feeling that she had extracted about as much information as she was going to get from her Commander on the subject. As she was walking away, Haidar called out to her.

"By the way, Master Fox—" he said, making Carmen stop and look back at him, "—if any of the other students ask…the preceding conversation never took place."

Fully understanding his concern for Natlek's privacy, Carmen nodded.

"Of course."

CHAPTER THIRTEEN
THE SECRET BENEATH THE SEA

Carmen and Blaze returned to the castle, unconvinced by Haidar's words that they were safe while Natlek was present. Though Haidar had given them his reassurance of his watchful eye, Carmen was still feeling ill at ease at the thought of Natlek Foretsam, and of his bizarre introduction to her. She was still searching her brain to try to remember who he reminded her of, but she was convinced that she had never met him prior to Haidar's class.

"There's just something about him that creeps me out," Carmen said, as she and Blaze approached their room on the third floor. "I can't quite figure out what it is."

"I think that we should pay a visit to the school library," Blaze suggested. "There are public records on Parliamentary figures there. If we could track down his family tree, maybe it would tell us something."

Carmen opened her door, turning to look at the Sarcan.

"Let's do that as soon as we can," she told him.

Carmen and Blaze were welcomed back from their first day of class by Glamis, Stellar, and Anubis sitting and waiting for them at the meal table. The castle staff had delivered a lunch tray of bread, meats, insects for Glamis, and cheeses that now sat in the middle of the group of friends.

"So, how was day one of Advanced Training?" Stellar asked, as Carmen put down her wand and sat next to him.

"Uh...it was...different," she said slowly, reaching for two pieces of bread to make herself a sandwich. "Haidar is teaching us Kelmarsian magic to combat the Keltan fighters.

We learned some defensive spells this morning…and he gave us the rest of the afternoon off."

"Wow, you don't hear *that* too often," Stellar remarked, amazed that Haidar would permit a break in their training. "You guys really must have impressed him."

"Something like that," Carmen replied, taking a bite of bread. "And there's a new student, too."

"A new student?" Glamis asked, leaning forward with interest. He had a plate full of multicolored insects in front of him. "Who is it?"

"Some guy named Natlek Foretsam," Blaze said, as he sliced the rind off a small wheel of cheese with his claws. "Apparently, he's the nephew of a Senior Parliament Member."

"How did he get into Advanced Training?" Stellar asked. "Is he a Sarcan Master?"

"No, and he didn't have any other creature with him, so we really don't know," Carmen said. "Haidar says that he's here to observe the Masters and Sarcans train, and to learn about our techniques…. He seemed really strange though, and he even told Blaze and me that he knew us from somewhere…. We've never seen him before."

Anubis and the others swapped looks of concern.

"We *both* sensed a strange presence about him," Blaze informed his friends. "We're going to research his name in the library and see if anything comes up."

"That is a wise idea," Anubis said, licking his mouth clean of some remaining crumbs. *"On another note, I have been thinking about how we are going to locate the first Secret…. Because we do not know how long it will take to find it, I have considered time travel as an alternative to spending hours, or possibly days, searching in the present."*

"Go on," Carmen pressed, continuing to eat her sandwich.

She and the others had traveled through time with Anubis before. It was one of the most useful and fascinating powers that he possessed, and it had helped them with many things previously, including Carmen's eventual defeat of Desorkhan.

"You and Blaze attend class five days a week from dawn until dusk, which essentially leaves us only the weekends to work on finding and deciphering the Secrets," Anubis reminded her. *"So because time is of the essence, I reasoned that if you wanted to search on a weeknight for Kelmar's Secret, we could approximate its location, and I could then take us there—to a time a couple of days before the present. That way, even if we need to spend several hours there, we could return to Sarcanian Valley without having actually lost any time. The both of you would never miss a class, and we could get more accomplished."*

"Sounds like a good plan to me," Blaze said, between bites of his meal.

"I agree," Carmen said. She wiped her mouth with her napkin. "We just have to figure out where exactly we have to go."

"Ah, I have already taken care of that," Glamis said cheerily, rapping one of his hooves on the table. "While you and Blaze were at training, I took the liberty of researching the location detailed on Merlin's Kelmarian map. After looking at the map yesterday, I had a fairly good idea of where the spot might be. So this morning, I visited the library and compared it to an all-encompassing map of Kelmar…. I found the site of the Secret to be beyond the Ferantay Mountains in East Kelmar…in the Sea of Elverion."

"A sea?" Carmen asked. "You mean underwater?"

"That's right," Glamis confirmed. "It is at the base of the sea—about two hundred feet down."

Carmen gaped at him.

"How are we supposed to get to it then?"

"We can't—not without using a little of *my* magic," Glamis said, with a gleam in his eye. "If you recall, I'm a highly adept swimmer. I can afford you and the others some of my powers of the Water to enable you to swim to such a depth and hold your breath long enough."

"Are you positive that it would work?" Blaze asked. He sounded somewhat nervous at the thought of diving so deep.

"Why, of course I am," Glamis said, chuckling. "It is an ingenious plan, if I do say so myself."

"Well, I guess that it's decided then," Carmen said, leaning back in her chair. She trusted Glamis and his powers very much, and so she didn't feel much of a need to worry about his ability to grant all of them his powers for a day.

"So…now that we know where we have to go and what needs to be done, when do we want to leave?" Blaze asked the group.

"If you desire, we can leave right after we eat," Anubis said. *"I have more than enough strength to get us to East Kelmar and back…. Perhaps we should utilize this time that Haidar has granted us."*

"I'm with you on that," Stellar said. "Opportunities like this don't come around every day."

Carmen grinned at him.

"And who's to doubt fate?" she mused.

Carmen changed into her sorcerer robes and stuffed a folded, blank piece of parchment, a quill, and a brass inkwell into her inner pocket, but not until after casting a waterproofing spell on all three objects under the direction of Glamis. She also waterproofed Merlin's map. She would keep the cipher disk hidden under her bed in her room, as she would not be deciphering the Secret until she returned.

The quill and paper that she would take with her would be used to write down the ciphertext Secret when they found it. And so once she had gathered together her things, Carmen joined her Souls at the base of the grandfather clock in the corner of her room.

Anubis stood with his eyes closed and his back to the ancient clock, whose face was decorated with flying Sarcans on a rotating background displaying the sun, the moon, and the stars. Carmen and the rest of her friends gathered in a circle around Anubis and waited as he focused his energy.

After a brief time, Anubis opened his spellbinding golden eyes. The others stared back at him...and seconds later, the room around them began to spin. Beyond Anubis's gaze, Carmen could see the face of the grandfather clock.... The hands were racing backwards.

Quickly, blackness overtook Carmen and her friends. Vivid explosions of color and light danced around them in the dark...as images and memories flashed past at speeds unattainable by man.

All of a sudden, a white portal of light rushed toward Carmen's group—and brought forth the sight of sprawling gray-blue sea waves crashing up against a rocky shoreline in the soft light of early morning. The cool smell of saltwater filled their noses.

Carmen and her Souls of Destiny stood on the sands of the chilly beach, beyond which lay a dark stretch of trees fortifying the treacherous Ferantay Mountains. A light mist was falling from the half-darkened sky, casting a ghostly fog over the forsaken shore.

"Before us lies the Sea of Elverion," Anubis reported to his friends, as they stared out at the body of cold water encircled by a barren beach. The sea breeze was blowing back his golden ribbon collar.

While not tremendously powerful, the sea's currents were fairly treacherous. Other than their own voices, all that Carmen and her Souls could hear were the tumbling waves washing ashore.

"Are the tides here always this powerful?" Carmen asked Anubis, brushing away her hair, which was blowing into her eyes.

"It depends on the hour of day," the Jackal said. *"Here, low tide occurs at dawn. Hence, the reason why I chose this time to come. The tides later in the day are much more hazardous than they are now."*

Carmen glanced over at Glamis. His red velvet cape was billowing in the wind as he gazed out at the murky sea. He seemed at peace with what they were about to do. When he noticed Carmen looking at him, he turned to her.

"Shall we get started?" he asked her respectfully.

"Whenever you're ready," Carmen said.

Glamis smiled, and then pranced ten long steps ahead of his companions.

When he reached the center of the beach, he turned around to face them.

"So, the first thing that we must do is protect ourselves from the frigid cold of the sea," he said, nodding toward Carmen. "While your robes already provide a magical barrier against severe temperatures, in these waters, an extra layer of defense is necessary for all of us. Carmen, please come join me up here."

Carmen did as he asked and plodded ahead through the sands. She walked past Glamis, just for a moment, to kneel down and feel the water temperature. As the rushing tide came ashore, Carmen allowed the water to wash over her out-stretched hand.

The bitterly cold water stung her skin. She promptly retracted her hand and walked over to position herself at Glamis's side.

"Now, this Protective spell is called the *Aquatic Shield*," Glamis told her. "You will place your non-dominant hand atop my back, and point your wand at the others.... You should then feel a cool sensation travel from my body, up through your arm, and into your own body. When you feel cold throughout, recite the incantation, *Aquatic Shield*."

Carmen made sure to follow Glamis's instructions carefully. With her left hand on the Boarax's smooth cape, she directed her wand toward Blaze, Anubis, and Stellar, who were standing directly across from her. Glamis lifted his head toward the sky...and Carmen felt an abrupt surge of cold sear through her palm and race up her arm.

Noticeably fast, a shiver ran throughout her body. It was hard for Carmen to keep her wand arm steady.

The instant she felt cold from head to toe, she shouted, *"Aquatic Shield!"*

With that command, a huge, watery blue bubble grew out from the crown of Carmen's wand. The bubble rose up into the air, and then came down to enclose her and Glamis.

Carmen watched through the semi-transparent wall of the bubble as a second bubble emerged from her wand. It expanded to nearly ten feet in width, breaking free from the one enveloping her and Glamis, and drifting over to the remaining Souls of Destiny. The giant magical bubble slid over the three creatures, and engulfed them within its protective walls.

Carmen's wand hand tingled for fifteen seconds before she felt warmth slowly climbing up her arm. She stopped trembling before long, as the calming heat consumed her entire body. She looked down to see that she and Glamis had each become encased in a protective azure light. Blaze and the others had as well.

Glamis slowly lowered his head, and both bubbles burst with a sharp *pop!*

The Boarax King praised her as she lowered her wand. "Ah, well done, Carmen! Now we shall all be protected from the frigid temperature of the Elverion."

Carmen looked back over her shoulder at the churning sea. She wanted to test the water to be positive that the spell had indeed worked.

"Try giving the water a feel now," Glamis suggested.

Glad that he'd had the same idea, Carmen walked to the edge of the beach and bent down. The sea rushed up onto the sands and over her glowing hand. Gazing through the water, she marveled at the fact that her hand now felt wet, but not at all cold.

Glamis grinned at Carmen as she stood up and returned to his side.

"We have just two more spells to perform before we're ready to take our dive," he said.

And so, under Glamis's direction, Stellar, Anubis, and Blaze lay down on their stomachs in a circle in the sand. Next, the Boarax had Carmen lie down the same way, next to Blaze. After all of his friends were in place, Glamis lay between her and Stellar.

"So, Stellar, place your left paw over Anubis's right, and Anubis, place your left paw on Blaze's right," Glamis requested.

When that task was complete, Carmen took Blaze's left paw in her right hand, and Glamis's right hoof with her left hand.

Glamis held Stellar's right paw with his left hoof to complete the circle. Dagtar's claw felt warm against Carmen's neck.

"Excellent," Glamis said, smiling at his friends. "So, this next spell is known as *The Stroke of the Boarax,* and it enables less practiced swimmers to swim with the power and grace that we Boarax do. We have to lie down so as to mimic the act of swimming."

With her hands occupied, and her wand lying in the sand behind her, Carmen knew that this spell must call on Glamis's powers more than her own.

"Everyone, please close your eyes," Glamis instructed.

Seeing only darkness now, Carmen heard birds calling in the distance as she lay there with her elbows in the sand. The smell of the saltwater was more overwhelming with her face just inches from the ground.

Glamis grunted a string of words in the Boarax language. No more than thirty seconds later, Carmen felt herself being gently lifted up out of the sand by an enchanted wind that swirled around her and her Souls. Glamis continued to utter his incantation as the five friends rose higher and higher into the sky, slowly spinning and still hand-in-hand. Carmen felt an unusual burning sensation in her arms and legs while she remained suspended in the air.

Wanting desperately to open her eyes, she waited impatiently for such an order from Glamis. She couldn't tell how high up they were, or what was happening around them.

Glamis's chanting eventually ceased, and he and the others opened their eyes to find themselves floating about fifteen feet above the beach, beneath a hovering magical ring of white light created by their bond to one another. Dagtar's claw was floating on its chain out in front of Carmen, as though the Dragon were also a part of the circle with them. The burning sensation in Carmen's arms and legs had gone away.

"You have each been gifted with the swimming abilities of the Boarax," Glamis said, as the circle of friends continued to leisurely rotate. "These capabilities will last from the time that we enter the water until we are back on dry land."

"Splendid," Stellar muttered, staring down at the slowly revolving shore. He appeared a tad dizzy as he looked up at Glamis. "Uh…and how do we get down from here?"

Glamis chuckled.

"We must use our legs of course!" he said, as though it were blatantly obvious. "We cannot break our hand-to-hand connection, or risk breaking the spell and falling," he told his companions. "With your new Boarax swimming abilities, your legs are powerful enough to allow all of you to kick to lower us to the ground. So, let us commence!"

The others didn't hesitate in following Glamis's lead. They each kicked up and down as though they were swimming…and little by little, they were all lowered to the ground on their own power.

When Carmen and her Souls touched the sand, the magical ring of light overhead vanished, and Dagtar's claw stopped floating. The friends stood up and brushed the sand off of them.

Without a warning to anyone nearby, Stellar shook himself off, inadvertently sending some of his sand flying into Blaze's face. Blaze made sure to let him know that he didn't appreciate getting the scratchy particles in his eyes by throwing a fresh handful of his own sand at Stellar's back.

"There is just one other spell that we must cast, and it is simple to execute," Glamis said. *"Undying Breath.* It provides humans and creatures not born of Water with the ability to breathe beneath the sea, beginning at the moment that the moisture touches the skin. It expires when the individual emerges from the lake or sea."

Glamis marched over to Carmen and asked that she kneel down before him.

"This will only take a moment," he said, closing his eyes before pressing his nose to Carmen's.

Glamis's bright orange snout sparkled, and Carmen's nose grew warm against his.

After a minute or so, Glamis pulled away. He then walked over to Carmen's other Souls and did the same with each of them.

"Well, I believe that we are thoroughly equipped to handle the mysteries of the deep!" Glamis proclaimed, once he had finished. He strode across the beach. "What say you all? Shall we venture into the waters of the Elverion?"

Carmen grinned and Returned her wand to its Key form. More than ready to take on this next challenge, she and the others hastened to join Glamis at the edge of the water.

"Does anybody know what kinds of creatures live in this sea?" Carmen asked, slightly nervous, as she let the tide wash up on her boots.

"An assortment of beings ranging from harmless Arakives and Orkafish, to a handful of more...substantial creatures," Anubis informed her.

"Are the substantial ones a threat to us?" Stellar asked.

Anubis's eyes glittered.

"I would think not," he said. *"But just to be certain, we will keep to ourselves, and not linger. The single reason that we are here is to find the first Secret. As soon as we have it in our possession, we will leave. Understood?"*

Carmen and the others immediately agreed.

Glamis waded into the water first, followed closely by his friends. As he had studied the map of the sea so closely earlier in the day, he would be the one to lead them on this journey.

One by one, Carmen and her Souls dove under the water—and entered into the domain beneath the cold sea.

The world of the deep was hauntingly quiet as Carmen and her Souls drifted downward. Their breathing caused bubbles of air to whoosh out from their mouths. Schools of orange and red fish swam past them, but the cloudy water made it impossible to see anything even remotely distant.

Carmen was amazed by how much faster and stronger she felt with Glamis's swimming abilities. Her robes swished around her as she traveled with ease through the waters. The Boarax led her and the others forward for about three miles, toward the center of the sea. Below them lay a shadowy, pebbly landscape.

After a while, they took a progressive dive down toward the sea floor, and as they swam, fresh sights emerged from the darkness.

There were jungles of twisting green seaweed blanketing the stone-covered seabed, and something great and dark was spread across the middle of the pebbly ground. Glamis pointed at the large shape, indicating to his friends that they should move in the direction of it. With their eyes wide open, they swam deeper and deeper, struggling to see through the dim, gray-blue water.

A school of shimmering, bluish green Deltacarp flitted past them and vanished into the shadows. Bigger forms drifted near them from time to time, but the objects were all determined to be pieces of wood or clusters of tree leaves.

Carmen and the others followed Glamis down toward the base of the sea, all of them straining to see what the huge object on the rock-strewn floor below them could be. They swam farther and farther down until they came upon a sight that none of them expected.

Just twenty feet beneath them lay the relatively intact remains of an ancient shipwreck, sprawled across a wide bed of seaweed.

The five friends drew nearer to the great wooden ship, which was covered in thick green mold from its bow to its stern. It was lying on its side, and had become partially buried by silt and the overgrown weeds that snaked up all around the hull.

Carmen and her Souls swam down to the craft. Beneath the layers of mold and decay, they could see peeling red and blue painted designs that swirled across the ship's waterline. The foremast had been snapped in two. The tattered remains of the vessel's navy blue and black sails billowed eerily in the current.

The group of Kelmarians stared at the once majestic ship, wondering both how it had sunk, and if it indeed held the Secret for which they were searching. Anubis pointed over the hull.

"I will search the deck for any clues. The rest of you should investigate the outer portion of the ship."

Anubis swam up and over the portside of the craft to begin his hunt for anything that might direct them to the Secret as his friends made their way around the outside of the ship. Just what they were looking for remained a mystery, but Carmen imagined that she would recognize something important if she saw it.

There were some moments as Carmen's group explored the ship for signs of the first Secret in which Carmen thought that she heard movement behind them. But when she looked around, she saw only swaying seaweed, and the occasional passing fish.

Having moved steadily around the rest of the sunken vessel, Carmen, Blaze, Stellar, and Glamis turned the corner around the bow. Carmen stared at the worn and discolored wooden planks of the ship's stem.

Peeking out from behind a coating of silt deposits, it looked to her like there were letters carved into the wood. She reached out and wiped the palm of her hand across the slippery plank. As she brushed away the remaining sea soil, a series of engraved words were revealed to her.

Carmen and her friends took a few moments to study the message. Then Carmen turned and looked somewhat skeptically at Blaze.

"Do you think this is it?" she asked, able to speak hundreds of feet under the sea because of her Boarax gifts of the Water.

"Remember," Blaze said, *"with ciphertext, each letter is a placeholder for another letter to be revealed by the cipher disk. The Secret's true meaning doesn't read the way that it does now."*

Carmen gazed back at the sentence for a short time, and then dug through the pocket of her robes to retrieve her quill and parchment.

With a shaky hand, she dipped the quill into her inkwell and scribbled down the message exactly as it was written on the ship. She hoped that this simple sentence was really what they had been searching for. On the surface, the words didn't appear to be very significant, but she also knew from experience that sometimes even the smallest piece of wisdom could help to change the world.

The unexpected sound of wood snapping behind her caused Carmen to freeze. Anubis darted over the side of the ship and swam quickly over to her and her other Souls.

"We are surrounded on all sides by Sea Dragons," he warned them. *"I saw them moving in the thickets. They camouflage themselves amongst the seaweed. They are very territorial creatures, and if we don't depart soon, they will see us as menacing."*

Alarmed, Carmen pointed to the ship's bow.

"We found the Secret!" she showed him. *"So we can go now."*

"Excellent," he said, gazing closely at the message. *"Let us leave now then."*

Anubis asked Glamis to lead them back to the shore. The Boarax readily obliged.

Carmen and her friends swam upward and back the way they had come. They were about thirty feet away from the site of the shipwreck when a roar louder than a tidal wave carried through the waters.

Carmen turned around instantly. The seaweed just beyond the sunken ship quivered…and a collection of giant, glowing blue-green creatures emerged up from behind the brush.

Each about half the size of an adult Sky Dragon, the Sea Dragons' powerful bodies were covered with gleaming cerulean and jade scales. A ghostly green glow sheathed each of their forms.

All of the beasts had tall, serpentine necks and gills, as well as dark golden fins around their faces that matched their eyes. Their four legs ended in great blue and gold fins, and they possessed long, finned tails that whipped behind them in the water.

"You will not leave with the Secret!" one of the large males growled. *"You have entered our territory without permission. The consequence for such dishonor is death."*

"We don't want to hurt anybody," Carmen told him hastily, her heart beating rapidly. *"We came here only to retrieve the Secret so that we can save Kelmar and the World of Light."*

"Your reasons matter not to us," the Sea Dragon hissed. *"We care only about protecting our own kind. You have entered into sacred seas and caused our females and offspring much distress. This is an unforgivable offense, and gives us reason to destroy you."*

A moment later, the five Sea Dragons were racing toward Carmen and her friends.

Carmen scrambled to summon her wand. When she had it in hand, she cast the *Lightning Shield* spell to protect her and her Souls from the approaching beasts.

In a flash, lightning struck the surface of the water above them and enclosed Carmen and her friends in a sphere of electrified golden light.

"Carmen, give me your wand!" Blaze said urgently, swimming to Carmen's side. *"I can carry it in my mouth so that you can swim!"*

Without even thinking about it, Carmen handed Blaze her staff, and he clasped it tightly in his jaws. Carmen's group then turned and swam as fast as they could to escape the shoal of angry Sea Dragons.

They raced through the waters at breakneck speed, using all of the energy and stamina that Glamis's gifts had provided them. The Sea Dragons chased them at an equally swift pace, all the while spewing powerful torpedoes of venomous water from their gills.

Carmen and her friends steered clear of the attacks, diving and swimming sideways to avoid them. As she flew through the water, Carmen was extremely grateful to Blaze for his quick thinking. With him carrying her wand horizontally in his jaws, it allowed her to swim freely. If she'd had to swim while toting the wand, there was no way that she would have been able to move fast enough to evade the Sea Dragons' assault.

Glamis led his friends ahead through the foggy waters. They propelled themselves forward for almost half an hour, and had gotten just shy of three-quarters of the way to the beach when Stellar cried out.

Carmen stopped and looked back, hearing her pulse pounding in her ears.

One of the Sea Dragons had somehow managed to swim ahead of the others. Its jaw was latched on to one of Stellar's back legs. The Keinen was trying desperately to break free from the Sea Dragon's unrelenting grasp, but the creature would not let him go. The other Sea Dragons were rapidly closing in on him as well.

Carmen grabbed her wand back from Blaze and sped toward Stellar. But being smaller and more agile, Blaze swam ahead of her to attack the ocean beast first.

Blaze threw back his head and used his horn to launch a jet of lightning at the commanding Sea Dragon.

The hulking creature roared and protected itself with an *Ocean's Guard* defense. Blaze's lightning struck the shield and disappeared.

Unfazed, Blaze swam toward the Sea Dragon and drove his horn into its flank. The Sea Dragon screeched in pain, finally releasing Stellar's leg from its jaws. Fresh blood from Stellar's wound drifted upward.

The Sea Dragon that had attacked Stellar promptly retreated back to its group. Blaze helped Stellar to swim away as Carmen hurried toward the advancing creatures.

"I'll take it from here, buddy!" she shouted, as she rushed past the Sarcan.

Carmen pointed her wand at the oncoming pack of Sea Dragons.

"Lightning Spark!" she shouted.

Swishing her wand through the water, Carmen released a torrent of electricity that sailed from the crown of her staff to the Sea Dragons directly across from her. The lightning lit up the gloomy water and slammed into the gathering of creatures with explosive force. An instant later, the struggling beasts' furious roars carried throughout the sea.

Carmen watched briefly to confirm that the spell had weakened them enough to allow her time to escape. She then turned around and swam back to Blaze and the rest of her Souls.

The gash in Stellar's leg was still bleeding. Carmen made use of the *Healio Ingatia* Healing spell to seal it up. Once that was done, she Returned her wand to its Key form.

Not knowing just how long the *Lightning Spark* spell would hold the Sea Dragons at bay, Carmen and the others continued on their underwater sprint toward the shore.

The sea became increasingly shallow the closer they got to land. If the Dragons did resume their pursuit of them, they never got close enough to harm them. The friends voyaged onward for twenty more minutes until they could see the gray sky above their heads.

With great relief, Carmen and her friends emerged from the sea and trudged out onto the beach. The blue light encasing their bodies faded as they slogged up the shore for five feet. That was before everyone but Glamis suddenly collapsed into the sand.

Carmen closed her eyes and grabbed her legs in agony, still breathing heavily from the lengthy swim. Her muscles burned as though she had just run a marathon around the world. She was sore all over, particularly in her legs and arms. And judging by the faces of the others...all of them were experiencing the exact same pain. With Glamis's spell wearing off, they found themselves weakened physically beyond anything that they had ever felt. Glamis himself, of course, was perfectly fine.

"Oh dear...I should have known this would happen," the Boarax King said unhappily, as he looked over his fatigued friends. His face was drawn with sadness. "I'm afraid that I don't know of a Healing spell to ease the hurting.... I feel just terrible now."

"Don't worry about it, Glamis," Carmen croaked, straining to open one eye to look at him. "When do you think this will pass?"

"I would imagine that it should let up within less than an hour," Glamis said, trying to sound soothing. He sat down beside her. "Just don't move, and let the muscles rest. Your muscles aren't really strained; they're just trying to catch up to all the work that you did…. Even with magic, our bodies have their limits."

"If we didn't already know that before, we certainly know it *now*," Stellar choked. His eyes were tightly closed as he winced in pain.

Carmen, Blaze, Stellar, and Anubis lay resting in the sand beneath the smoky-colored sky for close to forty-five minutes, waiting for the throbbing in their limbs to subside. They were finally beginning to feel some relief after that time; their aching bodies were no longer preventing them from getting into seated positions.

Carmen got up to wipe the sand off of the side of her face and shake the granules out of her hair. Slowly…she and the others were able to stand, and it appeared that they would finally be fit to travel back to their present time in Sarcanian Valley. Glamis was enormously pleased when his friends were back in form, and though he still admitted to feeling at fault for their conditions, Carmen and the others were just grateful to have the first Secret of Kelmar in their possession.

"I can't wait to see what the Secret actually means," Carmen said to Blaze, as she squeezed the last of the water out of her robes.

"Same here," Blaze replied, shaking to dry his fur. "I hope that the Secrets in the afterworlds aren't so exhausting to acquire."

"Oh, Blaze, don't even mention *them* yet," Carmen pleaded, waving her hand to stop him as she thought back to what Keltan was like. "I don't even want to imagine."

Minutes later, Carmen, Blaze, Glamis, and Stellar were standing before Anubis on the beach. The Jackal met their eyes, and swiftly made the world around them turn to darkness.

In a matter of moments, Carmen and her friends were traveling through a spinning tunnel of light and color. The days flashed by them in mere seconds, and before they knew it, they were standing back in their room in the castle of Thunder Academy.

Carmen dashed over to her bed to retrieve Merlin's cipher disk from beneath it. Then she and the others gathered around the table to begin working on deciphering the message from the sunken ship.

Carmen placed the disk in the center of the table so that all of them could see it. The crystal lights in the ceiling illuminated the engravings and produced shadows in the deeper set patterns that decorated the wooden surface. The large bottom plate contained the alphabetic sequence, while the smaller plate on top represented the Great Seal of Kelmar encircled by a ring of randomized letters.

Carmen unfolded the square of parchment that she had stuffed in her robes and laid it out next to the cipher disk.

To Dance the Song, every note I Skip.

Carmen stared at the wooden disk.... She touched the center circle ever so lightly, and found it to be movable on the central pivot that mounted it to the bottom plate. She frowned.

"How can we figure this out?" she asked her friends. "The smaller plate can move.... We can turn it to line up with the letters on the bigger disk practically any number of ways."

They all thought for a few seconds.

"Did Merlin give any additional instructions with the maps?" Blaze asked. "Maybe we should take a look at them again."

"No, there was nothing else with them," Carmen said, reaching into her pocket to get the parchment out to show him. "Here, see for your—"

She froze…staring at the paper in her hand. There was handwriting scrawled across the back of the maps that wasn't hers.

Carmen unfolded the parchment and read the lone sentence, which was written in shining black ink.

To begin to decipher the first Secret, rotate the movable disk two and one-half turns clockwise.

"That wasn't on there before…." Carmen said slowly, passing each of her friends the note to read. "Do you think that it could be Merlin's writing?"

"*Yes. He must have enchanted the parchment to let it reveal his instructions once each Secret has been found,*" Anubis said, looking up from the note. "*Quite a clever idea for use with a cipher disk such as this. I would say to follow his directions and see what happens.*"

Carmen gazed down at the magical wooden disk. With trembling fingers, she carefully turned the smaller circular plate to the right two full revolutions. She then moved it a half a turn more.

She looked at the ciphertext message that was written on the slip of paper, and then back down at the cipher disk. The first letter, *T*, on the smaller circle corresponded to the *O* on the outer ring of letters. She scribbled this down beneath the *T* of the ciphertext message that she had written on the parchment.

The next letter in the message was *o*. It aligned with the letter *f*. *To* had deciphered to *Of.*

Carmen continued on with the next word—*Dance.* She checked each letter as she went, and in time had deciphered the word to *Light.* She was about to move ahead to the following word when Blaze tapped her on her shoulder.

Carmen followed his eyes down to Merlin's parchment. The sentence that the Master of Kelmar had written had vanished, and another sentence was magically scrawling across the paper in the same silky black ink, as though an invisible hand and quill were writing it.

Now rotate the movable disk one full turn counterclockwise.

Carmen rotated the smaller top plate as directed, and *the* quickly deciphered to *and*. Merlin's message disappeared again, and was replaced by another.

Rotate the movable disk one-quarter turn clockwise.

Song soon became *Dark.*

Carmen followed Merlin's exact commands for each word, or set of words, turning the movable plate as needed. Her Souls of Destiny watched as she precisely aligned the two circles according to the written instructions.... It was only minutes before she had deciphered the entire inscription from the ship at the bottom of the Sea of Elverion.

Carmen and her friends stared down at the new, plaintext message that was written on the parchment; one of three passages whose words had been a closely guarded secret for nearly 3,000 years.

Of Light and Dark, there sets a Dawn.

CHAPTER FOURTEEN
THE DREAM

Carmen went to bed that night with her mind still spinning with questions. After deciphering the first Secret of Kelmar earlier in the day, she and her friends had spent most of the afternoon trying to uncover the meaning behind it. Through their endless discussions and debates, which had stretched on well into the evening, they eventually decided that without the other two Secrets, this one had virtually unlimited possibilities.

"It could represent literally *anything!*" Blaze said, before they went to sleep. "*Light* and *Dark* likely refer to Kelmarsia and Keltan, but there's no way to know for sure."

"*The deciphered sentence reminds me of a line from* The Legend of the Worlds Triad," Anubis said. "'*There came a morning that brought with it an improbable fate—a fate that while unforeseen by most, was one shared by all born holding the gift of magic,*'" he recited. "*I believe that there may be a link between the two verses.*"

"Why can't these kinds of tasks ever be straightforward?" Stellar asked. "Would it hurt for someone to just tell us in plain language what it is that we need to do to save our world?"

"Nonsense! That would spoil the fun of the hunt!" Glamis said, clapping Stellar on the back with his hooves. "It is our duty, after all, to solve these sorts of problems for the sake of Kelmar."

Carmen smiled wearily. "You know, sometimes I wish that this job *did* come with an instruction book. It would certainly save a lot of time and frustration."

At daybreak the next morning, Carmen and her classmates returned to Haidar's class to be greeted by the sight of their Commander standing and reaching his arm up into the sky as he stood in the middle of the dueling fields. He was balancing his wand on its base in his palm so that it stood with its crown pointing straight up in the air.

With his back to them, Haidar muttered an incantation under his breath, and the wand slowly began to spin around.... It completed five full rotations in his hand as a delicate white cloud drifted across the sky overhead.

When the cloud was stationed above the Sarcan instructor, it showered down a brilliant white light, which washed over Haidar's wand and infused it with powers unknown to Carmen and the rest of the students. It wasn't until Haidar pointed his staff at a boulder ten feet across from him that she and the other Sarcan Captains realized the spell's purpose.

A silvery white flow of light expelled from Haidar's staff and wrapped itself around the rock, enclosing it in a sparkling, translucent glow.

"What you just saw was another example of a Kelmarsian Protective spell," Haidar said, turning around to face his class, which had gathered behind him. *The Sentinel's Defense* is a Protective spell that can be used to safeguard inanimate objects from physical or magical harm. It will not work in protecting any *living* being, however."

The students peered over at the rock, which continued to shine in the sunlight that was escaping through the fleeting clouds over the valley.

"As you can probably imagine, this Protection requires tremendous balance," Haidar noted, lowering his wand. "In order for you to cast *the Sentinel's Defense,* you must first be able to balance your wand in your hand the way I just did. I would like all of the sorcerers to now attempt to do that."

The Sarcan Masters summoned their wands. Carmen glanced down the line of students at Natlek. He had summoned his wand before getting outside, but seemed to have no intention of using it, as he left it lying on the ground at his feet. Perhaps sensing Carmen's stare, he looked over at her, his steely brown eyes resolute. She promptly retreated from his gaze.

Haidar observed the human Captains closely as all of them attempted to balance their wands. The sporadic clanking of metal against rock carried through the air as many of the students lost their grip on their wands and dropped them to the ground.

The Sarcan Commander didn't seem at all upset when none of them could hold their staffs steady in the palms of their hands for any length of time. After five minutes or so, he cleared his voice and raised his hand, indicating that he wished for them to stop.

"This spell is deceptively simple," he said, once the Captains had picked up their wands and refocused their attention on him. "But it demands the magic user to possess a deep, inner sense of balance that cannot be utilized without first searching themselves for peace from within. Such peace is achieved through the art known as meditation."

Haidar directed the Sarcan Captains to get down on their knees. As instructed, the sorcerers held their wands horizontally in their dominant hands, and then closed their eyes, listening for Haidar's next set of directions. Their Sarcans knelt next to them.

"I ask you to empty your minds of anything that is not a peaceful thought," Haidar said calmly, as he stood in front of the students. "Release your tensions and fears…for from this moment on, you will experience nothing…but peace."

Carmen breathed in…and then exhaled. She had never been one to meditate, so she would have to concentrate very intently to allow her usually active mind to work itself into a state of relaxation.

"Envision yourself standing at the edge of a pier at sunset," Haidar continued, in a tranquil voice. "You are staring out at the calm blue ocean…watching the waves wash up onto the shore beneath you."

Carmen wrinkled her nose. After spending so much time in the waters of a murky sea as she sought the first Secret, this was hardly the vision of peace that she wanted to imagine. So instead of visualizing the ocean, she chose to see a quiet woodland, where sunlight was shining down through the trees to the forest floor….

The Captains knelt in silence for what must have been at least fifteen minutes. Most of them seemed relieved when Haidar finally asked them to return from their meditative states. Though the sorcerers' knees were padded in their uniforms, they still ached from holding up their weight on the hard ground.

"So, let's try this again," Haidar said, motioning toward the sorcerers' wands as all of the students stood up. "Don't lose sight of your vision, and allow the wand to balance in your palm. If you are hesitant or indecisive, your wand will magically sense that, and it will not stand. Once the staff *is* properly balanced, you will state the incantation, *the Sentinel's Defense,* and direct your spell at that boulder over there." He pointed off toward the large red rock that he had made use of earlier in his demonstration. "Begin."

Following a fair number of attempts, Kamie was the first Captain to get *the Sentinel's Defense* spell to work. Her classmates, who were spread out from one another across the dueling fields, applauded as she launched the spell that effectively draped the boulder in a protective sheet of silvery, glittering light.

Soon after, more than half of the other Captains were able to accomplish the feat as well, but Carmen was still struggling. Despite focusing her hardest to cast the spell, she simply could not balance her wand, no matter what she tried.

Carmen groaned. "Ugh, I can't do it!" she told Blaze, bending down to pick up her fallen wand for what felt like the hundredth time. "This is absurd. My wand won't listen to me!"

Blaze looked sympathetic to her troubles.

"Maybe you're not relaxed enough," he reasoned. "You know that the spell won't work unless your mind is at peace."

"I'm not relaxed *because* I can't summon this spell!" she snapped.

But then she sighed.

"I almost feel like giving up," she muttered.

"Umm…I could help you," Shea said quietly.

Carmen had been so busy complaining that she hadn't noticed her sandy-haired classmate, Shea, standing behind her with his Sarcan, Gia. Her face instantly flushed with embarrassment.

"Oh…sure," she said offhandedly. ".… That would be great."

Shea had successfully cast *the Sentinel's Defense* after very few tries, an achievement that only a handful of his classmates could claim. He seemed more than happy to help Carmen learn how to do it, too. She was just as grateful to receive his advice.

"I think the reason that the spell may not be working for you is because you're too focused," Shea said, gently taking Carmen's wand into his hands. "Usually that's a good thing, but with this spell, I found that I had to *not* think about it so much to get it right."

"That's all?" Carmen asked, imagining that the problem must be more complicated than just her inability to lose focus. "So I should think more about the ocean scene that Haidar described?"

"Right, or whatever you *want* to think about," Shea said, with a smile. Carmen had never noticed before how much his blue eyes sparkled when he smiled. "Think about whatever makes you feel at peace."

Shea handed Carmen back her wand. With his advice in mind, she looked down at the ground and closed her eyes. For some reason, all that she could see in her mind at this moment was Shea's kind face.

Carmen tried to shake Shea's image from her thoughts, and remembered back to the forest that she had first visualized.

The still forest scene came slowly back into her mind…but it now included the sight of a relaxed Shea standing at the base of a great tree. He was smiling as he leaned back against the bark, calmly looking out into the trees, the sun illuminating his face and the beautiful woodland around him.

At last feeling at peace, Carmen opened her eyes and tried to cast the spell yet again. This time, it took only seconds for her wand to balance itself in the palm of her hand.

Momentarily stunned, Carmen murmured, *"The Sentinel's Defense."*

Just as Haidar's had done, Carmen's staff performed five slow revolutions in her hand while a cloud of light glided over her head.

The cloud rained down a mist of bright white light, which subsequently enchanted the crown of her wand.

Carmen gripped her staff and pointed it at the boulder across from her. She then released the light from her wand in a straight path to the target…and soon, it had the red boulder wrapped in a glistening silver covering.

Shea applauded as Carmen lowered her staff.

"That was terrific!" he said, grinning. "I knew that you could do it!"

Carmen smiled sheepishly.

"Thanks for your help," she said, feeling somewhat awkward, especially after seeing Shea in her last vision of the forest. "I don't think I would have been able to cast the spell without...your advice."

Shea smiled. Carmen couldn't refrain from observing that his eyes were sparkling again.

"You're always helping other people," he said. "It was nice to help *you* for a change."

Carmen opened her mouth to speak. Just what she was going to say, she didn't know, but at the same time, Haidar called his class back together.

"Well, back to work I guess," Shea said, with a sigh.

Carmen, Blaze, Shea, and Gia walked back over to stand in formation with the other Captains on the edge of the dueling fields. Carmen was glad that she could now get her mind on something other than Shea.

"I'm confident to move on with the lesson now that you've all successfully cast *the Sentinel's Defense*," Haidar announced. "If you were not able to master it to your greatest ability this time around, I expect you to continue to practice it on your own. But for right now, we're going to go ahead to focus on Kelmarsian attack spells. For the remainder of the class, you will be learning ways to effectively combat powerful Keltan curses."

Haidar went on to explain a number of unique Kelmarsian battle spells, and then demonstrated them to all of the students. And though she was listening and taking in her Commander's words as best as she could, Carmen's mind occasionally wandered. She wondered what her other Souls were doing, and tried not to think about Natlek and his possible intentions, or Shea and his blue eyes.

"…. This is important to remember," Haidar said, around midday, breaking one of Carmen's lapses in concentration. "When you are not in Kelmarsia, Kelmarsian spells demand more of your magical energy than Kelmarian spells do. Therefore, it is vital that you conserve your energy whenever you can. Keep this in mind for the coming days and weeks."

The Captains were dismissed for lunch a short time after that, and returned an hour later for the last exercise of the day.

"We will now practice the Kelmarsian attack spells that I spoke about this morning," Haidar declared, once all of his students were standing in formation. "I am going to pair each Master and Sarcan team with another. Because we now have an odd number of students, one group will have *three* Masters."

Natlek's attendance was to blame for the uneven pairing. As Haidar went down the line, pairing off students two at a time, Carmen hoped that he would pair her with anyone but the outsider.

Fortunately, she got her wish, as Haidar ended up teaming her with Kamie Lonvan and her Sarcan, Dall. Natlek was put in a group with Draven, Flint, Max, and Kai.

After he was finished dividing up the teams, Haidar assigned every other pair of Captains to a dueling field and sent them off to practice dueling with their partner team.

Together, Carmen and Kamie walked up to their spots with their Sarcans. Haidar had sent them to one of the farthest dueling fields from the castle. As Blaze and Dall chatted high in the air above their Masters' heads, Kamie looked back over her shoulder before whispering to Carmen.

"So, what's going on between you and Shea?"

Carmen nearly tripped.

"What do you mean?"

"I saw him walk over to you before," Kamie said, with mild interest. "What were you talking about?"

"Oh…he was showing me how to cast *the Sentinel's Defense*," Carmen said, feeling a little relieved. "I was having trouble balancing my wand, and he told me to relax…and then it worked."

Kamie looked somewhat surprised.

"Didn't you meditate when Haidar had us do it together as a class?" she asked.

Carmen shrugged.

"I'm not really good at meditating," she admitted. "It's not one of my strongest skills."

"Well, you can't be good at *everything*," Kamie said, flipping back her long brown hair with her hand. "At least you got it eventually."

"Yeah," Carmen said with a smile. "I'm glad."

They were almost to their dueling field when Kamie looked over at Carmen again. "Are you sure that was all he said?" she asked, curious. "Shea, I mean."

"Yes…." Carmen replied honestly. "Why?"

Kamie arrived at her end of the dueling field. Carmen waited for her to give her an answer before she would walk to her spot on the opposite side of the space.

"I saw the way you were looking at each other," Kamie said. "It almost seemed like—"

"Oh, no," Carmen said, shaking her head. She knew what Kamie was thinking. "No. We're just friends."

Kamie smiled, clearly not believing her.

"Okay, Carmen. Whatever you say."

Carmen was beginning to feel annoyed.

"I'm not lying," she said flatly.

Then she turned to march to her side of the dueling field. When she was in position with Blaze, she gazed across at Kamie.

"Can we get on with practice now?"

Carmen and Blaze dueled with Kamie and Dall for the rest of the class. Carmen felt less angry with Kamie the longer they dueled, as her thoughts about Shea gradually slipped from her mind. The sorcerers each used the Kelmarsian attack spells Haidar had taught them that day, making it a point to cast all of them at least once. Among the more potent spells they tried for the first time were *Storm of the Heavens, Golden Lightning,* and *Everlasting Flight.*

In casting *Storm of the Heavens,* the spell caster's wand would cause the clear sky to turn into that of a raging storm. When used against a real opponent, the spell had the potential to inflict serious damage.

Golden Lightning brought forth a perfect strike of lightning, and *Everlasting Flight* allowed the sorcerer and creature to fly for an infinite time without wearing down their magical energies.

When class was over for the day, Kamie invited Carmen and Blaze to have dinner with her and the other Captains on Sunday. Carmen politely told Kamie that they would think about it, and that if they weren't busy collecting another one of the Secrets, they would join them.

"Great!" Kamie said, her eyes lighting up with her bright smile. "I really hope that you can come.... You're always so busy saving the world and all that, you never have time to hang out with us."

Carmen chuckled.

"We'll try our best to make it, Kamie," she promised.

Back in her room with Blaze and her other Souls later that night, Carmen sat at her table and wrote out a letter to her grandfather. She had been meaning to pen the letter for the past several nights now, so she decided to make good use of her time on this quiet evening. The sound of her quill pen scratching across the parchment helped to keep her on task. As she worked, her Souls of Destiny sat around the room and talked in low voices about various subjects of relevance to them.

After a little while, Carmen dipped her quill back in its inkwell. Then she leaned back and read the letter that she had drafted.

Dear Pop,
I know that Haidar already sent you a message telling you that I was okay, but I wanted to write to you and tell you that myself.

I'm fine, and I don't want you worrying. The last few days here have been a little chaotic, but everything's calmed down now. Blaze and the others are great.

I saw Mom and Dad in Kelmarsia. They wanted me to tell you that they're fine and that they miss you. I saw Grandma there, too. We all ate dinner together, and we talked a lot. It was an incredible experience.

My Souls and I also met Kelmari, Merlin's sister, and Blaze and I even got to meet Merlin himself. Kelmari told us the story of Kelmar's creation. I know that this will be hard for you to believe, but she and Merlin are Desorkhan's siblings.

As Inpu probably told you afterward, my friends and I traveled to Keltan from Kelmarsia and retrieved Merlin's cipher disk, which was hidden in Triedastron's fortress. We've since started our search for the three Secrets of Kelmar. We'll need

to decipher them to restore the balance of power between the spirit worlds.

Yesterday, we followed the map that Merlin gave us, and traveled to the Sea of Elverion. We found the first Secret of Kelmar there, and we were able to decipher the message to plaintext. We're not really sure what the Secret means, but we're hoping that when we find the others, it will make better sense. Each of the last two Secrets are located in one of the realms of the afterlife, so we'll be traveling to both places in the coming days.

Commander Haidar is teaching the Sarcan Captains Kelmarsian spells. He wants all of us to be prepared for battle with the Keltans. Everyone in the valley is hoping that it doesn't come to that, but Haidar seems to think that it will.

There's a new boy in our class. He's really more of a visitor than a student, but he comes to training every day. His name is Natlek Foretsam, and it seems that he's the nephew of a Senior Parliament Member. I'm really suspicious of him, Pop. It's complicated for me to explain, but something about him doesn't seem right. If you know anything about him or his uncle, Remnor, please let me know.

The weather has been fine so far here in Sarcanian Valley. How are things where you are? If it's okay with you, I'll come by Mortrock Forest this weekend. I can help you with the house repairs.

Keep me posted of any news. I hope that I can see you soon.

Love,
Carmen

Satisfied, Carmen folded up the parchment and stuffed it into an envelope. She then laid the sealed letter down on the table next to her written request to receive *The Kelmarian Re-*

view newspaper. She planned to mail both letters out the following morning before class.

"So, when do we start searching for the next Secret?" Stellar asked Carmen, as she walked over to sit on the edge of her bed. "We'll have to go to both spirit worlds to get the last two."

Carmen sighed. "I don't know," she said. "I'm still trying to figure that out myself."

She looked over at Anubis.

"Have you been in touch with Inpu lately?" she asked.

"I have," Anubis replied. *"I spoke to him earlier today."*

"Did you ask him if he could help us get to the afterworlds again?" Blaze inquired.

"Yes," Anubis said, *"and he assured me that he would come here to Sarcanian Valley as soon as he can. With all of the disorder taking precedence in the spirit worlds, he's had quite a time carrying out his obligations as the Opener of the Way. In addition to ushering the new spirits into the afterlife, Merlin has been keeping him busy with some additional work on a new spell that he is developing. My father has also been helping to combat Triedastron's fighters, who terrorize the Kelmarsian nights."*

"Are they *still* getting into Kelmarsia?" Carmen asked. "I thought that a new Protective spell was put into place at the barrier. And the weather in Kelmar hasn't been bad like it was before."

"Regrettably, even with the Protection, I have been told that fighters still find ways to get in," Anubis said, understandably disappointed. *"The difference now is that* fewer *of them are making it through. That is why we haven't experienced any new storms lately. There is still fighting, but it is currently not at the level that it was before, thanks to the new Protection."*

"Well, there's some good news," Glamis said, trying to be optimistic.

"But it won't stop completely until we discover the final two Secrets," Carmen reminded him. "And even after that, I'm really uncertain as to what to expect…. I still don't know what I'm supposed to do with all three of the Secrets."

"I wouldn't be too concerned about it yet, Carmen," Blaze said. "Believe in yourself, and sooner or later you'll figure it out. You'll see."

Carmen and her friends went to bed a couple of hours later. Surprisingly, Carmen fell asleep easily, even with all that was on her mind. Sometime close to midnight, she rolled over in her sleep, and was transported to a place far beyond her current realm.

Feeling something cool and rather bumpy against the side of her face, Carmen opened her eyes to the sight of a sunlit, deep blue sky speeding past her.

A giant, green scaled wing rose up to the side of her and came down again. Alarmed, she sat up, and felt the base of a Dragon's neck beneath her hands…. She was gliding through the air on the back of her fifth Soul of Destiny.

"Dagtar…?" she leaned over the Dragon's neck and saw his crystal blue eyes flicker back at her.

"Yes, Carmen, welcome back."

"Welcome back?" she repeated blankly.

She looked over his flank to see rolling hills of glittering green grass and pristine rocky mountainsides zipping by far below them. She could hear the most beautiful music playing somewhere off in the distance as she stared down at the magnificence of the landscape beneath her….

"Where are we?" Carmen asked, immediately alarmed. If she was where she thought she was, that could mean only one thing: She was dead.

"What am I doing here?"

Dagtar laughed, which sounded more like a noise between a snort and a growl.

"Do not worry yourself, Guardian," he said, in a serene voice. *"I am taking you to a place that you cannot travel to in your conscious state. I have some people who wish to speak with you, but you have my word that I will return you to your world well before class tomorrow."*

Carmen leaned back on the suede saddle that was strapped to Dagtar's back as the Dragon soared north over snow-blanketed mountains. The cool wind thrashed through her hair and across her face, making for a chilly yet refreshing ride through the sky. Before long, a grand, russet-colored mountain, which cast a colossal shadow over all of its surroundings, came into sight.

"Mount Landrea, Kelmarsia's tallest peak," Dagtar observed. *"That is where we are headed."*

It was only minutes after catching the first glimpse of the mountain that Dagtar began his slow descent. Carmen held tight to his saddle as he flew through the mountainsides and on toward the greatest peak of them all.

As they approached their destination, they came upon a stunning waterfall that cascaded down the north side of the mountain and emptied into a lake hundreds of feet below. The way in which the sun sparkled off the tumbling white falls breaking over the side of the cliff was surely one of the most spectacular sights in all of Kelmarsia.

Dagtar crossed over the lake and flew on toward the waterfall. Carmen could feel the wonderful breeze of the rushing water against her face as they drew nearer. That was the moment in which Dagtar whispered, *"Look up."*

Carmen gazed toward the sky, and her mouth dropped open…just before a huge smile spread across her face.

Above them spanned a flawless and radiant rainbow. Sparkling translucently in the light of the day, its multicolored arch stretched all the way from a mountain on the opposite side of the lake to the one for which they were headed. The purest of joy and delight filling their hearts at its sight, Carmen and her Dragon flew beneath the rainbow and across the glistening body of water.

Dagtar issued a low growling noise as he came up to the waterfall. In response, the flowing waters magically parted like a huge stage curtain, revealing a mountain cave that had been hidden behind the gorgeous falls.

With a graceful dive, the Dragon glided through the large opening in the center of the waterfall and into the darkened cave.

Light from the torches mounted on the stone walls flickered across the rocky interior of Mount Landrea, and dripping stalactites hung in various spots of the roof. The small and shadowy cave didn't go very far into the mountain, but the darkness at the back of the cavern made its depth appear more ambiguous.

Dagtar lay down on the cold stone floor of the cave. Behind him, the falls closed up again, preventing anyone outside of the mountain from seeing through to the entrance of the secret cavern.

Upon the Dragon's request, Carmen carefully dismounted, and stood beside him, looking ahead toward the back of the cave. She stared into the darkness, unsure of what she was supposed to be seeing. The rushing sound of the waterfall behind her was all that she could hear.

"We've arrived," Dagtar called out, gazing past the shadows. *"Come out and see your daughter."*

Carmen felt her heart skip a beat. She cast a fleeting glance at Dagtar, searching for answers, before staring straight ahead of her again. She heard footsteps coming toward her. The outlines of two figures were walking out of the darkness.... As they emerged into the light of the torches, she suppressed the urge to shout.

William and Isabella Fox, their faces aglow with the warmest of smiles, came forward and into Carmen's embrace. Overwhelmed with happiness, Carmen hugged her parents as tightly as she could. She fought hard not to cry, as she knew that once she started, she wouldn't be able to stop.

"How...?" Carmen struggled to speak as she looked up at them. "How are you here?"

"It doesn't matter, Carmen," her father said, patting her shoulder. His green eyes were radiant as he gazed down at her. "What matters is that *you* are here. Your mother and I have important knowledge that we need to share with you."

"That's right," Isabella said in a soft voice, as she and Carmen released themselves from each other's arms. "We know that you're about to begin your search for the second Secret.... For this one, you must travel back here to Kelmarsia."

"Like the Secret in Kelmar, Kelmarsia's Secret is guarded by powerful creatures that will try to prevent you from obtaining it," William explained. "The Secret is hidden inside an ancient shrine atop a mountain beyond Merlin's castle—Mount Alberik."

"What types of creatures are protecting it?" Carmen asked, her heart still racing as she spoke with her deceased parents. "Do you know?"

Isabella shook her head.

"We don't," she said disappointedly. "We have never been to the shrine, but others have told us that getting inside is an impossible task...impossible for anyone, except the Chosen One."

William Fox glanced up at the waterfall behind Dagtar, and then looked down at Carmen again.

"We have little time left with you," he said, taking his daughter's hands into his. "Please listen carefully to our words."

Carmen nodded, staring up into her father's eyes.

"To acquire the second Secret, you must be prepared to face these protectors, and do as they request of you to gain access to the shrine," William told her. "If you can prove to them that you are worthy of owning the Secret, they will allow you passage into the shrine. Stand by your friends throughout."

"There is nothing stronger than the bond of your friendship," Isabella reminded her. "Keep that in your heart, and no one shall ever be able to truly defeat you."

Carmen nodded once more, unable to look away from the sight of her parents, who looked just as genuine and loving as they had when she'd first met them.

"Can I see you again after this?" she asked, her heart aching at the thought of having to leave them. "When can I come back?"

"I'm sorry, Carmen," Isabella said, gently brushing her hand across her daughter's forehead. "But we cannot come with you on your journey to the second Secret. Only you and those you love from Kelmar can make that sacred trip."

William looked once more toward the waterfall before gazing back at his daughter.

"I'm afraid that your time here is nearly up," he said, sounding regretful. "For now, we have to bid you farewell."

"But…" Carmen reached out to her father, as though she could hold on to him and stay here forever.

She couldn't bear the idea of departing Kelmarsia without her parents for a second time…. It felt like someone had just stolen a piece of her heart, and would keep it locked away from her for the rest of her life.

Dagtar walked up next to Carmen, nuzzling the side of her face.

"It is time to go, Carmen," he said, his sadness for her heavy in his voice. *"We must return you to Kelmar."*

"I…I…can't…." Carmen said, choking back tears as she gazed into her departed parents' faces. "I don't want to leave you again."

William and Isabella shared one final embrace with their daughter, their love for one another unbroken, despite the boundaries of the worlds that divided them. They whispered their heartfelt goodbyes, and though none of them ever wished for the moment to end…Carmen finally let her parents go.

Her heart was aching with renewed loss, but she knew that she had no choice. She had to depart for the realm that was home to her.

Carmen smiled at her mother and father through her tears…. She was painfully reminded of how much she hated saying goodbye, but she would do what she had to do.

As Dagtar lay beside her, Carmen mounted his back. The Dragon then turned toward the waterfall and spread his wings. The waters parted to allow him to pass through once again.

Carmen wiped the fresh tears off of her face and looked back at her parents as Dagtar flew out of the tunnel. The last things that she saw were their shining, smiling faces as they waved to her. She made sure to wave back.

"I'm proud of you, Carmen," Dagtar said, as he and his friend soared through the waterfall and back up into the azure sky. *"I know that these brief meetings with your ancestors are hard for you to endure. But I promise you that you will look back one day and see that you have emerged stronger because of what you have been through in this life. We learn from our pasts…and we grow from them."*

Carmen and Dagtar sailed across the snowy mountaintops and back over the grass-covered knolls and never-ending fields of sun-kissed flowers.

"Thank you for bringing me here, Dagtar," Carmen said, in spite of her sadness, as they rose up into the clouds.

Moments later, she saw a round, bright white light appear in the sky ahead of her.

Dagtar smiled as he flew her toward the light, which grew larger by the moment.

"Here is where we part, my friend. I will see you soon. Until then…be well."

Carmen and Dagtar flew on into the white light…. The world around Carmen vanished from view as its radiance engulfed her.

But just then, an unexpected vision suddenly flooded her sight…. It was the horrible, gaunt face of Natlek Foretsam.

The appearance of the boy's wrathful brown eyes and his most atrocious smile nearly made Carmen scream. But as hard as she tried…she couldn't escape from his stare—he was going to kill her!

Carmen awoke with a start back in her darkened room in Thunder Academy. She was out of breath, and her face was damp with perspiration. She abruptly sat up in bed, trying to get her mind aligned with where she was. Blaze stirred in the darkness beside her.

"Carmen, what happened?" he asked, his large eyes searching hers. "Did you have a nightmare?"

Carmen buried her face in her hands, her mind still spinning. It took her a couple of minutes to become fully aware of what had just happened, and to mentally return to her conscious state.

"It was all a dream…" She sighed, staring into her dark room. "I can't believe it…."

Blaze looked at her with concern.

"What did you see?" he asked. "The unrest in your subconscious caused *me* to awaken as well."

As difficult as it was to explain, Carmen proceeded to give the details of the dream to Blaze, who listened with fascination as his Master retold of her voyage with Dagtar to the World of Light. She told him about seeing her parents, and the knowledge that they had shared with her. Then she told him how she had seen Natlek's face right before she woke up.

"I had this feeling like...he wanted to kill me," Carmen said, suppressing a shudder at the memory of the boy's devilish look. "I don't think it was my imagination."

Blaze was nodding thoughtfully.

"Well, I'm not sure why you saw Natlek, but I do have some theories on the rest of the dream," he said. "Do you remember the incantation for *Death's Eternal Sleep?*"

"Uh...vaguely..." Carmen said, her mind still hazy.

"One of the lines in the incantation is this: *And while each of us is inevitably bound to experience loss by death's hand, in living we are without limits in exploring the frontiers of death in sleep,*" Blaze recited. "We're free to explore the realms of the afterlife in our dreams.... This is exactly what *you* just did."

"Hmm...you could be right," Carmen said slowly. "But it somehow seemed...so real."

"My other idea was that this trip might have been a simple visitation dream brought about by Dagtar," Blaze said. "He did it once before...back when he first told you about the war in Kelmarsia and Keltan."

"I remember that well, but *this* dream was different," Carmen said, with certainty. "What happened before I woke up...wasn't a vision. It definitely occurred in real life. But regardless, Dagtar has helped us out yet again.... Now we know where we have to travel to find the second Secret of Kelmar."

Blaze nodded.

"The World of Light."

As Blaze spoke those last words, Carmen noticed that her room didn't seem as dark as it had been when she'd first woken up. She got on her knees and turned to gaze out through the window over her bed.

With the departure of the evening stars, the golden sun was rising over the eastern Barahir Mountains that bordered

Sarcanian Valley, illuminating the rocks below in striking shades of red and orange light. A new day had begun.

CHAPTER FIFTEEN
NATLEK FORETSAM

Much to Carmen's relief, Natlek was absent from training the rest of the week. Haidar informed his Captains that the boy was off visiting his uncle in Pyramid City. As he was not a student, he could come and go from the valley as he pleased. Carmen wasn't sure whether she believed a visit with his uncle to be the real reason behind Natlek's nonattendance, but she was nonetheless glad to have him gone, even if it was just for a few days.

While he was away, the Sarcan Captains continued on with their studies of Kelmarsian battle spells. The weather remained stable, and so the Captains held class outdoors every day, as usual. Carmen had told the rest of her Souls of Destiny about her dream the night after it had occurred, and they tended to agree with Blaze that what she had gone through had indeed been real—a visitation dream made real by her ability to travel to the worlds of the afterlife in her sleep.

Two days after sending out her letter to her grandfather, Carmen received a note back from him. Excited, she tore open the envelope, which had arrived by messenger bird along with her first copy of *The Kelmarian Review*.

> *Dear Carmen,*
> *I am so happy to hear that you and your Souls are well, and to learn of your success in the afterlife and in finding the first Secret. That's my girl!*
> *I believe you're right about the Secrets; I'm sure that once you discover the others, they will all come together and make sense.*

It's thrilling for me to hear that your mom, dad, and grandmother are happy and together in Kelmarsia! I can't wait to hear more about your trip the next time that I see you.

Reoc is wise to be training you and your classmates in Kelmarsian magic. Word from Inpu is that the peace in Kelmarsia is deteriorating daily. Merlin and his forces are working to employ yet another new Protection at the Impassable Barrier. I'm sad to say that the defenses are only a temporary fix. Eventually, the chains will be broken, and we may inevitably face all-out war in the afterworlds.

With these Protections, we are essentially buying ourselves time—time to mobilize our defenses and for you to collect the remaining Secrets. I know that you are already under stress to track down the Secrets, and I don't want to put any added pressure on you. However, as your grandfather, I must be honest with you. If Triedastron finds a way to get into Kelmarsia, he will then try to come after <u>you.</u>

I am highly disturbed by the individual about whom you spoke in your letter. I know his uncle from my dealings with Parliament, but never have I heard him mention the name of this supposed nephew of his.

I have asked around, and no one I have spoken with knows of him either. Should you continue to feel uncomfortable around him, you must alert Haidar immediately. Trust your senses; do not be misled by the improvement in the weather, for dark forces continue to remain at work in the worlds beyond.

If you can take the time to come to Mortrock Forest this weekend, I would love to see you. We have a lot that we need to catch up on. Thunderbolt and I finished up the last of the repairs on the house yesterday. I believe our home looks even better than it did before the storm!

Stay in touch, Carmen. I look forward to seeing you soon.

Love,

Pop

Once she had finished reading, Carmen put down her grandfather's letter and unfolded the daily *Kelmarian Review*. She read its headline aloud.

THE SKIES CLEAR, BUT FOR HOW LONG?

Beneath the headline was a photograph of a grassy field beneath a sunny, cloudless sky.

Carmen and Blaze read the article, and then passed it around to the others for them to look at. The piece examined the weather patterns over the past several weeks, and noted how the conditions had improved dramatically, with little explanation provided by Kelmarian officials. There were also photographs of earlier storm damage, including shots of beaches blanketed with snow, tornado-ravaged remains of forests, a sea storm over a western ocean, and hail pummeling a small northern town.

The article contained a quote from Head of State, Danuvius Dorvai, in which he essentially reported that new and more effective measures were being undertaken in Kelmarsia to guard against a Keltan invasion, just as Blaine had described, and that Kelmarians have no cause for concern. He did suggest, however, that Kelmarians take extra precautions when traveling, especially at night. There was no telling when the battles in the afterlife would escalate again, and this meant possibly unpredictable weather, and the small chance of Phantom Warriors entering into Kelmar. The article didn't give Carmen and her friends much new information, but it did show them that few were aware of just how critical the situation in Kelmarsia was becoming.

When Sunday morning arrived, Carmen and her Souls rose early to get a head start on the busy day ahead. They skipped breakfast at the castle in favor of paying Carmen's grandfather and Blaze's father a visit in Mortrock Forest.

They left their room shortly after 7AM and walked down to the main corridor of the school. With Carmen and Blaze's classmates and most of the castle's other inhabitants sleeping in, the stone halls were unusually silent.

They were about to walk down the last flight of stairs to the first floor when a middle-aged woman with long and wavy dark brown hair walked around the corner downstairs and began to climb up the steps. There was a female Sarcan flying just above her shoulder.

The woman looked up at Carmen and her friends. Her eyes were copper-colored, sharp and pretty. Upon seeing the group standing at the top of the stairs, she smiled, her violet and gold robes swishing behind her. Carmen noticed that there were a number of military medals pinned to the fabric.

"Carmen Fox and the Souls of Destiny, am I right?" the woman asked courteously, bowing her head with respect as she stood on the step below them. "I'm Officer Faelyn Sheridae, the Sarcan Basic Training Instructor. It's a pleasure to meet you."

"I'm Swift, Faelyn's Partner," her Sarcan added politely. She had purple and red star-shaped markings in her light golden fur.

"Oh...right, hi," Carmen replied, bowing back to both of them with her Souls. "It's a pleasure to meet you, too."

"I've heard a lot about you from Commander Haidar," Sheridae said. "He says that you're one of his best students."

Carmen smiled modestly.

"Well, he has a *lot* of good students," she informed Sheridae. "The entire class is really talented, actually."

"Ah yes, so I've been told," she said, with a cool smile.

"How are the new Sarcan Cadets doing?" Carmen asked. "I see them walking down to Thunder Canyon in the mornings."

Sheridae's face lit up with a grin.

"I'm pleased to report that they are doing splendidly thus far," she said, with much pride. "They are truly making my first year as an instructor a joy."

Sheridae's dedication to her craft and to her students was apparent in her eyes, which shined noticeably as she talked about her experiences in Sarcanian Valley up until now.

"I was a Sarcan Officer in the Kelmarian Army for many years, and it's an exciting new challenge for me to be teaching the magical leaders of tomorrow," she explained. "And Commander Haidar has been an immense help along the way. His undying support throughout this transition has been nothing but a blessing to me."

"That's great," Carmen said cheerfully. Sheridae's infectious smile was making her feel happy as well. "I'm so glad that you're enjoying it here."

Sheridae walked up to the landing with Swift. Then she sighed as she gazed around the empty hallway behind Carmen and her friends.

"Don't you just love this time of day? It's so peaceful and quiet…." Sheridae observed. "I was just out taking my Sunday walk around the valley. It helps me to relax, and prepare my mind for the week ahead."

"Yeah, it is nice," Carmen agreed, noticing the calm silence of the castle even more now that she had pointed it out.

"So, where are you off to on this fine morning?" Officer Sheridae asked.

"We're going to visit my grandfather," Carmen said. "He lives in Mortrock Forest."

"How lovely," Sheridae replied, another smile breaking across her fair face. "Give all my best to him. He's nearly as famous as you are, being the grandfather of the Guardian of Kelmar."

Carmen laughed.

"I will," she said.

Sheridae pulled up one of the sleeves of her robe and checked her watch.

"Well, I'd best be on my way," she said. "I don't want to hold you up any longer, and I have to prepare for tomorrow's lesson anyway. It was so nice meeting you and your friends."

"Yes, I'm really glad that we ran into you," Carmen said, with a grin. "Good luck with your class."

"Thank you, Guardian," Sheridae said, still smiling warmly as she turned to walk down the corridor.

Carmen and her friends descended the rest of the stairs to the first floor and ambled out the front doors of the castle.

Even though it had just recently turned to autumn, the outdoor air was beginning to feel of the colder months. There was a noticeable chill in the breeze as Carmen and her friends crossed the grounds of Sarcanian Valley and entered into the dense neighboring forest.

As they walked through the woods, Carmen thought about Officer Sheridae, and how very kind she seemed. Still, Carmen knew that there was toughness deep down inside of her that ultimately made her the ideal blend of compassion and strength for a Sarcan instructor. As far as teachers went, Sheridae seemed to balance Haidar out quite well.

Carmen and her friends walked north for almost ten minutes. The chirping of morning birds and the barking of flying Talsonca dogs rustled through the green foliage. The peace and natural beauty of this forest were things that Carmen loved returning to.

In next to no time, a beige stone cottage with a gray roof appeared out of the shadows, nestled in the shade of the ancient trees.

Carmen knocked on the wooden front door, and a moment later, she was in her grandfather's warm embrace. Thunderbolt flew out from inside the house and hugged his son with equally fond affection. He always looked to Carmen like an older version of Blaze. He possessed the same large blue eyes that his son did, and though his blue markings weren't shaped like flames, as Blaze's were, they too were on his wings and legs.

"I've missed you so much," Blaine said, as he released Carmen from his arms. "It feels like ages since I've seen you."

"I've missed you, too," Carmen said, smiling up at him. He was wearing his favorite red robes with golden trim. "Can we join you for breakfast?"

"Of course! Come in, come in," Blaine said. He gladly let Carmen and her friends inside, greeting each one of the Souls of Destiny with cheerfulness.

"Thunderbolt and I were just setting the table," Blaine said, as he closed the door after them.

Carmen and her friends passed through the familiar living room, finding that it looked just as welcoming and comfortable as they remembered it. The twin green sofas and antique rocking chair were placed around a thatched rug, upon which stood a wooden coffee table and a lamp. Flames were flickering in the stone fireplace.

They then walked into the kitchen and came upon the partially set table as the sweet smell of pancakes filled their noses. There were also two omelets cooking on the stove, and toast warming up in the toaster atop the counter.

Blaine kept this room in immaculate condition. Everything was kept in its place, with the dark wooden cupboards stacked neatly with plates, cups, utensils, and stocks of food. The beige tiled floor was always sparkling clean. There was a refrigerator standing next to the stove against the wall, and a spotless white sink beneath the window.

"Have a seat, all of you," Blaine said, gesturing toward the wooden chairs around the table. "Thunderbolt and I will have breakfast ready shortly."

"Don't you need any help?" Carmen asked, as her friends seated themselves.

"Oh no, not at all. You just sit and relax, Carmen," Blaine said, moving toward the cabinets and pulling a couple of them open. He began to remove a handful of glass jars filled with colored magical dust, which he would turn into food. "So, what would you like? We've got all sorts of things to eat."

Carmen smiled.

"We'll have whatever you and Thunderbolt were going to have. It smells really good in here already."

Blaine got out three more cast-iron pans and placed them on the stove. He opened all but one of the jars from his cupboard and threw handfuls of sparkling dust into each pan.

He then flicked his wand at the stovetop—and within an instant, the dust had transformed into three sizzling omelets. Blaine sprinkled the remaining dust into the toaster. As he worked, Thunderbolt flew around the table with teacups and utensils and set the remaining places for Carmen and her Souls.

Once the trio of omelets was done, Blaine moved them from the pans to white plates, and then made two more, before opening up the last jar that he had retrieved from the cabinet. About thirty seconds later, half a dozen pancakes were browning in the final large pan.

In the end, Blaine made more than twice that amount, along with a teapot of sweet Perterale tea. The entire undertaking took less than five minutes.

After placing a full plate in front of each of his guests, Blaine sat down across from Carmen to eat his own meal.

"As I told you in my letter, Carmen, Thunderbolt was able to help me with the last of the repairs yesterday," Blaine said, smiling at his granddaughter as he pulled his chair up to the table. "With magic and a little hard work, we can achieve great things."

Carmen sliced her omelet with her knife and then shoveled a thick forkful into her mouth. The omelet was so delicious and filling that she didn't know how she would ever finish the entire thing *and* the pancakes and toast that lined her plate.

"So…what is Kelmarsia really like?" Blaine asked, his blue eyes wide with curiosity. "Is it true that the World of Light is wondrous beyond anything in our world?"

"It is," Carmen said, swallowing her sizable bite of omelet. It was difficult for her to think of how to adequately describe the true splendor of Kelmarsia, but she tried her hardest to give her grandfather a broad sense of what it was like.

"Kelmarsia looks just like Kelmar, except that everything is even more beautiful…if you can believe that," she said slowly. "It's an amazing place filled with forests, mountains, and rivers…and all of our ancestors live there together."

Blaine had a faraway look in his eyes as he imagined the sight of the pristine spirit realm.

"Ah…and how were your mom and dad?" he asked, finally snapping out of his daydream. "You were much too young when they died to have remembered what they were like."

"Yes, but they were…just like I had always pictured them," Carmen said, feeling a grin spread across her face at the simple thought of them. "They were kind and loving, and…they looked like me."

Blaine nodded slowly, completely absorbed by her words.

"You are very much like the both of them, in more ways than one," he observed. "That is excellent that you got to see them…. What a truly priceless experience. You will remember it for the rest of your life, Carmen, I guarantee you that."

Carmen smiled as she continued to eat her food, even more aware now than she was before of how lucky she was to have been able to meet her parents in the legendary land of Kelmarsia.

She, her grandfather, and their friends ate in silence for a couple of minutes, until Carmen inquired about the latest news.

"Have you heard anything from Renalda?" she asked him. "I haven't gotten the chance to speak with Haidar about her.... And what about Alazar?"

Blaine swallowed his bite of toast.

"Our last conversation was three days ago," he recalled. "Renalda spent an extra day at her parents' home after you left for Kelmarsia. The storms made it too dangerous for her and Alazar to travel back to Amera Island. But as soon as the weather returned to normal, the two of them went home. From what Renalda said, she and Alazar are both doing well, and she asked me to give you their best wishes. Renalda plans to come visit everyone here in the valley as soon as she can. She's a teacher to very young children back on Amera Island, and so she can only come on the weekends or over the holidays."

"Mmm...is there any news from Parliament?" Carmen asked, as she continued to eat her omelet. "I just started receiving *The Kelmarian Review* at the castle today."

Blaine took a drink from his cup of Perterale tea.

"A few of my friends in Parliament tell me that there's a hearing being planned for Eli Elezar," he said in a dark voice, as he lowered his cup. "Maidak Kalvaro is the one leading the investigation. He's out to prove that Eli acted with full awareness and intention in what he did to you."

Carmen swallowed abruptly, almost choking on the chunk of omelet that she had consumed.

"That's not true though," she croaked, reaching for her teacup to force down the last of the egg. "Inpu and Haidar believe that Eli was under the control of someone else when he gave me the poisoned amulet. Haidar mentioned the name of the curse...."

"*Devious Manipulation,*" Anubis reminded her, looking up from his food.

"I believe that also," Blaine said firmly, as Carmen sipped her tea. "Eli is a well-regarded Kelmarian Seer, and a man with the highest of moral standards.... I've known him myself for nearly ten years. He is one of the last people that one would ever suspect of treachery."

"When is the hearing scheduled for?" Glamis asked.

"The final date has yet to be set, but from what it sounds like, it will be any day now," Blaine informed him and the others. "Maidak and his team of Parliamentary investigators are finalizing their case. It sounds like Maidak is out for blood, and he appears determined to prove Eli guilty."

Blaine looked toward Carmen.

"You should expect to receive notice in the mail requesting your presence at the hearing in Pyramid City," he told her. "Because the alleged act of treason was committed against you, you will need to testify in the case. Your Souls will probably also have to appear, as witnesses."

Carmen felt a nervous twinge in her stomach. She stopped eating.

"What should I say when I go there?" she asked. She had never been to a hearing, or a trial of any kind, for that matter.... Her initial reaction to the idea of testifying in front of a Parliamentary jury was one of unease.

Blaine's blue eyes were reflective.

"You tell the truth," he said, in a soft but forthright voice. "If you speak from your heart, justice shall prevail."

"You have nothing to worry about, Carmen," Stellar said, gazing down the table at her. "You've done nothing wrong, and we'll be there to support you."

Carmen sipped her tea again, allowing the warm, sweet taste to linger on her tongue. The thought of defending Eli in front of Parliament was not something that she would look forward to, but she trusted her grandfather's judgment. She could not allow an innocent man to go to prison, or suffer an even worse consequence for a crime that another had committed. The only problem was that she did not know who cursed Eli. She hoped that this would not prove to be the deciding factor in convicting him.... But unless she could find out who was responsible, her defense of Eli would likely fall on deaf ears.

"If the mind controller was indeed one of our own, that Kelmarian will eventually be found as the true traitor," Blaine said. "In due time, the truth always comes out."

Carmen resumed eating her breakfast, her stomach still feeling slightly unsettled. If the pancakes her grandfather had made hadn't been so delectable, she probably wouldn't have wanted to eat any more.

"So, how is your training coming along?" Thunderbolt asked Blaze and Carmen, seeming to sense Carmen's disquiet. "Have you learned some new techniques?"

"It's been excellent so far," Blaze said with a smirk, passing Carmen an encouraging glance. "We're focusing mostly on Kelmarsian spells right now, and then I think that we're going to learn some more advanced Kelmarian magic as the term progresses."

"Blaine told me about the new student," Thunderbolt said, biting off a piece of his toast. "How has he been?"

"He wasn't in class most of the week. He's been out visiting his uncle," Blaze told him. "We're pretty glad of that."

"Yes, you never know what's going on these days with the whole mess in Kelmarsia," Thunderbolt said, a suspicious expression on his face. "It is good that he's gone. When he returns though...I would mention something to Haidar again."

"I had a dream about him the other night," Carmen said, almost without thinking.

Her grandfather and Thunderbolt both looked up from their food. They seemed very interested in what she was about to say. Now feeling the need to explain herself further, Carmen put down her fork and looked between them.

"It was a really good dream before I saw him," she said. "Dagtar visited me, and he took me to see Mom and Dad.... They told me to look for the next Secret in Kelmarsia. Then they gave me an idea of where it was located, and how I could get to it. I'm convinced that it wasn't just a dream; that it actually did happen."

Carmen paused for a moment, as Blaine and Thunderbolt were listening to her every word.

"So after I spoke with them, Dagtar flew me back to Kelmar.... And that's when I saw him...Natlek Foretsam, just before I woke up. He looked...evil."

"I see...." Blaine was leaning forward, studying Carmen closely. "And did he say anything to you?"

"No. He was just smiling...in the creepy way that he always does during class," Carmen said, shaking off the thought. "This was different though. This was more...sinister."

Blaine and Thunderbolt exchanged expressions of concern.

"This is certainly a fascinating development," Blaine said pensively, scratching his chin as he gazed at Carmen. "I'm not an expert on dream interpretation, but it sounds to me like your subconscious is trying to make you aware of something that perhaps you don't see in your waking hours. It's trying to alert you of a possible threat.... That's why it was the last thing that you saw before you woke up."

Carmen spent a few minutes considering that idea, and then reasoned that her grandfather's notion was indeed a logical conclusion.

"So in light of this dream…" she said slowly. "Do you think that I should go talk to Haidar?"

Blaine thought for a moment, but then shook his head.

"For right now, I think that your time would be better spent trying to locate information about this boy on your own," he said. "Pay a visit to the school library. It has files on political families that date back hundreds of years. Look up his surname, and see what you uncover."

"We were actually planning on doing that this afternoon," Blaze said, cleaning his face with a cloth napkin.

Blaine smiled and tapped his temple.

"A wise idea from a wise young mind," he said with approval. He then looked toward Carmen, who was finishing up the last of her pancakes.

"On a more positive note, it's wonderful that you were able to see your mom and dad again," Blaine said, his eyes glistening. "I wish that I could have been there, too."

As Carmen and her grandfather caught up, Blaze talked with his father for a time about their family back at Dormien's Rock. Shortly before they were done eating, there was a knocking on one of the windows in the living room.

"I'll get it," Blaine said, wiping his mouth with his napkin before getting up from the table. "I have a feeling I know who this is."

Blaine left the room and walked to the living room. Within only seconds of him opening up the window, Cherub soared into the kitchen and sang a cheery "Good morning!" to her friends.

Though Carmen had just seen her at Haidar's wedding, it was still hard for her to take in how much the pretty young Sarcan had grown since she and her friends had rescued her during the Third Challenge here in Mortrock Forest last year.

Back then, she had only been an infant—a tiny ball of white golden fur. And though she had grown, and her fur had darkened to its adult golden color, it was still light and feminine. Her bright green eyes sparkled in the early daylight.

"How is everyone?" she asked affectionately, as Blaine walked in after her.

"Everyone's fine, Cherub," Carmen said, grinning at her. "How are you doing?"

"Oh, very well, very well!" she chirped, in her high and pleasant voice. She sat down on the end of the table next to Stellar, wrapping her claws over the edge of the tabletop. "Blaine told me that you would probably be coming over today, so I wanted to make sure that I saw you before you left."

"Would you like anything to eat?" Blaine asked his new guest courteously, beginning to gather up the used breakfast dishes.

"No, but thank you, Blaine," Cherub replied, batting her eyelashes at him in a friendly manner. "I just ate not that long ago. There was a big new school of Arakives in the pond where I usually fish."

Carmen helped Blaine clean up, and neatly deposited the dirty dishes in the sink. Then she and her grandfather sat back down with their companions.

Cherub was eagerly chatting away with Stellar, who was her closest friend in the room.

"Blaine and Thunderbolt were kind enough to let me stay here during the storms," she told him. "I'm thankful that the bad weather is finally over.... It was scary for a while there."

"Let's hope that the worst of the storms are behind us," Stellar said, sounding less than positive. "It can get really dangerous. You have to be careful."

Cherub nodded.

"Word around the woods is that the Sarcan Council is trying to push a bill through Parliament that will declare Sarcans to be an endangered species," she reported.

"An endangered species?" Carmen asked, prior to apologizing for interrupting her conversation. "Why would they do that? There's lots of Sarcans around."

"Not anymore," Cherub said, shaking her head sadly. "In some areas of Kelmar, the Sarcan population has taken a hit from the treacherous weather. Hundreds of Sarcans that couldn't escape the storms have been killed."

"What?" Carmen gasped. "No way."

She stared down at her empty plate, stunned. She couldn't imagine mere weather fronts being responsible for so many casualties of a species as powerful as the Sarcan.

"Noel tells me that Dormien's Rock didn't suffer any fatalities as a result of the storms," Thunderbolt informed her. "Luckily, there *is* some good news amidst all of the tragedy."

Concerned, Carmen patted Blaze on the shoulder, feeling his soft golden fur beneath her fingertips.

"Let's try our best to keep the good news coming," she said quietly.

When Carmen and her Souls were getting ready to leave Blaine's home, late morning was turning into early afternoon. After spending the first part of the day with Blaine, Thunderbolt, and Cherub, Carmen and Glamis washed and put away the dishes. Then they all walked outside and took in the tranquility of the forest in the warmth of the daylight. It had been a great start to the day, and it was hard for Carmen to want to return to Sarcanian Valley. She hugged her grandfather, Thunderbolt, and Cherub before saying her goodbyes. Blaze did the same.

"Once Advanced Training is over, I'll come back here to live with you," Carmen promised Blaine, as she stepped back from him. "I would live with you now if the Sarcan Council didn't require Captains to live in the school."

"I know that you would." Blaine smiled. "But it's safer for you and the others to stay in the castle, and your studies are very important. I'll always be here for whenever you need me."

"I'll *always* need you," Carmen said, staring up into her grandfather's eyes with the deepest admiration. "I'll come visit every weekend."

"Unless you're out saving Kelmar of course," Blaine said with a wink.

"Right." Carmen grinned back.

She and her friends bid everyone farewell and got on their way back to Thunder Academy.

This trip across the valley was far more pleasant than the one earlier in the day had been. The fall sun, shining down through the clouds, had warmed up the rocky gorge very nicely. There were even some Cadets training out on the dueling fields.

Carmen's group walked back up the mountain staircase and into the castle, returning to their room for lunch and a restful afternoon before they would head to dinner with the class of Sarcan Captains. As she and her Souls would not be able to travel to Kelmarsia for the second Secret until Inpu could come to Kelmar for them, Carmen would follow through on her promise to attend Kamie's dinner with the other students.

After entering her room, Carmen dug out her three swords so that she could polish them, something that she had been reminding herself to do for a while now. She didn't know when she might have to utilize them again in battle.

Carmen used a soft cloth to meticulously shine up the blades and hilts of her three sabers—the Guardian Sword, and the Light and Dark Swords. In their own way, each of the swords told a unique story.

The Guardian Sword was a saber with a silver blade and a gold hilt, the latter of which was encrusted with blazing sapphire stones. The hilt was engraved with the initials of her Souls—*BSGAD*. Blaze's mother, Noel, had presented it to her as a gift early on in her journey in Kelmar.

The Light Sword had a gold hilt covered with red stones. She had received it after the Magicon War, during the victory celebration in Pyramid City. The blade was inscribed with the words, *The Light that Rose out of the Darkness.*

The third and final saber, the Dark Sword, had many previous owners and a deadly history behind it. It was a gleaming red saber, possessing a silver hilt inlaid with rubies. Glamis and the rest of her Souls had given it to her last Christmas, and it was the weapon that she ultimately used to stab *The Book of Kelmar,* destroy Desorkhan's soul, and defeat the Magicon.

When she was done cleaning all of her swords, Carmen kneeled down to store them back in their respective leather scabbards in a lower drawer of her dresser.

As she stood up again, she found herself staring at the framed photograph of her and her parents that sat atop that very dresser. It was her favorite picture of them—the one that she had always looked at with regret before she came to Kelmar.

William and Isabella Fox stood proudly at the front of their beloved printing factory with their newborn daughter. Isabella was cradling her baby girl in her arms, her face light and blissful. William had his arms wrapped warmly around his wife and his daughter, and both parents were smiling the most beautiful smiles that only two people in love ever could.

Now, when Carmen looked at the photograph, she felt a sadness that was different from the one she had experienced prior to coming here. When she lived in the non-magical realm, she knew that only in death would she ever have the chance to see them again. She had been right of course, but in Kelmar, she had been given an early glimpse into that sacred eternity.

After experiencing what it was like to be with them, Carmen felt regret in a different way. She no longer regretted the fire that had taken their lives, as she had no control over that. Instead, she now regretted that she could not spend all of her days with them in Kelmarsia—a perfect paradise of unending happiness.

Although she was more than content with her life here in Kelmar, there would always be that missing part of her that could never be replaced. She almost wished that she had never seen her parents in the afterlife, for it made her miss them even more.

Carmen counted her blessings for her friends and her grandfather, who made every moment of her life worth living to the fullest. She did not wander through each day in sadness. Rather, the grief was something that returned every so often, but only to be remedied by the company of her companions, the calling of her destiny, and the promise of brighter days ahead.

All of these thoughts, and countless others, carried through Carmen's mind as she studied the old photograph. She finally forced herself to look away, feeling more ready to enjoy an afternoon with her friends in Thunder Academy.

She and her Souls opted to venture to the library after Kamie's dinner, as they assumed that it would be less crowded then. Even though Natlek had taken an indefinite leave of absence from Thunder Academy, Carmen was no less determined to find out all that she could about him. So she and her friends stayed in for the remainder of the day, and ended up leaving their room just past five to go to the party.

Kamie's dinner was taking place out on the castle's southern terrace. It was a place that provided a space for larger gatherings of guests, and it had played host to many events and parties throughout the years.

Kamie had already taken the liberty of ordering the Sarcans who delivered the castle meals to take all of the food for the Captains up to the terrace. Carmen had never been there, and so she counted on Blaze to lead her and the others to it.

The southern terrace was accessible through a doorway located on the highest floor of the castle. Carmen and her friends walked up to the corridor and through the pair of glass doors at the end of the hall.

From there, they were led out onto the spacious terrace, which offered a spectacular view of the surrounding valley. A white stone balustrade ran along the balcony, as did carved statues of white Sarcans, obelisks, and spheres on plinths. There were also assorted potted plants lining the patio. A long table covered with a white tablecloth contained a buffet spread for the twelve Sarcan Masters and their Partners.

When Carmen and her Souls walked outside, all of the other Captains had already arrived. By now, most of them had gotten their dinner and were seated two or three pairs each to round, dark metal tables that were scattered around the space.

"Carmen, Blaze, you're here!" Kamie got up from her table and rushed over to them, her bright turquoise robes blowing in the breeze. "We didn't think you'd make it," she said, excited.

"I promised you we would come if we could," Carmen reminded her, with a polite smile.

"I hope you don't mind that all of us came," Blaze said, on behalf of the rest of Carmen's Souls.

"Of course not! Come on and get something to eat," Kamie insisted, pulling the two of them over to the buffet table before ushering Carmen's other friends in the same direction. "There's more than enough for everyone!"

Carmen took a warm dish from the pile and proceeded to put together plates for her Souls. All of the food was stored in deep silver trays that kept it hot as long as the Captains needed it. There was a wide selection of everything from fresh bread and salad to Kelmarian meats, cheeses, and fish.

"We have an empty seat at our table," Kamie said, on her way back to eat. "You're welcome to come sit with us."

"Great," Carmen said, placing a large Arakive on Blaze's dish. "Thanks, Kamie."

Carmen asked each of her Souls what they wanted to eat, and then filled their individual plates. Stellar, Glamis, and Anubis all carried their food across the terrace to the foot of Kamie's table, which was near the glass doors of the castle.

As Carmen loaded her own dish with helpings of roasted Falconave, steamed vegetables, and bread, an anxious thought entered her mind. She was thankful that all of the carefree Captains around her were talking and laughing loudly enough so that they wouldn't hear her whisper a request to Blaze.

"Can you check to see who else is sitting at Kamie's table?" Carmen muttered to the Sarcan sitting atop her shoulder.

Blaze shot a glance back at the table, under which his three fellow Souls were eating their dinner.

"It's Jayden, Rose, and Dall," he informed her.

"Oh, good," Carmen said, breathing a sigh of relief.

"Why do you ask?"

"Uh...no reason really," Carmen murmured. ".... I just thought that Kamie might have been setting me up."

"Setting you up?" Blaze asked, confused. "What do you mean?"

"Never mind," Carmen said, with a shrug. "It's nothing important…. It's actually pretty silly."

Carmen finished getting her food, and then she and Blaze brought their plates over to Kamie's table.

Of the three other individuals sitting here, Jayden was the sweet, red-haired, and freckle-faced girl who happened to be the tallest sorceress in the class. Her Sarcan, Rose, had light golden fur and pink markings that almost looked like flowers. Kamie's Sarcan, Dall, was also a female, and possessed slightly darker fur that was speckled with silver and blue.

As Glamis, Anubis, and Stellar munched on their food under the table, Kamie, Jayden, Carmen, and their Sarcans soon found themselves lost in lighthearted conversation.

"So, I'm telling you, if Haidar makes us learn another impossible Kelmarsian Protective spell, I'm just dropping out of Thunder Academy," Kamie proclaimed at one point, stabbing at the meat on her plate with her fork. "I mean, really, enough is enough. That last one with the wand balancing was just ridiculously hard!"

"Hey, what are *you* complaining about?" Jayden asked, hitting Kamie lightly on her arm. "You were the first one in the class to get it right!"

"Only because I was determined not to drop my wand on my head!" Kamie argued. "I don't think that any of us will ever use that one…. It's difficult enough to cast it in a quiet setting. How in the world would we be able to use it out on the fields of battle? What would we say to our enemies? Oh, hold on a minute before you attack me. I have to meditate so that I can balance my wand."

Jayden laughed.

"That is a good point," she conceded, placing her napkin up on her empty plate. "It does seem pretty impractical now that you mention it."

"I think Haidar just wants us to have a broad range of knowledge on different kinds of spells. He probably doesn't expect us to use *all* of the ones he teaches us," Carmen said, after swallowing a mouthful of cooked Kelmarian vegetables. "He probably reasons that the more we know, the better prepared we'll be for unexpected challenges. Merlin knows we've had a few of those around here."

Kamie set down her glass of Snotree juice and chuckled.

"You've got that right, Carmen. It has been some adventure, hasn't it?"

All of the food that had been prepared for the dinner was delicious, just as it always was at Thunder Academy. As the Captains finished eating, they circulated around to one another's tables to chat. Carmen and Blaze got the chance to talk with nearly every one of their peers that evening; and as it got closer to sunset, Carmen glanced over at Draven Kalvaro, who was sitting at the far end of the terrace.

He was the only one that she hadn't seen making the rounds. His Partner, Flint, was off talking in a group of Sarcans in another corner, while Draven's two closest friends, Amaris and Luke, as well as their Sarcans, Sorin and Zay, had left him to talk with others. Draven was left sitting by himself at his table, looking sullen and distant.

"What's going on with Draven?" Carmen asked Kamie, as she sat at their table and watched him.

Kamie looked back over her shoulder at their classmate moping on the other side of the balcony. He was tall, with dark brown hair and a pale complexion, and at this moment, his dour brown eyes were staring down at his table.

"I've heard that he's been fighting with his father," Kamie said, brushing her bangs out of her eyes as she turned back to Carmen. "They don't get along very well."

"Really?" Carmen asked, taken aback. "I had the impression that they were close.... Draven seems to admire him a lot."

"He does, but they have their moments," Kamie disclosed. "Draven thinks very highly of his father, while he also sees his faults. It's when he points those out to his father that the two of them start to argue."

With Jayden off talking at another table, Carmen felt that she could dig a little bit deeper.

"What about his mother?" she asked. "Does Draven have a good relationship with her?"

"I'm not sure, but I know that his parents are divorced," she said. "He doesn't see his mother very often."

"Oh.... Well, I hope everything's okay with him," Carmen said, gazing over at her fellow Captain. "I think that deep down, Draven's not that bad of a guy. He just comes off that way sometimes."

"You're probably right," Kamie said, shrugging. "He doesn't like people to get close to him, but maybe it's because of his insecurities with his family."

Carmen nodded, finally looking away from Draven.

"Yes, that could be it."

Later that night, Carmen and Blaze had a nice talk with Akira and Keko. Carmen then got up to pour herself some more Snotree juice from the glass pitcher on the buffet table.

After Carmen got her drink, she wandered over to the side of the enclosed terrace. Leaning her elbows on the stone balustrade, she gazed out at the gorgeous Sarcanian Valley, taking in its natural magnificence as she sipped her juice.

The orange, late afternoon sun cast a serene glow on the red sandstone that encompassed the vast and ancient gorge. She could see the grand Thunder Stadium standing proudly beyond the dueling fields, where Sarcan Cadets and visitors to the castle continued to train in the shadows of the mountains. Carmen closed her eyes, feeling the warmth of the sun on her face. She inhaled deeply, breathing in the scent of the cool, early autumn breeze blowing through her hair.

As she stood there absorbed in the tranquility of the moment, another person joined her. Carmen opened her eyes, looked to her left, and found herself standing beside Shea.

"This place is beautiful, isn't it?" he remarked, leaning over the top of the balustrade, his glass in his hand. He was staring out at their surroundings with an admiration that rivaled Carmen's.

"Sometimes I forget just how amazing it is here," Shea said. "When you see it every day, it can get lost.... You don't appreciate it as much as you should. We take it for granted, and never stop to think that there's a chance it won't always be there."

"Yes...." Carmen said slowly, reflecting on his insightful words. "I guess we do."

Shea turned away from the early sunset sky to look over at her.

"It's sort of like why we're more grateful for peace during times of war," he mused. "It isn't until it's taken away that we realize how precious it is."

Carmen nodded, her thoughts too many to count. She continued to stare out at the valley in deep contemplation.

Shea looked back out with her.

"We humans tend to do that a lot with things that we love," he said.

But then he smiled.

"Gia, and others like her, remind me of how important it is...to tell those we care about how much they matter to us, before it's too late. Creatures are far better at doing that than we are."

"That's very true," Carmen said, finally turning to look at her classmate.

Shea seemed to have grown up a lot since she had met him last year. She always knew him to be considerate, kind, and intelligent, but it was almost as though the intensive training and all of his experiences in Kelmar had made him a much stronger and more thoughtful person than he had been prior.... Or perhaps he'd always had that side to him, but Carmen had never gotten the opportunity to appreciate it before now. As she watched the sunlight on his face, she wished that she could tell him all that was on her mind.

Shea gazed over at her, and the corners of his mouth spread into a warm smile as he met her eyes.

"I...uh...enjoyed dancing with you at Haidar's wedding." His face reddened as he ran his fingers nervously through his sand-colored hair. "Maybe...we can do it again sometime."

Carmen smiled back at him, recalling how much she, too, had liked dancing with *him*. And though she could think of no formal occasion where the two of them would ever get the chance to dance together again, she nodded.

"Sure," she said, her pulse beating faster than it should have. "I would like that a lot."

Shea smiled and raised his glass as he gazed at her. His blue eyes were sparkling in the light of the sunset.

Almost instinctively, Carmen raised her glass as well. At this point, she didn't care if anyone was watching them. Shea picked up a knife off of the nearest table and tapped his glass with it.

Soon, the other Captains stopped talking—and looked over toward him and Carmen.

"If I may, I'd like to propose a toast," Shea announced to the group, slowly strolling inward to the center of the terrace. "Let's all raise our glasses...to the amazing world of Kelmar."

The Masters and Sarcans gladly rose from their seats and gathered around Shea. Carmen walked over from the balustrade to join the circle. She and the others raised their glasses together and listened closely to Shea's words.

"Here's to not being afraid to tell what's in your heart," Shea proposed. "To our Unit...to our school...to Kelmar...and most of all, to everlasting peace in our world."

Shea tipped his glass forward.

"Cheers," the Captains said together.

As the golden sun disappeared beneath the horizon, Carmen and Shea clinked their glasses together. They then did the same with the rest of their classmates before drinking their juice to the hopeful prospect of harmony in their magical realm. At the conclusion of the toast, the Sarcan Captains applauded. The pleasurable evening had come to a fittingly optimistic close.

Still in high spirits from the party, Carmen and her Souls strolled down to the castle library. The hallways through which they passed were relatively quiet on this night, with only the occasional sorcerer or Sarcan roaming the corridors. As they walked, Carmen's group swapped amusing stories about the dinner, their voices echoing through the arched stone halls.

It was only a little while before they reached the heavy doors of the library. Carmen and her friends walked inside and passed by a tall, standing mirror that was leaning against the wall just past the circulation desk on the left, behind which sat a spectacle-wearing Sarcan. The mirror had been there last year, but Carmen hadn't paid much attention to it then. On this night though, the tarnished gold frame around the glass glittered in the light from the grand chandelier that hung from the high ceiling.

The library was also illuminated by several desk lamps, which were lit with hanging crystals. As a whole, the sunlight and crystals furnished the space with a soft glow that proved to be adequate for reading and studying.

Aisles of shelved books occupied the better portion of this large and often-used space. The library had a white marble floor, which had a large, gold Great Seal of Kelmar carved into the center of it. Countless paintings of past and current Sarcan Council members were displayed around the walls.

There were a handful of younger students studying at long tables that could be found throughout most of the room. A few more library visitors were browsing the shelves. Carmen and her friends found themselves an empty table near one of the back corners of the library.

"So, where should we start?" Carmen asked Blaze.

"In the reference section there's a collection of volumes containing Kelmarian family trees," Blaze informed her. "Let's head over there first."

"And I'll join you!" Glamis said eagerly. "I love studying charts on ancient ancestry. I'm well practiced at reading them."

"Fantastic," Blaze said, with a grin. Then he nodded to Stellar.

"As we're searching there, you and Anubis should check out the history section," he suggested, pointing in that direction. "Grab biographies of government leaders and anything that you find on Parliament."

"Right. No problem."

With that, the members of Carmen's group parted ways to search the library's substantial assortment of books for information about Natlek Foretsam. Carmen, Blaze, and Glamis walked to the opposite side of the library and thumbed through heavy genealogical encyclopedias. While they were doing that, Anubis and Stellar searched amongst two rows of books on the Kelmarian political system.

In about fifteen minutes, Blaze's trio returned to their table to look over what they had found. They put down their books and took their seats around the long desk. Carmen's arms ached from carrying the stack of cumbersome books all the way across the library.

After she got seated, she jotted down Natlek's full name on a scrap of paper and stared at it for thirty seconds. She reasoned that this exercise would help her to find his name in the books faster, as it would be more likely to jump out at her from the pages.

Glamis would begin his search of the books by first turning to the index in each volume. If he didn't find the Foretsam surname listed, he would close the book and put it in the discard pile, but not without first breezing through the pages and pausing every so often to study a particular family tree that he found to be fascinating for one reason or another.

Carmen could somewhat understand Glamis's interest in these charts. As she flipped through the pages of her own books, she observed how detailed many of the trees were, and just how far back in history they went.

All of the family trees presented the oldest generations at the top of the chart, leading down to the most recent generations at the base. Most of the family trees were plain, but some—especially those with descendants of royalty—were more elaborate, and detailed with illustrations of coats of arms and individual portraits.

Anubis and Stellar joined Carmen and the others before long. It took them a total of four trips to bring back their entire collection of books.

When they finally had all of their hardbacks on the table, the pair sat down with their friends and carefully scanned through each volume for any mention of the Foretsam family.

The five of them went through nearly all of their books within an hour and a half. Together, they found a total of three references to Natlek's uncle, Remnor Foretsam, all of which were short entries in an historical collection of volumes on Kelmarian politics.

There was nothing written about Remnor that stood out to Carmen as being deviant from the norm. He had been serving in Parliament for fifteen years, and prior to that, he had attended the South Kelmar Institute and served in the Kelmarian Army with his Komozale dragon.

During his term in Parliament, Remnor had worked to protect the rights of Kelmarian creatures, and pushed through a series of bills that demanded harsher punishments for those who infringed upon those rights. There was no mention of his family members, but in the total two pages or so that there were on him and his career, Carmen and her Souls didn't discover anything that was unexpected.

They had spent nearly two hours searching in vain amongst the bookshelves of the library for information on Natlek Foretsam. They were tired, frustrated, and nearly ready to call it a night. But then, sometime after nine, Blaze discovered exactly what they were looking for.

"Here it is, right here!" he said, excited.

Instantly refreshed, his friends hurriedly gathered behind him to read over his shoulder.

The Foretsam family tree was drawn across two pages of the lineage registry that Blaze had found. It was one of the more complete family trees in the book, with the earliest record of family members dating back to three hundred years ago. The tree had many branches, which included countless relatives, both close and distant.

Blaze traced his claw down the bloodline to Remnor Foretsam. He then searched all around his name, following every line leading from him. He had a married brother and a married sister, but neither of them had a child.

After staring at the chart for longer than he had to in order to realize that there was no mention of Natlek anywhere, Blaze sat back in his chair.

"This is the only documentation of the Foretsam family, and Natlek isn't on it," he concluded, sounding disappointed.

"Well, this tells us that he's not who he claims to be," Carmen said, picking up her books to put them away. She could honestly say that this finding didn't surprise her. "Our suspicions have been confirmed."

Carmen and her friends gathered up the volumes on the desk and returned them to their proper shelves, deciding it was about time that they retired to their room for the night.

In revisiting the shelves of books, Carmen came upon a hardbound book that sounded like an interesting read: *Great Battles Throughout Kelmarian History.* She reasoned that she could study it in her spare time—however little of that she had. Being that it was so late in the evening now, she planned to tell Haidar of her conclusion about Natlek's lack of ties to the Foretsam family the next morning before class.

Suppressing a yawn, Carmen walked up to the circulation desk with her Souls to check out her history book. She had the thick volume under her arm, beneath the scrap of paper containing Natlek's name.

As she waited in line behind three other patrons, Carmen examined her reflection in the antique, full-length mirror standing alongside them. That was when she saw something that caught her attention.

She edged a tad closer to the gold mirror, so close that there were mere centimeters separating her from the flecked glass.

Carmen stared at the reflection of her writing on the shred of parchment.... Natlek's full name stood out to her like it never had before.

The moment she realized what she was seeing, Carmen was unable to look away, or even speak. A chill ran down her spine.

Her heart pounding in her ears, she read Natlek Foretsam's name as it was reflected backwards in the mirror.

MASTER OF KELTAN

CHAPTER SIXTEEN
TRIEDASTRON'S REVENGE

Carmen didn't remember much of what happened after that, but the next thing she knew, she and her Souls were running as fast as they could through the corridors of Thunder Academy on their way to Commander Haidar's office. Heavy rain was pouring down over the school, and crashes of thunder resonated through the castle every few minutes.

Statues, suits of armor, and rows of tall windows whizzed past Carmen in a blur as she raced down the empty halls. It was vitally urgent that she get to the Commander's office. She had to tell Haidar about Natlek before it was too late.... She shuddered at the thought of what could happen should she not find her instructor before morning.

Carmen and her friends reached the top of the stairs in the south tower in record time. Winded and shaking, Carmen pounded her fist on the wooden door of Haidar's office. Her head was spinning—both from running up the tall spiral staircase and from the revelation that she had stumbled upon in the castle library. She hoped that Haidar was still awake....

In less than fifteen seconds, Haidar opened his door, instantly sensing that there was trouble. He stared at Carmen and her friends.

"What's wrong?" he asked, his voice full of concern as he watched them struggle to catch their breath.

"Natlek!" Carmen choked, leaning over against the wall to steady herself. "He's not really Remnor's nephew! His name...spelled backwards...is Master of Keltan. He's somehow connected with Triedastron!"

Haidar's brown eyes widened with shock. For a moment, he seemed unable to take in what he had just heard. Then, quite quickly, he put his hands on Carmen's shoulders and stared deeply into her face.

"Listen to me, Carmen. You are to follow my orders exactly as I give them to you," he said, in a most pressing tone. "You need to go down to your room, grab the cipher disk, and bring it back here at once. Have your Souls go with you for protection. Don't stop for anything or any*one*. Do you understand me?"

Carmen nodded right away.

"Yes."

"Good," Haidar said. "Now go!"

Carmen promptly straightened up, and without looking back, she and her friends hurried back down the spiraling stairway, their pulses racing at rates that matched the pounding of their frantic footsteps on the stone steps. The thunderstorm blowing outside sounded like it was gaining strength.

They hurtled down to the third floor of the castle without a word to each other. All they knew was that they had to retrieve the cipher disk from their room before something terrible happened. For whatever reason, Haidar seemed to believe that it was in immediate jeopardy.

Carmen and her friends ran down the vacant, darkened corridor leading to their room. As they sprinted toward their door, the wooden interior shutters adorning the hall windows magically slammed shut one after the other as they passed by. The banging of the wood echoed through Carmen's ears and made her already speeding heart beat even faster. Who or what was closing the castle shutters, Carmen didn't want to imagine.

She burst through the door of her room and flicked on the light. Without delay, she knelt down and reached under her bed for the precious wooden object. When she didn't feel it beneath her fingertips, she peered into the darkness under her bed…and a sick feeling sank into her stomach.

They were too late. Merlin's cipher disk was gone.

"It's not here!" Carmen told her Souls, panic-stricken as she got up from the floor. "Someone stole it!"

Her friends were at a loss for words; the shock and fear frozen on each of their faces spoke for them instead.

"Let's search the entire room!" Blaze suggested, as his Master looked hopelessly toward the window. "It could still be in here somewhere!"

Taking no chances, Carmen and her friends tore through the room in just shy of two minutes, searching every corner and space where the object could possibly be hiding. Carmen dug through all of her dresser drawers as her friends rummaged hastily through the rest of the space. When none of them could find the cipher disk anywhere, they met at the center of the room.

"We have to tell Haidar," Carmen decided, though she dreaded the mere thought. "We don't have any choice. The sooner we tell him, the sooner he can lock all of the doors and we can start searching the rest of the castle for it…. He's waiting for us to come back."

"She's right," Blaze told the others. "Let's go!"

Carmen and her friends nodded to one another—and ran back out into the hall without argument. But there, they came upon a sight that nearly made their hearts stop.

Natlek Foretsam was standing in the center of the hallway, leering at them in the most menacing way imaginable. A magical flash of lightning struck down behind him and illuminated his form. He held up the cipher disk in his left hand.

"Looking for this, are we?" he asked in a spiteful voice, as the winds continued to howl outside. "I only stole back what you stole from me. Now, that's not so bad, is it?"

Carmen just continued to gape at him, too stunned to speak. Standing there in his Sarcan Captain uniform, Natlek was looking at her in the same murderous way that he had in her dream. She suddenly felt numb all over, and wobbly from having run so far.

"I can't believe that it took you this long to recognize me as the Master of Keltan," Natlek said cruelly. "I would think that someone with as flawless a reputation as yours in fighting off Dark forces would have figured it out sooner."

Carmen opened her mouth to reply, but she still could not find the words to answer him.

"Natlek Foretsam was the perfect alias, don't you agree?" he said triumphantly. "I practically gave myself away to you. But lo and behold, here we find ourselves, I with the cipher disk, and you, with nothing."

"How are you here?" Carmen finally asked, trying to keep her voice even. "If you're really Triedastron...that means you're dead."

Natlek laughed.

"Death is merely a state of mind," he growled. "The extent of my power reaches far beyond mortal comprehension.... It was that which enabled me to seek an escape back into the realm of the living, and persuade one with the means to make the crossing into servitude.... See for yourselves."

Natlek took off his discolored gold necklace and summoned his wand. His twisted staff was now crowned with Triedastron's magic circle—which was comprised of a sharp *K* surrounded by flames, horns, and monstrous beasts. Natlek tapped his wand to his forehead, and then pointed it at Carmen's group.

A bright white light shot out of Natlek's staff—slamming into the startled Carmen and Souls of Destiny and flooding their vision, momentarily blinding them.

Seconds later...a smoky vision of Inpu battling Triedas-tron flashed before their eyes.

The Jackal was alone in a dark place, cornered by Triedas-tron, and a cluster of his masked fighters behind him. Triedas-tron attacked Inpu with a curse...but the Jackal fought it off with a defensive shield. The creature then tried to run, but there was no fleeing from his aggressors.

Soon, the Phantom Warriors had him surrounded—blocking him from sight. Carmen and her friends heard Inpu cry out.

The light and the horrible scene slowly began to dissolve away, but the scars that the memory left on the minds of Carmen and her friends did not fade with it.

"Where is my father?" Anubis shouted. His usually placid demeanor was replaced by immense anger as he glared at Natlek. *"What have you done to him?"*

"After a fair amount of persuasion, he assisted me with my escape into Kelmar," Natlek replied, the corners of his mouth curling into an unpleasant smile. "Normally, I would have just let him go afterward, as I have no further use for him." He shrugged. "But I know too well that he has the intention of helping all of you to find the remaining two Secrets, and I have thus taken it upon myself to prevent that from happening. Accordingly, he remains in my custody...and he is not alone. My prison in Keltan is full of meddlesome Kelmarsian captives just like him. He and his friends have the rest of eternity to spend together.... I have no intention of ever releasing them."

Carmen's head was throbbing painfully, a result of the combination of outrage and pure loathing that she was feeling toward this vile man. There was no way that Inpu would have agreed to transport Triedastron to Kelmar unless he was threatened with death.... He must have been tortured beyond anything that she could fathom…. Oh how Carmen wished she could have helped him….

"Because of your failure to protect the cipher disk, it will be returning to Keltan with us," Natlek announced to Carmen and her Souls. "Had you just paid closer attention, you would have known that we were coming for it before tonight."

"*We?*" Carmen asked, her stomach twisting into a knot. "You're not alone?"

Natlek's face broke into a horrible grin that made him look even more like a devil in human form. He waved his wand…and became engulfed in an explosion of black smoke that appeared out of thin air.

Carmen coughed as the smoke billowed out from around Natlek and filled the hall. Waving it away with her hand, she could see Triedastron in his adult form now standing before her and her friends.

Wearing his brocade burgundy robes, the Master of Keltan was tall and gaunt, with silvery-black hair and dark brown eyes. His malevolent glare was piercing.

"He's a Shape-Shifter!" Blaze gasped, as he and his friends gaped at Triedastron.

"Perhaps you still don't understand why I'm here," Triedastron mused, walking a few steps toward Carmen and her Souls. "I failed to mention to you that while I was absent from your training, I was out gathering together my most elite forces and preparing for this very meeting."

With that last revelation, Triedastron stopped walking and tapped the base of his wand to the floor three times.

Carmen and her friends watched in horror as the window right beside Triedastron shattered. Through a shower of splintered wood and broken glass, the Dark Master and Singe came crashing into the hall—landing smoothly on their knees before sauntering over to stand beside Triedastron, the fierce wind and rain blowing in through the gaping remains of the window.

One by one, the rest of the windows in the hall smashed in succession. Through each window came a pair of Phantom Warriors, all of the sorcerers armed and wearing black hooded cloaks.

Present now were Lucifer Mondalaus and Narcista, Sevadia Nankarsa and Syth, Oalyn Sarisin and his Skelyote, Valsera Vermae and her Decodore, and Ruan Thor, Audric Harthan, Dorsan Denethor, Dezra Razok, and Morik Galdor, with their respective Dragons. Finally, Lucia, Triedastron's Chimera, pounced through the remains of the nearest window and walked to her Master's side.

At that moment, Carmen wished that she were anywhere other than the third floor corridor of Thunder Academy.

"No, no, no, why would I have come alone when *all of us* could relish the priceless expressions on your faces right now?" Triedastron remarked, smirking along with his fighters at Carmen and her Souls' overwhelmed looks. "Besides, there is much more work to be done here. Stealing back the cipher disk wasn't our only reason for coming to this miserable realm. Oh no, we have far grander plans than just that."

"I guess I should have seen this coming, right?" Carmen asked Blaze in a flat voice.

Triedastron raised his wand.

"I hope that you've enjoyed your stay in Kelmar, Carmen," he said, "because after tonight, this world, and all who inhabit it...shall be no more."

Carmen fumbled for the Key around her neck. She suddenly heard many sets of running footsteps coming up from behind her. Triedastron had his staff pointed in her direction.

"Keltania Transtarna!"

In a flash of red and gold, Haidar dashed in front of Carmen, pointing his wand at Triedastron's oncoming curse.

"Flaming Shield!"

A wall of fire sprang up around Carmen and her friends, melting the red light of the Keltan curse before it could reach them.

Carmen looked back down the hall. Officer Faelyn Sheridae, the Sarcan Captains, and the Sarcan Cadets were racing up from the rear of the corridor to help their classmates. Sheridae was shouting encouragement to the students.

"KEEP GOING!" she ordered. "MOVE, MOVE, MOVE!"

Carmen summoned her wand, and the hallway exploded into pandemonium.

With their own wands raised, Haidar and Sheridae charged past her and rushed toward the Phantom Warriors alongside her classmates. There was shouting and banging as the two sides clashed, and wind and rain were blowing in through the shattered windows and blustering throughout the hall. Glass, wood, and stone debris littered the floor. Flashes of lightning and cracks of thunder were occurring nearly nonstop.

Carmen and Blaze braced themselves for battle with Triedastron and Lucia. Carmen then motioned toward her three remaining Souls.

"Help the other Captains," she told them, not taking her eyes off of the Master of Keltan and his three-headed beast. "Blaze and I can handle things here."

Knowing better than to question Carmen's judgment, Stellar, Glamis, and Anubis did as she asked and ran ahead to assist the rest of the Kelmarians. Triedastron, meanwhile, was looking at Carmen and Blaze with the hunger of revenge.

"I will kill the both of you now," he said, sneering as he raised his wand.

"Seltopiansanka!"

A bright fireball burst from Triedastron's wand and rocketed toward Carmen. Lucia stampeded past her Master, all six of her eyes focused on the Sarcan ahead of her.

"Golden Lightning!" Carmen shouted.

As the enemy flames shot at her, a bright bolt of lightning came down through the ceiling and struck the fireball in midflight. Triedastron's spell promptly exploded into a cloud of dense black smoke.

As Lucia neared Blaze, her lioness head roared a ferocious breath of fire upward at him. Blaze managed to elude the searing hot flames by spiraling higher into the air toward the ceiling. His horn lit up with a golden light, and he aimed and fired a bolt of lightning back down at the Chimera.

Though she was quick on her feet in spite of her large and imposing form, Lucia was barely able to escape Blaze's attack. Seeing this, Triedastron commanded her to remain alert and to follow his orders closely. Carmen decided to take advantage of her opponent's momentary loss in concentration.

"Sarcanto Mentolia!" she cried.

A sapphire beam of light released itself from the crown of Carmen's wand. She directed it at the Master of Keltan, who was standing directly across the way.

Carmen's spell soared through the air, headed straight for Triedastron, but this man was all too prepared to defend against it.

Without even flinching, Triedastron cast the *Dark Guard* defense to protect himself against the attack. The hazy black wall rose up from the floor...and concealed the Master of Keltan and his Chimera from sight.

Blaze flew up and over the magical shield, trying to see past it to get a shot at Lucia. But shortly after he disappeared from Carmen's view, he howled in pain.

Jolted, Carmen ran toward the shadowy wall of protection.

"BLAZE!" she shouted, fearing that he could be badly hurt. "What's wrong?"

Triedastron laughed insensitively, parting his shield with a wave of his wand. Carmen came to a stop about ten feet in front of him. Blaze was pinned between one of Lucia's front paws and the stone floor. The monstrous creature had the Sarcan trapped.

"Lucia eats creatures bigger than this one for appetizers," Triedastron scoffed, looking down at Blaze in disgust. "Go ahead and have a bite, Lucia."

"NO!"

Carmen pointed her wand at the creature.

"Fires of the Sarcan!"

A flaming Sarcan burst from the gold staff and galloped toward the Chimera. Lucia's two heads of a lion and a goat looked up from Blaze to stare irritably at Carmen. The creature's serpent tail hissed. Triedastron moved to block his Partner from the attack with an *Almighty Keltan* Protection.

"Oh no you don't!" Carmen shouted indignantly, before his shield could fully materialize. She pointed her wand at Blaze. *"Eiruk!"*

With the help of Carmen's *Release* spell, Blaze slipped out from under Lucia's paw and flew quickly back to his Master.

"Are you okay?" Carmen asked him.

"Yes, I'm fine," Blaze assured her. "She caught me off guard.... I didn't know that she could move so fast."

The *Fires of the Sarcan* spell ran into Triedastron's flaming Protection. Carmen and Blaze watched as the giant pocket of fire exploded and extinguished.

Lucia released a fuming roar. Triedastron's defense had only moderately protected him and his Partner from the attack.

After three minutes, the two Keltans emerged from the cloud of smoke, looking unkempt and rancorous. There were scorch marks in Triedastron's burgundy robes, and Lucia's brown lioness fur was darkened in certain spots. Both fighters were glaring at Carmen and Blaze with fresh hatred.

As a flash of lightning illuminated the hall, Triedastron thrust his wand at Carmen.

"The Master's Supremacy!"

There was a deafening crash of thunder, and then a smoky sphere of darkness began to form at the crown of Triedastron's wand.

With each passing moment, the orb grew steadily larger. Uncertain of what was happening or how to respond, Carmen and Blaze just stared at the dark Keltan orb, trying to ready themselves for what could possibly be coming.

When it was nearly twice the size of the enemy wand's crown, Triedastron's magical orb detonated—sending deadly fragments of the curse flying through the hall.

"Invisible Shield!" Carmen ordered.

The curse's shower of black, poisonous spikes that soared across the corridor was approaching Carmen and Blaze at an unparalleled speed. Carmen's *Invisible Shield* expanded from her wand and grew around her and Blaze...but it was not enough.

In a rush of darkness, *The Master's Supremacy* daggers punctured through the front of Carmen's Protection and slammed into her and her Sarcan, knocking both of them roughly to the floor.

Carmen screamed as a scorching hot pain shot through her body. It felt as though she had just been thrown headfirst through a burning window. She began to shake uncontrollably...and her vision blurred so much that she could see only fuzzy outlines of the forms around her. She could hear Blaze crying in agony on the floor beside her....

Carmen then heard someone scream her name, but she was so blinded by the stabbing pains tearing through every inch of her that she could not tell who it was. As she lay there convulsing on the floor, just inches from her wand, she sensed that someone was leaning over her.

Seconds after that recognition, she felt the cold metal of a wand against her cheek and a steadying hand on her shoulder. A woman was rapidly uttering a sequence of words in Keltongue as she held her wand to Carmen's skin.

Carmen heard yelling and mayhem around her, but all she saw were bleary shadows and shapes of people and creatures.... She wished that she would lose consciousness so that she could escape the pain. It was when she was right on the verge of blacking out that she heard the woman's familiar voice again....

"Stay with me, Carmen! Stay with me!" she pleaded. "You're going to be all right!"

Only a moment later, Carmen felt medicinal warmth transfer from the crown of the woman's wand into her cheek.... And slowly, very slowly...the curative properties of the spell began to take effect.

Fighting now to *stay* conscious, Carmen lay on the floor and allowed the magic to flow through her body.... Almost a full five minutes passed before she finally stopped trembling, and the shooting pain was reduced to a bearable ache. With her vision gradually returning, Carmen recognized the violet and gold robes of the person crouched down at her side. Officer Faelyn Sheridae was the one who was healing her.

"Swift is healing Blaze," Sheridae told her calmly, as she continued to work on her. "The both of you are going to make it."

"Thank...thank you...."

Carmen gazed beyond Officer Sheridae and saw bright bursts of light as spells bounced off of an *Invisible Shield* that was protecting all four of them. The Sarcan instructor must have summoned it.

"Why didn't mine work?" Carmen asked in a raspy voice.

Sheridae smiled at her.

"You're still young," she said matter-of-factly, gently pushing Carmen's golden hair off of her face. "You're very strong, but Triedastron has thousands of years experience on you.... There's only so much that one can do against an opponent like him. Plus, that curse that he just used on you is one of the most powerful forms of Keltan magic in existence. He's likely the only sorcerer who can use it."

"I wish I had known that before I cast *Invisible Shield*.... I should have summoned a stronger Protection," Carmen said, feeling physically better with each minute that went by.

She looked at Sheridae's wand as it leaned against her face. It was gold and white, with a crown of a magic circle with wings, lightning, and stars.

"It's likely that no defense would have been strong enough against *that*," Sheridae reminded her. "Our powers are limited by our age and years of practice. Your skills are at a far more advanced level than those of your classmates, Carmen, but Triedastron's are in a different world completely."

Sheridae carefully lifted her wand off of Carmen's face. She smiled as the young sorceress sat up.

"I've fully restored you, and freed you of all of the curse's effects," Sheridae informed her, as Carmen rubbed the back of her head, which was still a little sore from her fall to the stone floor. "Do you feel back to normal now?"

"Yeah," Carmen said with a nod, surprised at just how much better she felt. "Thank you again for helping me."

"You're quite welcome, Carmen," Sheridae said with a smile. Then she glanced behind her as Blaze flew over to them with her Partner, Swift. Carmen beamed to see her Sarcan looking like his usual self.

"We got lucky again, Car," Blaze said, with a matching grin. "Are you ready to go back and fight for Kelmar?"

"I'm ready," Carmen said. Without pain, she stood up, picked up her wand, and gazed around the hall through the walls of Sheridae's *Invisible Shield.*

Stellar and Haidar were trying to defend themselves and others against Triedastron, an act of bravery that they no doubt undertook when she and Blaze went down. Draven, Flint, and Glamis were taking on the Dark Master and Singe as Shea, Gia, Akira, and Keko were engaged in a battle with Denethor and his Dragon.

Anubis, Kamie, and Dall, meanwhile, were dueling with Mondalaus and Narcista. The rest of the Sarcan Captains and Cadets were all off in their own small groups, fighting the remaining portion of the Phantom Warrior army.

The castle emergency alarm was sounding through the halls, but it could barely be heard over the constant noise of the struggle. Everywhere that Carmen looked, there were masses of humans and creatures battling one another. Spells and curses flew back and forth across the third floor corridor. Though the Kelmarians outnumbered the Keltan combatants present here tonight, neither side showed that they were gaining an advantage on the other, but nor did they show signs of surrender. Carmen didn't know where the Sarcan Councilors and the rest of the school's inhabitants were, but she could only guess that Haidar had advised them to isolate themselves in a safe part of the building so that he and the students, as the castle's first line of defense, could work to drive the intruders away and protect the school.

"We have to take over for Stellar and Haidar," Carmen told Blaze, finally looking away from the other battles. "Triedastron is *our* responsibility."

"Right," Blaze said. "Let's go for it!"

"You can dissolve the shield, Officer," Carmen told Sheridae, giving her a look of determination. "We're ready."

"Very well then," Sheridae said, also appearing prepared to head back out into the battle with her students. "Swift and I will go help the Cadets. Good luck, both of you!"

Sheridae's *Invisible Shield* instantly vanished from around her, Swift, Carmen, and Blaze.

Sheridae and her Sarcan then hurried off toward Nankarsa and Syth, who were firing curses at a handful of the younger students, while Carmen and Blaze rushed ahead to relieve Haidar and Stellar from their duel with Triedastron and Lucia.

The Master of Keltan shot a sharp curse toward Haidar, which the Sarcan Commander blocked as Stellar sidestepped a blast of fire from the jaws of Lucia.

"We're here!" Carmen shouted, as she and Blaze ran toward their friends, making Stellar and Haidar glance back at them. "Let us take over now!"

Triedastron chuckled to himself.

"Oh, isn't this cute?" he said derisively, as Carmen and Blaze sent Stellar and Haidar away to stand in their place. "I see that you two haven't had enough of a taste of my power just yet.... Allow me to change that."

Triedastron raised his wand.

"Devilancatolum!"

"Illumina Hesquel!"

This time, Carmen's defenses didn't let her down. After crisscrossing her wand through the air, she watched with relief as her *Light Shield's* interlocking beams of light protected her and Blaze against the dominant fires of Triedastron's curse.

Carmen and her Sarcan carried on their duel with Triedastron and Lucia as their classmates and instructors battled the many other ruthless enemies from the caverns of Keltan.

When Stellar and Haidar left the able-bodied Carmen and Blaze, they went on to challenge Oalyn Sarisin and his

Skelyote. Sarisin was a short and stocky man with auburn hair, a round, rough face, and dark, narrowed eyes.

Haidar used a string of Lightning and Sky spells against Sarisin, but the brutish man and his Partner continued to put up a tough fight.

Sarisin's Skelyote, a dark gray wolf-like creature with scarlet eyes and a trio of curling white horns and tails, flew through the air using its great black and gray skeletal wings. It combated Stellar's Land attacks with those of the Sky, and Stellar could never attack it with enough force to defeat it, at least as of that time.

Haidar stayed on the offensive against Sarisin for a while, until the man was finally struck by one of Haidar's Lightning spells, weakening him to the point of relative significance.

And while this battle was taking place, countless others just like it were as well. Glamis had joined up with Draven and Flint to clash magic with his old adversaries, Desorkhan and Singe. The three Kelmarians made a surprisingly strong team against the Dark Master and his Partner. During the brief moments that Carmen could look away from her duel with Triedastron, she witnessed the Boarax and the Sarcan working together against Singe as Draven made progress against Desorkhan.

Glamis would shoot blasts of Water spells up at Singe as Flint chased him through the air overhead and launched Lightning attacks at him. Glamis and Flint's spells would intermittently hit the enemy Sarcan, and thus forced him to keep summoning magical defenses to protect himself. His Master wasn't spared any breaks from *his* foe either.

Though Desorkhan would try to psychologically and magically intimidate Draven, the Sarcan Captain stood his ground and didn't give in to his threats.

Carmen was impressed by how well Draven was able to handle himself against such a formidable opponent. He battled with strength and courage that few would have had when facing the Dark Master.

Just fifty or so feet away from Draven and Desorkhan, Shea, Gia, Akira, and Keko were fighting Denethor and his Dragon, Maladack. Shea and Akira concentrated their efforts on weakening Denethor while their Sarcans battled his Dragon.

Dorsan Denethor was a Magicon Commander in his late thirties. He was tan and trim, and had a narrow black goatee, black hair, and a long nose. One of the more highly skilled Magicon leaders, Denethor dueled Shea and Akira using a mix of Keltan curses and fiery attacks.

His Partner was an aggressive black Dragon with scarlet eyes and leathery wings. Together, Keko and Gia were able to confront Maladack by attacking together, and then splitting up when Maladack moved to return fire.

Carmen blocked an attack by Triedastron and stole a quick glance in Anubis's direction. He was at the far end of the hall with Kamie and Dall. The three of them had forced Mondalaus and Narcista back, but the infamous Magicon duo was not about to admit defeat.

Mondalaus, a tall, blonde-haired man with harsh blue eyes, chose a progression of prevailing Keltan spells with which to fight off his challengers. Narcista, his Zelthrel Partner, was a hideous, Dragon-like creature with a muscular body that was covered in slimy, acid green scales. The creature kept spitting venom at Dall and Anubis, but the two creatures were both more agile than the lumbering Zelthrel, and thus were able to dodge the poisonous strikes.

As Carmen's other classmates tussled with the rest of the Phantom Warriors, Carmen herself was faced with finding a way to defeat Triedastron and reclaim the cipher disk.

She ducked to avoid a curse fired at her by the merciless Master of Keltan while Blaze fled from the snapping jaws of Lucia's trio of heads. Carmen had been taking a lot of things into consideration whilst in battle with Triedastron, and the solution for a victory that she would arrive at was to use the strongest spell that she had mastered so far.

"Blaze, I think I'm going to go with *Fires of Lightning*," Carmen muttered to her Sarcan, as he hovered above her out of earshot of Triedastron. "I don't see any other way out of this."

"Normally I would tell you to avoid using that spell, but in this case, you're likely right," Blaze replied. "I'm ready on your word."

Possessing an apparently unlimited arsenal of attacks, Triedastron was getting ready to cast yet another curse—surely one that would inflict serious damage on an unguarded opponent. So before he could utter the incantation, Carmen hastened to execute her own strategy.

"Fires of Lightning!" she shouted.

Upon her command, Carmen's wand illuminated, and a glaring explosion of fire-infused electricity erupted from the crown. Simultaneously, Blaze flew up into the air as his horn began to glow. He threw his head forward and fired a piercing bolt of lightning as a potent fireball grew at the back of his throat and shot from his jaws. In a luminous blast of fire and lightning, the dual spell lit up the hallway and sped toward Triedastron and Lucia.

Without the time to summon a defensive spell strong enough to protect against such powerful magic, Triedastron and Lucia swiftly became engulfed in their opponents' intense blast of flames and electricity.

For the next thirty seconds or so, Carmen and Blaze tried to see through the fire, but they couldn't make out their two enemies' forms behind the blistering inferno.

They then heard Triedastron laughing, and the fire abruptly disappeared, along with the two Keltans who were inside of it. Carmen looked anxiously around the hallway, but Triedastron and Lucia had vanished.

"Ah my pathetic Kelmarian foes, is that really your best effort?" Triedastron asked, his voice sounding far away. *"I'll show you what a real fire looks like. Take a peek outside."*

Carmen and Blaze exchanged distressed glances. They raced to the other side of the corridor to gaze out through one of the broken windows. But before they could get there, Desorkhan and Singe stopped them in their tracks.

"You didn't think that you would die without first facing the Dark Master again, did you?" Desorkhan asked coldly. "Defeating your little friends is more than satisfying, but I simply couldn't resist finishing off my two most hated adversaries."

"I just love sweet revenge," Singe said, smiling wickedly as he rubbed his claws together.

Desorkhan pointed his wand at Carmen.

"Splificer Donesta!"

"Lightning Strike!"

Carmen, Desorkhan, Blaze, and Singe dueled one another for nearly twenty minutes, with no end in sight. They fired spells and curses across the hall at each other just as magic from all of the other ongoing duels flew through the air around them.

Carmen was eventually able to thwart Desorkhan and Singe's attacks with a *Lightning Knives* spell, which sent them running to escape the electrically charged blades that escaped from her wand and Blaze's horn. It was just after that when someone in the hall screamed.

"THUNDER STADIUM IS ON FIRE!"

Carmen's heart came to a sudden stop. Instantly sick with dread, she ran across the corridor to one of the broken windows with Blaze.

Together, they looked out into the valley through the torrential rain and witnessed the horrible sight. It was a scene far more awful than anything Carmen could have anticipated.

At the other side of the gorge, the majestic Thunder Stadium was ablaze in cursed, destructive flames. Giant plumes of black smoke and embers were billowing high into the starless night sky.

The dangerous rainstorm continued its assault on the valley, but it was not making any impact in dousing the flames that had engulfed the arena.

With their enemies temporarily distracted, Carmen and Blaze bolted from the window to hunt down Glamis. They both knew that they would need his powers of Water to have any chance of saving the stadium.

They ultimately found the Boarax King near the end of the hall, in combat with Officer Sheridae and Swift against Sevadia Nankarsa and Syth. When Sheridae had forced Nankarsa to throw up a magical shield to protect her from her *Lightning Strike* spell, Carmen pulled Glamis aside.

"Glamis, you have to come with us!" she said straight away. "Triedastron set Thunder Stadium on fire. If we don't put out the flames, and fast, it will be destroyed!"

A look of alarm passed over Glamis's face. He shot a fleeting glance at Sheridae and Swift.

At this point, they would be able to handle Nankarsa and Syth without him. They would have to. He turned back to Carmen and Blaze.

"By all means, let's hurry!"

Glamis galloped down the hall at the sides of his two friends. Carmen cast *Thunder Shield* to protect the three of them from enemy spells as they darted through the masses of fighters. Fortunately for them, the intensity and magnitude of the fighting allowed them to slip away from the battle without drawing attention. Carmen had to hope that Desorkhan would move on to deal with other Kelmarians in her absence, and not follow them outside.

Carmen, Blaze, and Glamis ran down a few flights of stairs, and then out into the central corridor of the first floor. They burst open the front doors of the school and scampered down the staircase leading to the base of the valley, cold wind and rain pounding their bodies.

Once they reached the bottom of the gorge, they sprinted across the dueling fields toward the glow of the massive stadium. The muscles in their legs burned as they neared the site. Blinking the rain out of her eyes, Carmen could feel the heat from the searing flames against her face.

Now soaking wet and gasping for breath, Carmen, Blaze, and Glamis stood before the burning building and stared up into the flames, all of them working frantically to think of a way to extinguish the huge fire.

As they remained there gaping at the flames, Triedastron sauntered out from around the other side of the stadium, wand in hand. The light from the fire flickering off of his face suited his devilish appearance.

The Master of Keltan stood no less than three feet in front of the stadium, a twisted smile warping his face.

"Now *this* is a fire!" he declared, spreading out his arms to showcase his work. He glanced proudly over his shoulder at his inferno before leering at Carmen and her friends.

"You brought this on yourselves," he said, pointing at them accusingly. "And this is only the beginning. Starting tonight, we Keltans begin the task of engulfing *all* of Kelmar in a deadly firestorm."

"You won't get away with it," Carmen promised Triedastron, glaring at him. "We're not going to let you come here and destroy our realm.... This fight isn't over."

Triedastron raised a black eyebrow. Lucia tramped out from behind the blazing arena and stood beside her Master, growling at him to show her pleasure. The monstrous beast appeared content with what Triedastron had done.

"Ah, Guardian, you are even more of a fool than I thought," the Master of Keltan said, stroking Lucia's fur. "You fail to remember that history is on *my* side. If you know anything about the Legend of the Worlds Triad, you'd know that Keltan has already been destined as the winner of this war." He sneered. "Kelmarsia shall be the first to fall...and then it will be *your* turn. The clock is ticking for the world of Kelmar, and your time to stop it has all but run out."

There was sudden commotion out on the dueling fields. Carmen and her friends looked over to see that the fighting from inside the castle had spilled out into the valley. The rain hammering down on them, all of the Sarcan instructors and students were battling their Keltan foes across the grounds of the school.

Carmen spotted Anubis and Stellar running through the madness toward her, Blaze, and Glamis as they stood at the base of the burning stadium. She was relieved that they were not hurt.

"CARMEN!"

Her thoughts racing, Carmen turned and glanced toward Mortrock Forest. Her grandfather and his Sarcan, Thunderbolt, were jogging toward them from the woods. Blaine had his wand in hand, ready to come to his granddaughter's aid. His red robes were blowing in the wind as he ran.

"Well, *this* should be fun," Triedastron said, eyeing all of the approaching Kelmarians with hatred. "More blood spilt ensures us of less resistance as we move forward with our conquest of Kelmar. Go get them, Lucia!"

"No—wait!"

The robust Chimera charged past her Master and on toward her family and friends. Carmen could do nothing but watch.

"Keep going!" Stellar called to Anubis, as he ran beside him in the direction of Lucia. "I'll take care of this monster. You go and help Carmen!"

Anubis nodded and continued on toward his friends, evading the snapping jaws of Lucia's serpent tail.

"I'll stay with Stellar!" Thunderbolt shouted to Blaine over the rain and winds, splitting up from his Master to fly to the Keinen's side and face Lucia.

When Blaine reached Carmen, he put his hand on her shoulder and stared severely across at Triedastron.

"I'm your new challenger...." he told him, his voice even in spite of the long run. "You will leave my granddaughter out of this and duel me like a man."

Triedastron shrugged, but a malicious smile was playing across the thin lines of his face.

"Have it your way, Fox," the Master of Keltan replied. "I'll gladly kill you first if you so choose."

The two sorcerers barely bowed to each other, and then Blaine raised his wand.

"Thunder Ray!"

"Instundo!"

With the duel underway, Carmen ran from her grandfather's side to help Glamis put out the fire. They, Blaze, and Anubis hurried to get as close to the stadium as they could without getting burned.

"What's our plan?" Blaze asked, as they stood before the burning walls. "There's nothing that I can really do as a Sarcan.... I can't use Water spells."

"You should go help your father and Stellar," Carmen decided. "Anubis, Glamis, and I will be fine."

"Are you sure that you'll be okay without me?"

"Positive. Go and help them," Carmen told him. "Lucia is a tough opponent."

Confident that his Master would be in safe hands, Blaze flew over to where Stellar and Thunderbolt were combating Lucia. Carmen couldn't worry about him; she knew that he would protect the others.

"Let's get started," Glamis said, staring up at the fire. "I'm going to use the *Sea's Fury* spell first. If that does not work, we'll try something else. Follow my lead!"

Glamis lifted his head…and then shot a torrent of magical blue water at a pocket of flames along the stadium's northern wall. Carmen put her left hand on Glamis's back and pointed her wand to the same spot.

"Sea's Fury!" she shouted.

A gush of cerulean water blasted out from the crown of Carmen's wand and collided with the flames, diminishing them into nonexistence.

Carmen and Glamis moved around the outside of the stadium, repeating this exercise over and over again until they began to see some progress. The smoke and the burning cinders had begun to irritate Carmen's throat by the time they had accomplished dousing just under a quarter of the flames.

"I believe that it's working!" Glamis informed Anubis, as he and Carmen saturated yet another section of the fire.

"Yes, but the blaze is spreading much too quickly," Anubis observed, gazing upward as he studied the flames. *"It will be impossible to keep up at this rate. If we retain our current pace, it will take all night to extinguish the fire, and by then the stadium will surely have burned to the ground."*

"Do you have any other ideas for what we could do?" Carmen asked, shooting another gush of water up at the stadium as the rain streamed down her face.

"*I do,*" Anubis said, walking up to her. "*Though it will take much of my strength, I can freeze time to allow you and Glamis to gain an advantage on the rapidly advancing flames.... I think that you should fly over the stadium while Glamis works from the ground.*"

Glamis's face lit up.

"That gives me a brilliant thought!" he said. "Carmen, if you fly over the stadium, we can utilize magic known as *Ocean Swell.*"

"And what does that do?"

"Your wand will bring a colossal tidal wave of water down from the mountains that will wash over the entire stadium," Glamis said, his face bright with hope. "That could very well be our answer."

Carmen couldn't begin to visualize any wave that would be tall enough to reach over the walls of a several thousand-seat arena, but it seemed that this was their only chance to save the stadium now. She had to trust Glamis on his idea.

"Okay...I'll do it," Carmen said slowly.

There was no ocean near here from which such water could come, but she knew better than to question Glamis's knowledge of spells. She summoned her wings.

"I'll go up and wait for your signal, Anubis," she told her friend.

Carmen flew up into the dark sky, blinking her eyes to see through the pounding rain that was falling over Sarcanian Valley. She held her breath to keep from inhaling the smoke, and positioned herself high above the center of the stadium.

Anubis looked up at Carmen, his golden eyes seeing her through the black smoke. His entire body became radiant in an amethyst-colored light as he performed the *Time Lock* spell.

Within just seconds, the world around Carmen came to a total standstill. She stared in awe at the sparkling raindrops hanging in midair.... She reached out and touched a cluster of them near to her with her fingertips, scattering them into tiny crystal droplets of stationary water in the darkness.

The flames engulfing Thunder Stadium had stopped spreading, and the thick plume of smoke above the building had turned into a stagnant, floating black mass. The fighters below were completely immobile—the dueling Keltan and Kelmarian forces all frozen in time. Blaze and Stellar peered up at Carmen, purposely not affected by the spell's powers.

"Use the spell now, Carmen!" Glamis called up to her.

Carmen took a deep breath. Concentrating hard, she raised her wand high above her head, maintaining a tight grip around her staff with both hands.

"Ocean Swell!" she cried.

For nearly an entire minute, there was silence.... And then came the unmistakable roar of an ocean. Carmen's wand glowed blue just as she heard a huge wall of water rushing from somewhere outside of the valley.

Her body aching, she looked ahead toward the southern Barahir Mountains and observed a spectacle like she'd never imagined.

A blue tidal wave was gushing down the side of one of the mountains, bringing thousands of gallons of pure crystal water toward Sarcanian Valley.

In only minutes, the water cascaded down the rocky peak and washed over the treetops of Mortrock Forest as though they were a child's pool toys.

As the water headed into the valley, Carmen pointed her wand down at the stadium, hoping to direct the wave there.

Just as she had hoped it would, the tremendous swell moved in a direct path to the burning stadium. Carmen and the others watched as the blue and white tidal wave rose up into the air, and broke over the top of the stadium, drowning the arena beneath an ocean of sparkling water.

Then, fairly soon after saturating the blazing building from top to bottom, the waters vanished.

Anubis unfroze time, and the booming noise and action of the battle in Sarcanian Valley resumed. Carmen thanked her lucky stars…. The spell had worked. The fire destroying Thunder Stadium was out.

The light gray stone walls of the arena had been scorched to a charred black color. The tall, metal light posts towering over it had melted and warped, and many of the seats inside had been damaged beyond repair. And although the formerly magnificent arena remained a burned-out shell of what it had once been, it was still standing. For this, Carmen was extraordinarily grateful.

It didn't take long for the other fighters to notice that the stadium was suddenly no longer in flames. Triedastron briefly gawked up at the structure's smoking remains before a look of rage deformed his face. As an exhausted Carmen flew down through the rain and joined Glamis and Anubis at the foot of the arena, the Master of Keltan pointed at them, his fury evident.

"YOU THINK THAT YOU'VE WON, DON'T YOU?" Triedastron snarled, blinking away the raindrops that were tumbling down into his eyes. "I'm sorry to disappoint you, but saving a dilapidated building will no more hinder your demise than your defeat of the Dark Master prevented him from returning to life. This night marks the beginning of the end for Kelmar…*and* Kelmarsia."

Triedastron pointed his wand up into the night sky, his brown eyes devoid of any compassion.

"Keltanasia Stelkantum!" he shouted.

Carmen and her friends watched in disbelief as the skies over Sarcanian Valley transitioned from black to an unnatural and disconcerting scarlet red. The other battles out on the dueling fields all came to an abrupt stop when everyone in the gorge gazed up into the ominous sky over their heads.

"I hereby unleash the Phantom Warriors with me on this night into the realm of Kelmar!" Triedastron bellowed into the blood-colored sky. *"I allow them to travel freely amongst the realms of the Worlds Triad, and by means of this, I order them to initiate the destruction of my enemies!"*

At the Master of Keltan's command, jets of snaking black lightning fired down from the red sky and struck each and every Phantom Warrior, giving new life to the deceased spirits.

Lucia trotted back over to her Master. Cipher disk in hand, Triedastron mounted the beast's back.

"No...." Carmen gasped, unable to accept what was happening....

"I bid you farewell, Carmen," Triedastron said, bowing his head as he and Lucia began to magically rise up into the sky. "Never fear though. You won't even have the chance to miss me. My comrades shall be staying behind in Kelmar to deliver you and your friends and family early deaths.... The next time that I will see you will be in the afterlife, if you even make it that far."

Like a sliding door parting the atmosphere overhead, the cursed red and black sky opened up to accept the Master of Keltan and his vicious Chimera. Moments after, the newly born Phantom Warriors transformed into shadowy demons and fled off into the woods, just as Triedastron escaped back to the World of Darkness with Merlin's cipher disk.

CHAPTER SEVENTEEN
THE TRIALS OF MOUNT ALBERIK

It rained for nearly a week straight following the battle in Sarcanian Valley. As a result, no outdoor training could take place. All classes were cancelled for five days to allow for the cleanup of the castle, the searching of the grounds for any lingering Phantom Warriors, and the recovery of the students and teachers. Thunder Stadium would remain as it was until a team of inspectors from the Kelmarian Parliament would come to assess the fire damage the following week. The Kelmarians were fortunate not to have suffered any major injuries or losses in the conflict, but everyone, particularly Carmen and Blaze, still desperately needed the few days of rest.

The Kelmarian Review ran a front-page article about the attack the day after it happened. The main headline was printed in bold typeface across the top of the paper.

THUNDER ACADEMY COMES UNDER ATTACK BY TRIEDASTRON

The story stretched on for two pages, detailing who had been present, and everything that had occurred. It even described how Triedastron had been able to gain access to the valley and escape with the most important of all objects— Merlin's cipher disk.

Reporters came to the valley late that night to interview the Sarcan Councilors, instructors, and students. Fortunately, Haidar declined the reporters' repeated requests to question Carmen, her Souls, and the other Captains and Cadets, having swiftly ushered them all back to their rooms after the Keltans disappeared into the woods.

Reluctantly, Carmen read the article, a fresh stab of pain shooting through her for every sentence that she read about Triedastron's successful mission. Surely Kelmarians near and far would be terribly distraught to read that their defeated enemies from the Magicon War and the Master of Keltan were on the rise, and that the Guardian of Kelmar had failed to thwart the theft of the invaluable cipher disk. The article would surely come as an unwelcome surprise to the many Kelmarians who were not aware of the extent of the war's severity.

Letters of concern from Blaze and Glamis's families had arrived with the paper that morning, only two of dozens for those living in Thunder Academy that were flooding the bags of the messenger birds.

Carmen had been feeling miserable ever since that harrowing night of defeat. Guilt and regret ate at her. She had much trouble sleeping, and when she finally did sleep, she was plagued by nightmares about Triedastron destroying Kelmar and her parents being disappointed in her inability to stop him before he gained control of the Worlds Triad. Blaze remained the greatest source of encouragement to Carmen throughout her struggle with grief over what had happened, often staying up with her until the early morning hours to comfort her, and more importantly, to listen.

Carmen's other friends had also made it a persistent effort to shake her from her depression. Though Carmen rarely left her room during the five days following the battle when no classes were held, if one of her classmates did happen to run into her in the hall, they would each give her their sincere words of support and encouragement. They and her Souls reminded her over and over again that it was not her fault that Triedastron had gotten away with the cipher disk; it was purely a loss that nobody could have seen coming.

But no matter what anyone said, Carmen continued to blame herself for the Keltans' victory. In addition to finding and deciphering the Secrets, it had been her responsibility to protect Merlin's cipher disk from harm. Now it was back in the hands of the sinister Master of Keltan, and there was nothing that she could do at the moment to retrieve it. And with Inpu locked away in Triedastron's prison, there was no one to escort her and her Souls to Kelmarsia to obtain the second Secret. That was what she and her friends believed, at least, until Anubis could speak with his father.

"I was finally able to reach my father today," Anubis told his friends one evening, late in the week following the battle with Triedastron. *"I had not been able to tap into his stream of thought earlier because Triedastron's torture had weakened him so much. He is still imprisoned in Haesnost Prison in Keltan, but he is feeling stronger now. He even has some good news for us."*

"What's that?" Carmen asked, looking up from her dinner.

"Now that he is well again, my father is able to lend me some of his Opener powers to enable me to transport all of us to Kelmarsia and Keltan," Anubis informed her. *"Through thought, he can transfer a portion of his magic to me.... This is an opportune chance for us, as Triedastron is not aware of this ability, which is unique to Jackals."*

"Are you serious?" Carmen asked, feeling a little hopeful for the first time in days. "Now we can go and save him."

"Yes, but he has asked us to wait," Anubis said, surprising all of his friends. *"He persuaded me that going after the second Secret in Kelmarsia must be our first priority. He wants out of Haesnost, but he feels that we should secure this Secret before traveling to Keltan for him and the third one. Triedastron isn't paying as much attention to making his prisoners suffer now that he has reclaimed the cipher disk. My father will be fine until we can get*

there to break him out, secure the third Secret, and take the cipher disk back from Triedastron."

Carmen thought carefully about what Anubis said…and then nodded.

"I'll do what the two of you think is right," she replied. "How soon can we leave for Kelmarsia?"

"Tomorrow," Anubis said. *"By then, my body will have accepted the magic transfer from my father, and I will be able to execute the Opener spells properly."*

"How do the rest of you feel about that?" Carmen asked her other Souls, who were all seated around the table with her and Anubis. "Will you be up to making the trip to Kelmarsia tomorrow?"

"You bet," Blaze said with a smile.

"Definitely," Stellar echoed.

Glamis slurped down the last of the fat blue Slugthores on his plate.

"Yes, of course!" he subsequently declared.

Carmen smiled—something that she hadn't done in quite a while.

"Well, I believe that we have our decision then," she said.

Because the weather had forced classes indoors, the Sarcan Cadets met in the basement training room that the previous class had utilized last winter. The Sarcan Captains, meanwhile, held their classes in a specially designed chamber on the uppermost floor of the castle.

Unlike its cellar counterpart, this training room had substantial light pouring in through the wide skylights that stretched across much of the ceiling. There was a set of wooden bleachers sitting against one of the side walls, and a blackboard standing opposite them, just like the basement room had. The room also featured a selection of advanced training tools, and provided sufficient space in which the students could learn.

The first day back to training proved to be atypical of the standard class. When his students arrived at the new classroom shortly after dawn, Haidar instructed them to seat themselves on the bleachers. Because of the early hour and the rain that pattered down on the glass skylights, the rows of crystal lights running across the ceiling of the training room were all turned on.

Haidar met all of his students at the door and waited for them to get seated before taking his place at the front of the class. Standing as still as a uniformed statue in front of the blackboard, Commander Haidar faced his Captains with a solemn expression. They could tell from the tightness of his face and his body language that he was about to deliver an important speech.

"Just five days ago…our school came under the attack of Triedastron and the upper ranks of his army," Haidar began, confirming the students' presumption. "This was a carefully planned ambush, and one that had clearly been in the making for some time."

Haidar's eyes rested on Carmen and Blaze for a moment.

"Now, let me be very clear," he continued. "There was no way to have prevented this attack, as no one on our end could have foreseen it happening. This was a plot that was devised in the World of Darkness, and hence…there is no one sitting in this room right now who could have known of its existence."

Haidar then took a passing glance up at the black sky beyond the glass windows over his head.

"These thunderstorms are due to fresh fighting currently taking place in Kelmarsia," he said. "When Triedastron returned to Keltan, there was a resurgence in violence between *his* forces and those of the World of Light."

Carmen felt chilled, thinking about Inpu trapped in the Master of Keltan's cold and torturous prison with numerous other Kelmarsians.

"Sarcanian Valley is guarded with many of the most powerful Protections known to magical kind," Haidar explained to his class, watching them attentively. "This recent attack is proof that no defensive system is powerful enough to inhibit every catastrophe. That is why we must all remain aware of what is happening around us. If you see anything suspicious, you must report it to an adult immediately. It was because one of you spoke up before the Keltans arrived that we were able to mobilize a defense that prevented loss of life and limited physical damages.... We should all be exceptionally thankful that we are still here to recognize that fact now."

There was a short-lived break in Haidar's address following his last statement, which seemed to convey the importance of his message to his young students. Carmen understood exactly what Haidar meant, and while she *was* grateful to be alive, she could not truly appreciate being here without first thinking about what she could have done differently that might have caused the battle to have an even better outcome—one that included the preservation of the cipher disk.

"Unfortunately, Triedastron was able to escape with a very important object—the magical cipher disk belonging to Merlin Cloud," Haidar said, as if he had read Carmen's thoughts. "With that said, this inopportune theft does not spell the end for Kelmar and Kelmarsia, as I trust that we will be regaining it very soon. After that happens, Carmen will be able to decipher the final two Secrets of Kelmar. And let me remind you that our future rests not on the mistakes of the past but on the discovery and the deciphering of those Secrets."

Carmen felt the passing gazes of her classmates, but she remained staring straight ahead at Haidar.

"On a lighter note, I couldn't be more proud of the courage and determination that was displayed by everyone here on the night of the battle," Haidar remarked, clearing the tense air. "Because of *your* efforts and *your* bravery...tragedy was averted."

With that simple yet poignant acknowledgement, the spirits of those gathered in the training room seemed to collectively lift a bit.

"Together, we put up a strong front against our enemies, and we showed them that any attempt at committing heinous acts of war on their part will be met with the strongest resistance our world has to offer," Haidar said. "Triedastron has slain more innocent beings over the years than I care to imagine. But because we united against an unrivaled evil that night, we were able to stop this murderer from taking any *more* lives, and you should all feel tremendously satisfied to have contributed to that cause."

There was a momentary pause. Then a small number of the Captains nodded. The others were listening carefully in reflective silence.

"Today at 1:00 PM, there will be a mandatory school-wide assembly in Sarcan Hall," Haidar announced. "The Sarcan Council will speak to all of you about the Keltan attack and its aftermath in greater depth. You will also be briefed on new security measures presently being undertaken to ensure that this kind of invasion does not happen again."

Haidar glanced momentarily toward the door, and then gazed out at his class again.

"Considering the circumstances, I do not intend to hold a regular class today," Haidar said. "Do any of you have questions before I dismiss you for the day?"

When nobody raised their hand, Haidar released his students, reminding them that he would be present at the assembly as well if they wished to speak to him there.

The Sarcan Captains shuffled out of the room, but Carmen stayed behind with Blaze, feeling the need to speak with Haidar alone.

Carmen rose from her seat and walked toward the Sarcan Commander. She was glad that Blaze was with her for support.

"Yes, Carmen?" Haidar asked, as she approached him.

Carmen bit her lip. She didn't want to say the wrong thing.

"I'm sorry that I couldn't have done more to stop Triedastron," she finally began. "If I had known earlier—"

Haidar put up his hand to stop her.

"Exactly. *If* you had known," he said calmly. "But you didn't, and that's not your fault. You never could have anticipated such a thing."

"But I sensed something wrong about Natlek prior to that that should have been my warning," Carmen said. "I even had a nightmare about him just days earlier. That's why my Souls and I went to the library to try to find out more about him.... When I saw his name backwards in the mirror...I came straight to you. But in the battle, I could've fought him with my grandfather instead of trying to save Thunder Stadium."

Carmen looked at her Commander with shame.

"I can't help thinking that if I had acted more sensibly than I did, maybe the end result would have been different."

Haidar leaned over and put his right hand on Carmen's shoulder, gazing into her eyes in earnest.

"Carmen, there is no sense living with regret," he said quietly. "You are ashamed when in truth you should be proud...proud that you had the foresight to see past Triedastron's facade when others, including myself, did not. You also had the awareness and resolve to rescue an historic building—one that represents all of us as Kelmarians. I promise you, that stadium will be rebuilt one day, and it will exist to forever remain a symbol of our undying strength, and the bravery that embodies who we are. You are a part of that, and this is something that you must never forget."

Carmen was nodding slowly...feeling rather selfish now for the way that she had been acting over the past five days. Having spent nearly all of her time moping and feeling sorry for herself, she suddenly realized that she owed her friends an apology.

Haidar straightened up to salute her and Blaze.

"I will see the both of you at the assembly," he said. "Until then, you are dismissed."

After lunch, Carmen and her Souls left their room to go down to Sarcan Hall, but not before Carmen asked for her friends' forgiveness for her inconsiderate behavior.

Haidar's concise and powerful talk was just what she needed to snap herself out of her despair and remind her of how important it was for her and the others to stay together as Kelmarians. And being the great friends that they were, of course, Carmen's Souls had accepted her apology without hesitation.

They walked downstairs and then into the grand Sarcan Hall, a room that Carmen had been in on only a handful of occasions. The ornately furnished chamber was wide and circular, with rows upon rows of dark wooden bleachers lining the walls and climbing high into the uppermost portion of the space.

This room was usually reserved for meetings of the Sarcan Council, the bimonthly summits of the Sarcan Delegates, and gatherings of other large groups visiting the castle. On this particular afternoon, however, the seats were occupied by the Sarcan Captains and Cadets, as well as a small group of adult Masters and their Sarcans who were given clearance to train in the valley on the weekends. Though not all of the students had arrived yet, the better portion of the bleachers would remain empty. Those that were here already were talking in hushed voices as they waited for the assembly to get started.

At the back of the hall, the four Sarcan Councilors sat beneath a blue and gold banner showcasing the school's coat of arms. The sorcerers here were all dressed in matching royal blue robes with the Council symbol patch stitched into the chest—a golden lightning bolt set within a pair of wings. Their golden chairs were placed behind a long table that was home to the gavel and sound block used to signal for attention and maintain order. Commander Haidar and Officer Sheridae sat at opposite ends of the table beside the Councilors, dressed in their scarlet and gold Kelmarian Army uniforms.

Carmen and her friends took their seats beside Akira Melkor and Keko at the end of the second level of bleachers and peered over in the direction of the Councilors' table. It was the first time that they had seen the three newly elected Sarcan officials seated alongside the familiar Councilor, Peruveus Seth. As Carmen watched them with interest, Akira filled her in on the newcomers' names and their backgrounds, having learned about them from a past article in *The Kelmarian Review*.

Seth had taken the central Head Councilor's seat, a position previously held by the disgraced Faran Kantour. Seth was somewhere in his mid- to late fifties, and had thinning brown hair lined with gray. He wore horn-rimmed glasses that were constantly sliding down his pointed nose, just as they were this afternoon as he read through a handful of papers that he had stacked in front of him.

Seth had proven himself to be a highly courageous man, having worked to protect Carmen the previous year from the wrongdoings of his then fellow Councilors. He had been of particular help to her against Sylvine Yokaro, who had posed as a Sarcan Councilor while acting as a Magicon spy and second in command to Desorkhan.

Seated between Seth and Haidar today was one of the new Councilors—Elmeric Maradon. He was only slightly older than Seth, but his patchy white hair would lead one to think that he was much higher up in years than he was. He had tranquil blue-gray eyes, an arched nose, and moderate wrinkles all throughout his face. Maradon had previously served as a Sarcan Delegate for ten years following his service in the Kelmarian Army. At the moment, he was chatting with Haidar and motioning toward the door with his hand.

On the other side of Seth was Brielle Kovelir—a woman in her late forties with fair skin, bushy, shoulder length red-brown hair, and light brown eyes. She had a round face and a short nose. Kovelir was a retired schoolteacher, as well as a Sarcan scholar. She had studied at Thunder Academy under Commander Haidar's father, and gone on to serve in the Kelmarian Army for three years prior to becoming an educator. Kovelir gazed peacefully around at the students as they filed into their seats.

Between Kovelir and Officer Sheridae was the final new Councilor—a tall and slender sorceress named Shermane Glynn, who was nearing the age of sixty. She had noticeably spiky gray hair and sharp hazel eyes that stared out from behind her rectangular glasses. Glynn was a strong-minded woman with an extensive history in Kelmarian politics. She had previously served as both a Kelmarian Security Expert and a Sarcan Ambassador before being elected as a Sarcan Council member this past summer, along with Maradon and Kovelir. She looked focused and intense as she leafed through a small notebook that she had tucked under the desk.

Once the last of the students had taken their seats in Sarcan Hall, Councilor Peruveus Seth whispered something to his colleagues and then pounded the gavel to the sound block in front of him three times.

The low roar of talking hastily ceased as those assembled in the chamber collectively focused their attention on the Head Sarcan Councilor, who was now standing.

"I thank you all for coming," Councilor Seth said graciously, his voice carrying throughout the hall. "Before I proceed with the meeting, I would like to introduce the newest of our Council members, as well as our instructors."

Seth turned halfway and motioned toward each Sarcan Councilor respectively.

"Please welcome to our school, Councilor Elmeric Maradon, Councilor Brielle Kovelir, and Councilor Shermane Glynn."

The Councilors each delivered a wave or a bow, and the students and visitors gave the officials a respectful round of applause.

"Also here with us today are our Sarcan instructors," Seth said, gesturing toward his pair of teachers. "Advanced Training instructor and Honorary Council Member, Commander Reoc Haidar, and Basic Training instructor, Officer Faelyn Sheridae!"

The two Sarcan instructors saluted their students, and another loud ovation came from the Sarcans and their Masters.

After the clapping had quieted down, Councilor Seth retook his seat. A few moments passed before he spoke.

"My fellow Councilors have called you to this meeting with regards to the devastating attack on our school and our homeland five nights ago," Seth explained. "Triedastron made use of his abilities as a Shape-Shifter to disguise himself as a student so that he could infiltrate the castle walls and steal the cipher disk of Merlin Cloud. Following much careful planning, he and his militia of Phantom Warriors crossed into our world…and nearly brought about the demise of this school. He fooled *all* of us on that fateful evening, and thus the blame for what happened lies with no one individual. This was a collective oversight, and had we not been so lucky…it could have cost us far more than the physical damages that it did."

Seth's eyes wandered across the room, seeming to meet those of each person and creature gathered in the hall.

"I'm certain that many of you are wondering what happened to the Phantom Warriors after Triedastron escaped back to Keltan," he continued. "Just before he left, Triedastron cast a spell that gave his Phantom Warriors the freedom to roam between our world, Kelmarsia, and Keltan. Where *exactly* they are now, we do not know. There has yet to be a documented report of the Phantoms being spotted in Kelmar since coming to the valley, but we cannot allow this fact to make us feel any more safe," Seth noted, his expression grave. "Just because they have not been seen does not mean that they have moved on to Keltan or Kelmarsia. So Merlin forbid they strike in our world again, smaller governments all across Kelmar have been mobilizing their armies and preparing to protect lives and historic landmarks, should they need to act. Lives and symbols of Kelmarian leadership and strength will be the most likely targets of additional Keltan attacks. Accordingly, the Kelmarian Parliament is collaborating with regional government authorities to ready everyone for the possibility of Phantom ambushes. These fiends wish to destroy anyone and anything representing our solidarity as Kelmarians, and as one of the Worlds Triad."

Councilor Seth cleared his voice, and then went ahead with his speech, his predominantly young audience sitting very still as they listened to his every word.

"We have been working with the Kelmarsians to try to create a spell to counteract the effects of Triedastron's, and get the Phantom Warriors back into Keltan permanently," Seth revealed, sounding cautiously optimistic. "But until such a spell is produced…I'm afraid that we in Kelmar…will have no choice…but to face these bloodthirsty entities on our own soil."

The silence that descended after those last words was overpowering. The entire student body was staring at Seth and the rest of the Councilors, clearly uneasy. Appearing to sense the apprehension in the room, Seth resumed his speech before the questions could arise.

"Since the last attack, the grounds of Sarcanian Valley, Thunder Canyon, and Mortrock Forest have all been thoroughly searched," he informed his audience. "There has been no sign of the Phantom Warriors in any of the aforementioned locations, and this Council and the Kelmarian Parliament have begun to work in partnership to build up the magical defenses around the valley. We have since applied a number of the most effective Protections known to resist Dark Magic. And though the search of Mortrock Forest turned up no evidence that the Phantom Warriors remain near, from this day forward, students will be forbidden from traveling into the forest for any reason."

"What?" Carmen mouthed, as she sat beside her friends in shock. Her grandfather lived in Mortrock Forest with Blaze's father.... How would she be able to see him now?

"Should any of you attempt to cross into Mortrock Forest, there will unquestionably be severe consequences," Seth declared. "I apologize for any inconvenience that this may cause...but we implement this rule for the well-being of everyone. Mortrock Forest is not under the control of the Sarcan Council, and thus, we have no jurisdiction when it comes to what Protections can be placed on it. Lacking the full means to secure the area, we cannot allow our students access into a potentially dangerous setting."

Carmen had to resist her immediate urge to stand up and argue against the new law. If she ever wanted to visit Blaine, she would somehow have to sneak out of the valley and avoid being caught. Eventually though, she decided that she could not risk any sort of consequences unless her reason for seeing

361

him outweighed any type of punishment that she could receive. She could still write to him in any case, but she hoped that this new regulation would be lifted after enough time had passed devoid of any confrontation with the Keltans.

"I will now turn this assembly over to Councilor Glynn, who will go over the rest of the latest security measures that are now in place," Seth told those assembled in the hall.

Glynn remained in her seat as she proceeded to explain a collection of castle laws that would be put into practice from the moment that the Sarcan students left the hall. There were easily fifteen rules pertaining to the Captains and Cadets, as well as fresh restrictions on who could visit and train in the valley on the weekends. While she spoke, Glynn occasionally glanced down to reference her notes, meticulous about reading through every single one of them.

"As of today, Sarcan Cadets will be required to be in their rooms by 10:00 PM each night, and Sarcan Captains, by 11:00 PM," Glynn said, gazing above her rectangular glasses. "If there is any need to be out later than that, students must be accompanied by an instructor at all times. Captains and Cadets alike will be subject to random questioning if suspicious activity has been detected. In addition, the Sarcan Council reserves the right to search through individual rooms and belongings for the same reason. Also, no one will be allowed to leave the valley unless there is a crisis situation, even if an instructor has granted clearance. Classes will continue on as planned, but we must all be extra watchful of our surroundings and report anything out of the ordinary to the proper authorities."

Carmen listened attentively as Councilor Glynn carried on with the rest of the new rules. None of the up-to-date security measures bothered her aside from the one prohibiting passage into Mortrock Forest. The home that she shared with her grandfather and Blaze's father was there, and she would not stay away if she had to get to it. Should there be some kind of emergency with either Blaine or Thunderbolt, no threat of disciplinary action would keep her from getting to them to help.

"We are implementing these measures for your own safety," Councilor Glynn reminded the students, once she had finished. Most of those gathered in the hall were looking sullen after hearing all of the recent decrees.

"If you will all now direct your attention to my colleague, Councilor Kovelir, she will discuss how each of you can protect yourselves from the new threat that we face every day with the Keltans present in our world."

Councilor Kovelir thanked Glynn, and then looked out at the students and castle visitors.

"Good afternoon, everyone," she said, doing her best to sound friendly, perhaps to soften the tone of all that had come before. "We want you to know that there are simple yet effective ways that you can guard against the Dark Magic of Keltan, and we're going to briefly run through some of those practices together."

Kovelir rose from her chair and strolled out from behind the table. She began to walk leisurely around the room, using helpful gestures as she spoke, so as to better connect with the students and visitors.

"Should you ever find yourself in a position in which you could choose to run or fight, you need to know your own strengths, and make the call that you feel will save *you,* and possibly the lives of others," Councilor Kovelir told them. "There is no shame in running from a situation that puts you in potential danger. Speaking specifically to the Sarcan Captains and Cadets, we believe that you are capable of making your own decisions, so never be afraid to use your better judgment in such a scenario."

Kovelir marched past where Carmen and her friends were sitting, brushing her bushy auburn hair away from her face as she continued to talk.

"As Councilor Seth alluded to earlier, you can all protect yourselves and each other by reporting any kind of unusual activity to an instructor or a Councilor," she said. "Students, your instructors will be training you further on defensive spells and Protections in the coming weeks and months. We expect all of you to take these lessons seriously, and to use your knowledge to aid you during real life predicaments. I thank you for listening...and I wish everyone the best for the remainder of the term."

Kovelir turned her back to the students to return to her seat. Seth briefly muttered something to her, and then spoke to the group once more.

"Before I conclude this assembly, I wish for Councilor Elmeric Maradon to say a few words of significance on behalf of this entire Council."

With that introduction, the white-haired man with the sharp nose stood up and gazed across the chamber through restful blue eyes. The vast hall was uncomfortably quiet, but the crowd's ambivalence did not seem to bother the experienced sorcerer.

Councilor Maradon ambled around the table and out to the center of the floor. There it felt like he was more a part of the greater group.

"My fellow Councilors did a marvelous job in getting our message across to you, so there is not much that I wish to add." Maradon bowed his head to his colleagues before gazing back around at the students and castle guests. "I only desire to share with you my parting thoughts."

Maradon's blue eyes glistened in the light of the crystals.

"I believe that we can overcome this army of demons that has entered into our world," he said, "and I feel that our success depends on our ability as Kelmarians to remain unified."

Councilor Maradon raised an index finger.

"It has been proven...countless times throughout history...that realms in which there is a strong sense of harmony amongst the inhabitants survive and prosper the longest," Maradon told them. "Staying together is the fundamental basis to getting through periods of war...and emerging from the aftermath as the more able victors. The unyielding resistance of armies who fight as one can defeat even the most formidable of foes."

There was a reflective pause before Councilor Maradon concluded his speech.

"You as individuals are more than just who you are today," he said to them all. "You are born into the magical inheritance that makes you Kelmarians for life. Be proud of your heritage...and fight back against those who try to steal it from you, as it remains the decisive advantage that we maintain over our foes. The Keltans derive from a past poisoned with hate and darkness, whereas you were created to restore the good, and rebuild from the ashes of their destruction."

Maradon granted Carmen and her friends a subtle bow of his head, and then shifted his gaze back to everyone.

"We advance each day toward a future of hope," he declared, his silvery blue eyes bright. "Our opponents seek to turn our aspirations over into the depths of despair. Should we surrender, we shall lose everything. I ask you to now take a look around you...and think about what you would miss if Kelmar ever fell to the forces of evil.... Remember what you saw as you go about your daily lives. Our future, and the future of our ally, Kelmarsia, depend on you—the next generation of Kelmarian leaders."

Councilor Maradon bestowed a look of confidence upon his audience, and then walked back to his seat beside Seth and Commander Haidar. Seth beat his gavel on the wooden block on the table, and the sound carried through the hall and silenced the rumbling of voices that followed Maradon's speech.

"We thank you for joining us today," Head Councilor Seth told the students and visitors, leaning over the table.

Then he hit the sound block one final time.

"I hope that you will bear Councilor Maradon's wisdom in mind as you move forward in the trying months ahead. This assembly is now dismissed."

There was a flutter of movement as the Sarcan students and castle visitors slowly exited the chamber. Carmen and her Souls left Sarcan Hall with the others. Maradon's inspiring words continued to run through Carmen's mind, on top of an abundance of other thoughts. She was so mentally distracted that she didn't even notice her own grandfather and his Sarcan waiting to meet her out in the central corridor.

Carmen came around the corner and found herself looking up at Blaine, who beamed at her as she nearly walked into him. His Partner, Thunderbolt, grinned at his son, Blaze, from just above Blaine's shoulder. Carmen and Blaze smiled back.

"That was some speech from Councilor Maradon, wasn't it?" Blaine remarked. "We just caught the end of the assembly, but it sounded like you got an earful of information."

"Yeah…. It was interesting," Carmen said, debating whether she should tell him how she planned to visit him in Mortrock Forest in spite of the Council's new rules. "So, what are you guys doing here?" she asked, looking between him and Thunderbolt. "Did you come just for the meeting?"

"Ah no, we're actually here to give you some good news…. Well, *we* think that it's good news anyway. We'll see what you think," Blaine said, glancing at his Sarcan with a smile.

He then returned his gaze to his granddaughter.

"Thunderbolt and I wish to come with you and your Souls to Kelmarsia to help you find the second Secret."

"*What?*" Carmen's mouth dropped open. "Are you kidding? You would do that?"

"Yes, I've been thinking about it for a while," Blaine said. "And if it's all right with you, we would like to join you on this journey."

"Of course it's all right with me!" Carmen said at once, smiling broadly. "That's terrific! I would love for you to come with us."

But then she remembered the key difference between her first trip to the spirit worlds and this one.

".... Would you be able to take the both of them with us, Anubis?" she asked the black Jackal standing at her side. "I know that this will be your first time in your father's role as the one to transport us to the afterlife.... Do you think that you'll be strong enough to do it?"

As long as I have full use of my father's powers, it makes no difference how many people we bring with us," Anubis said. *"If I can transport the five of us successfully, I can certainly transport seven. The magic has no limitations in that respect."*

"Superb! That's just what I was hoping to hear," Blaine said cheerfully. "So when exactly were you planning to leave?"

"We were planning to go today, just as soon as we got back to our room, actually," Carmen said. "Would you be ready to come now?"

Blaine laughed.

"I imagined that it would be that soon, hence my reason for attending the Council's assembly uninvited. But I won't hold us up any longer," he promised. "Let's be off on our way!"

Carmen and her group hastened to return to their room on the third floor of the castle. As they walked back upstairs, Blaze filled his father and Blaine in on what else the Councilors had said during the meeting.

Once they were all safely up in their bedroom, Carmen closed and locked the door. Anubis then gathered everyone together in a sitting circle at the center of the space.

"*As is required for living beings to travel to the afterlife, I will have to cast all of you into Death's Eternal Sleep,*" Anubis told the group, taking his place in the middle of the circle. "*Since I am borrowing my father's powers as the Opener of the Way, I will not be under the effects of the spell this time. After you are all asleep, I will perform the Opener's Sacred Duty to lift our spirits up into Kelmarsia.*"

Anubis gazed patiently around at his friends.

"*I will need everyone to lie down so that we may commence with the voyage.*"

Carmen and the others lay down on the floor, their minds alert, but calm. They had not a single doubt that Anubis would be capable of casting the two distinct spells required of the Opener. He was a wise and powerful creature, and not one to overestimate his abilities. And so not a word of concern was spoken as Anubis prepared himself to utilize his father's powers and escort his friends to the afterlife.

Anubis closed his eyes…and there continued to be complete silence as he spoke the first incantation through his stream of thought.

"*Death be not the final separation in the tale of one's life, but the start of life renewed and made whole,*" he recited. "*And while each of us is inevitably bound to experience loss by death's hand, in living we are without limits in exploring the frontiers of death in sleep…. The waters in the realms of the departed are not sailed by those of flowing blood and breath-filled lungs, but by those who invite death to their own being, and those who give way to death. With this hand, I grant you death's impermanent form, but keep you of sound mind and body to one day return to your worldly existence. I hereby bestow my magic on thee to cast you into Death's Eternal Sleep!*"

Staring up at the stone ceiling of her room, Carmen soon felt her eyelids becoming unnaturally heavy.... And before she knew it, she was asleep.

It was shortly after slipping from consciousness when Carmen experienced that strange feeling of floating above her body. Anubis was whispering the incantation for *the Opener's Sacred Duty,* but his words were impossible for her to make sense of.... Her eyes remained closed as her thoughts settled into a state of haziness.

But then, without warning, a bright white light flooded her vision. She opened her eyes.

She was rising up toward the ceiling as a spirit, beside those of her grandfather and her friends. She saw their bodies lying peacefully asleep on the floor of her room in Thunder Academy.... A strong wind suddenly gusted around her and her companions...and they began floating quite quickly up through the higher floors of the castle.

Having been through this transformation once before, Carmen was not surprised to see herself and the others as ghostly, translucent spirits. This was a new experience though, for her grandfather and Thunderbolt. She watched them gaping at their silvery, vaporous forms with shock and fascination. Out of all of the travelers, Anubis looked the least like a ghost, but this was because he was fulfilling Inpu's role as the Opener of the Way. He was glowing in a divine light just as his father had, and was still solid in form.

Carmen and the others passed smoothly through the floors and ceilings of each level in the upper part of the castle, and then out through the roof. It was still raining in Sarcanian Valley, but as spirits, they could feel neither the cold raindrops on their skin nor the biting wind against their faces.

Anubis led his friends up through the darkened sky and into the far reaches of the heavens. High in the utter blackness of the uppermost atmosphere, they saw the magical golden line of light drawn across the sky...the Impassable Barrier.

As they got closer to it, Carmen and her friends heard the beautiful music coming from the World of Light...a seamless orchestra of heavenly voices and instruments. It was the most wonderful, perfect sound ever to reach mortal ears.

The music grew louder as Anubis and company soared through the barrier—and then a brilliant light of warmth and peace welcomed them into Kelmarsia. They soared over scenic meadows and flourishing green forests, whose treetops glittered in the afternoon sun. Far ahead of them lay Merlin's grand white castle atop the cliff overlooking the lands.

Beyond the castle stretched mountains and tiny villages of white homes scattered throughout the forests. The azure sky through which Carmen and her friends flew was dotted with delicate white clouds.

With its endless span of gorgeous sights to behold, Kelmarsia remained as magnificent as it had been the first time Carmen had seen it. But for newcomers Blaine and Thunderbolt, this glimpse into the afterlife was especially incredible.

"Carmen, this world...is amazing," Blaine said, his voice full of wonder as he gazed around him. "In all my years, never did I think that I would ever see a place such as this.... It's..."

"Absolutely stunning," Thunderbolt finished, equally in awe.

Blaine and his friends glided over the valley through which flowed the River of the Departed Spirits—the waterway that ferried the newly deceased Kelmarians into the World of Light. With Inpu trapped in Keltan, Carmen looked down to see that another Jackal had taken over his duties of guiding new spirits into Kelmarsia. Slighter in stature than Inpu, this white, female Jackal wore a golden ribbon collar decorated with flawless white diamonds. She stood at the bow of the ferryboat full of spirits as it sailed on toward Merlin's castle. She possessed the same pointed ears and equally striking golden eyes of Anubis....

"My mother, Nephthys," Anubis said, as he led Carmen and the others over the river and on toward the forests. *"She is the Protector of the Spirits—a Healer who cares for Kelmarsians. Merlin has summoned her to the river to fulfill my father's role until he is freed. She knows that we are here."*

Anubis continued to lead his friends in the direction of the northern forests as Nephthys ferried her spirits upriver.

"I would introduce you to her, but she needs to get the young spirits right to Kelmari so that she may accept them into Kelmarsia," he explained to his fellow travelers. *"There can be no delay in their passage, as these spirits must be released into the world before darkness falls."*

Anubis escorted his own spirits in the direction of Mount Alberik—the mountain that Carmen's parents claimed to be home to an ancient shrine in which the second Secret of Kelmar was located. The group floated over the enormous towers of Merlin's castle and approached more distant mountains. The peak for which they were searching eventually came into sight.

Mount Alberik was a tall mountain, with a spiraling stone path snaking up to its crest. And standing there in the snow at the top of the mountain was a small, golden bricked shrine. It was too high up for Carmen to see any creatures that might be guarding it. She would have to wait until she reached the summit to catch a glimpse of the beasts of which her parents had spoken to her about.

Carmen and her companions collectively began a gradual descent, and touched down in a small meadow not far from the base of the mountain. Tall pink, yellow, and blue flowers were in full bloom all through the grass, blowing softly in the mountain breeze, almost as though they were dancing to the harmo-

371

nious music that was continually playing throughout the lands. Kelmarsian creatures, all of which lived in Kelmar as well, were roaming freely amongst the trees.

Carmen observed a duo of sparkling creatures called Bursen Hounds passing through the neighboring forests. The four-legged beasts, each of which looked like a combination of a small deer and a dog, had striking purple eyes, the lean brown bodies and hooves of deer, and fluffed, dog-like tails. Their heads had features of both animals, and they each possessed a pair of antlers, as well as wide and pointed ears.

There were also Feneltoffs fluttering and singing out in high chirps in the trees. These navy blue birds had silver beaks and sweeping feathers that had violet and green-blue tips, and rounded patterns of plum-colored markings.

Also among the creatures living in this part of Kelmarsia were gray, four-legged beings the size of ponies with bright green eyes, long tails, and wings similar to those of Dragons.... They had slender bodies and serpent-like heads. Peaceful creatures by nature, these animals, which were known as Meldacots, inhabited mountainous regions and foraged for plants and insects to feed on.

As Carmen was taking note of these captivating new beings, an old friend came flying overhead, landing smoothly on the grass in front of her and her friends.

"Dagtar!"

Carmen grinned at the sparkling green Dragon, who was her fifth Soul of Destiny. Even while he was sitting on the ground, he still towered high above the trees. He had to lean down in order to speak with his friends.

"Hello, everyone," Dagtar said, with a bow of his great, spiked head. *"It is wonderful for me to see you all here safe and sound after what occurred in Sarcanian Valley. I fear for your safety now that the Keltans can travel freely between your world, theirs, and ours. I hope that this defensive breach will be remedied*

before the Keltans can do the kind of damage in your world that they've already committed here."

"I hope so, too," Carmen replied, saddened at the thought of what Dagtar must think of her failing to protect the cipher disk from Triedastron.

"Well, in any event, I am most pleased by the way that you fought that night, Carmen," Dagtar said. He was looking more positive, which came as a surprise to her. "You proved yourself for all of the Worlds Triad to see. Your parents can't be with us today, but they wanted me to tell you that they are very proud of you as well."

"Thank you," Carmen said, feeling quite small standing before the enormous Dragon.

"Blaine, Thunderbolt, welcome to Kelmarsia," Dagtar said, nodding toward them. "It appears that you've made the voyage here to help Carmen claim the second Secret.... I'm here for the same reason."

"Really?" Carmen asked eagerly. She hadn't expected that Dagtar would be able, or even allowed, to help her. "That would be great!"

Dagtar laughed, which sounded more like a deep snorting noise.

"I'm delighted to hear that this makes you happy," he said.

"So where do we go exactly?" Blaze asked him. "We checked the map yesterday, and it led to the top of Mount Alberik."

"That is correct," Dagtar said. "It is the mountain just behind me, and you will need to climb it in order to get to the shrine. I will fly with you as you scale the peak, should you need any help along the way, though I trust you will have no difficulty with this climb. You've scaled your fair share of mountains in the past."

"That's true," Carmen said, with a chuckle. But before Dagtar directed them to the mountain, she longed to ask him something about which she had been wondering for days.

"Dagtar..." she said slowly, "is Merlin very upset about the loss of the cipher disk?"

Dagtar gazed insightfully at her.

"No, Carmen," he said. *"My Master is not the least bit concerned about his cipher disk, for he knows that you will get it back for him. He is only concerned for* you *and your* safety. *He does not wish for you to be injured in your quest to return it to Kelmar, but he has faith that you will make it through.... He trusts that you will not disappoint him."*

For her own peace of mind, Carmen had to believe that Dagtar was telling her the truth.

"Please let him know that I'll be okay," Carmen requested. "I *will* get the cipher disk back and decipher the final two Secrets...no matter what it takes."

Dagtar nodded.

"I will tell him," he vowed. *"But I have a feeling that he already knows."*

Dagtar stood up, smiling as he looked down at Carmen and the others.

"Follow me," he said.

Merlin's Dragon led Carmen and her friends through the meadow, and over to the base of Mount Alberik. Carmen gazed up at the daunting, gray-brown mountain, unsure of what she would find upon reaching the top. She was more curious than scared.

"Here we are," Dagtar said, staring toward the peak, which had a fairly wide walking path cut into the rock, snaking all the way up to the summit.

"Just follow the path until you reach the top. If any of you get tired along the way, we will all stop and rest. I will be flying next to you as you go. I believe that we should reach the shrine within a couple of hours."

More than eager to track down the second of the three Secrets, Carmen, Blaine, and the others walked ahead onto the path as they began their hike up the snow-tipped mountain. The path was wide enough so that two of them could walk side-by-side, with the Sarcans flying over the shoulders of their Masters. They marched over the ancient rocks together as Dagtar flew next to them. Carmen summoned her wand just in case she should need it. Blaine did the same.

The Kelmarians trekked one step at a time up the path that wound around the mountain, making steady progress as the afternoon went on. They were fortunate to have beautiful weather for the climb, though Carmen had yet to see anything less than a perfect day here in Kelmarsia.

The group made it to the halfway point about forty-five minutes after beginning the hike, putting them on track to reach the summit in less than two hours, just as Dagtar had reasoned they would.

As they climbed, Carmen and her friends talked about a range of topics of interest, their moods relatively joyful and optimistic. They had not come across any creatures living on the mountain yet; leading Carmen to believe that whatever challenges awaited them in acquiring the second Secret likely lay at the top.

Dagtar kept Carmen's mind occupied with lighter thoughts, conversing with her and her other Souls about everything from his favorite foods, to his existence in Kelmarsia. In that single trip up the mountain, Carmen and the rest of her friends bonded with Dagtar in ways that they had never gotten to before. It was nice for them to finally get to talk to him without the threat of imminent danger looming.

"…. I rise with the sun each morning, just as you do," Dagtar said. "At first light, Merlin and I go out for our daily flight around Kelmarsia, and we greet all of our friends and the new spirits from Kelmar. After we come back, Merlin takes care of his *responsibilities as the Master of Kelmarsia, some of which, I help him with. We examine how Kelmarsia is faring, and we maintain the magic that supports this world, as well as repair anything that needs fixing."*

Carmen listened with much curiosity, having always wondered how Dagtar spent his time while she and the others were living in Kelmar.

"In the afternoon, Merlin and I work on creating new spells, potions, and more recently, improved Protections for Kelmarsia," Dagtar continued. *"Before the night stars appear, we secure Kelmarsia's borders with any new defenses that we have developed, and then...on most nights, we sleep. As spirits, theoretically, we don't have to, but the peacefulness of sleep allows us to better empty our minds for the day ahead."*

When Dagtar's friends were nearly three-quarters of the way to the summit, snow appeared beneath their feet. The muscles in Carmen's legs had begun to burn with fatigue, but she made the mental decision to keep going. She was determined to reach the top within the hour, and with the urgency of finding the second Secret in mind, she didn't want to slow down the advancement toward that goal.

She and her companions pushed ahead, tramping through the powdered white snow in the light of the afternoon sun. They could soon see the walls of the golden shrine as they drew nearer to it. Carmen and Blaine led the way up the remainder of the path, maintaining a stable pace as they neared their destination high in the clouds. By the time they reached the top of the mountain, the troop of steadfast Kelmarians had climbed several hundred feet.

Carmen and her friends came around the corner to the summit of the mountain, and it was instantly evident that the carefree portion of the climb was over.

Ahead of them lay the small gold shrine standing atop the snow-blanketed peak. It was a relatively plain and small brick building, with a brown tiled roof. The carved wooden entry doors were engraved with the Great Seal of Kelmarsia; a magic circle containing clouds, the Kelmarian Elements, and an image of a flying Dagtar. It was not the shrine that intimidated Carmen and her friends, but rather the pair of demons guarding it.

Known as Ammits, each of these horrid-looking creatures had a body that was half-adult lion and half-hippopotamus, with the head of a crocodile. Pale golden fur covered the better part of their forms, and they possessed thick brown manes that framed their crocodilian skulls. One Ammit sat on either side of the entry doors on the shrine's covered porch.

On guard, Dagtar and the Kelmarians inched toward the shrine. Approaching these fearsome demons, Carmen was glad that she had summoned her wand earlier, should they try to attack. When she and her friends were standing only ten feet away from the entrance, the Ammit sitting on the right side of the doors spoke in a deep voice.

"Beyond us lies the Secret that you seek," it said, revealing a set of white, razor sharp teeth. *"But in order for us to allow you to pass into the Shrine of Secrecy, you will first need to convince us that you are worthy of gaining entrance."*

"We will require you to answer a series of three questions," the other Ammit told Carmen. *"Those who are with you are allowed to help you. However, if you do not answer all of our questions correctly, we will devour you as spirits, and you will henceforth be lost between the two afterworlds for the rest of eternity."*

Carmen remained where she was, in a state of shock, trying to imagine what sorts of questions these two creatures could possibly give her to test her competence to acquire the second Secret.... She tried to shake off the thought of what would happen should she answer the questions wrong. It was fortunate for her that she would be able to ask her companions for help if she needed it. Without them, she would be feeling even more helpless now.... She had to believe that between the eight of them, she and the others would be able to formulate the correct responses.

"I agree to your test," Carmen said with a nod, gazing into the scarlet eyes of both of the Ammits. "Please give me the first question."

The first Ammit rose to its feet and stared out at Carmen's group. The creature appeared even more menacing when standing.

"If you ever came upon a Gorfelrod, where specifically would you be?"

It didn't take much time for Carmen to recall her experience with the answer to this question. Nonetheless, she double-checked with Blaze before speaking.

"The mountains of North Kelmar," she said, thinking back to the powerful Gorfelrod that she had encountered in Mortrock Forest last year.

"Very good," the second Ammit replied, standing up with the other. *"But keep in mind that our questions will get progressively more difficult. Next you must tell us this: Which curse will result in distortions of the mind?"*

Carmen thought hard.... She had been the victim of a number of such curses at the hands of her enemies in the past, but she could not decide which one would be the likely answer. She turned to her friends for help.

"Do you guys have any ideas?" she asked hopefully. "I'm a little perplexed on this one."

Anubis looked up at Carmen with a contemplative expression as he stood in the shadow of Dagtar.

"If my fluency in Keltongue serves me correctly, I believe the curse that they are looking for is Distotus Psychea," Anubis said quietly. *"The spell translates to 'Distort Psyche'. I vividly remember Nankarsa casting it during your First Challenge last year."*

Carmen felt like slapping herself on the forehead as the recollection finally came back to her.

"That's it!" she said.

Carmen turned back to face the Ammits.

"Distotus Psychea," she told them.

"That...is correct," the first Ammit said, bowing his long head. *"Here is your final question."*

The Ammits looked at each other, and then spoke their request together.

"What do you consider to be your greatest accomplishment?" the demons asked.

Carmen gaped at them. It was a trick question, and one whose answer would seem to be more of an individual opinion.

Unlike the previous two questions, there was no asking others for their ideas, or recalling specific encounters from her past. The first thought that came to Carmen's mind was her managing to stay alive throughout the numerous brushes with death that she had experienced as the Guardian of Kelmar.

In all seriousness though, there were many answers for which the Ammits could be looking. Carmen considered getting accepted into Thunder Academy a big accomplishment, as well as her victories in battles against the Magicon, with her defeat of Desorkhan being her most important victory to date. Yet even with all of this in mind, for some reason, she couldn't pinpoint her one single most impressive feat. Perhaps it was because she had never given much thought to the idea before.

Carmen spent nearly ten minutes lost in her search for the ideal response...until she turned around and saw her grandfather and her friends standing behind her. They were watching her with trust, their faces glowing with smiles. Seeing her companions all here together was the sight that convinced Carmen that she would not have achieved any of what she had if she had been without them.

"You know the answer, Carmen," Blaine told her calmly, his eyes sparkling in the light of the snow. "Listen to your inner voice."

Carmen thought back to what her parents had told her in her dream…. Then she gazed around at all of her friends and realized that her greatest accomplishment stood here on the mountaintop with her.

"There is nothing stronger than the bond of your friendship…. Keep that in your heart, and no one shall ever be able to truly defeat you."

"My mom was right," Carmen whispered to herself, before meeting the eyes of the Ammits. She stared down the duo of demonic creatures with confidence and courage.

"My greatest accomplishment…is this group of individuals here by my side," Carmen said, motioning toward her accompanying travelers. "My friends."

Carmen's Souls of Destiny exchanged beaming smiles with Carmen before she returned her gaze to the Ammits.

"I wouldn't have arrived at where I am today if it weren't for them," she said. "They are instrumental pieces in my life, and none of what I have done would have been possible, or even mean anything, if I had been alone. For this reason…I believe that my friendship is priceless, and my greatest accomplishment by far."

The Ammits were nodding as Carmen spoke. When she finished her answer, they conferred, murmuring to each other, for nearly a minute—sixty seconds of agonizing anticipation for Carmen, in which she prayed to Merlin that the shrine's protectors would accept her answer as the correct one.

Finally, the Ammits sat down and spoke to Carmen and her friends together.

"Congratulations," they said. *"We have determined you to be worthy of entry into the Shrine of Secrecy. You may pass through the gates behind us."*

The wooden doors at the front of the shrine magically swung open...and an enormous sense of relief washed over Carmen.

"Thank you," she said, as she gestured toward her friends to follow her.

"I will wait for you here," Dagtar assured Carmen. The shrine was much too small to allow the full-grown Dragon to fit inside.

"Sure. We'll be right out," she promised.

Carmen, Blaine, and the others strode ahead through the snow, past the seated Ammits and into the Shrine of Secrecy.

The interior of the shrine was decorated with oil paintings of Merlin Cloud at various stages in his life. Seeming to be in chronological order, there was a painting of him studying magic as a teenager, another of him in a duel with a sorcerer whose face was hidden in shadow (Carmen presumed it to be Desorkhan), and farther down, there was a painting of Merlin and Dagtar speaking to a gathering of Kelmarsians out in the forest.

There were also collections of small magical relics belonging to Merlin lining shelves along two of the walls. Precious stones, pieces of jewelry, and bottles of colored potions were among the items there. And sitting in the center of the back wall were the most predominant objects in the shrine—a miniature wooden altar placed beneath a large square of smooth, shining golden blocks. These blocks were mounted higher up on the wall, each one marked with a red, abstract design.

Having not found the ciphertext Secret written across any other surface, Carmen and her fellow Kelmarians carefully walked over to the altar. The wooden platform was built to the right height to allow a human to stand atop it and touch the golden blocks. After just a moment of indecision, Carmen climbed up onto the platform with Blaze.

She stared at the mysterious golden blocks on the wall, touching two of them ever so gently with her fingertips.... The pair of blocks that she touched magically shifted. That was when she reached a surprising conclusion.

"This is a puzzle," Carmen said, her eyes flickering from block to block. "If we can put the blocks together in the right order...they should create a single image. I'm guessing that we won't find the Secret until we do that."

"That is a brilliant observation, Carmen," Blaine said, peering up at the blocks. "Start moving some of the tiles...and try to organize them in different ways. If you can get even a small number of the blocks to line up, perhaps we'll be able to figure out the rest of the image."

Carmen leaned her wand against the side of the altar and began to randomly slide the movable golden blocks across the wall. She stared at the red images on the tiles, trying to discern any part of the greater illustration.

After shifting the blocks around for five minutes, she could see a single tree painted with sweeping red brushstrokes, which a handful of them had created.

With that part of the puzzle complete, she left those blocks where they were and continued working around them. It was only about ten minutes before she had put together a forest of neighboring trees, the bottom portion of a river, and then the clouds and sun in the upper rows of blocks.

She was more than halfway through assembling the puzzle when she realized that it represented a picture of Merlin's castle and the surrounding landscape.

Carmen worked swiftly to piece together the remaining golden blocks...and in a short while, she and the others found themselves looking at a stylized painting of central Kelmarsia.

Just as the final tile slid into place, the edges of the golden blocks lit up and rose slowly up the wall, revealing a square hole about the size of a shoebox cut into the bricks. Carmen carefully reached in and removed a narrow piece of parchment, upon which a message was scrawled. She instantly recognized the handwriting as that belonging to Merlin Cloud.

The music is the Best, art won me tonight.

Once she had finished reading the ciphertext message and showed it to her grandfather and her friends, Carmen pulled out a piece of parchment and a couple of other items from the pocket of her robes. She removed the lid of her inkwell and dipped her quill pen in it.

As soon as she was done copying the message exactly as it read, she placed the original parchment back in the hole in the wall and watched as the golden blocks slid securely down over it, before scrambling themselves into a jumbled puzzle again.

Her task complete, Carmen put away her things, picked up her wand, and left the shrine with her Souls, Blaine, and Thunderbolt, feeling amazing to have secured the second Secret of Kelmar. But when she came outside to see Dagtar waiting for her on the other side of the mountain in the warmth of the sunlight, a sudden cloud of sadness drifted over her.

"What's the matter, Carmen?" the Dragon asked, as she and the others walked over to him. *"Did you not find the Secret?"*

"Oh, no…we found it," she said dully. When she looked at him, she could feel her unexpected sadness worsen. "I was just thinking how I wish that we could stay here with you a little while longer."

Dagtar smiled affectionately at her as he floated beside the mountain.

"I wish that you could, too," he said, *"but we will see each other again."*

"Promise?"

"Of course."

Still not looking forward to bidding Dagtar farewell, Carmen turned to Anubis.

"I guess it's time to go back to Kelmar then, huh?"

Anubis nodded.

"Yes...I believe that it is time," he answered. *"We can leave right from here if you wish."*

Carmen sighed.

"Okay...." she said. Then she reached up and stroked the side of Dagtar's face.

"I guess this is goodbye, for now...." she told the Dragon, taking note of how the sun glistened off of his emerald scales. "Thank you for coming with us."

"Be well, Dagtar," Blaze said, smiling at him. "We appreciate you bringing us up here."

"I had a great time," Dagtar replied, as he raised his head and looked down at the entire group.

"I know that I leave Carmen in very capable hands.... It was an honor seeing you all again."

The Kelmarian spirits graciously echoed his sentiments. Then they gathered together in a circle and prepared to depart for their own world.

Their undertaking a veritable triumph for Kelmar, Carmen and her companions floated without hurry up into the air as they waved goodbye to Dagtar, who watched them respectfully whilst Anubis led them away from the snowy mountaintop. With the sun shining brightly in the boundless blue heavens of Kelmarsia, the spirits soared through the sky once more on their way back to their home, the second Secret of Kelmar safe in their possession at long last.

CHAPTER EIGHTEEN
MAIDAK KALVARO

The spirits of the seven Kelmarians made it back to their world and returned to their bodies without any difficulties. They had floated down into their sleeping forms and then awakened just as they had been prior to traveling to Kelmarsia. All things considered, it had been a very successful trip. Carmen had obtained the second of the three Secrets of Kelmar, and while she could not decipher the message without the cipher disk, she still felt better knowing that she was one step closer to remedying the difficulties plaguing Kelmarsia and her own world.

It continued to rain on and off in Sarcanian Valley for the next three weeks, causing the students to have to train indoors on most days. The depressing weather indicated to Carmen and her friends that the fighting in Keltan and Kelmarsia was ongoing. Though the storms had lessened in intensity following the turbulent week of the attack on Thunder Academy, there remained some remnants of the enduring struggle.

Carmen planned to journey to Keltan to search for the third Secret, get back the cipher disk, and rescue Inpu just as soon as Anubis received news that it was safe enough to travel there. The Kelmarsians had launched an invasion into the World of Darkness to free some of their own being held captive by Triedastron a week after Carmen returned with the Second Secret. The mission had been more of a success than a failure, with the Kelmarsians freeing more than half of the innocent spirits trapped in Haesnost Prison, but Inpu was unfortunately not among those who were rescued.

But this movement, coupled with the fallout from Carmen's discovery of the second Secret in Kelmarsia, had caused an upsurge in the fighting in the afterworlds. Because of these new battles taking place, Inpu asked Anubis to wait to come for him until there was a lull in the combat. Although he had not been lucky enough to be one of the Kelmarsians freed in the strike, the Jackal remained unharmed after recovering from Triedastron's initial hours of torture. Yet even as he had seen others around him escaping the largest prison in Keltan, he was patient enough to have Carmen stay in Kelmar until it was safer for her and the others to come save him. He was truly a creature with remarkable strength of heart.

There had been a handful of Phantom sightings throughout Kelmar since Triedastron had released them into the realm, and two recent acts of war committed by the Master of Keltan's forces.

Mondalaus and Denethor, together with their Partners, had burned down half of a forest in West Kelmar before able Kelmarians could arrive and extinguish the blaze. The four Phantom Warriors had eluded capture by transforming into demon spirits and fleeing the scene before the Kelmarian fighters could secure the area. In a separate incident, Desorkhan and Singe had set fire to an entire street of homes in the town of Feroewolf in East Kelmar before escaping in the same way that their fellow Warriors had.

All of the Phantom strikes were detailed in *The Kelmarian Review*, which arrived daily to Carmen's room in Thunder Academy. Each morning before unfolding the paper, Carmen hoped that there would be no bad news for the day, and was upset every time word of yet another attack made the front page of the publication.

It seemed that with every sighting of Phantom Warriors, a fresh wave of consternation soured the mood of those in the castle. Only adding to the ubiquitous sense of dread amongst the students were the new security measures that had been implemented a few weeks earlier. Even such innocent acts as walking the halls past 8:00 PM, or well before dawn, would frequently result in questioning from a Councilor or an instructor, who patrolled the halls of the castle more often than usual as of late. Consequently, the Sarcan students were left feeling like more and more of their freedoms were being taken away with each passing day.

For the most part, the Cadets and Captains didn't complain, understanding that the new rules were present for the sole purpose of their protection. Carmen didn't know how the castle visitors were affected by the increasingly tight security policy, but she imagined that they were not as impacted by it as she and her peers were.

Just more than a month after her expedition to the World of Light, Carmen was greeted one morning with a letter from the Kelmarian Parliament accompanying her newspaper. She had a feeling that she knew what it was even before she tore open the seal. Her grandfather had told her to expect a letter requesting her presence at Eli Elezar's hearing any day now, and this was most likely that very document.

Carmen carefully opened the envelope and unfolded the single piece of parchment that was inside. The Great Seal of Kelmar was stamped in the upper left corner of the paper. The letter, which was dated a day earlier, was written in scarlet ink.

DEAR MS. FOX,
ON NOVEMBER THE THIRTEENTH, THE KELMARIAN PARLIAMENT WILL BE PRESIDING OVER THE HEARING OF MR. ELI ELEZAR FOR HIS ALLEGED CONSPIRACY TO POISON YOU WITH A COUNTERFEIT COPY OF THE SEER'S AMULET BACK IN SEPTEMBER OF THIS YEAR.
THE CHARGES PENDING AGAINST MR. ELEZAR STAND AS FOLLOWS: CONSPIRACY TO COMMIT MURDER, BETRAYAL, AND ATTEMPTED MURDER.

By Kelmarian law, you are obligated to testify in the case, as you are the victim of the suspected crime, and the key individual in helping us to conclude this investigation. We are thus calling on you to provide honest and true testimony in this formal hearing, which will take place in the South Chamber of Parliament. In addition to you, your Souls of Destiny are also required to attend the hearing as witnesses to Mr. Elezar's actions.

For your convenience, we have arranged your transportation to and from Pyramid City. At 9:00 AM on the morning of November the thirteenth, you and your Souls will leave by chartered airship from Sarcanian Valley, and be flown directly to the capital. You will report to Parliament by 12:45 PM. The hearing is scheduled to begin at 1:00 PM sharp, and is not expected to take more than three hours.

If you have any questions regarding your participation in the hearing of Eli Elezar, please contact us prior to the hearing date. We look forward to seeing you on the thirteenth.

Sincerely,

Danuvius Dorvai

Danuvius Dorvai
Head of State
Kelmarian Parliament

Carmen read the letter over a couple of times. Eli's hearing was only three days away. She showed Blaze the note before they left for class that morning. After reading it over, he shook his head.

"It's on Monday," he said, as he handed Carmen back the letter. "I hope that Haidar will let us out of class."

"I was thinking the same thing," Carmen admitted. "We'd better ask him today."

"There will be no Advanced Training taking place on Monday," Haidar reported to his students, after all of them had gathered on the bleachers in the training room for their last class of the week. "I will be out of town all day on Parliamentary business, and shall return for class on Tuesday," he said. "The Sarcan Council will also be out of town on Monday, but a team of Senior Sarcan Delegates will fill in for them until they return the following morning."

"Well, there's our answer then," Carmen whispered to Blaze, as they sat in the bleachers. "I wonder if we're all flying together."

"Today, we're going to resume our work on Kelmarsian defense spells," Haidar said, as he stood in front of the blackboard. "We will start out with a group spell that will require everyone's equal participation.... But before we can perform the spell as a class, I need all of you to stand up and position yourselves off to my right, and turn so that you can see me."

The Sarcan Captains climbed down off of the wooden bleachers and walked past Haidar. Once in place, they turned around to face their Commander and await his instructions.

"The defense that you're about to learn is called *the Spinning Ribbon*," Haidar said. "It is a Kelmarsian defense against curses, both Kelmarian and Keltan. When cast by an individual sorcerer, it will protect both them and their Partner from attack. When cast by multiple magic users of a joint company, the spell takes on the power of each member, and collectively guards the entire group against harm. I will first demonstrate how to cast the spell as Master and Partner pairs, and then we will come together and perform the spell as a Unit."

The Captains watched as Haidar summoned his wand, and then raised it up high above his head. Concentrating, Haidar closed his eyes and spun around three times on one foot.

"The Spinning Ribbon!"

A silver ribbon of light snaked out from the crown of Haidar's wand and effortlessly wound itself around his body, forming a magical protective cage over him. When the floating shiny band had him covered from head to toe, Haidar lowered his wand and spoke through the gaps in the ribbon.

"This is the form that the spell should take when cast correctly," Haidar pointed out.

He then allowed his students some time to closely study how the spell looked before he dissolved it away with a flick of his wand.

"Do we understand?" he asked, lowering his staff.

A number of the students nodded.

"Excellent," he said. "You shall now each practice *the Spinning Ribbon* on your own. I will watch to make sure that all of you have it mastered before we attempt it as a class."

Haidar looked out at his students with a watchful eye.

"Begin."

With that order came the sound of a dozen young voices echoing through the spacious room as Carmen and her sorcerer classmates summoned their wands. In his usual fashion, Haidar had completed the spell with minimal effort, but with decades of magical training under his belt, he made practically *everything* look natural.

At their own paces, the Sarcan Captains imitated Haidar's stance of holding their wands high in the air, and then they each completed three smooth turns with their eyes shut.

"The Spinning Ribbon!" Carmen shouted.

A winding ribbon of silvery light meandered down from the crown of her wand...and warmth swept over her body as the spell came to fruition.

Carmen glanced to her right. The end of the ribbon broke off into a second strand, which immediately wrapped itself around Blaze's form. She then watched through the openings in her own shield as her other classmates worked on completing the spell. The light from most of the students' magical ribbons was fading before it could fully develop.

Overall, it took most of the Sarcan Captains two tries to get the spell down perfectly. But after they had finally completed their Kelmarsian defenses, Haidar called them all to the center of the room and asked them to form a circle.

Carmen and Blaze assembled alongside Kamie, Akira, and the rest of their peers in the middle of the training space, listening for their instructor's next set of directions. Commander Haidar crossed to the center of the circle and looked around at his students.

"On my signal, each sorcerer will cast his or her spell in the same manner as before, but instead of focusing only on yourself and your Sarcan, you will take *all* of your classmates into consideration," he instructed. "Imagine that you are in battle as a Unit, and an attack has been launched against the whole group.... In order to protect yourselves, you must work together. Keep this in your thoughts as you cast the spell this time around."

Haidar then raised his own wand.

"Ready...." he said slowly. "Now!"

The Sarcan Masters pointed their wands skyward and closed their eyes. Then they each twirled themselves around— three quick turns on one foot.

"The Spinning Ribbon!" they summoned in unison.

With a brilliant burst of energy, bands of silvery light flooded the room as the sorcerers' spells grew from their wands.

But then, instead of each ribbon enclosing the sorcerer who had conjured it, along with their Partner, the ribbon extended to the right, and wound around the neighboring Master and Sarcan.

When the spell was finally complete, all of the ribbons had joined end-to-end and wrapped around the entire circle of students, creating a giant ring of dazzling, silver-white light that illuminated the wide space. It was a beautiful sight, and one that was justly representative of the students' collaboration as a Unit.

"What teamwork!" Commander Haidar said, applauding as his students stared around them in wonder at the silver circle of light. "Excellent job, Captains. This is how it's done. I would challenge any army of Keltans to cast such a spell."

Haidar gazed at his students with approval as the light from the spell faded away.

"Only harmony amongst members of a common good could bring to life the potential of magic such as this," he said.

Carmen hoped that the same principle would hold true when it came to their struggle against Triedastron.

After training ended that night, Haidar held Carmen and Blaze back.

"I have been summoned to Eli's hearing to serve as a witness to the effects of the poisoned amulet," Haidar informed them. "As you are Sarcan students, the Sarcan Council is coming to oversee the proceedings with the Parliament Members. I will be flying out at 7:00 AM from the valley with the Council.... I've been told that you and your Souls will travel separately aboard a later flight."

"Yes, that's right," Carmen said.

"The flight from the valley to the capital is about three hours. I will meet you at the airfield in Pyramid City upon your arrival," Haidar said. "We will eat lunch in the city, and then walk over to Parliament together."

"That sounds great," Carmen replied. "Thank you."

Haidar dismissed her and Blaze not long after that, and the duo retired to their room for the evening.

Carmen and her Souls would go on to spend a quiet weekend indoors, as the rain carried on for most of the two days. Content to finally have a little time to herself, Carmen got some reading done and visited with some of her classmates. On Saturday, she penned a letter to her grandfather regarding her upcoming trip. He replied promptly with his own note wishing her luck and reminding her to get plenty of rest the night before she left.

When Monday morning arrived, the sky over the valley was a dreary, dull gray color. Thankfully, the rain had finally ceased, affording Carmen and her friends a clear day for flying. Carmen had taken her grandfather's advice and gone to bed earlier than usual the previous night, leaving her feeling well rested and ready for the day when she and the others awakened shortly before 8:00 AM. The group consumed a hearty breakfast of eggs, toast, and Perterale tea in their room before heading out the front doors of the castle into the valley.

They could see the Parliament airship sitting at the southern edge of the gorge. It was a long wooden craft that looked just like a boat with scarlet and gold sails, embellished with the Great Seal of Kelmar. The name of the ship was carved into the wood framing the bow—*The Allegiant.* There was also a giant pair of dark brown wings affixed to the sides of the ship, which powered the vessel through the air. As was commonplace with airships, there was no captain. The magical ship could direct itself to the intended destination with no assistance from those on board.

Carmen and her four Souls of Destiny crossed the empty dueling fields and passed by the damaged Thunder Stadium. The building had undergone its share of repairs since the battle with Triedastron, but they were not yet complete. The ancient wood and stone of the exterior structure had been replaced, leaving the arena looking even better on the outside than it had prior to the fire. New seats and light posts still needed to be installed inside though, and the halls running around the stadium required extensive renovation to be useable.

The five friends boarded the chartered airship and settled themselves into individual cushioned wooden seats that were installed in a row on the deck. After they were all safely seated, the side door of the craft closed and sealed itself shut. Then the airship rose smoothly up into the cool, overcast sky, and the vast Sarcanian Valley soon shrank to a distant canyon of red sandstone far below them.

Regardless of the happenings that awaited Carmen in Pyramid City, flying aboard the high-speed airship with her friends was an incredible experience in and of itself. Sitting in an end seat, she could peer over the side of the craft and see the lands, rivers, and lakes speeding past them as they traveled north. She observed an assortment of creatures living throughout the countryside—including horned Yeslyans, which looked similar to mountain goats, wild black Thersan horses, and red-furred Leafoxes.

The colors and forms of the landscape more or less blurred together once the airship got up to full speed, but they still made for a stunning, ever-changing visual display that Carmen admired at different points during the trip. She had traveled in airships before, but never aboard one that flew so fast. It got colder the farther they soared north, but the skies were gradually lightening for every hour they moved beyond Sarcanian Valley.

Carmen had been to Pyramid City only once before as a teenager—for the victory parade following the conclusion of the Magicon War. She looked forward to visiting the capital again, but only wished that she were going there for a less serious reason. It would have been nice to visit the city and see the sights without having to worry about testifying in a criminal hearing. But even with this thought in mind, Carmen tried to enjoy the outing with her Souls. It wasn't until they got to within an hour and a half of the city that Carmen turned the conversation to the impending event.

"How do you think the hearing is going to go?" she asked Blaze, just more than halfway into the trip. "It sounds like Kalvaro really wants to see Eli convicted…. We'll probably have a hard time proving his innocence."

"I know what you mean," Blaze muttered, looking up at her from his neighboring seat. "It will be especially difficult without Inpu there to back up Eli's story."

"My father indicated to me his desire to attend the hearing as a witness," Anubis said, chiming in. *"But given his present circumstances, this is, of course, impossible. It's a shame though…. He is a dear friend of Eli and would have readily stood up for him."*

"Does he have any ideas as to who could have cursed him?" Carmen asked.

Anubis shook his head.

"I asked him that very question, and he has put a great amount of thought into who the potential assassin might be," he said. *"The man had no enemies to speak of…but as we know, at any moment, there are an indeterminable number of Dark loyalists lurking among us. My father is convinced that whoever did it is still out there—a killer, who's most likely some kind of servant to Triedastron."*

Disturbed enough by that idea alone, Carmen looked out over the side of *The Allegiant.* She and her friends were flying over the dark green treetops of the dense Oldac Forests, heading toward the Torena Mountains, on the other side of which lay Pyramid City. Flocks of brightly colored Snarebirds were flying in formation far below the airship. The light from the sun peeking through the clouds shined against their silky feathers.

"Where do you suppose Commander Haidar is taking us for lunch?" Glamis asked his friends, attempting to distract Carmen from her worries. "I know of a few good restaurants in town that we should visit. One of them is just down the street from the Parliament building."

"If they serve only insects, I'll just wait for you outside," Stellar told him flatly.

"Oh no, they have a very diverse menu!" Glamis insisted, sitting up straighter in his seat as he gazed over at Stellar. "It's called The First City Café. I've been there countless times in my travels."

"Well, that's a relief," Stellar replied. "I was starting to get a little nervous there."

"I could tell," Glamis said with a chortle. "But you have no need to fear. I'm certain that Haidar will take us to a place with a wide assortment of foods for you to choose from."

Stellar grinned, passing Carmen a knowing glance from a couple of seats down from her.

"We can hope, can't we?"

In the next hour, *The Allegiant* passed through the mountain clouds, and Pyramid City came into view. Carmen watched from above as the airship soared over the tall golden buildings and beige cobblestone streets.

Many sorcerers and creatures were out strolling the sidewalks of this lively town. The high sun, warming the streets on this dry and breezy afternoon, made for fine conditions to shop and walk to and from work. Carmen could see the town square in the center of the city, with its sparkling crystal monument of Dagtar towering proudly over the open area.

There were countless different sizes, shapes, and types of buildings in this city, but every single one of them had been built with golden bricks. The town was home to an abundance of businesses, restaurants, and shops. It also had the highest population of Kelmarians of any city in the entire realm.

Pyramid City had been the first metropolis ever founded here in Kelmar, close to three thousand years earlier, and it had remained its capital ever since. The city was named for the Parliament building, which was a golden pyramidal structure standing at the top of a tall staircase that overlooked the entire city, located a short distance away from the town's central square.

The Allegiant began a slow descent toward the Pyramid City Central Airfield. The collection of lit runways, which was enclosed by a tall, chain-link fence, was only five blocks away from the Parliament building. As they drifted downward, they could see a windowed control tower to the north, and three other airships sitting on adjacent landing strips. The uniformed Commander Haidar was standing beside the fourth and final runway, watching *The Allegiant* come down.

The magical wooden aircraft landed smoothly on the asphalt. Carmen and her friends then got out and met Haidar near the fence. He smiled as they approached him, undoubtedly pleased to see that they had arrived safely.

"How was your flight, Master Fox?" he asked. "No problems, I assume?"

"None at all," Carmen said, smiling.

"Excellent," Haidar replied. Then he checked the sky to determine the time.

"What do you say we have a meal before we head to the hearing?" he asked. "There's a café just blocks from Parliament that should meet the nutritional needs of all of us."

"That would be super," Carmen said, before winking at Glamis. "We're pretty hungry from the trip."

Haidar led Carmen and her Souls through the gates of the airfield, and then out onto the streets of the capital city.

Carmen spotted a painted wooden sign announcing that they were on Sun Star Street. The group moved briskly up the sidewalk to cross at the intersection, and then marched five blocks toward Pyramid Avenue, the street home to the Kelmarian Parliament. As they walked, Carmen noticed that for all of the people and creatures who lived here, the streets of the city were impeccably clean.

Carmen and the others made their way through the crowds of sorcerers and creatures out shopping, and passed rows of stores displaying their products and services in their large, eye-catching windows. As they walked, Carmen took note of a family-owned business specializing in wand repair, a school that gave lessons in swordsmanship, and a small second-hand bookshop that reminded her of the one that her grandfather had owned back in the non-magical realm.

She and her friends arrived at the doors of The First City Café within fifteen minutes. The café was a small, gold restaurant tucked between a shoe store and a bank. It was a rather whimsical-looking structure, with a green tiled roof and abstract blue diamond designs climbing up the edges of the building. The café's name was written in large cursive letters above the door. Carmen and her Souls could see Masters and their Partners eating and drinking tea at round tables on the other side of the glass windows.

The five of them followed Haidar inside, squeezing through the seated diners into the lengthy line of hungry customers. The popular café was nearly filled to capacity with the lunch crowd.

The chatter of the seated customers made it difficult to hear anything other than the almost constant sound of chairs scraping against the hardwood floor, and the clanging of dishes coming from the kitchen. Tall, round tables were placed sporadically throughout the restaurant, most of them currently occupied with two or more customers. At the front of the line of patrons was a long counter, behind which stood a creature unlike any that Carmen had ever seen before.

Standing upright like a human, this tall, long-necked being was covered in red scales and possessed a horned head somewhat similar to that of a Dragon. The beast had a slender build, with long legs, short arms, and a snaking tail. His bright, narrow eyes were ginger in color. On his back, the beast had a hard natural shielding that was brown and spiked. This creature, which was known as a Beltlasan, according to Blaze, handled the orders of the customers.

There was a window over the Beltlasan's shoulder that led into the kitchen, where a single, gray-haired sorcerer dressed in a white chef coat was doing all of the cooking. Carmen and her Souls studied the menu that was hanging from the ceiling over the counter as they waited in line. Glamis recommended that Carmen try the café's famous Harklefly salad, but after seeing a customer pass by with a large bowl of the leafy green salad sprinkled with the slimy winged bugs and smothered in a crushed insect salad dressing, she politely declined his suggestion.

The line of hungry customers was moving up surprisingly quickly. As the Souls of Destiny swapped ideas on what to get to eat, Carmen gazed over to her right and studied an artistic tiled mural of the city, which covered the entire side wall.

When Haidar and the others eventually got to the front of the line, the Beltlasan smiled courteously.

"What can I get for you today?" he asked, in a surprisingly pleasant voice.

The Sarcan Commander placed his order first.

"I'll have the Arakive sandwich with a glass of Snotree juice, please."

Haidar then turned to Carmen, who was digging in her pocket to get out the money that she had brought with her.

"Lunch is on me today," he told her. "Order whatever you want."

"Oh...okay," Carmen said, suddenly flustered.

She looked up at the Beltlasan.

"Uh…I'll also get the Arakive sandwich with Snotree juice," she decided.

Blaze, Stellar, Glamis, and Anubis stepped forward and placed their orders next. The Beltlasan wrote each one down on a small notepad, and then tore off the sheet and passed it through the window to his Master and chef.

As promised, Commander Haidar paid the Beltlasan, who deposited the money in an antique metal cash register sitting on the counter. Then, with a *clang*, the Beltlasan shut the drawer and went over to the kitchen window. When he turned around, he was holding a sizable tray of food in his claws.

"Here you are," he said kindly, handing over the tray to Haidar. "Have a fine afternoon!"

Haidar thanked the Beltlasan and directed Carmen and her friends over to a couple of empty tables next to one of the front windows. Glamis, Anubis, and Stellar seated themselves at one table so that Carmen, Blaze, and Haidar could sit together. After Carmen's friends were settled with their food, Haidar sat down across from his two students.

"How are you feeling today?" Haidar asked Carmen, watching her with concern. "Are you nervous?"

"Um…I'm trying not to be," Carmen replied, avoiding his eyes as she unwrapped the silver foil that was around her fish sandwich.

Haidar nodded.

"You shouldn't worry. Nothing that you could say today could implicate an innocent man," he reminded her. "As long as you're honest and forthright, you have no reason to fear testimony."

"That's what my grandfather told me, too," Carmen murmured.

Carmen bit into the soft roll and tasted the fresh bread and the tender cooked Arakives inside. The fish were red, moist, and luscious. Blaze was seated next to Carmen at the table, sipping spoonfuls of Deltacarp soup from a ceramic bowl.

For the most part, the meal was a silent one, with each member of Carmen's party quietly enjoying the food that they had selected off of the menu at the café. Glamis was munching on his substantial Harklefly salad as Stellar chewed his steak next to him. Anubis was eating slices of herb-roasted Qwethral and drinking from his tall glass of Snotree juice with a straw.

Carmen gazed out the window and watched the passersby on the street as she ate. Even being in the city for only the second time in her memory, it was plain to see that everyday life here was a stark contrast to that in Sarcanian Valley. Pyramid City was a loud, crowded, and bustling place populated with humans and creatures of all kinds. This single metropolis was illustrative of just how diverse Kelmar was as a whole.

"Maidak Kalvaro is meeting us in the entrance hall of Parliament," Haidar told Carmen, toward the end of lunch. "I would advise you not to take offense to anything he might tell you. He can come off as somewhat...condescending to those who aren't familiar with him. He's fairly well known for his often patronizing manner, so I don't want you to be taken aback if he is not one of the most congenial individuals that you've ever met."

Carmen wiped her mouth with her napkin, and then laid it down on her empty plate. She remembered how Kamie had revealed to her that Maidak regularly fought with his son, Draven. She also keenly recalled Renalda referring to him as a "pretentious, arrogant dirtbag" following his argument with her husband and his initial refusal to summon an emergency session of Parliament to discuss the fighting between Kelmarsia and Keltan.

401

"Do you know Maidak to be a good man?" Carmen asked her Commander. "Is it true that he used to be a member of the Magicon?"

Haidar raised an eyebrow; seeming surprised that Carmen would have awareness of such a fact. After that, he appeared to be giving a lot of thought to his answer before he spoke.

"It is true that he was a follower of Desorkhan," Haidar said, looking Carmen straight in the eyes. "As for how I feel about him personally..."

He paused briefly to consider his next words.

"In truth, I do not feel that I know him well enough to justly vouch for his character," he admitted. "From what I *do* know of him though, I see no reason not to trust him. In all of his years in Parliament, it is my understanding that he has never once engaged in any act that would suggest unscrupulous intentions."

Carmen just listened, feeling anxious to meet this man and see what he was like for herself. That impartial response was likely all that she was going to get out of Haidar. She understood why, of course. As an instructor and an Honorary Council Member, he couldn't simply suggest a fellow Kelmarian leader was guilty of any wrongdoing unless he had concrete knowledge of such offenses.

"Do you have any other questions for me before we leave?" Haidar inquired. "We likely won't have much of a chance to talk again until after the hearing is over."

Carmen considered for a moment, but then shook her head.

"No, that was it," she said. "Oh, and thank you for lunch," she added. "It was delicious."

Haidar smiled.

"You're quite welcome, Master Fox."

Carmen's Souls finished eating a little while later, and then they, Carmen, and Commander Haidar left the café together.

The group walked five blocks up the sidewalk under the midday sun, the striking gold Parliament building looming larger with each step.

"Expect tighter security as we approach Parliament," Haidar told his companions. "Though we cannot see *all* of the security that has been employed, Pyramid City currently has the most defenses in place of any location in Kelmar. With the Phantom Warriors on the loose, the capital requires the strongest protection of any area.... It is home to the central government, and is symbolic of Kelmar's stability. Hence, it is likely the most desirable target of an attack by the Keltans, as one of their central aims is to dissolve physical and emblematic representations of Kelmarian rule."

Haidar and the younger Kelmarians crossed at the intersection of Pyramid Avenue and Citadel Boulevard after waiting for a cluster of Pegasus-drawn carriages to pass by.

There were dozens of uniformed guards stationed all around the perimeter of the Parliament building's square courtyard. Lining the outside of the tall stone walls, they stood at the ready with sabers suspended from their belts and their wands held diagonally across their bodies. These guards served as additional security on top of the surely numerous magical Protections defending this historic landmark, and the larger city.

As she and her friends walked into the expansive stone courtyard of the Parliament building, Carmen couldn't help feeling intimidated by the grandeur of the building that she was about to enter. This mountainous gold structure had stood proudly for three thousand years, and had remained the central emblem of the Kelmarian government throughout. It was in the chambers of this most distinguished edifice where new laws were created and influential leaders met and worked to better the lives of their constituents. Many of the greatest moments in Kelmarian history were made right here. The Kelmarian Parliament was both a beautiful piece of architecture and a classical museum that was unrivaled in terms of its prestige and significance.

The Kelmarians climbed the golden staircase, which must have contained at least two hundred steps by Carmen's estimate. They gazed up at the massive golden pyramid as they walked up to it. The entrance of the building was lined with a row of tall, white marble columns that supported a gold overhang.

When they finally reached the top of the stairs, Carmen and her friends had to pause to catch their breath before they walked ahead toward the heavy wooden entry doors that stood between the marble columns.

In addition to those out in the courtyard below, there was also a duo of uniformed Kelmarian guards flanking the entrance. The two men were each dressed in the same scarlet and gold military uniform that Commander Haidar always wore, but both were less decorated with badges and medals than his was. Their heads were crowned with golden, spiked helmets embellished with the Great Seal of Kelmar.

The otherwise still guards saluted Haidar and the others as they passed. Haidar opened one of the front doors, and allowed Carmen and her friends to get their first steps into the entrance hall of the Kelmarian Parliament.

Carmen gazed around at the cavernous space that opened up around her. The golden Great Seal of Kelmar was inlaid on the white marble floor, and a long hall of doors at the back of the gallery led off into the inner chambers of Parliament. Sun peeked in through the tall windows that lined the sloping room.

Hanging around the walls were old paintings and black and white photographs of past and present Parliament Members and other public officials. The majority of the framed art was made up of portraits of individual leaders and paintings of historic events that had taken place in these very halls.

Blaze showed Carmen the words of the original Guardian Prophecy, which were carved into an ancient stone tablet mounted above the front doors of the building. She gazed up at the tall, smooth gray and black stone in wonder, and it sent a chill through her as she thought about how that simple object, discovered more than one thousand years before, had been the start of her journey to Kelmar and all that had happened since.

Carmen turned around as she heard a pair of voices echoing out from the corridor leading to the entrance hall.

"I told you that I wanted my tea *HOT,* and *this* is what you bring me? A cup of *ICE COLD* tea!" a man snarled.

There was a loud crash as a ceramic teacup was thrown and shattered to pieces on the marble floor.

"How many times must I repeat myself?" the man asked impatiently. "Honestly, I would drill it into your skull if I could."

"I'm...I'm so-sorry, sir," a younger man said, his voice quivering. "It won't happen again."

"See that it doesn't," the first man said in a harsh voice. "Unless you want to find yourself back out on the streets where I found you."

"Yes, sir," his assistant squeaked. "I'll get it right away."

Then came the patter of hurried footsteps as the young boy scurried off and slipped through a door at the end of the hall to retrieve the other man's tea. He would have to get that first before he could clean up the mess left by his first attempt at satisfying the needs of his elder.

The man who had yelled strode out into the entrance hall, his deep scarlet and gold Kelmarian Parliament robes billowing as he walked. Looking to be in his late forties, he was tall and slender, with a narrow, pale face, dark brown eyes, and long bronze hair that ran just past his shoulders. His lips were thin, and his ears were slightly pointed. Carmen noticed that the Great Seal of Kelmar was stitched into the upper left chest of his ceremonial robes.

"Good afternoon, Maidak," Haidar said, with a respectful bow. "Having a stressful day, I assume?"

Carmen walked a couple of steps behind Haidar with her friends, feeling fairly apprehensive. If first impressions were anything to go by, at the moment, this man was someone who Carmen would be much happier not to meet.

"You have no idea," Kalvaro muttered, bowing back to the Sarcan Commander. "You wouldn't believe the incompetence of these new interns…. Sometimes I feel like I'm working with a bunch of *children*."

"I can imagine," Haidar said, nodding. He was obviously obligated to be agreeable. "Is everything in place for the hearing to begin on time?"

"Unless any of these fools hold us up, I believe so," Kalvaro said, before checking his watch. "In ten minutes, I'll expect to see the entire Parliament and Sarcan Council seated in the South Chamber. We will bring in the accused shortly after."

He then peered over Haidar's shoulder, a suspicious look in his eyes.

"Who did you bring here with you?" he asked.

Haidar stepped aside and motioned for Carmen and her Souls to come forward.

"This is Carmen Fox," he informed Kalvaro. "As you probably remember, she's the Guardian of Kelmar."

Carmen bowed instinctively. Maidak Kalvaro was staring at her through his narrowed brown eyes. She couldn't tell what he was thinking.

"And her Souls of Destiny: Blaze, Stellar, Glamis, and Anubis," Haidar said, introducing them individually.

Maidak bowed back to all of them together.

"It is a pleasure to meet you," he said, though the coldness in his eyes told a different story. "I would hope that you have arrived today prepared to provide open testimony. Before the hearing begins, you will be required to take the Oath of Honesty, which will call for you to speak nothing but the truth throughout the duration of the hearing," he informed them, seeming to be speaking more to Carmen than to any of the others. "Should you mislead any of the Kelmarian officials, you face a potentially harsh punishment, no matter the outcome of the hearing. Do you understand?"

"Yes," Carmen answered, making sure to meet his eyes.

"You won't have any problem with that," Haidar assured Kalvaro. "Carmen and her friends are Kelmarians of the utmost integrity. I speak from having known them for quite a while."

"Well, that's certainly good to hear," Kalvaro replied, but his eyes remained dull. He watched Carmen as she admired a painting of a Dragon across from her. An idea seemed to strike him just then that lightened his mood considerably.

"As long as we have some time, how would you all like a short tour of Parliament before the hearing gets started?" he asked her and her Souls. "I can show you around while Commander Haidar gets situated in the South Chamber with the Councilors.... You wouldn't mind that, would you, Reoc?"

Haidar appeared momentarily stunned that Maidak would ever willingly volunteer to take his young companions on any kind of tour, or anything even remotely close to that, for that matter.

"No, of course not," he said, still looking put off as he gazed toward his student. "Would you be interested in doing that, Carmen?"

"Umm...sure," she replied.

She would have been significantly more enthusiastic if the tour were being given by virtually anyone else, but with the thought of the impending hearing looming over her, she felt that it was in her best interest to agree to it, and stay on Kalvaro's good side.

"Brilliant," Kalvaro said. His steely eyes were gleaming as he steered Carmen and her friends toward the hallway.

"We will meet you in the chamber in a few minutes, Reoc."

Carmen glanced back over her shoulder at Haidar, who watched them attentively for a brief time as she and the others walked away. Then he made his way over to the first door in the hall, which led into the South Chamber.

Maidak directed Carmen and her Souls down the main corridor of the building, which eventually branched off into two shorter hallways, as well as rooms accessible through heavy wooden doors, all of them presently closed. As they walked, Maidak explained where each door led, but he did so in a brusque and indifferent manner.

"Over there is the office of the Head of State, Danuvius Dorvai," he said, pointing toward a door on their left about midway down the hall. "The next room is *my* office, and so on…. The highest in Parliamentary rank are located closest to the entrance hall."

In addition to the offices, the group also passed a room called the Hall of Greatness, in which stood a collection of statues representing illustrious individuals prominent in the histories of the four corners of Kelmar. There were five statues from each of the four areas—North, South, East, and West.

Near the end of the hall, Carmen spotted the evidence of Maidak's rage taken out on the innocent teacup, its remains scattered as shards of glass on the marble floor.

When they reached the two corridors leading off of this one, Kalvaro directed Carmen and her Souls down the hallway to the left.

"There's a terrific little secret that you really should see right down here," he said, pointing toward a door just ahead of them.

When Kalvaro and his visitors reached the apparently significant door, Kalvaro opened it a crack and peeked inside.

"Ah, yes…this is the one," he said, turning toward Carmen and her friends. "Have a look in here."

Kalvaro opened the door wider, and then ushered his guests toward it.

The room was a dark, walk-in closet lined with coats and robes hanging along two of the walls. Carmen turned and stared at Kalvaro.

"What is this?"

"Oh, you're not seeing it?" Kalvaro asked, seeming surprised. "At the rear of this closet is a hidden passageway that leads back to the entrance hall. It's been here for years, but not many know that it exists. Take a couple of steps inside. You'll see it there on the back wall."

Carmen and her friends edged warily into the closet. They really didn't feel the need to see this supposed passageway, but with the intimidating Kalvaro breathing down their necks, they had no choice but to look a little bit closer.

"That's it. Just go a tad farther inside," Kalvaro urged, gradually forcing them all into the cramped space.

Carmen stared into the darkness of the closet.

"I don't see any—"

BANG!

The closet door slammed shut, and Carmen and her Souls were standing in complete darkness. Kalvaro summoned his wand.

"*Rovenlock!*" he ordered.

Carmen heard a sharp *click* as the door locked itself shut. Instantly unnerved, she moved to wrench open the doorknob, but it would not budge.

"Oh dear, it seems that the door won't open!" Kalvaro said, feigning concern as he fiddled with the knob of the closet out in the hall.

"Get us out of here!" Carmen shouted angrily, continuing to try to break open the door. She pounded her fist repeatedly on the wood, her pulse racing. "WHY ARE YOU DOING THIS?"

"Sorry, Carmen, but I can't have you interfering in my campaign for Head of State," Kalvaro said cruelly. "Eli is guilty, and shall be sentenced to life imprisonment for his betrayal, leaving me as the obvious choice to defeat Dorvai in the next election. You and your friends shouldn't be so quick to judge people. Let this be a lesson to you."

Carmen heard the scrape of metal against wood as Kalvaro touched his wand to the narrow crack separating the wall and the closet door.

"Oceanazarka!"

Seconds later, a stream of cold water came gushing in through the crack in the door, cascading down to the floor of the closet. Carmen hastily summoned her wand, illuminated it, and pointed it down at her feet. The water was rapidly rising...and would soon fill up the entire space. If she didn't act fast, she and her Souls would all drown.

Carmen pointed her wand at the door.

"Lockstra!" she shouted. *"LOCKSTRA!"*

The door didn't unlock. Maidak's spell was more powerful than hers.

"LET US OUT!" Carmen bellowed through the door, as the water climbed up toward her knees. *"NOW!"*

Carmen continued to shout after Maidak for a time, but no response came from the other side of the door.... He had left them there to die.

It was hard for Carmen to keep from panicking as she stood in the frigid and swiftly rising water. She turned to her friends for their advice.

"How are we going to get out of here?" she asked them, trying her best to stay calm in spite of the circumstances. "The water's coming up too fast!"

"We have to use a spell that will have enough force to break down the door," Blaze said at once.

They all thought for a moment.

"What about *Rushing Stampede?*" Stellar suggested. "Anubis, Glamis, and I can all perform that one!"

The freezing waterfall continued to gush down into the closet.... It was almost up to Stellar's chin.

"We can all use my magic to breathe beneath the water also!" Glamis said, moving hastily through the closet to press his nose to those of his friends for the *Undying Breath* spell.

"Okay, let's do it!" Carmen said, as the water rose up to her neck. Her body was beginning to numb with the cold as Glamis finished performing the spell on her and the others.

With Blaze at her side, she pointed her wand at the door while the rest of her friends swam to the back of the closet.

"Rushing Stampede!" Carmen bellowed.

As the water rose just over her head, the bodies of Glamis, Anubis, and Stellar were lit by a powerful green light. An instant later, the three of them darted forward like speeding torpedoes rushing through the water.

In a blast of sound, the three creatures crashed into the closet door and burst it open. The water that had entrapped them poured out of the room, and the five of them collapsed out into the hallway in a heap, shaking from the cold and gasping for air.

They lay there on the floor, shocked and troubled...trying to regroup from the terrifying incident. Though
they weren't speaking to one another, the same thoughts were
undeniably running through all of their minds.

What was happening? Why had Kalvaro attempted to
drown them? What were they going to do *now?*

After a while, Carmen got unsteadily to her feet. If she
weren't careful, she could easily slip on the polished marble
floor. She and the others were dripping wet from head to toe.

"We have to tell Haidar," she decided, as her friends got
up off of the floor. "I don't know what's going on, or why, but
I know that...that man just tried to kill us."

"Come, we must get to the South Chamber," Anubis said,
walking gingerly toward the main corridor. *"The hearing has
probably already started!"*

Carmen Returned her wand, and then she and her Souls
walked back up the main hall as quickly as they could without
sliding on the floor. Water was dripping from their bodies with
every step. As they neared the entrance hall, they could hear
Haidar and Kalvaro talking.

"Where are they?" Haidar demanded. "What do you
mean *'they got lost'?"*

"They wanted to explore off on their own, and I haven't
seen them since!" Kalvaro told him, in an unruffled voice. "I
haven't the slightest idea where they could be. They know that
the hearing was scheduled to begin ten minutes ago. We'll just
have to start without them."

"Don't be ridiculous," Haidar said, his tone sharp and
agitated. "You cannot expect to begin without them here....
I'm going to go look for them."

"You don't have to," Carmen said, as she and her water-logged friends emerged from the corridor and crossed the gallery.

Haidar gawked at them. He promptly rushed to meet them in the center of the entrance hall.

"What happened to you?" he asked, his face lined with his distress as he looked over the five of them.

"*He* locked us in a closet and tried to drown us," Carmen said, keeping her voice steady even as she shivered from the cold. She nodded toward Kalvaro, who was staring at her in disgust.

"I did no such thing!" Kalvaro said defensively, as Haidar turned and gaped at him. "Why in the name of Merlin would I carry out an atrocious act like that?"

"Because you don't want us to testify," Carmen asserted furiously, pushing her wet hair off of her face. "You want to convict Eli so that you can run for Head of State uncontested. This is all one twisted plot for you to get yourself elected to higher office."

Kalvaro bristled.

"How *dare* you accuse me of such despicable crimes?" he seethed, pointing at Carmen as he marched up to her. "I challenge you to speak to me like that in my chamber. I'll have your testimony thrown out!"

Haidar had to step between the two of them to prevent their argument from turning physical.

"That's enough," the Sarcan Commander said in a firm voice, holding Kalvaro back from moving any closer to his students. "Whatever happened here deserves a full investigation...and that cannot happen with the present inquiry hanging over us. Eli deserves a fair trial. Once it is over, we will deal with this. Do I make myself clear?"

Kalvaro forced himself free from Haidar's grasp, but moved no closer to Carmen. He was clearly incensed that the

Sarcan Commander would even think of speaking down to him.

Indignant, Kalvaro marched past Carmen and her friends and threw open the door of the South Chamber.

"We have waited long enough," he declared. "The hearing for the alleged Keltan mastermind, Eli Elezar, begins *now*."

Still furious, he threw his dark bronze hair over his shoulder and stormed into the chamber.

CHAPTER NINETEEN
THE TRAITOR'S HEARING

Carmen and her friends entered the chamber behind Commander Haidar a minute or two after Kalvaro with a never-ending assortment of reservations about what to expect of this inquiry. If Maidak Kalvaro truly was the manipulative lowlife that Carmen thought him to be, there was little likelihood that the outcome of this hearing would result in their favor.

The South Chamber was a wide room designed specifically for the purpose of criminal investigations. Tall, wooden panels covered the gold walls, and though the ceiling was illuminated with rows of crystals, the space seemed significantly darker than the sunlit hall from which Carmen and the others had come.

The Kelmarian Parliament and the Sarcan Council sat in rows of tiered wooden benches at the back of the room, and there was a pair of long wooden tables with chairs sitting in the center of the chamber. Eli Elezar was seated alone at one of them, his back to the hall door. The table next to his was designated for the victim and witnesses.

Carmen, Haidar, and the Souls of Destiny walked in and looked in the direction of the public officials seated in the benches. Maidak Kalvaro was sitting to the right of Danuvius Dorvai in the middle of the first row of seats, his expression unreadable. Kalvaro's cup of hot tea was sitting in front of him.

Dorvai was slightly shorter than Maidak. He was a thin, fair-skinned man with high cheekbones and ginger hair. He wore dark-rimmed glasses over his hazel eyes and had a neatly trimmed goatee. He looked to be somewhere in his early fifties.

On Dorvai's left was an elderly sorceress with a wrinkled face and messy black and gray locks of hair. She was staring harshly at Eli through her silver-blue eyes.

"Victim and witnesses, please be seated," Dorvai said, motioning for Carmen and the others to come forward.

The Head of State and the twenty-four other Parliament Members were all dressed in the same deep scarlet and gold-colored robes adorned with the Great Seal of Kelmar. All of them were staring at Carmen and her friends with stunned expressions as they walked toward them, wondering why in the world they were soaked to the skin. A handful of the sorcerers were whispering to those seated next to them.

Haidar, Carmen, and the four Souls of Destiny sat down at their table, anxious for the hearing to start. After getting over the initial shock of seeing the victim and four of the five witnesses looking like they had just come from a dip in the ocean, most of the Kelmarian Parliament Members were now gazing out at Carmen and the defendant's tables with stern faces. But some, mostly the Sarcan Councilors, just looked interested.

Before Dorvai could speak again, Carmen snuck a glance over at Eli. The older man with thinning white curls of hair and calm blue eyes was sitting with his hands folded on top of the table. He was wearing navy blue robes decorated with golden moons and stars. If he was nervous, it didn't show in his body language. Sitting up straight and looking directly at the politicians in front of him, he looked alert, yet at peace with what was happening.

"We have assembled here today on the thirteenth of November for the criminal hearing of Mr. Eli Elezar of South Kelmar," Dorvai declared, his deep voice carrying throughout the chamber. "On September the seventeenth of this year, the defendant allegedly attempted to take the life of Ms. Carmen Fox of North Kelmar, through the use of a poisoned amulet. Under the Kelmarian Code of Law, the three charges against the accused stand as conspiracy to commit murder…betrayal…and attempted murder."

There was then a short-lived pause before Dorvai went on to read the roles of those present from a list on the desk in front of him.

"I, Head of State, Danuvius Dorvai, will be presiding over this hearing," he announced. "Senior Parliament Member, Maidak Kalvaro, is serving as the Lead Investigator."

Kalvaro looked smug as Dorvai read his name. He sipped his tea. The Head of State nodded to him and continued on with the witnesses.

"The defendant in this case is Mr. Eli Elezar," Dorvai stated. "The victim of the alleged crimes is Ms. Carmen Fox. And finally, the witnesses in this case are as follows: Mr. Reoc Haidar, Anubis, Blaze, Glamis, and Stellar—all of North Kelmar."

Dorvai laid his paper down on the table and looked out at Eli and Carmen's tables.

"I will need all of you to now rise, and sorcerers to raise your right hands, so as to recite the Kelmarian Oath of Honesty."

Carmen and her friends stood up, and Dorvai read the oath through one line at a time, requiring the defendant and witnesses to each speak the pledge through in its entirety.

"I, Carmen Fox, from this moment forward, do hereby promise to speak the whole truth as I know it," Carmen recited with the others. "I vow to maintain my integrity and my honor throughout the course of this judgment. And if a lie shall ever escape my lips, I resolve to fully accept the consequences of my actions."

The oath complete, Dorvai asked all of them to sit. He began to read from another parchment in a clear voice that rang through the chamber.

"This investigation has found that on September the seventeenth of this year, Mr. Eli Elezar allegedly gave Ms. Carmen Fox the amulet in question after telling her that it would protect her from the Dark Magic of Keltan," he recited. "The protective powers of which he spoke belong to the legendary Seer's Amulet.... But by all accounts, the amulet that Mr. Elezar supplied was *not* the genuine item; rather, it was a false one, produced to fool even the most well trained magical eye."

Dorvai's gaze momentarily fell on Carmen's friends.

"Instead of protecting the wearer from harm, this twin amulet slowly poisoned the victim...and had swift intervention not occurred, the poison would have killed her," Dorvai went on to say. "In attempting to murder a fellow Kelmarian, Mr. Elezar committed betrayal of the most heinous kind."

A handful of the Kelmarian Parliament Members were whispering to one another. Most though, remained straight-faced. Kalvaro took another sip of his tea, a subtle smile curling his thin lips.

"If this hearing finds that Mr. Elezar acted with intent and complete awareness of his offenses, he will be sentenced in accordance with his crime," Dorvai said, in a flat voice.

He then glanced to his right.

"Master Kalvaro, please proceed with the questioning."

"Thank you, Master Dorvai," Kalvaro said slowly. "I will start with the defendant, Mr. Elezar."

Kalvaro shuffled his papers and looked coldly toward Eli.

"Please explain to this assembly just what happened on September the seventeenth," he requested. There was no emotion in his tone.

"Well, when I woke up on the morning of the seventeenth, I wasn't feeling like myself...." Eli began, gazing steadily into Kalvaro's eyes. "I felt weak...and more tired than usual, but I was still able to complete my chores, and so I went about the rest of my day as usual."

"And since then, have you determined why you weren't feeling right that morning?" Kalvaro asked.

Eli shook his head.

"No, sir. I haven't the slightest idea."

"Very well," Kalvaro said. "Please continue."

Eli nodded.

"So, around mid-afternoon, I experienced an unexpected vision of Carmen Fox...struggling to battle a Dark enemy in Keltan," Eli told him. "I had never even met Carmen before, so it came as a complete surprise when I had a vision of her.... But oh, it was a terrible sight...just terrible.... To this day, it still pains me to remember it."

Eli glanced sadly at Carmen, and then closed his eyes for a moment before continuing.

"Later that evening, my dear friend, Inpu, stopped by my home in Sirranon and asked me for an urgent favor," Eli said, meeting Kalvaro's gaze. "He told me that Carmen would be traveling to Keltan to retrieve the cipher disk of Merlin Cloud. He then asked me if I could provide her with a sacred object that I'd had in my possession for a long time—the Seer's Amulet. I gladly obliged with his request. He also asked me for one additional act of assistance."

Eli sat up straighter in his chair. The Sarcan Councilors and Parliament Members were all observing him closely.

"Inpu asked me to come with him to the town of Brandec to perform *Death's Eternal Sleep* to cast Carmen and her Souls into unconsciousness, so that they could make the journey to the afterlife with him," Eli explained. "Once again, I told him that I would be honored to help.... And that night, Inpu and I traveled through a Gateway of Truth to Brandec and met Carmen and her Souls in the back room of Tedra and Adelin's Artifacts and Ancient Relics."

"Ah," Kalvaro said, leaning forward. "And then what happened there?"

"Inpu introduced me to Carmen and her Souls," Eli answered, motioning toward them at the other table. "Inpu told Carmen that I had brought an important item with me that would help keep her safe in Keltan. After that, I shared with her my vision from earlier that day.... Later on, I gave her the amulet, explained its protective abilities, and subsequently put her and her friends to sleep. Inpu escorted their spirits to the afterlife while *I* hid their bodies from sight. Once I had fulfilled my obligations, I returned to Sirranon. It was late when I got home, so I went to bed shortly after I returned."

Eli had finished his speech, but Kalvaro was still staring at him as though there were more to his story than what he was telling. His dark brown eyes narrowed; he flexed his fingers and glared at Eli.

"That was quite an interesting little story," he said condescendingly. "But, tell me, where exactly did you *find* the Seer's Amulet that you gave to Carmen?"

Eli blinked.

"I discovered it in the ruins of the Lightning Temple in West Kelmar five years ago. When I found it, I knew that it was the real thing," he said, sounding confident. "In addition to being a Seer, I'm also a magical treasure hunter, you see. I seek out ancient artifacts that help us to piece together the long and fascinating history of Kelmar. I donate most of them to museums and—"

Kalvaro waved his hand at Eli, motioning for him to stop talking.

"Yes, yes, we're well informed on that subject," he said, a sharp edge to his voice as he gestured toward his fellow Parliament Members.

Then he cast his cold gaze onto Carmen.

"I now wish to question the victim and the witnesses," he announced to the assembly.

Feeling chilled as she stared back at Kalvaro, Carmen tried to ready herself for his questioning. Her stomach was feeling tight, and she had a dry throat as a result of the tension that she was feeling.

Had Kalvaro not attempted to drown her just prior to this meeting, perhaps she would have been in a better mental state. She restlessly patted down her damp and tangled hair.

Her sodden robes were heavy on her body. It seemed like a while before Kalvaro spoke; further testing Carmen's nerves as she imagined the types of things he might ask her.

Acting as though nothing unusual had happened on the way to this trial, Kalvaro looked down at Carmen and proceeded with his questioning.

"Tell me, Ms. Fox," he said calmly, "in your words, what happened to you on September the seventeenth."

Taking a deep breath, Carmen spoke slowly and clearly.

"My Souls and I were in the town of Brandec after escaping from some Phantom Warriors that had entered into Kelmar that night," she began.

These few words alone ignited a flurry of muttering amongst many of the Kelmarian Parliament Members. The restless chatter went on for almost five minutes. Carmen continued with her testimony, pretending that she didn't notice.

"We went to Tedra and Adelin's Artifacts and Ancient Relics, and Inpu and Eli arrived through a Gateway of Truth," she told Kalvaro. "Eli showed me his vision of me in Keltan...and then presented me with the amulet. I wore it around my neck as my Souls and I traveled through Kelmarsia and Keltan."

"And when did you first realize that something was wrong?" Kalvaro asked.

"After I was in Keltan for a little while, I began to feel sick...like I was going to faint," Carmen recalled, feeling cold at the thought of that horrible sensation. "I collapsed, but I never lost consciousness completely," she said. "Blaze and Anubis healed me with *Dolen's Heart* until I could get back to Kelmar. Commander Haidar fully cured me of the poison there."

"And where is the amulet now?" Kalvaro inquired.

"I destroyed the amulet," Haidar told him, as Carmen didn't know the answer to this question. "I did not want it to fall into the hands of another innocent sorcerer, so I disposed of it before it could do any more harm."

Kalvaro shuffled the stack of papers in front of him, and then pushed a couple of strands of his long bronze hair out of his eyes.

"It's a shame that we no longer have it," he said, sounding bored as he gazed down at Haidar. "We could have used *the Tracer Enchantment* to trace the amulet back to its original source."

"I attempted to use that very spell before doing away with the item," Haidar informed him. "My first concern after healing my student was to find the owner of this poison-laden object.... It was evident to me that whoever provided her with that amulet did so with the intention of killing her. The toxicity of the poison inside of it was that potent. But regrettably, it appears that the killer was a highly experienced assassin. He covered his tracks by utilizing a concealing spell that would prohibit anyone from tracing it. Knowing that there was no longer a means to discover the owner of the amulet, I destroyed it."

Kalvaro looked at Haidar with displeasure before resuming his questioning of Carmen.

"Ms. Fox," he said, addressing her in a formal tone, "having been the victim of this alleged crime, how do you feel about these allegations against Eli? Do you feel that they are justified?"

Carmen stared at Kalvaro, full of suspicion.

"No," she said. "I feel terrible about what's happened to Eli."

Kalvaro appeared somewhat surprised to hear this.

"And just why would you testify as a witness to Mr. Elezar's defense?" he pursued. "Have you no negative feelings toward him for what he did to you?"

"No…because I know that he didn't act with the knowledge of what was happening," Carmen said. "Someone working for Triedastron took the real amulet and gave him the poisoned one to give to *me*."

Kalvaro raised an eyebrow in disbelief. Councilor Shermane Glynn murmured something into the ear of Councilor Elmeric Maradon.

"And why would an innocent man accept the amulet from such a person?" Kalvaro asked.

"Because he was under mind control," Carmen replied, unable to hold back from saying what she truly believed. "The same person who possessed the poisoned amulet either did it without his knowledge or cursed him to make him accept it."

A skeptical smile warped Kalvaro's narrow face.

"Fair enough. I'll play along," he said, sounding rather amused. "And exactly what curse do you believe that this hypothetical individual used?"

Carmen glanced over at Haidar, who nodded his approval. She turned back to Kalvaro.

"Devious Manipulation," she answered.

There was a sudden rumble of voices as close to half of the Kelmarian Parliament Members began to speak fervently with their neighbors. Danuvius Dorvai had to pound his gavel to the sound block in front of him to quiet them. Kalvaro's look of amusement faded.

"Do you have any proof of this supposed plot to falsely incriminate Mr. Elezar?" he asked.

Carmen frowned. She had no physical proof of such a conspiracy. Her idea was merely educated speculation garnered from Commander Haidar and Inpu, among others. She did not regret speaking it though, as she believed deep down that Eli was not the true killer.

"And what do *you* think of Ms. Fox's claim of a deeper plot, Mr. Elezar?" Kalvaro asked the elderly sorcerer, after Carmen failed to answer his question. "Is this indeed what happened?"

Eli was looking both perplexed and frightened at the thought.

"I...I don't know," he said, in a shaky voice. "I don't recall...."

"Well, there you have it," Kalvaro concluded, before Eli could finish. "I think it's safe to say that we can move on now."

"He wouldn't be able to remember!" Carmen shouted, standing up. She couldn't bear to keep quiet any longer. *"Devious Manipulation* wipes clean the memory of its victim."

"He would have no recollection of being put under control of the curse, or knowledge of what he was doing while he was experiencing its effects," Blaze added, flying up from his chair.

"Silence! You will not speak out of turn in my chamber!" Kalvaro bellowed, pointing at them in a hostile manner. "One more outburst like that and I will dismiss you from this hearing."

Carmen and Blaze sat back down, but both were filled with anger over the unfair turn that the trial was taking. Carmen was particularly frustrated that she couldn't even speak up for what Kalvaro had done to her and her Souls before the meeting started without risking being thrown out of the hearing, and increasing the likelihood of Eli's conviction.

Kalvaro took a sip of his tea and peered down toward Carmen's Souls of Destiny.

"Starting with Blaze, I would now like to hear each of your own accounts of the events that occurred on September the seventeenth," he said.

One at a time, Blaze, Anubis, Glamis, and Stellar offered their versions of the day's events, which of course, coincided with Eli and Carmen's stories. It was then Haidar's turn to deliver his testimony, and before his turn to speak was over, he spoke in full support of both Carmen and Eli.

"Master Dorvai, Master Kalvaro, Parliament, and Sarcan Council," Haidar said, his hands folded neatly on the table. "As you deliberate on the verdict of this trial, I only ask for you to consider the personal histories of all of us who sit here before you.... You have a well-respected Seer and educated Kelmarian historian, who has contributed decades worth of knowledge to our society," he said, motioning in the direction of Eli. "Sitting beside me you have two good students, the Guardian of Kelmar and the Blaze of Fire. And finally, you have three more of the legendary Souls of Destiny," Haidar continued, gesturing toward each of them. "All of those of whom I just spoke have served Kelmar with bravery and dignity.... They have saved countless lives, and worked to prevent the destruction of our world by the forces of Darkness."

Haidar paused briefly to allow his words to sink in.

"Would any of these true Kelmarians, who have proven their honor time and time again, sit here in the capital building and lie to you?" he asked the assembly. "What could we possibly gain from risking the loss of the trust and respect that we have earned from the good people and creatures of Kelmar? The answer...is nothing. We have no reason to perjure ourselves. Please think about this, and remember that we continue to serve Kelmar, as both law-abiding citizens and sworn protectors of these lands."

When Haidar reached the conclusion of his testimony, Kalvaro did not seem to be nearly as moved by his words as those around him. He maintained his icy stare even as most of the other Parliament Members were talking quietly around him. Nearly all of them already held Haidar in high regard, and they now appeared to be looking out at him with noticeably more admiration than they had when he first walked in.

"Thank you for that *rousing* speech, Mr. Haidar," Kalvaro said over the chatter, not even trying to conceal the acidity of his tone as he roughly put down the papers he'd been holding. "But before we break for deliberations, I have a few more questions for Mr. Elezar."

The discussion amongst the seated officials gradually died down. Kalvaro eyed the defendant sourly and went ahead with his interrogation.

"Mr. Elezar, I see here that you were involved in some rather suspicious business transactions involving priceless relics that you found during your numerous searches for treasure," Kalvaro said, glancing momentarily down at his notes. "In my investigation, I found there to be quite a number of questionable dealings in your past…. Do you care to fill us in on those?"

Eli's mouth was opening and closing as he struggled to formulate a response. He seemed to have no idea what Kalvaro could be referring to.

"I…I don't know what you're talking about," he said honestly.

Kalvaro smiled at him.

"Perhaps that suspected curse was used on you more than once in your life," he said unsympathetically. "Allow me to refresh your memory."

Maidak flipped through his notes, and soon came to the page that he was looking for.

"Ah, here's one," he said, gazing up at Eli before reading from the parchment. "On the night of July the tenth of this year, you were allegedly involved in a transaction with a gentleman from East Kelmar named Fellador Sedgely. He presented you with an artifact dating back to the early days of Kelmar's founding—a pearl necklace belonging to a woman named Kelmari Cloud. Do you deny this?"

"No, I don't," Eli said. "I did see him that day, but—"

"And what did you give him in exchange for the item?" Kalvaro asked.

Eli looked confused.

"Nothing. He—"

"You gave him *nothing?*" Kalvaro asked, intentionally cutting Eli off. "For such a valuable item? Surely the necklace was worth a considerable amount of money."

"Fellador is a *friend* of mine," Eli said, obviously irritated that Kalvaro wasn't allowing him to speak. "He's a magical treasure hunter, too.... We've known each other since we were teenagers. He found the necklace while on one of his expeditions, and offered it to me as a gift that night. He didn't expect any money in return for it."

Kalvaro sneered.

"How opportune for you."

"What is he getting at?" Carmen whispered to her Sarcan.

Blaze shrugged. Kalvaro proceeded to move on with his inquiry.

"Enlighten me, Mr. Elezar, on how many different occasions were similarly precious objects given to you as 'gifts'?" he asked.

Yet again, Eli appeared to be at a loss as to how to produce an answer that would be satisfactory to Kalvaro.

"I...don't know *exactly* how many times I've received gifts from colleagues and friends...but I can assure you that those that I did accept were never sold to anyone for profit. A small quantity of them remain in my personal collection. The rest I have donated, with permission from the previous owners, to assorted museums throughout Kelmar."

"I would hope that you have not provided this assembly with false testimony," Kalvaro said. "I'll have you know that committing perjury is a very serious offense, punishable by Kelmarian law."

Eli stared at Kalvaro with bewilderment. He looked understandably shocked at the interrogator's inability to accept any of his words as the truth. But then he nodded.

"I understand."

Finally content, Kalvaro changed the subject, but kept his questions focused entirely on Eli.

"Did you or did you not create the poisoned amulet that you provided to Ms. Fox on the evening of September the seventeenth?" he asked.

"No, I did not," Eli said, in an unwavering voice.

"If you did not make the false amulet, then where did it come from?"

Eli took a minute to consider his answer before speaking.

"I don't know," he eventually replied. "All I know is that I never intended to harm Carmen, nor would I *ever* plot to harm her, or anyone else."

"How did you feel when you heard what happened to Ms. Fox as a result of you giving her the amulet, Mr. Elezar?" Kalvaro asked. "She nearly died, you know."

Eli took a deep breath before answering.

"I felt sick," he said, his voice cracking.

Eli's eyes were glistening with tears as he met Carmen's at the table next to his.

"When Inpu told me what had happened...I almost wanted to die. I've been so distraught, I haven't gone on any expeditions since that day...and have decided to give up treasure hunting for good. But I do believe..." he said slowly, and with more strength, "that the amulet I gave to Carmen had been switched with the real one at some point. Just who switched them, and when, I do not know. But the original amulet was not created for the purpose of murder; it was created to defend humans and creatures of Light against the venoms of Darkness."

Insensitive to Eli's words, Kalvaro sighed and sat back in his chair.

"Well, regrettably, Mr. Elezar, unless you can produce evidence supporting this plot that you, the victim, and the witnesses speak of, we will likely have no choice but to convict you," he said, in a falsely disappointed voice. "You remain the sole suspect in this case."

Carmen was feeling unusually nauseous.... She couldn't believe that the Kelmarian Parliament would convict an innocent man of murder. That just couldn't happen...especially after hearing Eli's sincere testimony, and that of her and the others who came to his defense.

"The examination portion of this hearing is complete," Danuvius Dorvai proclaimed, much to the relief of everyone. "This assembly will now break for deliberations. Please wait here. We will return within the hour with a decision, and the hearing will then be adjourned."

Dorvai and the rest of the officials slowly got up from their seats and shuffled over to a door behind the benches. The Kelmarian Parliament Members and the Sarcan Councilors moved into the small deliberation room one by one and shut the heavy door behind them, leaving the defendant alone with the victim and witnesses to await his fate.

It seemed like hours before the elected Kelmarian officials returned, though it was actually only forty-five minutes. Carmen and her friends were all on edge. They had shared only a handful of words with Eli during the break, as they waited for the Kelmarian officials to come back and hand down the verdict. But in the brief time that they had talked, Carmen and her friends tried to reassure Eli that Parliament would judge him fairly. They also expressed to him their confidence that, eventually, the real conspirator would be caught.

Eli apologized profusely to Carmen for what had happened, though she knew that it was not his fault, and he begged her to believe him that he would find a way to make all of this pain and unnecessary stress up to her. He also wished her the best of luck in finding the remaining Secret of Kelmar and freeing his friend, Inpu, from Haesnost Prison.

When the members of the Kelmarian Parliament and Sarcan Council finally walked back into the chamber and retook their seats, their expressions were impassive. There was no telling from their faces what decision they had reached. Danuvius Dorvai muttered a sentence or two to Maidak Kalvaro just after the both of them sat down. Dorvai then looked out at the defendant, victim, and witnesses.

"We thank you for your patience," Dorvai said, acknowledging all of them. "This was a very difficult decision for us to reach…but we are confident that on this day, justice will be served."

The rest of the room was silent and still as Dorvai spoke. It seemed that everyone in attendance was impatient for the verdict to be read.

"The charges against Mr. Eli Elezar in this case were among the most serious of crimes under Kelmarian law; conspiracy to commit murder, betrayal, and attempted murder," Dorvai reminded all of those present, in a sharp voice. "After careful deliberation, and much discussion, the verdict stands as follows: We find the defendant to be…"

The entire room held its breath as Dorvai looked down at his paper.

"Guilty on all three charges."

Carmen's heart sank down to her stomach. The color drained from Eli's face.

"As punishment for his crimes, we hereby sentence Mr. Eli Elezar to life imprisonment in the Mount Zhalore Prison in East Kelmar," Dorvai announced. "He will spend the remainder of his days in jail for the monstrous crimes that he committed against Ms. Carmen Fox."

Carmen winced as the sentence was read. She felt dazed…. It was hard for her to contain her fury as she stared across the room at Kalvaro. She almost wished that a well-aimed lightning bolt would come through the ceiling and strike him dead for what he had done. The Lead Investigator looked more than pleased as he peered down at Eli with a twisted half-smile.

On cue, the doors of the South Chamber opened, and two armed Kelmarian guards walked in from the entrance hall. Without a word to anyone, they marched up to the defendant's table and proceeded to fit a pair of heavy metal manacles around Eli's wrists.

Dorvai hit his gavel to the wooden sound block as Eli stood up, the guards securing his upper arms.

"This hearing…" Dorvai confirmed to the victim and the witnesses, "…has now concluded."

As though all of the life had just been drained out of the room, the chamber fell eerily silent. Carmen, Haidar, and the Souls of Destiny could do nothing but watch powerlessly from their seats as the Kelmarian guards turned Eli around and led him away in shackles.

CHAPTER TWENTY
THE UNDERGROUND CAVE

Over a month had passed since the hearing that sent Eli Elezar to jail for crimes that he did not commit. Crisp red and brown autumn leaves had fallen and been swept away by the cold winds, which would eventually invite in the first snowfall of the winter season. The extreme weather patterns that had been brought on by the war between Kelmarsia and Keltan gradually faded into more normal conditions, allowing the students in Sarcanian Valley to train outdoors until the snow arrived.

The morning after Eli's trial, two articles about the proceedings appeared in *The Kelmarian Review*. The lead story was an unbiased report of the hearing, while the other was an opinion piece that praised Kalvaro for his thorough investigation, and for working tirelessly to convict a highly dangerous man and give him his due sentence.

The first headline, which stretched across the width of the paper's front page, read:

SEER ELI ELEZAR CONVICTED OF
CRIMES AGAINST KELMAR

Beneath the headline were two photos. One image showed Maidak Kalvaro standing behind a podium on the steps of Parliament, addressing the Kelmarian reporters. Alongside that picture was a shot of Eli being escorted down the staircase by the pair of Kelmarian guards who had taken him from the South Chamber. His head of white hair was hanging, and his face was etched with weariness. The article started just below the photos and ran on to a second page.

> *Pyramid City—Yesterday, in a shocking turn of events, the Kelmarian Parliament convicted Master Eli Elezar of South Kelmar with three severe crimes; conspiracy to commit murder, betrayal, and attempted murder. Even after listening to what many Kelmarian officials present described as "moving" and "heartfelt" testimony from the defendant, the victim, and the witnesses, the Kelmarian Parliament handed down a guilty verdict, sending Elezar to jail for the rest of his life....*

Carmen read both articles with revulsion, particularly the one that praised Kalvaro's efforts as the Lead Investigator in the case. On their way out of the hearing, Carmen had told Haidar about Kalvaro's attempt to drown her and her Souls in a closet right before the start of the trial. Haidar was stunned by what he heard in Carmen's retelling of the incident. He promised her that he would speak with Kelmarian officials before they left the building, and speak to them he did. As Carmen and her friends waited for him in the entrance hall, Haidar met with the other Parliament Members while Kalvaro spoke to the press outside.

Haidar and the Parliament Members returned to the closet where the confrontation had occurred, only to find that the door was closed and undamaged, and the space itself was bone-dry. There was not a doubt in Carmen's mind that Kalvaro had magically restored the closet to normal before heading out to the front steps to talk about the hearing to reporters. Because this was so, there was little that Haidar and Carmen could do to prove that Kalvaro had indeed carried out the attempted drowning. And with his seniority and strong alliances within the Parliament, there was little chance of the altercation coming under investigation.

It made Carmen feel sick to think that Kalvaro was out on the front steps of Parliament playing up his role as a hero who had just put a killer behind bars, while he, in fact, was a criminal himself. Defeated and downcast, Carmen, Commander Haidar, and the Souls of Destiny snuck out a back door of the building to avoid the press, and returned to Sarcanian Valley.

Ever since the conclusion of the hearing, all of them had been feeling equally disgusted and disappointed by Eli's incarceration. Haidar was just as dissatisfied by the unjust outcome of the hearing as Carmen and her friends were. They were all but certain that Kalvaro had persuaded the other Parliament Members to convict Eli for his own political gain. Haidar told Carmen on the flight back to the valley that under Kelmarian law, Eli could appeal his conviction, but a review of the trial was unlikely to happen until after the holidays, if ever. Kalvaro would also likely try to block any type of appeal that Eli could request.

There had been a total of four Phantom sightings over the one-month span from the time of the hearing, all of which had occurred in West and South Kelmar. In each of the attacks, a handful of Warriors had attempted to destroy homes and forests, and though they had done some damage, no Kelmarian fatalities were reported. Fortunately, there had been no attacks on individual Kelmarians as of yet, which remained the single piece of good news in this long-lasting war.

Carmen and her friends had been forced to wait to travel to Keltan, as periodic fighting there carried on for a few more weeks following the hearing. Inpu kept in contact with Anubis every day, telling him just what was happening in the World of

Darkness, and restoring confidence in him that he was doing well.

Anubis, similarly, kept his father up to date with what was going on in Kelmar. Inpu was greatly saddened to hear of Eli's unfair conviction, and promised his son that he would try to help Eli draft an appeal to Parliament just as soon as he was free from Haesnost. Anubis's mother, Nephthys, continued to fulfill Inpu's role as the Opener of the Way until Inpu could return, so that new spirits could cross over from Kelmar into Kelmarsia.

But now, just days before Christmas, the fighting in Keltan had finally died down, and Carmen and her Souls could at last make the voyage to the World of Darkness to free Inpu, claim back the cipher disk, and locate the third Secret of Kelmar. Such a tremendous expedition, however, would require strategically careful planning, which is just what Carmen and her friends did on the night of Christmas Eve.

A tall, decorated Christmas tree stood in one of the front corners of Carmen's room, and beneath it were half a dozen packages wrapped up in glittering silver and gold paper. Sitting around the table in their room with steaming mugs of hot chocolate, Carmen and her Souls plotted out their journey to Keltan in the light of the fireplace. Merlin's map showed the last Secret of Kelmar as being located in a long underground cave that ran under Triedastron's fortress.

"Our first priority should be to locate the last Secret," Blaze said, after mulling over the idea for a little while. "Once we have the Secret, Carmen and I need to find a way to sneak into Triedastron's fortress and get the cipher disk.... While we're doing that, the rest of you can start to head over to the prison—" he pointed to the illustration of the gray jail with high stone walls a short distance northwest of the Dark castle, "—and we'll meet you there."

Stellar nodded.

"That seems like the most logical order of things. When Triedastron realizes Inpu has escaped, we'll want to be long gone."

"Precisely," Blaze said. "I feel that doing it like this will minimize the chance of Triedastron finding out that we're there. We'll have only limited time to elude the guards and get back to Kelmar after we free Inpu, so we want to make that prison our last stop."

"Do we know how we will get down into the underground tunnel that's home to the Secret?" Glamis wondered, leaning over the map. "This drawing doesn't seem to show an entrance."

Carmen sipped her hot chocolate and took a closer look at Merlin's map. The line snaking up from the bottom of the drawing of Keltan led through a winding tunnel to a spot beneath the center of Triedastron's castle. There was a rectangular box around the end point of the line. It was unclear whether the rectangle represented a physical box, or was simply a symbol highlighting the exact location of the Secret.

"There must be an entrance located somewhere along the tunnel, as there had to be a way for the Secret to be placed there," Anubis said, studying the map attentively. *"If this map does not show it…we will have to find the entrance for ourselves."*

"I'm just worried about time," Carmen said uneasily. "When we get there…every second will be crucial. If we have to take a lot of time to find a hidden entrance…it could seriously hinder our chances of breaking Inpu out before being discovered."

Carmen and her friends took some time to think through what they could do to possibly save a few precious minutes in their quest. They were sitting in the quiet of the moment when Carmen began to feel Dagtar's claw growing warm against her skin.

Suddenly feeling more alert, she sat up straighter. Sensing that Dagtar was trying to reach out to her, she closed her eyes.

"Time shall not be an issue in this crossing. I will be there to help you find your way through the World of Darkness," Dagtar promised.

"You will?" Carmen asked, astonished. With the Dragon's promise, she was already starting to feel more hopeful about their chances of success....

"When you arrive, I will cloak you into invisibility and lead you to the tunnel's only accessible entrance," Dagtar told her. *"And I will stay with you until you are safely back in Kelmar."*

"Thank you...." Carmen replied, relaxing a bit. *"I appreciate it a lot."*

"I will see you in Keltan, Carmen," Dagtar said, his voice fading away. *"Farewell until then."*

"Bye...."

The claw became cold again, and Carmen opened her eyes.

"Was that Dagtar?" Blaze asked.

"Yes, it was," Carmen cheerfully informed him and the others. "He said that he'll show us where the entrance to the tunnel is, and that he'll help us out with what we have to do."

"Outstanding!" Glamis said brightly. "We seem to always be able to count on Dagtar to come through when we need assistance.... He is such a kindhearted creature."

Anubis looked toward Carmen. *"As tomorrow is Christmas, I believe that we should stay in, and travel to Keltan the following day. The holidays are risky days to travel on, if you recall what happened last year."*

"Yeah. I agree," Carmen said, thinking back to the Magicon raid on Thunder Academy that had occurred last Christmas night. She looked at the four of her Souls.

"Well, we have our strategy for our journey to Keltan," she said. "Does everyone agree that we've figured out the best way to go about it?"

Once they had all decided to go ahead with their latest plan, Carmen sat back in her chair.

"All right. So I guess this means that we can rest a little, until we journey to Keltan," she said, before drinking the last of her hot chocolate. "We should get a good night's sleep.... We've got a big day coming up."

The inhabitants of the castle woke up the next morning to discover that a blizzard had blanketed Sarcanian Valley in two feet of heavy, wet snow. Even though they were in the north, a snowstorm of such a high accumulation was very uncommon. Carmen hoped that this unusually strong weather event didn't mean that the battles in the afterlife were intensifying again.

She and her Souls exchanged their gifts right after breakfast. With permission from Commander Haidar, Carmen had traveled with her grandfather by airship to Pyramid City to buy her gifts for her friends earlier in the week. Blaine had arranged for the ship to come pick them up at the southern entrance of the valley, and the two of them had spent the afternoon shopping and eating in the city.

Carmen purchased a package of fresh Deltacarp each for Blaze and Stellar, and a metal polishing kit for Glamis to shine his crown. For Anubis, she bought a new star map that featured recently discovered constellations, and for Dagtar, Carmen had bought a silver bracelet engraved with an image of fire, which she planned to give to him the next time they met.

Unsure of when she would get the chance to see her grandfather again, Carmen had bought him a new sweater, and gave it to him that very same day.

Once all of her friends had opened their presents, Carmen unwrapped the group gift that her Souls had given her together. Beneath the silvery gold wrapping was a small, white ceramic jar. The metal lid of the magical jar was sculpted in the form of a seated golden Dragon.

Known as the Jar of Protection, Blaze and the others explained that if Carmen placed an object inside of it, only *she* could open the container to retrieve it. The jar was also unbreakable by physical or magical force.

A knock on the bedroom door shortly after brought Naomi and Kamie bundled up in robes and winter coats, asking Carmen and her Souls if they wanted to come out and enjoy the snow with them.

Without even a moment of indecision, Carmen and the others hurried eagerly out of their room and down the stairs to the main floor of the castle. From there, they walked out as a group into the frozen landscape of Sarcanian Valley.

Standing at the top of the castle stairs, the Sarcan Captains and the Souls of Destiny gazed around in wonder, seeing their breath in the cold air. The great red sandstone gorge was almost unrecognizable beneath a deep layer of perfectly white snow, which was sparkling in the late morning sun. The Eldron Canal was frozen over just as the walls of Thunder Canyon were coated in ice. There were fresh snowdrifts built up around the edges of the valley, and icicles were hanging from the tall light posts of the newly refurbished Thunder Stadium. The branches of the ancient trees in Mortrock Forest were bent beneath the weight of the heavy precipitation.

The steps leading down into the valley had not yet been cleared, making the march down the tall mountain staircase fairly treacherous. Treading carefully, it took Carmen, Naomi, Kamie, and their creatures nearly twenty minutes to get down the stairs. The snow came up to Carmen's knees, but it was nearly at chin level for Stellar, Anubis, and Glamis, making it especially difficult for them to walk through.

When at last they reached the base of the gorge, Carmen and her friends observed the pure magnificence of their surroundings. None of them had ever seen the valley under such conditions…. The untouched snow and ice glistening in the sunlight was a peaceful and outright beautiful sight.

They weren't outside for very long when they turned and saw the rest of their schoolmates beginning to make their way down the front steps of the castle. Carefully, the wide-eyed Sarcan Captains and Cadets climbed down the stairs and plodded out into the snow-covered valley.

As Blaze flew over to greet the other Sarcans, Carmen met up with Akira and Shea to wish them a Merry Christmas. She was caught completely off guard when Shea handed her a silver gift-wrapped box, inside of which was a blue and gold scarf. An image of a Sarcan was stitched near the edge of the fabric, beside the golden fringe.

Highly embarrassed that she had not gotten him anything, Carmen thanked him for the gift, and then awkwardly apologized that she didn't have one for him. She had not expected him, or anyone else in her class to get her anything for the holiday. Shea laughed and told her to think nothing of it. Akira quietly clued Carmen in that Shea had given scarves to all of the sorcerers in their class because his mother loved to knit them, and that most of their classmates had been surprised by the gifts as well.

Still feeling foolish for not having bought an extra gift for just this kind of situation, Carmen put on the scarf, which was very soft and warm. She wished that she had known of Shea's generosity with presents before now.

"Thanks again, Shea," she said. Kamie was tugging at one of her sleeves to show her something. "I'll make this up to you."

"Oh, you're very welcome," Shea said graciously, his blue eyes shining in the sunlight. "I hope that you and your Souls have a wonderful Christmas."

He smiled and waved as he walked away with Gia to talk to a couple of his other friends. Carmen and Akira then went off with Kamie, who demonstrated to both of them how she had crafted a perfect snowball with a special sphere-forming spell that Dall had shown her. Carmen was joking with Kamie and Akira when she heard her grandfather calling her name from somewhere off to her left.

Blaine was trekking toward her through the snow, a flat package wrapped in glossy green paper in his hand. His face was slightly red from being out in the cold, but his eyes were bright and full of life. Thunderbolt was flying over his shoulder. Carmen and Blaze hastened over to them.

"Ah, this is for you," Blaine said warmly, handing his granddaughter her present as she met him at the center of the valley. "Merry Christmas."

Carmen hugged him tightly.

"Thank you!" she said, smiling as she let go of him. "Should I open it now?"

Blaine spread out his arms.

"Why not?" he said, grinning. "In fact, considering what I got you, I would say that now is the perfect time to open it."

Excited, Carmen tore back the paper and removed the lid of the box. Wrapped in white tissue paper was a pair of leather gloves lined with silky faux fur.

"Oh, these are excellent!" Carmen said, slipping the gloves over her cold hands.

They were a perfect fit. She held them up for Blaine to see.

"I will definitely use *this* gift!" she said. "Thanks again!"

But little did Carmen know that her new gloves would be put to use right there in the next five minutes. Kamie threw a snowball at a Sarcan Cadet's back, and that simple act ended up launching an hour-long snowball fight between the Cadets and Captains. With all of the students taking part in the friendly scuffle, Carmen, Blaine, and their creatures readily participated with the Sarcan Captains. It was a fun and carefree way to spend the morning.

Eventually, the Sarcanian Valley snowball battle was declared a draw. With every one of the students tired and dripping wet from enemy fire, the Sarcan Captains and Cadets returned to the castle around early afternoon to warm up and have lunch. Carmen and her Souls said goodbye to Blaine and Thunderbolt before they hiked back to Mortrock Forest. They told the pair of their intended trip to Keltan the next day, and Carmen promised to write to Blaine after they got back.

The remainder of the Saturday Christmas went by quietly in Sarcanian Valley. Carmen and her Souls stayed inside the rest of the afternoon and got to sleep at a reasonable hour, in anticipation of getting an early start to the following day. They didn't know just how many unavoidable obstacles lay ahead of them.

Upon awakening the next morning, Carmen and her friends ate breakfast and prepared themselves for their departure for Keltan. Carmen gathered together Merlin's map, her quill pen, and parchment, and tucked them all into her pocket. Then she lay down on the floor of her room beside Blaze, Stellar, and Glamis.

Tapping once again into his father's powers, Anubis stood over his friends and cast them into *Death's Eternal Sleep*. Carmen felt her eyes slowly drift closed as her vision faded....

Minutes later, she was floating above her body as a silvery translucent spirit, alongside those of her Souls. Their bodies remained sleeping peacefully on the floor below them.

Fairly well accustomed to the distant and ghostly feeling of being spirits by now, Carmen and her friends followed Anubis upward, through the ceiling of their room and those of the higher floors of the castle—and eventually out through the roof.

They floated swiftly up into the darkened early morning sky, rising higher and higher every moment. Carmen was doing her best not to fret about what they would be met with in Keltan. She had not been to the World of Darkness since she had recovered Merlin's cipher disk for the first time. So now with an army of Phantom Warriors having been unleashed into Kelmar, and Triedastron continuing to battle with the Kelmarsians in the afterworlds, it was even more pressing to secure the cipher disk for the final time.

Anubis and the others eventually came to the Impassable Barrier high in the heavens of Kelmar, but instead of flying straight up toward the soft, serene music echoing from Kelmarsia, Anubis led his friends downward.

They glided through the underside of the golden line of light, passing through a tunnel of complete and utter darkness before experiencing that horrible jolt of frigid cold that told them that they had arrived in Keltan.

Carmen and her Souls descended through the dark stone ceiling, and soon touched down on the ground in the center of the shadowy and cavernous world of Keltan, whose ponds of boiling magma were glowing in the light of the fire contained by the tarnished torches that lined the dusty stone walls. Carmen looked out toward the northern mountains and the dark tunnels that led off of this vast cavern. Stalactites hanging overhead were dripping grimy water down to the floor, creating dark puddles that would eventually grow into stalagmites.

Keltan sorcerers were constantly leading lines of newly departed spirits away through the tunnels in chains and shackles for judgment on what type of punishment they would have to endure in Keltan. Carmen was relieved that neither they nor any of the Dark creatures that inhabited these caves had noticed that she and her Souls had appeared in the realm.

Distracted by the internal question of what she should do if anyone *did* eventually see them, Carmen had to suppress a startled shout when Dagtar floated down through the ceiling of the cavern right over her head. The sparkling green Dragon looked calm as he descended through the air and cast himself into invisibility, before sweeping over Carmen and her friends on the ground for the same reason.

Under the *Dragon's Invisibility* spell, Carmen and her Souls would remain out of sight to everyone in Keltan but themselves, and be protected from the Darkness of the realm that would otherwise harm them. Dagtar gazed down at the others as he flew over them.

"Did you all have a merry Christmas?" he asked in a kind voice.

"Oh yes, we did," Carmen told him, grinning up at him. "Thank you for asking."

"I am glad," Dagtar said with a smile. *"So…are you ready to find the third Secret of Kelmar and Merlin's cipher disk?"*

"Lead the way," Blaze said.

Carmen, Blaze, Stellar, Glamis, and Anubis moved quickly off in the direction of the colossal Fortress of Darkness, with Dagtar flying just ahead of them. They could see the tall, silver pointed fence, just behind which, Triedastron's angry Chimera guarded the premises.

About halfway north to the Fortress of Darkness, Dagtar pointed his nose down at a large gray boulder.

Carmen and her other Souls approached the rock and examined it closely.

"You have to move the boulder toward the castle to reveal the entrance to the underground tunnels of Keltan," Dagtar told them. *"It is far too heavy for one individual to push alone, so we must move it together."*

Carmen laid her wand down on the ground. Then she planted her feet firmly on the stone ground and placed both of her hands against the rock, ready to push it once everyone else was in place. Her Souls gathered around her, allowing room for Dagtar to lean his great head against the boulder with them.

"Ready..." Carmen said. "Go!"

Utilizing all of their physical strength, Carmen and her friends forced the boulder forward.

But even with their collective might, the group struggled to shove the boulder toward the fortress.... Little by little, they pushed it about six feet ahead of them...and in so doing, uncovered a square, metal door with a heavy iron handle in the floor of the cavern.

Dagtar and his friends backed up and allowed Carmen to kneel down and lift up the handle. It took another impressive feat of strength just for her to wrench open the door with a sharp *creak.*

A musty smell rose up into Carmen's nose as she and her friends peered down into the dark depths of Keltan's underground world. Carmen illuminated her wand and pointed it into the black tunnel below their feet. The light revealed a fixed, tarnished silver ladder leading down into the dank maze of stone passageways.

"Refer to your map to follow the tunnels to the Secret," Dagtar instructed Carmen and her companions. *"Be very careful as you move through them.... Triedastron likely employed traps to deter potential thieves and intruders. You must always remain mindful of your surroundings."*

"Oh, terrific," Stellar said sarcastically.

"We cannot keep the door propped open without risking discovery by any Keltans who might be walking by," Dagtar decided, glancing around him. *"These tunnels eventually lead up into the basement of Triedastron's fortress. After you get the Secret, you should find a door that will take you up into the dungeons."*

Dagtar nodded in the direction of the castle gates.

"Anubis, Stellar, and Glamis, sneak out through the front doors of the castle and past Lucia while Carmen and Blaze are locating the cipher disk. I will have unlocked the gate for you by then. As soon as I see you out on the grounds, I will take you to the prison so that we can gauge the situation there.... Carmen and Blaze, promise me that you will reclaim the cipher disk and get out of Triedastron's fortress as fast as you can."

"We will," Carmen vowed to the Dragon.

She looked around at her other friends before handing Blaze her wand.

"Let's get down into the tunnels before it gets too late."

Carmen descended the silver ladder first, her stomach churning nervously. Blaze flew next to her, holding her wand over her to light her way into the underground cave.

Once the two of them reached the bottom, about twenty steps beneath the ground surface, Blaze handed Carmen back her wand and helped the rest of her Souls as they climbed down the ladder.

Carmen pointed her wand straight ahead of her. The darkened stone walls of this ancient passageway were covered in a thick coating of dust and smelled strongly of mold.

After Glamis, Stellar, and Anubis were safely inside the tunnel with her and Blaze, Dagtar gazed down at them from above.

"I'm going to move the boulder back into place so that nobody knows that you're here," he said. *"Good luck, all of you. I will see you outside."*

Carmen nodded up at him, and with Merlin's map in hand, she led her friends forward through the tunnel as Dagtar slid the rock over the entrance.

They moved at a cautious pace, all of them wary of the potential for traps. The farther they moved ahead, the more connecting tunnels that appeared out of the darkness off of this one, but they made sure not to stray from their path. Making even one wrong turn could easily result in getting lost.

Carmen kept her eyes and ears alert for any sign of danger. It was uncomfortably silent down in the tunnels, making her more aware, and feeding her fear that something intense was going to happen at any moment. She couldn't believe that they would be able to make it to the momentously significant third Secret of Kelmar without first facing some kind of potent defense that guarded it. Her senses heightened by her conscious effort to locate traps, Carmen marched onward, periodically referencing Merlin's map to estimate how close they were to reaching the Secret.

After twenty minutes or so, they arrived at what was the tunnel system's halfway point in Carmen's mind. They continued walking as Carmen glanced down at the map. Stellar took a step, and a small square section of the floor abruptly sank in beneath his foot.

The surprisingly loud scraping sound of the sinking rock made Carmen and the others freeze. They immediately glanced around them.

A horizontal line of softball-sized holes magically appeared halfway up both walls of the tunnel. Pure instinct prompted Carmen to scream, "DUCK!"

Carmen and her friends dropped to the floor just in time as violent blasts of red fire shot out from the holes in the walls. Their hearts pounding, they crawled quickly on their stomachs through the rest of the hall, feeling the heat from the flames on their backs. With her pulse beating loudly in her ears, Carmen guided her Souls farther on into the maze of tunnels.

Once they had gotten a safe distance past the tunnel where the trap had gone off, they stopped to catch their breath. While none of them could honestly say that they hadn't expected to be ambushed, they were all nonetheless stunned and reasonably frightened after almost being burned alive.

"Dagtar was right," Stellar said, between gasps for breath. "I didn't even see anything on the floor.... It just sank without warning."

Carmen was also still breathing heavily from the scare.

"That's probably how all of the traps are," she said, wiping the perspiration from her brow. "We just have to stay together.... There's no telling what else is down here."

And so, after they had all recovered from the scare, they tramped ahead, their goal of finding the final Secret outweighing their fear of falling into another one of Triedastron's traps. The group walked for another ten minutes through the dark tunnels without stumbling upon anything threatening. Their worries eased a tiny bit with every step closer to the end of their underground journey.

Carmen directed her friends on their advance toward their destination by following Merlin's map closely, and it wasn't until she saw movement in the darkness out of the corner of her eye that she told everyone to stop.

Carmen pointed her wand at the floor. The light illuminated a brown and black striped scorpion-like creature crawling up toward the wall. The Scepthropod had sizeable claws and a long, arched tail that ended in a sharpened barb—likely used to inject its prey with deadly venom.

"Stay away from it, Carmen," Blaze warned, gently pulling her back. "Scepthropods are fast...and their venom can kill within minutes."

Never one to take Blaze's guidance lightly, Carmen promptly moved on from that spot.

She and her friends hiked ever deeper into the tunnels of Keltan, the minutes passing very slowly as they ventured through the seemingly never-ending labyrinth of damp passageways. When they were nearly three-quarters of the way to the third Secret, Carmen and her Souls turned a corner, and came upon a scene that would make even the bravest of explorers cringe in fear.

Carmen shined her light straight down the tunnel. Both walls were covered from top to bottom with live Scepthropods. Their bodies were packed so tightly together that they almost made the stone walls look like they were covered entirely in textured brown and black tiles.

"This is another trap," Blaze said, as he and his friends gaped down the hall at the hundreds of stationary creatures. "If we walk through here…they'll move to attack us."

"What should we do?" Carmen asked, unable to look away from the disturbing sight.

The group considered their options. If they used an attack spell to try to get past them, there was no telling how well the creatures would be able to defend themselves against it…. They would have to make use of a Protection if they were going to escape this corridor unscathed.

"Lightning Force Field," Carmen eventually decided. She had used that spell only once before, but it had done its job of protecting her and her friends as they ran from enemy fire.

"That's a good thought," Blaze said, nodding his head in agreement. "I think that we should go with it."

The others also agreed. And so, taking a deep breath, Carmen took a minute to focus on what she was about to do. When she was ready, she threw her wand up into the air like a baton, allowing it to spiral up above their heads.

"Lightning Force Field!" she shouted.

A magical wind swirled around her and her Souls, and they ran ahead through the tunnel, Carmen's wand floating over them, near to the ceiling. There was instant chaos and frenzied movement as the Scepthropods scurried down the walls, launching themselves at Carmen and her friends.

The leaping Scepthropods flew through the air and hit the stone walls as they were deflected off of the magical shield of wind surrounding Carmen and her friends. The powers of the spell prevented any of the creatures from touching a single member of Carmen's group, just as they had hoped.

To maintain the spell, Carmen had to keep her eyes locked on her spinning wand, even as she sensed the motion and heard the angry hisses of Scepthropods all around her. The Kelmarians galloped down the dark hall, made a right turn, and finally left the walls of enraged Scepthropods behind them.

As soon as Blaze alerted her that they were safely past the trap, Carmen broke eye contact with her wand and allowed it to fall down into her hands.

"Phew…. I'm glad *that* worked," Carmen said, leaning over, struggling to catch her breath. "I think I've had enough of these traps for one day…. Come on, let's get that Secret before anything else tries to kill us."

Carmen and her friends wearily resumed their journey through the tunnels…and eventually, a long, gray stone box lying on top of a matching pedestal came into sight at the end of the hall just ahead of them. There was a fixed metal ladder along the back wall of the tunnel that led up to the underside of a square, steel drain grate in the ceiling. On the other side of that grating was Triedastron's dungeon.

"That must be it," Stellar said, as Carmen shined her wand's light down to the end of the passageway. "The Secret must be inside of that box."

Carmen hesitated.

"Don't bad things usually happen in threes?" she asked, before taking a single step in the direction of it.

"Let's try not to think about that superstition," Glamis said. "The Secret is right here before us! We must go to it!"

Carmen sighed.

"You're right...." she admitted. "Let's go."

Carmen and her Souls walked toward the stone box, keeping an eye out for anything suspicious. As they got closer to it, they were disturbed to realize that this box was actually a casket. They could see that the lid and sides of the coffin were engraved with snaking designs and shapes reminiscent of the symbols in Triedastron's wand.

When they reached the casket, Carmen handed Blaze her wand. With trembling hands, she slid the flat stone lid forward just enough for her to peek down through the crack into the casket. Then she took back her wand to point the light down into the box. Engraved at the bottom of the empty coffin were the words of the final Secret of Kelmar.

Be loved to run Back, Dance the Song with friends in tow.

Carmen memorized the phrase, and then straightened up to retrieve her parchment, ink, and quill from her pocket. Quickly, she dipped her pen into the inkwell and jotted down the phrase before she could forget it. Experiencing a wonderful feeling of accomplishment, Carmen then tucked the paper back into her robes.

"We did it, guys!" she said, excited. "We've got the last Secret!"

Carmen and her friends took a brief, joyous moment to savor their first success on this voyage to Keltan. That was when something went terribly wrong.

The hallway began to rumble, as though it were weakening under the stress of a powerful outside force. The Kelmarians gaped at the walls around them. As a result of them obtaining the ancient message, the cursed walls of the tunnel were now quickly closing in around them. The corridor was becoming more and more narrow, the walls inching ever closer to Carmen and her friends....

A jolt of panic came over Carmen. If they didn't get out of here now, they would be crushed!

Carmen and her Souls ran around the stone casket to the rusted metal ladder mounted on the back wall. Carmen held her wand between her teeth and began to climb. Her hands were wet with perspiration as she raced to the upper rungs.

Frantic, and conscious of the fact that she had to get her friends up with her as fast as possible, Carmen pressed her hands up against the drain grate in the ceiling that led into Triedastron's basement. With an upward thrust, she pushed the grate aside so that they had an opening to get up into the castle. She then tossed her wand up into the dungeon.

Carmen got back down the ladder in a flash to help her Souls flee up into the fortress. Blaze flew upward and took Anubis's front paws into his as Carmen pushed him up through the ceiling of the tunnel. Next, they helped Stellar get out...and lastly, Glamis, who was the heaviest and most difficult for Carmen and Blaze to lift, even together. All the while, the walls were rapidly drawing within centimeters of Carmen's body.

With her Souls safely up in the basement of Triedastron's fortress, Carmen scrambled up the ladder just before the walls made a final lunge forward to crush the casket. She leapt up onto the moist, grimy floor of the dungeon and collapsed onto her stomach. Blaze slammed the steel floor drain back down into place after her.

The crash of stone on stone echoed throughout the dungeon as a cloud of dust rose up through the drain hole.

Fighting to regain her composure, Carmen lay there, dazed and fatigued, trying to catch her breath and slow her racing heartbeat. She had somehow escaped being crushed to death by mere seconds.... She didn't want to think about what would have happened if she had moved even a little slower than she had.

"I told you that bad things always happen in threes," Carmen said, as she got up on her hands and knees.

Her hair was damp with sweat and moisture from the tunnels, and her robes were smudged with dirt and dust from lying on the green, slimy dungeon floor.... She was still shaking from the scare.

As her pulse gradually stabilized, Carmen gazed around her.... She and her Souls were in the middle of a damp, dimly lit dungeon. There were torches running along the walls, and the expansive space had a high, vaulted ceiling. Heavy, barred doors guarded the individual cells that lined both sides of the hall. The dungeon was completely silent, as all of the Kelmarsian captives were currently locked in the separate prison to the west of the castle. This room merely served as a holding space if there were ever an overflow of prisoners. Carmen imagined that Haesnost Prison must look at least somewhat like this dungeon did.

Carmen got up from the cold floor and glanced around the corner. A winding stone staircase led up to the higher floors of the castle.

"Let's head to Triedastron's study," she told her Souls, as she picked up her wand. "If I were to guess, I would say that he's probably storing the cipher disk there."

Blaze nodded.

"He's far too arrogant to have moved it anywhere else."

Carmen and her Souls walked across the vacant dungeon, their footsteps echoing in the damp and spacious chamber. When they reached the top of the stairs, Carmen extinguished the light from her wand, and she and her invisible friends walked out into the entrance hall of Triedastron's fortress.

All was quiet on the main floor of the castle. There were a handful of Dark sorcerers dressed in hooded black robes roaming through the corridors, but none were moving with an urgency that would suggest that they knew of the Kelmarian plot currently being carried out right here in the Master of Keltan's stronghold.

"You should go now," Carmen murmured to Anubis, Stellar, and Glamis. "Blaze and I will go get the cipher disk and meet you at the prison."

"Yes, we will go find Dagtar," Anubis said, in keeping with the plan, as he and the others moved toward the front doors of the fortress. *"Good luck."*

Carmen and Blaze watched as their friends snuck out onto the castle grounds. They then crossed the suit of armor-lined entrance hall and tiptoed down the corridor home to Triedastron's study.

Just like last time, Carmen unlocked the door near the end of the hall with *Lockstra*. After that was done, she and Blaze crept into the candlelit room and gently shut the door behind them.

But *unlike* the last time that they were here, it appeared that Triedastron had been in this room not long before they had arrived. The candles of the chandelier, as well as those placed around the room, were still burning, and there were fresh pieces of parchment scribbled with notes and maps scattered about on Triedastron's desk. On guard, Carmen peered around the bookshelves to make sure that they were alone before she and Blaze moved farther into the room.

As they hunted for the cipher disk amongst the rows of books, they kept a careful eye out for any indication of a hidden compartment similar to the one in which the object had originally been stored. They knew that they had to move swiftly, but they couldn't afford to overlook any small element that could help lead them to their objective.

In the midst of their search, Carmen spotted a tall wooden display case with a pair of glass doors standing in the back corner of the room. This was new; she hadn't noticed it the first time that she had been here.

Curious, she walked over to it and gazed up through the doors. Merlin's wooden cipher disk was leaning on its side against the back of the cabinet, in the middle of the highest shelf.

"There it is!" Carmen called to Blaze, pointing up to it. "He's incredibly vain…. He didn't even *try* to hide it."

Blaze flew over and gazed up at the cipher disk. He examined the heavy, bronze circular lock situated halfway up the doors of the cabinet, between the tarnished handles.

"I don't think you're going to be able to unlock this with just *Lockstra*," he said. "I know of a stronger unlocking spell that works more effectively if the lock has additional Protections placed on it."

"What is it?" Carmen asked.

"*Mosenca*," Blaze answered. "It means 'disengage.' Just point your wand at the lock and state the incantation. It will use more of your magic than *Lockstra*, but in this case, it's worth it."

Carmen agreed. She raised the crown of her wand up to the lock and murmured, "*Mosenca.*"

Carmen's wand illuminated the doors of the cabinet, casting a red-orange glow. An instant later, the heavy lock clicked and fell down. Blaze hurried to catch it before it could hit the stone floor.

With no time to waste, Carmen got up on her tiptoes and stretched to reach inside the display case for the cipher disk. Once it was in her grasp, she handed it to Blaze. But just as she was about to shut the cabinet, the door of the library suddenly creaked open. Carmen felt her heart stop.

Triedastron strode into his study, his dark eyes gazing in the direction of his desk. Without looking up, he strutted over to it and flipped through some of the papers on the table in search of something, the deep creases in his forehead accentuated by the shadows produced by the candles.

Carmen and Blaze stood frozen in fear—Carmen leaning over into the cabinet, and Blaze holding Merlin's cipher disk in his claws. Though *they* were invisible, it would only take one quick glance for Triedastron to notice that the doors of his display cabinet were wide open. It seemed like an eternity before Triedastron found the paper that he was looking for.

Finally, with the parchment in hand, the silver-haired sorcerer swept out of the room, shutting the library door with a *bang*. Triedastron's pounding footsteps soon faded away, and Carmen and Blaze both exhaled the breath that they had been holding.

"We've had some close calls before…but *that* was one of the worst," Carmen said, shaking a little as she stepped back from the cabinet.

"You don't have to tell *me*," Blaze said, looking drained as Carmen shut the glass doors and fitted the lock back on to them. "Let's hurry and get out before he comes back."

Carmen took the cipher disk from the Sarcan and cast *the Sentinel's Defense* Protection on it to protect it from possible harm. Then she and her Partner ran over to the door of the library.

Blaze pushed the door open just a crack and peeked out into the hallway. Triedastron's muffled voice carried out from behind the closed door of his meeting room on the other side of the grand staircase.

Seizing their ideal opportunity to escape, Carmen and Blaze dashed up the corridor and across the entrance hall. Once at the front doors of the fortress, Carmen pulled open one of them, and she and Blaze slipped outside.

Lucia was napping at the foot of the silver fence, her muscular chest rising slowly up and down as she breathed. The eyes of her lioness, goat, and serpent heads were all closed.

Just as Dagtar had promised, the lock on the ornate iron entrance gate had been lifted, allowing Carmen and Blaze to escape the courtyard of Triedastron's fortress. But in order to reach the gate, they first had to sneak past the sleeping Chimera.

As quietly as they could, Carmen and Blaze inched down the path leading to the gate, praying that the Chimera wouldn't be able to hear the stressed pounding of their heartbeats. With great care...they crept past Lucia and cracked open the gate just wide enough for them to fit through.

Once out on the common grounds of Keltan, Carmen and Blaze turned and looked out toward the west, to the distant gray and black mountains that rose up toward the ceiling on the cavern. They could see the crumbling, shadowy towers and walls of Haesnost Prison looming there amongst the peaks. Faint candlelight was flickering in the barred windows. That was where they were headed next.

Lucia suddenly stirred behind the fortress gate. Knowing better than to linger, Carmen and Blaze broke into a sprint toward the prison. They were painfully aware that if anyone were to discover them, their most critical mission in Keltan would inevitably come that much closer to failure.

CHAPTER TWENTY-ONE
HAESNOST

Carmen's nose stung with the odor of the thick, red magma that flowed in rivers through the rocky landscape as she and Blaze galloped toward Haesnost. When they finally reached the base of the ominous-looking western mountains, which effectively surrounded the prison on all sides, Carmen summoned her wings and flew up toward the facility with Blaze.

Haesnost was an old and crumbling gray castle that had barred windows, towers, and a high outer wall to prevent prisoner escape. There were predatory black birds circling over the jail, which stood at the top of one of the tallest peaks. Carmen spotted a group of the feathered scavengers feasting on another creature's carcass on the ledge of an adjacent mountain.

As Carmen and Blaze soared around the eastern side of the prison, they came across Dagtar flying there, looking through the windows of one of the countless towers. Anubis, Stellar, and Glamis were riding on his back.

"Have you found a way in yet, Dag?" Carmen asked, as she and Blaze approached the Dragon.

Dagtar looked over at her but shook his head.

"The magical forces guarding this prison were implemented specifically to prevent escape," he said, sounding frustrated. *"Creatures known as Sentry Hounds are stationed at every entrance. They have a keen ability to sniff out intruders, even if they are invisible. In addition to them, armed guards regularly patrol the halls of Haesnost. There is also a Protection placed over the castle doors that prevents anyone from entering or leaving the facility without either a guard's key, or permission from Triedastron."*

Dagtar then noticed Merlin's cipher disk, which Carmen was holding under her arm. Almost instantly, he looked more encouraged.

"The others told me of your success in obtaining the third Secret. Did you have any problems in getting the cipher disk back?"

"We almost got caught, but luckily Triedastron was distracted with something and didn't notice us," Blaze replied. "We were very fortunate to get away."

Dagtar smiled.

"Well, you did just what you came here to do," he said, full of pride. *"You should be very happy about that."*

Carmen nodded. In truth, she was overjoyed about retrieving Merlin's cipher disk, but pressed for time, her thoughts had already shifted to the all-important matter of freeing Inpu from Haesnost. Anubis looked like he wanted to say something.

"Do you have any ideas on how we can break into the prison?" Carmen asked him.

"Yes. I spoke with my father just before you and Blaze got here," he said. *"Because of the Sentry Hounds and Protections defending the doors, he told me that we should enter Haesnost by breaking the bars on his window and gaining access to the rest of the prison through his cell."*

Carmen and the others listened closely.

"Once we get inside, my father will wait for one of the guards to approach, and then pretend that he is ill, so that the guard will come in and check on him," Anubis continued. *"When the guard enters the cell, Carmen can grab the ring of keys off of the man's belt, and we can sneak out into the hallway.... Then, after the guard leaves, we will be able to unlock our door and free the other Kelmarsian prisoners."*

"We're going to free *all* of them?" Stellar asked. "I thought that we were just here for Inpu."

"As many as we can," Carmen said on the spot, almost surprising herself with how fast she agreed to the new plan. "As long as we're here, we should help to the greatest extent that we can…. There's no way that Kelmarsia will win this war if Keltan keeps holding their people as prisoners. They need all of the able fighters that they have if they're going to stand up to Triedastron."

Understanding her logic, Stellar then concurred with Anubis as well.

"After you have the captives freed, you must direct them back out here *to avoid the Sentry Hounds,"* Dagtar said, motioning toward the building. *"I will wait just outside the window, and then take the freed prisoners back to Kelmarsia a few at a time. I promise to come back for all of you as soon as everyone else is out."*

"What about the armed guards?" Stellar asked. "They're bound to notice that the cells are magically emptying as they walk by."

"That's where you and Glamis come in," Anubis explained, clearly having thought out the plan for this operation while Carmen and Blaze were recovering the cipher disk. *"I will handle the communication between those of us in the halls and my father. We will need to keep in touch with each other to report on the progress of freeing the prisoners, and to check on where the guards are at any given moment. Meanwhile, you will both need to act as the diversion while Carmen and Blaze are freeing the prisoners,"* he finished, gazing at Stellar and Glamis.

"Very well, but how exactly will we do it?" Glamis inquired. "We are invisible to the Keltans."

"Precisely," Anubis said. *"As the situation allows, you will need to make noises, throw objects, and so forth—anything to draw their attention away from the escaping prisoners."*

"Got it," Stellar confirmed.

Then he turned and looked back at the Boarax seated behind him.

"I think that we can handle that…. Right, Glamis?"

"But of course!" Glamis answered. "We shall do whatever needs to be done to ensure the accomplishment of this escape."

"Good," Anubis said, nodding his head. *"Let us then commence with the plan."*

"Yes," Carmen said decisively.

Anubis closed his eyes and listened briefly to his father's voice in his head tell him where in Haesnost he was located…. Once he got his answer, he directed Carmen and the others around to the opposite side of the prison.

Row upon row of barred windows covered the dingy, gray prison walls and climbed up the towers that stretched up toward the dark ceiling of Keltan's central cavern. Carmen and her Souls were overwhelmed by feelings of despair as they flew around the grounds of Haesnost…. It was as though the ancient prison itself had been cursed to exist in the same eternal state of misery that its prisoners did.

They flew up to a window about halfway up the wall on the western side of the jail. Carmen and the others gazed through the bars and saw Inpu lying on his stomach on the stone floor, which was covered in hay. His golden eyes gazed out at them. As always, there was a soft white light encasing his body that made the multicolored jewels on his gold collar glitter.

The cell that contained Inpu was small, and held only a handful of illuminated crystals—barely providing enough light to see. There was a stone bench running along the side of one of the walls, and a set of black metal chains with shackles hanging on the opposite wall. Heavy iron bars guarded the arched doorway that separated the cell from the hallway.

Inpu stood up and bowed his head to his friends, making full use of his inherent ability to see through invisibility spells. He then walked up to the window, which was just low enough to allow him to see outside.

"Thank you for coming for us," he said. *"Anubis told me of your plan."*

He then looked into Carmen and Blaze's eyes.

"My son also informed me that you've already secured both the final Secret of Kelmar, and Merlin's cipher disk. Well done."

"How are you doing?" Carmen asked him, concerned. The Jackal appeared to be in perfect health, but she knew better than to assume.

"I am fine," Inpu assured her. *"We get fed twice a day, and though the food is about as terrible as you might expect, it is enough to sustain us. Spirits in theory do not need to eat anyway, which is a good thing for most of those here. I am not a spirit in the true sense of the word, but I've gotten by anyway."*

Inpu took a fleeting glance behind him to make sure that no guards were coming down the hall.

"The worst part about being held here is that we are unable to leave our cells," he said sadly. *"For a creature like me, who loves to travel, the sameness of these walls can get a bit unbearable at times."*

Carmen instantly sympathized with him. She could only imagine how difficult the last couple of months had been for the Jackal.

"Has anyone tried to hurt you since Triedastron attacked you and brought you here?" Carmen asked.

Inpu shook his head.

"No. The guards have threatened us at times, but so long as we behave, they generally leave us alone."

"Well, you won't have to suffer here any longer," Carmen promised him, leaning her wand against the bars of the window. "Stand back," she advised. "We'll have you free in no time."

Carmen waited as Inpu moved a safe distance away, to the front of his cell. There, he took one more look out into the hallway to check for guards walking by. When he gave Carmen the signal that all was clear, she pointed her wand at his window. She would use an advanced Kelmarian spell that Haidar had taught the Sarcan Captains just days ago to break the bars.

"Force of Strength!" Carmen ordered.

With a thunderous *BANG,* the metal bars blasted out of the window and tumbled down into the hay, which cushioned their fall and prevented them from making a loud noise when they made contact with the stone floor.

Carmen held on to the windowsill and Returned her wings. Then she climbed through the gaping hole into Inpu's cell and jumped down, landing on her feet in the hay. Blaze flew in right behind her.

Dagtar rested his body up against the outside wall of the tower to enable Stellar, Glamis, and Anubis to climb in behind Blaze.

After they were all inside, the Dragon peeked his head in through the window.

"I'll be here when you get back," he vowed, his blue eyes glistening.

Carmen walked to the front of the cell and looked out through the barred iron door. At least two dozen identical square cells lined the two sides of the long gray hallway. An aged metal lock was mounted high up on the door of each of the units. There were Kelmarsian sorcerers and creatures being held in almost every cell, usually one or two of them per space. From those that Carmen could see, she didn't recognize any of them.

She then looked to the end of the hall and observed two gruff, broad-shouldered male Keltan sorcerers standing there. They were talking in low voices near the stairs that led down to the lower floors of the jail. Both were wearing gray and black uniforms.

One of them was listening with his arms folded, leaning against the wall, and the other man was motioning with his hands as he spoke. The first man had a coarse mustache, short black hair, and hollow brown eyes. The other man was slightly younger, with brown hair, oily skin, and a similarly empty expression. The guards both had scabbards fitted to their belts; the silver hilts of their swords were glittering in the light of the ceiling crystals.

"I don't know if these guys are easily fooled," Carmen murmured, turning back to Inpu. "This might be trickier than I originally thought.... Are you sure that you'll be able to convince them that you're sick?"

Inpu smiled at her reassuringly.

"I believe that I can put on a fairly believable act," Inpu said, a glint in his eyes. *"Have a look for yourself."*

Carmen crept a short distance back from the door as Inpu walked to the center of the cell. The Jackal lay down on his side in the hay—and abruptly released a howl that could easily have been taken for a cry of immense pain. Most of the neighboring prisoners got up from where they were sitting and gazed out through the bars of their own cells to see what all of the commotion was about.

Inpu continued to howl for close to a minute before the pair of guards stopped talking and looked down the hall for the source of the noise.

"I'd better check and see what that is," the younger man told the other guard in an aggravated voice. "I swear, these Kelmarsians are driving me mad. I can't wait for Triedastron to come and quiet them for good. I just might put a silencing spell on them myself in the meantime."

The guard marched down the corridor, his silver ring of keys clinking on his belt with each step. When he got to Inpu's cell, the Jackal was lying in the hay with his eyes completely closed, still crying loudly. The man leaned over and peered in through the bars of the door.

"So, what's your problem?" he asked. There was not an ounce of sympathy in his voice.

Inpu released another agonizing moan.

"I.... I need.... Please...."

Inpu's voice wavered in such a believable manner that Carmen had to keep telling herself that he wasn't actually dying.

"What was it, Randore?" the other guard called from the end of the hall.

Randore took his keys off of his belt, selected the right one, and unlocked Inpu's cell.

"Don't know," he said. "This Jackal here doesn't look too good."

Randore opened the door and took a few steps into the cell. As he bent down near Inpu, Carmen approached the man from the side and reached for his ring of keys...careful not to breathe too loudly and give herself away. Glamis quietly scooped up a bushel of hay in his jaws a couple of feet away from them.

Ever so gently, Carmen unhooked the ring from Randore's belt. Then, with the keys in hand, she slipped out through the cell door behind the guard—Blaze, Anubis, Stellar, and Glamis on her heels.

Carmen, Blaze, and Anubis waited just outside Inpu's cell while Glamis and Stellar jogged down the corridor toward the second guard. Randore was watching Inpu closely as he rolled on the floor, howling in pain.

Glamis trotted down the hall and tossed the hay forward. It landed at the older guard's feet, just as the Boarax had wanted it to. The puzzled officer crouched down, staring dumbstruck at the clump of hay that had appeared out of nowhere, allowing Glamis to squeeze past him and tiptoe down the first three stairs. Stellar approached the guard next, and promptly sank his teeth into his lower leg.

The guard let out a shout of distress and collapsed to the floor, hugging his throbbing leg to his chest.

"AHHHHH!"

Stellar dashed by him and joined Glamis on the stairs. Randore immediately looked up and turned his head back toward the hall.

"What happened, Tortbold?" he yelled.

"Argh, something just bit me!" the injured man barked, as he lay in a pained position on the floor. "But there's nothing here!"

Randore straightened up and gazed down the hall at his wounded comrade. Feeling the need to tend to *him* before he did the obviously ill Inpu, the young guard brushed the hay off of his boots and hurried toward the door.

"Hold on, I'm coming!" he shouted, leaving Inpu's cell and shutting the door behind him. The door locked automatically with a sharp *clang*.

As Randore hastened down the hall with his hand on the hilt of his sword, Carmen searched through the ring of keys to find the one that fit Inpu's cell.

After trying just a couple of them, she located the correct key. She unlocked the cell door as Inpu continued to howl to cover up the squeal of the door opening.

As soon as Inpu's door was ajar, Carmen, Blaze, and Anubis ran to the opposite end of the corridor. Carmen fumbled with the keys, and tried fitting various ones into the lock of the first cell on the right, where a sad elderly sorceress and her Talsonca dog were sitting on the stone bench inside. All of the keys were long and silver, so there was no way to tell which one fit each door without using simple trial and error.

Randore worked quickly to ease Tortbold's discomfort by utilizing a Keltan Healing spell. Once Tortbold was able to get back to his feet, Glamis jumped heavily up and down on the stairs behind the pair of guards before he and Stellar turned and scampered loudly down the steps.

Gazing dumbfounded at the visibly vacant staircase, Randore and Tortbold each appeared to be growing increasingly agitated.

"What is it with this place tonight?" Tortbold asked, his irritation apparent in his tone as he and Randore tramped down the stairs after Stellar and Glamis.

Carmen finally found the right key for the first cell on the right side of the hallway. She turned it in the lock and opened the door.

The sorceress and her Partner sitting on the bench stared at the gaping door, staggered as to how it had opened by itself. Carmen spoke in a fairly low voice, so as not to scare the two Kelmarsians.

"Listen, I'm Carmen Fox, the Guardian of Kelmar," the invisible Carmen said from out in the corridor. "My Souls and I are freeing as many of the prisoners here tonight as we can. Come into the hall and I'll lead you out. Merlin's Dragon, Dagtar, is waiting outside the window of one of the cells to take you and the others back to Kelmarsia."

The white-haired sorceress, who was wearing shimmering, light green robes, cupped her hand to her mouth in complete shock. Her Talsonca barked in surprise.

"Can it be true?" she asked, her voice shaking with hope.

"Yes," Carmen said at once. "Please trust me."

Sensing the urgency and the earnestness in Carmen's voice, the woman and her Talsonca stood up and rushed out into the corridor. Carmen took the sorceress's hand to guide her to Inpu's cell as fast as she could. Before taking off, she tossed the ring of keys back to Blaze so that he could get to work on another door while she escorted the pair of Kelmarsian prisoners to their destination.

When Carmen and the others got to Inpu's cell, the Jackal showed the sorceress and her Partner to the window.

"Good work, Carmen!" Inpu said, as he helped the both of them climb up the wall. *"Keep going!"*

Not needing to be told twice, Carmen darted back down the hallway and watched Blaze turn the appropriate key and open up the next cell in the row. This one contained a young boy and his Frelark.

Carmen told the boy who she was in a gentle voice, and then brought him and his Partner out into the corridor just as she had the first two prisoners. Inpu now stood beside the door of his own cell. The original duo of prisoners was safely outside on Dagtar's back. Carmen urged the two captives to run to the Jackal, promising them that he would take them to safety.

With the second set of prisoners off on their way, Carmen and Blaze proceeded to unlock one cell door after another as Anubis stayed with them—freeing countless captives desperate for an escape from Haesnost Prison. They alternated between the cells on the left and right sides of the hall, and the more people and creatures they freed, the more animated the still incarcerated prisoners became. Seeing the newly released captives running eagerly past their cells, the remaining prisoners looked out through the bars of their doors to watch an ever increasing number of cells opening, and their fellow Kelmarsians escaping.

The confined detainees in neighboring cells began speaking feverishly with one another. But as word moved through the hall that Carmen was the one who was breaking out the captives, many of those still waiting in their cells began calling out desperately for her to come to them.

"Please!" one distressed young mother cried through her door. "I miss my son! Please get me out of here!"

"Help us!" shouted an older man in a nearby cell. "We cannot stand it here anymore!"

The screaming grew louder and more despondent as the minutes passed. It was agonizing for Carmen to hear the chorus of frantic cries for help.... She just couldn't bear to listen to their suffering wails as she wrestled with Randore's keys to unlock yet another door, sweat running down her face. She was enormously relieved when Inpu ordered the prisoners to stay quiet so that the guards on the other floors wouldn't hear them. The realization that their escape depended on their complete cooperation finally made them settle down.

In the newfound silence of the hall, Carmen heard a loud crash downstairs while opening a cell door about halfway down the corridor. She hoped that the noise had come from Glamis and Stellar working to distract the guards, and was not something more pressing.

Carmen and Blaze swiftly worked their way through the entire hallway—freeing all ages and species of prisoners in their effort to empty the prison of as many innocent Kelmarsians as they could. They were able to evacuate all of the cells on the current floor in less than half an hour's time, and just as they freed the final prisoner—a middle-aged sorceress at the end of the corridor—a look of alarm crossed Anubis's face.

"The two guards are attempting to come back upstairs!" he said, gazing up at Carmen and Blaze with genuine fear. *"We have to get downstairs. Stellar and Glamis are telling me that there are four prisoners on the floor below who still need to be freed. Come!"* He ushered his friends toward the staircase.

Carmen and Blaze followed Anubis down the steps, their hearts pounding as they sped to the prison's lower level. They had no idea what awaited them in the basement of Haesnost. All they knew was that they had to get there.

When they arrived downstairs, Randore and Tortbold were standing back-to-back in the center of the hall with their sabers drawn as they searched for the elusive Glamis and Stellar.

The two invisible friends were standing at the far end of the corridor. When Glamis and Stellar saw Carmen and the others, they nodded toward the two cells nearest to them on the left, indicating that these were where the last of the prisoners were being held.

"We know that you're here, intruders," Tortbold warned in a slow, deliberate voice, as he stood with his back to Randore. "NOW SHOW YOURSELVES!"

When Carmen and her Souls remained silent, the duo of Keltan guards split up—each one running toward opposite ends of the hall, their swords raised over their heads.

Not seeing another option, Carmen Returned her wand, drew her own saber, and mentally prepared herself to battle the oncoming Tortbold.

"Give me the keys!" Blaze insisted. "I'll go free the final captives!"

Carmen promptly handed him the silver ring of keys. With great urgency, Blaze flew through the air over the heads of the guards to the pair of cells beside Glamis and Stellar. The two Souls on the ground pressed their bodies against the cell doors on either side of the hall to avoid Randore's sword as the guard came rushing by.

A couple of feet from the stairs, where Carmen stood, Tortbold swung his sword blindly through the air. The blade of the Light Sword collided with that of Tortbold's saber, and the booming clash of metal on metal echoed through the vast space.

"THEY'RE HERE!" Tortbold bellowed to Randore, as the young man turned around at the other end of the hall. "GET OVER HERE!"

On the orders of his superior, Randore ran back up the corridor as Blaze gaped into the two cells beside Glamis and Stellar. For a few moments, the Sarcan seemed unable to accept the sight behind the metal bars, but then he hastily began rummaging through the keys to find the appropriate one for each of the cell doors.

Carmen couldn't imagine who could possibly be inside those cells that would cause Blaze to look so shaken. Normally, she would call out and ask him who was there, but she was too hassled with dealing with Tortbold and Randore to speak with him now.

Carmen thrust her sword at Tortbold and began to duel with both of the guards. Being invisible, she had a major advantage over them, but she still had to fight to buy time for Blaze to set the final prisoners free.

As Carmen worked to fend off the guards, Anubis backed up several steps to stay out of her way. He kept in constant contact with Inpu upstairs, as it was crucial for him and the others to communicate in coordinating the successful breakout of Haesnost.

Randore pointed his sword at Carmen.

"Revealio!"

Carmen blocked the *Reveal* spell with her blade, and effectively avoided coming into the sight of the Keltan guards. She then unleashed a *Lightning Blade* attack on Randore, who was barely able to dodge the spell, just about losing his balance and falling to the floor as he ducked the sharpened edge of Carmen's invisible, electrically charged saber.

Next, Tortbold fired a *Black Sword* curse at Carmen. She fought it back with a *Light Barrier* defense.

The duel continued on for close to fifteen minutes as Blaze struggled to find a right key at the other end of the hall. Carmen glanced up at him on a handful of occasions while she was in battle. She couldn't understand why it was taking him so long to find the correct keys to unlock the two doors. At this rate, they would never get out of here in time.

"Sound the alarm!" Tortbold ordered, as he thwarted a strike from Carmen. "We need backup!"

On command, Randore dashed to the wall near the stairs and threw up a red switch, which caused a siren to blare through every single hall and room in Haesnost Prison.

With time now even *more* of an issue, Carmen had to break free from this sword fight and go help Blaze, who still had not yet been able to unlock either of the cells.

"Go to him!" Anubis urged, sensing Carmen's need to come to the aid of her Partner. *"I will manage against the guards until you can return."*

"Thanks, Anubis," Carmen said, as she shielded the two of them from another one of Tortbold's blows.

Carmen chased Tortbold and Randore back with a flaming *Karsthra Murtog* spell, which sent a scorching blast of fire into their faces. She then raced past the retreating guards and on toward Blaze.

The Sarcan was flying outside the last two cell doors, still tussling with the ring of keys. Anubis waited on the landing of the stairs to attack the guards the instant they advanced in his direction.

Carmen slid her sword back into its scabbard and soon arrived at the two neighboring cells. Without even thinking to look through the barred doors, Carmen immediately questioned Blaze.

"What's happening?" she asked. "None of these keys work?"

"Carmen, you're here!"

For a split second, Carmen thought that she was going crazy, as she turned her head at the sound of her mother's voice.

"Mom?"

Isabella Fox and her Sarcan, Airian, were standing at the cell door and gazing through the bars at her.

In the cell next to theirs, Flare was flying beside William, who was smiling cheerfully out at his daughter, whom he could not see from behind his door. All of them appeared to be unharmed, but Carmen was nonetheless appalled to see them here in this horrible prison in the World of Darkness.... She was suddenly feeling overwhelmed with sadness.

"How.... Why did they capture you?" Carmen asked, her voice trembling as she put her face to the bars of her mother's cell.

"We were detained just three days ago," Isabella said. "A small group of Keltans got across the Impassable Barrier, looking to capture Kelmarsian adults to help stifle Merlin's front against Triedastron.... We were out walking in the forest one morning last week when we were ambushed. There were ten other people taken with us."

"They brought us down here because the floor above this one was filled," William explained.

"It's vacant now," Carmen informed both of them, trying her hardest to remain calm. "We came here tonight to free Inpu, and all of the others that we could.... I'm going to break you out of here."

"We need Tortbold's set of keys," Blaze told her. "I've tried every one of Randore's, and none of them fit."

Her hope dipping just a little, Carmen glanced back at the two Keltan guards. Anubis was using a selection of mind spells to cause them to temporarily forget where they were, and why they were there. She had to hurry and grab Tortbold's keys while she had the chance. Any minute now, additional guards would be arriving from other parts of the prison.

Carmen sprinted up the hallway without a second thought, her eyes fixed on the keys fastened to Tortbold's belt. Tortbold staggered back as Anubis attacked him with a *Telepathic Strike* spell. The Haesnost guard instantly staggered, then fell backwards to the floor.

Carmen ran to his side and unlatched the ring of keys from his leather belt. Tortbold's dark eyes were unfocused, his mouth was agape, and a narrow stream of saliva was running down the side of his face. Before he could recover from the attack, Carmen got up and jogged back down to Blaze, Glamis, and Stellar.

When she got to her mother's cell, she slid the first silver key into the lock of her door and turned it. No luck. She then tried the same key on her father's door.... It didn't match that lock either. Carmen moved on to the next key without delay.

As Carmen tried to find the matching two keys, the prison alarm endlessly boomed through the corridors of Haesnost, adding to her stress.

Following more than ten failed attempts, she finally found the matching key for Isabella and Airian's cell. She turned it and unlocked the door, and the two Kelmarsians came rushing out. Carmen gave her mother a brief hug.

Isabella and Airian stood beside Carmen as she worked the next key into William and Flare's door. Just then, Carmen heard the pounding of footsteps moving quickly through the upstairs hallway.

The rest of the guards! she thought, terror-stricken. *We need to move fast!*

Carmen placed key after key into the lock, but she just couldn't locate the right one for her father's door. She was becoming ever more frustrated as her precious seconds slipped away with nothing achieved.

"Inpu says that more guards are on their way downstairs!" Anubis told Carmen, confirming her suspicion. *"We need to get your parents and their Sarcans out of here, now!"*

"I know!" she shouted back to him, as the now delirious duo of Randore and Tortbold were lying on the floor, fighting to stay conscious. "I'm trying to find the last key so that we can leave!"

"You'll get it!" William said, his green eyes twinkling. "I believe in you!"

"Don't give up!" Stellar added supportively. "It's got to be *one* of these."

Carmen's body was strained by her nervousness. Her hands were shaking, and beads of perspiration were rolling down her face. There were only three keys left now. If none of these were the right one, she would never be able to free her father and Flare.

It was difficult to say the least...but Carmen eventually pushed past her doubts and shoved the first of the final group of keys into the lock and hoped.... It would not turn.

There was shouting coming from the jail's upper level, but the thick stone of the prison floors and walls muffled the words. The loud siren was starting to make Carmen's ears ring, but she couldn't hear it over the noise of the high-pitched alarm.

She fitted the second to last key into the cell's keyhole, but this one didn't work either. That left only the final key....

All of a sudden, a small army of Keltan guards, followed by a pair of Sentry Hounds, came charging down the stairs at the opposite end of the corridor. Anubis had to rush into the hallway to get out of their way.

With a soft *click*, Carmen turned the key in the lock of her father's cell. William Fox and his Sarcan, Flare, pushed open the door and ran out. And though he couldn't see her, William was still somehow able to find Carmen's face and kiss her lightly on the cheek.

"That's my girl, Carmen," he said proudly. "Thank you. You're amazing."

"You're welcome," Carmen said with a grin, wiping a layer of sweat from her brow. But her happiness would be short-lived.

The four new Keltan guards and the two Sentry Hounds were standing at the bottom of the staircase. All of the guards were male, and had the same burly appearances as the first two.

The Sentry Hounds were brown muscular dogs with large heads and eyes the color of blood. Their teeth were curved and sharp. The creatures were staring at Carmen and the others, simply waiting for their Masters' commands to attack.

Tortbold and Randore were unconscious on the floor as a result of Anubis's powerful mind spells. The Jackal was standing to the side of them, gazing across at the adversaries who had just arrived.

"How are we going to get past them?" Carmen asked her friends, her confidence wavering.

"We fight our way through," William decided, drawing a saber from the scabbard beneath his blue and silver robes.

When he had his sword in hand, he fixed his eyes on the enemy sorcerers and creatures, squaring his shoulders in determination.

Isabella bravely drew her own sword from the belt that she wore under her matching robes. So long as they were able to fight, she and her husband were clearly not going to let Carmen and her friends go into battle alone. It was that courage that granted Carmen the strength to fight on.

Feeling stronger now than ever before, Carmen unsheathed the Light Sword...and she and the others charged forward.

There was shouting and the clashing of swords as Carmen, her parents, and their friends combated their opponents. The creatures worked jointly against the Sentry Hounds while the sorcerers dueled the Keltan guards.

Carmen and her mother confronted a couple of the guards together. William battled with the other two Keltans alone, stepping over the lifeless bodies of Randore and Tortbold as he crossed blades with the active guards.

They had to keep moving, as Carmen and her companions didn't know if any more guards were on their way. Anubis continued to communicate with Inpu upstairs throughout the fight, even as he battled alongside his friends. For now, it seemed that the upper floor was calm.

The conflict carried on for almost twenty minutes, with Carmen and her group advancing slowly toward the stairs. They were just about to the first step...when an unexpected shout of fury cut through the air.

"THIS IS WHAT HAPPENS WHEN I ALLOW WEAKLINGS TO CARRY OUT THE *MASTER'S* WORK!" Triedastron roared from the upstairs hallway.

Horrorstruck, and momentarily petrified with fear by the sound of Triedastron's voice, Carmen was nearly stabbed in the side by one of the Keltans' swords, but Isabella stepped in and threw up a magical shield just in time.

As much as Carmen dreaded the thought of facing Triedastron, it was crucial to get upstairs right now.... But she knew that in order to escape the basement, she had to cast a potent spell that she would only use when absolutely necessary.

Carmen ran one complete circle around the group of battling figures to enable her spell to affect each and every Keltan fighter present.

Pointing her sword at her targets, she shouted, *"Fires of the Sarcan!"*

In a bright burst of scarlet flames, Carmen's fiery Sarcan exploded from the point of her sword and stampeded down the hall. The Keltan guards and Sentry Hounds were forced to scatter to escape the speeding spell.

Now with a clear path to the stairs, Carmen, her parents, and their friends hurtled up the steps and out into the upstairs passageway.

When they emerged in the hall, Triedastron was standing in the middle of the corridor of empty cells. His lined face was the same shade as his burgundy robes, and contorted with utter rage. He had his wand pointed steadily at Carmen and her companions.

"Your journey ends *here*," he said, in a fatally serious voice. His dark brown eyes were livid. "No one steals my prisoners and leaves alive…. Prepare to meet your death, *kelscum.*"

Then he raised his wand.

"The Master's Supremacy!"

A huge shock of thunder rocked the stone prison. Seconds later, a rapidly growing dark sphere appeared at the crown of Triedastron's wand.

Not again! Carmen thought, panicked.

The cursed black sphere suddenly exploded. Without thinking, Carmen lunged forward.

"Force of Strength!" she cried, slashing her sword through the air.

As the dark onslaught of poisonous daggers fired from Triedastron's wand, a huge gust of wind rushed from Carmen's sword and blew the Master of Keltan's curse back toward him—like a speeding missile firing across the hall.

Before he could escape, the two spells crashed into Triedastron in a blast so intense that it sounded like a huge cannon being fired, sending him flying backwards down the corridor. He smashed hard into the stone wall at the end of the hall with a *BANG*—producing a cloud of ashen dust that billowed throughout the passageway.

Not waiting around to see Triedastron reemerge out of the dust storm, Carmen and her parents and friends raced to Inpu's cell, where the Jackal was waiting with Dagtar. Once inside, they climbed out through the window and onto Dagtar's back one by one. It was a tight squeeze…but all ten of them somehow found a way to fit.

Just as soon as everyone was aboard, the shining emerald Dragon swiftly flew Inpu, Carmen and her parents, and their friends away from Haesnost—back up toward the darkened ceiling of Keltan. Though they were all exhausted and over-wrought from what had just transpired, Carmen's Kelmarsian ancestors were so thrilled to be free that it made for the most joyous flight that Carmen and her Souls had ever taken to-gether.

While they were flying south toward the Impassable Bar-rier, Carmen suddenly remembered that she still had to give Dagtar his Christmas present, and so she took the silvery brace-let engraved with the flame out of her pocket.

Holding steady to Dagtar's saddle, she leaned down over his shoulder and fitted it to his right front leg. Though he wouldn't get the chance to admire the gift until he returned to the World of Light, she wanted him to have it before she and her friends left the realms of the afterlife once again, as none of them knew just when they would be back.

Nearing the golden line of light at the southern end of the cavern, Inpu enlightened his friends with the news that they had managed to free all of the prisoners from Haesnost that night. And so it was with much elation that Carmen and her Souls parted ways with Inpu and the rest of the Kelmarsians at the Impassable Barrier to return home to Kelmar. Their jour-ney to the sanctum of evil, however terrifying, had been worth every moment.

CHAPTER TWENTY-TWO
A CLASS IN THE AFTERLIFE

The first thing that Carmen did after she and her friends got back to Thunder Academy was work on deciphering the final two Secrets of Kelmar. She had already deciphered the first Secret a few months ago, and now with the last of the Secrets and Merlin's cipher disk in her possession, she could put the pieces together, and with any luck, restore order to the Kelmarian spirit realms.

Carmen sat at the table in her room with her Souls of Destiny, Merlin's cipher disk in front of her. She also had his maps, on the back of which would appear his instructions, and the parchment that she had used to write down all three Secrets in their ciphertext forms, as well as the plaintext version of the first one. Carmen and her friends were worn out and weakened from the long trip to Keltan, but each of them still found the strength from within to push ahead, working to solve the Master of Kelmar's puzzle that very same day. Their ambition to finally end the war between Kelmarsia and Keltan served as their motivation to get through this last challenge.

Carmen read the second Secret over again to refresh her memory before she started to decipher it.

The music is the Best, art won me tonight.

With that ciphertext phrase in her mind, she unfolded Merlin's instructions, which he had magically written on the back of his drawn maps of Kelmar and the two afterworlds. As Carmen gazed down at the paper, words began scribbling across the surface of the parchment in glossy black ink—instructions for deciphering the second Secret of Kelmar.

To decipher the first word of the second Secret, rotate the movable disk three full turns clockwise.

Carmen reached for the cipher disk, and then carefully turned the smaller top plate as instructed. She matched up each of the three letters of the first word with the corresponding letters on the stationary bottom plate.

The became *But.*

Carmen wrote down the new word beneath the original one, and then glanced down to read Merlin's next set of directions.

For the second word, rotate the movable disk one full turn counterclockwise.

Carmen did as she was told, and *music* turned into *ahead.*

She continued on with the rest of the message, turning the movable disk in different directions, and with varying quantities of rotations, every one or two words. After ten minutes, she had the second Secret deciphered in its entirety. Carmen read the new message aloud to her friends.

But ahead of the Dawn, the sky is darkest.

Before Carmen and her Souls got the chance to even begin considering the possible meaning of the second message, Merlin's words of praise appeared on the parchment beneath his previous set of directions.

Very good. This just leaves the third Secret.

Carmen and her friends realized that it was of greater importance that they decipher the third Secret before thinking about the second one in depth, and so they waited anxiously for the last set of instructions to appear. Their adrenaline was keeping them going, their exhilaration at the idea of deciphering the final Secret filling them with hope even though their minds and bodies were severely fatigued from their adventures in Keltan. Carmen was especially excited. In a matter of minutes, she would have the solution for restoring harmony in the Worlds Triad. While awaiting Merlin's subsequent instructions, she read the third ciphertext message over again.

Be loved to run Back, Dance the Song with friends in tow.

Shortly after this, Merlin's second group of directions for the day began to appear.

To decipher the first word, rotate the movable disk one-half turn clockwise.

With her fingertips trembling, Carmen moved the top plate.... *Be* on the movable disk lined up with *To* on the fixed one. As always, she wrote down the plaintext word under the ciphertext one.

Now make two and one-half turns clockwise.

Loved then became *bring,* and *to* became *on.*

Carmen worked diligently to decipher the third Secret, her Souls watching with anticipation as she completed the very last rotations of the top plate. Once she had deciphered all of the words, Carmen put down her quill and read the new sentence out loud.

To bring on the Dawn, Light and Dark must coexist as one.

Carmen stared at her own handwriting on the parchment...unsure of what to think. To help her make better sense of the deciphered Secrets, she read all three messages together. Her friends listened attentively.

Of Light and Dark, there sets a Dawn.
But ahead of the Dawn, the sky is darkest.
To bring on the Dawn, Light and Dark must coexist as one.

"That's *it?*" Stellar asked, after she had finished. "What does that even mean? I was under the impression that the Secrets were supposed to be some grand collection of knowledge that would tell us how we could bring about the end of the war...or *something* like that. This is basically just a poem, right?"

Carmen silently read the messages over one more time. Stellar had a valid point.... How were they supposed to use these phrases to save Kelmar from the wrath of Triedastron? Merlin had made no mention of that to them. She could already feel a headache coming on as she continued to stare blankly at the plaintext messages on the parchment.

"I don't understand either," Blaze admitted, reading over Carmen's shoulder. He sighed, disappointed. "There must be something to this that we're missing.... We just have to think about it."

"These sentences alone don't make much sense," Carmen said, leaning her heavy head in her hand. "Why would Merlin protect and treasure these phrases so much if they had no significance to them?"

"We must read beyond the words to uncover their true meaning," Anubis said, placing his paw up on the parchment. *"Things are not always what they first appear to be. Let's say, for example, if one were to look past the apparent simplicity of the sentences.... In theory, we could derive deeper meaning from the basic choice of words, and the order in which they are placed.... These phrases appear to be laden with symbolism, and the key words are capitalized."*

Carmen studied the Secrets more closely, and then tried to observe the words in ways that she hadn't before, in an attempt to draw new information from them. She hadn't even given much thought to the fact that some select words were written in uppercase.

"I'm guessing that Light and Dark refer to Kelmarsia and Keltan," Carmen said, thinking out loud. "Light and Dark together make Dawn...but before Dawn comes, the sky is the darkest that it ever is the entire night. This could be taken literally...or it could be saying that before the end of the war, the sky is very dark in Kelmar because of the storms.... *To bring on the Dawn, Light and Dark must coexist as one...."*

"What *is* the Dawn, exactly?" Glamis wondered. "Perhaps the Secrets are using Dawn in a figurative sense to describe the resolution to the crisis in the Worlds Triad."

"That could be," Carmen said. "I'm not really sure."

"We just need to figure out how this information can help us to defeat Triedastron," Blaze said. "It's only beneficial to us if we know how to use it."

"No matter...I think that, at this point, we should all rest for the evening," Anubis suggested, glancing at the starry sky outside the window. *"We've done all that we can tonight. In the coming days, our minds will be more refreshed...and we can come to some more definite conclusions."*

"I second that thought," Stellar agreed, looking weary as he jumped down off of his chair. "Let's get some sleep."

Carmen sighed as she folded up her papers and tucked them away in the pocket of her robes. She stood up.

"Well, I'm happy with what we did today," she told her friends, in spite of tonight's disappointment. "We accomplished some amazing things."

"Indeed. We did," Anubis said. *"My father tells me that the Kelmarsian prisoners that we freed returned safely to the World of Light with Dagtar. He and the others also wanted to thank all of us for our help.... My father is now working with Merlin to seal up the Impassable Barrier once again."*

"That's great to hear," Carmen said with a tired smile, as she walked over to the back of the room and sat down on the edge of her bed. She began taking off her boots. "I expect that they'll have better luck with the Protections this time around."

"They should. We've certainly done *our* part," Stellar said. "Now it's up to them to make the changes that will keep their world safe."

"Yeah...we have enough on our hands in keeping *Kelmar* safe," Carmen concurred. "Being responsible for two worlds is pretty daunting."

Spring rolled into Sarcanian Valley with a mixture of warm and cold days, a good amount of rain, and consecutive weeks of windy mornings. Carmen had written a letter to her grandfather the night after she and her friends had gotten back from Keltan with the final Secret. She told him how they had escaped Triedastron's attack, and been able to free all of the prisoners trapped in Haesnost with the assistance of Dagtar. Though she hadn't had much of a chance to talk with her parents, Carmen told Blaine how she had saved *them* from the prison as well.

In the days following Carmen's return, there were thunderstorms all throughout Kelmar, not caused by fighting, but by Triedastron's anger at losing his valuable prisoners and the chance to kill Carmen and her friends that night. Nobody knew for certain when exactly the Master of Keltan had discovered that Carmen had taken Merlin's cipher disk back, but judging by the intensity of the storms in the five days after, it certainly seemed like he had already by that point, and was seething with bitterness because of it.

Carmen had spent countless long evenings talking with Commander Haidar, her grandfather, and several others concerning the meaning behind the deciphered Secrets of Kelmar, but the months slowly passed with no new leads. So, unsure of what else to do, Carmen and her friends carried on with their daily activities in hopes that something would eventually trigger a realization within one of them as to what to do with the trio of Secrets.

There had been no Phantom sightings in Kelmar in the months since Carmen's trip, and while this was outwardly good news, it also made many Kelmarians uneasy about what was happening with the Master of Keltan and his forces. It remained a fear that the Phantoms were regrouping, and planning for another major strike. Kelmarian officials remained on watch for any signs of impending attacks, or rumors of new plots. Carmen continued to monitor *The Kelmarian Review* for daily reports on Phantom activity.

With the coming of April, most of the training in Sarcanian Valley took place outdoors. Commander Haidar taught the Captains new, advanced Kelmarian magic, in addition to Kelmarsian Healing spells. He also trained them more thoroughly in flight by putting them through a series of flying drills. Carmen suspected that Officer Sheridae was keeping the Sarcan Captains busy with their own progressively more demanding lessons.

One warm and sunny mid-April morning, the Advanced Training students were assembled in a line out on the dueling fields as usual, waiting for their instructor to arrive. The class was buzzing with excitement on this particular day, as there was talk that Haidar was going to take the Captains somewhere outside of Sarcanian Valley for their lesson; something that he hadn't done once yet this year.

Shortly after dawn, Haidar soared down from the rooftop of Thunder Academy to meet his students as he normally did, landing effortlessly in front of them.

"Good morning, class," Haidar said, greeting the Captains calmly, as he stood before them dressed in his scarlet and gold military uniform. "Today, we're going to do things a little differently than usual. We're going to take a field trip to Caldrenon—a small town just north of Mortrock Forest."

The Captains exchanged energized looks with those around them. They had never before traveled anywhere outside of Sarcanian Valley and Mortrock Forest for training.

"We will be visiting two people who will be teaching you about death and the afterlife," Haidar continued. "Because we will be battling Phantom Warriors and other Keltan fighters again sooner or later, you will need to learn how to properly combat opponents who cannot die. These people who will be speaking to you today know much about this subject, and have many important lessons to share with you."

Several of the Sarcan Captains began whispering spiritedly with one another. Haidar waited patiently for his students to quiet down before he delivered the remainder of his instruction.

But without even a word from the well-respected Commander, the low roar of talking promptly quieted, and Haidar resumed speaking.

"Before we go, I would like you to think about what you will be faced with in the future," he said. "As I'm sure you remember, in Kelmarsia and Keltan, the sorcerers and creatures are already deceased. Hence, your strategy for combating Triedastron's fighters, as well as your mindset for battle, must both change accordingly. If you are in battle against an opponent who cannot be killed, what do you do? You may very well find yourself in this precise situation, with which you are still unfamiliar and untrained to deal with. After today, I believe that you will be better equipped to prevail in battles under these types of circumstances."

Haidar began to walk slowly down the line of Captains as he carried on with his talk.

"The afterlife will be unlike anything that you've ever experienced," he said, his eyes flickering to Carmen and Blaze. "You can't afford to make the mistake of thinking that you will be victorious there using the same strategies that you would employ against mortal opponents. The sorcerers and creatures that exist in these realms have a different way of thinking than we do...particularly those in Keltan. With the addition of the Magicon, Triedastron and the other Keltans believe that they are indomitable."

Haidar's expression was that of disgust. He clearly despised the attitude of many of those inhabiting the World of Darkness.

"The environments are also infinitely different in Kelmarsia and Keltan," he went on to explain. "Each realm favors the beings indigenous to that world, but *both* worlds favor departed spirits over the spirits of the living. Thus, no matter which of the two realms we are fighting in, we are *always* at a disadvantage to our enemies."

Not feeling particularly uplifted by this speech, the Sarcan Captains listened to their Commander's words with growing skepticism about their chances of success in overpowering Triedastron and his armies.... Their enthusiasm about the upcoming field trip had faded quite quickly with Haidar's fairly depressing talk.

Perhaps sensing his students' confidence slipping, Haidar concluded his opening lecture on a more inspiring note.

"Captains, this war is not yet over," he said, determined. "We still have a long way to go to triumph over our adversaries, but we have progressed that much closer to our goal over the many months that we have spent together. I am exceptionally proud of the growth that I have seen in each of you."

Haidar gazed over his class with confidence.

"We will now depart for Caldrenon together," he announced. "Masters, please summon your wings. All of you will follow me."

The Sarcan Masters did as they were told, and flew up into the cool spring air with their Commander and their Sarcans. They rose high above the red sandstone valley, and then turned toward the north. Flying in formation, the Masters and Sarcans followed their instructor over the green treetops of Mortrock Forest, which were bathed in stunning shades of orange light as the sun rose over North Kelmar.

Beyond the forests, they passed over rolling hills of bright green grass and moss-covered rocks, and soon, the peaceful village of Caldrenon came into sight beneath the passing clouds.

Standing in the shadows of the Barahir Mountains, the town of narrow and winding roads was lined with small, stone houses and shops with pointed roofs. Caldrenon was one of the oldest towns in all of Kelmar, and it had retained its rustic, appealing qualities even as the centuries had passed and ushered in new generations and traditions.

Haidar and his Sarcan Captains soared to the northern edge of town, to a tiny, one-story home on the corner of a side street. They touched down in the middle of a stone-laden path that snaked up to the front door.

The old house was square, and covered from top to bottom with rounded gray, white, and brown pebbles. A stone chimney rose up from the wood shingled roof. It was a lovely little home, and although it had undoubtedly been there for decades, it looked just as nice as it had when it was first built. There was a mellow, welcoming quality about it that made Carmen and the others want to go inside and stay for a while.

Haidar led his Captains up to the doorstep. The Sarcan Commander knocked on the painted green door and stood back on the porch with his students.

They soon heard shuffling footsteps inside the house, and seconds later, a short, plump man with white hair and light brown eyes answered the door. He was wearing sepia robes that had dark gold trim around the edges of the sleeves. The man had deep-set wrinkles lining his face, and his hands were spotted with age, yet he wore a radiant smile across a face that could easily have been mistaken for that of a man half his age.

"Commander Haidar, the Sarcan Captains, welcome!" the man said warmly, as he opened his door wider. "My wife and I are so honored to be able to speak with you."

He bowed to them.

"Hello, Irwick," Haidar replied graciously, returning him his own deep bow. Then he turned and looked around at his class. "Students, this is Master Irwick Malcoff."

"It's just wonderful to meet all of you," Irwick said, beaming at the young sorcerers and Sarcans. "Come in! Come in!"

Haidar and the Sarcan Captains crossed the threshold into the living room of the quaint home, and Irwick closed the door quietly after them.

There was a beige loveseat in the center of the scuffed hardwood floor, neighbored by two red plaid couches placed perpendicularly to the smaller sofa. A stone fireplace stood at the back of the space, as well as a pair of antique wooden chairs—one sitting on either side of the couches. A doorway at the back of the room led off into the kitchen.

Irwick's wife emerged from the kitchen as Haidar and his students moved farther into the living room. The sorceress wore pastel pink robes that had a purple floral design. She was just a little taller than her husband, and had bright blue eyes and thick white hair that fell just below her ears. It was easy to see that she had been very pretty when she was young.

"Well hello, everyone! Oh, it's so nice to have visitors," she said in a joyful voice, as she walked to her husband's side and bowed to their guests. "I'm Laurelin Malcoff. Please have a seat." She motioned politely toward the couches. "We put the extra sofas out just for you."

Irwick and Laurelin walked about ten steps and sat down on the loveseat as Haidar marched to one of the two antique chairs. The Sarcan Masters fit comfortably on the two plaid couches. Their Sarcans sat in a line atop the back of each couch.

"So," Haidar began, gazing toward the elderly couple, "the reason that I asked you to speak with my students to-day…is because the both of you have an unusual amount of experience and knowledge regarding death and eternal life. You also have a deep understanding of these topics that few others possess. I believe that the Captains will benefit from your story, and in having you talk to them, I hope that they will come away with greater insight into these subjects, which I alone could not have taught them."

Haidar then looked out at his students.

"I am going to interview the Malcoffs to get their views on a variety of topics related to the afterlife," he informed them. "Feel free to ask questions at any time. I would like for

491

this to be an interactive experience, as opposed to just a lecture."

"Yes, that's right," Irwick agreed. He leaned forward in his seat and made eye contact with the students, keenly aware that they were watching him with all of their attention.

"Irwick, please enlighten my students about your...condition," Haidar said. "As promised, I have not told them yet."

"Oh, yes, of course," Irwick replied. He took a deep breath before speaking again.

"Well, you see, Captains..." Irwick began, glancing briefly at his wife. "Laurelin and I...are both immortal."

Carmen swallowed and nearly choked. The room then fell unnaturally silent.

The students gaped at Irwick with bewilderment, many of their mouths falling open in shock. None of them could believe that immortals really existed in their world.

"And how did you become immortal?" Haidar asked, in a composed voice, apparently having known of the Malcoffs' secret.

Irwick sat back in his chair. Laurelin rubbed his shoulder supportively.

"Ah...I remember it vividly," he began. "One afternoon, my wife and I were sitting out on a bench in the middle of Caldrenon...when a young, pale man with short black hair emerged from an alleyway and approached us. We had never seen him before. He must have been...in his early twenties, I would say," Irwick recalled. "The streets were unusually quiet that day. The three of us were the only ones out in that part of town.... I later learned that this was no coincidence. The stranger had magically forced everyone else to stay indoors for the afternoon without their knowledge."

Carmen didn't like where this story was going.... It sounded like this young man had come with a purpose—one that was menacing in nature.

"As he walked up to us, he had his wand drawn...and there was a strange glint in his dark eyes that immediately made me highly suspicious of him," Irwick said. "I asked him what he wanted, but he just continued to stand there, no more than ten feet away from us, with an iniquitous smile on his face. And the longer he stood there...the more strongly I sensed that he had destructive intentions."

Irwick took a reflective pause, peering thoughtfully out through the sunlit windows on the wall behind the Captains.

"So this went on for about fifteen minutes," Irwick said. "Finally, just out of pure intuition, I summoned my own wand. I stood up and demanded to know why this man was watching us. But then...in one smooth motion, the man took one step back...raised his wand with one hand, and arched his other arm like a rearing serpent. He cast a deadly curse known as *the Unleashing of Darkness,* and Laurelin and I dove to the ground to escape the spell. But instead of the curse hitting us, it flew over our heads and struck a circular mirror that was mounted on the lamppost standing next to the bench. The curse bounced off of that mirror, and in doing so, developed the opposite effect of its originally intended purpose. So, when it did come back and hit us only seconds later, instead of killing us...it made us unable to die."

Irwick gazed at the students, perfectly composed, and then spoke to them in a softer voice.

"This was close to three thousand years ago," he murmured. "One day, centuries after this had happened, I learned that that young man...was Triedastron."

Carmen and a number of others released audible gasps. Carmen felt like someone had just dropped an iron weight on her head. It was a full two minutes before Irwick resumed his story.

"After three more unsuccessful attempts to kill us, Triedastron ran from the scene, cursing in anger over his failure. That was when we realized what had happened to us," Irwick said. "Any one of those attacks that followed the first should have destroyed us just as soon as it struck us.... But none of them did. That was because Triedastron had unintentionally turned us into what we are now…immortals."

"Has anything like this ever happened since then?" Amaris asked. "It seems really strange for a spell to change its objective once it's already been cast—especially one that strong."

Irwick shrugged.

"Not that I'm aware of, but who knows? I would tend to believe though…that if similar incidents *have* occurred, in which people became unable to die, there are very few who would admit to being like us," he said. "It can be a very isolating existence, as Laurelin and I know firsthand."

Irwick's wife nodded in agreement.

"If we didn't have each other to talk to, and grieve with when our friends and family members passed away…it would be horrible," Laurelin said, placing her right hand over her husband's left. Her blue eyes glistened with sorrow. "It would be…utterly unbearable."

Carmen looked sadly at the elderly woman seated beside her husband. She couldn't begin to imagine all of the tragedies and difficult times that she had been forced to live through as a result of her situation.

"Why did Triedastron target you?" Carmen asked, unable to hold back her question. "Do you have any idea?"

Laurelin and Irwick looked at each other. Irwick spoke first.

"In truth, we didn't know for years…and that's what made it even harder to accept," he replied. "After the attack...we gave a lot of thought as to why it had happened to us, out of all of the people who he could have picked."

"What we eventually realized was that Triedastron had likely selected us as the perfect target because of our advanced age," Laurelin added. "Neither of us came from a privileged family, and we are certainly not descendants of any famously powerful sorcerers. He chose us simply because he assumed that we would be less physically able to resist."

"He likely watched us for days, and then followed us to that spot in town," Irwick said. "We were just the unfortunate victims of Triedastron's attempt at trying out a new spell.... He probably wanted to test out this curse on a couple of living sorcerers who he believed wouldn't put up much of a fight. He wished to see just how potent it was before he used it against one of his true enemies."

"That's awful...." Carmen said, feeling genuinely sorry for what the two elderly sorcerers had gone through. "Aren't you angry over what he did to you?"

"Yes, for *an entire century* we were, in fact," Irwick admitted. "Shortly after it happened, Laurelin and I knew that we would lead an unnatural existence from then on.... It's not normal, or right in any way, for people to live forever. It destroys the whole meaning of life itself."

Haidar listened closely. He took a little time to consider the Malcoffs' words before posing his next question.

"What else can you tell us about your existence as immortals?" Haidar asked. "How are your daily lives different than they were before the accident?"

"It's a shame to say, but we don't value day-to-day life the way that we used to," Laurelin answered, her tone filled with regret. "We can't truly appreciate each day as mortals should, because for us, the days have no beginning and no end. We just drift through the months and years as shadows.... We don't grow any older, and we never change. We remain...exactly as we were, nearly three thousand years earlier."

"Our Partners, our family, and our friends have since passed away, and yet we carry on without them as empty shells of ourselves. This is not the life that we would have chosen for ourselves. *Nobody* would want this," Irwick said, shaking his head. "It's sad...and lonely."

"That's why we were so happy when Haidar told us that he wanted you to come see us," Laurelin told the students. "We don't have many friends left anymore.... Hardly anyone wants to associate with people like us. Most see us as inhuman—and they believe that they could never relate to us."

There was a long and difficult pause, during which Carmen could feel the misery hanging in the air.

"Generally speaking, the average person would consider it the greatest of blessings to be immortal," Irwick remarked. "How many individuals do you know who say they would love to live forever? But in reality...this life is more of a curse than the one that Triedastron attempted to murder us with."

Carmen listened to the Malcoffs' story with a blend of sadness and fascination. She had never even considered what life would be like for someone who couldn't die.... The few times that the thought had entered her mind before now, she had imagined it with the immaturity of those that Irwick described—believing that living forever would be the ideal existence. This class was beyond doubt an eye-opening glimpse into a most abnormal reality.

"Is there anything that you can tell my students about the psychology of how immortals think?" Haidar asked. "In due course, my students will be battling Keltan sorcerers and creatures that, while not immortal in the true meaning of the word, are already dead, and thus cannot die again."

Irwick took a couple of moments to think about his answer.

"I'm not sure if Keltan thinking would be exactly the same as ours," Irwick said slowly, speaking candidly to the Captains, "but essentially what it comes down to with any immortal being is that...they have nothing to lose. No matter what you do to them, or how hard you fight, they will continue to exist in their spirit forms evermore. You, as mortals, on the other hand, still risk dying at the hands of the Keltans, just as you would anyone else. Although you will be fighting as spirits in the afterlife, you will not exist forever unless *you* die, too. Your motivation and purpose for fighting is dramatically different from your opponents'. You have to fight to stay alive—not to destroy your enemies."

"But how can we win in a war against an unconquerable enemy?" Shea asked.

"Now I never said that the Keltans were unconquerable," Irwick reminded him, glancing over at the blue-eyed Sarcan Captain. "I just said that they couldn't *die* under any circumstance. You have to find another way to defeat them; one that doesn't involve killing them."

Irwick then looked out at the rest of the students, a contemplative expression on his face.

"I've been alive for far more years than any man ever should, yet I still do not have all of the answers," Irwick finally said, sighing. He ran his fingers through his white hair before adding, "What I do know...is that if you take chances and believe in what you're doing, eventually, the answers usually come. Sometimes all you have to do...is ask for the help in finding them."

Carmen shivered. It was almost as though Irwick were speaking directly to her and her current dilemma with the Secrets of Kelmar.

The Sarcan Captains quietly absorbed Irwick's words and remained still. Laurelin then shared a piece of her own wisdom with the young students.

"As you're battling the Keltans, bear in mind that, while they have the advantage in being able to survive forever, you can still *outsmart* them," she said. "Everyone, immortal or not, has weaknesses. To conquer any enemy, you have to take the initiative to *find* their weaknesses, and capitalize on them, even when all hope seems lost."

Irwick nodded.

"*That* is the moment in which you have to look into the eyes of the enemy and say, 'I may not have the means to defeat you...but I can still obtain victory.'" He gazed around at the Captains, and smiled.

"We feel that if you believe in yourselves, the Worlds Triad can be restored to what it was always meant to be...and a new era of harmony can arise."

Irwick and Laurelin looked at peace as they sat across from the students. Irwick had his arm around his wife's shoulder, and when the two of them turned and gazed at each other, it was with an admiration that was rarely seen in society, let alone between two people who had been together for thousands of years.

In a showing of respect and appreciation, Haidar applauded the couple, as did all of the Sarcan Captains. Carmen fully understood why Haidar had brought her and her classmates here.... The point of this trip wasn't just to learn about immortality, or to get a small look into the realities of two people who live through it every day; rather, it was to gain motivation from their story, and to realize that no enemy is truly unstoppable.

At the Malcoffs' invitation, the students stayed for lunch before they would return to Sarcanian Valley in the afternoon. Irwick and Laurelin continued to speak with them as they ate, and the generous couple even invited them back anytime that they wished to come.

It was bittersweet for Carmen and the others to leave. They had been so touched by the couple's incredible tale of hardship and unending strength that they almost wished they could stay with them for a longer time. As young and open-minded students, they did not judge the Malcoffs the way that most others did, and just as Haidar had promised, they walked away from this meeting with insight that they otherwise would not have obtained.

As Haidar and his students were gliding back over the Barahir Mountains that encircled Sarcanian Valley that afternoon, the Sarcan Commander turned to look back at his students flying behind him.

"Just as you learned this morning, living forever is not the fantasy that most believe it to be," he said. "But the wisdom that one gains over an existence of so many years can reward us with a new appreciation for life."

That wisdom, and the mark that it left on each and every one of them, was something that Carmen knew she and her classmates would never forget.

CHAPTER TWENTY-THREE
RISE OF THE PHANTOMS

O ne evening near the end of June, Carmen was awakened in the middle of the night by a frantic knocking on the door of her bedroom in Thunder Academy. She could hear the wind howling outside her window, and her friends stirring in the darkness near her. She blindly turned on the lights—and then stumbled across the room, rubbing her eyes.

Carmen opened her door to Head Councilor, Peruveus Seth, who looked pale and nervous. His eyes were bloodshot behind his horn-rimmed glasses, and his thinning gray-brown hair was disheveled, as though he had just woken up himself. He was wearing a royal blue and gold robe over his night-clothes.

"There's been a Phantom sighting just south of Pyramid City," he said urgently. "We need our Sarcan Captains to head them off before they can break through the gates. The capital has substantial Protections on it, but we fear that the Phantoms have been plotting their capture of the city for the past several months now."

"What?" Carmen asked, suddenly wide-awake. "How will we get there?"

"There is an airship waiting for you and your classmates out on the dueling fields," Seth said quickly. "Commander Haidar is already there."

Taking a moment to allow her body to catch up with her speeding mind...Carmen glanced back over her shoulder into her room. Her Souls of Destiny were all sitting up and staring out the door at Seth, their faces alert and aware.

"We wish you the best for a safe return," Seth said, wrapping his hands around Carmen's shoulders. "Pyramid City is preparing its defenses, should the Phantoms cross through the border. But we would like to avoid that scenario by any means possible."

"Yes, certainly," Carmen said at once. "We'll get ready and meet the others outside just as fast as we can."

Carmen shut the door of her room as Seth hurried off to alert the rest of the students of the news. She then rushed into the bathroom through the door near the back of her room to change out of her pajamas and into her sorcerer robes. Her Souls were hastily rising from their beds or the floor and stretching out their legs.

Less than a minute after Seth left, an early breakfast was delivered to Carmen and all of the other Captains in time so that they could eat before they left for battle.

Carmen and her friends shoveled in their food at a much faster rate than usual, with no time to enjoy the meal. They could hear the wind still gusting with substantial force out in the valley.

When they were finished eating, they left their empty plates on the table and rushed out of the bedroom, closing the door behind them.

In the hall, they ran into Akira, Naomi, and their Sarcans. Devoid of the need for conversation, they galloped down the stairs together to the school's main floor, and then out through the front doors of the castle.

As they expected, a large airship was sitting in the middle of the dueling fields beneath the darkened sky. The vessel was crafted of light, beige-colored wood, and had sturdy gray wings and three scarlet sails decorated with the Great Seal of Kelmar. The ship was lined with twenty-five cushioned seats arranged in five rows of five chairs each, most of which were already filled with Sarcan Captains—the Masters in the seats and their

501

Sarcans sitting either next to them, or atop the backs of the sorcerers' chairs. Commander Haidar was standing watchfully next to the craft, whose name was written across its bow in red paint—*The Fearless.*

Carmen and her friends walked swiftly down the front steps of the castle, all of them feeling reasonably nervous—but as prepared as they could be to meet Triedastron's army of Phantom Warriors. They had combated these foes before, most recently in the corridors of their own school when Triedastron had come to steal Merlin's cipher disk earlier in the term. In many ways, that battle seemed like it had taken place a very long time ago, yet it was still vividly etched in each of their minds, as though it had happened only yesterday.

When the students arrived down at the dueling fields, Haidar pointed them toward the wooden stairs leading up into the ship.

"We will be leaving very shortly," he said, his voice steady. "The Phantoms can travel at speeds that cannot be matched by airship, but *The Fearless* is among the fastest in the Army's fleet. With any luck, we should be able to intercept our enemies' route before they reach the entrance to the city."

Their minds spinning with thoughts about what was to come, Carmen and her friends marched past Haidar and climbed aboard the aircraft. They observed that the only seats grouped together that were left were three seats in the last row. The rest of the remaining seats were all individual ones scattered throughout the first four rows.

Carmen suggested that Anubis, Stellar, and Glamis sit next to one another in the final row, and that she and Blaze would share one of the empty seats in the row in front of them. Naomi, Akira, and their Sarcans claimed *their* seats in the front two rows.

As Carmen walked toward her seat, she realized that Shea was sitting next to the lone vacant chair, which she was headed toward. She hadn't talked to him at length in a while, but was excited at the thought.

The wind blowing her hair into her eyes, she walked past the other Captains to her chair, which was right up against the side of the ship. As she crossed the deck to her seat, she thought about how silly it was that she was so eager to sit next to Shea. She liked him as a friend…but nothing more than that.

"Hey, Carmen. Hey, Blaze." Shea greeted them with a friendly smile as they walked by him. Gia was seated atop the back of his chair. She was a light golden Sarcan with diamond-shaped green and cherry-colored markings.

"Hi, Shea. Hi, Gia," Carmen said, taking her seat. She had to keep pushing her hair behind her ears to stop it from flying into her face when a strong wind would pass through.

"That was something when Councilor Seth came to our rooms, wasn't it?" Shea remarked, as Carmen glanced over at him. "I have to admit, I was somewhat startled to see him standing in my doorway." He laughed. "Somehow that was what woke me up instead of the winds. I was still in my pajamas when I met him."

Carmen laughed.

"Yeah, me, too," she said. "I was pretty scared actually…. I knew that there was only one reason why Seth would come to see me; there had to be trouble somewhere."

Commander Haidar climbed up into the airship, and the door of the craft closed and locked automatically after him. He walked to the front of the ship and turned to face the Sarcan Captains. His expression was tense.

"Good morning, Captains. As Councilor Seth alluded to, we are heading to the Oldac Forests, which are just to the south of Pyramid City." Haidar raised his voice to be heard over the wind. "The Phantom Warriors are on their way to the capital as we speak. We must work to push them back, and foil their plot to attack the city."

Haidar paused for a moment, seeming to weigh his next words carefully.

"It is...rather crucial...that we stop the Phantoms here and now," he finally said. "If they can get into Pyramid City, we face a major threat not only to our own security in Sarcanian Valley but also to the security of the entire realm of Kelmar."

Just then, a strong gust of wind rushed through the ship's scarlet sails, a sign that all was not well in the Worlds Triad. The students remained silent as Haidar continued to speak.

"Our plan of attack is this," he said slowly. "As we approach the forests, I will cloak *The Fearless* into invisibility so that we catch the Phantoms off guard. We stay aboard the ship for as long as possible.... We are much safer in the air than we are on the ground, so we do not land until we have the enemy in our sight. After we have found them, we will land in a secure location, and move through the forests together as a Unit. We battle with the goal of driving the Phantoms as far away from Pyramid City as we can. The more we can weaken them, the easier this task will be.... Are we clear?"

"Yes, sir," the Captains replied.

With a satisfied nod, Haidar saluted his students and took his seat at the center of the first row of chairs. He then raised his right hand, indicating that the ship would be taking off.

Powered by its great wings, *The Fearless* rose up into the dark, early morning sky...and the Kelmarians of Thunder Academy flew off toward the north.

The ship started out slowly, but it didn't take much time for it to reach its peak speed. The warm, late spring wind rushed past the students' faces and through their hair as the ship soared ahead.

Carmen soon understood why Haidar had named this ship as one of the fastest in the Kelmarian Army's fleet. When she was flying, she usually liked to peer over the side of the airship and observe the scenery below, but as she looked down over *The Fearless,* it was hard to see much of anything. The ship was traveling at such a high speed as it flew over rivers, trees, and mountainsides that the continually changing landscape faded into a rush of colors.

"So, how are you doing?" Shea asked Carmen politely, as she sat back in her seat.

Carmen sighed. "Um…fine, I guess. I have no complaints. I just wish that I knew how to use the Secrets of Kelmar…. Then I could finally put an end to this war."

Shea listened calmly.

"I wouldn't worry too much about it," he said, sounding relaxed.

Then he motioned toward their classmates in front of them.

"We all trust that you'll figure it out when the time comes."

"Thanks," Carmen said shyly. "I hope so."

"Oh, I meant to ask you…" Shea said, "have you talked with your grandfather recently?"

"Yes, mostly just through letters, though," Carmen replied. "Why?"

"I was just wondering because of a note that I got from my parents yesterday. I thought you might want to know about it." Shea lowered his voice. "They told me that they've heard some disconcerting rumors about Maidak Kalvaro."

Carmen's eyes widened, and immediately, she was even more interested in what Shea was about to say than she was before.

Fortunately for both of them, Draven was sitting all the way up in the front row of seats, and most of the other Captains around them were also talking, so Carmen and Shea didn't have to worry about their classmate overhearing their conversation about his father.

"What did they say about him?" Carmen asked.

"Well, it looks like a lot of people are talking about Maidak going ahead and blocking Eli's appeal for a retrial," Shea whispered. "This happened a couple of weeks ago. It hasn't been in the paper because Maidak has pressured reporters to refrain from publishing an article about his latest move. He's trying to keep them mum about anything in regards to Eli.... He convinced them that any such article would compromise *your* safety."

"That's crazy. He's just making that up," Carmen said, knowing very well that Kalvaro couldn't care less about her safety, after trying to kill her himself. "So does this mean that Eli can't appeal again?"

"Yeah, it doesn't look like it," Shea muttered. "I think that he would need the support of at least half of Parliament for them to proceed with a retrial. With Maidak there, that's unlikely to happen. It's too bad.... I think that Eli is a good guy who's just had some bad luck."

"It sure is," Carmen said sadly, looking down at the deck of the airship. This disclosure that Kalvaro had blocked Eli's appeal was not good news to her at all.

Shea gazed sympathetically at her, and then tried to cheer her up a little.

"Things like this have a way of always working themselves out," he said supportively, his blue eyes sparkling. "Eli's situation shouldn't be any exception."

Carmen glanced at him, filled with appreciation. She had told Shea and a couple of other close friends how she believed that someone had cursed Eli, and forced him to give her the poisoned amulet. It meant a lot to her to know that Shea believed *her,* and not the government that had convicted Eli without sufficient evidence.

"You're right," she said, sitting up straighter in her seat. "We just need to stay positive."

The Fearless soared over the trees at the northern edge of Mortrock Forest. Blaze was talking with Gia and Carmen's other Souls about the impending battle while his Master conversed with her sorcerer classmates.

The Kelmarians would glide over the Oldac Forests within the next hour, and the conversation on board was instantly hushed by Haidar's raised hand at the front of the ship. Haidar summoned his wand, and afterward, instructed the other sorcerers to do the same while he cast the airship and everyone aboard into invisibility using *Inviscreen*.

As they sailed on over the trees, the ship slowed down significantly. There were still a couple of hours until sunrise, so the forests remained shrouded in the darkness of night.

Carmen and most of the other students sitting in the outer seats along the sides of *The Fearless* gazed down and tried to observe any movement below. They would end up spending nearly twenty minutes drifting slowly over the treetops before there was any sighting of the Phantom Warriors.

"I wonder where they are," Carmen whispered to Blaze. "Do you think that they're invisible?"

"No, I would doubt it," Blaze replied. "They don't know that we're coming, so there would be no reason for them to waste their magic on becoming invisible."

"There's someone over there," Shea murmured, pointing over the side of the ship.

Carmen and the others followed his eyes down to a clearing, where three hooded sorcerers dressed in long black robes were standing closely together and talking in low voices. Haidar observed them from the front of the ship, but the craft was too high up in the air to allow him to see their faces, which were cloaked in the shadows.

The Fearless flew noiselessly over the trio of Phantoms, and then beyond a cluster of trees toward another clearing. This one was empty. Haidar turned around to face his class.

"We are about to land," he told them, as the ship descended smoothly down to the patch of open grass. "Once on the ground, we will advance together toward the small group of Phantoms that we just saw. If they are here, the others can't be far away. If and when they make a move toward the north...we attack."

The Fearless touched down quietly on the grass. Haidar, the Sarcan Captains, Stellar, Glamis, and Anubis then climbed down one at a time off of the ship.

Haidar led his group silently through the trees, holding his wand out in front of him for protection. It was difficult for him and the others to see in the darkness, but any light from a wand would give them away to their enemies. They also had to be careful not to snap any branches, or make other distinct sounds that would suggest to the Phantoms that they had company.

As the Kelmarians drew closer to the Keltan sorcerers, a queasy feeling settled in Carmen's stomach. She heard the voices of Desorkhan, Lucifer Mondalaus, and Sevadia Nankarsa as those coming from the trio of hooded Phantoms.

"I just spoke with Denethor. There is a considerable quantity of Protections placed around the city," Mondalaus reported to the other two Magicon. "The Kelmarians must be aware of our presence."

"Let them have their little defenses," Nankarsa said in her shrill voice, with an unconcerned flip of her hand. "They have nothing strong enough to stop us from getting past the gates."

"Yes, I have no expectations for failure, Lucifer," Desorkhan said sharply to the sorcerer next to him. "Before long, the kelscum will see their precious golden city crumble...and that is just the start of it. Their days left to live are numbered to few."

Carmen and the others guardedly edged a little closer to the group of Phantoms. Desorkhan had his back to the Kelmarians.

"Well, let's get moving then!" Nankarsa said impatiently. "It's almost daylight!"

But just as she moved to walk away from the other two Phantoms, Desorkhan held his arm out to stop her.

"What is it?" Nankarsa snapped.

"We are no longer alone," the Dark Master murmured.

Desorkhan turned around and pointed his lit wand into the trees where Carmen and the others were hiding. They could see his pointed face and dark eyes beneath his hood.... Haidar motioned to his students to hold their fire. Nankarsa and Mondalaus gazed warily around Desorkhan's shoulders into the darkness.

"*Revealio!*"

A flash of silvery light burst from Desorkhan's wand and rushed through the trees. The Kelmarians instantly scattered in a dozen different directions, ducking down behind bushes and shrubs to escape the spell. Surprisingly...it worked.

When Desorkhan's spell failed to reveal any of them, the Dark Master lowered his wand, a confounded look on his face.

"You saw something?" Mondalaus asked. His voice was emotionless.

"No. I felt it," Desorkhan replied tersely. "Kelscum. I can sense their presence from miles away.... They're here in the woods."

Lucifer and Nankarsa stared into the darkened forest around them.

"You're right," Mondalaus said, a moment later. "I feel it, too. There are a number of them...at least twenty."

"If they think that they've got us outnumbered, they're in for a nice little surprise," Desorkhan said, in a louder voice. Then he raised his right hand and snapped his fingers.

Carmen and the others watched with dread, as one by one, the rest of the twenty Phantom Warriors that Triedastron had set free into Kelmar appeared out of individual bursts of smoky vapor. The sorcerers were all dressed in identical, black hooded robes. They and their creatures now had the Kelmarians surrounded in one enormous, inescapable circle.

"Ready to show yourselves, yet?" Nankarsa asked, as Haidar and the others searched hopelessly around them for a way to break out of the circle of Phantoms.

"It looks like we'll have to smoke them out," Desorkhan decided, feigning indifference.

When the Kelmarians stayed quiet, Desorkhan pointed his silver wand crowned with the Magicon symbol at the nearest tree.

"Demise by Fire!" he ordered.

A sharp burst of red and black flames erupted from the crown of Desorkhan's staff, which the Dark Master then used to set fire to the tree.

In only a matter of moments, the cursed flames began to spread rapidly to the neighboring woods. It took less than two minutes for the flaming ring of trees, in between which stood the Phantom sorcerers and creatures, to encircle the fighters from Sarcanian Valley.

Now faced with no choice but to reveal himself and his students to their foes, Haidar gazed around at his Captains, who were standing on either side of him.

"The time has come," he told them bravely. "We must fight to save our capital."

Carmen glanced around at her classmates. There was not a single one of them that didn't look tense...but collectively, they stood together ready for battle. Haidar pointed his wand at each of his students and Carmen's three additional Souls before using *Revealio* to bring all of them into sight.

Once every one of the Kelmarians was visible, Desorkhan and the other Phantom Warriors stared at the sizeable group of their enemies standing before them. Each of the sorcerers in both armies was holding his or her wand at the ready.

"Well, well, this is quite the shocker, isn't it?" Desorkhan said with a dark laugh, as the trees around him burned. "I should have expected that the kelscum would be stopping by for a visit."

Then Desorkhan flashed a vindictive smile at Carmen.

"So I heard that you were poisoned and nearly killed by an amulet given to you by a friend," he said, in a taunting manner. "I should really just leave you in the hands of your fellow Kelmarians and let them do away with you. It would seem that you're even less popular with them than you are with us."

A handful of the other Phantoms chuckled. Carmen made the decision to remain mute, and not give Desorkhan the satisfaction of a response.

"Enlighten me, Guardian. What exactly is your grand plan this time around?" he said, his dark eyes staring into hers. "I would hope that you didn't waste time agonizing over a strategy to destroy us, because I can give you your solution right now in words that you can understand. We are immortal spirits, and *you* are not. Consequently...we hold the only advantage over you that we would ever need. It is that which we are about to use to enter your beloved Pyramid City and destroy it so that nothing remains."

"Why not tell me something that I don't already know?" Carmen replied harshly. "Although you're wrong on the last part. You're not getting into Pyramid City...not unless you can defeat us first. It's pretty obvious that you have a selective memory, or else you would recall that we've defeated you plenty of times before."

Desorkhan laughed.

"Oh, I'm just *terrified*," he said. He nodded toward the rest of the Phantoms.

"The kelscum want to play," he told them. "The least that we can do is have some fun with them before we kill them, am I right?"

Desorkhan snapped his fingers yet again. In the next moment, bedlam arose as the Phantom Warriors and the Kelmarians charged in more than a dozen different directions toward their respective opponents.

Carmen and her Souls broke free from the Sarcan Unit and ran around the bush in the direction of Desorkhan, Mondalaus, and Nankarsa. Haidar and the other Kelmarians focused their efforts on the Phantoms standing amongst the flaming trees.

Carmen pointed her wand at Desorkhan as Blaze flew toward Singe.

"Fire Shock!"

The crown of Carmen's wand lit up as it shot a bolt of flaming lightning at the Dark Master.

Desorkhan quickly summoned a *Dark Guard* defense.

Once Carmen's spell was reduced to nothingness after striking his wispy black Protection, Desorkhan put down his shield and cast a *Petripulous* curse.

Carmen effectively blocked the dark energy that fired from Desorkhan's spell with a *Lightning Shield*. Blaze shot an intense gust of fire at Singe, who put up his wings to protect himself from the flames.

"I don't think that you're really at your best unless you're angry, Blazey," Singe teased. Then he darted around back of Blaze and bit him on his tail, prompting the Sarcan to cry out and whip around to chase Singe through the black sky above Carmen and Desorkhan.

"Lightning Strike!" Carmen shouted.

"Lightning Strike!" Desorkhan countered.

Two identical bolts of lightning fired from the sorcerers' wands and raced toward one another in a blinding flash of light.

When the two spells collided, there was a loud crack of thunder—and then the lightning strikes destroyed each other.

Frustrated, Carmen glanced upward to see that Blaze and Singe were firing shots of lightning back and forth from their horns. Their spells were also of equal strength, so when they hit, all that each accomplished was canceling out the enemy attack.

"You see?" Desorkhan said, pointing up at the Sarcans as Carmen met his eyes again. "Your attempt to defeat us is nothing but a waste of all of our time. We both know that there is no way for you to win...so why don't you just give it up already?"

"Can we skip the monologue for a day?" Carmen asked crossly. "Just keep quiet and duel."

Desorkhan shrugged.

"It appears that you enjoy the taste of defeat," he said. "Who am I to starve you of what you hunger for? Besides, it is *you* who has the life to lose here—not me."

Carmen and Desorkhan resumed their battle as Blaze and Singe carried on with their own struggle in the sky overhead. Meanwhile, many more duels were taking place throughout the rest of the forest whilst Desorkhan's fire continued to spread from tree to tree.

Stellar and Anubis had teamed up to challenge Mondalaus and his Zelthrel, Narcista. Stellar was fighting Lucifer as Anubis focused on combating Narcista. The Keinen was fighting hard against his opponent. As Mondalaus shot curses at him, Stellar utilized an assortment of magical shields, as well as his speed, to dodge his enemy's attacks.

"Ever regret joining up with the kelscum, Stellar?" the Magicon Officer asked, putting up his own shield to block a sequence of Stellar's spells. "You were one of our most promising young spies in a previous life, and just look at how far you could have come with us."

Stellar ran to avoid another curse from Mondalaus.

"The only regret that I have is that we were ever on the same side in the first place," he replied resentfully.

"Ouch. That one stung," Mondalaus said coldly, putting his hand to his heart. "Incidentally, you never did tell me what made you decide to leave the Magicon. Do you care to share your reason?"

"No. I don't," Stellar answered sharply. "It's not of your concern."

Stellar was wise not to allow Mondalaus to know anything about him that he could ever use against him. But it was evident that the Magicon Officer was not going to let up on his attempt to psychologically intimidate his challenger.

Mondalaus smiled and then fired a *Eurorkaisia* spell at Stellar, forcing him to duck to steer clear of the attack, which materialized as a small but powerful explosion of blue energy shot at him from Mondalaus's wand.

"No matter. I can always just use your friend's abilities to tap into your mind and find out for myself," Mondalaus said casually, as he watched Stellar get up from the grass. His cool blue eyes then shifted in the direction of Anubis.

Suddenly, Lucifer pointed his wand at the Jackal, who was standing no more than twenty feet away from him.

"Surrender thine powers to me!" he commanded.

A rusty bronze jet of energy blasted out of Mondalaus's wand and sped toward Anubis. The Jackal had just performed a mind control spell on Narcista to make the giant, slimy green creature stop attacking him temporarily. That was when Lucifer's unexpected attack struck him in his side.

"ANUBIS!" Stellar yelled.

But it was too late. Anubis stiffened and stared straight ahead of him as the spell worked its magic....

Without Stellar even feeling anything...Anubis searched through the Keinen's mind under the orders of Mondalaus, and found Stellar's painful last memory with the Magicon.

"Ah, it was my killing of the young Keinen mother and the capture of her baby," Mondalaus said, a horrible smile curling his face as he recalled the event and saw the image that had been transferred from Stellar's mind to Anubis's, and then into his own.

"I'll bet that you're still wondering what happened to that baby," Mondalaus mused, as he gazed across at Stellar. "Well, I'll gladly tell you. He grew up with the Magicon...and then foolishly tried to escape one day, just like you. But he never made it out alive.... Oh, I made certain of that."

Mondalaus lowered his wand, snapping Anubis out of his trance. Stellar flinched, beginning to shake with irrepressible anger.... He ran at Mondalaus and pounced on the Magicon Officer, sending him crashing to the ground.

Stellar tore relentlessly at Lucifer's robes with his saber teeth, trying to break through to his skin, tearing off shreds of fabric even as Mondalaus roughly tried to push the Keinen off of him.

Following Mondalaus's attack, Anubis was not strong enough to come to Stellar's aid just yet, and so he continued to defend himself against Narcista. He had the advantage over her in that he was smaller and faster on his feet. As she spit poisonous arrows at him, he ran through the clearing using *Inviscreen* to conceal himself from her view while he used a progression of mind spells against the Zelthrel.

"I will have you defeated before the morning light appears," Anubis vowed, after stunning Narcista with one of his more potent attacks.

Narcista eventually recovered, and then roared irritably at him. Her slimy scales were glinting in the light of the fire as she lumbered across the grass. Though she had wings, she elected to stay on the ground so as to give the various battling Dragons in the skies more space.

As all of this was going on, Glamis was dueling with Sevadia Nankarsa and Syth not far away.

"Come on, Syth, let's crush this porker," Nankarsa said, as Syth floated down from the sky after trying in vain to strike Glamis with a *Psychstra* curse.

"You shall not succeed!" Glamis declared, pounding his hoof on the grass in defiance. "You are merely puppets in Triedastron's quest for power...and you do not possess the motivation that we Kelmarians do. We fight to save our friends, our families, and our home, while you fight for power unattainable by devastation and hate."

"Silence, now!" Nankarsa hissed, glaring across the clearing at the Boarax. "You are *nobody* to speak down to me. Kill him, Syth! *Selkanthia!*"

The Syntor's body enclosed itself in a red glow of light. He flew toward Glamis, his scarlet eyes blazing.

Glamis swiftly reacted by summoning a *Land Shield* spell, conjuring a cylindrical glittering wall of silver stone around him.

Just as the Syntor neared Glamis, he was forced to fly above the wall to get to him. But when Syth opened his jaws to release the curse, Glamis raised his head and fired his own *Sea's Fury* spell up at him.

Syth took a direct hit, as the strong flash of blue light struck him and sent him crashing down into the grass.

"Rise! NOW!" Nankarsa commanded of her Partner.

But when Syth struggled to get up, a momentary look of fury engulfed Nankarsa's face. Her purple-blue eyes flickered dangerously under her hood.

"If you can't destroy the pig, then I'll finish the job myself!"

Nankarsa pointed her wand at Glamis. The red stones decorating the electric blue staff glittered in the light of the burning trees.

"Teldandrum!" she ordered.

A silvery blast of energy exploded from the crown of Nankarsa's wand and discharged in the direction of the Boarax.

Glamis didn't panic. Instead, he charged forward into the oncoming curse, his body glowing green with the power of the *Rushing Stampede* spell.

The Boarax ran headlong into Nankarsa's curse in an explosion of purple and green smoke. And after a few worrisome minutes...he emerged from the cloud unharmed, having been protected by the effects of his own magic.

Meanwhile, Reoc Haidar was engaged in a fierce sword duel with Dorsan Denethor on the other side of the clearing. The Magicon Commander was dueling Haidar with a determination that rivaled that of his opponent. The black-haired, long-nosed sorcerer met Haidar's strikes with equally strong blows, but being the highly experienced swordsman that he was, Haidar made use of his quick footwork to stay ahead of his opponent. Denethor's black Dragon was flying overhead, waiting to attack Haidar upon his Master's command.

"Karsthra Murtog!" Haidar ordered.

When the fiery blade of his sword met Denethor's, the heat from the spell radiated down into the hilt of the Magicon's saber.

Denethor shouted in pain, dropping his sword and cursing at Haidar.

"You'll pay for that," he said bitterly, clutching his burnt hand. He looked up toward his Dragon, who had sharp, scarlet-colored eyes.

"Thardos!" he called up to him. "Give him a sampling of *our* fire!"

The adult Dragon roared and flew down through the air. Haidar remained where he was. He pointed his wand upward at the approaching beast.

"Sky Guard!" Denethor summoned.

Thardos sent a huge breath of red fire down at Haidar, just as a glowing domed shield formed at the crown of Haidar's wand and grew to encase the sorcerer.

The Dragon's flames grazed the solid shield, but couldn't break through to Haidar, forcing Thardos to retreat back up into the air.

Haidar dissolved his defense with a wave of his wand, and prepared to go on the attack.

"Lightning Blade!" he shouted.

In the next instant, a brilliant strike of lightning discharged from the dark sky and struck the Dragon in mid-flight. Thardos howled desperately as the electrical properties of the spell weakened him. In time...he found the strength to fly farther away over the trees and await direction from his Master.

The rest of the individual members of Haidar's Unit had paired up with other students to confront up to four Phantoms at once. Sarcan Captains Jayden, Rose, Neal, and Vix had joined together to battle Dezra Razok and his Dragon, Zolabar. Neal, who was short, with dark brown hair and brown eyes, teamed with Jayden against Razok as their Sarcans dueled the Dragon.

Jayden had her crimson and gold wand pointed defensively at Razok while Neal ran around her to fire a *Lightning Spark* spell at Zolabar. The Dragon had grabbed Rose by the tail as she flew by and had her pinned to the ground beneath his claws, forcing Neal to flee from his duel with Razok to come to her aid.

The bolt of lightning that erupted from Neal's wand forced Zolabar to retreat, but Rose remained motionless and injured on the ground.... Jayden had to tend to her before she could help Neal combat Razok.

Jayden dashed over to the Sarcan and knelt down at her side. She then muttered a Healing spell that would fix her wounded leg and tail, both of which were bleeding due to deep bites from Zolabar. But while Jayden worked on Rose, Neal was having a difficult time keeping up with the veteran sorcerer, Dezra Razok, who was tall and thin, with sharp brown eyes.

"*Takolra!*" Razok ordered.

"*Thunder Shield!*" Neal shouted.

A bright orange-red light burst out of Razok's wand. Neal's shield soon materialized in front of him...but Razok's spell was too powerful.

The light of the curse punctured Neal's mighty shield, hitting him at nearly full strength. Neal screamed and collapsed to the ground.

Jayden looked over at him straight away to see that he was in distress. His eyes were tightly closed, and he was fighting to stop shaking as the curse ripped through his body.

"Neal, I'm coming!" Jayden called out, as she got up from the grass and ran toward him. The fully healed Rose flew back up into the sky to rejoin Neal's Sarcan, Vix.

"Oh no, you're not!" Razok shouted, pointing his wand at her. "*Stakardon!*"

Razok's purple beam of energy sped across the clearing, but Jayden was determined to reach Neal. She raised her wand.

"*Invisible Shield!*" she cried.

A clear, protective bubble of magic swiftly grew around her. Razok's spell deflected off of the shield and disappeared into the trees.

Jayden reached Neal in next to no time. She crouched down and placed her right hand on top of his, then closed her eyes.

With great concentration, she squeezed his hand and allowed her healing magic to flow from her body into his as she performed the spell known as *Lightning Rescue.*

After about forty-five seconds, Neal opened his eyes…and his body stopped trembling. Jayden helped him to his feet just as he uttered a fast but sincere thank you.

"You kids are idiots if you expect to defeat me," Razok said, mocking them as they turned and faced him. "I've got more experience at dueling than you and the rest of your little friends combined."

"That's what *you* think anyway," Neal retorted. He turned to Jayden.

"Let's show this guy what we've got."

Jayden nodded in agreement. After deciding on their next spell, the duo launched their joint attack against Razok.

"Firejolt!"

Jayden and Neal touched the crowns of their wands together…and their combined strength caused a pocket of lightning-fueled fire to form. The sorcerers thrust their wands forward and released the dual spell, and their red and golden fire, ignited with electricity, blazed across the clearing.

Razok had no chance to plan an escape; the spell cut through the air with such speed that it seemed like only milliseconds had passed before Razok was engulfed in the fires of the Kelmarian attack.

As he screamed from inside the ball of flames, Rose and Vix released their own breaths of fire at Zolabar, who was flying just above them.

The Dragon unleashed a deafening roar. The fire was searing the dark scales on the underside of his huge body.

At least for right now, in this duel, it seemed that the Kelmarians were slowly gaining the winning advantage over the Phantoms. But elsewhere in the forest, signs that just the opposite was actually happening were everywhere.

Arianna and her Sarcan, Ezri, together with Kamie and Dall, were struggling against Oalyn Sarisin and his Skelyote, Yastar. Arianna was doubled over in severe discomfort as a result of being hit with Sarisin's *Portollsa* curse, which caused its victim to suffer crippling stomach pains. There was nothing that Arianna could do but wait for the pain to pass, but every excruciating second in which she was rendered incapable of moving undoubtedly felt like a lifetime.

Kamie was fighting the hefty Sarisin back with a range of Lightning spells, but Sarisin was not surrendering to his younger foe in any way.

"Arickio!" Sarisin shouted.

"Sarcanto Mentolia!" Kamie countered.

In a fraction of a second, the flashes of red and blue light collided, and Sarisin's attack negated Kamie's.

Kamie looked visibly stressed after her spell shrank into nonexistence.

She glanced at Arianna, who was just now able to straighten up. Arianna's dark hair was matted against her fair face, which was wet with perspiration.

Ezri and Dall were fleeing from Sarisin's Skelyote in the sky. Yastar was fast and strong, and outmatched his opponents' collective power. The Sarcans frequently tried shocking Yastar, but every time they attacked, the Skelyote would shield himself behind his skeletal black and gray wings. Yastar was a wolf-like creature, with dark gray fur, scarlet eyes, and three long tails. His head was crowned with three curling white horns.

Arianna told Ezri to use her claws and teeth instead of her lightning against Yastar, but it was difficult for the Sarcan to get close to the Skelyote without being scratched or bitten herself.

Captains Max, Kai, Luke, and Zay, in the meantime, were having problems of their own with Ruan Thor and his black Dragon, Nylan. As slow and lumbering as he was, Thor had been able to force Max and Luke to produce defensive spell after defensive spell to combat the constant inundation of curses that he fired at them. The Magicon sorcerer was large and balding, possessing dark brown eyes and an ever-present scowl.

"What's wrong, boys?" Thor asked, after firing yet another fierce curse at them. "Is fighting someone who's an immortal spirit a little more challenging than you thought it would be?"

Max, who had a round face, green eyes, and brown hair, cast a *Storm Shield* defense to protect Luke and himself. Luke was tall and lean, and had blue eyes and auburn hair that he kept short and spiky.

"We should use a Sky spell," Max muttered to Luke, as Thor waited on his opponents' next move. "His Dragon is fast, but Kai and Zay are faster."

Luke concurred with his classmate's idea. "Thor isn't the quickest on his feet either."

Kai and Zay got their orders from their Masters through thought. The Sarcans then flew higher up into the air, over Nylan, who was watching them closely through his scarlet eyes.

Max and Luke exchanged brief glances. They had already chosen the exact spell that they wanted to use.

"Tunnel Wind!" they shouted in concert.

Kai and Zay flew in circles over Nylan's head. Their small bodies were moving so fast that they looked like golden balls of light racing through the dark sky. In only seconds, the speeding Sarcans formed a giant tornado that swallowed Nylan up in its forceful, swirling winds.

Minutes later, Max and Luke's wands released their own squall of wind, which ultimately joined into one—creating a second tornado that blew across the clearing and swept Thor up in its winds before the Phantom Warrior knew what was happening.

Thor disappeared up into the funnel cloud just like his Dragon. Max, Luke, and their Sarcans watched from below as the two tornadoes spun side-by-side. Before long, the tornadoes blew together to form one greater storm, knocking down nearby trees and tossing rocks and debris throughout the clearing. Thor and Nylan remained trapped inside the tornado's dominant winds, unable to escape.

The gusting storm went on to rotate for ten minutes, until a sudden burst of light blasted out from its center. Thor emerged through the side of the tunnel using his Dragon *Wings of Flight*. Nylan flew out after him.

To the Kelmarians' dismay, the two Phantom Warriors had somehow found a way to break out of the immense magical tornado unharmed. Thor launched a flaming curse at Max and Luke while Nylan chased Kai and Zay, and the battle began all over again.

Shouting and flashes of light carried throughout the Oldac Forests as the soft light of early morning arrived. Nearly all of the battles had reached impasses. The members of Triedastron's small but dominant army of Phantoms were unyielding, and it would take more than just magical force alone to bring them to defeat.

A little farther away from the other duels, Draven and Flint had paired with Shea and Gia to battle Valsera Vermae and her Decodore, Garlenon.

Vermae was tall, with long gray and white hair that ran halfway down her back. Her eyes were brown and cold, much like those of her Decodore, Garlenon, who was a huge, black lion-like creature with a flowing black mane and a muscular body.

Draven and Shea fought unexpectedly well together. They seamlessly alternated firing spells in turn against Vermae. Their Sarcans, Flint and Gia, were similarly able to handle Garlenon well enough. Gia distracted Garlenon by flying in a dizzying manner over the trees of the forest, and forcing him to follow her so that Flint could remain on the offensive against him. Draven ordered Flint to stay with Gia at all times.

Draven himself was standing strong alongside Shea as the two of them dueled with Vermae. The pair of Sarcan Captains shared the responsibility of carrying out spells as individuals, but Draven allowed Shea to make the calls as to just which spells they would cast as a team.

"Let's see how you counter this one, boys," Vermae said with a sneer, twirling in a circle and thrusting her wand at them.

"Rezanja!"

A bolt of red lightning flew out of the crown of Vermae's violet wand. Shea turned to Draven right away.

"I'll handle it," he said, before raising his wand.

"Lightning Shield!"

Upon Shea's command, a jet of lightning plummeted down through the sky over his head and Draven's, warping to create a magical shield around them. Vermae's curse struck the shield and diffused into nonbeing.

"Nice one," Draven said.

"We've got to keep it going though," Shea reminded him. *"Thunder Ray!"*

And so, Draven and Shea continued to duel Vermae while Flint and Gia battled Garlenon. Gia discharged a bolt of lightning at Garlenon, but the creature fought back using its powers of Fire, Water, and the Sky. Flint flew around the Decodore and stabbed him in one of his rear legs with his horn. Garlenon responded by attacking Gia with a violent breath of fire.

"Had enough yet?" Desorkhan asked harshly, as Carmen fell to her knees in fatigue, breathing heavily after fighting off the Dark Master's unremitting curses for the past two hours.

"Face it, Carmen, you can't keep this up forever," Desorkhan said. "Your time is running out.... Unlike us, your magic and body are wearing down with every spell you cast. The longer we fight, the weaker you become, and the more forest that gets destroyed. If you really wanted to save these woods, you would surrender before there is not a single tree standing."

"I'm quite aware of how this works," Carmen said angrily, forcing herself to stand back up. Her legs felt impossibly heavy, and there was an uncomfortable burning in the back of her eyes from the black smoke that rose up from the burning trees and into the slowly lightening sky. She was trembling from exhaustion.

Blaze wasn't faring much better than his Master. His wings were aching from chasing Singe throughout the skies for the better part of the battle. He had used his lightning and fire on numerous occasions, and was just as tired by this point in the conflict as Carmen was.

At the present, Carmen had no idea how they and the others would be able to drive the Phantom Warriors away from the gates of Pyramid City. As much as it pained her to admit it, Desorkhan was right.... As the Kelmarians worked to combat the Phantoms, they were getting weaker all of the time, while the Phantoms were losing virtually no strength whatsoever in fighting them back. No matter how long and hard the Kelmarians battled, they were not making any progress against their foes. It had become increasingly clear over the course of the battle that without a miracle, the Phantoms would storm the gates of Pyramid City.

With all of these thoughts haunting both of their minds, Carmen and Blaze waited to see what Desorkhan would do next. The Dark Master and his Sarcan were currently observing their opponents from across the clearing, as though trying to decide on the spell that was the surest to bring them to defeat. Carmen, for the time being, was at a loss to find a solution that would spare Pyramid City from the wrath of the Phantoms.

"Well, Singe, as long as we're here wasting time, why don't we give our old friends a lesson in battle?" Desorkhan remarked to his black Sarcan, before his face bent into a nasty grin as he stared across at Carmen and Blaze. "This one will teach you that in the end, we always win."

"I like this idea," Singe said, with an equally spiteful smile.

Carmen tightened her grip on her wand. Blaze's eyes were locked on their adversaries.

In the next second, Desorkhan raised his wand.

"Perhaps you'll remember this spell," Desorkhan said slowly. *"Fires of Lightning!"*

Carmen gasped. Her heart instantly began beating faster than it had all morning. Briefly stunned, she had to think before she reacted. *Fires of Lightning* was the strongest Dual Elemental spell that she knew, and knew too well.... Her mind racing, she ultimately chose to use a commanding Kelmarsian spell to combat Desorkhan's magic.

"Golden Lightning!"

As the blast of fiery lightning energy broke free from Desorkhan's wand, Carmen's staff glowed in a heavenly white light...opening up the early morning sky above her.

A flawless gold lightning bolt shot down through the air, striking Desorkhan in a blinding flash of light that illuminated the entire clearing. He crashed to the ground, temporarily paralyzed as the magical current rushed through his body. Blaze's horn then released an identical bolt of forceful lightning, which accordingly struck Singe.

But despite its success, the use of the advanced Kelmarsian spell had taken more out of Carmen than she had anticipated. As Desorkhan's *Fires of Lightning* spell continued to charge toward her, she suddenly began to feel faint. Her extremities went numb, and she was sure that her wobbly legs would give out from beneath her at any second. The *Golden Lightning* spell had been too much for her to handle in her already weakened state…and now her body was suffering the cost.

"Carmen!" Blaze said, urgently shaking her shoulder, as his Master swayed back and forth in a daze. "Carmen, summon a shield—quickly!"

But Carmen couldn't move, and Blaze, also weakened from the battle, didn't have the strength to produce a shield powerful enough to protect the both of them from the mighty *Fires of Lightning* that was headed their way. Carmen was fighting just to stay conscious as she stood there in the path of the enemy attack. If she cast a defensive spell, it would surely not be enough to protect them from Desorkhan's attack, and would probably knock her out completely, sealing her and Blaze's fate in this most critical battle.

Frantic now, Blaze looked toward Shea and Draven, who were dueling Vermae and her Decodore a short distance away. Shea was watching Draven intensely as he fought off another one of Vermae's curses and prevented it from striking them.

"SHEA, HELP!" Blaze shouted, waving desperately across to him as he remained at Carmen's side.

Shea immediately glanced back at the Sarcan, and then saw Carmen's pale and dazed appearance. Without even a glance at Draven, he raced over to her, shouting for Gia to follow him.

Carmen turned her head at the sound of her classmate's footsteps.... She saw him coming, but didn't even have the strength or awareness to form the words that would tell him what was happening. Desorkhan's electrically charged ball of flames was rapidly coming within twenty feet of her and Blaze....

A moment later, Carmen felt Shea shove her out of the way of the spell whilst he pointed his wand at the enormous wall of fire.

"Catch her, Blaze! *Invisible Shield!*"

Carmen staggered, her wand slipping from her grasp and falling into the grass. Dizzy and disoriented, she was about to fall down to the ground beside Shea when Blaze caught her. At the same time, an invisible dome was growing out of the crown of Shea's golden wand. Gia took Blaze's place while he helped Carmen to lie down in the grass. An extra invisible dome expanded out from Gia's horn and joined together with Shea's shield to make the magical defense twice as strong.

Carmen watched helplessly from the ground through blurred vision as the huge, blazing fireball smashed into Shea and Gia's shield in a blistering explosion in front of them. The roar of the wind and the flames rushed through Carmen's ears as the wall of fire surrounded her and her friends. Shea held tight to his wand with both hands, staring into the fires with tremendous focus while he maintained his shield using every last ounce of strength that he had left.

Eventually...the fires died down, reduced to a lingering black smoke that drifted throughout the entire clearing. When the smoke finally dispersed, it revealed a sight that made Carmen's stomach turn.

The other Kelmarian fighters displayed noticeable signs of severe fatigue. They were not fighting the Phantoms with the same level of power that they had been earlier. It seemed as though they had exhausted most, if not all, of their physical and magical abilities, just as the realization that victory was now an impossible goal was truly sinking in.

Now that the fires of Desorkhan's attack had been extinguished, Shea lowered his wand and looked down at Carmen with concern.

"Carmen, are you okay?" he asked, as he knelt down next to her, his face filled with worry. "I'm sorry that I had to push you, but I had to get you out of the path of the spell."

"Yes...." Carmen said slowly, still feeling somewhat light-headed and shaky. "I'm fine. Thank you for protecting us.... That was really brave of you."

Shea smiled wearily. He extended his hand to Carmen and helped her to her feet. He was perspiring, and his eyes were unusually dull and tired. He, Carmen, and their Sarcans looked sadly around at their drained classmates. It wasn't hard to see that their time was running out.... Even Commander Haidar was slowing down.

Desorkhan and Singe had both been hit directly with Carmen and Blaze's *Golden Lightning,* yet as they rose back up off of the ground, they appeared only to have suffered minimal harm. Desorkhan's expression was still confident, and his body looked to be functioning normally, as though nothing at all had happened. He even had the audacity to laugh in the faces of Carmen and her three friends.

"So, how does defeat feel?" he asked them cruelly. "You must be getting accustomed to it by now."

When the young Kelmarians didn't answer him, Desorkhan smiled.

"That last spell finished this battle for you," he said coldly, gazing most penetratingly at Carmen. "I can see it in your eyes.... You have lost."

Desorkhan snapped his fingers, a sound that was magically amplified in volume to reach the ears of all of the Phantoms.

All at once, the rest of the Phantom Warriors turned their attention toward the Dark Master. Therefore, so did the other Sarcan Captains, Haidar, Stellar, Anubis, and Glamis.

"Well, it appears that we have reached the turning point in this contest," Desorkhan announced, as he gazed around at his associates through the smoke of the burning trees. "We are here for one purpose, and one purpose only...and that is to bring Kelmar to an early end for our Master, Triedastron," he said boldly. "These kelscum who had the nerve to get in our way are too weak to continue to pose a threat to us, meaning that our work here is complete. It is now time to descend upon Pyramid City."

"No...." Carmen was gripping Shea's upper arm tightly, both for emotional support and to prevent her from collapsing again. "They can't do this.... They just can't."

"Ah, yes, we can, actually," Desorkhan arrogantly informed her. "We have arrived at the defining moment of this war.... Just as the Legend of the Worlds Triad predicted, before long, Keltan will take control of Kelmar and Kelmarsia to welcome in the dawning of the next age in magical history...an age in which the Keltans will rule over all three realms into the coming centuries. The destruction of the first empire in the Worlds Triad...begins now."

Desorkhan snapped his fingers once more, and the Phantom Warriors each became encased in a dark glow, and shot up into the sky. The Dark Master flew up with them, pointing his fellow fighters toward the north.

"To Pyramid City!" he ordered.

Carmen and her friends watched as Triedastron's Phantom Warriors transformed into shadowy spirits. The ghostly army promptly turned in the direction of the capital...and flew away from the Oldac Forests at speeds unsurpassable by any living being.

The fire tearing through the woods crackled and hissed as the smoke and embers burned in the backs of the Kelmarians' throats. None of them could believe or accept that the rise of the Phantoms had begun. But as the fighters stared up into the darkness of the predawn sky overhead, there was an unsettling awareness among them that they alone could not stop Triedastron and his undying forces. It would take magic far beyond what they presently had to save both Kelmar and the World of Light from an untimely downfall. And for the moment, it seemed that victory in this ongoing war was as far out of their reach as it had ever been.

CHAPTER TWENTY-FOUR
THE UNEXPECTED REINFORCEMENTS

As the Phantoms raced across the northern skies to the Kelmarian capital, Carmen and her classmates used the remainder of their magical energy to put out the fire that Desorkhan had set at the beginning of the conflict. It took Commander Haidar and his students nearly twenty minutes to douse the powerful cursed flames that were eating away at the ancient trees of the forest. By the time they were finished, the fire had destroyed nearly one-quarter of the woodland.

Haidar took time to assess the damage, and then gathered his students together in the center of the clearing where the battle had taken place. He would need to provide a full report to the Sarcan Council on what had happened during the clash upon returning to Sarcanian Valley, but that seemed to be the least of his concerns as he addressed his students.

"I know that this isn't the outcome that all of us had hoped for when we arrived here this morning," Haidar told his somber students, in regards to their defeat at the hands of the Keltans. "But know this: Though we have found ourselves now facing a significant setback, we have *not* lost this fight.... I am going to send a Herald Guard to Parliament officials in Pyramid City to alert them that the Phantoms are on their way. They need to prepare themselves and the city's other inhabitants to combat the Keltans."

Haidar closed his eyes and raised his wand. It was quiet for a brief time while he mentally put together the message for his Herald Guard spell to carry.

After Haidar had spoken his entire message through his stream of thought, he opened his eyes and flicked his wand.

"I hereby summon my Herald Guard to me!"

With that, a golden burst of sparkling light in the form of a Sarcan grew out of the crown of Haidar's wand. The young adult Sarcan, which was a representation of Haidar's deceased Partner, soared up into the air to a height of twenty feet. He then turned his head and nodded back at Haidar, giving Carmen and the others a glimpse of his youthful, friendly face before he flew off to Pyramid City.

It was the first time that Carmen and her classmates had gotten to see what Morin had looked like when he was alive. Carmen could only wonder if seeing the Sarcan in this beautiful but impermanent form brought renewed pain to Haidar, who had once confided in her that he missed his beloved Sarcan, whom he had lost in a violent struggle with the Magicon many years ago, every day of his life. His emotions were often difficult to read.

"The Herald Guard will deliver the message to Pyramid City before the Phantoms get there," Haidar assured his class in a steady voice, as he gazed over all of the Captains. "In the meantime, we need to fly back to Sarcanian Valley, where we belong. We are too weak at this point to be of any use to the Pyramid City fighters, so the wisest course of action is to return home and recover. We have to formulate a plan for how we will move on from this loss and challenge the Keltans again.... Time is crucial, for the longer the Phantoms remain here in Kelmar, the more death and destruction they will cause. We must find a way to transport them back to the World of Darkness, and we will need to work quickly and effectively to minimize the damage that they will undoubtedly produce in the coming days."

Commander Haidar promptly led his weary students back to *The Fearless,* which was sitting on the other side of the trees in another clearing. Most of the sorcerers and creatures looked like they were ready to faint as they marched through the woods to the airship. Despite their extensive training in magical battle, there was no escaping the inevitable exhaustion that resulted from consecutive hours of intense warfare.

The students lumbered up into the airship and collapsed into their seats. Haidar took one final glance around the Oldac Forests, and then climbed aboard after them, the wooden door on the starboard side of the ship closing behind him. The Sarcan Commander took his seat at the front of his craft, and the airship lifted off of the ground and drifted up into the sky.

The flight back to Sarcanian Valley was long and subdued. In the back of each of the young Kelmarians' minds was the question of how they would ever be able to defeat Triedastron and his seemingly invincible Phantom Warriors. They needed a new weapon that the Keltans could not contend with, or at the very least, an extraordinary boost of strength that would take them over their untiring foes.

Though she didn't want to show it, Carmen was probably the most concerned out of all of them. The Secrets of Kelmar, which were her responsibility as the Guardian of Kelmar to utilize together, were supposed to be that very weapon. But as of this morning, she still hadn't found a way to use them to the Kelmarians' advantage. She wished that she knew of a way to contact the spirits of her parents, or Merlin himself, to get their assistance.... Her task of solving the meaning behind the Secrets was beginning to look like a hopeless undertaking.

On the quiet return trip aboard *The Fearless,* several of the Sarcan Captains fell asleep. Carmen herself nearly dozed off on at least five separate occasions, but each time, her restless mind prevented her from taking that final slip into unconsciousness. She was feeling better following her near blackout during the duel with Desorkhan, but was still far weaker than usual.

It was midmorning when the students flew over Thunder Academy and landed at the southern edge of the valley. The bluish skies had lightened considerably as the sun peeked out from behind the hovering, late spring clouds.

Haidar stood up and turned to face his students before he allowed them to walk up to the school.

"As you might expect, training is canceled for today," he announced to his exhausted class. "I want all of you to return to your rooms and rest…. Later today, you will be summoned to assemble with the younger students to get an update on what's happening in Pyramid City. But I must first meet with Officer Sheridae and the Sarcan Council to determine the best plan for victory going forward. So, until the assembly, you are dismissed."

Slowly, very slowly, the Sarcan Captains traipsed down off of the airship, and began their long march across the dueling fields. The winds that had been tearing across the landscape earlier in the morning had died down to a mild breeze. Overall, it was developing into a clear and warm day, but the lovely weather did nothing to help ease the students' troubled minds, nor did it make them feel any less defeated after failing to prevent the Phantom Warriors from advancing to the gates of Pyramid City.

Once they were all out of the ship, Haidar walked swiftly past the worn-out Captains and made his way up to the school. He was at the top of the mountain stairs in less than ten minutes, and then disappeared inside the castle as he hurried off to track down his colleagues.

Carmen, her Souls, and her classmates trudged up the front steps of Thunder Academy, their sore legs aching as they climbed higher. Without more than a word or two to one another, the Sarcan Captains entered the castle and went their separate ways up to their rooms.

"Thanks again for helping me out," Carmen muttered to Shea, just before she left him, Akira, and their Sarcans to open her door.

Shea smiled modestly as Carmen let her Souls into their room.

"It was nothing," he said, with a slight twinkle in his tired eyes. "I'll see you around."

Carmen walked into her bedroom after her Souls and shut the door. Then she crossed the room to her bed and collapsed face first into the softness of her mattress.

"Ahh...." She breathed in deeply and savored the warmth, burying her head into her pillow. "I'm so tired...."

Carmen sighed and turned to look at her Souls.

"You guys must be drained, too," she said, reaching down and rubbing the side of Blaze's face as he stood beside her bed with Stellar, Anubis, and Glamis. She smiled at all of them in spite of what they had been through.

"I'm so proud of you," she said. "You did a great job back there.... Everyone did. Unfortunately, it just...wasn't enough to stop the Phantoms."

"Well, as Commander Haidar said, it's not over yet," Blaze calmly reminded her. "We're still here, so that means that they haven't won everything."

Carmen rolled over onto her back and stared up at the stone ceiling, lost in her thoughts.

"You're right," she said, as she pondered what their next move should be. "I just don't think that we can win this war by ourselves anymore. This is unlike anything that we've ever faced.... We need help."

Carmen lay there in contemplation for a couple of minutes, and then decided to take a short nap to try to regain some of her energy. She took off her boots as Glamis and Stellar climbed into their beds and Anubis curled up on the floor. None of them had suffered any serious physical harm during the battle, but their magic had been reduced to very low levels due to their tremendous efforts in fighting off the dark forces of Keltan.

Blaze climbed into bed beside Carmen, and was asleep even before his Master. Carmen smiled at him and leaned over the bed to set her boots down on the floor. Her head throbbing and feeling rather heavy, she pulled the quilt over Blaze and herself, and fell asleep.

A few hours later, Carmen found herself gaping at the grandfather clock that was standing in the corner of her room. Although she had planned to sleep for only an hour or so, it was shortly before 1:00 in the afternoon when she awakened.

Feeling well rested and much more alert than before going to sleep, Carmen went to the bathroom to brush her hair and wash her face. While she was cleaning up, Blaze and the other Souls of Destiny rose and stretched their legs. Not long after, a pair of Sarcans appeared at the door with lunch. They carried the large, covered silver tray of food into the room and set it down on the round table.

Carmen gladly joined her friends for lunch. She munched on a thick Arakive sandwich, and drank a tall glass of milk with it, feeling noticeably better with every bite that she took. The rest and the food had left her Souls also feeling very much restored. The friends took their time consuming their meal, and it was just as they were finishing that there was a knock on the door.

Carmen got up and answered it. A young Sarcan messenger was flying in the hallway.

"Your presence is required in Sarcan Hall in ten minutes," the male Sarcan said. "You *and* the Souls of Destiny."

"Okay…." Carmen said slowly. "Can you tell me what's happening there?"

The Sarcan nodded.

"Commander Haidar is holding a school-wide meeting to inform everyone on his strategy for challenging Triedastron and his army," he explained. "You will be given additional details when you get downstairs."

"Oh, right," Carmen said, wondering how she could have forgotten about the planned assembly that Haidar had mentioned earlier this morning. "Well, thank you for letting us know. We'll start heading down there right now."

The Sarcan bowed respectfully to her, and then flew down to the next door.

"Well, you heard him," Carmen said, as she walked back to her table and looked around at her friends. "Haidar's got a plan together.... Let's hope that it's a good one."

Carmen and her Souls took the last bites of their food and promptly left the room for Sarcan Hall. When they arrived downstairs, they found a line of students waiting out in the corridor to enter the chamber, whose pair of wooden doors was closed.

Observing that the sorcerers and Sarcans were in a random order, Carmen and her Souls slid into the end of the line behind Max and Kai. While they waited for the hall doors to open, the last pair of students filed into the line after Carmen's group. Carmen noticed that just like her, all of the other Captains looked visibly more rested than they had aboard the airship on the return flight to the valley.

Following only about five minutes of waiting, Officer Sheridae came out through the two heavy wooden doors of Sarcan Hall. The Basic Training instructor, who had long, dark brown hair and copper eyes, was dressed in her scarlet and gold Kelmarian Army uniform. As she strode out into the corridor, she kicked a couple of doorstops into place so that the hall doors would remain open. She had a blue velvet box of parchment tucked under her left arm, and a single rolled up piece of paper in her other hand.

"Welcome!" Sheridae said, greeting the students, silencing the handful of them who had been talking quietly with their friends. "As you walk into the hall, I will be handing each Master and Sarcan pair a map. Do not let this map out of your sight!" she instructed, waving hers in the air. "You will need your map for this informational session, as well as for after. When you get inside, seat yourselves amongst the middle rows of seats."

Sheridae stood in front of one of the doors with the velvet box, and handed the first duo of students their map from inside it. The students then marched past her and into Sarcan Hall.

The line moved up relatively quickly as each pair of students received their rolled up map, which was tied with a blue ribbon and featured their names. When Carmen and her friends got to the doors, Sheridae gave Carmen the map with the ribbon that was stitched with her name, as well as those of each of her four Souls present. Upon passing into the hall, they saw Commander Haidar sitting at the back of the room with the Sarcan Councilors. An empty gold chair to Haidar's right was reserved for Officer Sheridae.

Carmen and her Souls walked to the left and climbed up the wooden bleachers. They sat down between Max and Kai and two female Sarcan Cadets, opposite of the Councilors and Haidar.

"So what do you think Haidar's going to say?" Carmen asked Blaze, as the rest of the students gathered in the hall.

"I don't know, but if it's anything like his speech before last year's battle on the Island of Dark Magic, it will be thorough," Blaze replied. "This is an entirely different set of circumstances though. We don't know where the final battle of the war will take place.... It could be in any one of the three magical worlds. And just where it happens makes a major difference in what tactics we would use."

"And what about the Secrets?" Stellar asked. "We still haven't figured out how to use them."

"Well, we can reason that they'll be a huge factor in the entire strategy," Blaze said. "They really could end up making all the difference. We just don't know *how* yet."

Glamis looked down at Haidar, who was taking the empty velvet box from Sheridae and muttering a few words to her as she sat down next to him and the Councilors.

"I'm certain that Haidar has considered the Secrets in putting together his battle plan," the Boarax remarked. "He's likely already discussed it with the other officials."

Anubis nodded in concurrence.

"Yes, he is well aware of the fact that we haven't reached the solution for the Secrets' utilization just yet. But that does not mean that he is not taking their potential powers into account."

After all of the students were seated, Haidar hit the wooden gavel to the sound block on the table in front of him to silence the low rumble of voices. The room soon quieted down, and Haidar rose from his chair.

"Thank you for coming," he said, his booming voice carrying throughout the chamber. "We have gathered all of the Sarcan Captains and Cadets here this afternoon for an essential purpose.... For those of you who do not already know, late last evening...the Phantom Warriors resurfaced in the Oldac Forests."

Almost immediately, a handful of the Cadets began whispering amongst themselves.

"The Sarcan Captains and I were dispatched there to try to prevent them from reaching their ultimate destination—the gates of Pyramid City," Haidar said, over the noise. "But regrettably...we were incapable of hindering their mission. The Phantoms arrived in Pyramid City at sunrise."

Haidar paused, and then took a deep breath before continuing on.

"As it stands right now, Triedastron's forces have broken through the gates of the most heavily fortified area in all of Kelmar," he announced. "The Kelmarian Parliament's guards, the city militia, and civilian fighters are currently assembled in the streets, and working to drive the Phantom Warriors out of the capital. But it is no small task…as the Phantoms are restricted by neither the physical nor the magical limitations that we mortals are."

Many more of the Cadets now murmured words of trepidation with their neighbors. The Captains remained quiet as they listened to the rest of Haidar's address.

"The latest news, as of this afternoon, is that the fighters from Pyramid City have so far been able to hold off the Phantoms from getting very far into the capital. But unless we act swiftly, and with intention, the Keltans will eventually find a way to capture the city. This is why we have assembled here today…. We must review the plan that Officer Sheridae and I have developed for what we hope to be the final phase of this war. Please unroll your maps."

There was the sound of rustling paper as the Sarcan students untied their ribbons and unrolled their maps on the benches in front of them. Carmen stared down at her map, and held the edges down flat so that she and her Souls could read it.

This diagram was divided into three side-by-side maps, similar to the way that Merlin's hand-drawn ones were laid out. Kelmarsia was on the left, Kelmar was in the middle, and Keltan was farthest to the right. But unlike Merlin's map, Haidar's version of the Worlds Triad was drawn in silvery purple ink. It was even more detailed than the Master of Kelmar's map, as it featured all of the cities, natural landmarks, and buildings in each world. Everything was clearly labeled.

Haidar pounded the sound block yet again to redirect the students' attention to him. He had his wand pointed toward the ceiling, and his eyes were *also* focused upward. His map was clipped to the crown of his wand.

"Representatio!" Haidar summoned.

A white beam of light shot from the crown of Haidar's wand and through his paper map, projecting an image of a giant, three-dimensional upside-down map on the ceiling of the hall.

Officer Sheridae dimmed the lights in the chamber so that the students could study the magical, illuminated map as Haidar spoke. Haidar kept his wand directed up at it.

"I am going to run through each of our battle strategies as they are relevant to the individual realms," the Sarcan Commander explained. "Listen carefully, as we will only have the chance to go over this once as a group."

Suddenly, there was knocking on the closed doors of Sarcan Hall that captured everyone's attention. Haidar peered cautiously over in that direction. Councilor Elmeric Maradon glanced indecisively at Head Councilor Seth, who nodded at him. Councilor Maradon pointed his wand at the center of the two doors, and swished it down through the air. This caused the heavy wooden doors to swing open.

Carmen leaned forward, along with the other students, to see a small army of individuals marching into the room. Haidar's wife, Renalda, and her Frelark, Enn, were leading the group. Just behind them were Blaine, Thunderbolt, Alazar, and Redge. Following those four were Renalda's parents and their Starclaws. Bringing up the rear were armor craftsman, Rishaw Sivetsky, and his assistants. All of them were dressed in polished gold and silver battle armor.

Haidar stared at Renalda and the others as they arrived at the center of the hall. This visit was apparently as much of a surprise to him as it was to everyone else in the room.

"We've come to help," Renalda announced to the Sarcan officials and students, the light from the overhead map sparkling off of her long black hair that tumbled down over her shoulders.

"You can't expect that you'll be able to defeat the Phantoms alone...." she said slowly. "That's why we're here."

The initial look of shock left Haidar's face, replaced by one of disapproval. Sheridae brought the lights in the room back up.

"Renalda, this is an extremely dangerous situation that we're in," he said. "Why would you travel all the way to the valley to put your life at risk? You should have stayed where it is safe."

"I read the urgency in your letters, Reoc. I sense the darkness in what's happening all across our world," Renalda said, her resolve clearly showing on her delicately lined face. "The signs are everywhere. If we don't take a stand together *now*...we may not have many tomorrows left."

Haidar's expression softened a little, but his brown eyes remained fixed on her.

"Commander Haidar," Rishaw said, addressing him with a respectful bow, finally making Reoc's eyes flicker to him. "I have developed a special kind of armor that can withstand the curses and spells of immortal spirits better than typical armor can. My assistants and I have brought supplies with us to fit everyone in the castle with this new armor for use in the realms of the afterlife."

Haidar listened carefully...and then nodded favorably at the older man, who had long white hair, silvery-blue eyes, and a kind face.

"This comes as wonderful news," Haidar said. "Thank you, Rishaw."

Alazar was the next to step forward. Though his head of gray and russet hair was thinning, there was a noticeable glint of determination in his green eyes.

"Reoc, you know that you are not getting rid of us," he said, with a grin. "As Kelmarians, we owe it to our Kelmarsian ancestors to fight with all of the resources that we have. And as soon as we can send the Phantoms back to Keltan, we need to make sure that they never invade our world again."

Despite his initial anger when Alazar and his companions had appeared, Haidar's face finally broke into a slight smile.

"I couldn't agree more," he admitted.

He gazed around the room and motioned toward the empty seats in the upper benches, having already made up his mind about what to do with his new collection of fighters.

"Please come forward," he requested, "and join us."

The hall was quiet for a few minutes as each of the unexpected reinforcements approached Haidar. The Sarcan Commander conjured them each a map out of thin air by pointing at the individual sorcerers and muttering a spell under his breath.

Once the newcomers had their maps, they walked up the stairs to their seats. As Alazar climbed up the bleachers with Redge, Blaine, and Thunderbolt, he winked at Carmen and her Souls. Carmen returned all four of them an appreciative smile. After speaking briefly with Haidar, Renalda and Enn climbed up behind them to sit down next to their friends.

Never one to be easily distracted, Haidar dimmed the lights in the hall and returned his gaze to the magical map floating on the ceiling.

"Our first step in winning this war is to force the Phantoms out of Kelmar," he said, pointing his lit wand up at the representation of his world. "It is difficult to track the Phantoms' movements...but we can realistically assume that they will try to attack the major cities and kingdoms within the realm first. Pyramid City was just the beginning."

Haidar pointed his wand to the capital on the map, which was represented by a drawn pyramid with a star at its center.

"From the capital, they will likely move to the next most guarded and renowned location in Kelmar...." Haidar said, pointing his wand south. "Sarcanian Valley."

With that deduction, a heavy silence hung in the air, like an enormous weight crushing whatever remained of the students' confidence after their last battle.

"By our estimation, Pyramid City should have enough manpower and supplies to fight the Phantoms for three full days," Haidar said. "That means that in three days' time...we must be prepared to fight again—this time, to defend our own home."

With a lump in her throat, Carmen gazed around at her classmates. Some of them looked realistically frightened, but *all* of them had endured their fair share of storms and battles during their time here.... If Sarcanian Valley needed to be defended, she was positive that there was no one else more up to the challenge than they were.

"If our predictions are correct, and the Phantom Warriors descend upon Sarcanian Valley in three days, we will need to implement a different strategy from what we have employed in the past," Haidar said.

He then illuminated the icon of the castle encircled by mountains, which represented Sarcanian Valley.

"Rather than battling our foes on the ground, we will instead fight them...in the skies."

Haidar flicked his wand, which subsequently made a triangle of red dots appear over the illustration of the castle. The dots represented the Sarcan Unit flying in formation. Then he flicked his wand once more, prompting a cluster of black dots to appear in the northern portion of Mortrock Forest. These dots were a depiction of the twenty Phantom Warriors.

"Triedastron's Phantoms will most likely approach Sarcanian Valley from the north, meaning that we will need to fly directly over the castle to meet them. As soon as we catch sight of them, we advance toward them as a group. We do not wait for them to get to us.... *We* must attack first in order to begin the battle with the momentum shifted in our favor."

Haidar sliced his wand forward, causing the Sarcan fighters on the map to rush toward the oncoming Phantoms.

"I am confident that we will be capable of weakening the Phantoms enough to transport them back to Keltan," Haidar declared to the Captains and Cadets. "This time, we will have not only our family and friends who have joined us today, but also the Sarcan Council battling with us. It has often been said that when fighting to defend the home, we discover strength that we would not otherwise possess. This is *our* land, and if we don't protect it from these invaders...we will have nothing worth fighting for when all is said and done."

Haidar looked out at all of his students. A few of them nodded in agreement.

"To accomplish our goal, we will use the strongest magic that we currently have at our disposal," Haidar said. "I have spoken with Kelmarsian sources close to Merlin, and all of them have told me that if we are able to weaken the Phantoms to the point that they are unable to defeat us with *their* magic alone, Triedastron will be forced to summon them back to Keltan to restore their strength."

Haidar thrust his wand in front of him in an *X* pattern, causing the Kelmar portion of the Worlds Triad map to darken.

"With the Phantoms back in Keltan, we will have to coordinate ourselves for travel to the World of Darkness," Haidar told the students. "Your classmate, Carmen Fox, is currently working on determining how we can make use of the Secrets of Kelmar to restore the balance between the Worlds of Light and Darkness…. But until she finds the definitive answer, we must prepare ourselves to fight as though the Secrets of Kelmar did not exist, and by this I mean using Kelmarsian magic to keep the Keltans from crossing the Impassable Barrier into Kelmarsia…. We do not know in which of the two spirit worlds the Secrets of Kelmar will come into play, but in any case, we have to do all that we can to prevent Triedastron's capture of Kelmarsia. I cannot say how many Kelmarsian fighters will join us if we fight in Keltan, so we have to be ready to work alone if need be."

Haidar illuminated Triedastron's fortress on the map of Keltan.

"In all likelihood, this is where the battle in the World of Darkness will be centered," Haidar said.

Then he moved the light from his wand south, down to the horizontal line representing the Impassable Barrier.

"We will enter Keltan here, and then make haste to the Fortress of Darkness, where our objective will be twofold—stay alive, and deter the inhabitants of Keltan from reaching the Impassable Barrier. This magical boundary is what separates the three realms in the Worlds Triad from one another."

Haidar then turned the map of Keltan dark, leaving Kelmarsia as the final world to discuss.

"If it so happens that we are unable to inhibit the Keltans from crossing the barrier, and the Protections placed there fail, we will have no choice but to travel to Kelmarsia to assist its inhabitants in defeating their enemies," the Sarcan Commander said, illuminating Merlin's castle and the surrounding land.

"In the World of Light, our best hopes for victory lie in our ability to restore harmony to the Worlds Triad by defeating Triedastron and utilizing the Secrets of Kelmar," Haidar said decisively. "Nothing is guaranteed in Kelmarsia...and we just don't know what will happen when it comes to the Secrets. But our most dependable plan for success is to keep our friends near, battle with heart and with honor, and always remember that we have the power to decide the fate of our world. If we fail to help Kelmarsia and Keltan resolve their differences...it is certain that we will not have a home to come back to."

The map of Kelmarsia dissolved into darkness. Haidar then disbanded the entire three-dimensional map with a wave of his wand before restoring the lights in the chamber. The hall was hushed as Commander Haidar lowered his wand and gazed around at the Sarcan students. There was a steadfast look about his face as he spoke.

"As Kelmarians, we have a difficult journey ahead of us," he promised, "but I believe that together, we will see it through to the end."

CHAPTER TWENTY-FIVE
THE PRISONER'S MESSAGE

P*HANTOM WARRIORS INVADE PYRAMID CITY.*
The bold headline that was printed across the front page of
The Kelmarian Review the following morning was not the
one that Carmen had hoped to be greeted with.

After handing Blaze and Glamis letters from their families, Carmen sat down at the breakfast table in her room and
read the article as she nibbled on a piece of toast. A black and
white photo, taken just inside the gates of the capital, showed
the Pyramid City fighters clashing with the Phantoms.

> *At daybreak yesterday morning, a faction of
> Triedastron's army stormed the gates of Pyramid City.
> The Master of Keltan had released the army of twenty
> fighters into Kelmar several months ago, and the spirits
> have been causing sporadic destruction throughout the
> realm ever since. But this most recent invasion of
> Pyramid City marks the Keltans' boldest effort so far in
> attempting to destroy the Kelmarian infrastructure.*
>
> *Despite a heroic effort by the Sarcan Captains of
> Sarcanian Valley, the Phantom Warriors, led by the
> notorious Dark Master, broke into the city, where they
> were met with armed resistance from the capital's
> forces. As of press time, the Phantoms and the Pyramid
> City Militia remained locked in combat less than five
> miles from the Parliament building. Parliament re-
> mains the most heavily guarded structure in the entire
> city.*

At noon yesterday, Head of State, Danuvius Dor-
vai, confirmed early reports that a sector of the Phan-
tom brigade had made its way into the heart of the city.

"We have moved all residents into temporary safe
houses while we mobilize our defenses," Dorvai said,
from his own secure location. "Under no circumstances
will we surrender to these monsters and allow our city
to fall to them."

While the Head of State's words would suggest
confidence, there remains the question of just how long
the Pyramid City forces can maintain stability in the
capital. Dorvai refused to provide specifics on the num-
ber of fighters protecting the city, but wished to reassure
all Kelmarians that he is doing everything within his
power to save the capital from suffering major damage.

"We are the largest and strongest city in all of
Kelmar," Dorvai declared. "Residents have no reason to
fear. Our fighters are working around the clock to pro-
tect our homes and establishments."

But like flames rushing through a field of dry
brush, fear is spreading, and spreading rapidly. Kel-
marians can only wonder when this violent and de-
structive struggle playing out in the Worlds Triad will
finally cease.

Carmen sighed, a heavy feeling in her chest as she put
down the paper. Blaze and Glamis had just finished reading
their letters and were eating with Anubis and Stellar.

"Any news from your families?" Carmen asked the Sarcan
and the Boarax, before consuming the rest of her breakfast.

Blaze wiped his mouth with his napkin.

"My mother is worried that the Phantom Warriors will
travel to Dormien's Rock sooner or later," he told her. "That's

why she didn't come here with Renalda…. She and Skythorn are needed there in case of an invasion."

"It's a similar situation back at my burrow," Glamis said, as he chewed his insects. "Sabriel and Daryan are understandably fearful, particularly for us. They're curious to know what's been happening with the Secrets since we've acquired all of them."

"I wish that we had something encouraging to tell them," Carmen said, scratching her head.

"You don't have to write back to them right now," Anubis quietly pointed out. *"Why not wait to see what the day brings? Who knows? Perhaps we will stumble upon a breakthrough."*

Stellar abruptly gaped at him.

"That's exactly what I was just thinking! Not in those exact words but…. Did you just read my thoughts without telling me?"

Anubis smiled.

"Perhaps. But I was thinking much the same thing. Great minds, you know."

There was a knock on Carmen's door, and seconds later, Blaine Fox peered into the room. He was wearing a new set of golden battle armor over his robes. Thunderbolt was also dressed for combat.

"I heard voices, so I knew that you were all up," Blaine said, as he walked in with Thunderbolt.

He grinned at his granddaughter.

"How are you feeling this morning, Carmen?"

"I'm all right," she said, with a convincing smile. "Did you eat breakfast already?"

"Oh yes," Blaine replied, approaching the table. "I had nearly forgotten how delicious the food is here. I guess it's been a long time since I was a student."

Blaine and Thunderbolt had slept in a vacant bedroom across the hall the previous night, after coming to the castle

551

with Renalda, her parents, and friends. It was the first night that he had spent in the castle since he was a Sarcan Cadet.

"So, are you ready to get fitted for your armor?" Thunderbolt asked his son. "Rishaw and his assistants are in the upstairs training room fitting the Sarcan Captains for their new armor now. They asked us to come and get you."

As it was Saturday, Carmen and Blaze didn't have to worry about going to class.

"Ah, fantastic," Blaze said, swapping a smile with his Master. "We'll head up there then."

Soon after finishing their meal, Carmen and her Souls said goodbye to Blaine and Thunderbolt, and left their room to walk up the steps to the highest floor of the castle. When they emerged in the sunlit upstairs hall, they could see Renalda, Alazar, and their Partners standing and talking just outside the open door of the training room at the far end of the corridor. Renalda was dressed in orange robes, and Alazar, in a cerulean blue cloak.

"Alazar, Renalda!" Carmen called out to them, waving as she and her friends marched up the corridor to them.

Renalda turned at the sound of Carmen's voice and ran to meet her in the middle of the hall. There was a wide smile across her face as she hugged Carmen tightly.

"Sorry we didn't get a chance to see you after the meeting yesterday. I had to catch up with Reoc," she said, as she released Carmen from her arms and hugged Blaze. "It's been so long since I've gotten to talk to you! How are you doing?"

"We're doing pretty well," Carmen replied, as she hugged Alazar. "You both came all the way from Amera Island, right?"

"That's correct!" Alazar said. "Thank goodness for airships. It would have taken us far longer to swim here."

Carmen and her friends laughed. They realized at that moment how much they had missed Alazar's quirky sense of humor.

"Speak for yourself, Alazar," Renalda said, playfully shoving him. "I happen to be an excellent swimmer."

"So, how are things back on the island?" Blaze asked. "Is there anything new?"

Alazar and Renalda exchanged knowing glances. Then Renalda shrugged.

"Morale isn't at its highest with the attack on Pyramid City," she admitted. "Frankly, most who weren't familiar with the Phantoms' abilities were shocked that the Sarcan Captains couldn't have stopped the attack on the capital. They were naïve to have expected that you would've been able to prevent the invasion."

"No one was more shocked than we were," Carmen said, still feeling a bit upset about it. "It was horrible. We felt like...we had failed Kelmar. We're *still* feeling that way to some extent."

"But you didn't fail," Alazar reminded her, gazing earnestly into her eyes. "If you couldn't stop them, nobody could have. The Phantoms have countless advantages as immortal spirits, unluckily for us. They came with a mission, and they succeeded. It's as simple as that. We're just fortunate that Pyramid City is so well defended."

"But on a more uplifting note, Reoc told us that you've found all three Secrets," Renalda said, her eyes bright as she looked at Carmen and her Souls. "We're so proud of all of you."

"Thanks," Carmen replied, returning her a small smile. "It would certainly be much more impressive, though, if we knew what to do with them. We're pretty baffled as of right now."

A thoughtful look found its way to Alazar's face.

"Did you ever ask Merlin about it?" he inquired.

Carmen stared at the thoughtful, green-eyed sorcerer.

"How...exactly would I ask Merlin something?" she inquired.

Alazar's question reminded her of what the immortal man, Irwick Malcoff, had told her and her classmates about reaching out for assistance when they needed it.

"What I do know...is that if you take chances and believe in what you're doing, eventually, the answers usually come. Sometimes all you have to do...is ask for the help in finding them."

Alazar smiled.

"Think hard about what you want to know," the sorcerer said simply. "See his face in your mind, and then ask him. We Masters can take a cue from creatures with telepathic abilities," he said, acknowledging Anubis. "Just give it a try. There's nothing lost in the effort."

"Okay. I'll do it," Carmen said, willing to try anything that might help her find a way out of her predicament.

She closed her eyes for a brief time...and imagined Merlin's lined but exuberant face. Moments later, she saw his sparkling blue eyes and silver hair. He was standing in his castle in his long scarlet, white, and gold robes...smiling as he awaited her question. Trusting that this vision in her head was real, Carmen reached out to him.

How can I use the Secrets of Kelmar? Carmen asked him through thought. *I want to help my friends defeat Triedastron, but I'm afraid that we won't be able to until I discover what to do with the Secrets.... Please help me find the answer.*

Carmen waited. Merlin just continued to smile at her, but said nothing. Finally, she opened her eyes.

"He may not answer you right away," Alazar explained, when Carmen looked disappointed. "But it's always been my experience that if you ask for something that you strongly desire and deserve, you will ultimately receive it. At the very least, you'll be given a sign that Merlin is working to fulfill your request."

"Okay. Well, we'll see if anything happens," Carmen said, unsure if she really expected anything to come of this little exercise. "Thanks, Alazar."

"Let's go and get you fitted for your armor," Renalda suggested, motioning toward the door of the training room. "We don't want to keep Rishaw waiting."

Renalda and Alazar escorted Carmen and her Souls up the hallway and into the Captains' classroom. A handful of Carmen's peers were standing on stools beside desks scattered throughout the space, where half a dozen of Rishaw's assistants were measuring them. The master craftsman himself was standing at the far end of the room, showing Commander Haidar a shining golden helmet in the light of the windows. Carmen noticed that the metal armor appeared to glisten unnaturally bright in the sun.

She then spotted a young female assistant with short brown hair, who was just finishing fitting a set of golden armor on her classmate, Akira Melkor. Akira was admiring the armor in a standing mirror across from her while she thanked the assistant for her help. The glistening gold plate armor was detailed with intricate silver designs. Merlin's magic circle was engraved into the center of the breastplate.

After the assistant had completed her work, Akira stepped down off of the stool with Keko and walked toward the door. The petite girl, who had a gentle face and large brown eyes, grinned when she saw Carmen and her Souls standing just inside the room.

"Hey, Carmen, I didn't know that you were here," Akira said, as she approached her.

"Oh, that's because I just came in," Carmen explained. "Am I the last one?"

Akira shook her head.

"No, there's still a bunch of Captains who haven't gotten here yet."

"Ah. That's good to know," Carmen said, relieved that she was not late.

"Go and head over to Ebany," Akira said, pointing to the girl who had equipped her and her Sarcan with their new armor. "She'll measure you and get you what you need."

Akira and her Sarcan, Keko, bid Carmen and her Souls goodbye as their classmates crossed the room to meet the assistant. Alazar and Renalda came along to make sure that Carmen was provided with the right kind of protection.

Rishaw's assistant, Ebany, had sweeping dark brown bangs and long eyelashes. She was pale, and wore pastel blue robes covered by a suede apron with pockets. A single piece of measuring tape was wrapped over the back of her neck.

"Carmen Fox, right?" Ebany asked politely, as Carmen approached her, following a respectful bow. "Step right up. I'll fit you and Blaze first. I'll do the same for the rest of your friends after I'm through with both of you."

Carmen stepped onto the stool. Blaze flew higher above her shoulder than usual to allow Ebany to take her measurements.

Very carefully, Ebany assessed Carmen's height and waist, as well as the width of her shoulders. She also measured the length of her legs. After she had meticulously obtained all of the measurements, Ebany recorded them in a small spiral notebook on a desk next to her.

It took the young woman less than two minutes to gather all of Carmen's numbers. When she was done, she had Carmen step off of the stool so that she could measure Blaze. After a short time, she had all of *his* measurements documented as well. She then walked over to the heavy trunks of armor that were lining the opposite wall of the training room to retrieve pieces that matched their sizes.

While Carmen and her friends waited for Ebany to come back, Rishaw crossed the room and greeted them with a bow. He had a partial set of armor draped over one of his shoulders.

"Why, hello, Carmen, Blaze," he said courteously, his blue eyes shining much like his armor. "It is an honor to serve you again."

"It's very nice to see you," Carmen said graciously, bowing back to him. "Thank you for coming and helping us get ready."

"Oh, it's my pleasure, Carmen," Rishaw said, in a considerate voice. "Let's see what Ebany has picked out for you."

Rishaw turned Carmen toward his young assistant, who had her arms full of silver and gold human and Sarcan battle armor.

"This is made of a special Darkness-resistant metal," Ebany said. She laid the armor on the floor and knelt down to strap a pair of greaves onto Carmen's legs as she stood on the stool. "When a living being travels to the afterlife, his or her body has to endure countless forces that do not exist in our world. Rishaw crafted this armor specifically to combat these forces, particularly those in Keltan."

"The Worlds of Light and Darkness were built to sustain spirits, not living beings, so it is important to be equipped with protection against the intensive energies that travel through these realms," Rishaw added, as Ebany stood up to fit the metal breastplate onto Carmen. "This shielding ensures that you will be at your best when in battle. You will not have to worry about casting Protections or defenses to guard yourself against the elements, as this armor will do that *for* you. You can instead just focus on defeating your opponents."

"This type of defense is of course in addition to the strength of the metal, which provides sufficient protection against physical and magical attacks," Ebany explained, now scrupulously adjusting Blaze's breastplate. "This armor is equally as strong as any of our other armors in that respect."

Ebany stepped aside, allowing Carmen and Blaze to observe their reflections in the tall standing mirror.

Carmen smiled. The armor that Ebany had provided fit them perfectly. It was lightweight, yet sturdy and durable. Each set of armor was primarily gold, but had the same elaborate silver engravings that Akira and Keko's had, as well as Merlin's magic circle.

"How does it feel?" Renalda asked.

"It's amazing," Carmen said, turning around to see how the greaves were strapped to her legs.

Blaze nodded.

"Flawless," he said, smiling.

"Wonderful!" Rishaw said contentedly, also admiring the armor on Carmen and Blaze. "Armor should feel like a second skin when fitted properly."

He then turned to his assistant.

"Another fine job, Ebany."

Ebany smiled in gratitude. "I learned from the master," she said.

Stellar, Glamis, and Anubis were equipped with their protection next. Each was provided with the same special armor that Carmen and Blaze wore, and Ebany worked to find pieces that fit their individual body types. Within less than an hour, she had all of them equipped.

"All finished," Ebany said proudly, as she stepped back from the three creatures. "You are ready for battle."

"Thank you, Ebany," Carmen said, grinning at the reflection of her Souls of Destiny in the mirror. "We really appreciate you doing this for us."

"You're welcome! It was my pleasure," Ebany said, with a cordial bow. "I wish you nothing but success on the rest of your journey."

Carmen and her friends prepared to leave the training room just as the last of the Sarcan Captains came inside to receive their armor. Before they walked out, Commander Haidar informed Carmen and Blaze that he would keep all of the Captains updated as to when the Advanced Training classes would resume. Renalda and Alazar stayed behind to speak with the Sarcan Commander before they would venture downstairs to ask the Sarcan Councilors' permission to live in the castle for the next two months.

Shortly thereafter, Carmen and her Souls walked downstairs and returned to their room, where they planned to store their armor under their beds until they would need it.

Carmen opened the door of her bedroom on the third floor to see a small orange messenger bird standing on her windowsill—a letter clasped in its long beak. There was a leather mailbag hanging from its neck.

The bird flew across the room and dropped the note that it was carrying down onto Carmen's table.

"I apologize. I forgot to deliver this letter this morning," the bird chirped. "I just found it at the bottom of my bag."

Carmen walked over to the round table and picked up the letter. The yellowed envelope had her name written across it.... There was no return address.

"Thank you," Carmen called to the messenger bird, as it turned and flew back out the open window.

Very curious as to what this letter could be about, Carmen broke the envelope's seal and unfolded the parchment that was tucked inside. The pages were covered in scratchy handwriting that was difficult to read. But before looking over the contents of the letter, Carmen flipped to the very last page and glanced down at the signature at the bottom of the paper. Her eyes widened.

"This is from Eli Elezar," she said, her gaze now glued to the parchment.

Carmen's Souls shut the door behind them and hurried to gather around her as she read the letter aloud.

"Dear Carmen," she read. "I hope that you and your Souls are well. Please excuse my poor penmanship. As I write this letter, it is the early morning. The sun has not yet risen, and it is very dark in my cell. I am also writing quickly, as I am very excited to tell you about a dream that I just had involving you, and the Secrets of Kelmar."

Carmen squinted to read the second paragraph.

"In the dream, I was sitting on the edge of my bed back home, admiring the pearl necklace belonging to Kelmari Cloud that my dear friend, Fellador Sedgely, had given to me almost a full year ago. I was holding the necklace in my hands, when out of the corner of my eye, I saw a stunning flash of white light. I glanced to my left and saw a beautiful young woman with silvery blonde hair, sparkling blue eyes, and porcelain white skin standing there. She was wearing flowing silver and white robes, and had a glow about her that told me she was not of this world."

Carmen held the parchment closer to her face to read the third and fourth paragraphs. The writing seemed to be getting sloppier as the letter went on.

"I stared at her, trying to figure out where I had seen this girl before. She looked so familiar. And as I watched her, awestruck, she moved toward me, more so gliding than walking. Then she reached out and placed her hand over the necklace that I was holding.

"'Thank you for keeping my necklace safe,' she said in a charming voice. 'My brother, Merlin, gave it to me as a gift. After I lost it, I was worried that I would never see it again.'

"It was at that point when I came to realize that this young woman was none other than Kelmari Cloud."

Carmen exchanged a surprised glance with Blaze before continuing.

"I asked Kelmari if she wanted her necklace back. But she shook her head and said, 'No, this gift is with you for a reason. If you agree to keep it, you must promise me that you will share it with someone else.'

"'Okay,' I said, confused. 'Who do you want me to share it with?'

"Kelmari lifted her hand, and I noticed that there were now a series of words engraved into the pearls where she had touched them, but I couldn't read the message. It was like a fog had drifted over my eyes.

"'Carmen Fox,' she said. 'I have just carved the fourth and final Secret of Kelmar into the necklace. You must get this to her before it's too late to save the Worlds Triad.'

"'I will do as you ask,' I pledged, as I bowed my head to her, still stunned by what was happening. 'Thank you for coming. I know that Carmen will be most grateful.'

561

"'There's one more thing as well,' Kelmari said. 'If this necklace should somehow fail to find the eyes of the Guardian of Kelmar before it does anyone else, she will no longer be able to read its Secret. After it has been read once, the message will disappear, and be lost forever.'

"'Very well. I understand,' I said. 'I will make sure that no one else sees it.'

"Kelmari smiled at me.

"'You have a pure soul, which is why you have my trust,' she said.

"Then she vanished, and I woke up."

Carmen flipped over the parchment to read the final three paragraphs of Eli's letter.

"Kelmari's necklace is inside the top, right-hand drawer of the dresser across from my bed at home. I obviously cannot return there to get it for you, so you will need to travel to Sirranon to retrieve it. My address there is 15 Telgone Street.

"You should have no trouble using Lockstra to unlock the door, but I would suggest slipping through a back window instead. Be certain that you are cloaked in invisibility the entire time. You never know who might be watching the house. I cannot promise that Kalvaro won't be snooping around trying to gather more 'evidence' to convict me of further crimes I never committed.

"Please come for the necklace as soon as you can, as there's no telling if anyone in Keltan knows of the necklace, and the lost Secret. Write to me when you return to *let me know that you've gotten it. Be discreet, though. The prison mail system is monitored.*

"Best of luck,

Eli."

Carmen looked up at her Souls.

"Do you realize what this means?" she asked, her heart pounding. "There are four Secrets, not three! That was a visitation dream that Eli was talking about...and it actually happened, just like the one I experienced with Dagtar. We have to get a hold of the lost Secret before Triedastron or anyone else does!"

"This was the key phrase that was missing," Blaze said eagerly. "Without it, the other Secrets mean nothing.... This is exactly the answer that we've been searching for."

"Well, it looks like Alazar was right," Stellar said reflectively, as he stared down at the letter. "All you had to do was ask."

CHAPTER TWENTY-SIX
THE LOST SECRET

What's the fastest way to get to Sirranon?" Carmen asked Blaze, as she stuffed Eli's letter back into its envelope.

The Sarcan took a minute to consider the possibilities.

"High-speed airship," he finally decided. "If the ship that we took to the Oldac Forests is still here, we can ask Haidar if we can use it. But if not, we'll have to mail in a request to the airfield in Sirranon to get one sent up here.... It likely wouldn't be here for a few days though."

Carmen tucked Eli's letter into her pocket for safekeeping. She already knew which of the two options she would rather exercise.

"Okay, let's go track down Haidar and see if he can help us."

Carmen then looked at Stellar, Glamis, and Anubis.

"Can you guys find my grandfather, Renalda, and Alazar, and tell them what's going on? I don't want them to worry if we're gone tonight or tomorrow with no explanation."

"No problem, Car," Stellar said. "I'll go to Blaine. Anubis and Glamis can track down Renalda and Alazar."

"Thanks," Carmen said, walking quickly toward the door with Blaze. "We'll meet you back here in a little while."

Carmen and her Souls left the room and split up. Carmen and Blaze climbed the stairs to the Captains' training room; Stellar walked across the hall, and Anubis and Glamis hastened downstairs to the Councilors' meeting chamber on the lowest floor of the castle.

When Carmen and Blaze arrived in the upstairs hallway, they saw Commander Haidar emerging from the training room at the end of the hall with Rishaw, who was moving out the last trunks of armor on a rolling cart. Haidar shook the craftsman's hand and muttered his words of thanks.

Rishaw bid Haidar farewell before proceeding to make his way down the stairs to meet with Officer Sheridae's students, pulling his trunks of armor behind him. The trunks hit each step with a heavy thud.

Carmen and Blaze dashed down the corridor to meet Haidar before he left. They were glad that both the hallway and the training room were otherwise empty. Haidar looked toward them as they approached.

After exchanging greetings with her Commander, Carmen launched into a brief explanation of the letter that she had just received, knowing that she could trust him not to reveal its critically important contents to anyone else. Haidar listened closely as she spoke, asking no questions, but nodding occasionally throughout her talk.

".... So, that's what's going on," Carmen said, at the conclusion of her story. "Is *The Fearless* still here in the valley?"

"Ah, unfortunately, it is not," Haidar said, sounding genuinely disappointed. But then he appeared to come to another idea.

"I will go ahead and send in a request for a smaller high-speed airship for you and your Souls," Haidar decided. "I have an old friend who works at the Sirranon Airfield.... I would guess that he should be able to have the ship here by tomorrow morning. With all that's happening in Pyramid City, it would normally take twice as long."

"Uh...okay, great," Carmen replied. She would have to be satisfied with Haidar's plan, as she had no other means to leave the valley any sooner than the following day.

"Thank you, sir," she said, as she turned to go. "That would be wonderful."

"Master Fox," Haidar said, making Carmen turn back around a couple of steps away from him. "Be careful. What you are about to do may seem to be a straightforward task...but let me remind you that our duties as Kelmarians aren't always as easy as they first appear."

Carmen stared at him. She knew all too well what the Sarcan Commander meant. Over the past two years, life's unpredictable twists and turns had taken her on an incredible ride that she never could have envisioned prior to its beginning. Nobody had promised her before the start of this great journey that it would always be easy; she just knew that in the end, it would be worth all that she had gone through along the way.

"Take care, Carmen," Haidar said, nodding to her. "I will see you soon."

Carmen and Blaze turned and walked back up the hall. As they descended the stairs at the end of the corridor, Carmen sighed.

"What is it, Car?" Blaze asked.

"I just hope that we make it to Sirranon in time...." Carmen said. "We always have to worry that someone will get there before us."

Blaze looked thoughtful.

"Well, we always have our challenges," he said, as he and Carmen walked to their door on the third floor. "But one way or another, we always get through it.... Just believe that whatever happens, everything will eventually come together for the best."

Carmen and her Souls woke up shortly after 8:00 AM the next morning to a warm and sunny first day of summer in Sarcanian Valley, but the weather was not at all fitting with what was taking place only three hours north of the gorge that was home to Thunder Academy.

Carmen received *The Kelmarian Review* from her messenger bird before breakfast, only to be met with a disturbing photo of a street in Pyramid City filled with Phantoms battling uniformed Kelmarian fighters. A pair of buildings was on fire behind them, and the formerly beautiful cobblestone street was nearly unrecognizable beneath the layer of debris that littered the ground beside puddles of fresh blood. The photo was centered beneath the newspaper's headline.

PYRAMID CITY ABLAZE AS PHANTOMS ADVANCE FARTHER INTO CAPITAL

Carmen sat down at the breakfast table with her friends and read the article, her heart sinking more and more with every sentence.

Following two full days of intense fighting, Triedastron's Phantom Warriors have made a steady advance toward the center of Pyramid City. As they progress, smoke from the fires that the Keltan spirits have set blackens what were once serene blue skies over the Kelmarian capital.

Since the Phantoms' arrival, the Pyramid City defenders have been working without rest to drive the Phantoms away and return safety to the streets, but as of the end of the conflict's second day, there seems to be no end to the fighting in this city, which has survived a number of large battles over the years.

The historic golden buildings that line the streets of the capital are all at risk for destruction if the city militia cannot hold the Phantoms back. At the time of this release, a handful of structures have already fallen victim to the Phantoms' path of devastation, and more will surely share the same fate unless the Pyramid City forces can hinder the enemies' progress.

The next twenty-four hours will be critical as the Kelmarian fighters maintain their defense of Pyramid City. The resiliency of the residents here will continue to be tested, and their collective strength and determination called upon, in this intense and enduring clash. Only time will tell whether Pyramid City will stand to survive another 3,000 years.

Carmen put down the paper. She didn't want to read any more about what was happening in Pyramid City, as it disturbed her to know that she was powerless to help the Kelmarian fighters there. Until she came to own the lost Secret, there was nothing that *anyone* in Sarcanian Valley could do to be of assistance to his or her fellow Kelmarians.

Carmen and her friends ate their breakfast quietly, their minds cluttered with thoughts and fears about the coming days. The Souls of Destiny passed the newspaper around the table and read the front-page story one at a time. After they had all finished reading, Carmen looked up from her plate of half-eaten scrambled eggs.

"I've been thinking about a plan for today," she said, as she set down her fork.

Her friends listened with interest.

"I think that we should take the Jar of Protection that you got me for Christmas with us…to hold the necklace," Carmen began. "In case there's a person out there who might want to steal it, I think that we should put it in the jar and bring it back to Sarcanian Valley with us. Nobody can open that jar but me, and it's me who has to read the last Secret."

Glamis was the first to agree.

"That is a brilliant idea, Carmen," he said jovially, a piece of cooked insect dangling from his jowl. "And I believe that Eli would want you to keep the necklace."

"It makes perfect sense to me, too," Stellar said. "Whenever there's something that valuable around, there will always be someone who wants to steal it."

"We need to get it before anyone else finds out about it," Blaze added.

There was a momentary glint in Anubis's golden eyes as he observed something in his mind that none of the others could see.

"Go ahead and get the jar, Carmen," he said. *"If my vision is correct, our airship is waiting for us outside."*

Carmen hastily finished the last of her eggs. Then she piled up all their empty breakfast dishes for the Thunder Academy Sarcan servers, who would come by at lunchtime to collect them. After that chore was complete, she walked over to her dresser and bent down to open the bottom drawer.

Carmen reached in and felt the smoothness of the ceramic Jar of Protection beneath her fingers. She promptly lifted out the white container, whose lid was sculpted in the form of a sitting golden Dragon, and carried it back over to the table.

"Are we ready to go?" Carmen asked her friends, as they got up from their seats.

"Absolutely," Blaze said, speaking for everyone.

Carmen and her Souls closed the door of their room behind them and walked downstairs.

The halls of Thunder Academy were fairly quiet this morning, which was ideal for Carmen, who was anxious to get to the airship bound for Sirranon as quickly as possible. She and her friends would pass a total of only four other students and castle visitors walking through the corridors that led down to the front doors of the school.

Carmen emerged from the castle with her Souls and looked across the valley. A small wooden airship was sitting at the southern edge of the dueling fields. The light wooden craft had a set of white sails and gray-brown wings. The bright morning sun fell on the ship's name adorning the bow—*The Purpose*.

Carmen and her friends crossed the unoccupied dueling fields and boarded the ship. There were five seats on the vessel, which was just enough for their group. Carmen and Blaze took the two front seats, while Glamis, Anubis, and Stellar sat behind them.

About thirty seconds after they had boarded, the group heard a click as the door of the ship locked shut. *The Purpose* then rose up into the sky and turned south. Carmen sat back as the airship soared over the green trees of Mortrock Forest, and flew off to Eli's hometown of Sirranon.

Trees, mountains, lakes, and rivers rushed beneath Carmen and her Souls as *The Purpose* flew three hundred miles south. The ship maintained a steady speed, which felt to be equivalent to that of the ship that had taken Carmen and her friends to the Oldac Forests.

The sun was pleasantly warm on Carmen's face. Near the end of the reasonably long flight, she closed her eyes and allowed the sun and the light breeze to relax her. Clutching the Jar of Protection in her lap, she fell asleep for a short time.

When Blaze woke Carmen up, she peered automatically over the side of the ship to see an unfamiliar city through the clouds below. Very old houses and businesses with colored slate roofs comprised the town. Many sorcerers and creatures were walking throughout the cobblestone streets.

"We're almost there," Blaze told her.

Just a minute or so later, the airship began its slow descent to a grassy park in the center of Sirranon. Several of the sorcerers and creatures who were out walking on this beautiful summer day gazed up at the airship that was flying down to the town square. Some of those passing through the park even gathered around the perimeter of the stone plaza amid the trees to watch the ship land.

The Purpose touched down smoothly in the heart of Sirranon at 11:15 AM, according to the brick clock tower that stood at the northern end of the town square. Eager to find Eli's home and retrieve Kelmari's necklace, Carmen and her Souls climbed down off of the ship as the small crowd of curious sorcerers and creatures watched them.

Carmen caught the eye of a middle-aged sorceress, whose thick, curly gray hair draped past her shoulders. She decided to approach her.

"Excuse me," Carmen said politely, walking up to the woman. "Can you tell me how to get to Telgone Street?"

The sorceress pointed straight up the central street of the city.

"Just head up Main Street for about five blocks," she said, "and then make a left onto Lantern Avenue. Go to the end of that road, and you'll see Telgone Street right off of that."

"Lantern Avenue, got it," Carmen said. "Thank you."

Carmen rejoined her Souls at the foot of the airship, and then the five of them left the park and wandered up the western sidewalk of Main Street, which was congested with Pegasus-drawn carriages and young children on bikes. The sidewalks were also quite busy, with throngs of sorcerers and creatures walking up and down the streets, taking advantage of the balmy weather.

Carmen and her friends strolled past stores, small cafés, and schools as they made their way up to Lantern Avenue.

Carmen could smell the refreshing salty scent of an ocean somewhere nearby.

They marched for five full blocks through the city before they came upon Lantern Avenue. Carmen and the others then made a left turn down the narrower side street, which was much quieter than the busy town's main road.

Just as the resident sorceress had promised, Carmen and her companions saw the sign for Telgone Street upon nearing the end of Lantern Avenue. As they walked through the shadows of the tall buildings on either side of them, Carmen cast all of them into invisibility, and they hiked the rest of the way to the end of the road.

The group turned right onto the one-lane Telgone Street, which was lined with small, Victorian-era houses painted in unusually bright colors and spaced equally apart on square lawns. Carmen stared at the number on the house directly across from her. It was 7, and the number on the one to the left of that was 8, meaning that they would have to walk past a few more residences in that direction in order to get to Eli's.

Reading the house numbers as she strolled by, Carmen couldn't help noticing that all of the homes on this street were not only very old but had also been repainted at some point over the years to maintain their original charm. There were houses that were painted purple, with light pink shutters and violet roofs. There were also rich green houses, bright yellow houses, and ones in nearly every other color as well.

Carmen's group finally reached the house adorned with the number 15. Eli's home was lavender and had navy blue shutters and a sea-green slate roof. Like all of the others on the street, it was a Victorian-era home, with front steps and a covered porch.

After observing that the small house appeared to be unoccupied, Carmen and her friends hiked up the stone walkway, and then around to the back of the residence. They planned to take Eli's advice and slip inside through a rear window to avoid attracting attention.

As she and the others walked around the yard, Carmen noticed that Eli had an old wooden lawn swing and an antique stone birdbath sitting near the edge of his property. Both looked like they had been there for close to a century.

There were four windows running along the lower floor at the rear of Eli's house. Blaze flew up and peeked through each of them, all of which were about five feet above Carmen's head.

"The room on the far left is the bedroom," Blaze reported, as he flew back down to his friends. "I saw the dresser next to the front window."

"Okay," Carmen said, looking up at the fairly small window.

"It's probably best if you and I just go in and get it," she told Blaze, before looking around at the others. "The rest of you should keep watch out here."

After the rest of them had agreed, Carmen summoned her wings and flew up to the window, handing Blaze her wand and the Jar of Protection.

Once there, she lifted up the glass, and then the mesh screen underneath. She took her wand and the jar back from Blaze and followed him through the open window.

Eli's bedroom was painted in a light yellow color. The bed, which had a heavy wooden headboard and a dark blue quilt, was placed against the back wall. There was a closet off to Carmen and Blaze's right as they stood next to the bed, and a dark wooden dresser sitting beside the front window.

Carmen and her Sarcan hurried to the other side of the room. When she arrived at the dresser, Carmen placed the Jar of Protection on top of it and leaned her wand against the wall. With shaking hands, she pulled open the uppermost right-hand drawer.

Lying there on top of a dusty, antique box of quill pens was a perfectly white string of pearls, which seemed to sparkle in the sun coming in through the window.

Carmen reached her hand into the drawer and gently picked up the necklace, as though afraid that a rough touch would destroy the delicate piece of jewelry.

She stared down at the ancient necklace in her hand. She could see the tops of silver words engraved into the other side of the pearls.... She was just going to turn the necklace over to read the message when Anubis suddenly cried out to her and Blaze, causing both of them to jump.

"GET OUT OF THE HOUSE, NOW!"

Only a second later, the front door of Eli's home opened with a sharp THUD!

Carmen's heart stopped. Her blood pounding in her ears, she wrenched open the gold Dragon lid of the Jar of Protection and dropped Kelmari's necklace inside. She then quickly screwed the lid back on, shut the dresser drawer, and grabbed her wand. There were footsteps just outside the door.

Carmen and Blaze exchanged uneasy glances. But just as they were about to race to the window, the bedroom door flew open, and Maidak Kalvaro swept inside.

The two of them froze, their heartbeats thumping loudly in their chests. A younger man with blue eyes and a thin face framed by fine brown hair came in after Kalvaro. Both men were dressed in red and gold Kelmarian Parliament robes, and the boy had a large burlap sack clutched in one of his hands.

"My guess is that the most valuable objects would be stored in here," Kalvaro told his young accomplice. "Check the closet. I'll search the dresser."

Their heads throbbing and their bodies aching, Carmen and Blaze moved quietly to the left to get out of Kalvaro's way as he strode over to Eli's dresser and began pulling open the drawers.

Carmen desperately wanted to fly across the room and out the window to safety, but she couldn't risk Kalvaro feeling the breeze created by her wings. Looking much like a deranged madman, Kalvaro dug through each and every drawer, carelessly throwing the contents, most of which were clothing, onto the floor.

After failing to find anything of significance, Kalvaro slammed his hand down on the top of the dresser, furious.

"It's not here!" he hissed to his associate, who had been equally unsuccessful in uncovering anything of value in Eli's closet. "They've beaten us to it! The necklace is gone!"

Carmen felt her blood turn cold.

"Are you sure that you went through everything?" the young man asked.

Carmen recognized his voice. This was the new intern Kalvaro had screamed at for failing to get him a cup of hot tea just before Eli's trial.

"Of course I'm sure, Hazrond!" Kalvaro snapped. He stepped over a pile of Eli's robes as he stalked over to him. "The Master will not be pleased by this. Now *I'll* have to figure out what we're going to tell him."

Hazrond frowned. Then he happened to glance over at the open window. He looked from the window to the incensed Kalvaro standing before him.

"Maybe they're still here," he muttered, jerking his head toward the only way out of the room.

Kalvaro stared across at the open window...and then turned and looked right to where Carmen and Blaze were situated, just feet away from him. His dark brown eyes were gleaming as his pale, narrow face twisted into a horrible smile.... Carmen couldn't hesitate for another second.

Kalvaro removed a gold ring from his finger and summoned his wand in a flash of light. Carmen and Blaze rose up off of the floor and flew across the room. Immediately feeling

575

the wind from their wings, Kalvaro pointed his wand up at them.

"*Wingdasarum!*"

Carmen felt her wings disappear just when Blaze's stopped beating. They both tumbled awkwardly down through the air onto Eli's bed, causing it to sag. The Jar of Protection slipped out of Carmen's hands.

Kalvaro tramped over and pointed his golden wand at the indentation in the bed, his long bronze hair blowing out behind him.

"*Revealio!*"

Instantly, Carmen and Blaze became visible. Kalvaro lowered his wand, a smug expression on his face. Kalvaro's eyes then fell on the Jar of Protection, which had rolled to the end of the bed. He suddenly glared at the young Kelmarians.

"What exactly is going on here?" he demanded.

"I could ask *you* the same question," Carmen retorted, sitting up. She knew that she had to grab the Jar of Protection, but she couldn't make a move toward it until she found out what Kalvaro wanted with the item inside.

Kalvaro frowned.

"I'm patient enough to wait my turn," he said, in a low but menacing voice. "And unless you can provide a reasonable explanation as to why you have broken into a convicted felon's home, I will be forced to escort you down to Parliament for questioning."

Carmen considered her options. She debated whether she should tell Kalvaro the truth…. Something about the strangeness of the situation was making her believe that she would have to be honest, but she would be careful not to elaborate too much on her real reason for being in the house.

"We came here to get something for Eli…." Carmen said slowly. "Something that he wanted us to keep safe until he's released from prison."

Kalvaro raised an eyebrow.

"You must have put a great deal of thought into fabricating such an imaginary tale," he replied stiffly, clearly unamused.

Kalvaro then pointed his wand at the Jar of Protection.

"What's in the jar?" he asked brusquely.

Carmen shrugged.

"I don't know."

Kalvaro looked unconvinced.

"I'll see about that," he said.

And without hesitation, Kalvaro leaned over the bed and picked up the jar. He wrenched the gold Dragon lid as hard as he could. A pulsing vein was visible in his forehead as he worked to force open the jar.

Carmen held her breath. But no matter how vigorously Kalvaro turned the lid, the jar would not open.

After trying in vain to open the jar with physical force, and then magic, Kalvaro glared at Carmen. Then he abruptly threw the jar down to the floor with enough force to shatter even the sturdiest ceramic object.

BANG!

The jar hit the hardwood floor but remained intact. Kalvaro bent down, picked it up, and stared at it...only to see that there wasn't a mark anywhere on it. That was when he appeared to realize something.

"This...is a Jar of Protection," he told Hazrond, who was standing just a few steps away from him. "Only the owner of the jar can open it."

Kalvaro's eyes drifted slowly back to Carmen. Then he carelessly tossed her the jar, which she caught before it could hit the bed. Kalvaro pointed his wand at her.

"Open it," he ordered.

Carmen glared at him.

"Not until you tell us what you're doing here."

Still staring at her, Kalvaro lowered his wand slightly. Then he and Hazrond exchanged self-assured glances. The young intern had apparently come a long way since Eli's hearing to become Kalvaro's personal assistant.

"We are collecting evidence for a second investigation into crimes involving Mr. Elezar," Kalvaro said calmly. "If my suspicions are correct, the item that is inside this jar is the very one that we require as a part of our investigation.... The relevant item in question is therefore the property of the Kelmarian Parliament. Now *open it.*"

Carmen looked from Kalvaro to Blaze, trying to decide what she should do. Even if Kalvaro was being truthful, which she doubted very much, she nevertheless couldn't open the jar and risk him reading the message on Kelmari's necklace before she did. And if Kalvaro was lying, as she thought him to be, it was all the more reason for her to run. Potential consequences disregarded, she had to do what was best for Kelmar.... That was why she had been chosen as Guardian, after all. She had made up her mind.... She and Blaze had to get out before Kalvaro and Hazrond could force her to reveal the lost Secret.

Kalvaro was watching Carmen closely as she clutched the Jar of Protection. She glanced fleetingly up at the ceiling as she prepared to make her escape.

"*I summon the Wings of Flight!*" she shouted.

Carmen's wings appeared a moment later, and Kalvaro made a desperate leap toward her. He threw aside his wand and grabbed the Jar of Protection—attempting to pry it from her grasp. When she wouldn't let it go, Kalvaro seized her right hand and tried to force her to open the lid.

Blaze flew over and bit Kalvaro on the wrist. Kalvaro immediately retracted his injured hand, recoiling in pain.

Carmen and Blaze scrambled off of the bed and ran to the window. Blaze flew out first. Hazrond pointed his wand at Carmen just as she was all set to fly out behind her Sarcan.

"Instundo!"

"Invisible Shield!"

Much to Carmen's good fortune, her invisible dome protected her from the enemy spell, and securely encased her as she soared out through the window. On the lawn below, Glamis, Stellar, and Anubis were waiting nervously with Blaze.

"Let's get out of here!" Carmen shouted to them.

She swiftly touched down on the grass, and she and her friends sprinted around the house without looking back. Kalvaro's shouts of rage followed after them.

They galloped up Telgone Street and back through Lantern Avenue. Turning the corner onto Main Street, Carmen and her Souls rushed down the sidewalk, steering their way through the crowds as they ran toward the town square.

"Come on, we're just about there!" Carmen yelled, as the white sails of the airship came into view in the park.

Their legs burning, Carmen and her friends crossed the street into the tree-lined town square. With haste, they climbed aboard *The Purpose* and collapsed into their seats. The wooden door of the ship closed and locked with a soft *click*. Then the wings of the vessel began to beat…and lifted the ship up into the air.

Still struggling to catch her breath, Carmen looked down over the side of the aircraft. Kalvaro and Hazrond hadn't followed them…or if they had, they were too far back to be seen from the center of town.

The Purpose couldn't leave Sirranon fast enough for Carmen. As the city shrank to a meager speck of color beneath her, she sat back in her seat and closed her eyes, feeling as relieved as she was exhausted. But then she unexpectedly found herself laughing as she looked over at Blaze and the rest of her friends.

"We did it...." she said, struggling to catch her breath. "We managed to escape...again."

Blaze was smiling as well.

"We can do anything, can't we?" he remarked.

Carmen briefly glanced down at the Jar of Protection in her lap before looking back up at Blaze.

"Do you think that Kalvaro was telling the truth?" she asked, "about needing the necklace as evidence?"

"I'm not sure," Blaze said. "But you made the right decision to flee.... It was the only wise choice."

"Why don't you take a look at the necklace, which you were almost killed trying to get?" Stellar suggested, as *The Purpose* soared away from the city.

Carmen grinned.

"I guess I should."

She placed her hand on the golden Dragon sitting atop the lid of the jar.

"Here I go."

Blaze and the other Souls of Destiny looked away as Carmen reached into the jar and removed Kelmari's pearl necklace so that they wouldn't accidentally read the Secret before her. Carmen laid the piece of jewelry in her hand and silently read the message, which was engraved in flowing, cursive handwriting on the back of the pearls.

Set free the doubts, echo the songs of days afore.

Carmen memorized the sentence, and then wrote it down on the parchment she'd removed from the pocket of her robes. Once she had the lost Secret documented, it vanished from Kelmari's necklace. She slipped the item back into the jar and met the eyes of her friends.

"I hate to say this, but it looks like we still have to decipher it," she told them.

Blaze didn't seem disappointed.

"I'm not surprised, actually. At least we have it," he said, in a positive tone. "After we get back to the castle, we'll work on deciphering this last Secret...and hopefully save Kelmar."

A mild summer breeze rustled through the white sails of *The Purpose* as Carmen and her friends flew north to Sarcanian Valley. Carmen smiled, leaning back and looking up into the blue afternoon sky while she reflected on Blaze's words.

"Now, if only it could be that simple," she said, sighing.

CHAPTER TWENTY-SEVEN
THE FLIGHT OF THE DARK MASTER

It was early afternoon when Carmen and her Souls arrived in North Kelmar. Before reaching Sarcanian Valley, they'd had to fly through a thunderstorm centered over the southern portion of Mortrock Forest, and as a result, the five of them were left sopping wet from head to toe in frigid rainwater as they soared into the sun-drenched sandstone gorge.

Exhausted, Carmen and her friends climbed down from *The Purpose* and trekked across the dueling fields, where half a dozen Sarcan Captains and Cadets were practicing dueling with one another. Among the students out on the fields were Kamie, Dall, Max, and Kai. They all stared at Carmen, Blaze, and the others as they walked past them to return to the castle.

"Oh, don't even ask," Carmen said, putting up her hand before one of them could question her and her friends regarding their disheveled appearance. "We flew to South Kelmar to obtain another one of the Secrets, and there was a thunderstorm on our way back...but the trip was well worth it."

Carmen briefly explained the story of the lost Secret to her classmates, and then she and her Souls climbed the mountain steps and upstairs to the third floor of the school.

With the sun peering in through the tall windows of the corridor, Carmen walked down the hallway with her friends to the door of her bedroom.

She opened her door only to find her grandfather and Thunderbolt waiting for her and the others inside their room. They both looked up from their conversation at the meal table when the group entered.

"You're back!" Blaine said, his blue eyes shining.

Then he stared at Carmen's rain-soaked clothes with concern.

"What happened?" he asked.

"Don't worry. We just flew into some rain on the way back from Sirranon," Carmen explained. "The weather was fine for most of the trip.... It was when we flew over Mortrock Forest that the storm came up."

Blaine chuckled.

"The weather has a mind of its own."

He then rose from his seat at the table.

"I hope you don't mind that we came in while you were away," he said, on behalf of him and Thunderbolt. "*Someone* had to make sure that the Sarcans delivered your lunch," he explained, motioning toward the covered tray of food on the table.

"No, of course not!" Carmen said, grinning. "Thanks for coming."

"It was the least we could do," Blaine said, with his own kind smile. "So, how did it go? Did you find the necklace?"

"We did," Carmen replied brightly. She held up the Jar of Protection for him to see. "It's right inside here. Though we almost didn't get it in time.... Kalvaro came to Eli's house to try to seize the necklace as evidence against Eli...supposedly for a new investigation."

"You're kidding," Blaine said, frowning in disbelief. "And how did you convince him to let you have it?"

"Uh...I didn't. Blaze and I just left with it," Carmen admitted. "Kalvaro had no intention of allowing us to keep it, even if I had told him the complete truth, so we did what we had to do."

"Carmen simply needs to decipher the message, and then we'll have all four of the plaintext Secrets in our possession," Blaze said.

Blaine and Thunderbolt both beamed at Carmen and her Souls.

"You should all be very proud of yourselves.... That is quite an achievement," Thunderbolt said. "Now come get dried off. We'll have a late lunch together."

Carmen went to the bathroom to grab a handful of towels. She tossed one of them to Blaze, and then used the rest to dry off her other Souls by vigorously rubbing them through their fur. Once she was done with that, Carmen dried off her hair and her robes before penning a quick note to Eli to let him know that she and her friends had successfully retrieved Kelmari's necklace. She planned to mail it out to him the next morning.

Finally, Carmen and her companions sat down to eat their sandwiches, which had been prepared by the castle cooking staff. Blaine had brought in a couple of additional chairs from his room so that he and Thunderbolt could eat with her and her friends.

"I can't wait to find out what the final Secret says," Carmen said with a smile, in between bites of her Deltacarp sandwich. "I hope that it provides us with a clue as to how to make use of all of the Secrets together."

"I have a feeling that *this* Secret will be the most telling of the four," Blaze remarked, after swallowing a mouthful of fish. "There's a reason that so few people knew that this one existed.... Most everybody always thought there to be only *three* Secrets of Kelmar."

"Excellent point, Blaze," Thunderbolt said, putting down his sandwich. "It was kept hidden for centuries, most likely to prevent Dark forces from acquiring it."

"It was very wise of Merlin to keep it within the family," Glamis said.

Fifteen minutes later, Carmen and her friends were calmly finishing eating when Carmen noticed that Anubis had his eyes closed. His plate had only a couple of crumbs left on it.

"Is something the matter, Anubis?" Carmen asked.

The Jackal, who was sitting in the chair to her right, opened one eye to look at her.

"No. I am merely concentrating," he said, before closing his eye again. *"I have just been sensing something strange outside since we got back to the valley.... I'm trying to get a better idea of what it is."*

Reasonably alarmed, Carmen looked around at the rest of her friends.

"Are any of you sensing the same thing?" she asked. "I don't feel anything...."

There was silence for a short time as each of Carmen's Souls attempted to feel the unusual presence that Anubis was sensing.... Blaze was the first of them to speak.

"I didn't feel it before, but I do now," he said. "It's outside...beyond the valley, and it's getting stronger."

Glamis and Stellar were both nodding slowly.

"Yes...there is, undoubtedly, an abnormal force present," Glamis observed.

"Definitely," Stellar agreed.

Thunderbolt looked at his Master.

"It's Dark," he told Blaine. "Without question."

Blaine and Carmen stared at each other.

"Kelmarian creatures have a keener sense of awareness than we do," Blaine reminded his granddaughter. "It's likely still too far away for us to feel."

It was an uncomfortably quiet end to the meal. Carmen and the others ate the remainder of their food with heightened senses. Carmen tried with much effort to tap into her magical consciousness as she took her last bites....

585

Suddenly, the room darkened noticeably. It was as though the light of day had abruptly turned to night. That was the moment in which Carmen felt the exact same thing that her friends had been feeling all along. She instantly jumped up from her chair and ran to the window. Her grandfather and her friends followed.

Carmen knelt on her bed and gazed outside.... Her jaw dropped as she gaped at the sight of the magnificent Sarcanian Valley cast under a blanket of darkness. An enormous, snaking black and gray shelf cloud had descended over the gorge, swallowing up the bright blue skies that had been present just minutes ago. High up in the atmosphere above the wall-like cloud, a threatening thunderstorm was rumbling through the heavens.

The shelf cloud, whose underside was turbulent and gusting, was rising over the valley from the north, overtaking everything in its path. The sky grew darker and darker with each passing second. Carmen and her friends stared, mesmerized, at the rapidly blackening sky, their thoughts racing with the speed of the oncoming storm.... What was happening?

A sudden, sharp rapping on the door gave all of them a start.

Carmen immediately tore her attention away from the window, leapt down off of her bed, and hurried back across the room. She answered the door to see Commander Haidar standing before her. He was wearing his new gold and silver battle armor over his Kelmarian Army uniform.

"The Phantoms are on their way to the valley," he alerted Carmen.

Then his eyes flashed into the room in the direction of her companions.

"I need all of you to get into your armor and meet me on the roof. Our enemies are substantially weakened from the battle in Pyramid City.... We fight with the goal of driving them out of Kelmar permanently."

He then locked eyes with Carmen again.

"I must now go and alert the rest of the students. Move quickly."

"We'll be right up," Carmen promised. She could feel her heart pounding in her chest as she shut the door and hastened over to the other side of the room to retrieve their armor from beneath the three beds. Blaine and Thunderbolt met Carmen's eyes as she threw the pile of armor up onto the top of her own bed.

"We'll leave to get dressed, and then we'll come back to help you get your Souls into their armor," Blaine promised. "We'll get back as fast as we can."

Carmen nodded, and hastily began to slip on her greaves and breastplate. She amazed herself with how easily she could get her new armor on by herself for her first time. After she was completely dressed, she started to help Blaze and the others get ready. She had to fight the urge to look out the window every couple of seconds at the looming storm. But in record time, she had Blaze in his armor, and then got to work on the rest of her Souls.

Blaine and Thunderbolt returned to the room in under three minutes, dressed in their armor and ready for battle. With speed that none of them knew they had, Carmen, her grandfather, and Thunderbolt got Stellar, Anubis, and Glamis into their armor.

Carmen grabbed the Light Sword in its scabbard and attached it to her belt, her pulse sharply accelerated in anticipation of the impending clash with the Phantoms. Before she left, she hid the Jar of Protection under her bed. As much as she wanted to decipher the lost Secret here and now, it would have to wait until after this battle was over. So with everyone dressed and prepared to leave, Carmen and her companions dashed out of the room, shutting and locking the door behind them.

Out in the hallway, there was organized chaos as the Sarcan Captains and Cadets emerged from their rooms and gathered in the corridor, all of them wearing their new armor, as well as looks of readiness. The Sarcan Councilors, all of them in armor, too, were ordering the students to line up and follow them to the rooftop of the castle. Alazar and Renalda somehow found Carmen and her Souls in the crowded hallway and wished them good luck. As neither of them could fly, they would not be going into battle on this day. Carmen and her friends hurriedly joined the crowd of students headed upstairs, and in less than five minutes, they were on their way up to the roof.

As Carmen climbed the steps with her grandfather and her Souls, there was a nervous fluttering building inside of her, just as about a hundred different questions flooded her mind.

What would happen if she and the others couldn't defeat the Phantoms and force them out of Kelmar today? Surely Sarcanian Valley would be captured before daybreak tomorrow.... She didn't even know what had happened in Pyramid City yet. Had the capital forces driven the Phantoms out of their city? Or had the Phantoms merely defeated their opponents and moved on to Sarcanian Valley? The glorious Pyramid City could lie in smoldering ruins right now for all that Carmen knew....

In about fifteen minutes, the Kelmarians made it to the top floor of the castle, where they marched halfway down the hall and made a right turn down a narrow corridor.

At the end of this passageway were a staircase and an open door in the ceiling leading out onto the rooftop of Thunder Academy. All of the Kelmarians could see the black and stormy sky on the other side of the doorway.

Blaine, Thunderbolt, and the Sarcan students followed the Sarcan Councilors down the corridor. At the end of the hall, they climbed the relatively narrow stairs two at a time, and then walked out onto the gray shingled castle roof. The Sarcan Councilors climbed out first, followed promptly by the Captains and Cadets.

Carmen and her Souls climbed up right after Blaine and Thunderbolt, in the middle of the line of sorcerers and creatures. As Carmen ascended the stairs, a bitterly cold breeze stung her face. Only seconds later, she and Blaze walked out onto the rooftop.

Commander Haidar and Officer Sheridae were standing with the Councilors at the opposite end of the roof, in the shadow of the giant, metal golden lightning bolt that crowned the school. They were watching attentively as their students emerged from inside the castle.

Carmen, Blaine, and their creatures marched out to the center of the rooftop, where the rest of the Sarcan students were gathered. They looked up into the dark clouds churning and billowing over their heads.... It was unusually cold outside, and as the fierce winds blew past their faces, it felt much more like late evening on a stormy winter night than the middle of an early summer day.

"All of you, come forward and assemble beside Officer Sheridae and me," Haidar ordered of the Sarcan students.

The Captains and Cadets swiftly joined Haidar, Sheridae, and the Sarcan Councilors and lined up along the front of the castle. The Captains stood beside Haidar—the Cadets beside Sheridae. Each of them then turned around and faced the north, waiting to catch sight of the onrushing Phantom Warriors.

"Pyramid City is still standing," Haidar informed the students, continuing to stare out at the storm caused by the Phantoms' approach. "The residents of our capital did an amazing job in fighting off our foes for this long.... Now it is *our* turn to protect *our* home, and to send these devils back to the World of Darkness for the final time."

Sheridae glanced down at her students standing alongside her.

"Stay in flight throughout the battle," she told them. "Keep to the strategy that Haidar went over with you during the assembly. These skies are our territory, and we know them better than anyone else."

"Masters and Partners, work together as always," Haidar reminded both the Captains and the Cadets. "This will likely be our last chance to rid our world of the Phantoms' presence. We cannot afford to fail our fellow Kelmarians today."

Upon those words, the black silhouettes of flying humans and creatures came rising over the distant trees at the northern edge of Mortrock Forest. As they flew ahead toward the castle, Haidar ordered all of the students to summon their wings.

Carmen and her classmates did as they were instructed, and soared up into the sky with their Commanders, Blaine, Thunderbolt, and the Sarcan Councilors. Stellar, Glamis, and Anubis would have no choice but to remain on the roof, as none of them could fly. But even if they were limited in how they could contribute in this particular battle, Carmen was nevertheless insistent that they be here. She was always thankful for anything that they could do to help, even if it was just cheering her and Blaze on, and being there in case of trouble.

The Kelmarians watched as Triedastron's Phantom Warriors drew nearer. Desorkhan and Singe were the ones leading the army of Phantoms into Sarcanian Valley. Carmen squinted into the darkness, trying to see how the Phantoms looked after three straight days of fighting in Pyramid City.

The Keltan fighters were approaching Sarcanian Valley with great speed. If they had indeed been significantly weakened from their previous battles, as Haidar had said, it was certainly not evident in the hungry smiles on the faces of the sorcerers or their creatures as they flew in the direction of Thunder Academy. Most of the Masters had tears in their robes, and some had new scars on their faces and hands...but other than those imperfections, physically, the Phantom Warriors appeared to be no more weakened than the last time the students had seen them.

Carmen drew her saber. Her sorcerer classmates summoned their wands. Blaine had his own sword in hand, as did the Sarcan Councilors and instructors.

Carmen motioned for her Souls to get ready, then she braced herself as the ten Phantom sorcerers raised their weapons, which were a mixture of wands and sabers.

Commander Haidar and Officer Sheridae exchanged glances with the Sarcan Councilors. Haidar then raised his right arm.

"Get ready...."

Haidar and his forces watched as the Phantom Warriors advanced toward them.... Carmen's heart was beating loudly in her ears.

"ATTACK!"

With a huge gust of wind, the Kelmarians rushed forward. Swords and wands clashed, and colored light burst throughout the sky as the Kelmarians and the Phantom Warriors came to blows.

Carmen and Blaze flew toward Desorkhan and Singe, Carmen slicing her sword through the cold air at the Dark Master. Their blades met with explosive force, sending silver sparks flying through the sky. Blaze exhaled a breath of fire at Singe, burning the enemy Sarcan's wings.

"Couldn't wait to have another go at it, could you?" Desorkhan asked, as he dueled with Carmen. "I hope that you weren't planning to travel to Pyramid City in the near future. I doubt that you would recognize the place after the redecorating that we've done to it."

Carmen ignored him. She knew that this kind of talk was one of Desorkhan's many ways of trying to intimidate her, but it wasn't happening on *this* afternoon…not when there was so much at stake for the Kelmarians in the greater conflict.

"Fire Sword!" Carmen cried.

The blade of her sword ignited in flames. Carmen dodged a strike from Desorkhan and thrust her sword at his shoulder.

Carmen's fiery blade ripped through Desorkhan's robes and instantly set them ablaze. Desorkhan bellowed in pain, hastily dousing the flames with a Fire Healing spell.

"Lightning Blade!" Desorkhan ordered.

A bolt of lightning shot from Desorkhan's sword. Carmen summoned a *Flaming Shield* without delay to protect Blaze and herself.

As this and the other duels proceeded, it gradually became more apparent that Desorkhan and the rest of the Phantoms were not battling at full strength…. Their reactions were slower, and their attacks were less potent and precise than they had been in the battle in the Oldac Forests.

The Sarcan Councilors were each dueling a pair of the most experienced Phantom Warriors, and the rest of the Sarcan Captains and Cadets fought together against the remaining portion of the Keltan Army. Stellar, Glamis, and Anubis were watching the battle unfold from below. Being outnumbered in the sky alone, the Phantoms had yet to challenge them.

The Kelmarians had been battling with the Phantoms for over an hour when Carmen used the *Sword of Light* spell against Desorkhan, just as he moved toward her.

The blinding burst of white light struck the Dark Master in the chest, knocking the wind out of him. He staggered in midair, and Carmen took the opportunity to attack him with the very same spell one more time.

With a forward slice of Carmen's sword, Desorkhan was hit head-on with the powerful beam of light energy, and was sent crashing down to the rooftop. The cold winds thrashing her hair across her face, Carmen pointed her sword at Desorkhan as he fell through the darkness.

"Wingdasarum!"

The Dark Master was in no position to block Carmen's last spell. His wings vanished less than ten seconds later, speeding his descent to the roof of Thunder Academy.

Singe flew away from Blaze and sped after Desorkhan, but his Master was falling far too fast for the Sarcan to reach him before he hit the gray shingles.

With a heavy *THUD,* Desorkhan crashed to the center of the hard rooftop. Carmen and Blaze observed Stellar, Glamis, and Anubis as they gathered cautiously around his limp body…. If he made a threatening move toward them, they would attack.

Desorkhan lay there, facedown on the shingled roof, for nearly a full minute before he stirred.

The Dark Master got back up slowly, first on his hands and knees, and then rising to his feet. After picking up his silver sword, which had fallen a couple of feet away from him, he turned and glared back up at Carmen and Blaze.

The left side of Desorkhan's face was red and deeply scored from where he had hit the roof. Fresh blood glistened on his cheek. Carmen and Blaze prepared themselves for him to fly back up and resume his duel with them.

But Desorkhan looked away from his opponents. He strode to the front of the rooftop, his black robes swishing behind him in the wind. Carmen and her friends watched him, on guard, dumbfounded as to what he could be doing.

When Desorkhan reached the gigantic golden lightning bolt standing at the edge of the roof, he stopped walking and slid his sword back into its scabbard. Then he quickly climbed up the diagonal metal sculpture that was the symbol of Thunder Academy.

Standing now at the narrow tip of the lightning bolt, Desorkhan turned around and looked up to face the battling Kelmarians and Phantoms. He raised his arms in the air and motioned toward his own fighters, uttering a Keltan spell that Carmen could not hear from where she was.

Right away, all of the Phantom Warriors in the sky stiffened. A silvery mist drifted from each of their bodies to the hands of the Dark Master, who appeared to be magically borrowing some of their power to assist him with a spell of his own....

Once he had gathered enough of his comrades' strength, Desorkhan summoned his wand and pointed it down at the rooftop shingles, a vicious smile twisting his face.

"Fiery Death!" he commanded.

Roaring red fire suddenly sprang up around the entire perimeter of the rooftop. Unnaturally swift, it began spreading inward. Carmen gasped in horror.

"NO!" she cried.

The fire was moving rapidly. If she couldn't get Stellar, Glamis, and Anubis off of the roof, the cursed flames would soon consume them—and eventually destroy the school. But she couldn't carry more than one of her Souls at once, and Blaze still had Singe to contend with.

Her thoughts now moving a mile a minute, Carmen flew to the Kelmarian sorcerers fighting nearest to her. Both of them had temporarily forced their opponents away from them with well-executed Kelmarsian spells. Carmen tapped her two classmates on the shoulders and made them turn around.

"My Souls are trapped by the fire down there!" she told Shea and Draven quickly, pointing at the roof several feet below them. "You've got to help me save them.... I can only hold one of them at a time, and the fire is spreading too fast for me to get them all out by myself!"

The pair of Captains immediately glanced down at the rooftop. Then Shea looked up at Carmen.

"We'll get them, Carmen, don't worry!" he promised.

In the next second, Shea, Draven, and Carmen were racing down to Thunder Academy, just as the flames were closing in around the three creatures, who were gathered together in the center of the roof. The Dark Master stood atop the gold lightning bolt, using his wand to direct the magical flames closer and closer to them.

Carmen was the first to land, and she ran straight away to the closest creature, which happened to be Anubis, scooping him up into her arms. Shea landed right behind her, and made the brave choice to carry Glamis, who was by far the heaviest of the trio. With a heave of strength, he lifted the Boarax up into his arms as Draven came down and rescued Stellar.

"LET'S GO!" Draven yelled, over the noise of the battle above, cradling Stellar in his arms.

Feeling the heat from Desorkhan's approaching fire on their faces, Carmen and the two boys soared up into the air with the three Souls of Destiny. In a momentary break in his own duel with Mondalaus, Haidar witnessed his Captains flying up from the uncontrolled fire. He called out to them.

"ALERT THE COUNCILORS OF THE FIRE!" he shouted, just as Mondalaus charged back toward him. "THEY MUST EXTINGUISH IT BEFORE IT DESTROYS THE CASTLE!"

Quite aware that every second was crucial in preventing the destruction of their school, Carmen and her classmates flew as fast as they could to each of the Councilors and informed them of the devastating fire that was threatening to destroy Thunder Academy. Nearby Captains and Cadets courageously took over the Councilors' duels as the elder sorcerers soared down to the burning school. Unable to do much of anything while carrying the Souls of Destiny, Carmen, Shea, and Draven then flew higher above the other fighters to keep themselves safe from harm while the Kelmarians and Phantoms continued to battle.

Carmen's eyes darted about the dark sky. There was near nonstop action as the two armies dueled each other. But though the fighting was ongoing, the Sarcanian Valley defenders were clearly outdoing their enemies, with the Phantoms looking weaker and weaker as the minutes passed.

Then, at one point, there was a shout of rage from below that made Carmen and her friends look down. The Sarcan Councilors had somehow put out Desorkhan's fire, and were moving in to attack the Dark Master as he stood at the top of the metal lightning bolt with his wand drawn.

"If you think that you've won this fight, you're in for an unpleasant awakening," Desorkhan said. "If we can't defeat you today...we'll simply come back tomorrow."

Then he snapped his fingers—a magically loud sound that made all of the other Phantoms stop dueling and turn to look at him for direction. Consequently, the Kelmarians each turned and stared at Desorkhan as well.

"Phantoms, we leave Sarcanian Valley until tomorrow night," Desorkhan told his followers. "When we return at full strength...we shall deliver our foes the end that they have had coming to them for a great many years now."

Desorkhan then gazed up at the Kelmarians mixed in amongst the Phantoms. His face was still blistered and red with dried blood.

"Until next we meet, kelscum," he said with a curt, disingenuous bow. "Farewell!"

Desorkhan summoned his wings and soared up into the sky, and was soon rejoined by his Partner, Singe. The Phantoms flew past their Kelmarian opponents to follow him, but Haidar and the rest of Sarcanian Valley's inhabitants had other ideas.

If the Kelmarians let the Phantoms get away, they would just go to a safe place to rest for the day, and return the next night, refreshed and at their strongest. This battle that was taking place over Thunder Academy was the Kelmarians' one and only chance to defeat their enemies and send them back to Keltan. Under no circumstances could they allow the Phantoms to escape now that they were so close to defeating them.

Haidar pointed at the twenty Phantoms fleeing toward the south.

"FOLLOW THEM!" he ordered.

Invigorated and more determined than ever, Haidar flew after the Phantoms. The rest of the Kelmarians followed, chasing the Phantoms across the darkened sky over Sarcanian Valley, the gusting wind helping to carry them faster through the cool air. Shouting and small explosions of light rang through the sky as the Kelmarians fired spells at the escaping Phantoms.

In the midst of the pursuit, Carmen made a bold decision. She found her grandfather in the center of the Kelmarian formation and darted her way through the other fighters to get to him, Blaze flying at her side and Anubis cradled in her arms.

"Pop!" she called, soaring over to Blaine. "I need you to hold Anubis for me…. I'm going after Desorkhan."

Blaine slipped his sword into its scabbard and took Anubis into his arms without another word. His eyes were alert and confident as he gazed at his granddaughter.

"Go get him, Carmen!"

With that, Carmen and Blaze flew away from Blaine and raced ahead of their classmates, their eyes on Desorkhan and Singe, who were leading the Phantoms away from the valley.

They had to fight past the cold winds, which were constantly swiping at and burning their faces.

Carmen reached her sword arm out in front of her as she neared Desorkhan from behind. Now was her moment. If she were ever going to drive the Phantom Warriors back to Keltan, the time for it to happen had come at last.

Carmen and Blaze were just two feet away from their foes, flying slightly higher than they were. Carmen raised the Light Sword as she dove down behind Desorkhan. He glanced back over his shoulder when he heard her come within reach of him, and his dark eyes widened in shock.

"Sword of Light!" she cried.

The blade of Carmen's sword produced a dazzlingly bright glow that encased its entire form. Blaze's horn lit up the same way. Carmen sliced her sword straight down into Desorkhan's back as Blaze stabbed Singe's wings with his horn.

In an instant, Desorkhan became rigid. There was a sharp crack of sound—and then he and Singe disappeared in a burst of white light.

Then, as though a collection of fireworks were exploding across the sky over North Kelmar, each of the accompanying Phantom Warriors vanished in identical striking explosions of light.

The menacing black shelf cloud that had snaked its way through the atmosphere beneath a raging thunderstorm slowly disbanded, revealing a beautiful, brilliant blue sky. A world away, Triedastron was standing on the Keltan side of the Impassable Barrier, furiously accepting his fighters back into the World of Darkness.

CHAPTER TWENTY-EIGHT
UNLOCKING THE SECRETS

The Kelmarians celebrated their hard-fought victory over the Phantoms with aerial hugs and high-fives. A rousing cheer greeted Carmen and Blaze as they turned around at the front of the flying formation. Blaine was the first to rush up to Carmen from the crowd of sorcerers and creatures gathering around her, embracing her as best as he was able to while cradling Anubis in his arms. Thunderbolt came up from behind him and hugged his son, Blaze.

"That was phenomenal!" Blaine said, as he released Carmen. The smile on his face was wider than it had been in a long time. "You and Blaze are *some team!*"

"Thanks," Carmen replied, with a modest grin, glancing toward her Partner. "I just knew that we couldn't let them escape."

"You made sure of that!" Thunderbolt remarked, beaming at her and Blaze.

Commander Haidar and Officer Sheridae approached Carmen and Blaze only moments later.

"Excellent work, Captains," Haidar said, as he flew over to his pair of students. "Thanks to your swift and astute actions, Kelmar is no longer in the path of the Phantoms' destruction."

"Normally, we would rejoice with this victory, but there is still much that needs to be done," Sheridae said, her copper eyes gazing into Carmen's. "You still need to decipher the last Secret to restore the balance between Kelmarsia and Keltan. Until you do that, we cannot rest soundly here in Kelmar."

"But for now, I want you to return to your room and take it easy for the remainder of the day. Do not worry about working on the Secret tonight," Haidar said, before Carmen could argue. "At dawn tomorrow morning, the Captains will meet out on the dueling fields for the final lesson of the term. After that…you have my permission to decipher the last Secret."

"Okay," Carmen said, knowing better than to go against Haidar's wishes. "Then I guess we'll go back to the castle now."

She, Draven, Shea, and their creatures flew down to the roof of the school through a sea of applause and cheers from their classmates, their instructors, and the Sarcan Councilors. When they touched down on the gray shingles, Carmen thanked both of the boys for helping her to save Glamis and Stellar from the fire, and for taking care of them while she and Blaze moved to strike Desorkhan.

"No problem," Draven said with a nod, after placing Stellar down on the rooftop.

He then turned and began to walk down the steps with his Sarcan, Flint, to the top floor of the castle. Just before he disappeared from Carmen's view, he peered back up at her.

"Kelmarians always stick together, right?"

Carmen looked thoughtfully at him…and nodded.

Shea smiled after Draven as he descended the stairs. When he returned his gaze to Carmen, his blue eyes were sparkling in such a way that Carmen couldn't look away from him.

"You're quite welcome," he said courteously. "Just promise me that you and your Souls will stay safe from now on."

"Well, with what *we* do, I can't guarantee anything," Carmen said, grinning appreciatively at him. "But we'll try our best."

Shea smiled, the sun continuing to shine in his eyes. Then he walked quietly past Carmen and strolled down the steps with Gia.

Carmen took one final glance back up at the stunning azure sky. The rest of the Kelmarian fighters were flying down to the rooftop. Feeling tired, but all the more content, she followed Blaine, Thunderbolt, and her classmates down the staircase into Thunder Academy.

Carmen and her Souls went to bed earlier than usual that evening, and awoke shortly before dawn the following morning to eat their breakfast. On this day, their plates were filled with grilled Iyderfish, toast, fried eggs, and fresh fruit.

After sending Eli's letter off with the messenger bird, Carmen took sips from her glass of Snotree juice between bites of her food. It had taken her a while to fall asleep the night before, with her mind buzzing with thoughts and questions regarding what lay ahead for her the next day.

But of all of the ideas that popped into Carmen's mind as she struggled to sleep, one of them was certain. She would decipher the final Secret of Kelmar today, and with any luck, receive her solution to reinstating the peace between the spirit worlds. Just exactly what would happen once she deciphered the lost Secret would remain a mystery until such a time. But as she continued to ponder the possibilities in the morning, Carmen found herself feeling oddly tranquil and alert, in spite of the looming uncertainties. It was as though someone had cast a highly effective calming spell over her to make her relax.

"So, today's the day," Blaze said cheerfully, as he and his friends ate breakfast. "By tonight, we'll have precisely what we need to bring things back to normal around here."

"We *hope*," Carmen said, correcting him.

"How are you feeling this morning, Carmen?" Stellar asked, leaning over his plate of half-eaten food to look across at her. "Did you sleep last night?"

"I'm feeling good today," Carmen answered. "I slept pretty well." This was a lie, but she didn't want to worry him.

"I am also feeling rather wonderful today," Glamis said merrily, grinning at his friends. "I have a feeling that this is going to be a splendid day."

Carmen grinned in response.

"Your senses are usually much more accurate than mine, so I trust you to be right on that."

Anubis had just finished eating the last of his meal. He lifted his head and looked toward her.

"Our senses are no more advanced than yours," he said. *"Believe in your inner voice."*

At the conclusion of breakfast, Carmen and Blaze left their companions to join their classmates out in the valley for Haidar's final lesson. Half of the class of Sarcan Captains was already assembled in the center of the dueling fields when they arrived at the base of the gorge.

It was a lovely, clear day. The sun was peeking in and out of the white clouds that continuously floated through the pale blue skies overhead. Carmen and Blaze exchanged greetings with a couple of their friends, and took their place in line next to Akira and Keko.

Facing the front doors of the castle, Carmen and the others watched as the rest of their classmates emerged from the school and strolled down the mountain stairs to the dueling fields. It was only seconds after the last Master and Sarcan team had joined the class when Commander Haidar appeared on the edge of the castle rooftop.

He stood there in the shadow of the giant golden lightning bolt, looking down at his Captains as the light from the sunrise glistened off of the medals that adorned his red and gold uniform. Haidar observed his students below for a short time, and then summoned his wings and flew down to them.

The Sarcan Commander landed smoothly in front of his line of students. In his typical composed and serious manner, Haidar bowed to the Captains, who intuitively bowed back to him.

"Good morning, Captains. We have come to our final lesson of the term," Haidar said. "Before we get started today...I first must tell you how very proud I am of the extraordinary progress that we have made over these past months."

Many of the students smiled at those simple, sincere words. It meant a great deal to them that Haidar acknowledged their hard work and perseverance, especially as it came in the midst of a strenuous and enduring war.

"This morning marks a critical point in our history," he continued. "At the conclusion of this lesson, you will have completed your second year of training, and you will thus graduate to become Sarcan Majors. You should be tremendously pleased with what you have achieved over the past two years. I cannot tell you what an honor it has been for me to have been your instructor during this time.... You are all worthy of the titles that you hold...and I see only bright, new undertakings in the days and years ahead for each of you."

Haidar beamed at the students, meeting each of their gazes. Carmen wasn't sure how all of the other Captains felt, but she knew that she did feel proud of what she and her peers had accomplished as a class. They had grown up very much over the two years that they had spent in Thunder Academy...and it was gratifying, yet bittersweet to think that in a matter of days, they would be graduating together for the second time, and then moving on to bigger and better things.

"What will also happen at the end of this lesson..." Haidar went on to say, "is that your classmate, Carmen Fox, will decipher the final Secret of Kelmar. This is immensely significant to all of us, because according to the infamous Legend of the Worlds Triad, the Secrets of Kelmar hold the key to our success in reestablishing peace across the three magical realms."

Haidar nodded to Carmen before continuing.

"For our final lesson today, I am first going to go over our strategy for possible battles in Keltan and Kelmarsia once more. After we're through with that, I am going to impart a bit of wisdom as it pertains to the ways of good and evil. There will be no formal instruction or practice dueling today. All I ask…is that you listen."

Haidar summoned his wand. Then he drew a large, invisible rectangle in the empty space to the right of him.

"Summonsio!"

A moment later, the rolling chalkboard from the training room appeared out of thin air beside the Sarcan Commander.

"So," Haidar began, "as we discussed back in Sarcan Hall last week, I have laid out a battle plan for each of the two spirit worlds. Depending on what transpires following the decipherment of the last Secret, we could likely find ourselves traveling to either of the two worlds, or possibly both, to defeat Triedastron."

Haidar turned and tapped his wand to the smooth surface of the blackboard, causing a pair of maps to draw across the board in white chalk. The map closest to Haidar was that of Kelmarsia, and the one next to it was of Keltan. Both maps featured labeled landmarks and important structures in each of the realms.

"We'll start with the World of Darkness," Haidar said, using his wand as a pointer. "Up here is Triedastron's fortress." He pointed to the drawing of the black castle with the tall silver fence on the northern portion of the map. "It's probable that we will need to enter the fortress in order to challenge Triedastron, unless he makes the decision to join his fighters outside. But no matter what scenario we come across…we will undeniably need to keep the Phantoms from escaping through the Impassable Barrier that separates Keltan from Kelmarsia."

Haidar then went on to describe the types of creatures that the Captains might come across in Keltan, most of which Carmen had already seen throughout her trips to the realm. In the World of Darkness, she and the others would be facing a much greater army than the one that had come to Kelmar, including *all* of the Magicon, numerous other Dark sorcerers and creatures, and the Master of Keltan himself. As Haidar talked, Carmen glanced up and down the line of Captains. She could see the expressions of mild fear developing on a number of their faces. They would have to prepare themselves to encounter an assortment of both new and old foes on their journey to the afterlife.

"Now that we've gone over the strategy for Keltan, we'll move on to Kelmarsia," Haidar said, pointing the crown of his wand at the map nearer to him. "*Should* we not defeat Triedastron in the World of Darkness, he will be apt to attempt to claim the World of Light as his own. Our job will then be to make certain that he does not reach the Castle of Merlin.... For if he does, there is little chance that we will ever be able to overthrow him and his followers."

Haidar paused, his silence telling of the seriousness behind his words.

"The Kelmarsians will come to our aid as they work to save their world from capture," Haidar promised, "but it will take our collaborative efforts to conquer this enemy."

Haidar pointed to the meadow surrounding the River of the Departed Spirits on the map.

"Upon entering Kelmarsia through the Impassable Barrier, we would arrive here," he said, before looking out toward Carmen.

"Master Fox, if and when the time comes, you will have to speak with Anubis. He needs to tell Inpu to make sure that the Kelmarsians are assembled on the grass and ready for battle when we get there."

Carmen nodded.

"I will do that, sir."

"Good."

Haidar then directed his students' attention to the forests that surrounded the central meadow in the World of Light.

"The forests in Kelmarsia serve as both an advantage and a curse, dependent upon how well we make use of them," he explained. "The ancient trees can provide us with protection and camouflage in case of an ambush...but they can be an equally useful hiding place for our opponents. We will count on our Kelmarsian allies and our maps to help us navigate through the forests.... There is also a secret path and a bridge leading up to Merlin's castle that is hidden amongst the trees. *At no point* can we allow the Phantoms to use this path," he said, with particular emphasis. "Merlin's castle is the most sacred and powerful place in all of Kelmarsia. It is where Merlin Cloud reigns over the Worlds Triad. A Keltan takeover of that castle could very well end in disaster for Kelmar."

There was another heavy pause in Haidar's speech. The Captains all seemed to take their Commander's words in earnest as they listened to his plan.

"To conclude, we will work to keep Triedastron and his fighters away from the castle and Merlin Cloud," Haidar said. "If we can do that...perhaps our efforts will allow the Secrets of Kelmar to guide our way to victory."

With a wave of his wand, Haidar made the blackboard next to him vanish in a puff of white smoke. All that was left now was for him to share his knowledge on the interactions of Light and Dark, which he had mentioned he would do at the start of the lesson.

"Good and evil..." he began, "seem like two completely separate, utterly opposite entities. But what it really comes down to is not what makes good and evil different...but rather, what makes them the same."

Haidar looked at each and every one of the Captains as he spoke.

"Good and evil, Light and Dark, are each equal parts of a world that exists only when the two sides are present and balanced," he said. "Neither one can be without the other. And it is when one side overpowers their equal that catastrophe strikes, just as it has in the Worlds Triad as of late. Triedastron, as an example, is a Shape-Shifter. He can assume the form of any man or creature, living or dead. But while he, and the evil that he embodies, can take on many different forms, beneath the mask...he does not change in accordance with his appearance. His ideals, and who he is as a person, remain the same— no matter what identity he chooses to accept. But to counteract his darkness, and the darkness of others like him, we have people like ourselves...who do our best to be good, and fight back against the constant threat of evil."

Haidar nodded to himself.

"Both sides—Light and Dark—bring out the best and the worst in each other," he said. "When the two combatants go to war, as they so often have throughout history...we see acts of both compassion and neglect from both parties. So in looking at the perpetual struggle between Light and Dark objectively, we can observe that while the two sides are different in their core values and purposes...they are, in essence, equal. Both good and evil see their opponent as detrimental to their cause, just as each one sees the other as their adversary, as opposed to their mirror reflection."

Carmen absorbed Haidar's words with great interest...quite fascinated by all that the Sarcan Commander was saying. She had never given much consideration as to how the members of good and evil armies interacted in the world...and how in fighting each other, they worked together to make the universe whole.

"As it would be impossible to tell the night from the day without experiencing the rising and setting of the sun...without evil, how would we gauge what constitutes good?"

Haidar paused to let his students consider his words before continuing.

"Similarly, without the presence of good, how do we decide what is truly evil? How would we measure it? The answer...is that we simply couldn't. In reality, we wouldn't be able to tell the two sides apart, and hence, *neither* would exist."

Haidar glanced briefly up at the sky, and then met his students' eyes again.

"The point that I'm trying to make is this," he said. "If one could isolate the cause of this war down to one reason, it would be that the roles of Light and Dark have shifted, while their identities have remained the same. To bring an end to the fighting, we must dispel the darkness that has overtaken the good...and bring Light and Dark into balance again. This fight is not about eliminating evil—it is about good and evil coexisting together peacefully."

There was an insightful glint in Haidar's deep brown eyes as he gazed across at his Captains.

"I have watched all of you learn and grow over the past two years, and I am confident that you will not disappoint Kelmar in this, or any other war. You truly are the future leaders of our world...and I am humbled to have been a part of each of your lives."

Haidar saluted them one final time.

"That concludes today's lesson. Please use the afternoon to review your maps of the afterworlds. I hereby dismiss you for the remainder of the day."

The Sarcan Captains returned the gesture, and then slowly departed the dueling fields to return to the castle, muttering quietly to one another. Before Carmen and Blaze could leave with their classmates, Haidar held them back.

"I just wanted to wish you good luck with the final Secret," he said, stepping forward and resting his hand calmly on Carmen's shoulder. "I'm going to come by your room and check on you in an hour or so, once you've deciphered it, should you need assistance with anything."

"Oh...okay, thank you," Carmen said, wondering what Haidar could think that they would need after deciphering the last of the Secrets. "We'll see you later then."

She and Blaze turned and hiked back to the school with the rest of the students. When they reached the mountain, Carmen glanced back over her shoulder. Commander Haidar had remained on the dueling fields, his hands folded behind his back. His gaze steady, he watched as the Captains passed through the front doors of the castle. When he noticed Carmen looking back at him, he gave her a slight nod, as if to say that even though her formal training was over, he would always watch over her as an instructor and as a friend. Carmen nodded back, and then refocused her eyes ahead of her, so as not to walk into anybody as she and Blaze entered the school and made their way upstairs.

When they got back to their room, they found Glamis, Anubis, and Stellar seated around the meal table. A pile of untouched spaghetti on a sizable silver tray sat in the center of them.

"It was difficult, but we waited for you!" Glamis said, smiling as Carmen and Blaze approached the table. "We're all very hungry!"

"Aw, you didn't have to wait," Carmen said, sitting down with Blaze. "How did you even know when we'd be getting back today? The last lesson of the term is always different from all of the others."

Glamis and Stellar both looked at Anubis.

"I might have listened in on your minds...just a little," Anubis said with a wink.

The group of friends laughed as they each took helpings of the spaghetti. The mood was surprisingly light throughout the meal. The Souls of Destiny shared stories from the term in Thunder Academy while Carmen spent the time looking over her maps.

As Carmen took the final bites of her pasta, the thought of the last Secret reentered her mind, taking her focus away from the lighthearted discussion. She stared out the window of her room as she waited for Glamis and Stellar to finish their food, abruptly feeling a strong desire to go see her grandfather, who was back at his home in Mortrock Forest.

Even with the Phantoms' return to Keltan, the Councilors had decided to prolong the rule that forbids students to travel outside of the valley, until Kelmarsia and Keltan were completely at peace again. But Carmen had now decided that she wanted her grandfather to be with her when she deciphered the remaining Secret...and she suddenly felt so strongly about it that she was willing to break the castle law.

As she was thinking about how she and her friends could take a trip into the forest unnoticed using *Inviscreen,* another thought unexpectedly entered Carmen's mind, just when Dagtar's claw became warm against her skin. That thought was that she and her Souls should all wear their new armor when they went down to Mortrock Forest.

"So, shall we decipher the lost Secret now?" Glamis asked, wiping his mouth with his white linen napkin after slurping down the last of his spaghetti.

"Yes, but I want to do it at my grandfather's house," Carmen said, finally breaking out of her semi-trance. "I want him to be there when we decipher it."

"All right...." Blaze said slowly. "Are you ready to go down there now?"

"Not until we all get into our new armor," she replied.

Blaze stared at her, perplexed.

"Why would we do that?" he asked.

"Um...I don't know," Carmen admitted. "It's...just a feeling that I have."

Carmen and her Souls got dressed in their armor and left the castle for Mortrock Forest no more than ten minutes later. Carmen grabbed the cipher disk, her quill, parchment, and Merlin's maps on her way out the door.

Once outside, she and her friends crossed the eastern border of the valley, and Carmen cast all of them into invisibility, just as a precaution, in case the Sarcan Councilors or instructors were out in the woods.

It was a gorgeous day for a stroll through the forests of North Kelmar, but Carmen could hardly enjoy the marvelously warm and bright afternoon on this early summer day, with her thoughts focused solely on deciphering the last Secret.

When the group reached Blaine's cottage, which was nestled in a small clearing in the trees, Carmen knocked on the front door, not wanting to scare Blaine by walking in unannounced.

Blaine answered the door after only a few seconds, staring out through Carmen and her invisible friends.

"Pop, it's us. We're invisible," Carmen whispered. "I didn't want anyone to see us. Can we come in?"

"Oh, of course," Blaine said, looking rather surprised as he opened the door for them. "Come on in."

Carmen and her friends ambled into the middle of Blaine's small living room, and Carmen gave the okay for her grandfather to shut the front door. Thunderbolt was sitting on the top of the couch across from the fireplace, looking curious. As soon as Blaine had the door closed, Carmen brought the members of her group back into sight again.

"What's going on?" Blaine asked, looking troubled. "Why are all of you in your armor?"

"I wanted to decipher the last Secret here with you," Carmen explained, as Blaine and Thunderbolt stared at her, the worry evident upon their faces. "And…something told me that we should wear the armor, and that you and Thunderbolt should, too."

"Carmen, are you feeling well? I'm afraid I don't understand why you would think that…."

"Just trust me on this, Pop," Carmen said, sounding determined. "You and Thunderbolt need to go and get into your armor, and I'll set up the cipher disk in the meantime."

Blaine and Thunderbolt exchanged bewildered glances, but then went upstairs to get dressed. Carmen marched over to the coffee table in front of the squashy green couch. She laid the cipher disk down on the table and sat on the sofa next to Blaze.

"Come on, guys," Carmen called over the back of the couch to her other Souls. "Come sit down."

Stellar, Glamis, and Anubis wandered past the sofa and warily sat in a circle on the floor around the coffee table, occasionally glancing back and forth from Carmen to the cipher disk.

A couple of minutes later, the staircase creaked as Blaine and Thunderbolt walked down to the living room, both of them dressed in their armor.

Blaine crossed the room and sat in his antique rocking chair across from Carmen. Thunderbolt perched himself on one of the wooden arms.

With everyone now in place, Carmen pulled Merlin's maps out of her pocket and placed them on the table. Then she took out her quill pen, ink, and parchment, and set those down next to the maps.

"Okay…here we go…." Carmen told her companions, as she leaned down to begin deciphering the final message.

She was feeling both nervous and excited for what she was about to do.

"The moment of truth," Blaze said, nodding.

Carmen inhaled deeply to calm her nerves, and read the message from Kelmari's necklace, which she had written on her paper beneath the other Secrets.

Set free the doubts, echo the songs of days afore.

She then glanced over at Merlin's parchment. Little by little, instructions for deciphering the lost Secret were scrawling across the back of the maps in the legendary sorcerer's handwriting….

To decipher the first word, turn the movable disk four full turns clockwise.

Her hands shaking slightly, Carmen delicately rotated the top plate of the cipher disk as directed, and observed how the first three ciphertext letters lined up with the plaintext letters that were on the larger bottom disk.

Set had become *You.*

Carmen immediately wrote down the new word beneath the original one on her parchment.

For the first letter of the next word, turn the movable disk one-quarter turn clockwise.

Carmen followed this guidance…and then the rest of the instructions of the individual words to eventually decipher the first half of Kelmari's message.

You hold the answer,

Carmen's eyes widened. Certainly the second half of the message would be that very answer…. With her fingers trembling even more now, she deciphered the next word.

Echo turned to *cast.*

A single word at a time, Carmen deciphered the second portion of the message, writing down each new plaintext word beneath the ciphertext word. When she was finished, she stared at the newly deciphered Secret for nearly a full minute, trying to fathom what it could mean.

"*Well?*" Blaine pressed, as he sat at the edge of his chair. "What does it say?"

Carmen exhaled. She hadn't realized that she had been holding her breath for the better part of sixty seconds. She slowly read the plaintext version of the lost Secret, as it was written in her own handwriting, aloud to her friends.

"*You hold the answer,*" she recited, "*cast the spell in your heart.*"

All of a sudden, the edges of Merlin's cipher disk began to glow in a blindingly bright light.

An instant later, a beam of that very same white light shot up from the Great Seal of Kelmar at the center of the disk, reaching all the way up through the ceiling.

No sooner had that happened than the room began to shake violently. Carmen and her friends scrambled to their feet, their pulses racing. The lamp that was standing next to the couch toppled over with a *BANG,* and the coffee table was sliding little by little across the hardwood floor. Ceramic plates and glasses were falling and shattering in the kitchen.

"WHAT'S HAPPENING?!" Carmen shouted over the noise, struggling to stay on her feet.

Blaine gaped at the glowing cipher disk on the vibrating coffee table. In the next second, he appeared to realize something. He looked up at his granddaughter.

"CARMEN, THIS IS A VANISHING POINT!" he yelled to her, as pots and pans crashed down from the cabinets in the next room.

"WHAT?"

"MERLIN MUST WANT TO TAKE US SOME-WHERE.... WE ALL NEED TO GRAB A HOLD OF THE DISK TOGETHER!" Blaine shouted. "ON THE COUNT OF THREE!"

Carmen was glancing frantically around at her friends, but none of them seemed to have any more of an idea of what was going on than her grandfather did.

"One...." Blaine began, staring around at all of them while he and Thunderbolt leaned over the table. "Two...."

Carmen and her friends moved in closer together as they gathered around the cipher disk.

"THREE!"

Carmen thrust her hand forward and grabbed on to the edge of the disk. Suddenly, she felt her consciousness leave her, and she collapsed to the floor, asleep.

Sometime in the next several seconds, Carmen felt herself drifting up from her body, her spirit slowly rising into the air. She opened her eyes and saw the silvery, translucent spirits of her grandfather, Thunderbolt, and her Souls of Destiny float-ing around her.... Carmen then looked down and saw all of their unconscious bodies lying on the floor of the living room.

615

Not knowing what else to do, Carmen and her companions drifted toward the beam of white light that was shooting up from the cipher disk...and floated into its radiance.

There was no sound. Blackness abruptly engulfed them. Though Carmen and the others were not physically moving, all of them felt as if they were traveling incredibly fast through a long, black tunnel. As they flew ahead through the darkness, they could see a warm, golden line of light straight ahead of them....

Moments later, the seven Kelmarians passed through the Impassable Barrier. The heavenly warmth unpredictably turned to bitter cold at the same time that the rotting stench of magma overwhelmed their senses. The tunnel of utter nothingness around them gradually began to dissolve, transforming into the lifeless cavern walls of the World of Darkness.

CHAPTER TWENTY-NINE
THE ARMY OF THE IMMORTALS

Carmen was shivering as she gazed around at the shadowy landscape of Keltan. Blaine and Thunderbolt were gaping at their surroundings.... This was their very first look at the World of Darkness. Carmen and her companions were standing at Keltan's southern edge.

Unlike in past times, there were no Dark creatures wandering through the tunnels and prowling the stone grounds; but there were still rivers of magma that pooled in lagoons of varying sizes throughout the cavern, and water dripping from the stalactites hanging from the ceiling. The Kelmarians looked north toward Triedastron's fortress...and their hearts sank to their knees.

The doors of the black castle were propped open, and armored Keltan fighters were pouring outside, marching ahead through the open wrought iron gate. Very quickly, the stone-faced sorcerers and creatures were assembling in a line along the front of the sharpened silver fence that enclosed the Fortress of Darkness.

The Masters were each dressed in black robes decorated with orange and red flames, and all of them had their wands drawn and sabers in the scabbards at their belts. The Keltan creatures were dressed in silver and black armor, looking as frightening as they ever had. Carmen could barely stand to watch as the army of the immortals grew by the dozen every few minutes.... She finally had to look away and turn to her friends for their thoughts.

"What should we do?" she asked them, trying her best to keep her composure. "Without the others from Sarcanian Valley...we're in serious trouble."

"Don't worry, Carmen," Blaze said reassuringly. "Remember what Haidar told us? He was going to go check on us in our room after lunch.... As soon as he sees that we're gone, he'll know that something happened, and he'll come for us."

"We will not have to wait for that," Anubis chimed in. *"I have just informed my father of where we are. He is going to find Haidar, and transport him and the others to Keltan. He should be here with the rest of our friends from Sarcanian Valley shortly."*

Only somewhat comforted by this news, Carmen glanced toward Triedastron's fortress once more, still feeling anxious.

Why had Merlin's cipher disk brought her and her friends to Keltan of all places? Could this be a part of the plan for the Secrets of Kelmar? And how had she known before she left Thunder Academy that she and her friends would need their armor to protect them once she deciphered the last Secret? The only explanation Carmen could think of was that someone had tapped her mind to let her know....

The minutes crawled by as she and her friends watched the Master of Keltan's army gather out on the grounds. Though she was a good distance away from them, with her magically enhanced vision, Carmen could see Mondalaus, Yokaro, Nankarsa, and countless other familiar foes emerging from within the fortress. It was only a matter of time before Desorkhan, and ultimately, Triedastron, would come out to lead them.

Eventually, Carmen again had to force herself to turn away from the scene. She was conscious of the fact that even with the Sarcan instructors, Councilors, students, and

Renalda's small militia, they would still be massively outnumbered here in Keltan—easily three to one.

As Carmen stood there, contemplating their chances of defeating their enemies without the help of a more powerful force, Dagtar's claw became warm against her neck. Seconds later, she felt a strong gust of wind against her back, and her hair lifted and fell in the breeze.

Carmen turned around immediately. Dagtar was flying nimbly downward through the ceiling—drifting to a height of about fifteen feet above the ground. He gazed at the Kelmarians below through his calm, crystal blue eyes. The Dragon was wearing a beautiful set of golden armor that Merlin had made for him. The hard gold plates covered most of his shining green scales, from his neck down to his tail. Carmen noticed the silver bracelet that she had given him for Christmas around his right front leg.

"I believe that a congratulations is in order, as well as a thank you for your lovely gift," Dagtar said, nodding down at Carmen. *"Your presence indicates to me that you have deciphered the last of the four Secrets of Kelmar.... I had no doubt that you would succeed, Guardian."*

Carmen stared up at him, curious about many things that only he could answer.

"Was it you who made me decide to go see my grandfather when I deciphered the final Secret, and to wear my armor?" Carmen asked, wanting desperately to get some answers to what had just happened. "And why did the cipher disk transport us here to Keltan?"

"This is where our opponents are gathering together for the final battle," Dagtar explained, briefly glancing off to the north. *"My Master is the one who made the cipher disk a Vanishing Point, but yes, I am the one who communicated to you through subconscious thought to wear your armor, and to go to your grandfather so that he could come with you to Keltan."*

"I still don't know what the Secrets mean," Carmen said bluntly. "The last one said that I have to cast the spell in my heart…and as soon as I read it aloud, we were brought here. I don't understand…. What spell do I have to cast? And what will happen then?"

Dagtar tilted his head sympathetically.

"I am sorry, but I am forbidden to reveal that answer to you," he replied. *"If I were to tell you, it would ruin everything that you have worked toward. You will need to figure it out on your own by listening to your heart, just as the Secret suggests. That is the one and only way for the spell to work."*

"Does that mean that whatever spell it is I'm supposed to cast…will help us to victory?"

Dagtar couldn't answer, but the glimmer in his blue eyes suggested that it was yes.

"Fair enough," Carmen said, sighing. She knew that she couldn't expect any further help from Dagtar at this time. "So…can you stay to help us fight the Keltans?"

Dagtar smiled.

"That is the exact reason that I am here," he said. *"The rest of the Kelmarsian Military is currently preparing for battle in the World of Light…. They will be ready for combat, should we be unable to stop the Keltans before they invade. Triedastron cannot claim control of the entire Worlds Triad unless he can first conquer Kelmarsia."*

Carmen peered over her shoulder at Triedastron's forces. The line of Dark fighters had stretched to more than twice the width of the castle, but the Dark Master, Triedastron, and their Partners were still noticeably absent.

"Where do you think that Desorkhan and Triedastron are?" Carmen asked Dagtar.

The Dragon shook his head.

"You know by now how cowards act in times of danger," he said darkly. *"Most likely, they are still inside the fortress. They*

send their minions into battle for them...and they will wait until the very last moment to join their fight. The two probably think that we will be easier to defeat after their warriors have already weakened us. They're almost certainly plotting their takeover of the Worlds Triad, as they prematurely assume a victory.... Is that confidence, or stupidity? I suppose it is all a matter of perspective."

Carmen and her friends observed the remaining Keltans marching out of the castle and into line with the others. The door behind them shut magically with a deep, rumbling *BOOM.*

Dagtar was right. Desorkhan, Triedastron, and their Partners would come out only after their fighters had weakened the Kelmarian forces for them.

Something suddenly floated down from the ceiling just to Carmen's right. She gasped in surprise, and then stepped aside as the spirits of Inpu and Commander Haidar drifted downward to the floor of the cavern. Officer Sheridae, the Sarcan Councilors, Renalda, Alazar, and Rishaw and his assistants soon followed. Following them were the Sarcan Captains and Cadets.

Carmen smiled gratefully as her allies from Sarcanian Valley joined her and her friends in the World of Darkness. All of them were dressed in their new battle armor, and looked fully ready to fight in this final effort to stabilize the Worlds Triad and save Kelmar.

"So *this* is Keltan," Alazar said, gazing around the darkened cavern. "I wouldn't have selected these colors, nor the creepy ambiance of this cave, but perhaps that's just me."

"You have no idea how happy I am to see you," Carmen said, grinning at him and the others. "Now we might actually stand a chance."

Haidar walked out to what was more or less the center of his army of fighters. The light from the torches hanging around

621

the cavern walls was flickering off of the badges that adorned his scarlet and gold military uniform.

"Gather around, everyone," he ordered.

The Kelmarians and Kelmarsians swiftly formed a circle around Haidar. For the time being, their adversaries stood by, ready to challenge them outside of Triedastron's fortress.

"It is up to us to make the first move," Haidar told his army. "The Keltans have to go through *us* to reach the Impassable Barrier, but we have to go through *them* to get to Triedastron…. If we don't advance toward them first, we'll begin at a disadvantage. We fight our way through their forces, and Carmen and her Souls will enter the castle if need be. Carmen," he said, looking over at her, "have you determined how to implement the Secrets?"

Carmen bit her lip. Everyone's eyes were on her now.

"Uh…sort of," she lied. "I think that when the moment comes, I'll know what to do," she said, in a more convincing voice.

Haidar stared at her. Carmen knew that he could see right through her less than certain answer, but he gave her an unexpected nod of faith nonetheless.

"You always do," he replied.

Carmen was relieved when Haidar finally shifted his gaze back over the entire group.

"We line up side-by-side, and march in the direction of the fortress," he announced. "Sorcerers, summon your wands…. Partners, stay with your Masters. Be prepared to use your magic at any time…. We don't know how our enemies will react when they see us moving toward them."

The Kelmarians, Inpu, and Dagtar promptly assembled in a line around Haidar and Sheridae. The Captains stood at the side of Haidar, and the Cadets stood with Sheridae, the sorcerers with their wands at the ready. Carmen positioned herself between her Souls and her grandfather, not far from Haidar.

She and her companions stared across at their stationary challengers as they waited for Haidar's signal to move.... After everyone was in place, Haidar raised his right arm, and then sliced it down through the air.

"MARCH!"

And so, with Haidar's order, the members of the unified line of Kelmarians and Kelmarsians marched in step with each other, progressing at a quickened pace toward their Keltan opponents.

It was disturbingly quiet as they walked across the World of Darkness.... Other than the dripping of the stalactites and the flames dancing in the torches on the walls, the caves were noiseless and stagnant. The Keltan Army remained immobile, watching with cold expressions as their enemies approached.

In less than ten minutes, the Kelmarians were halfway to Triedastron's fortress. It was then, as though someone had thrown a switch, that there was a burst of movement. The Keltan Army raced to meet their adversaries in the center of the cavern, the sorcerers with their wands raised.

"RUN TO THEM!" Haidar ordered in response.

The line of Kelmarians and Kelmarsians rushed forward, their footsteps echoing through the vast cavern. As they drew closer to their foes, they could see the hunger for victory in their eyes.

An explosion of sound rang throughout the World of Darkness as the Keltan and Kelmarian Armies clashed, about a quarter of a mile from Triedastron's fortress. Chaos was everywhere that Carmen looked when she and her Souls of Destiny met Desorkhan's Secret Guard, Sylvine Yokaro. The short and elderly black-haired sorceress had a sullen face and icy eyes. Without exchanging even a single word with Carmen, Yokaro launched her first attack.

"Fires of the Sarcan!"
"Illumina Hesquel!"

A fiery Sarcan burst from the crown of Yokaro's brown and purple wand. An instant later, Carmen's staff released bands of golden light that snaked up into the air and formed an intertwined web around her and Blaze.

The flaming Sarcan galloped forward to leap through Carmen's shield. But the rays of light from the defensive spell sliced the fire apart and extinguished the flames.

"Golden Lightning!"

As her shield disappeared, Carmen pointed her wand at Yokaro. A perfect bolt of lightning sped down from the ceiling of the cavern.

Yokaro was not fast enough to summon a defense. The lightning struck her in a blaze of light, and she collapsed face first down onto the stone floor.

Yokaro shrieked as her body shook uncontrollably. Carmen watched her slowly weaken with every second that the lightning's energy remained inside of her…. After a few minutes, she could finally get to her feet…and when she did, she glared at Carmen, her matted hair hanging in her eyes.

"I might not have succeeded in killing you last year as a mortal, but it's an entirely different game in the afterlife," she warned. "You are outmatched in ways beyond your comprehension."

"It's nothing but foolish to fear a *place*," Carmen replied, unfazed by Yokaro's threat. "As long as you play by the rules, we're stronger than you are."

Yokaro's lined face twisted into a dark grin.

"You should know by now that we never play by the rules here."

Carmen braced herself as Yokaro raised her wand.

"Siayetha!"

Red light erupted from Yokaro's wand and hit Carmen like a speeding train.

"AHHHHHHEEEEE!"

Carmen could feel the blood pulsing in the back of her skull as pain from the mind curse blinded her. She dropped her wand and grabbed her head, wishing desperately for the searing pain to stop. It felt like her brain was on fire.... She couldn't stop screaming.

"Carmen, hang in there!" Blaze pleaded, as he hugged her shoulder supportively. He was powerless to put a stop to the mind curse's effects; he could only stay with his Master until the pain finally ceased.

Carmen closed her eyes, still shrieking in agony. She couldn't think or see, and had no way to protect herself from further attack....

At some point later on, the pain finally faded away. Carmen couldn't tell exactly how much time had passed. Her vision had returned...though still hazy, and the throbbing in the back of her head was reduced to a tolerable level. Carmen had fallen victim to this powerful mind curse before, but it didn't make it any easier to handle.

Now finding herself back in the present, she realized that she was lying on the ground, looking up at the dark ceiling of the cavern.... Drips of water from the stalactites were falling down onto her face. She had evidently fallen down while trying to fight off the pain of Yokaro's curse, but she hadn't felt herself collapse.

Blaze helped Carmen to her feet and picked up her wand for her, and then the two of them gazed toward Yokaro...trying to get some idea as to what her next move would be. But Yokaro was just staring back at her opponents.

"Ready to give up yet?" she asked harshly.

Carmen felt her face redden in anger. She still had a headache, but she refused to give her enemy any indication that she was even slightly weakened from her attack.

"Not in *this* lifetime," she said sharply.

Carmen and Yokaro resumed their duel in the next instant, just as so many others were taking place all around them.

The nearest battle to Carmen, Blaze, and Yokaro was that of Stellar against Dorsan Denethor and his black Dragon, Maladack. Without Carmen or another Master to duel alongside, Stellar found himself with a major shortcoming against the Magicon Commander. But even outnumbered two to one, Stellar was not yielding to his challenger's spells.

After dodging a string of curses from the experienced sorcerer, Denethor, Stellar would then have to use even more energy to summon magical defenses to protect himself from Maladack's attacks. When Stellar did get a chance to go on the offensive against the Keltans, he used his powers of the Land to combat Denethor and Maladack's Sky and Fire abilities.

It was a challenge for Stellar, but every time Carmen caught a glimpse of him, he was moving with speed and attacking with power. On one occasion, he even blocked a forceful *Redentum* curse from Denethor, and afterward, he used the *Cerkatra* spell against both of his challengers.

In that last blast of orange light, both Denethor and Maladack were hit with Stellar's spell and spiraled backwards through the air. Denethor slammed his head against the hard ground.

The Magicon Commander lay there for a short time...momentarily stunned. Stellar stared at the motionless sorcerer, waiting. Maladack shook off the spell and flew over to his Master, gazing down at him through his scarlet-colored eyes.

Denethor eventually stirred and was able to get back up, but as he rubbed the back of his aching head, his face twisted in fury. Acting as though nothing had happened to him, he hastily snapped back into attack mode.

With a quick but skillful flick of his bronze and black wand, Denethor launched one of his strongest curses upon Stellar.

"Psychea Confound!"

A beam of brown and silvery energy discharged from Denethor's wand. Stellar cast a *Land Shield* Protection at once, and a glittering wall of stone sprang up around the Keinen. But before Stellar knew it, Denethor's curse had smashed through his shield, hitting him in a diluted yet still potent form.

Stellar staggered, dizzy and confused, as he struggled to remain standing. His armor had protected him from the more severe effects of the curse...but he was still left unable to fight back. Denethor capitalized on Stellar's temporary lack of awareness by summoning yet another curse.

Carmen forced Yokaro to cast a *Thunder Shield* by attacking her with *Lightning Strike*. With a fleeting glance over at Stellar, Carmen could see that he needed help, so she fired a *Lightning Spark* spell at Denethor just before he could shout the incantation for his next curse intended for Stellar.

A jet of lightning exploded out of Carmen's wand and struck Denethor's metal breastplate with great force, knocking him to the ground.

Stellar shook his head. His body was now finally clear of the previous curse. He nodded toward Carmen, grateful for the help.

"Thanks, Car!"

"No problem!" Carmen yelled back, over the noise of the duels around them. Observing that Stellar was fit for battle again, Carmen restarted her duel with Yokaro.

The other Souls of Destiny were engaged in all-consuming duels of their own. Glamis was standing strong against Valsera Vermae and her Decodore, Garlenon. Vermae was utilizing her Decodore's ability to fly to try to overpower Glamis, who was limited to fighting only on the land in Keltan. Glamis didn't let his limitations hold him back though; he battled hard against his foes, even as Vermae commanded her Decodore against him. While Garlenon used his fire to attack Glamis, the Boarax doused the flames with watery defenses.

Garlenon flew in a slow, wide circle above Glamis, leering down at the Boarax as he waited for his Master's next order. Glamis watched him cautiously from below.... Decodores could move fast when they had to. He would have to be just as agile to dodge the potential attack.

But Vermae was staying silent. She would apparently let her Partner select the spell that he wished to use against Glamis, so as to give the Boarax even less of a warning as to what was coming.

Garlenon circled two more times. Then, halfway into the third circle, the black lion-like creature dove down at Glamis and released a blast of fire from his jaws.

Glamis didn't flinch. As the flames rushed down through the air, he cast a *Water Shield*—a defense that encased him in a slick, protective coating from head to toe. The magical defense was subtle, and hardly visible, but highly effective when used in the proper situation.

Carmen looked over her shoulder as she summoned an *Invisible Shield*. She felt her heart stop as she witnessed the seemingly unprotected Glamis being consumed by a huge ball of fire.

But a split second later, the fire extinguished as it hit Glamis's water-coated skin, and the Boarax was left unharmed by Garlenon's spell.

Carmen sighed with relief.

"You nearly gave me a heart attack just now, Glamis!" she shouted to him from where she stood.

Glamis snorted with laughter as Garlenon angrily turned and flew back up into the air.

"Sorry about that!" Glamis called to her.

On the other side of Glamis, Anubis and his father were dueling Oalyn Sarisin and his Skelyote, Yastar. The two Jackals worked brilliantly as a team, with Inpu focusing his efforts on Sarisin, and Anubis on Yastar. Because Anubis and his father could speak with each other through thought, they could keep their communications and strategies secret from their foes.

Sarisin went after Inpu with a barrage of daunting curses, but his opponent could read his mind before he summoned each spell, and thus react with the perfect spell to counteract it. This invaluable advantage of Inpu's frustrated Sarisin from start to finish. Carmen took a peek over at the battle and noticed that Sarisin was covered in perspiration as he pointed his dark silver wand at Inpu.

"*Petripulous!*" Sarisin shouted.

Inpu lifted his head and closed his eyes. The dark energy from Sarisin's spell was firing toward him. With his command, a magical wind billowed around the Jackal's form, enclosing him. Sarisin's curse soared across the grounds of Keltan and through the heavenly windstorm, breaking up inside Inpu's defense, failing to reach the Jackal himself.

Initially, Carmen didn't know what spell Inpu cast next, but whatever it was, it caused Sarisin to scream in pain an instant later. Anubis communicated to her afterward that Inpu's mind spell was forcing Sarisin to see random and erratic images in his mind, disorienting him, as well as giving him a stabbing headache.

Meanwhile, Anubis was also fighting off Yastar with his own selection of mind spells. Though Yastar could fly, he could not always escape Anubis's attacks.

Anubis leapt up as the Skelyote flew by and bit his leg. Yastar barked in pain. Next, Anubis used *Psychic's Hypnosis,* which caused Yastar to experience a sequence of distressing memories. The enemy creature flew about in circles near the ceiling of the cavern, wincing as he was weakened by the spell bit-by-bit.

When Yastar was finally able to carry on with the duel, he fought back with startlingly greater strength, making the most of more efficient attacks against Anubis. From that time on, Anubis was kept on the defensive for much of the rest of the battle.

Just north of Anubis and Inpu's duel, Dagtar was combating Lucifer Mondalaus and his Zelthrel, Narcista. Narcista, while not a Dragon, was very similar in her abilities and appearance. Dagtar was much larger than her, though, and so when it came to dueling, he had the edge in terms of pure physical strength. But with Carmen still occupied in her duel with Yokaro, Dagtar also had to fight Narcista's Master, Mondalaus.

"Show this old beast how true champions duel, Narcista," Lucifer called up to his Zelthrel, as she followed Dagtar through the air over the battlefield.

Narcista roared and sent a blast of fire at Dagtar's back. Dagtar flew higher to escape the flames, and then turned back around and released his own breath of fire at his foe.

Narcista fanned the flames back with her enormous, slimy green wings as she continued to chase him. The two flying creatures went on to share quite a few more fiery exchanges before an impatient Mondalaus decided to step in.

"Binds of Death!" he shouted.

Green vines shot up from the crown of Mondalaus's black wand. As they darted into the sky after Dagtar, the Dragon grabbed the ends of the wriggling vines in his jaws, allowing them to wrap themselves around two of his bottom, sharp teeth.

Then Dagtar jerked his head upward, yanking so hard on the vines, which were still attached to Mondalaus's wand, that the sorcerer could barely keep a grip on his staff. Narcista snarled at Dagtar and moved to attack him again. In the next second, Dagtar flew off as fast as he could, with the tops of the vines still clasped in his jaws.

"ARRRRGGGHHH!"

Mondalaus was swept up off the ground and sent flying through the air, dangling twenty feet below Dagtar as he held on to his wand.

Dagtar turned and circled above the battlefield, swinging Mondalaus along with every aerial maneuver that he made. The Dragon continued to pick up speed as he performed a series of dives, spins, and turns, all while evading Narcista.

Mondalaus struggled to keep a grip on his wand.... His hands, slick with sweat, were sliding farther down the staff with every sharp movement. He was shouting with fury up at Dagtar and his own creature as he was unwillingly taken on this dangerous ride through the air.

Narcista unleashed a ferocious breath of fire at Dagtar—causing the Dragon to soar upward, putting the green vines of the *Binds of Death* spell in the direct path of the flames.

Dagtar raced ahead and made another sharp turn just as the fire destroyed Mondalaus's vines. Mondalaus screamed—flying sideways through the air and falling freely back down to the battlefield.

Narcista rushed down to try to catch him mid-descent, but Mondalaus was plummeting much too fast. The Magicon

Officer crashed down to the rocky grounds of Keltan with a spine-crushing *THUD,* near the center of the fighting, producing a plume of dust that billowed up from the site of his plunge.

Still locked in her own duel with Yokaro, Carmen couldn't look to see what happened after that. She hoped that that fall had defeated Mondalaus for the last time.

The battle between the Kelmarians, Kelmarsians, and Keltans raged on for hours as the two sides fought to gain control. While Carmen and her Souls of Destiny dueled their enemies, countless additional conflicts were taking place all across the barren landscape of the World of Darkness. And in every single one of the battles, each opponent was fighting with the keen awareness that the outcome of this very battle would decide the future of the Worlds Triad.

Commander Haidar had taken on the colossal challenge of dueling Dezra Razok and Ruan Thor together with their Dragons. With no living Partner of his own, Haidar faced a considerable disadvantage—but even so, he dueled his adversaries with honor and courage, just as he always did. Calling upon his years of training and experience, Haidar carefully planned out each of his moves before acting, and took on the sorcerers and their Dragons as individual challengers. This way, he was free to use each of their weaknesses to help him select the strongest spells against them.

A couple of hundred feet away from Haidar, Officer Sheridae and her Sarcan, Swift, dueled Sevadia Nankarsa, Syth, and Morik Galdor and his Dragon, Tailabar. Sheridae allowed Swift to choose her own spells against the Dark creatures. Sheridae dueled the two sorcerers on her own.

The Kelmarian duo's strategy was working reasonably well against their immortal opponents, but the question of just how long they and their allies could sustain their efforts as the night wore on hung over their heads.

Throughout the World of Darkness, there was already evidence that the Keltans were barely weakening at all in proportion to the Kelmarians' progressively dwindling strength. Blaine and Thunderbolt bravely dueled Audric Harthan and his Dragon, Saedor, but their energy was declining. They had been dueling these and other Keltan fighters for many hours by now, and age and fatigue were starting to catch up with them.

Perspiration was flowing down Blaine's face as he and Harthan battled. Harthan had the upper hand in the duel by being both young and a Keltan immortal. Although Blaine was in shape, and a much more capable dueler than most sorcerers his age, he was understandably beginning to tire as the battle entered its later hours. Despite his fighting spirit, it was difficult for him to keep on fighting off his skilled foes.

Alazar Friar, Renalda Haidar, and their Partners had teamed together against Zorlan Xoncarg and his Keinen, Tas. The Kelmarians, who were lifelong friends, used their friendship to work well together in keeping Xoncarg and Tas from pushing them farther back from Triedastron's fortress.

The Camersleys and their Starclaws came to Alazar and Renalda's aid when they could step away from their duels with other members of Triedastron's army.

Xoncarg was young, but was also one of the stronger Keltan fighters. The thin, pale boy with black eyes and straggly brown hair fought with the tactical skill of a seasoned sorcerer, and was relentless in forcing Alazar and Renalda to summon defenses to protect themselves from his commanding curses. Tas was just as unrelenting as he fought Enn and Redge.

To the south, Rishaw and a group of his young assistants were battling Randore, Tortbold, and their Sentry Hounds.

Rishaw dueled with Randore and his Sentry Hound while his assistants fought together against Tortbold and *his* Partner.

In each of the rest of the duels, the Sarcan Councilors, Captains, and Cadets fought bravely throughout the course of the massive battle. Carmen and her fellow Kelmarians each combated an array of Keltan opponents as the fighting reached a peak. The duels were grueling and intense, but with their worlds at stake, the Kelmarians and Kelmarsians alike battled with great intention. A loss in this conflict was almost certain to result in the destruction of both Kelmarsia and Kelmar. They had come too far, and fought for too long, to allow their realms to fall to the darkest forces in magical existence. The relationships that they had built, their lives, and the lives of their family and friends, were worth every ounce of pain that they suffered in the final push to save it all.

But though the Kelmarians and Kelmarsians were fighting with every last drive of their heart and strength, in the later hours of the battle, they came to realize that the Keltans were gradually pushing them farther and farther away from the Fortress of Darkness. Carmen looked up from one of her numerous battles only to see that she and her allies were closer to the southern edge of Keltan than they had been when the battle began. Throughout the arduous hours that she and the others had spent engaged in battle with their enemies, Carmen recognized that in spite of how strong the Kelmarians, Dagtar, and Inpu were together, they could not defeat their foes without the help of sorcerers and creatures even more powerful than they were…. They needed the help of the rest of the Kelmarsian Military.

Nevertheless, in the face of this recognition, Carmen continued to fight on alongside her friends, her spirit refusing to fall in defeat to these adversaries, both old and new. She was exhausted, and fighting off pain like she had never known before, but as long as she was breathing, she would not surrender. She would do all that she could to save her home, her family, and her friends. As the Guardian of Kelmar, this was her most important duty.

BANG!

A sudden crack of sound, which could be heard even over the noise of the ongoing battle, echoed throughout Keltan. Only seconds later, a red beam of light shot up from the roof of Triedastron's fortress.

The Kelmarians, Kelmarsians, and Keltans all stopped what they were doing and turned to look toward the dark castle.

The front doors of the fortress slowly swung open, and Triedastron and the Dark Master emerged from inside. Desorkhan was wearing the same black robes with orange and red flames that the other Keltan sorcerers wore, but his were also stitched with Triedastron's magic circle on the chest. Triedastron wore his signature burgundy robes.

The duo of Dark sorcerers sauntered ahead through the gate. Their Partners, Lucia and Singe, marched beside their Masters. The four of them stopped walking when they were thirty feet past the silver fence enclosing the Fortress of Darkness.

Triedastron, Desorkhan, Lucia, and Singe stood a safe distance away from the other fighters, but at this moment, all of the eyes and ears in the cavern were on them.

Triedastron spread out his arms as he gazed around Keltan's central cave.

"My, what a delightful scene this is," he said, a look of approval on his face as he saw how worn-down the Kelmarians and Kelmarsians appeared.

Carmen felt sickened by the sight of his nasty smile.

"Well, now that our world looks even more like the supreme realm that it is, it would be only too fitting if we went ahead and took ourselves to a realm that needs the same…*transformation,* shall I say," Triedastron said, as Desorkhan's black eyes glinted unpleasantly.

"You heard our Master," Desorkhan said authoritatively, staring across at the rest of the Keltan fighters. "Day has surrendered to darkness in the World of Light…. Now is the time to invade Kelmarsia."

Looks of panic spread quickly throughout the Kelmarian Army, but that was even before most of them noticed that Triedastron was raising his wand.

Without thinking, Carmen dashed around Yokaro and raced toward Triedastron, in a last-ditch effort to stop him before he could utter what would surely be a powerful spell.

As Carmen sprinted across the rocky grounds of Keltan, she heard Blaze and several others yell out to her, and even felt a few Keltans try to grab a hold of her, but she was fast enough to escape their grasp.

Just before she reached Triedastron, Desorkhan smiled at her and threw up his hands in a gesture meant to stop her. Carmen ran hard into his *Invisible Shield* and crashed to the ground at his feet. Triedastron arrogantly grinned down through the defense.

"Silly girl, what *were* you thinking?" he asked, in an insincerely sympathetic voice. "When will you learn that the only people who succeed in this life are the ones who know how to manipulate their situation to tip the scales in their favor? Here's proof to you that only the gifted and merciless get what they want."

Triedastron pointed his wand up at the shadowy ceiling of the cavern.

"Sanandrum Celestio!"

A beam of dark energy exploded from his wand and vanished into the blackness above him. Less than thirty seconds later, a sizable gray boulder fell down from the ceiling over Carmen's head. Her eyes widened in shock. With lightning fast reflexes, Carmen grabbed her wand off of the ground next to her.

"Invisible Shield!"

The huge rock bounced off the top of Carmen's domed shield, less than two feet above her head, and hit the stone floor with a heavy *THUMP*.

Carmen gaped up at the ceiling.... Across the entire width of the cavern, a shower of those very same rocks was raining down through the darkness.

The rest of the Kelmarians and Kelmarsians hastily summoned their own shields as the bombardment of rocks, most of them boulders larger than basketballs, descended to the battlefield. Carmen maintained her shield and hurried to her feet.

She ran to find her Souls of Destiny, her eyes darting around the cavern through the rock shower, but soon she spotted Dagtar flying over Inpu and her other Souls, protecting them all with his own *Invisible Shield*.

The Keltan fighters abruptly charged past the preoccupied Kelmarians and galloped south to the Impassable Barrier.

Triedastron muttered a Protective spell under his breath, and he, Desorkhan, and their Partners became encased in a glowing blue force field as they calmly strutted ahead through the crowd of fighters.

Carmen knew that she had to stop them, but with boulders still tumbling down from the ceiling onto the Kelmarians, there was no way she could dissolve her shield and attack the four Keltans without getting crushed by one or more of the falling rocks.

Most of the other Kelmarians tried to run out of the way of the rocks at one time or another, but no matter where they fled, more and more boulders would come down over them. There was no escaping the deadly onslaught of rocks, which purposely avoided striking any of the Keltan duelers.

And thus, Carmen and her friends could do nothing but watch, ill with dread, as Triedastron, the Dark Master, Singe, and Lucia strode across the battlefield and followed their army of fighters to the Impassable Barrier.

It wasn't long before the Keltans reached the enchanted golden line that cut through the shadows at the southern wall of the cavern. Now facing no resistance from the Kelmarians, rendered helpless by the deluge of cursed boulders, Triedastron's forces crossed the Impassable Barrier and disappeared into the World of Light.

CHAPTER THIRTY
THE COMING OF THE DAWN

The Kelmarians stood in stunned silence, their bodies aching and their spirits half-defeated. The rocks stopped falling just as the last of the Keltans crossed over into Kelmarsia—a sign that Triedastron no longer saw his enemies as a threat to his ambitions. Carmen communicated to Anubis to have Inpu instruct the Kelmarsians to assemble on the grass by the River of the Departed Spirits and be ready for battle. She then turned and looked to Commander Haidar for his next order, although she already had a good idea of what it would be.

Haidar was staring across the cavern at the golden line of light that separated this realm from the next. Finally, he gazed back at his allies.

"This is it," he said in a steady voice. "Before us lies the final battlefield in this war. We follow our enemies to the World of Light...and it is there where the fate of our two worlds will be decided."

Keeping their heads held high, the solemn but determined Kelmarians and Kelmarsians turned and tramped south toward the Impassable Barrier. Carmen and her Souls walked side-by-side as they made their way to the southern wall of Keltan. Unprecedented warmth washed over the group of friends as they and their fellow combatants neared the perfect golden light less than ten minutes after the start of their march.

As the fighters floated through the barrier, the heavenly warmth that always welcomed them into the World of Light was accompanied this time by the sound of myriad murmuring voices. It wasn't the singing that accompanied the serene music always playing in Kelmarsia, but rather, more familiar voices....

Among them, Carmen heard those of her own parents standing out from the rest.

"Stay strong, Carmen," William said, over the countless other whispers. *"Though you may not see us, we're always with you, no matter where you are."*

"You are cherished by so many," came Isabella's soft and elegant voice. *"And you mean the world to us.... Our baby girl, we love you so much."*

Carmen tried to respond, but couldn't find her ability to speak. Seconds later, the magical utterances around her were silenced, and a picturesque view of Kelmarsia beneath a velvety black sky filled her eyes as she and her friends flew slowly down to the eastern side of the meadow adjacent to the River of the Departed Spirits.

The reflection of the full moon seemed to ripple the surface of the stream. The trees surrounding the meadow were dark and shadowy, and there was a soft breeze rustling through the branches. But the one most noticeable difference about Kelmarsia on this particular evening was that there was no peaceful music playing, as there had always been before now. That wonderful, inspirational melody had instead been replaced by the violent clamor of battle. This observation chilled Carmen, and made her feel quite sick, as this could only mean that terrible things were happening in this world tonight.

She and her friends peered watchfully into the forest on the opposite side of the river, and saw flashes of metal in the darkness as members of the Kelmarsian Military ran through the trees as they combated the Keltan forces. Their golden armor, which sparkled in the moonlight, was decorated with Merlin's magic circle, just as the Kelmarians' was. Shouting and the sounds of clashing blades carried through the warm night air as the Kelmarsians and Keltans fought for control of the World of Light.

"We have to help the Kelmarsians," Haidar told his own army, gathering the fighters around him. "Captains and Cadets, refer to your maps if you get lost. We will work to assist the Kelmarsians in any way that we can."

Then he looked toward Carmen.

"Stay with your Souls," he advised, his brown eyes cool and alert. "I need you to find your way to the path and the bridge that lead up to the Castle of Merlin. Triedastron is likely headed there.... We have to stop him before he reaches the Master of both Kelmar and Kelmarsia."

"I will show her to it," Dagtar said, edging in the direction of the eastern trees.

"Yes. We'll go right now," Carmen promised Haidar, looking determined.

She waved a hasty goodbye to her grandfather, Thunderbolt, Inpu, and the other soldiers of the Kelmarian Army, and hurried off into the forests after Dagtar and the rest of her Souls. The remaining section of the Kelmarian forces crossed the river and went off into the trees to battle Triedastron's forces alongside the Kelmarsians.

Dagtar flew up and over the substantial grove of trees. Carmen illuminated her wand to light her way as she and her four Souls followed Dagtar deeper into the forests.

Just as Haidar had warned, the woods of Kelmarsia were a dark and dense maze. Carmen had to be very careful to watch out for the tree roots and fallen branches that littered the forest floor as she ran. Shadows danced across the green foliage as Carmen raced past. Occasionally, a bird or similar creature would unexpectedly fly through the nearby trees, crackling the branches and startling Carmen and her friends. In the trees to the east and west, they could hear voices, swords clashing, and small explosions as opposing spells and curses soared through the air.

With Dagtar flying overhead, Carmen and her friends darted their way through the endless forests of the World of Light, swerving around ancient trees and squeezing between bushes as they moved north. It took them nearly half an hour to finally reach the stone-laden path at the edge of the woodland.

The trail, which lay just fifteen feet ahead of them when it came into sight, snaked up to a grand, white stone bridge that spanned across the River of the Departed Spirits and climbed up to the mountain that was home to Merlin's towering white castle.

"There it is," Dagtar told his friends, as he gazed down at them through the trees. *"This is the hidden path that Haidar spoke about."*

Carmen stared warily down the straight trail, trying to see through the trees that were near to the bridge at the end of the path. She was still breathing heavily from her sprint through the woods, and had to lean over to catch her breath and settle the shooting pain in her right side. For her own peace of mind, she needed to know for certain that there were no enemies hiding amongst the trees near the bridge before she willingly advanced toward it.

"Is it safe?" she asked the Dragon, pointing at the bridge. "Can you check?"

Dagtar nodded, and then flew ahead—circling slowly over the trees at the base of the bridge as he searched for any sign of movement. Once he had made certain that the area was free of any Keltan fighters, he soared back over to Carmen and the others.

"I do not sense anything," he said, appearing calm. *"I believe that we should advance to the center of the bridge, and remain there. No one will be able to enter the castle without us seeing him or her. The other entrances and tunnels leading into the castle were all secured yesterday."*

Feeling reassured by Dagtar's words, Carmen straightened up and decided to guide her friends up the hidden path. Stepping out of the trees, their feet crunched on the smooth, stone pebbles as they walked in the moonlight. Carmen remained on high alert, heart racing, constantly looking around her to confirm that they were still alone.

Carmen and her Souls soon came to the end of the quiet path and gazed up at the bridge that connected the forests to the island mountain, atop which stood the Castle of Merlin. With a deep breath, Carmen took a step up onto the white bridge, and instantly felt someone grab her around her neck from behind. She screamed. Blaze did, too.

"Revealio!" a cold voice ordered.

The now visible Desorkhan had Carmen pinned to him, her neck locked in the crook of his right elbow. Singe had Blaze in the very same chokehold. Desorkhan was clutching his wand in his left hand.

"Nobody moves until I say so," he said threateningly.

Carmen's heart was pounding. Stellar and the others were all on edge, staring at the Dark Master for what he would do next and readying themselves to react.

"We're going up to pay a little visit to the Master of Keltan so that he can defeat all of you for the final time," Desorkhan said, his black eyes flashing around at Carmen's friends. "If *any* of you kelscum attempt to attack or run, I will kill you myself.... Do we understand?"

Her heart in her throat, Carmen nodded as best as she could. Desorkhan and Singe forced her and Blaze forward, marching them up the bridge, their arms still locked around their necks. Carmen's remaining Souls were forced to follow behind them.

As they walked across the bridge, Dagtar flying at the end of the line, Carmen could see flashes of colored light and smoke out of the corners of her eyes as the Kelmarsians and

Keltans battled in the forests below. It was impossible to tell if either army was winning.... All that was clear was that the duels were intensifying as the minutes passed, and neither opponent would ever consider surrendering to the other, as there was far too much to lose for both sides.

At the end of the bridge, Carmen and her companions found themselves standing at the foot of the southern wall of Merlin's castle. Desorkhan and Singe steered their foes to the right, and then down a covered stone walkway. They strode fairly briskly along the walkway, which was lined on the open left side with white stone columns. At the end of the path, they turned left and passed beneath an archway that took them out into the castle courtyard.

Still restrained by Desorkhan and Singe, Carmen and Blaze, as well as their friends, stepped onto the green grass of Merlin's square courtyard. Carmen spotted the statue of Merlin, Kelmari, and Desorkhan placed in the corner of the lawn, near the canal meandering up from the River of the Departed Spirits.

Triedastron was standing with his arms folded across his chest at the opposite end of the moonlit courtyard, which was lined with white stone columns running along the perimeter of the outdoor space. Lucia was at her Master's side.

"It's about time you got here," Triedastron snapped at the Dark Master, the lines in his forehead deepening with displeasure. His black and gray hair was slightly unkempt. "I was beginning to think that I would have to find the girl and bring her here myself."

"The Kelmarsians have the castle well surrounded," Desorkhan curtly informed him. His tan, pointed face was unwavering, as was his sleek black hair. "But we're here *now*, aren't we?"

"Late, but yes," Triedastron replied stiffly. "I just got through with Merlin. He will not interfere with our work tonight."

"Did he put up much of a fight?" Desorkhan asked.

"No…but that was because I was conserving my energy for *this* very encounter," Merlin answered, surprising everyone present as he stepped out from the shadows behind a column to Desorkhan's right.

The Master of Kelmar was dressed in sweeping red and golden robes covered in the pattern of his magic circle. His blue eyes were radiant, and the moon was shining on his silver hair as the ancient, able-bodied sorcerer walked out to the center of the courtyard and shook his head at Triedastron.

"Honestly, Triedastron, enchanted rope?" he asked. "Did you really think that would be enough to hold me? Ah, I must say that you've always had a tendency to underestimate my abilities."

As Triedastron scowled at him, Merlin looked back at Desorkhan and Singe, who were still holding Carmen and Blaze against their will.

"Release them, now," he ordered, in a composed yet commanding voice.

"I am not your servant!" Desorkhan snarled, as he continued to restrain his foes. "And in case you haven't noticed, you're rather alone up here tonight. After these kelscum are vanquished, it will be four against one."

"Do what he says, brother," Kelmari said, walking out from the darkness near the eastern wall to join Merlin in the middle of the courtyard.

She was holding her golden staff as she marched around the columns. Her long, white blonde hair was quite bright in the light of the moon, lifting in the breeze as she strode across the grass. She was wearing white and gold robes embroidered with ornate designs that made her porcelain skin and blue eyes sparkle.

"Silence, Kelmari!" Desorkhan spat, glaring at his younger sister. "This matter does not concern you."

"Yes, it does," she said, an uncharacteristic edge to her smooth voice. "Let Carmen and Blaze go, and duel all of us with honor."

"Two can play at this game," Triedastron interjected, his lips curling into a smile as he nodded toward the columns behind him. "Maidak, show yourself. Some of your old friends are here."

If Desorkhan hadn't been holding Carmen up while he restrained her, her knees just might have buckled in shock as she watched Maidak Kalvaro walk out from behind the row of white columns to stand beside Triedastron. He was wearing the black Keltan robes with red and orange flames. His bronze hair was blowing in the breeze, and his tall and slender form cast a long shadow next to him. He had a narrow, pale face and dark brown eyes that looked particularly unpleasant tonight.

"What *is* this?" Carmen gasped, barely able to talk with Desorkhan compressing her windpipe. Her eyes shot from Triedastron to Kalvaro. "What are *you* doing here?"

Maidak smirked at her.

"Are you really so startled?" he asked, taunting her. "I always thought that you and your friends knew *everything*."

Triedastron himself was also smiling at the expressions of downright shock on the faces of Carmen and her Souls.

"Maidak is my apprentice, you see; my voice and ideals in a living, breathing form," Triedastron told them. "He's trained under me for the past decade…. He is the one who orchestrated the Phantoms' first appearance in Kelmar nearly a year ago, and it was he who convinced Haidar that I was the nephew of Remnor Foretsam so I would be granted access to

Sarcanian Valley. He is also the one who gave Carmen the now *legendary* poisoned amulet."

"*What?!*" Carmen just about screamed, her mind practically exploding with her racing thoughts. "IT WAS YOU WHO FRAMED ELI THEN!"

"Well, of course it was me," Kalvaro said, quite proudly. "I made the cursed amulet, and replaced the real one with it. I then cursed Eli with *Devious Manipulation* so that he would give it to you. Eli, of course, has no memory of this...one of the side effects of the curse. Oh, and do you remember the vision that Eli showed you of yourself dying in Keltan? You weren't dying from the Dark elements, as Eli was forced into leading you to believe; you were being poisoned by the cursed amulet, and *I* was the one in the vision who subsequently put you out of your misery."

Carmen felt her stomach drop down to her ankles. Haidar and Inpu had been right about everything, and her own suspicions had also proven to be true.... Her initial shock swiftly turned into burning anger.

"YOU TRIED TO KILL ME!" she yelled across the courtyard, still fighting to break free from Desorkhan's grasp. "YOU TRIED TO KILL *ALL OF US!*"

"Under a few different circumstances, yes," Kalvaro said, swollen with pride at the fact. "One of those times was back when you stole the lost Secret from Eli's home before I could beat you to it." His nostrils suddenly flared angrily. "I was also certain that the flooding of the closet back at the Parliament building would have done it, but unfortunately for you, those times are over.... *This* is the night when everything begins anew."

"But you're an elected *Kelmarian Parliament Member!*" Blaze shouted, pulling away from Singe. "The Kelmarians that you represent put their trust in you!"

"Ah, life is just full of disappointments, isn't it?" Kalvaro remarked, feigning sadness. "But none whatsoever will compare to the one that is about to take place here in this courtyard.... No, after tonight, the Kelmarians will have very little to celebrate."

"And what is it, exactly, that makes you believe that we are simply going to bow down to you?" Merlin asked sharply, gazing at both him and Triedastron. "This is my home, and the world that I alone created. By magical law, if you desire to take it from me, you will first have to defeat the coalition of Kelmarians and Kelmarsians gathered here on this night. Then, and only then, will you be able to claim control of the Worlds Triad."

"I expected such a formality to come from you, Merlin," Triedastron said bitterly. "But do tell me, what of the Guardian of Kelmar? As Kelmar's sworn protector, surely she, too, should have to fight."

"I *will* fight," Carmen said boldly, finding the strength to break herself free from Desorkhan's grip. "That's why I'm here.... I will fight you to the death if I have to."

"Fight to the death, how appropriate," Triedastron quipped, with a condescending laugh. "My guess is that this is how it will indeed end for you."

"*All* of us will fight," Kelmari said strongly, holding her wand at the ready. "Let's finish this once and for all, and may the true victors prevail."

Without a single word, Desorkhan stomped across the courtyard with Singe to stand with Triedastron, Lucia, and Kalvaro. Merlin and Kelmari then joined Carmen and her Souls at their end of the courtyard. When he approached Carmen, Merlin placed his hands on her shoulders and peered into her eyes.

"We have arrived at the final battle," he said quietly, as though she needed reminding of how very important this conflict of epic proportions was. "Are you ready to stand and defend both of our worlds?"

Carmen swallowed hard.

"Yes, sir," she answered. "I've been preparing for this day for a great while now."

Merlin smiled at her warmly. Then he leaned in closer so that their faces were only inches apart.

"Remember the Secrets," he whispered, his words, urgent. "When the moment is right...set them free. They will come to you only when summoned."

Carmen blinked.

They? she wondered.... *What does he mean they will come?*

"Oh, I have waited a long time for this night," Triedastron said with a confident smile. He rolled up his sleeves.

"Those battles leading up to this one were mere child's play. *This* is a challenge, and who am I to turn down a challenge?"

Carmen and her allies exchanged customary bows with the Keltans, and then all of them but Kelmari summoned their wands.

Her head spinning with contradictory ideas and uncertainties, Carmen charged across the grass with Blaze. They would battle Triedastron and Lucia while Merlin and Dagtar dueled Desorkhan and Singe, and Kelmari dueled Kalvaro. The rest of the Souls of Destiny ran with Carmen and Blaze to stand with them against their opponents.

Carmen and Triedastron raised their wands at the same moment, but the spells that they cast against each other were as different as the sorcerers themselves.

"Fires of the Sarcan!"

"Noxious Venom!"

The crown of Carmen's wand burst into flames, releasing a fireball in the form of a Sarcan. A gaseous, toxic purple cloud expanded out from Triedastron's staff.

Carmen's flaming Sarcan ran through the *Noxious Venom* haze, disappearing inside its vapors midway between her and Triedastron. The magical flames cleared the air of the potent poisonous gas but fell short of reaching the Master of Keltan.

Blaze's body glowed as he flew through the air at Lucia. The Sarcan shot a powerful breath of fire at the Chimera, but she opened her jaws and unleashed her own breath of *Noxious Venom* at the oncoming fire.

Blaze flew up to escape the deadly fumes, which cut through his fire and evaporated up into the atmosphere. Triedastron aggressively moved to initiate his next spell.

"Splificer Donesta!"

A blast of dark energy erupted from Triedastron's wand. Carmen had to scramble to counter it, as Triedastron's curse fired across the courtyard with speed that she rarely saw.

Carmen tossed her wand sideways up into the air. When it was directly above her head, she shouted, *"Eternal Gates!"*

Carmen watched as her wand slowed…and a set of white, magical iron gates materialized in front of her. She caught her wand from behind the shield.

Triedastron's curse slammed into Carmen's gates with explosive force. The gates swayed dangerously. Carmen jumped back just in time, as the gates abruptly fell backwards and crashed down into the grass, vanishing in a cloud of white smoke.

Blaze soared over Lucia while her three heads watched him closely. When he came back around to attack her, Lucia's serpent tail hissed and unhinged its jaws, shooting a bronze beam of energy at the Sarcan.

Caught off guard by where the attack had come from, Blaze barely avoided getting hit with the curse. He veered to the left as he dove downward, and the curse missed him by less than an inch.

Carmen was anxious to regain momentum. She pointed her wand up into the night sky.

"Golden Lightning!" she bellowed.

Seconds later, there was a crack of thunder in the distance—and then a perfect bolt of gold lightning sliced through the darkness, striking Triedastron where he stood in a stunning blaze of light.

Triedastron toppled over, convulsing as the electricity surged through his body. Initially, he struggled against the forces…but it seemed that almost as soon as he had fallen to the ground, he was gingerly getting back on his feet. His face was now moist with perspiration, his silver-black hair was standing up on end, and he was still trembling a little.

In step with Carmen, Blaze flew ahead as Lucia ran after him, snapping her lioness jaws as she tried to bite off a piece of him. Blaze kept away from all three of Lucia's heads while he rose higher into the sky.

When the Sarcan was more than fifty feet above Lucia, a second bolt of lightning lit up the darkness over Merlin's castle and struck Blaze's horn. Blaze then directed his horn down at Lucia, and discharged the electrical energy into her body.

Lucia's legs shook violently for close to a minute before giving out from beneath her. She collapsed onto her side in the grass, the Lightning energy rapidly draining her strength.

"Fight it back, Lucia!" Triedastron ordered, standing over his weakening beast. "Rise, now!"

Lucia staggered but was able to stand up. Completely disregarding his Partner's tired state, Triedastron went ahead and pointed his wand at Carmen.

"Flames of the Chimera!"

Thick black smoke drifted out from Triedastron's dark gold staff, and then a sharp flare of searing red flames erupted from the crown.

Carmen hastened to summon a defense against the mighty attack. She raised her wand high above her head, closed her eyes, and spun around three times on her right foot.

"The Spinning Ribbon!" she yelled.

She kept her wand pointed straight up in the air as the silvery ribbon shield formed a protective cage around her, Blaze, Stellar, Anubis, and Glamis.

The wall of fire collided with the shining, silver protection no more than a foot away from Carmen's body, engulfing her shield in aggressively moving flames.

With intense focus and strength, Carmen worked to maintain her defense. If the *Flames of the Chimera* melted the shield, the cursed fire would critically burn her and her friends…. As weak and weary as she was, Carmen knew that she could not afford to let her shield fail her.

After five minutes of unsuccessfully attempting to break through Carmen's shield, Triedastron's flames gradually died down, and Carmen could finally dissolve her shield…but her problems were far from over.

Lucia charged ahead now, and by the way that she was breathing in, much deeper than usual, it didn't take Carmen long to realize that the creature was about to set free her own fiery assault. She concluded that her best chance to halt the flames was to fight fire with fire.

Carmen called for Blaze to fly toward Lucia. She then raised her wand as Lucia opened her lioness mouth.

"Dormien's Fire!"

Warmth crawled up Carmen's arms as she held tight to her wand. Lucia roared, setting free her concentrated breath of flames. Blaze opened his mouth and released his own gust of fire.

Carmen's wand shot its flames over Chimera, at Triedastron. The Master of Keltan cast a *Dark Guard* defense, which made a smoky black wall glide out from his wand and stand in front of him.

Blaze and Lucia's fires slammed into each other in an explosion of heat and power, sending a huge plume of black smoke rising up into the sky. Carmen covered her mouth with one of her sleeves to keep from choking as the smoke wafted across the courtyard. She tried to see Blaze through the smoggy air, but it wasn't feasible just yet.

The smoke lingered for nearly five disconcerting minutes, but after it cleared, Carmen and Triedastron could observe that their Partners' attacks had canceled each other out. Triedastron's *Dark Guard* had also protected him from Carmen's flames.

"Looks like we've got a nice, *long* evening ahead of us," Triedastron told Carmen, in a nonchalant voice. "I hope for your sake that you have the everlasting energy to match that of a leader of immortal spirits."

As Carmen silently wished for that very energy, Kelmari and Kalvaro remained engaged in an aggressive duel near to her and Triedastron. Kelmari was a highly gifted sorceress, and as the sister of Merlin, she shared many of his magical talents. She faced a competitive opponent in Kalvaro, though, and their combined skill levels made for an exceptionally volatile clash.

"*Fire Dragon!*" Kelmari shouted, pointing her wand at her opponent.

The crown of Kelmari's silver wand illuminated, and then a substantial, luminous burst of flames shaped like a Dragon grew out from it. The spectacular gold and red flaming Dragon raced through the air over the courtyard, leaving a trail of silvery smoke in the air behind it.

Eyeing the approaching *Fire Dragon* spell guardedly, Kalvaro waved his wand in a *Z* pattern in the air in front of him.

"*Keltan Shield!*" he commanded.

A dark glow swiftly climbed up Kalvaro's body, expanding from his feet to his head, enclosing him in shielding magical armor.

Kelmari's *Fire Dragon* flew down to the ground and snaked itself around Kalvaro. The Dragon roared as it constricted the sorcerer in its flames.

But after reaching the peak of their power less than a minute later, Kelmari's flames hastily extinguished, and the magical Dragon disappeared. Thanks to his effective defense, Kalvaro was left standing just as he had been before the attack.

"You're going to have to do a lot better than that if you want to defeat *me*," Kalvaro said contemptuously. "As one of the Cloud siblings, it should be no trouble for you to summon some of the more powerful magic that you undoubtedly have at your disposal."

Kelmari glowered at him.

"There's only so much air to breathe in the atmosphere," she said resentfully, "so it would certainly be of help to all of us if you stopped wasting it with your nonsensical remarks."

Kalvaro grinned—looking mildly surprised that Kelmari would speak back to him.

"You and your brother, Desorkhan, share the gift of a sharp tongue," he said. "I'm wondering what else you have in common with him. Clearly it's not intelligence, or else you would've had the cleverness to switch to the dark side a long time ago."

Kelmari continued to glare at him.

"Just shut up and duel, Maidak."

Kalvaro's grin was arrogant.

"Never say that you didn't ask for it," he said, raising his wand.

"Venomous Daggers!"

Ten acid green knives shot out of the crown of Kalvaro's staff, but Kelmari didn't appear panicked at all. She briefly watched as the knives flew toward her, and then threw her wand upward.

"Winged Shield!" she yelled.

Kelmari's wand froze in midair about three feet above her head, and a silver metal shield with white-feathered wings expanded from the sides of the staff.

As Kalvaro's poisonous knives flew in ten different directions upon approaching Kelmari, the sorceress's shield flew down to guard her. The *Winged Shield* darted in front of Kelmari and blocked each and every knife from reaching her. One by one, the knives bounced off of the shield with a piercing *clang*, and vanished.

"Impressive," Kalvaro conceded, as Kelmari's shield deflected the last of his knives.

Kelmari smiled confidently at him.

"There's the answer to your question," she said.

Kelmari then gazed up at the black sky.... The full moon was the only source of light for the courtyard, which was located at the center of Merlin's castle. She suddenly seemed to want to utilize that very light for her next spell as she pointed her wand up into the air.

"I call upon the Power of the Night!" she ordered.

The crown of Kelmari's wand glowed for a brief time before releasing a beam of gleaming white moonlight. Kalvaro extended his arm and held his wand horizontally over his head, casting a *Curtain of Darkness* defense. As Kelmari's spell rushed through the air, an enchanted black curtain tumbled down from Kalvaro's wand, concealing him from view.

Kelmari's *Power of the Night* spell slammed into Kalvaro's *Curtain of Darkness*—and shot straight through it. Kalvaro screamed, dropping his wand down into the grass.

With his shield destroyed, the wounded Kalvaro stumbled about in a daze, disoriented as a result of Kelmari's attack. Kelmari observed him as he wandered around in circles for a few minutes. But then…still in the midst of his daze, Kalvaro pointed his wand at Kelmari. His eyes were dull.

"*Dezvidenta!*" he shouted.

Kalvaro's wand expelled a maroon blast of energy.

Kelmari countered the curse with a *Perpetual Shield*. But just around the time that she defended herself against his magic, Kalvaro had recovered from the effects of the *Power of the Night* spell. He readied himself to cast yet another strong curse.

"*Tarcansol!*"

Not appearing to be even somewhat troubled, Kelmari pointed her wand back at him.

"*Storm of the Heavens!*" she cried.

With her command, a billowing storm blew up over the castle—and the courtyard lit up with explosions of light as the opposing sorcerers' spells met each other.

Only thirty feet away from his sister, Merlin was immersed in a similarly intense duel with their brother, Desorkhan, as Dagtar and Singe fought high in the skies over the castle without the orders of their Masters. It was Merlin and Desorkhan's first battle since the Dark Master had murdered his brother in the fateful duel in which he attempted to take control of Kelmar so many centuries before. And so, here they found themselves again tonight—this time, as spirits, and existing only in the magical afterlife, both still fighting for Kelmar.

"Did you ever think that you would find yourself in this situation again after our last duel?" Desorkhan asked, in the middle of their clash. Both he and Merlin had their wands pointed at each other, their arms steady.

"No, I can honestly say that it was not in my plans," Merlin replied, in an even tone. "But at that point, I was dead, and still am, just as you are now. Yet regrettably, even in death...we still somehow find ourselves divided."

"You can blame me for that all you want, Merlin, as you so often do," Desorkhan said sharply, "but it doesn't change the fact that you and Kelmari both disowned me following my decision to leave home and go out on my own."

Merlin gazed at his brother with what looked to Carmen like genuine sympathy and regret.

"We had no choice," the sorcerer said, in a bleak voice. "You were already lost by then as far as we were concerned."

"And were you right?" Desorkhan asked.

Merlin stared into the Dark Master's cold, black eyes. There was undeniable sadness and hurt behind his next words.

"Yes...I'm afraid we were."

Desorkhan shared one final, meaningful look with his brother. Then he shook his head.

"The past is nothing more than that," he said coldly, "and I'm about to show you how foolish you were for not joining me."

Desorkhan raised his wand.

"Fiery Death!"

Cursed flames instantly fired from Desorkhan's staff and sped across the courtyard at Merlin, who appeared ready for a prolonged and difficult fight.

"Flames of the Forgotten!" he shouted.

Merlin's wand illuminated, and orange and red fire erupted from the crown and charged through the air at Desorkhan's curse.

BOOM!

In an explosion of light and sound, Merlin and Desorkhan's spells collided, and the resulting outburst shook the castle around them, producing a plume of thick black smoke so enormous that it temporarily blinded the combatants in the two neighboring duels, rising up above the tallest towers of the building.

Carmen gaped up into the smoky air, where Dagtar and Singe were consumed in a sea of flames as they carried on with their own duel. She then saw the two enemy sorcerers standing in the aftermath of the blast below. Both had black ash coating their robes, and both were breathing deeply in momentary fatigue, but aside from that, Merlin and Desorkhan each looked prepared for more. Desorkhan pointed his wand up at the sky.

"Tolth Lumicatia!"

Not to be outdone, Merlin waved his wand and summoned his wings.

"Everlasting Flight!"

Merlin's green Dragon wings glowed with a white light as he flew up into the air and joined Dagtar. Seconds later, Desorkhan's *Swift Lightning* spell shot down from the black sky above Merlin. Carmen watched in awe as Merlin, with reflexes faster than any human she had ever seen before, pointed his index finger up at the approaching lightning bolt.

Without uttering a word, Merlin made the descending lightning decelerate to a crawl as it approached him.... So now, with Desorkhan's attack moving at an impossibly slow speed, it was easy for Merlin to fly out of its path before it could strike him.

Desorkhan cursed loudly. Singe flew down to him. From about fifty feet above the courtyard, Merlin directed his wand down at his challenger.

"The All-Knowing Light!" he ordered.

In the next moment, a glittering beam of multicolored light rocketed downward from Merlin's wand. Dagtar opened his jaws and released the same light upon Singe.

Desorkhan's eyes grew wide in disbelief. Quickly, he summoned a *Shield of Darkness* defense for both him and Singe. The Dark Master even went a step further and cast a subsequent *Invisible Shield* to encase the black wall that had materialized around them.

Merlin and Dagtar's spells struck Desorkhan's *Invisible Shield* with remarkable force, shattering through it to hit the *Shield of Darkness* in a powerful blast of colored energy.

Desorkhan kept both of his hands on his wand as he worked to preserve his shield. His arms shook, but his eyes remained focused ahead of him.... He refused to lower his defense and risk being struck with Merlin's potent attack, despite how much energy he was wasting in maintaining it.

It was a stressful several moments as Merlin and Dagtar's magic tried to break through Desorkhan's Protection. There was no telling what was going to happen from one second to the next....

All of a sudden, there was a piercing burst of sound as the energy from the *All-Knowing Light* was reduced to nonexistence.

Desorkhan could finally lower his wand, his arms still trembling. Merlin flew down and landed smoothly on the grass across from him. His wings vanished as soon as his feet touched the ground. Desorkhan's black Sarcan, Singe, flew up into the air after Dagtar once more.

"It would appear that time hasn't changed all that much," Merlin said insightfully, wiping a layer of perspiration from his brow. "We are still evenly matched when it comes to our degree of power."

"I wouldn't make that broad of an assessment so early on in the duel," Desorkhan said, in a flat voice. "We are far from the days of our youth, just as we are from naming a winner in this battle."

"True, true," Merlin agreed. "But no matter how much you may hate to acknowledge it, Desorkhan, we *are* brothers, and despite our marked differences...we will always share that connection."

Desorkhan's stare was still vacant—an emptiness in his eyes that could never be filled with the love and respect that caused Merlin's to shine. As Haidar had so wisely said, good and evil shared many things in common—in this case, even blood. But there was no mistaking that what separated Merlin from Desorkhan was far too deep for either one to change in the other.

And so, with no need for further words, Desorkhan and Merlin prepared to resume their duel. It was Desorkhan who made the first move.

"*Storm of Retaliation!*" he shouted, pointing his wand up into the night sky.

Merlin wasted no time in responding with his own spell.

"*Element Shower!*" he commanded.

Only a moment after that, the sky over Merlin's castle transitioned from pure black to a murky gray, and the light evening breeze warped into dominant gusts that blustered through the courtyard like a raging hurricane. Desorkhan's *Storm of Retaliation* spell was building in strength in the clouds of the upper atmosphere…and there seemed to be nothing that Merlin could do to stop it.

As Desorkhan's storm took shape, Merlin's wand fired red, yellow, green, blue, and white beams of light upward—one for each of the five Kelmarian Elements. Those glowing jets of light raced up into the stormy gray clouds overhead, where lightning strikes were now occurring every single second.

Merlin set free a continuous sequence of Element strands up into the clouds to combat Desorkhan's storm. Dagtar and Singe were still battling each other in the uppermost reaches of the turbulent sky as thunder roared outside the castle walls. The unsettled atmosphere looked like it was about to unleash a storm of driving rain and devastating lightning.

But then…the wind abruptly began to slow. Merlin kept on launching Element streams into the sky, and because of this, the enemy storm was steadily weakening. But unless Merlin could continue to carry on his spell further into the night, Desorkhan's storm would soon unleash its wrath upon him.

Carmen dove out of the way of Triedastron's *Demise by Fire* curse. She tumbled to the ground and rolled to the side, just escaping the scorching flames from the Master of Keltan's wand.

She promptly got back up and pointed her wand at her opponent.

"*Fire Shock!*" she ordered.

A blast of fire and lightning instantly discharged from Carmen's wand, zipped across the courtyard, and engulfed Triedastron in a pocket of magical, electrified fire.

Triedastron was yelling and thrashing about inside the flames. Blaze expelled simultaneous torrents of fire and lightning from his mouth and horn, which swallowed up Lucia just as Carmen's spell had Triedastron.

Then, suddenly, both fires extinguished, and Triedastron and Lucia emerged from the ensuing cloud of smoke. Triedastron's face was burned and blistering, and his burgundy robes had been singed to black. Lucia's brown fur was laden with embers. Triedastron ordered his Chimera forward.

"*Crushing Force!*" he hissed.

Lucia galloped ahead of him, her feet pounding heavily on the grass as she charged toward Blaze.

"*Lightning Horn!*" Carmen shouted, over another crack of thunder.

Blaze dove down at Lucia. Carmen summoned her wings and flew up to evade a huge eruption of force that exploded from Triedastron's wand.

Blaze pierced Lucia's flank with his horn—sending a surge of electricity into her body. In response, Lucia roared and slammed her huge lioness head into the Sarcan, knocking him down into the grass. Carmen became fearful when he didn't stir.

"Blaze, are you all right?" she called down to him.

Blaze lifted his head and saw Lucia standing over him. Almost at once, he was back on his feet, grimacing in pain. He flew up into the sky with his Master.

Significantly fatigued, Carmen and Blaze soared back to their end of the courtyard, above the chaos of the other two duels. Triedastron commanded Lucia to return to him.

The Kelmarians, Kelmarsians, and Keltans had been battling here in the World of Light for four hours, the trio of armies contributing every last bit of their strength to their respective causes, and it seemed that they had finally reached the critical moment that could shift the direction of the battle in one of two ways.

Triedastron stared at Carmen and Blaze.... There was fire flickering behind his dark and heartless eyes.

"I'm growing a little tired of dueling in my human form," Triedastron decided, in an eerily calm voice. "I think that the time has arrived for me to show you both another side of myself...a much more nefarious side."

Carmen tightened her grip on her wand. Her hands were already shaking. Triedastron held his wand directly out in front of him and closed his eyes.

"Demonsanthria!" he bellowed.

There was a shrill crack of thunder...and then a highly disturbing scene played out in front of Carmen's eyes.

Triedastron became rigid. His back arched as his pale skin turned to an ugly brownish-red, and his fingernails lengthened into curling black claws. His muscles bulged so large beneath his robes that it tore them in half. His human face deformed into that of a snarling, grotesque beast with sharpened horns and red eyes, and he grew a long, pointed tail.... Triedastron's true form as a Shape-Shifter...was that of a Keltan demon.

Triedastron looked over his new features with admiration, and then flashed a horrible, yellow-toothed smile at Carmen and her friends as they stared at him in utter horror. Perspiration was pouring down Carmen's face—her stomach turned upside down at the sight of him.

"Now we can have some *real* fun," Triedastron declared, in a deep, raspy voice.

He eyed the Souls of Destiny. Then he abruptly thrust his wand at the colossal, white stone columns behind them.

"DESTRUCTOS!"

Carmen ducked as a blast of dark red light shot from the crown of Triedastron's wand and slammed into the columns right at the back of her and her friends. She whirled around.

One by one, the entire row of columns smashed to pieces, sending dangerously sharp shards of rock flying through the courtyard.

"MOVE!" Carmen shouted, pushing Stellar and Blaze away from her.

But then she glanced to her left, and her eyes fell on the last column in the row. The top half of it had shattered, and now the unstable bottom portion was about to fall onto Glamis and Anubis, who were standing directly in front of it. In that split second, Carmen raced over to them.

With the last of her strength, Carmen shoved her two friends as hard as she could away from the column. An instant later, she felt something hard and heavy crash down onto her back, and she fell face first into the grass as excruciating pain ten thousand times worse than anything that she had ever felt rushed through her body. She screamed so loud that she was sure everyone in Kelmarsia could hear her.

"CARMEN!"

Blaze and the others were immediately at her side. The smell of the cool grass pressed against her face filled Carmen's nose as she lay there, dazed, aching, and on the verge of blacking out.... It felt like an elephant was sitting on her back. She was dizzy...and immense pain was shooting through every part of her body, making it very difficult to breathe. In those first few seconds, she saw her entire life flash before her eyes as the column crushed her body.

Then...just when she was sure that she could no longer endure the agony of the weight that was pinning her to the ground, she felt all five of her Souls of Destiny work together to lift the broken half of the stone column off of her back and drop it in the grass.... Quickly, she felt life return to her, and she could breathe, however painfully, once again.

The stone column had not broken Carmen's skin but had left an exceptionally deep bruise, and nearly crushed her to death. Drained now beyond magical and physical restoration, Carmen didn't even know how she would be able to stand up, let alone continue to fight in this condition. Every last inch of her was throbbing, and the unbearable pain was not going away.

"You're going to be okay, Carmen," Blaze promised her, his face just inches from hers. "Just don't move."

But even in her severely injured state, Carmen could hear the panic in his voice, and could sense his uncertainty. She managed to turn her head and look into his frightened blue eyes, but just that small motion caused a sharp pain to shoot up her neck, and then down her back. She winced, crying in pain as she looked back down into the grass.

Triedastron laughed loudly from across the courtyard, prompting the other combatants to stop fighting and turn to see what was happening.

"Well, I would say that we have reached the conclusion of this battle," the demon Master of Keltan smugly announced to the others. "This is where we end it all.... Have you any final words before I take your life, Guardian?"

Carmen's tearstained face was still flat in the grass, the pain on the verge of blinding her. In the darkness of that moment, she thought about many things.

She thought about her friends and her grandfather, about her home back in Kelmar, about her training, and all that had happened over the past year.... Finally, she thought about her parents, and how much she wished that she could see their faces one last time before she died.... It was when she thought of them that Desorkhan and Merlin's preceding words about the Secrets of Kelmar sunk in at last.

"...Merlin has formulated a new spell involving the Secrets...the likes of which none born of magic blood have ever seen."

"We in Kelmarsia have the utmost confidence that you will succeed. You just need to have faith in your powers, and trust your intuitions.... The Secrets of Kelmar won't reveal themselves unless you believe in yourself, and in your gifts. When the moment is right...set them free. They will come to you only when summoned."

After months of searching for the truth of the Secrets, Carmen finally found it here, as she lay in the dark, in plain sight of both her friends and her enemies, closer to death than she had ever been. Somehow, she gathered the strength to lift her head...and used her arms to steady herself as she got into a seated position.

Searing pain was stabbing at her body as she stared around the courtyard at Kalvaro, her Souls, and the trio of Cloud siblings. Each and every one of them was watching her. As her gaze passed from one to the next, Carmen realized that if she were wrong about what she was about to do, Kelmar and its sister world, Kelmarsia, were doomed to ruin.... But if she were right, maybe, just maybe, they would survive to see another dawn.

Still gasping for breath and cringing in pain, Carmen peered into Triedastron's scarlet eyes.

No matter what form he took at any given moment, Triedastron represented the culmination of evil, and the darkness that carried on for eternity, long after souls embodying its destructive force had wasted away into death. For the beautiful gift of life to rise out of that darkness, light had to bring forth the good, and that was what convinced Carmen now that she and only she could call upon the powers of the Secrets of Kelmar.

She struggled to keep her arm from shaking as she raised her wand.

"Of Light and Dark, there sets a Dawn," Carmen recited, straining to keep her voice steady. She gazed up into the black sky through watery eyes. *"But ahead of the Dawn, the sky is darkest."*

Suddenly…the crown of Carmen's wand glowed, radiating white light. A sense of incredible power began to radiate through her body, instantly making her feel more alive.

"To bring on the Dawn, Light and Dark must coexist as one," she said, her voice building in strength.

Abruptly looking more unnerved than Carmen had ever seen him, Triedastron pointed his own wand up at the sky.

"I SUMMON THE DARKNESS OF DEATH!" he roared.

The radiant moon that was hanging overhead vanished behind a black cloud, shrouding the courtyard in darkness. The only source of light that remained was that which came from Carmen's wand.

Right away, Carmen began to feel her life again draining from her as Triedastron's curse exercised its influence…. But as her eyes began to drift shut, seconds before she was about to lose consciousness, she reminded herself that she just *couldn't* die yet. No matter what happened, she had to finish what she started.

With her Souls of Destiny gathered around her, Carmen held tight to her staff, and summoned all of her remaining strength to speak the final verse of the Secrets' incantation.

"I hold the answer!" she cried into the night. *"I cast the spell in my heart!"*

With those final words, a brilliant ray of silvery white light shot from Carmen's wand, up into the black sky.

After momentarily disappearing into the atmosphere...the light plummeted down through the air and flew directly across the courtyard, crashing with tremendous force into the unguarded Triedastron—slamming him screaming against the row of stone columns behind him. Triedastron's hulking demon body smashed the columns to pieces, and he fell forward and collapsed to the ground.

That same silver-white light that had struck the Master of Keltan then darted around the entire perimeter of the courtyard, and wispy, glowing white spirits appeared one by one around the edges of the grass.

Carmen stared around her.... There were many people and creatures that she did not recognize. But then she looked to her right, and saw Anubis's mother and father standing alongside Glamis's grandfather, Stellar's father, Haidar's Sarcan, Morin, Blaze's grandparents, and Dagtar's mother.

A moment later, she felt someone standing on the other side of her. She looked up to see the glittering, silvery-white spirits of her own parents and their Sarcans smiling down at her. They looked more loving and peaceful than she had ever seen them.

"You called for us, Carmen, and here we are," Isabella said, in her unmistakable, kind voice. *"It's us—the Secrets of Kelmar."*

Carmen gaped at her...her heart racing. She couldn't believe it....

Still fighting off the brutal pain that was crippling her body, she stared up at her mother and father, unable to understand all that was happening.

"But...but *how?*" she stammered.

William knelt down and gently placed his shimmering hand on Carmen's injured back. Then he closed his eyes...and unexpected warmth suddenly gushed through her body as he proceeded to heal her.... After only a minute or so, the brutal pain that had nearly killed her was completely gone.

Carmen sighed, able to breathe deeply for the first time since the attack.... She was amazed by how unbelievably wonderful it felt just to smell the evening air, and to know that she would live beyond this night.

"You've done your part. Now it's our turn to help you," William said, rising to his feet again.

And without delay, he, his wife, and their Sarcans drifted back over into line with the ancestors of Carmen's Souls. All of the silver, translucent spirits standing around the courtyard were smiling the warmest and most perfect of smiles as they joined hands...and floated up into the dark sky as one.

Carmen and her friends watched in awe.... Slowly and gracefully, the spirits drifted ever higher together, and disappeared inside the dark clouds over the castle.

Then, there was a huge burst of white light as the darkness was shattered and the sky opened up—giving way to dawn.

From somewhere far beyond where she was, Carmen heard the joint voices of her parents and the other ancestor spirits who had just destroyed Triedastron's curse.... When they spoke together, it sounded like a single, magnificent and musical voice.

"Virtue and love transcend the boundaries of time and space," the Secrets of Kelmar sang. *"They can bring miracles that span across worlds, and change each of our lives in unimaginable*

ways.... They bring together dawns and sunsets that keep our worlds in balance, and it is they that allow Light and Dark to exist together in eternal harmony."

A beautiful pink light washed over the courtyard as the orange sun rose over the eastern mountains of Kelmarsia. Triedastron and his Keltan fighters vanished back to the World of Darkness in the light of the Kelmarsian sunrise.... Just like that, the balance between Light and Dark had been restored.

Shortly after the Keltans disappeared, a great silver cloud glided over the castle, releasing a cleansing shower of cool and pure rain.

"You've done it, Carmen," Merlin said, beaming at her as he strolled across the courtyard with his sister. He opened his arms to embrace her. "Congratulations."

Carmen smiled wider than she ever had as she hugged Merlin and Kelmari, raindrops mixing with the tears that were sliding down her face.

As Carmen and her Souls spent a few precious moments celebrating their great victory together in the rain, they could hear familiar voices carrying up from the meadow far below...the rest of their family and friends from Kelmar!

Carmen and her companions shared a final joyful glance with Merlin and Kelmari, who bowed gratefully to them, before they hurried out of the courtyard, down the bridge, and through the sparkling green forests to reunite with their friends and loved ones.

Within minutes, Carmen and her Souls emerged from the woods to meet their fellow Kelmarian fighters, all of whom were standing beside the River of the Departed Spirits, their faces glowing with smiles. The Haidars, the Camersleys, Officer Sheridae, Alazar, Rishaw and his assistants, the Sarcan students, Partners, Councilors...all of them were there.

With not even a word spoken between them, Carmen and her Souls rushed forward into the hugs of their friends and family members. It was because of their collective efforts that the Worlds Triad would come to exist in everlasting peace, and that Kelmar and all of its inhabitants would live on to tell this very story.

After sharing a long and tear-filled embrace with her grandfather and Thunderbolt, Carmen spotted Shea grinning at her through the rain a short distance away. Blinking through the raindrops as she and her grandfather released each other from their grasps, Carmen then ran headlong into Shea's outstretched arms. She beamed over his shoulder at Blaze and Gia embracing behind them. She had never felt happier than she did in that moment.

As Carmen and Shea stepped back from each other, the rain gradually slowed, and ceased. The orange sun illuminated Shea's smiling face as he gazed upward. His eyes widened in surprise.

"Wow," he said, glancing down at Carmen before directing her eyes up at the sky. "Would you have a look at *that*."

Carmen turned around...and found herself staring up at the most beautiful and perfect translucent rainbow that she had ever seen. It stretched high across the meadow and disappeared on the other side of Merlin's castle. Dagtar was soaring beneath its sweeping arch as he flew toward the field. His crystal eyes were shining when he bowed his head to her.

"Thank you."

Carmen beamed up at him.... And just then, the enchanting music that had forever played throughout the World of Light returned to the ears of the humans and creatures of Kelmarsia. An even wider smile broke across Carmen's face as she and her friends admired the prodigious rainbow in the pink and orange dawn sky, and listened to the music that gave new life to all who heard it.

Before long, she felt a light tap on her shoulder. She turned to look at Shea again.

"If it's not too much to ask," he said, smiling nervously as he held out his hand, "may I have that second dance that you promised me?"

Carmen grinned at him, and gladly took her friend's hand.

"I would love to," she said.

Shea smiled once more, his blue eyes sparkling.

Hand-in-hand, he and Carmen walked out to the center of the meadow.

Then, without thinking much about it, Carmen laid her hands atop Shea's shoulders as he placed his on her waist—and the two of them danced, slowly and effortlessly, as though it were something that they did together quite often. Carmen never wanted to forget the sheer bliss that she felt as she danced, content and free from care, on that fateful morning.

The Souls of Destiny, Blaine, Thunderbolt, Gia, and many others soon joined Carmen and Shea out on the open grass. Together, they danced with unmatched joy beneath the dazzling, everlasting rainbow to the heavenly music of Kelmarsia in the soft light of dawn. It was, in every possible way, a more perfect ending than Carmen ever could have imagined.

EPILOGUE
THE NEXT GREAT ADVENTURE

The sun was shining vibrantly against the azure sky on the day that the Sarcan Captains and Cadets participated in a joint graduation ceremony in the refurbished Thunder Stadium. The arena was filled to near capacity on this afternoon, upon which the Kelmarians also celebrated the restoration of harmony in the Worlds Triad. Commander Haidar and Officer Sheridae led the Thunder Academy commencement, and honored all of the brave individuals who had helped in defeating Triedastron and his army of followers.

A stage was erected in the center of the stadium, where the Sarcan Council awarded each Sarcan Captain and Cadet a Badge of Distinction for his or her service to Kelmar. Haidar and Sheridae shook their students' hands as they marched across the stage to the thundering cheers of the crowd. The Sarcan Cadets graduated to become Sarcan Captains, and the Captains graduated to become Sarcan Majors. Carmen smiled when Head Councilor, Peruveus Seth, pinned her Badge of Distinction to her Captain's uniform. The round, polished gold badge was marked with the Great Seal of Kelmar above the phrase *Greatness is earned through action.*

Blaze bowed his head to receive the same badge attached to a silk award ribbon, which he would wear around his neck.

After they received their awards, Carmen and Blaze waited for Glamis, Stellar, and Anubis to accept their own medals before they all walked across the stage in one another's company to a standing ovation from the Kelmarian audience in the seats.

Carmen couldn't stop grinning as she shook Haidar and Sheridae's hands. The allied victory over Keltan had been a hard-fought struggle, but they had made it through together, and together was just how they welcomed in the beginning of a new age in Kelmar's history.

Haidar whispered words of gratitude to Carmen and her friends, and then saluted them as they left the stage to return to their seats, which were located next to Alazar and Renalda.

The ceremony concluded in the early evening with a final gesture of acknowledgment to the Kelmarsians, without whom, the Kelmarians could not have saved either of their worlds from devastation. The ancestor spirits who were the Secrets of Kelmar had given Carmen the help that she so desperately needed to bring dawn to the World of Light.

And so, in honor of the Kelmarsians' bravery in the final battle alongside their Kelmarian allies in the forests and courtyard of Merlin's castle, Carmen and the thousands of other Kelmarians present raised their wands to the sky, and sent ribbons of golden light up into the heavens. Dagtar's claw became warm against the base of Carmen's neck, letting her know that he appreciated their thanks, and reminding her that his spirit would continue to be with her always.

Carmen had cleaned out her room in Thunder Academy earlier that day. As she packed up her belongings in cardboard boxes, she reflected on how very sad, yet satisfied she felt to be finished with her formal training. Sarcanian Valley had been home to her for the past two years, and it was hard for her to imagine life outside of it. She had made some of her strongest and most lasting friendships here, gone on adventures that helped to make her into a greater person, and learned and trained to become the sorceress and the young woman that she was today.

Would she miss her day-to-day existence as a Sarcan student? Yes, she was convinced that she absolutely would. She would miss rising at dawn and learning new spells with Commander Haidar; she would miss walking through the halls of the great castle; she would miss seeing her classmates each morning and afternoon; and perhaps most of all...she would miss seeing the beautiful sunrise and sunset over the red sandstone rocks of the valley. But though it would not be easy, she would move on—just as she had to. Time would no doubt change many things, but for the rest of her life, she would never forget all that Thunder Academy had given to her.

In the days and weeks following the conclusion of the war, the partially destroyed Pyramid City was rebuilt and restored to its original beauty and strength. The Kelmarian capital had been well defended during the Phantom Warrior invasion, and now with the Keltans securely back in the World of Darkness, the Kelmarians would never again have to worry about another Phantom attack on their realm.

The various other locations throughout Kelmar, which had been attacked earlier in the year, were also brought back to their former states of splendor. With Carmen's restoration of the balance between Light and Dark, Triedastron and his followers would be permanently confined to Keltan, just as they were supposed to be, and could not threaten the peace in Kelmarsia and Kelmar for the rest of eternity.

During the last phase of combat in the realms of the afterlife, Kelmar had suffered through some of the worst storms in its history, due to the intensity of the fighting that was taking place in the spirit worlds. Hundreds of trees had been knocked over in the tornadoes and thunderstorms that had swept across the lands at the height of the battle, and there had also been heavy rain that resulted in flooding in the low-lying areas of

Kelmar. Fortunately, despite the dangerous conditions, no Kelmarian lives were lost while the fighting in the afterlife raged on.

A massive cleanup effort to repair the storm damage was undertaken once the Kelmarians returned from the World of Light. It took a considerable amount of time and effort, but before Carmen knew it, Kelmar looked as naturally magnificent as it had prior to the start of the war.

These days, the weather in Kelmar was a far cry from that of the months' prior. Summer in Sarcanian Valley was defined by gorgeous days of golden sunshine, calm breezes, and the occasional rain shower in the later months. Finally, it seemed that Kelmar had returned to a state of peace and normalcy.

On Carmen's seventeenth birthday, she awoke to good news as she looked over at her bedside table in her room at Blaine's cottage. The front-page story in *The Kelmarian Review* that morning detailed Eli Elezar's release from prison, following the investigation into a wrongful decision made during his criminal hearing.

Carmen and her Souls had traveled to Pyramid City after returning to Kelmar to inform Parliament of Kalvaro's ties to Triedastron, and his admission of attempting to murder Carmen with the cursed amulet that he had made and given to Eli. Parliament, in turn, reexamined Eli's case, and found there to be not only a lack of sufficient evidence to charge him with any crime, but also that his accuser had knowingly framed him for a crime that he himself had committed.

Kalvaro disappeared after the battle in Kelmarsia, leaving Parliament unable to discipline him until he willingly resurfaced on his own, or they could locate his whereabouts. Carmen hadn't spoken to Draven since his father's disappearance, but she could only imagine how much pain her classmate was in over his father's betrayal. Only time would tell what would come of Maidak's actions.

Carmen spent her birthday with her grandfather and her Souls of Destiny in Mortrock Forest. They enjoyed a delicious picnic on the grass in the woods, which included the same insect cake with white frosting that Glamis had made Carmen for her birthday the year before. As they ate, Blaine still couldn't help smiling over what Carmen had achieved in Kelmarsia, and all that she and her friends had accomplished these past several months.

"You did it again," Blaine said proudly, as he ate his cake. "You saved Kelmar from destruction by our enemies.... What more could we ask of you?"

Carmen smiled back at him.

"But the difference is that we didn't do it alone this time," she pointed out. "Mom and Dad, and our other ancestors all helped us. *They* were the ones who brought the Dawn."

"Yes, but they couldn't have done it without *you*," Blaine reminded her. "You allowed their presence to come forth. The love that you have for them and your friends and your trust in your magic became the power necessary to break the spell of darkness. Only a light with that kind of power behind it could have freed us from Triedastron's curse.... And in the end, that's what gave life to the Secrets of Kelmar."

Carmen looked up from her piece of cake.

"You really think that's what did it?" she asked.

Blaine smiled warmly at his granddaughter. "There's not a single doubt in my mind."

At the conclusion of the picnic, Carmen felt like taking a walk. She'd had a lot on her mind since the Kelmarians' victory in the Worlds Triad War, and she thought that the tranquility of the forest would help her to settle her thoughts. She asked her grandfather if he wouldn't mind if she and her Souls met him and Thunderbolt back at the house in a little while.

Much to Carmen's relief, Blaine seemed to have no problem with her going off on her own. He collected the used dishes and then got up from the ground to walk back to the cottage with his Sarcan while Carmen and her Souls gathered together to wander deeper into the forest. Carmen smiled one last time at her grandfather before they left, just to let him know that they wouldn't go too far.

She wasn't sure exactly what she was looking for as she led her friends through the trees, but in walking through the quiet forest, she could already feel her worries easing. She and the others eventually stumbled upon a small clearing, which was open to the perfectly blue sky. Lovely yellow wildflowers were growing in the grass, and as soon as Carmen stepped out of the trees and into the tiny, flowering meadow, she knew that this was exactly where she wanted to be at this moment.

She walked to the center of the clearing and lay down on her back in the bed of flowers, finding herself staring up into the infinitely blue heavens as her friends rested in the grass next to her.

Blaze gazed over at his Master.

"What are you thinking about, Car?" he asked.

Carmen smiled and turned to look at him.

"Oh...I'm just thinking about my parents," she said wistfully. "I wonder...if they're proud of me."

The last time that Carmen had to say goodbye to her parents, when she and her friends left Kelmarsia after the final battle, was one of the most heartbreaking goodbyes she had ever experienced. A part of her wished she could have stayed there with them in the World of Light...but she also knew that that was an impossible fantasy. She missed them, and Dagtar, each and every day, yet just as they'd had a purpose to fulfill in Kelmarsia, so too, did she have a purpose here in Kelmar.

"Of course they're proud of you," Blaze said, without hesitation. "They always have been, and they always will be."

Carmen sighed, staring back up at the sky.

"In Kelmarsia, it almost felt like they were alive, because they were with me...." she said. "I just sometimes wish that they could be *here*, too."

Blaze nodded understandingly.

"A huge part of your life was stolen from you the day your parents died, Carmen," he said slowly, "but you must remember for all of time that on that very same day, we Kelmarians were given the greatest gift we could ever ask for...and that's *you*."

At those most sincere and heartfelt words, an appreciative smile came to Carmen's face. She looked over at the serene expressions on the faces of all of her friends, and she found her thoughts drifting from the past to the future.

Dagtar's claw was warm against her skin as she turned and peered up into the white clouds slowly passing across the sapphire sky. She felt a wonderful sense of peace wash over her.

"I don't know what's going to happen tomorrow," Carmen said, as she turned to Blaze, "but I wish that this feeling could last forever."

There was a reflective flicker in Blaze's thoughtful blue eyes as he gazed back at her.

"Think of tomorrow as the start of the next great adventure," he said quietly. "Forever, though, begins today."